The Best American
Mystery Stories 2000

The Best American Mystery Stories 2000

Edited and with an Introduction
by Donald E. Westlake

Otto Penzler, *Series Editor*

HOUGHTON MIFFLIN COMPANY

BOSTON • NEW YORK 2000

Visit our Web site: www.houghtonmifflinbooks.com.

ISSN 1094-8384
ISBN 0-395-93917-8
ISBN 0-395-93918-6 (pbk.)

Printed in the United States of America

QUM 10 9 8 7 6 5 4 3 2 1

Contents

Foreword

THE AMERICAN MYSTERY STORY is flourishing as we approach the new millennium (which begins, of course, on January 1, 2001, as I do not know of a single historical entity who lived in the year 0).

Mysteries have changed in both style and content, just as the rest of literature has changed, over the course of the genre's life, which is just a bit more than a century and a half (assuming that we're all agreed that the first true mystery short story was Edgar Allan Poe's "The Murders in the Rue Morgue" in 1841).

Mystery stories used to be mainly puzzles, then they seemed to be mainly private eye stories. Both kinds are still written, and sometimes they are very good, but more stories in this anthology (and the three that preceded it) are stories of character than one has been accustomed to seeing in collections of mystery stories. These are still mysteries, but they are more. In the words of the truly stupid reviewers who condescend when they write about a good mystery, they "transcend the genre." As readers have become more demanding, contemporary writers have stepped up and produced more complex, more textured, more stylistically original stories.

This evolution has been reflected in the Edgar Allan Poe Awards, given in the short story category by the Mystery Writers of America. Recent winners have been Tom Franklin's "Poachers" and Michael Malone's "Red Clay," neither of which could be classified as a traditional mystery story, and neither of which, I'd be willing to bet, could have been honored a half-century ago. Therefore, as you open this book and begin to read, be prepared for the unexpected, and be ready for some of the best prose being written today.

Not only do crime stories seem to be improving each year, but there seem to be more of them as well. For the first anthology in this series, I read more than 600 stories. The next year the number exceeded 800, and it went up the following year. For the calendar year 1999 I examined more than 1,100 stories — a task that would have been impossible without the help of Michele Slung, who looks at three times that many stories just to see whether they are mystery-related, much less any good. It seems reasonable to think that with a wider array of material from which to pick, more good stuff will float to the top.

This year's guest editor, Donald E. Westlake, demonstrated his professionalism yet again. He's the kind of writer who, if you ask for a story of 5,000 to 6,000 words, will give you one of 5,500. If you say you need it by the fifteenth of the month, you get it on the fourteenth. When I sent the fifty stories that I regarded as the best of the year to him, I apologized for being a little late, as there had been many late submissions. If you can read the stories and make your selections in a month, I hinted, that would be nice. He did it in just over three weeks. And wrote the introduction. And this from a man with more books and movie scripts waiting to be written than you can imagine.

This next paragraph is redundant only to those who have added previous volumes in this series to their collections — and who actually read the foreword. Mysteries are defined for this series as any story in which a crime or the threat of a crime is central to the theme or plot. To be eligible for this anthology, stories must be by an American or a Canadian author and published initially in an American or a Canadian periodical or book. Popular consumer magazines, specialty mystery magazines, literary journals, anthologies, or collections containing initial appearances — all and any can serve as the source for these stories.

To submit a story for consideration in this series, please send a copy of the published story (no originals can be considered) to me at the address below, or just drop me a note to let me know the name of a worthy story and where it has been published. Don't bother telling me about the mystery magazines and anthologies, as these are scrutinized carefully. I'm unlikely to miss anything in *Playboy* or *The New Yorker*, as these have been good sources for first-rate stories. If the story has appeared on the Internet, forward a printed hard copy to me, together with the name of the e-maga-zine, since I am unlikely to have encountered it. Well, *more* than un-likely: since I don't have a computer, it is impossible for me to see these. The earlier in the year I receive a story, the better.

Submissions and other correspondence may be sent to me at The Mysterious Bookshop, 129 West 56th Street, New York, New York 10019.

O.P.

Introduction

THE DURABILITY of the short story is astonishing, all in all. It does not these days make any reputations, nor are the financial rewards particularly lush. Today's slick magazines pay for a short story exactly what the slick magazines of the twenties paid for a short story; not adjusted dollars, real dollars. Scott Fitzgerald got the same pay from the magazines as today's writers in similar venues, but in his day that was enough to keep him in Paris, whereas today the same income is enough to keep you on the farm.

Today's digest-size magazines also pay just what their uncles, the pulps, used to pay. Up and down the market, this is the one and only example in the entire American economy of a durable and successful resistance to inflation.

Then why does the short story continue to endure? Given the way our world works, the modest financial return very strongly implies a modest readership; if the millions were clamoring for short stories as though they were Barbie dolls, the price would go up.

Still, there they are. The slicks still publish short stories, though nowhere near as many as they used to. The digest-size magazines toddle along, far fewer than the pulps of yesteryear but still alive and in good health. University publications produce a hefty number of short stories every year, including some you'll find in this volume, but that's probably because their content providers are in the main academicians, and it's a given that the writer of short stories will be keeping his day job.

So it must be love that keeps the form alive, the writer's love for the work. It has been said that jazz and the short story are the two

American contributions to the world of art, and they do seem to have at least this one thing in common: both are engaged in by the practitioner primarily for the love of doing it.

There's another link as well between the short story and jazz. Both are exemplified by the extended riff on a clean and simple motif. What the novel is to the symphony, the short story is to jazz. Like the best jazz solos, what the best short stories have to offer is a sense of vibrant imagination at work within a tightly controlled setting. That's what turns the writers on, and that's what maintains for the form a strong and knowledgeable readership. There is a joy in watching economy of gesture when performed by a real pro, whatever the art.

The short story evolved from several sources. The medieval *conte*, the tale meant to amuse the idlers at court (and the wanna-be idlers), and which more often than not involved a young wife and her lover putting one over on her much older husband, is one source. The traveler's tale, such as those in Chaucer and Boccaccio, twists of fate and reversals of fortune, morality lessons in which irony is mostly delivered by the hand of God, is another. The joke, particularly the shaggy dog story, of ancient lineage, is a third.

All of these sources came into the American psyche through the campfire yarns, the tall tales and frontier reports by which the early settlers tried to describe to themselves this new world they were blundering through. When these rowdy chronicles became tamed for print, by Mark Twain and Ambrose Bierce and many others, the American short story had begun.

What the short story shares with its forebears, and what it does not share with novels or movies or television plays (except in the early days of live television from New York), is a singularity of focus, of character, and of effect. Though a story might cover years, as does Barbara D'Amato's lovely "Motel 66" in this volume, or hundreds of miles, as does David Edgerley Gates's somberly beautiful "Compass Rose," its movement is nevertheless within the confines of the Aristotelian dictum that a drama consists of the playing out of one action. The short story is not a place for digression.

Which leads me to a second vein of short story writing that's been popular now for some forty years or more, but which needn't hold our attention for long, because you'll find none of them in here (though some of them are very good indeed). This kind of story establishes a mood or an attitude or a situation and stops when the establishing is done. These stories are more closely allied to painting than to narrative and can be very strong, emotionally, though a certain limpness is always a danger.

These other stories are frequently called slices of life, and from a narrative point of view they don't have endings, which is why I could find none of them to include here. A story in the mystery or crime or detective genre (I've *never* known an inclusive enough term for this particular corner of the literary world) by definition has to have an ending. One way or another, the story of the type you'll find in this volume begins with a problem and cannot end until that problem has been dealt with, though not necessarily solved. These stories slice life too, but lengthwise. While it is true that one cross-section of a river, shore to shore, will imply everything upstream and everything downstream, it is also true that as a general rule the river itself is more interesting.

Given the constrictions of length and of subject matter — there must, after all, be a crime *somewhere* in the story — it's still astonishing to me just how broad a range the mystery short story can cover. For instance, the American South has always been fruitful ground for stories of every length and kind, and here we have Thomas H. McNeely's harrowing "Sheep," Dennis Lehane's gothic "Running Out of Dog," Tom Franklin's gritty "Grit," and Shel Silverstein's rollicking "The Guilty Party." All are clearly and evocatively set in that part of America, all are steeped in the flavor of the region, but could any four stories be more unalike?

(It's a sad reminder also that, Shel Silverstein having died last year, long before his time, this is probably the last effusion we're likely to see from that wonderfully fertile and varied mind, but at least he certainly did go out on a roisterous high note.)

I am encouraged also when I see that the field is in no way stuck in yesteryear, though the traditions of fairness, cleverness, and excellence remain intact. Within those traditions, we find much that couldn't be more new. Here we have a story told to a video camera, a story that makes bizarre use of the latest telephone equipment, and a new way of seeing — look out for it — the ICU.

The venues where these stories first appeared remain, as always, as broad a spectrum of American periodical publishing as you're likely to find anywhere. Here we have the major mainstream magazines *Playboy* and the *Atlantic Monthly,* and here we also have the more specialized *Oxford American* and *Chattahoochie Review.* Plus we have selections from three fine anthologies, from *Mystery in the Sunshine State* assembled by Stuart Kaminsky, *Murder and Obsession* compiled by Otto Penzler, and *Murder on Route 66* edited by Carolyn Wheat. And of course we have the faithfuls, *Alfred Hitchcock's Mystery Magazine* and *Ellery Queen's Mystery Magazine,* principally the latter.

For nearly sixty years, *Ellery Queen* has been the polestar of the mystery short story, finding and publishing the newest writers, the latest expansions of the genre, everything that keeps the field exciting and fresh. *Ellery Queen's* Department of First Stories, the first published work by a brand-new writer, has been a staple of the magazine forever, and an amazing number of those stories have made it onto best-of-the-year lists. I'm happy to say we have one this year, "Jumping with Jim" by Geary Danihy, that is I think one of the best debuts ever, told with such assurance and skill that I had to keep looking back at the first page; yes, this is the Department of First Stories. Long may it continue.

It's been a long time since the mystery story was no more than a puzzle acted out by marionettes for the amusement of the cloistered Victorian mind. In the stories in this volume there are surprises galore, but they are surprises of character, of motivation, of story, not merely surprises of mechanical puzzle-playing. Although it is certainly possible for some writer somewhere to come up with a new and richer variant on, say, the locked-room story, there's no tired smoke-and-mirrors exercise of that former sort to be found here. Every one of our writers has more serious fish to fry.

And many show their awareness that they are writing at the end of the millennium, that, in a way, everything that was published in 1999, in any genre, served as a kind of summing-up. Even our Department of First Stories entry begins by contrasting past with present, the current narrator with Joseph Conrad's Lord Jim. At the other extreme, Robert Girardi's "The Defenestration of Aba Sid" and half a dozen of our other stories all draw a picture, clear and concise, of just where America found itself at the end of the twentieth century.

I suppose that must inevitably lead me into a discussion of the future of the mystery short story. Our genre began with the publication, in April 1841, of "The Murders in the Rue Morgue" by Edgar Allan Poe, so it is now entering its third century and its 159th year, so wouldn't I like to say where I expect it will travel next? "Whither," and all that?

Well, no. I'm terrible at predictions, always have been. I don't even know what *I'm* going to do next, so I'm not likely to be a particularly reliable oracle when it comes to the fate of an entire genre of popular fiction. Come to think of it, it's probably my inability to guess what's going to happen next that makes me such a fan of the mystery short story in the first place.

More a fan than a practitioner, I'm afraid. I've done a few short stories myself, enough to inform my admiration when I see the thing done well, but I admit I find it hard. In the novel I feel more at home, I can stretch and wander and take my time. In the short story, I can't be self-indulgent, I can't explain at length, I can't distract the reader with subplots or amusing but ultimately irrelevant characters and settings.

All of which, of course, is the point. A good short story is a jewel in miniature, as concise and carefully wrought as a fine watch, but at the same time alive. Like the stories herein.

DONALD E. WESTLAKE

The Best American
Mystery Stories 2000

DOUG ALLYN

Miracles! Happen!

FROM *Ellery Queen's Mystery Magazine*

A NEON SIGN on the mansion's sprawling lawn said: *Miracles! Happen!* I paused a moment, considering the idea. And my fingertips strayed unconsciously to the scars on my face.

Miracles? Not likely. The way my luck usually runs, I get warm and fuzzy when I catch an even break.

The guy who owned the estate knew a bit about miracles, though. Evan Grace Ministries. Radio, TV, national politics. Not bad for a preacher who'd been touring with tent-show revivals twenty years ago. A lifetime ago.

No tents for Evan nowadays. His Grosse Pointe palace sprawls across three waterfront lots on Lake St. Clair, a Victorian manor with a stable, a six-car garage, and a state-of-the-art broadcast studio. Evan can preach a sermon in the morning, take his fat-cat contributors out to lunch, and still sleep in his own bed.

With a friend of mine.

So perhaps Miracles do Happen. Sometimes. Not very often.

A black funeral wreath was hanging on the front door. I rang the bell beside it. Chimes played the first two bars of "Amazing Grace."

A linebacker opened the door — six foot four, crew cut, a two-hundred-fifty-pound hardbody in a perfectly tailored blue suit. Armani, from the look of it. A black armband around the bicep.

I was wearing a black canvas duster, jeans, and a face that had been seriously rearranged by a patch of concrete.

"Yes?"

"Hi. I'm here to see Mrs. Grace. My name's Axton."

"I'm sorry, there's been a death in the family. They aren't seeing visitors."

"I'm not visiting. Mrs. Grace asked me to come by."

The linebacker looked me over doubtfully. "Under the circumstances, another day would be better. If you call —"

"She called me two hours ago, sport. If she's changed her mind, fine. But why don't you check first? Please."

Another man, equally large, materialized at my shoulder. "A problem here, Mr. Klein?"

"Not yet," the suit in the doorway said. "Keep our friend here company, Jack. Because if you're a tab reporter, we're gonna haul you out back and show you the error of your ways. Sport."

He closed the door in my face. I glanced sidelong at the new arrival. Also crew-cut, but darker, Hispanic maybe, and his suit was strictly Sears, off the rack. He was wearing a miniature earpiece with a small curly cord that vanished beneath his collar. A professional security type, not just a college boy borrowed for the day.

"What's with the wreath?" I asked.

"Maybe it's for you," Jack said. He wasn't smiling. The door opened again.

"It's okay, Jack," Klein said. "Sorry about the mix-up, Mr. Axton. It's a bad day for all of us. Follow me, please."

I trailed him down a long entrance corridor into the living room, past a dozen people dressed in black or wearing armbands, clustered in small groups, voices subdued. A few glanced up curiously. I clearly didn't belong here today. But no one said anything.

Klein led me down a second corridor, rapped once on an ornate oak door, and showed me inside. A comfortable library, floor to ceiling bookshelves, leather chairs, a fire glowing in the grate. Krystal Grace, nee Doyle, was staring into the flames, lost in thought.

Her blond hair was shorter now, worn up in a bouffant. Understatedly elegant. As was her unadorned black dress. It had been nearly ten years. It could have been ten minutes.

"Hey, Ax," she said to the fire, not turning. She was holding a brandy snifter, swirling it slowly.

"Hey, Krystal. How have you been?"

She glanced up and realized Klein was standing just inside the door. "You can leave us, Jerry."

"Mr. Grace asked me to —"

"*Get the hell out!*"

"Yes, ma'am." He hesitated in the doorway, memorizing my face, then vanished.

"Sorry about that," she said.

"Krys, what's up? Is this some kind of a wake or what?"

She turned back to the fire, shadows playing on her face. "Don't you watch TV? It's been all over the news."

"I've been in Cincinnati. Just got back last night."

"The wake's for . . . my son Joshua, Ax. He died yesterday."

"God. I'm sorry, Krystal. I didn't know."

"Yeah, well, it's not like it came as a big surprise. He's been dying since the day he was born. Almost two years ago. Sandhoff's disease. The doctors told us he'd be lucky to last three months. He was a lot tougher than they thought. Miracles happen. Or so they say." She took a serious draught of brandy, showing perfect teeth at the bite of it. "Oops, I'm being rude. Would you like a drink? Bourbon was your thing, right?"

"Thanks, no, I'm okay." But Krystal wasn't. She was flushed and bleary. Half bagged.

Her eyes caught mine. Then she peered at me more intently, blinking. "Good God. What happened to your face, Ax?"

"Motorcycle accident."

"Damn. It looks like it hurt." She said it deadpan, but with a glint of the old mischief I remembered so well. And then she was in my arms and we clung together a moment. Not passionately. Desperately. Like sparrows in a tornado.

For a guilty moment I savored her embrace, the scent of her hair. But the perfume was different. A lot more expensive. And it had been ten years. And we weren't scuffling kids trying to get ahead in the music business anymore.

"Thanks, I needed that," she said, stepping back. "Don't worry, I won't fall apart on you."

"Fall all you want. You're entitled."

"No, I'm not." She frowned down at the brandy snifter. "That's the thing. I don't have the right to cry. I earned every bit of this."

"What are you talking about?"

"Sandhoff's disease. Do you know anything about it?"

"I've never heard of it."

"It's hereditary. Evan and I both have the gene. It's recessive, doesn't affect us, but the odds are three to one that any kids we have will be born with the dysfunction. Three to one. I can't watch any more babies die, Ax. That's why I called you."

"I don't understand."

"I heard you were working as a private investigator now."

"Sort of. I'm no Sherlock Holmes. Mostly I run down deadbeats and collect bad debts. Why?"

"I had another child once," she said simply. "I want you to find her for me."

"What child?"

"When I first met you, what, ten years ago? I was singing backup for Bobby Penn and the Badmen. Remember them?"

"Sure. I was managing the Roostertail when you played there. Thought you were one of the best damn singers I ever heard."

"Get real. I was strictly minor league."

"Wrong. When you sang alone the room always went quiet. People listened to you. It's a special talent, Krys."

"Maybe" — she shrugged — "but Bobby was the star and didn't let anyone forget it. I was living with him then. And I got pregnant. So I stayed behind when Bobby and the guys went on a Canadian tour. And I had a baby girl. I named her Cher." She took another long sip of brandy.

"A booking agent called, needed a backup singer for a gospel roadshow. The Evan Grace Ministry. I was flat broke so I left the kid with my landlady and took the gig. And it was . . . a revelation. Playing big churches and stadiums instead of rock joints. Everybody clean and sober. Listening to Evan preach every night, spreading the Word. It was so different from the life I was in. And I wanted it. And I wanted Evan too."

"Looks like things worked out. Some miracles must happen."

"But they come at a price. I . . . didn't tell Evan about my daughter. The people around him are pretty uptight. I figured if they knew I had a love child with a rock 'n' roller they'd stone me or something. So I kept putting off telling him. And then he asked me to marry him and it was too late to tell him. Afraid I'd lose him. And all this," she added, with a wave of her hand.

"What about Bobby?"

"When he came back from Canada he was drugging so heavy I

doubt he noticed I was gone. Until I married Evan and it made the news. And then he came around one night, wrecked. He had a picture of the baby, wanted money. For our kid, he said. I gave him all I had. A few hundred. Evan handles the money in the family. Bobby wanted more and we argued. I was angry about being held up, but mostly just angry with myself. And I'd been drinking. Always did have a problem with booze. Evan's security people threw Bobby out. I expected to hear from him again. But I never did. It's been nearly eight years."

"I see. Any idea where he is now?"

"No. I don't see anybody from the old days anymore. I thought you might know. You're still in the business, right?"

"I do some security work for promoters and road bands so I know a few people. But I haven't heard anything about Bobby or the Badmen for years. He was Canadian, right?"

"Yeah, and that's about all I knew about him. Except that he was a hunk. He was an orphan, or said he was. He told me once that artists can't be limited to the truth. I thought he was joking. He wasn't. But he was a wonderful liar. Very . . . creative."

"So you don't know doodley about his background and the little you know might not be true?"

"I'm afraid so."

"Terrific." I mulled that over. "Didn't Bobby and the Badmen cut a record once?"

"They had two local hits in the seventies before I joined them. Nothing big."

"Do you remember which label?"

"Something southern, I think. Raleigh?"

"Okay, that's a place to start. Can you think of anyone else who might know where he is?"

"Beans, maybe."

"Beans?"

"Fat guy, long black ponytail? Beans was the band's road manager and sound man. He and Bobby went way back."

"Yeah, I vaguely remember him. What was his real name?"

"God, I don't know. He was just . . . Beans. That's what everybody called him. I don't know if I ever knew his real name. You know how it was in those days."

"Pretty much the same as it is now. I'll be honest with you, Krys.

Even if I can turn Bobby up, and that's not a gimme, your claim to
the baby might be pretty shaky after all this time."

"Don't worry, I can handle Bobby. You sleep with a guy awhile,
you get a pretty good idea what he's about. Bobby was beautiful and
he could sing like a bird, but down deep . . ."

"What?"

"That's just it. There wasn't anything down deep. No soul.
Maybe he traded it for his looks, I don't know. You've got to find my
daughter for me, Ax. Please. I know I screwed up, but I can make it
up to her. I have to. I can't go on like this."

That much was true. If I've ever seen anyone on the lip of the
abyss it was Krystal Grace. I didn't know if finding her lost child
would help. What she really needed was rest and counseling and
support. Or maybe a Miracle! from the sign out front.

But considering my shambles of a life, I'm the last person who
can offer advice. Especially to an old friend in a world of hurt. So I
kept my mouth shut and set out to do my job.

I didn't get very far. Klein, the linebacker, met me in the hallway
and said Mr. Grace wanted to see me before I left. He didn't bother
to say please.

We took an elevator down to the broadcast studio in the basement. I'd seen Evan Grace's gospel broadcasts a time or two, usually at 3 A.M. on Christian stations. He's a terrific talker with a good
band who can bring a crowd to its feet. Or its knees. Or so I'd
thought.

The cameras and equipment on the soundstage were top of the
line, the latest and best from Sennheiser, Bose, and AKG. But there
was no seating area for an audience in the room. The front of the
stage faced a wide blue screen. Interesting.

Evan Grace's inner office was the size of my apartment: thick
carpeting, leather chairs, walls covered with gold-framed, auto-
graphed photographs. Evan posing with Nixon, with Pat Robert-
son, Tipper Gore.

The man himself was sitting at an antique desk, his face buried in
his hands. He glanced up when we came in.

He was in shirtsleeves and looked haggard. His usually flawless
silver pompadour was mussed, hanging in his eyes. Even so, he
was magnetic. Charisma, stage presence, whatever you call it, Evan
Grace had it. Bobby Penn had it too, as I recalled.

He eyed me a moment in silence, sizing me up. "What does the other guy look like?" he asked.

I smiled. At least he was direct. "The other guy was Eight Mile Road. Motorcycle accident."

"Very impressive. I imagine it helps you in your work."

"My work?"

"Intimidation is part of your line, isn't it? When Krystal said she wanted to hire you, I had you checked out, Mr. Axton. You have an investigator's license and a concealed-weapons permit. You do collection work for nightclubs and booking agencies, and occasionally hire out as a bodyguard. People you've worked for say you're honest and tenacious to a fault. And a little crazy."

"Sounds fair. So?"

"I'll be blunt. My wife is in no condition emotionally to make decisions that could affect her entire life. And mine. I'll be happy to reimburse you for your time and trouble, but we won't be requiring your services."

"Sorry, but it doesn't work that way."

"She can't pay you, Axton. I control the purse strings and I guarantee you'll never see a dime."

"Actually, Krystal and I never got around to discussing a fee, so I guess this one's on the house. Call it Christian charity."

"Are you mocking my beliefs, Mr. Axton?"

"Not at all. I have a question, though. That blue screen facing the broadcast dais? How do you morph the audiences in?"

He eyed me a moment, then shrugged. "We film the crowds when I speak at churches and halls. The congregations you see on television are mine, they just don't happen to be in the studio at broadcast time. A miracle of the electronic sort. Why?"

"Just wondered. Look, Reverend, I know this is a tough time for you and I sympathize, but Krystal asked me to do this thing, I agreed, and that's it. And right now she's alone and half plastered. You should be talking to her, not me."

"You intend to press on with this? Over my objections? Are you a Christian, Mr. Axton?"

"Probably not by your standards, no."

"I'm not surprised. I imagine genuine Christian values could be a drawback in your line."

"Actually, I think my line and yours are both a lot like making sausage, Reverend. The less people know about how we do it, the better off they are. Tell Krystal I'll be in touch."

Halfway between floors, Klein hit the elevator stop button and turned to face me.

"You shouldn't have talked to Reverend Grace like that."

"Like what?"

"Disrespectfully. When a man like him asks you to do something, you do it."

"If I was working for him, I probably would. But I'm not."

"Then I'll make it simple. When you say no to Reverend Grace, you're saying no to me. Your face has already been rearranged once. I could do it again."

"Maybe. But not in this elevator."

"Why not?"

"Because people are in mourning upstairs, Jerry. I doubt your boss would appreciate a dustup in the middle of it. No matter who won."

"I'm not afraid of you."

"Hell, you don't look like you're afraid of anything. Which makes me think you've led a pretty quiet life. Up to now. So? You wanna take your best shot? Or restart the elevator?"

"Maybe this isn't the time or the place, Axton. But your time's coming."

"I hope so. I'd hate to think it was past."

Krystal was half right. Raleigh Records was southern. Southern Michigan. South of Detroit, in Ecorse, to be exact. A rundown studio in a block of dilapidated warehouses off West Jefferson. Raleigh Productions: Rollie Newcomb, president, chief financial officer, salesman, packing clerk, secretary, janitor. Whatever. Strictly a scuffler.

I found Rollie working the phone in his second-floor office, trying to peddle the crates of CDs, tapes, and old LPs stacked in the open bay beyond. In the fifties and sixties, Rollie cut sides with Jackie Wilson, Mitch Ryder, and other Motown hometown heroes. A few hit it big later on, but not Rollie. He was stuck in Ecorse, selling second-rate recordings by stars who were nobodies at the time, or nobodies who stayed that way. Like . . .

"Bobby Penn and the Badmen?" Rollie said, eyeing me warily.

Rollie's fat, sixty, and still wears polyester leisure suits. And not because he's into retro styles. "Is business so bad you're down to working for the Badmen these days, Ax?"

"I thought they were defunct."

"Went belly-up years ago. But sometimes a member of a group tries to use the name. If you're looking for their royalties, you're out of luck. Penn made all the contracts in his name only. The Badmen weren't even named individually on the album jacket, which was just as well since he bagged two of 'em in the middle of the session. Bobby hired and fired people so fast if you lined all the former Badmen up they'd look like the Million Man March. Bobby's got some dough coming, though. He hire you?"

"No. Actually I'm trying to find him for somebody else."

"A drug dealer?"

"Hell no. Why?"

"Because the first couple of years after he split, at least a half-dozen slimeball dope dealers came around looking for him. He owed everybody."

"Since when do dealers extend credit?"

"Oh, Bobby was slick, I'll give him that. Kid could schmooze the Statue of Liberty out of her concrete skivvies. So what's up? You lookin' to bust his legs?" He sounded hopeful.

"Nah, I don't do that kind of work. I'm just trying to run him down. A matter of paternity."

"You're kidding. He reproduced? How? In a pond with the rest of the scum? I hope you burn him for every dime he's got."

"I have to find him first."

"Can't help you there, Ax, but I'm holding eighteen hundred bucks of Bobby's money. If you find him, maybe we can work something out."

"What money?"

"Royalty checks. I packaged Bobby with a dozen other lousy groups, called it *Garbage Band Nobodies,* and put it on the Internet for the collector market. It's been selling pretty well. His career's doing better since he quit the business."

"What makes you think he quit?"

"If he was still playing, somebody'd mention the record and three seconds later he'd be on the phone screaming for his cut and then some. He had a nose for a buck, that one."

"So you've got no idea where he is?"

"Not a clue. And no loss."

"What about his pal, Beans? Remember him?"

"Yeah, heavyset guy? Beans Marino?"

"Was that his name? Marino?"

"Yeah. He was Bobby's road manager, so he signed off on the equipment rentals for the studio. Not a bad guy. In fact, I tried to hire him, but he and Bobby went way back. Boyhood pals or something. Can't remember his first name but it was something like Beans. Dean or Gene or something."

Not Dean or Gene. After leaving Rollie's studio, I went back to my apartment office, fired up my computer, ran a couple of name searches, and scored. Benno Marino, Mr. and Mrs., lived upstate in the boonies, in northern Oakland County near the Mount Holly ski resort.

I called, got a lady with a delicious southern accent, told her I needed to talk to Benno about the royalties Rollie owed Bobby, and made an appointment for that evening.

Driving upstate is always a mindbender. Detroit's a sprawling rustbelt relic frantically reinventing itself. Casinos a-building, warehouses imploding, housing exploding everywhere.

But drive forty minutes north of the city and you're in Hicksville, U.S.A. — heavily wooded hills where transplants from Tupelo and Texarkana build replicas of the backcountry shacks where they were fetched up. Plus a few amenities like hot tubs, central air, and satellite TV.

The Marino place was a mountain ranch house sided in rough cedar. Perched on a bluff with a view of gently rolling hills to the south, it had an odd look as I approached. I didn't realize what was out of place until I pulled into the driveway. Instead of steps, a ramp led up to the broad front porch and another around to the side door. Wheelchair ramps.

The woman who answered the door resolved the riddle. She was in a power wheelchair, though she looked healthy enough to get up and run a ten-minute mile: chubby, rosy cheeks, dark hair trimmed in a pageboy bob.

"Mrs. Marino? My name's Axton. I called."

"I'm Jeanie. Ben's not home yet, but come in. Sorry about the ramps; a drunk driver clipped me seven years ago. This way." She backed away from the door and I followed her into a brightly tiled country kitchen, copper pots, a brick island in the center, everything waist high. Wheelchair height.

She offered coffee and I accepted, taking a seat at the long pine kitchen table. She looked at me oddly as she poured.

"I know you, right? Didn't you manage the Roostertail when we played there?"

"We?"

"I was a backup singer for Bobby Penn. The other backup singer," she added wryly. "Krystal's the one people remember — tall, blond, and talented. I was the short, chubby country kid. You called me Alabam, because of my accent. Remember?"

And I did. A bouncing bundle of eager energy with a southern drawl. For an instant I saw her as she was in the old days, so vital . . . and then I was seeing her now. The woman in a steel chair. And then our eyes met, and I realized with a jolt that she was seeing me exactly the same way.

"My God," she said wonderingly. "Look at us. Dick Clark hasn't aged a minute in twenty years and the two of us look like we've been chewed up by an alligator and crapped in a ditch."

She shook her head with an infectious chuckle that swept us both along until we were gasping. Sometimes life kicks you so hard all you can do is laugh. And she had the gift for it.

"Is something funny?"

Lost in the moment, I hadn't heard him come in. Wouldn't have recognized him anyway. Beans had lost most of his hair, slimmed down forty pounds, and was wearing a tailored three-piece suit. And toting a briefcase.

"Mr. Marino? My name's Axton."

"Right. Jeanie called me at the office, told me you'd be stopping by. Something about royalties?"

"Raleigh Records owes Bobby Penn back royalties, yes. Are you still in touch with him?"

"Slow down a minute. Can I see some ID, please?"

"Sure." I gave him my wallet and he looked over my license carefully. Jeanie watched, amused. Her normal state, I think.

"So why do you want Bobby? And skip the royalties garbage. Nobody hires private heat to find somebody they owe. Especially not Rollie Newcomb. We may live in the sticks, but we're not hicks. Either tell it straight or hit the door."

"Fair enough. Bobby's onetime squeeze, Krystal, hired me to find him."

"No kidding? After all this time? Why?"

"I'm afraid that's between Krystal and Bobby."

"It doesn't matter anyway. I haven't heard from Bobby in years. I've no idea where he is, and I wouldn't tell you if I did. For the record, Bobby and I not only worked together back when, we grew up in the same orphanage in Windsor. We were like blood to each other. What kind of a jam is he in?"

"Why do you think he's in a jam?"

"That guy was born in trouble. What is it this time?"

"He's not jammed up, but that's all I'm free to say."

"Okay, let's try another angle. Does Krystal really want to find Bobby? Or is she looking for the kid?"

I leaned forward involuntarily. "Do you know where the child is?"

"Nope, but I know what happened to it. It's the reason Bobby and I broke it off."

"How do you mean?"

"Bobby was always like a crazy little brother to me. He was a hell-uva talented singer, but he had a nose for dope along with it. Bailing him out of jackpots was my full-time job when we worked the road together. The Badmen played every hole-in-the-wall joint between Cedar Rapids and Toronto and I saw Bobby pull some crappy stunts, but I always figured, he's young, he'll grow up. But with Krystal and the baby he was so far over the line I realized he was never gonna change. A guy who could do that . . ."

"Do what?"

"He sold the baby," Marino said evenly. "His own child. Peddled it like a used car."

"There's a gray market for babies, especially healthy white kids," Marino explained. We were sitting at his kitchen table over coffee and sandwiches Jeanie whipped up. I offered to help, but Marino warned me off with a look. She might be in a chair, but she was far from helpless. In fact, I noted a short-barreled shotgun at the end of the counter behind the kitchen door. Jeanie caught me eyeing it.

"Insurance," she said. "We're a long way from help out here and one thing you learn on the road is, Lord, there are some strange folks loose in this world. No offense."

"None taken. I resemble that remark," I said, and she smiled. I shifted to her husband. "What can you tell me about Bobby selling the kid?"

"The group broke up after Jeanie's accident. We got married and I started working my way through Oakland U. driving a garbage truck on the night shift. I'm a purchasing exec with the highway department now," he added ruefully. "Go figure. Anyway, one afternoon Bobby showed up out of nowhere. He was strung out on smack, and he needed my help."

"To do what?"

"He said he wanted to do the right thing by his kid, give her a chance to be with a good family. Wanted me to go with him. You gotta understand, coming from the background we did, giving up his kid was a pretty heavy step. Still, Krystal dumped her on him, and he was in no shape to cope. He could barely take care of himself. Adoption seemed like the right thing."

"What happened?"

"We drove into Motown to the Renaissance Center, but instead of an agency, we go to a lawyer's office. Bobby told me the guy arranges adoptions, but two minutes into the conversation I realize they're not talking about whether the kid will have a good life. They're just dickering over the price. I couldn't believe it. I blew up. Big mistake. Two bruisers came busting in, told me I could leave by the elevator or the window, my choice. We were on the twenty-third floor."

"So you took the elevator."

"Out of that building. And out of Bobby's life."

"Do you know for a fact that he sold the child?"

"I only saw him once after that, just long enough to tell him to get lost. He didn't have the kid anymore."

"Do you remember the lawyer's name?"

"Zeman. Anthony Zeman."

He was watching my face for a reaction. "Damn," I said.

"Mr. Axton, are you expecting company?" Jeanie said, glancing out the kitchen window.

"No, why?"

"A white Cadillac's coming up our road. We don't get much company out here. I guess when it rains, it pours."

"Well, I'll leave you to your guests," I said, rising. "Thanks for your help."

Marino walked me out on the porch just as the Cadillac's doors opened. And four neatly dressed linebacker types climbed out: Jerry Klein, his pal Jack, and two more just like them. A matched set of muscle.

"Is the child here, Axton?" Klein asked, trotting up the ramp.

"No. These people have nothing to do with it."

"You'll excuse me if I don't take your word for it. We'll just take a quick look."

"Whoa," Marino said, "where do you think you're going?"

"Inside," Klein said. "We have reason to believe you may be involved in a kidnapping. Stand aside."

"The hell I will! Who are you people —?"

Without warning, Klein drove a fist into Marino's belly, spinning him face-first into the wall, dropping him to his knees. I yanked Klein around but before either of us could swing, a shotgun blast shattered the air, freezing everyone.

Jeanie Marino came humming around the side of the house in her chair, the short double-barreled shotgun cradled in her arms. The shot she'd fired had perforated the Cadillac in a dozen places. For a silent moment the only sound was the Caddy's rear tire wheezing flat.

"That's enough," Jeanie said quietly. "You boys had best git in your car and go. While you can."

"Lady, you'd better put that gun down —"

"Save your breath. Get moving. Now."

Klein licked his lips. "You've only got one round left in that thing."

"That's right. Who wants it? You?" She shifted the weapon to cover Jack. His eyes widened, staring down the double barrels.

"Jesus, lady!"

From his knees, Marino launched himself up at Klein, tackling him waist-high, tumbling him down the ramp into the dirt at Jack's feet. Without a word, Jack hauled Klein up and thrust him into the Caddy's passenger seat. The other two piled in as Jack slid behind the wheel, fired up the Caddy, and roared off, thumping down the dirt road on their flattened tire.

"Honey, are you all right?" Jeanie asked.

"Yeah, I think so. What the hell was all that, Axton?"

"Security types. They work for Krystal's husband. I'm sorry, I had no idea they were coming."

"Yeah, well, sorry doesn't quite cover it." Marino winced as he massaged his ribs and touched a cut on the corner of his mouth. "We've told you what we know, now I want you out of here. We've got a new life. We don't need any crap from the old days."

"Understood," I said. "And I really am sorry."

"Stuff happens," Jeanie said, humming up to me, offering a firm hand. "Maybe you can come back again sometime. Say in another ten years?" The twinkle in her eyes took the sting from the zinger.

"It's a date. In another ten years."

"Do you remember the lawyer's name?" Marino called after me.

"Yeah. I'm afraid so."

Afraid was the word. The name Zeman runs through the legends of the Motown mob the way Capone's does in Chicago. Only there were a lot more Zemans than Capones. Brothers, cousins, uncles. The grandfather was a member of the original Purple Gang, a stone killer who always carried three automatics. Or so they say. His grandsons pack law degrees or MBAs, which makes them a lot more dangerous.

Back in the late thirties, Capone sent two thugs to Detroit to talk to the Purples about an alliance. They disappeared. No warnings, no threats, no horse's head in a bed. They just vanished. The way Jimmy Hoffa would a few years later.

Damn! Why did I have to think of that story in the elevator heading up to Anthony Zeman's office?

The offices of Barrett, Arlington, and Zeman occupy most of a floor in the Renaissance Center. Twenty-three stories up. The place was busier than a wacko ward during a full moon, but I had no trouble getting in to see Tony Zeman, Jr. Just by saying I was a licensed investigator who wanted to talk about babies.

Zeman came around the desk carrying a golf club. A squat, powerful man, heavily built. Almond shirt and slacks, dark hair, thinning on top, blue jowls. Fortunately, the club wasn't for me.

"Do you mind? I've got a foursome at one." He lined up a few balls, squared his stance, and began putting them toward a narrow electronic cup against the wall. It beeped each time he scored. He never missed. "What can I do for you, Mr. . . . ?"

"Axton. I'm looking into an . . . adoption you arranged eight years ago or so."

Zeman shrugged, loosening up. "We handle some adoptions

through this office, but all data concerning them is confidential, as I assume you know. So why are you wasting my time?"

"Because there may be a problem with this one. My clients are wealthy and determined. If you blow me off, they'll go to the police and they have the political juice to make things messy. No one wants that. Just give me what I need and I go away. No problem."

He glanced up. Light gray eyes, cold as Rouge River ice. "If I thought you were a real problem you'd be gone already. What do you want? Exactly?"

"The man who arranged the adoption was Bobby Penn. Tall, scruffy blond hair?"

"A singer or something? Claimed he had a few hit records in the seventies?"

"That's the guy."

"Then I definitely can't help you. We didn't handle that case. I only recall it because Penn brought a buddy who kicked up a fuss. I had them escorted out."

"The pal says he was thrown out. But Bobby wasn't."

Zeman paused in mid stroke, frowning, then followed through. "Actually, he's right about that. Penn did stay a bit longer to plead his case. But we didn't do a deal."

"No?"

"No," Zeman said, straightening, examining the head of the putter. "Let me enlighten you about the work we do, Mr. Axton. When sufficient capital is involved, and those are the only cases we take, finding eligible children is no problem. Appalachia, Russia, former Iron Curtain countries, it's a buyer's market. So to speak. We arrange proper health care, cover hospital expenses, and the mothers have the comfort of knowing their babies will be placed with families who can afford our services. And if those families sometimes offer a . . . gift to soothe the young mother's anguish, that's no concern of ours. Are you with me?"

"So far."

"Good. Then you must see that the scenario I've just outlined has no place in it for your Mr. Penn. He was a junkie, so was the baby for all I knew, and it was seven or eight months old. We only deal in — excuse me, arrange adoptions for — newborns. It simplifies the paperwork."

"And an eight-month-old could have its name and footprints on file in the hospital where it had been born. Which could present problems if anything derailed later on."

"Exactly. Which is why I never seriously considered doing a deal with Mr. Penn. The man had trouble tattooed on his forehead. His pal got out of line that day and now you're here. I don't like problems, Mr. Axton. But I'm very good at solving them. Are you going to be a problem for me?"

"I don't know," I said. "I hope not."

Sulka tie and his precious Ping putter aside, Anthony Zeman was a thug, the son and grandson of thugs. And he was apparently still in the baby business, tap-dancing through legal loopholes to supply desperate people with the ultimate treasure. For a price. Doubtless using the same rationale his grandpop used to justify running booze across the Rouge from Canada during Prohibition, and numbers, drugs, and hookers since.

Victimless crimes. Unless you somehow get crossways of the Zemans, in which case they'll make you a victim in a heartbeat. Maybe even a vanishing victim.

I had no doubt Tony Zeman would lie like a pol on election night if it suited his purposes. But that didn't mean he'd lied to me. He wanted me gone with minimum fuss. If the truth would make me disappear faster than a lie, why not tell it?

And I was fairly sure he had. He was running a lucrative operation, judging from his pricey office and polished golf game. Would he jeopardize it for one junkie's kid?

Unlikely. Besides, Marino pitched a bitch in Tony's office. If the deal had closed, Marino could have posed a threat to the Zeman family business. And he probably wouldn't be breathing.

But he was. I found him at his desk in an open, airy second-floor office of the state highway department building in Pontiac. He wasn't pleased to see me. I didn't blame him. His jaw had an angry red souvenir of my last visit.

"I'm sorry to bother you again," I said hastily, before he could rip into me. "I only need a moment. Zeman didn't do a deal with Bobby that day, so I'm back to square one. You said you saw Bobby once after the thing with Zeman. Did he say anything about where he was living? What he was doing?"

"We didn't talk that long. And what makes you think Zeman didn't buy the kid? Because he said so?"

"I wouldn't take Zeman's word that the sun'll rise tomorrow, but I believe him about this. Bobby didn't make that deal. Can you think of anything that might help me get a line on him?"

Marino started to shake his head, then hesitated. "That last time, he was with another guy. A biker named Little Vern. One of the Mountain Outlaws."

"The Outlaws?"

"Yeah, toward the end, our band developed a biker following. They adopted us, like mascots. Which gives you some idea how far down we were. I never ran with those guys, but Bobby did. By their standards, he was a celebrity. So they shared their dope with him, and sometimes women. He and Vern were talking about going on a run that weekend. It was late summer, August, I think. I didn't care where they were going, I just wanted them gone. And now I want you gone."

"I understand and —"

"Don't say thanks, Mr. Axton. Just say goodbye."

It could have been worse. Bobby could have been running with the Manson family when he disappeared. The Mountain Outlaws, a.k.a. the Mounts, aren't the wildest dogs in the murky underworld of Motown motorcycle gangs, but they're close to it.

With over a hundred members, a private clubhouse, and their own bar, they're well-off by biker standards. But they're not a collection of misunderstood romantics.

The Mounts take the Outlaw half of their name seriously. They're major players in the amphetamine trade; they hire out as freelance muscle and drug couriers for the Five Families in Saginaw. The hard-core leaders are all ex-cons, and most of them are speed freaks to boot, the human equivalent of wolverines with hyperaggressive tendencies.

I'd met a few Mounts over the years, mostly when I bounced them out of various nightclubs I'd been running. Couldn't remember whether I'd made any lasting enemies. Hoped not.

For once, my road-burned face wasn't a drawback. When I wandered into the Mountain Lounge, the Outlaws' stomping grounds, I looked like I belonged. Almost.

It was an ordinary neighborhood bar — dim, two pool tables, a few pinball machines, and a jukebox against the wall. Formica tables carved with initials and obscenities.

The odd points were subtle but telling. High, narrow windows offered light but no entry, and the only doors were reinforced steel with hinged cross-braces. One second after they slammed shut, you'd have better luck trying to break in through the wall. And no way out at all.

Early afternoon, the place was nearly deserted. A couple of bikers were shooting pool while a buddy kibitzed. Four more, at a table near the jukebox, were playing euchre.

The bartender was a scrawny burnout, one-forty tops, scruffy brown hair styled with pruning shears, tattooed arms, watery eyes. He looked like a punk any high-school jock could mop the floor with. But if he was tending bar in a place like this . . .

I ordered a Bud Light. He made no move to get it.

"You're not from around here."

"Nope. But my beer is. It's in the cooler behind you."

"So it is." He reached into the cooler, retrieved a can, and slammed it down on the bar with a bang. "Whoa, don't open that, pal, it'll spray. Take it with you. Drink it down the road."

"Can't do that. Thing is, I'm looking for a guy. Not one of yours. A guy named Penn who used to hang with a Mount called Little Vern." I didn't catch the signal but suddenly I had a pool player on each side of me, still holding their cue sticks.

"Can't help ya," the bartender said, his eyes locked on mine. "Try the phone book. Might be a Little Vern in there."

"Or try Forest Lawn," one of the card players said, standing up, stretching. "That's where Vern is. Take him a flower. He probably doesn't get many. You're Axton, right?"

I turned to face him. He looked vaguely familiar but they all did, like wolves from the same pack. "Do I know you?"

"Not exactly. You threw me out of the Thirteenth Hour Club once."

"Could be. I worked there. You sore about it?"

He eyed me a moment, his face unreadable. He was taller than the others, pitted face, a leather Harley hat. And I was one second from the emergency ward. Until he smiled, showing broken teeth.

"Hell, you did me a favor, bro. I was ready to beat the bejesus out of a mama who wasn't worth the jail time. Maybe I owe you one. Why are you lookin' for Vern?"

"To ask him about a guy he ran with. Bobby Penn? Singer? Had a band called the Badmen?"

"Penn. Yeah, I remember that loser. Goes back a ways."

"To when?"

"I don't know. Seven, eight years ago. Vern brought him in, thought he was some kinda hotshot superstar just because he played in a band. Vern wasn't too bright, which is why he's dead. Passed on a hill. Met a cattle truck head-on."

"Sorry to hear it. What about Penn?"

"Last time I saw him he was crawlin' toward that door."

"Crawling?"

"Maybe Vern thought he was special, but he was just another junkie mooch to the rest of us. He got crossways of somebody, got decked, a few guys did the boogie on his sorry ass. Nothin' heavy. Like I said, he crawled out."

"What was the beef about?"

"Who knows? It don't take much for an outsider to get stomped in here. Probably just pushed his luck."

I didn't push mine. Pushed off instead. Headed out into a gray, overcast afternoon. After the dingy twilight of the bar the air seemed especially sweet. Sometimes just being alive is enough.

But the feeling only lasted seven or eight miles, then I realized I had no idea where I was heading.

The road goes on forever, but my hunt for Bobby Penn had zeroed out. The computer search had nothing current, no driver's license, no Social Security payments or welfare checks, no cars registered in his name. Nothing for the past seven years.

If Penn was a straight john I'd assume he was dead or in a witness-protection program. But the music business runs by different rules. Club owners pay under the table to duck taxes, players bunk with pals to avoid having a legal residence, singers change their names for professional reasons. Or no reason at all.

Seven years ago Bobby Penn hit rock bottom. Then what? A name change, a fresh start? Not likely. His name had some market value because his records were still selling a little.

A career change? Also unlikely. All he knew was the music business . . . and there it was. The answer.

Bobby Penn might be a loser, but he was also a professional musician. Whose records were still selling.

I drove aimlessly for a while, mulling over how that played out. But the bottom line was: I didn't know quite enough.

I killed an hour by driving into Detroit Metro Airport to ditch my car in long-term parking and rent an anonymous gray Chevy. Then I drove to Pontiac, parked down the street from the state employees' lot, and waited the half-hour until five.

Ben Marino came out promptly, fired up his van, and pulled out of the lot. I gave him a two-block lead, then followed. In the first quarter mile I knew he wasn't headed home. He seemed to be trailing a car that had left the lot just ahead of him, a guess he confirmed by turning left on Logan into the upscale Pinewood subdivision. Both cars pulled into the same driveway in front of a gray-brick townhouse.

I started to turn off, to avoid being spotted, but changed my mind when a miniature dervish came sprinting out of the house to throw herself into Marino's arms. He was swinging the child around as I cruised past. It had been years since I'd seen Bobby Penn, but I had no doubt the girl was his daughter. I'd always thought Krystal looked like an angel down on her luck. Her daughter looked like the real thing, baby Cupid in blue denim bibs.

I drove on a few blocks, then pulled into a driveway, turned around, and parked in the shadow of a tall hedge. I couldn't see the house, but I could still see the rear of Marino's van. Rather than risk a confrontation here, I decided to wait until he left. It wasn't long.

As I was settling in to wait, a figure suddenly stepped through the hedge, leaned down, and tapped on the passenger window of my rental Chevy. Marino. And he was tapping with the muzzle of a 9mm automatic.

Any thoughts I had of running for it evaporated when I read his eyes. I popped the electric door lock and he slid in beside me, the gun leveled at my midsection.

"Let's go," he said.

"Where?"

"Out to Twenty-four, then north." Not to his home then. Bad omen.

"Look, you can't —"

"Shut up and drive or I'll pop you right here. Your choice."

I shut up and drove, out of the business district on M-24, then north into the boondocks. The farther we went, the less I liked it, but there was nothing I could do. We were both belted in, and Marino kept the automatic on me. His eyes were somewhere else, though, in some inner place. Deciding what to do with me.

And then he relaxed a little, the decision taken. I tried to read his face with a glance, but it showed me nothing.

The few directions he offered took us farther into the empty countryside through barren fields, already harvested, a few isolated farms so widely scattered that a distant gunshot wouldn't raise an eyebrow.

The sun was setting when Marino suddenly tensed. "Slow down here, turn right on the next dirt road."

I did as he said, wheeling down a narrow two-rut lane that circled the base of a towering mound. The fading light dimmed, then we suddenly plunged into deep shadows as the hilltop blocked the sunset, engulfing us. I reached for the headlight switch but Marino shook his head.

"No lights. Stop here."

We climbed out of the car beside a tall, chain-link fence topped with barbed wire. Marino motioned me ahead, keeping his distance, his gun trained on my spine.

"Hold up right here."

In the dimness I could make out a gate secured with a padlock. He unlocked it, swung it open just far enough to let us pass, then motioned me through.

There was no place to go but up. As we climbed the hill in the gloom I could make out wider white shapes in the distance. And my heart sank. They vaguely resembled tombstones, but in a way they were even worse.

My calves were aching from the strain of the long climb when the shadows above me began to lighten, then glow, then suddenly we broke into the auburn light on the crest of the hill. The massive grassy hillside sprawled out below us for most of a mile, bathed in the glow of the dying sun, marked at regular intervals by white plastic pipes.

A landfill, a cavernous hole filled with a mountain of garbage, then covered with earth and seeded with grass. In these hills it could almost pass for a natural rise. Except for the PVC pipes that vented the gases generated by the corruption below.

I turned slowly to face Marino. "What now?"

"I don't know. You're a pain in the ass, you know that? I asked you to leave us alone. More than once."

"You also pointed me at two dead-end leads, hoping one or the other would run me off."

"Too bad it didn't work. So we're down to it now. You were dead set on finding Bobby. Here he is."

"Where?"

"I'd guess seventy, maybe eighty feet down. This wasn't a hill then, it was still a pit. I worked here in those days and had a key. Still do. It was night and I was pretty wrung out when I brought him here, so I don't have a real clear recollection of where I put him exactly. I remember carrying him through that gate, though, so we're close."

"What happened?"

"What I told you. He stopped by with that guy from the Outlaws. Bobby wanted to leave his dope stash with me so the bikers wouldn't rip him off. Figured he could mooch off them. And he said we had to come to a permanent arrangement about the kid. I knew he meant money, only I didn't have any. I was working my way through school, driving a trash truck on the night shift. Jeanie's legs were still in casts from the accident, but she was dragging herself around to care for the baby."

"The child was living with you then?"

"She's been with us since she was a few months old. Krystal took off to work with a gospel show and dumped the kid on her landlady. When the band came back from Canada, Bobby picked Cher up and left her with us. We're the only parents she's ever had."

"You never adopted her?"

"A garbageman with a handicapped wife? We didn't stand a snowball's chance in hell of keeping her without Bobby's consent. I was an orphan myself, I know the drill."

"And Bobby?"

"He came back a few nights later, roughed up pretty bad. Said some of the Mounts had worked him over. Hadn't fixed in a couple days, had the shakes really bad. Talking crazy. About how he'd use the money I'd pay him for the kid to get his career going. And if I couldn't pay him, he'd go back to Zeman, offer him a deal he couldn't turn down. Like a fire sale or something."

"What did you do?"

"I looked at him," he said simply. "Maybe for the first time, I saw what he'd turned into. We grew up together like brothers, but this wasn't about us, it was about a child, *his* child. And about Jeanie. She loved that kid more than her life. So I sat at the kitchen table with Bobby and dickered for the kid over a bottle of Cuervo. He was hurtin' pretty bad, so he killed most of it. And then he needed to fix, so I gave him his stash. He shot up, and I put him to bed on the couch. And, um . . ."

He looked away and took a deep breath. His eyes were unfocused, seeing something a long way off, a long time ago. And he was trembling. With pain or rage, I couldn't tell.

"A couple of hours later I heard him groaning. He was sick. Between the booze and the drugs and the beating, he should've been in a hospital. But instead of getting help, I . . . I asked him if he wanted another fix. For the pain. And he said yes.

"I took him his works but he was shaking so bad he couldn't do it. So I . . . did it for him. I shot him up. And he *knew.*

"He watched me load up. He knew what another hit would do on top of the junk he'd already done. And he didn't care. He looked in my eyes . . . and then he offered me his arm. He was my brother. And I put him to sleep like a dog."

He fell silent for a while. The sun dropped lower, pine shadows from the trees at the base of the hill crept up toward us. I didn't say anything. No point.

"I'll never get past what I did," he continued softly. "But I'd gotten to where I could live with it, to make a good life for Jeanie and Cher. Then I saw the news about Krys and her husband losing their kid and you called asking about Bobby. We figured something was up and stashed Cher with my in-laws. Only you wouldn't let it go. How did you know?"

"In my business, you learn to follow the money."

"What money?"

"Newcomb's royalties. Bobby was obviously on the skids, ready to peddle his own blood for a few bucks. But he was also a pro musician. He should have remembered that royalty money and tried for it. Since he didn't, I guessed he was probably dead. Only there was no record of that, so he didn't die in bed.

"Either Zeman or the Outlaws could have waxed him, but they talked to me. If they'd taken him out they would have stonewalled or run me off. The last time anybody saw Bobby, he was crawling, banged up pretty badly. I figured he'd go to you. He had nowhere else."

"And now he's here. Someplace."

"And so are we. You figuring to plant me with Bobby?"

He eyed me a moment, then swallowed. "That's why I brought you here. I almost killed you back in town. Maybe I should have."

"And now?"

"Hell, this isn't your mess," he said, lowering his weapon, "it's mine."

"Offhand, I'd say Bobby made most of it. You carried the weight for him his whole life and you still are. You're even raising his child."

"Up to now, you mean. What are you going to do?"

"I don't know. But I've spent as much time on this dump as I care to. Let's go."

"No. You go ahead. I think I'll sit here awhile. I don't come here often. Maybe I should. I've got a cell phone, I can call a friend for a ride. Go on."

"You sure?"

"Yeah. Funny, Bobby used to say someday he'd be so famous they'd put him on Mount Rushmore. This is as close as he got."

"Half a dream's not bad. Most of us never get that much."

I left him sitting on the crest of his trash mountain, his arms folded across his knees, staring into the last rays of the sunset. And far beyond it, I suppose.

The walk down the hill was easier than the climb, maybe because I figured to be alive at the bottom. But the drive back to the airport was troublesome.

What I'd told Marino was absolutely true. I had no idea what to do about this. In the end, it came down to the fact that I'd given Krys my word. That covered the situation as far as I was concerned. Somebody else would have to sort it out.

I set up a meeting with Krystal and Evan Grace in his basement office that night. The studio was abuzz when I arrived, twenty minutes to airtime. No problem. However things worked out, this wouldn't take long.

Evan was in shirtsleeves, sitting behind his desk making last-sec-

ond corrections on a script. His pompadour was broadcast perfect
and a makeup bib was draped over his collar to shield it from
smears. Jerry Klein ushered me in, then waited by the door, his eyes
locked on me like radar.

Krystal was pacing in front of the desk, elegant in a peasant
blouse and slacks. She looked like she hadn't slept at all, and one
more missed meal would bump her from stylishly slender to an-
orexic.

Judging by her cautious steps, the drink in her hand wasn't her
first. Or her second. Evan ignored me, totally focused on his work.
And making a point about our positions. I waited.

"So, Mr. Axton," he said, glancing up at last. "You asked for this
meeting. I assume you have something for us?"

I said yes. Or started to. Instead, I heard myself saying, "I'm
afraid there was nothing to find, Reverend Grace. The baby was
taken to a law firm that arranges adoptions. Their records are confidential and they have the legal muscle to keep them that way.
There's nothing more I can do. I'm sorry."

"No need to apologize," Evan said, trying to conceal his satisfaction. "We knew it was a faint hope at best. We'll just have to find the
strength to move on. I'm sorry to seem abrupt, but I'm due on the
set. Send me your bill, Mr. Axton. I'll see to it." He swept out of the
room with Klein at his heels.

"You're going to burn in hell, Axton," Krystal said quietly.

"Probably," I said, turning to face her.

"Definitely. Evan's a minister of the Gospel, and you just looked
him straight in the eye and lied your butt off. Didn't you?"

It wasn't a question. She knew. I don't know how, but she did.

"Look, I'm not angry but I want the truth, Ax. And don't waste
any more smoke. You're not a very good liar."

"I'll try to do better. Evan didn't seem to notice, though."

"Because you told him what he wanted to hear. What really happened? Did you find Bobby?"

"No. And no one ever will. He's gone, Krystal."

"I thought he might be. He was pretty strung out when I saw
him last. I expected him to hit me up for money again. When he
didn't . . ." She shrugged. "It's too bad. He was a beautiful man
once. What happened to him?"

I hesitated. "An overdose."

"God. What a waste. What a godawful waste. And the baby?"

"She's fine. She's happy and healthy and with good people."

"But you weren't going to tell me that, were you? You bastard!"
I had no answer for that. She was right.

She took a long pull at her drink, emptying the glass. Then
turned to face me. "It's all right, Ax. I was in so much pain when
Joshua died that I needed . . . something. A miracle, maybe. A reason to live. I thought Cher could give it to me. But thinking about it
the past few days, I realized it was all about me, not her. She's nearly
eight, but I didn't try to find her until *I* was in trouble. Some people are natural mothers. I'm not. But that doesn't mean I can't be a
friend. Does it?"

"No. Of course not."

"Then I want to ask a favor. I know I'm a mess. I have been for a
while. But I'm going to get some help to dry out and get myself together. If I do, will you fix it so I can meet her?"

"I can't promise that, Krys."

"I can't promise I'll get straight either. But if I do . . . ?" And for
just a moment the alcoholic clotheshorse was gone and I glimpsed
the girl I once knew. "How about it, Ax? Deal?"

"Yeah. Deal. We'll work it out somehow."

"Good. I've got to go; Evan has a fit if I'm not in the audience. So
he can keep an eye on me. Thanks, Ax. For being a friend."

"No charge. Hey, Krys? A minute ago you said you needed a miracle. But in a way you used to be a miracle. When you sang, you
touched people. It wasn't just your voice, it was . . . hell. I don't
know. But it was a gift. Maybe you shouldn't waste it."

"Some gift. Singing was never special to me, Ax. It was just a way
to pay the rent."

"Then it's an even better miracle. Because it meant a lot to
the people who heard you. Especially me. Anyway, think about it,
okay?"

"Yeah, I'll do that. I've gotta go. Take care, Ax."

I stopped on the lawn for a minute. Didn't know why. Then I realized I was listening. Like a complete idiot. What did I expect? To
hear Krystal cooking up a chorus of "Amazing Grace"?

But there I was. Standing in front of a neon sign: *Miracles! Happen!* Waiting for one. Stupid, right?

Or maybe not. Granted, most dreams never come through. The hope they offer is all we get. It's still better than nothing. And now and again, things actually do work out for the best.

A miracle? Dumb luck? Who cares?

Maybe the sign was hokey. That didn't make it wrong.

DAVID BEATY

Ghosts

FROM *Mystery in the Sunshine State*

IT WAS JUST BEFORE sunset in Biscayne Estates, and the Armstrongs were safe at home. Darryl paced around his study, sipped scotch, and listened on his cordless telephone as a client screamed threats at him in broken English. Finally, he said, "Narciso, old buddy, stay calm. This is a temporary setback." He kept his voice reasonable but firm. "You've been going on about killing me all week. What good would that do you?"

Darryl cleared his throat. He said, "And believe me, I understand your anger. Nobody likes to lose money. But you wanted to play with the big boys, remember? Then the market went limit down three days in a row." He paused, not certain of what he'd just heard. "What? Simultaneous buy and sell orders? Who told you that? That's a lie. I don't care who told you. I've never dumped a bad trade in your account. That one? You gave me a direct order. Well, no, I can't play it back for you because your order came over my untaped line." He winced and said, "Hey, c'mon, you're calling me at *home.*"

He took a greedy swallow of scotch and said, "Stop it. That's enough. I need a vacation from hearing about how I'm going to die. I'll hang up now, okay? But call me if you get any more crazy ideas. Don't sit there obsessing. We're going to work this out. You have my word on that, okay? Bye, bye." He lowered the telephone into its cradle.

While Darryl talked in his study, his wife, Caroline, drifted among the racks of clothes and shoes in her walk-in closet, searching for a simple blouse to wear. She wondered at the forces in her-

self that had driven her to buy so many bright, costly things. Who
was the woman who'd chosen them? Where was the exhilaration
and hope they'd represented? She couldn't visualize herself in
them now. The sight of them embarrassed her. When she looked
around the closet, she imagined an aviary of tropical birds.

Caroline had recently turned thirty-three, and now, with a rueful
laugh, she told friends that she was quickly closing the gaps: next
year she'd be eighty-eight! Last week she'd resigned from her civic
committees, her charities, her mothers' groups: places where she'd
been spinning her wheels. She felt herself changing. She was tired
of people who thought about money and not much else — and
that included herself. She yearned for a more spiritual life. She
wanted to break free.

At the moment, however, she felt blocked. A free-floating gloom
seemed to hang over her life.

The telephone was driving her crazy. It started ringing as soon as
Darryl came home from the office. When she answered it, the
caller hung up, but he stayed on if Darryl took the call. Then
Darryl would hurry into his study and shut the door. He pretended
that everything was fine, but she knew better. Worrying about it —
and how could she not? — kept her under the thumb of depression. Caroline turned again in her closet, sorrowing over the constant losses, the daily disconnections from hope, that seemed to define her life now.

Darryl, forced out of his study by the need for more scotch, signaled his availability to Kyle, age nine, and Courtney, age eleven, by
cracking open a tray of ice in the bar. They appeared behind him
in the doorway, energetic and needy.

He wondered when Narciso would call again. Silence was a danger signal. Silence meant: "Grab your wallet and go out the window!" Darryl poured scotch over the smoking ice in his glass. He
had to keep Narciso talking, had to draw off his anger, like draining
pus from a wound, or God only knew what that maniac might do.
He wondered, But what if my luck has deserted me?

He fled onto the patio with the children chattering at his heels
like dwarfish furies. He sagged into a white plastic chair and tried
to quiet Courtney and Kyle with the promise that if they ate all the
food on their plates and didn't give Mrs. Hernandez a hard time,
they'd get a big surprise after dinner.

"Oh, what surprise?" Kyle said. Feeling full of the idea of surprise, he danced around the patio. Courtney, who liked to mimic adults, folded her arms on her chest, struck a pose, and said, "Daddy, what on *earth* are you talking about?"

"Something of interest to you, my little madam." He talked to distract them, afraid that they could hear the voice of Narciso raging and threatening in his head. His children circled him — his fragile offspring, driven by such blatant needs. He felt the spinning pressure of their love. What have I done to them? he wondered and abruptly closed his mind against that thought. He offered them a face all-knowing and confident. "If I tell you, it won't be a surprise. Wait until after dark." He drank deeply.

"After dark!" Kyle shouted. "Wow!" Making airplane noises, he skimmed away. He ignored a barrage of furious looks from Courtney and settled into a holding pattern around the patio table. Courtney said, "But, Daddy, you didn't answer me."

Daddy's attention, however, had been captured by the sapphire beauty of his swimming pool, and by his trim green lawn, where sprinklers whispered *chuck, chuck, chuck* and tossed quick rainbows in the evening light, and by the *Lay-Z-Girl,* his sixty-foot Bertram yacht, which seemed to bob in polite greeting from its mooring on the canal. It was a typical view in Biscayne Estates, just south of Miami, and fragrant with the odors of damp earth and thrusting vegetation and the faint coppery tang of the ocean, but this evening its beauty and the achievement it proclaimed seemed like a trap to Darryl. Like one of those insect-eating flowers, but on a huge scale.

At one time, this life was all Darryl had hoped for. Now the prospect of working to sustain it made him think of a photograph he'd seen in *National Geographic,* of Irish pilgrims crawling on their knees over a stony road in the rain.

He felt, on his eardrums, the light percussion of rock music from next door, where Mr. Dominguez, a successful importer of flowers, fruits, and vegetables from Colombia, lived with his young wife, Mercedes, and a son Kyle's age, a sweet boy named Brandon. There was another son, from his first marriage, Jorge, a seventeen-year-old monster with shocking acne, who lived there too. Jorge was forever wounding Darryl's sense of neighborliness with his sleek red Donzi speedboat, his roaring Corvette, his end-of-the-world music, and his endless succession of guests, who used Darryl's lawn to drink and drug and screw and then left their detritus for Courtney and Kyle to puzzle over. Whenever Darryl trotted next door to complain, Mr. Dominguez laid a manicured hand over his heart and said, "I sorry, I sorry," and somehow managed to imply that he was apologizing for Darryl's bad manners, not Jorge's.

Jorge was a painful reminder that there were millions of teenagers out there having a high old time with their parents' money. Meanwhile, Darryl's resources dwindled away. If only he could get a tiny slice of what those parents were wasting on their kids. The idea of offering an Armstrong Education Fund shimmered in his mind, then faded. The word "slice" had turned his thoughts back to Narciso and his death threats.

Darryl didn't want to think about Narciso, so he let himself get angry with Jorge Dominguez. A door cracked open in Darryl's mind, and Darryl scampered down the rough stone steps to the dark arena where he played his special version of Dungeons and Dragons with his enemies. There, in his imagination, he passed a few delightful moments clanking around, teaching Jorge Dominguez to howl out his new understanding of the word "neighbor."

And then, from somewhere close by, Darryl heard the sounds he'd been dreading. He raced up from his mental dungeon to see the water empty from his swimming pool, and the swimming pool float into the sky and join the other clouds turning pink in the evening light. After that, the noises of a chain saw and a wood chipper came growling toward him and his gardenia bushes, hibiscus, sea grape, the low hedge of Surinam cherry that separated him from the Dominguezes, and all of his palms fell over, crumbled into mulch, and blew away. His lawn burst into flame and burned with the fierceness of tissue paper, exposing earth the color of an elephant's hide, dusty and crazed with cracks. The *Lay-Z-Girl* popped her lines and fled down the canal into Biscayne Bay. Behind him, Darryl heard glass shattering and sounds of collapse and rushing wind, and he knew that if he turned around he'd find empty space where his house had once stood. His world had vanished. Ashes filled his heart.

Then it was over. His vision cleared. He lifted his shaking hand and glanced at his watch and guessed that no more than half a minute had passed. He took a swallow of scotch and saw, with gratitude, Kyle circling the table and Courtney staring at him.

He looked away from them and regarded the *Lay-Z-Girl*. Another broken-down dream. At first, Darryl had retained a full-time captain, but when that became too expensive, he'd found someone less competent who was willing to work part-time. Now he couldn't even afford that. A week ago, without telling Caroline, he'd fired the man. Yesterday he'd called a yacht broker and put the *Lay-Z-Girl* on the market.

Tonight, however, he dreamed of sailing away with his family to a new life. Tortola. The Turks and Caicos. A home on the ocean wave. Yes. He said to Courtney, "Mommy knows I'm here?"

"Mommy knows," a voice behind them said. Caroline, barefoot, dressed in designer jeans and a white linen blouse, closed the sliding glass door on the greenish talking face of the television news announcer and stepped onto the patio, darting shy, uncertain glances at Darryl.

He said, "Baby, you look great." She brightened and gave him a smile and a kiss.

He sniffed the air between them. "Love the perfume too."

The children cut across their current, clamoring for attention. A moment of plea bargaining with their mother ensued, after which Kyle and Courtney trudged away toward the kitchen, where Mrs. Hernandez, a smiling Nicaraguan who was going to apply for her green card any day now, stood ready to dish out their supper before she began her trek out past the guardhouse and estate gates to the bus stop, and her night off.

"Any better today, sweetness?" Caroline asked, sitting down and taking a joint from her jeans pocket and lighting up.

The phone rang inside the house. Darryl lurched to his feet, saying, "I did okay in coffee. Made a buck or two. But I got hammered again in currencies. Big time." He stepped into the house, carefully closing the sliding glass door behind him.

"I'm sorry to hear it," Caroline muttered, watching him pick up the phone in the television room. She took a hit off her joint. When she exhaled, it sounded like a sigh.

She smoked and watched Darryl waving a hand and talking. Behind him, the colors on the television screen changed into electric blues, greens, and reds and became a map of Israel, Jordan, and Syria, which was replaced by the image of a handsome young man in a safari jacket talking into a microphone in a desert. Caroline wondered, Would he find me attractive? The correspondent's eyes narrowed, as if he were thinking it over. Then his hair lifted, like the wing of a bird, revealing a bald spot the size of Jordan. Caroline shouted with laughter.

Darryl paced around the television room: tall, red-haired, muscular, dressed in chinos and a blue Izod shirt, moving his right arm as if he were conducting the conversation. Still handsome, Caroline thought. She'd fallen in love with him when she was sixteen years old and he was twenty. He desired her still. She was as certain of that as she was of anything else in this darkening world. Lately, though, he had been making love to her with such a blind, nuzzling intensity that she felt herself recoiling from him. His need frightened her. At the same time, her response left her feeling inadequate and guilty.

Well, she would get him a nice safari jacket for his birthday. She watched the frown on his face and drifted into a fantasy: Darryl was talking to the correspondent in the desert. Together they were solving a knotty international problem. "I told Arafat that he better cut the crap." Something like that.

Darryl slid open the door and returned to slump into the chair next to her.

Caroline glanced at him. "What's happening, Mr. A?"

His face looked drained. "That client keeps calling to say that he's going to kill me."

Dread thumped on Caroline's heart. She blinked and fingered a button on her blouse. "Have you called the police?"

"It's under control."

"Control?" She sat up and flicked away her joint. "Whose control? He's calling you at home?"

"Well, he's upset."

"And you're not? He should be locked up."

"I've got to keep him talking. Calm him down."

"So, are we in danger? And damn you, Darryl, don't you lie to me."

"He'll calm down. And there's a guard on the gate and police on tap. We're safe."

"I don't feel safe. I mean — you're going to do nothing?"

"I've just got to live with it for a while. It'll blow over. Someday I'll kick his ass. He's a jerk. The market turned against him and he started hollering that I'd robbed him."

Caroline asked where the client was from, and Darryl said that, as far as he could make out, he'd begun in Ecuador but had ended up in Panama. Darryl shrugged. "He uses a Panamanian passport. But who knows? He hangs out in Key Biscayne when he's not in Panama."

"He's the only one complaining?"

Darryl looked darkly at her. "In a down market, everybody complains."

"But he says you clipped him? Why would he think that?"

Darryl shrugged. It wasn't what she thought. This guy loved playing the commodities market. Darryl had made a lot of money for him in the past. Last week, however, he'd lost big time — stopped out, three days in a row. Darryl had told him, "Cool off." But he was hot to jump in again. Well, he'd lost again, big time. Now he claimed it was Darryl's fault. He wanted his money back.

"And the threats?"

"You want his actual words?"

She looked away. She didn't want to hear the threats. "Well, anyway, this isn't Ecuador, or wherever he's from."

"Oh, no. Thank God we live in little old Miami, where everybody fears God and pays their taxes." Darryl nodded over his shoulder. "Like that nice Mr. Dominguez."

"This is not a sane way to live."

"Well, my choices are limited at the moment."

Caroline asked if maybe, just maybe, Darryl was getting too old for the commodities game?

Darryl bristled. "You don't like the style of life we have down here? I do it for you and the children. You want to go back to Chunchula, Alabama?"

She gave him a troubled smile. She told him that she surely loved him more alive than dead. And his children did too.

"Lover," he said, calming down. He took her hand and kissed it and admitted that maybe his life was a little too exciting now. That happened in his business. It was part of the adventure. As soon as he was clear of this little problem, they would think about changing things. Right now, he had to sit tight and roll with the punches.

Darryl told her a story about how Napoleon interviewed officers slated for high rank. The last question Napoleon asked was: Are you lucky? If they hesitated, or said no, he didn't promote them. Darryl grinned. "I damn well know what I would've told him."

Caroline had heard the story before. Tonight, it lacked its old

magic. An aggressive attitude to luck might help on a battlefield.
But in business? She worried that Darryl bragged about luck just to
keep himself moving through the scary scenarios he seemed bent
on creating for himself these days. Maybe bragging was a fuel. Or a
mantra. Or a charm. He'd always been addicted to danger, to the
edge, to the thrill of winning big. A little impromptu craziness had
made life interesting for him. It used to refresh him. Now it seemed
to her as if something else was going on.

She worried about Darryl's attitude toward other people's
money. She used to love hearing him romance a client: his voice
had carried a weird and beautiful music, rich and deep and sexy —
a "brown velvet" voice, somebody had once called it. But over the
years she had identified new sounds, less beautiful. Now when the
check changed hands, the music suffered a modulation too. She
heard dry notes of contempt in Darryl's voice. Darryl acted as if the
client had signed away his rights over his own money, and Darryl
resisted with bewilderment and outrage any client's attempts to
withdraw his account. He acted as if the client were trying to weasel
away his, Darryl's, property.

. Caroline worried that Darryl was growing addicted to the stronger jolt, the darker thrill, of losing big. She had been trying to identify the signs. Was she seeing another example tonight? She wasn't
sure. He'd deny it, of course. Could she tell before it was too late?
The fragility of their life worried Caroline, but it seemed to excite
something in Darryl.

"Lover?" he said. "Didn't you hear me? I said I'm thinking of
making some big changes."

"When?"

"Well, as soon as I get clear of these problems."

They looked at each other, and then away, toward the canal,
where the *Lay-Z-Girl* gently chafed at its moorings in the evening
breeze.

Courtney and Kyle returned to the patio just as the telephone rang
again. Their father went into the television room and returned immediately, shaking his head at their mother.

"So, Daddy," Kyle said. "What's the big surprise?"

His remark startled his parents. They stared at him.

"Surprise?" Caroline said, reaching up to finger the button at her
throat.

"Daddy," Courtney said, "you promised us a surprise."

"Oh, that surprise." Their father put his face in his hands and choked with laughter, and his neck flushed bright pink. When he didn't stop laughing, the children grew uneasy. They looked to their mother for guidance and saw her staring at the top of their father's balding head, as if there were something wrong with its color or shape. The phone rang and both parents moved, but their father was faster. His absence left everybody on the patio wordless and uneasy.

He was back in a moment. As he came out onto the patio, Darryl breathed out sharply, clapped his hands, and shouted, "Ghost!" That got everybody's attention. He said, "We're playing Ghost tonight. That's the surprise." He waited for the confusion to subside. They'd played it once before: after their dinner, Mommy and Daddy had turned out all the lights and come searching for Courtney and Kyle.

Caroline said, "Not tonight."

Courtney said, "I hate that game."

Kyle said, "What's the prize?"

"Something really nice," Darryl said. "Now listen up." They'd play for only an hour. Kyle giggled and said, "I'll hide at Brandon's house." No, Darryl told him, nobody could leave the house. Whoever remained free, or was the last to get caught, won the game.

"What's the prize?" Kyle said.

"It's a *su*-prize," Darryl said. The children examined this statement and rejected it as adult nonsense. Kyle gasped, "We're staying up late," and his mother said, "Not too late. School tomorrow. Tonight's special." Why was it special? the children wanted to know, and their mother directed them to their father for their answer. He winked and said that it was a secret. "Why is everything a surprise or a secret?" Courtney said.

"Is this necessary?" Caroline said. She sensed her evening sliding toward a dark corner. But she knew that marijuana stoked her paranoid tendencies, and she was confused about what she really felt, so she went out of her way to enunciate her doubts in reasonable tones. "Do we really need this tonight, honey?" They were eating on the patio. The children had been banished to the television room. Caroline served the food that Mrs. Hernandez had prepared — pork chops and rice, a salad of crispy greens, and a

bottle of Chilean cabernet — and then she brought out the portable television so she could keep an eye on a rerun of *Star Trek* while
she ate.

Darryl had drunk himself into a mood where he found life pi-
quant. "C'mon," he said. "I need a little lighthearted fun. It's just
a game." He laughed. "It reminds me of what my daddy said to
me at his own daddy's funeral: 'These are the jokes, so start laughing.'"

"Stop." Caroline put down her fork.

The image of Mr. Spock came on the television screen and said,
"Irritation. Ah, yes. One of your earth emotions."

"Darryl, this just doesn't sound right."

He shrugged. "Isn't it like life? You're in your house and it feels
safe, but suddenly it's dark as Hades, and out there are people who
are coming to get you."

"I forbid you to talk like that." Caroline blinked at the pale light
coming down over the canal and felt a heavy downward drop in her
emotions. "Let's just take the kids to Dairy Queen, okay?"

They wrangled quietly. "I was joking," Darryl said. "The kids
were bugging me. We'll play for an hour."

Caroline, unhappy and distrustful, looked over at the portable
television. Mr. Spock, wearing earphones, said, "This must be gar-
bled. The tapes are badly burned. I get the captain giving the order
to destroy his own ship."

Caroline told Darryl that she'd think about it. She busied herself
with her dinner, even though she wasn't hungry now, and pretended to concentrate on *Star Trek*. Captain Kirk was ordering a
twenty-four-hour watch on the sick bay.

And then she thought, Maybe I'm not being fair to him. Maybe
I'm not being helpful. He's so edgy tonight. He needs to play more
than the kids do. She wavered and then gave in. "Okay. Okay. But
only for an hour." He brightened immediately. She looked away,
feeling slightly creepy.

"Let's do it right this time," Darryl said. They discussed ways to
turn themselves into ghosts. "We need sheets," Darryl said. "You're
not cutting my good sheets," she said. "I'm talking about old
sheets," Darryl said. Caroline said that all their sheets were new.
She said, "Everything in this house is new."

"But what's a ghost without a sheet?" Darryl said.

From the television, Mr. Spock shouted, "We're entering a force field of some kind! Sensor beam on!"

"Hold it," Caroline shouted. "We're almost ready. But not yet, so you can't come in." Courtney and Kyle wouldn't stop tapping on the locked bedroom door, so their mother, whose hair had suddenly turned white and who was wearing the palest makeup she could find, burst out of the bathroom in her bra and panties, trotted across the bedroom, and shouted through the door for them to knock it off. The telephone rang and she picked up the receiver and said, "Hello?" She waited, and when nobody spoke she muttered, "Oh, fuck you," and dropped the receiver into the cradle and walked to her dressing table and looked at the image of herself with white hair. She shook her head, closed her eyes, and sighed. She felt exhausted.

She reached into a drawer and retrieved a small vial. She dipped her finger, applied it to each nostril and inhaled, rubbed the finger around her gums, and then replaced the vial and went back into the bathroom, where Darryl waited nude in the shower stall singing an old Pink Floyd number about money, and she finished powdering his hair with flour.

She wiped the flour off his shoulder with a towel, kissed him on the lips, tweaked his nipples, and fondled his penis. She stepped back, her eyes hard and sparkling, and considered her handiwork. From the shower stall, Darryl, smiling, red-faced, and drunk, blew kisses at her. "Hmmmnnn," she said. "Hmmmnnn what, baby?" he said. She said, "I just wanted to see how you'd look as an old white-haired cracker with a hard-on."

The children rushed through the doorway and halted just inside the bedroom and almost fell over with fright. In front of them, holding hands side by side on the bed, sat two laughing ghosts with pale, shiny faces, chalky white heads, and bloodshot eyes. They wore flowing white sheets. The ghosts raised their hands in the air, flopped them around and wailed, "Whooooooooo!" and Kyle turned and ran into the door frame.

A ghost jumped up and took Kyle's face in its white-dusted hands and said, "Honey, you all right?" Kyle looked up with one of his eyes shut and said, "Mom?" The ghost nodded. Kyle said, "You scared me." The ghost bent back Kyle's head to examine the bump over his eye and asked, "You sure you're all right?" Kyle nodded. "You want to play the game?" Kyle nodded again. "I guess so." "It's only for an hour," the other ghost said, and Courtney said, "Kyle's so spastic."

"So, if we're all okay . . . ," Darryl said. He reminded them that no lights or flashlights were allowed during the game.

"And Kyle better find his own hiding place," Courtney said.

Darryl told them that the ghosts would wait in this bedroom, then come out and search for the children, *ha, ha, ha.* Courtney pressed her hand to her forehead and said, "Dad, you're weird."

Darryl, noticing a look on Kyle's face, said, "And you can't just give up. If you're caught, you'll have to wait in the TV room — with the TV off. Under no circumstances can you go outside the house. OK?"

Kyle nodded and touched the bump on his forehead and said, "But what's the prize?" "A Peanut Buster Parfait at Dairy Queen," Darryl said. "Tonight?" Kyle said, in a rising voice. Darryl nodded. "Wow!" Kyle said, and even Courtney forgot herself enough to show enthusiasm. "So, we're ready?" Darryl asked.

From where the children waited in the TV room, they caught glimpses of the ghosts floating around the house, turning off lights. They heard, in the gathering darkness, one ghost remind the other about the alarm system. Then the ghosts returned to the doorway of their bedroom, their sheets billowing behind them.

Darryl called out, "Children, can you hear me? Can you hear me?" "Yes," the children shouted. They had ten minutes to hide themselves, he announced. He looked at his digital watch and called out, "From *now.*" He slammed shut the bedroom door, and he and the other ghost groped toward the bed and lay down side by side in the darkness.

He said, "Lordy, think of them creeping around out there like mice." Caroline said that she didn't know if she had the energy to spend an hour chasing the kids around a dark house, and Darryl reached over and touched her nipple and said, "Who says you have to do that? I've got a great idea. Want to hear?"

"Hmmmnnn — probably not," she said. "But tell me anyhow."

As he began to speak she sat up, moved off the bed, and found her way over to her dresser. She quietly opened the drawer, found her little vial, and applied some of its contents to her nostrils and gums, and when her husband paused to ask what on earth she was doing at her dressing table, she sniffed and told him that she was looking for her eye drops, because flour from her hair was irritating her eyes. "I'll take some," Darryl said. "Some what?" she said. "Eye drops," he said, and she said, "Coming right up!" A moment later she started swearing because, she said, she'd just dropped the container on the shag carpet and now she couldn't find it.

Kyle couldn't find a place to hide. Every spot he chose turned out to be too obvious, or it bothered Courtney, who seemed to be playing a game of her own, popping up behind him in every room he went into and hissing at him to *go away*. He finally returned to the living room and squeezed himself under the sofa. Kosmo the cat came over to keep him company and interpreted all of Kyle's efforts to shoo him off as invitations to play, and just when Kyle realized that he'd picked another stupid place to hide, he heard his parents' bedroom door open. His father's voice called out, "Ten minutes is up. This is now officially a *ghost house*. Only *ghosts* live here. Watch out, heeeeeerrrre we come!"

From under the sofa, Kyle looked over and saw the two ghosts standing in the doorway of his parents' bedroom. He whimpered when they laughed like those jungle animals from Africa Kyle had seen on TV. As they began searching through the house, flapping their sheets and making terrible noises, Kosmo finally ran away, and Kyle squeezed himself into the tiniest ball he could imagine and tried not to think about the throbbing bump on his forehead, or about all the places on his body that itched, or the fact that he badly needed to clear his throat, at least once. An hour seemed like forever.

The game glided over Caroline's imagination with the sinister smoothness of a dream bird. She felt more energetic now, and she put her best effort into it. Action kept her paranoia — the panic feeling that she was wavering like an old quarter around the edge of a bottomless pit — far enough away to be bearable.

They swept through the house making ghostly noises, and the first place they looked for Kyle was under the living room sofa, because they both remembered that when Kyle was a little younger he loved to crawl under this sofa and declare himself invisible. Caroline spotted one of his feet and pointed it out to Darryl, who nodded. They circled the sofa, moaning and flapping their sheets, and went on in search of Courtney.

Caroline's senses twitched when they passed the broom closet just off the kitchen, and they stopped and flapped their sheets outside that. While she was dancing around and tapping on the freezer next to it, Caroline felt a stronger twitch of intuition, and she led Darryl to the linen closet by the laundry room. She had remembered that Courtney loved the floral smell of the sachets slipped between the laundered sheets and towels to keep out the smell of mildew. The ghosts wept out her name, and Caroline rattled the linen closet doorknob and felt a sudden pull from the other side. She pulled harder, but the door wouldn't budge. She pictured Courtney obstinately hanging on to the doorknob, and a wave of irritation rose up in her, and she felt a wild urge to yank open the door and strike terror into her daughter's heart, and then she felt ashamed. She loved Courtney. Why should she want to terrorize her? Caroline was appalled at herself. This game had gone too far. She turned away and signaled urgently to Darryl. They made one last sweep through the house, then silently departed through the sliding glass door to the patio and fled across the lawn.

Courtney sat on a pile of towels in the linen closet and hung on to the doorknob with both hands. She wept as silently as she knew how. She had felt, through the door, the force of her mother's anger, and it had shocked her. What had she done to deserve it? She knew she was overweight and unlovely, but she couldn't help it. Her father was acting so weird too. She cried harder now, because she wanted to love him but he wouldn't let her, and she felt so alone.

Kyle strained until he thought his ears were going to pop, but he only heard the thumping of his own blood. He waited and waited and *waited* for the ghosts to make a noise, and finally he just had to move his legs, and then he had to scratch all his itches, and after that he couldn't stop himself and he cleared his throat. Time dragged by. He couldn't remember the house being this quiet, ever.

Caroline and Darryl threw cushions down on the dew-dampened afterdeck of the *Lay-Z-Girl* and tore off each other's sheets, T-shirts, shorts, and underwear and made love in the silvery light of an almost full moon, as if they were young again and back in a field outside Chunchula, Alabama. Ah, it was sweet and powerful, the best ever, they told each other afterward. Sweaty and relaxed, they dozed for a while, until the crisp growl of twin outboard engines, approaching in the canal from the direction of Biscayne Bay, awakened them. The outboard engines shut off close by, and they looked at each other and shook their heads. "Jorge?" "Jorge." Both of them had thought the same thing: young Jorge Dominguez was returning home. Darryl got up into a crouch, looked over the railing, and glimpsed two figures moving across the Dominguezes' lawn. He lay back down again next to Caroline. They decided that Jorge had taken his girlfriend out in his boat, to smoke a joint or fuck in the moonlight.

"Someday," Darryl murmured, lying on his back and tracking the blinking lights of a passing airplane, "I'll get me a sweet little .357 Magnum and take Jorge's heart for a spin over the red line. I surely will. I swear it on the grave of my Aunt Alice, who always had a strap handy for uppity children — I'm not joking," he said, turning toward Caroline.

"You're my big strong hero," she said, fondling him. "Sure you are."

Kyle flitted from room to room, growing more and more upset. He was alone, all alone in this dark house. They'd gone away and left him. Even the cat was gone.

Or maybe they were playing a joke on him? Yes, that was it, he thought with a burst of blistering hatred, because Courtney was a bully and she always got what she wanted and she loved to gang up on him, and now they'd taken her side. Now they were all together someplace, laughing at him. They were waiting for him to act like a baby. Well, he wouldn't. He wouldn't call out or turn on any lights.

But what was he supposed to do? Where was everybody? He'd checked everywhere — now he was coming out of his parents' bathroom, leaving a safe zone of damp towels and reassuring smells, the scent of his mother's perfumed powder, his father's cologne. He walked through a house now unfamiliar, pretending not to notice how the walls bulged out at him. It was hard not to shout with fear when he saw the dark hairy animals that had taken the place of the chairs and sofas he had known. He pretended he didn't see them, and the animals stopped breathing and watched with glowing eyes as he passed. He heard their hearts beating; they gave off a rank, rotten smell as they inched nearer in the darkness, on every side. He knew that they longed to touch him.

He slipped into the kitchen, quietly closing the door behind him, sniffing the air and finding faint traces of the pork chop and rice Mrs. Hernandez had served him for supper. He missed her and her kindly, rough hands. He felt so alone. He fetched up in front of the refrigerator, pondering his father's last words: "This is now officially a ghost house." Was that a secret message which Courtney had understood, but which he, Kyle, had missed? Would it be a ghost house forever? Did they have to abandon it? As Kyle repeated his father's words in his mind, they became alien and threatening. He opened the refrigerator door. The light was wonderfully bright and warm. He reached in, grabbed four slices of bologna, shut the refrigerator door, and stuffed the bologna into his mouth. He stood there in the dark, chewing.

The more Kyle thought about it, the more he grew convinced that they were all someplace together, Mom, Dad, and Courtney. Well, if they weren't inside, they weren't playing fair.

They were together outside. That had to be it. He pictured them sitting together on the back terrace, near the pool, waiting to see how long it would take dumb Kyle to figure out their big joke, and because this picture was the brightest thing in his world at the moment, Kyle accepted it as the truth. Courtney had gotten hold of his mom and dad. Now they were on her side.

So now he'd leave the house too. He'd sneak around to the terrace, where they were sitting around playing their big joke on him, and he'd leap out of the bushes and give them the fright of their lives. "Ha, ha, ha," he'd yell. He'd beat up Courtney. He'd wipe everybody out, *pow, pow, pow.* Then they'd be sorry. Boy, would everybody be sorry when Kyle the Avenger jumped onto that terrace. They'd see how Courtney had lied to them and they'd never ever play a stupid joke on Kyle again.

He grinned as he opened the kitchen door, slipped into the night, and began trotting toward the back of the house and the terrace. He was playing that scene over again in his mind, the one where Kyle the Avenger jumps onto the terrace and frightens the willies out of everybody, when he heard a noise behind him. He dropped down on the ground and froze against the side of the house. He looked back and saw two figures in dark clothes detach themselves from the Surinam cherry hedge. They had come from the Dominguezes' yard. They walked directly over to the kitchen door and opened it, silently entered the house, and just as silently closed the door behind them. Kyle stared at where they'd been. They'd moved so smoothly, so quickly, so quietly. Like ghosts. For a moment, Kyle found it hard to breathe. He felt dizzy and light-headed; he wanted to clear his throat, but he fought against it, and then he began to gag.

He jumped up and plunged through the Surinam cherry hedge and landed on his hands and knees in the Dominguezes' yard, where he quietly vomited up the bologna. He wiped his mouth with his hand and flopped onto his back in the grass and lay shaking in the darkness. Music poured from the Dominguezes' house, and it felt soothing and familiar to him. Dad hadn't told him there were other people playing the game. Where'd they come from? Why were they wearing dark clothes?

Lying in the Dominguezes' yard, Kyle looked up at the moon and thought of the ghosts in dark clothes. Boy, were they scary. He never wanted to play this game again. He closed his eyes and saw stars and felt dizzy, so he opened his eyes and stared up at the sky and wondered how long he'd have to wait until the game was finally over and he could go home and fall asleep in his own bed.

"Christ Almighty, would you listen to that racket?" Darryl said when the heavy metal rock music started up at the Dominguez house. Darryl and Caroline had dozed off again; the music had awakened them.

"I'm going to the head," Caroline muttered, "and then let's collect the kids. Don't forget we've got to take them to Dairy Queen." She kissed him, then groaned as she got off the deck. "I'm getting old, sweetness," she said, descending the stairs. "Old."

Darryl moved to a chair moist with dew. He looked up at the stars and over at the lurid night sky above downtown Miami. He felt better than he had in a long while. Getting out of the house and away from the telephone and making love to Caroline in the moonlight had brought him to a place of balance between the ever-tightening inner craziness of the last few weeks and a sense of future possibilities. He felt refreshed. Hopeful. He loved his wife and he loved his children. He stretched, feeling sexy and content and not at all drunk. He knew he could solve his problems. He was ready to fight the fight. "Fucking rock music," he muttered, staring at his neighbor's house. How could old Dominguez stand that shit? Was he deaf?

"That client — the one who's been threatening you?" Caroline was coming back up onto the deck.

Darryl sighed.

She peered up at the sky and began to pick up her clothes. "What are you going to do?"

"Make a deal."

"What kind of deal?"

"I'll make them happy. I'm thinking of a way to pay them back."

She stopped dressing and stared at him. "Them?"

"Yes." He looked at her. "I told you that."

"You did?" She began crying.

He touched her, but she moved away. He opened his mouth but didn't know what to say. He pulled on his shorts and T-shirt.

She zipped up her shorts, weeping. "What are we going to do?"

"I borrowed some of their money."

"Borrowed?"

"Something like that."

"Well, for God's sake, give it back." Her head emerged from her T-shirt.

"I don't have it right now."

"What have you done with it?"

"It's gone." He opened his hands. "I'm in a deep hole."

She wept again. "Oh, tell them — anything."

"I've been doing that."

She hugged herself. "This is too much."

"It's business. I can't panic, or they'll be on me like sharks."

"Aren't we talking about your life — our lives? Is it all some kind of a game to you?"

"No." He felt her receding from him and he wanted to set things right between them. He told her that he loved her, and he em-

braced her, breathing in her smell, waiting to feel her soften. She
didn't, so he stepped back and willed a smile onto his face. "Look,"
he said, "I screwed up, but I *know* a way to get out of it."

"How?"

"My luck's got to hold out a day or so, and then I'm clear. I want a
different life. I can't go on like this. And that's a definite promise.
We'll sit down and you'll tell me what you want and we'll make a
plan."

She stared at him. "You're never going to change, are you?"

He remembered the flour in his hair and felt self-conscious. He
must look absurd. "I'm changing," he said. "You'll see."

"I don't believe it."

"My biggest worry at the moment," he went on, rubbing his
head, "is how I'm going to get this gunk out of my hair. Go back to
the house and round up the kids and we'll go out to Dairy Queen.
I'll use the boat dock hose and be right there."

She climbed down onto the concrete edge of the canal and
then looked toward their house. It was dark and silent. Compared
to the Dominguezes', so bright, throbbing with music and energy,
her house seemed like the negative of a house. The children, she
thought, were being unusually patient and quiet. She looked up at
Darryl. She was angry at him and disappointed. "Oh, hurry up,"
she said.

"I love you," he said.

She gazed up at him, then turned and started into the darkness. Darryl tried, and failed, to find something reassuring to call
after her.

He stepped into the cockpit, groped around, found a key, fitted
it into the ignition, and tried to start the twin diesel engines.

The *Lay-Z-Girl* was Darryl's province, one in which Caroline was
not interested. She hated fishing, and she complained about sun-
burn and seasickness.

The *Lay-Z-Girl* badly needed repairs. Now the main engines
wouldn't start. He couldn't work the radio. The gauges for the
three fuel tanks were hovering near empty. He gave out a deep
sigh. How he had loved this boat. And what a mess his life had become. He had told Caroline the truth. He wanted to change. But
what was he going to do about Narciso? A solution seemed impossible but at the same time close, very close.

On his way back to the railing, he almost tripped over the sheets that Caroline and he had shed on the deck. He threw them over his shoulder, climbed down onto the concrete dock, turned on the hose, then changed his mind and turned it off.

He'd seen the Dominguezes' lawn explode into low fountains of water. Their automatic sprinklers had come on. In the light from their porch, Darryl saw droplets sparkling on their grass. It was a strange and beautiful sight. His own lawn was dark. So was the house. Caroline hadn't turned on the lights. He halted, uneasy, and stared at his house and around his backyard. He felt that something was wrong with it all, but he didn't know what it was.

His house was perfectly quiet. Darkness seemed to flow out of it toward him in dense waves. He felt a spurt of anxiety and fought to control it. Where was Caroline? Where were the kids?

"Caroline?" he called. There was no answer. He thought that he glimpsed a dark movement behind the sliding glass door to the living room. "Caroline?" he called again. Why didn't she answer?

Darryl studied his house. For some reason, it didn't look like his home. It seemed alien. He didn't like it. He glanced with irritation at all the bright lights illuminating the Dominguezes' house, and he wrestled down his anxiety.

He made up his mind: he'd had enough paranoia for one day. He was tired and he wanted this game to be over. There was, he decided, only one reason for the silence in his house. His family was waiting inside in the darkness to surprise him. Well, he'd play along, even though the notion of moving into that darkness gave him the creeps.

He wanted to be greeted by warmth and light and happy children. He had a vision of them standing just inside the door, holding their breath, waiting to switch on the lights and yell "Boo!" That vision propelled him forward, smiling.

Perhaps, he thought, as he walked up the lawn, rubbing the flour from his hair, perhaps when they got back from Dairy Queen, he'd switch on his porch lights and turn on his sprinklers and show the kids how beautiful water can be, even at night.

Spring Rite

FROM *Alfred Hitchcock's Mystery Magazine*

"WHICH IS even weirder yet," Gowen said. "But that ain't the best part."

At approximately which point, Kramer didn't want to hear any more. It had been a mistake to let Gowen get started. He went outside into the mild March evening to take a leak and get away from Gowen for a little while before hitting the sack.

"Seriously, I got the skinny on 'em," Gowen said, unzipping and joining him at the edge of the porch.

"Tell it to someone who gives a good goddamn," Kramer said.

The elder of the brothers and known his entire adult life simply by his last name, Kramer felled trees for a living, had a nagging pain in his right shoulder, had to get up before dawn, and felt certain the sources of Gowen's information would turn out to be his stoner drinking buddies down at the Trail's End Tavern. People from the Community Church used to get on Kramer about Gowen: do this for him, do that for him, this or that *about* or *to* him. Orphaned at age three, with only Kramer left, Gowen had been permitted the discovery of leisure, then self-indulgence, inevitably rebellion, and on down the line to a number of vices including drug use and actual dope peddling.

Kramer accepted that he had done a poor job with Gowen, who now as an adult in his mid-thirties still brought the law around on occasion and still had that tendency to get mixed up in things that were none of his business. Mr. Town Gossip was one of Kramer's nicknames for him. Arguably a clearer infraction of the social code than even dope peddling in a neighborhood of millions of trees

and few people, most of whom, even the straight ones, did something a little illegal from time to time, poached a deer or an elk,
a few salmon, a load of firewood out of the state forest, gossip
had from homesteader times actually gotten people killed. Gowen,
never one to back off an argument, purported to have read a magazine article somewhere that said that scientific research showed
gossip was seventy-five percent accurate.

"Amazing stuff happens right under your nose, Kramer."

"Gowen . . ." Kramer used the parental voice on him, and they
were quiet for a time. A lone housedog harooed somewhere in the
distance.

"There's Wes Greenly's dog. Figures. Word is that Wes is going in
with them."

This was standard Gowen. Kramer was supposed to ask, going in
with *who* on *what?* At minimum, experience in this country should
have led to a circumspect attitude as to who was doing what and
with whom, and even more generally what was coming from where.
Sense of direction itself was confounded here. Rescuing hunters
who got themselves lost in the twists and turns of river and ridge
was a local industry. A compass was useless because of the iron in
the hills, and with the unpredictable airs that ran upstream and
down over the surface of the Neslolo River, the suddenly uprising
mists, downrolling fogs, and various other phenomena of distinctly
odd and possibly magical nature depending upon your point of
view and maybe level of intelligence, the local acoustics fooled
even the natives. It was Gowen, for that matter, who was always
yacking it up, by way of proving any number of different points,
about how Mount St. Helens had blown her stack right on the eastern horizon and nobody there had heard a pop. It had been
Gowen, just the previous spring, who had found Jake Armbrister in
the river dead of hypothermia, pinned in the current by the limbs
of a snag but with his head above water so that obviously he had
screamed his lungs out in the hour or so before all his heat was
gone, screamed and screamed but was unheard by his wife at home
fifty yards away and for that matter by the Kramer brothers upriver
a quarter of a mile, who on any number of occasions had been able
to hear the Armbrister family in normal conversation in their yard,
sometimes been able to pick out several words.

The residents of the Neslolo Valley, in neighborhoods strung on
the meandering river like beads on a snarled string, were alter-

nately clustered together on benches of usable land and distanced from one another by passages of rapids and rifles. The fifty-three acres that were left of the original Kramer homestead were alone on the north bank of Kramer's Bend, a stretch of deep water that lazed westerly in a nearly hundred and eighty degree arc from the riffle beneath the Hinsvaark Bridge to a twisting, north-northwest-erly slide of whitewater, along which no one could live until the now-deserted Armbrister place. Neither could anyone live in the patchwork of Crown Corporation forest and clearcut directly across from the Kramers on the north side of Long Andrew Ridge.

There were two homesteads on the flat bench of the upriver shoulder of Kramer's Bend: Jensen's, currently being rented by a gang of Mexican treeplanters, and Old Frick's. The raucous music the Mexicans played during their Saturday all-day parties some-times sounded like it was right outside the Kramers' kitchen win-dow, while at other times it either seemed to be coming from the Armbrister place, in completely the wrong direction, or else was not heard at all unless the Kramers came out their front door and walked up to the Hinsvaark Bridge, where it was like the Spanish-language MTV they could get on the satellite dish but turned all the way up to ten. The Frick place was actually closer than Jensen's, but seldom was anything at all heard from that quarter. When Kramer as a kid had cut hay for Young Frick, his mother had been able to call him home to supper with a just-barely-raised voice as she stood on their back porch, yet he could shout and shout his re-turn to her and not be heard.

Old Frick's, as they still called it, was located in a natural cul-de-sac which Old Frick and then Young Frick had knocked themselves out farming or ranching or whatever they could do to make a buck, and which a succession of renters had also failed to turn into any-thing. The last renters at Old Frick's had installed professional-looking chain-link kennels for raising Afghan hounds. Now these new people kept wolves.

It was the new renters at Old Frick's, in fact, who were the object of Gowen's current preoccupation. Watching the wolves pace back and forth in the Afghan hound kennel and listening to them be-ing harassed by the neighborhood coyotes night after night, the Kramer brothers had at first found themselves in an unusual state of agreement. Neither of them would have admitted to any roman-tic notions about the forest that surrounded them or the creatures therein, which as a matter of fact had not included any freeranging wolves for at least a generation, but the penning up of such creatures was, in Gowen's word, "weird." The brothers had assumed that the new neighbors were the source of the flyers taped to the Vildefeld store window advertising WOLF AND WOLF-X PUPPIES FOR SALE, but then Gowen, Mr. Town Gossip, learned that the wolf-puppy seller was someone else entirely. The new neighbors weren't selling, just keeping, which was even weirder.

Beyond which Kramer was unwilling to listen. He had been down this road with Gowen too many times. He took a deep breath and let it out through his nose.

"You don't know whose dog that is, Gowen. The only way we know for certain where those goddamn wolves are is we can see 'em in the binocs. Jesus Christ."

"If it ain't Wes's dog, then whose dog is it?"

"Oh ja," Kramer said, imitating the great-grandfather he had known but Gowen had not. He zipped up and turned away.

Suddenly from the bottom of the yard their own dog, Bucket, started up. They both shushed him immediately. This was how it started every evening now. First one dog, then another, then the coyotes, and then the goddamn wolves.

"I'm going to bed now, Gow."

"I got the information on 'em," Gowen said again.

A single coyote sent a long wail out from some hillside — they could not have said which — and was answered from somewhere lower down, closer, possibly on their side of the river. Quickly more coyotes chimed in, followed by Bucket, unable finally to restrain himself. They let him go. Soon Bucket and the other dog dropped out, so that it was only pure coyote singing. The song rose to fill the entire bowl of the valley, transforming itself, as they listened, to a kind of wild laughter. Kramer was just opening the back door when the wolves joined in. Half in, half out of the doorway, he paused for that interval, now familiar, of uncertain duration but predictable conclusion, in which at some undetectable-to-human-ears cue the coyotes stopped suddenly, all together on a single beat, leaving the wolves to continue solo, forlorn, and ridiculous in their cages.

"Same coyote practical joke, night after night," Kramer said. "Why do you think they do that?"

"I know for a fact the wolf guy's running a meth lab up there,

right up there by Old Frick's Spring, right there by that big maple, remember? Remember that big maple? Thirty-five-foot trailer.
Can't see it, but it's there. Fishburn or Fishback or Fishman, some
goddamn thing like that, something with fish in it. Keeps a few
cows so he can pretend he's doing something over there, and the
wolves so people'll think he's real bad. Lives with some kind of
child prostitute or sex abuse victim or something."

It was Kramer, not Gowen the ladies' man, who saw the Fisher
woman first. He wouldn't have said she was a woman really but a
girl, and with her short hair Kramer thought at first she was a boy,
fourteen or so, soaked to the skin and white with chill, drying off in
front of Wes Greenly's stove. But then she had looked back at him
and arched her spine to the heat.

It automatically put Kramer one up, and the first half-thought
that went through his head was, wait till I tell Gowen.

Lately, with the national forests closing up because of the spotted
owl and all the environmental laws, and sawmills shutting down all
over the country, the valley was full of women and children who
had been deserted by their men. The Kramer family had the opposite problem: three generations of women had run off. Kramer
alone, having never actually had a woman, had avoided this rite of
passage. Gowen had been married, if only briefly, ten years before
and had subsequently had a string of girlfriends, but since the wife
he hadn't brought any of his women home and Kramer didn't
know any of them, although he might know their fathers or their
brothers or their estranged spouses.

Kramer didn't really know any single women, at least none that
he thought of as such. He had missed out on the few schoolgirls of
his youth, eight total in the sophomore class he had dropped out
of at age sixteen to go to work in the woods, and as the years had
gone by, there had been only a few widows or castoffs with children
who had caught his eye. But he'd had enough of child-rearing with
raising Gowen from age three, himself barely more than a child at
the time.

Kramer's temperament was anyway a more or less direct shot
from the great-grandparents, sawed-off Germans who'd migrated
from Schleswig-Holstein in the 1870s, tough squareheads who had
ruined their oxen dragging cuckoo clocks and carved bedsteads

over the shoulder of Nicolai Mountain to that bench of sandy loam created and perennially reclaimed by an obscure, crazy river the Indians avoided and called Neslolo. Whereas Gowen apparently could not have cared less about all that had been accomplished by that and two subsequent generations, Kramer had paid the taxes, repaired the fences, preserved Great-grandmother Grace's diary in German — only a few words of which he could translate — and her German Bible, and all manner of yellowed licenses, bills of lading, deeds, newspaper articles especially from the bootleg days, receipts for Roebuck shoes, seed corn, kegs of nails, lumber for barns and outbuildings long since washed down the Neslolo, and women's clothing in surprising quantity — they had all left in a hurry — some of which over the years had been transformed into unlikely school shirts, trousers, pajamas, work coats, and grease rags, while others, the very feminine items, rested in obscure crannies and boxes and on mute hangers pressed to the backs of closets.

Kramer had been nine and was still called Albert and Gowen was only just about to be born when Great-grandpa Jan, Old Kramer, more than one hundred years old and bent over like a horsecollar from osteoporosis yet still trundling baby-loads of firewood around the yard in his little wheelbarrow, had finally toppled over head-first directly into the wheelbarrow and died curled up like a tire standing on its tread. Within the family Old Kramer's demented belief that his wife would imminently be returning from Astoria — where she had gone fifty or so years before with money to pay their back taxes and instead had hopped a steamer for San Francisco — had become the butt of dark humor the point of which had not re-vealed itself to child Albert until that moment of looking down into the pale blue, dead eyes still open to the sky between the old man's legs. *Aha!:* you don't live forever. Albert in turn had been discov-ered standing over the dead old man by Grandma Elise. When he said to her, showing off his new insight, "He's still waiting for Grandma Grace to come back!" she had slapped him full across the ear and yarded him all the way back to the house by his hair.

This bellringing Kramer had retained as one of very few memo-ries of the paternal grandmother, who a year later, subsequent to Grandpa Walter's stroke and drowning in the river along with his D-10 Cat, had departed for California just as her mother-in-law had done. Of Grace, however, there were many almost-memories, vivid swatches of reminiscence from Old Kramer, who could and did read her diary out loud, of rounding the Horn in steerage, fending off the rats with her good silver soup ladle and the terrible thirst by drinking her baby's urine, of the panther crouching in the soft mud of the new road as she rode her white pony to Vildefeld. As to reasons Grace may have had for deserting husband and child there was nothing — since she was perpetually, hah!, coming right back — just as there was not a word, not of protest or even of surprise, when Grandma Elise left. Similarly, when Kramer and Gowen's mother, Jenny Bergersen Kramer, hit the road with a truckdriver in Kramer's thirteenth year and Gowen's third, there was no explanation offered and, with Frank Kramer into the bottle big-time then, none sought. When, all in that same year, Frank died right in front of the house in the path of a log truck, Uncle Curley was killed in the woods, and Aunty Gert had gotten "the hell out of here, boys!" the same day the insurance check arrived, that was it, the men were dead and the women had split.

The last female in the family hadn't even been properly in the family. Gowen had brought a bride home from the university where he had gone for a year on his G.I. benefits. She was an artist, the real thing, a painter in oils and watercolors who said the Neslolo was the most beautiful place she had ever seen. She had arrived in spring. Then winter and rain and darkness. Kramer had listened to her slow, cigarette-smoking footsteps go room to room, window to window in the wornout homestead house that rocked on its poles when the wind came up and had never quite come up with anything in particular to say to her. Yet he had understood the problem long before the groom. Women hated rain. They needed sun. They were something like tomatoes, which refused to ripen in that country because the nighttime temperatures were so seldom above fifty-five degrees. They craved the company of other women, which otherwise was a good thing, for where there was one there might come others.

Kramer, notorious tightwad that he was, had sprung for a new TV and satellite dish. But around Christmas she had split anyway, leaving half her stuff behind. Kramer hadn't understood why Gowen hadn't gone after her. He briefly considered it himself, but then what would he have said to her when he caught up with her? Kramer sensed without being able to put words to it that he had come to count on the status that went with having a beautiful young woman in the house. And by inertia of some obscure illogic he had come to believe that he too would soon find a wife. And now he had lived like a maiden aunt with his brother for an additional decade and the same logic dictated that the bride's name never be spoken.

It was a Saturday in April. Spring had turned around to play with winter, dumping pea-sized hail and cold rain here and there while up the road a warm sun was shining. It was raining where Kramer turned off the highway onto the rocky mainline that led through a second-growth fir plantation to Wes Greenly's driveway. There was an easterly wind, so it would be colder up high where Barber Logging Company's timber show was. Kramer pictured himself working Monday in wet snow. Maybe Barber would call a day off. How would he spend a day off? Wiping Gowen's butt, he thought. That's how I spend my time.

A week earlier Gowen had come back from steelhead fishing in a state of rage. The new neighbor with the wolves had run him off the north bank of the river with a shotgun. Kramer could see Gowen's argument — they had fished there their whole lives — but at some point Gowen just had to cool down. After all, the wolf guy was paying rent over there. Plus, without any doubt whatsoever, Gowen had been guilty of snooping around.

Kramer had followed Gowen as he went kicking and thrashing his way through the house and had nearly come to blows with him getting his pistol away from him. Kramer had locked up all the guns then, and Gowen, in the grand finale of his tantrum, had packed up and trekked over to the framed tent he kept on Long Andrew Ridge for tending his pot plantation. Kramer had spotted him up there in his binoculars the night before, his shadow sitting still on the surface of the tent for as long as Kramer watched. Old Frick's house was on the same ridge as the tent, about three-quarters of a mile away overland, and Old Frick's Spring was even closer, east and downhill, half a mile at most. Kramer had caught himself hoping the law would somehow get wind of what was going on, whatever it was that was going on. Kramer himself could never call the cops, but maybe somebody would.

Countering the steep slant of Wes Greenly's driveway, Kramer shoved his rear end into the back of the pickup's seat and feathered the brakes over the deeply potted track. The rain slacked off, and momentarily a sunbreak swept across the clearcut around him. It was not often he went to Wes and Jeanellen's these days, although he and Wes went back a ways and they still worked for the same gyppo outfit. More or less worked, since lately Wes hadn't even shown up on the landing half the time, and usually when he did at least one guy on the crew wanted to kick his ass for something stupid he had done or said.

About two years ago Wes had gotten into the dope-growing business just like Gowen, although they didn't seem to have much to do with each other. Barber had begun hassling Kramer because it was Kramer who had vouched for Wes way back when. "Go down and find out does he want the goddamn job or not!" It had already occurred to Kramer that Wes was the one to talk to anyway. Now he had a good excuse. Who else to ask about a doper but another doper? At least Wes was a doper he knew. He needed to talk to somebody. He sure as hell couldn't talk to Gowen.

Kramer went under big timber and descended through the cavernous space beneath the heads of the giant white fir and hemlock rooted on the riverbank below. The truck complained as it took the big bounce at the bottom of Wes's driveway and waded into an expanse of tan water that had been left behind by the receding river. Kramer kept his speed up, having negotiated this track many times in high water, until he made the rise that led into the Greenly yard. Jeanellen's milk goats followed him with their slit eyes as he went past and stopped at the laundry shack, where the lights were on.

The sky changed quickly again and dumped a hard shower on him as he got out. He skipped through the mud in front of the laundry shack and banged on the door briefly before letting himself in. Jeanellen was in there with Lydia, her fourteen-year-old daughter from a previous marriage. Jeanellen was feeding dungarees through her old ringer, which grunted away in the midst of the humming new automatic washer and dryer Wes had bought her with some of his dope money. Lydia was folding.

"Want to borrow my boat?" Kramer said. This was a reliable opener. Careless Wes had lost a succession of boats and canoes to the river, two or three of which had wound up in the Kramer pasture. So the boat joke was always good.

Lydia cut her eyes at her mother. Jeanellen did not look up, merely gave Kramer a brief wave of a plump hand that was not particularly hello any more than a gesture toward the rain on the metal roof. As he moved into the warm spot by the trash burner, Kramer thought he detected tears hanging in the corners of Jeanellen's eyes. He made sure not to stare. Women crying was anyway impossible to deal with. If Gowen had been there, Kramer would have done all right playing second fiddle. Gowen would have got her to talk or laugh.

"Your old man down at the house?"

Jeanellen waved again, taking in a larger portion of rain and roof.

"He's there," Lydia spoke up, something in her voice. Kramer went back out into the rain and down the planked path to the porch built onto the front of the trailer. How Wes got away with it he would never understand, keeping a wife and pretty daughter down in this wet hole with hardly any sunlight, unreliable electricity, crappy TV reception, no company. As Kramer went up the steps onto the porch, a shadow passed across the drawn front window-shade. He knocked.

Fifteen seconds passed and he knocked again. Another half minute and he knocked and gave Wes a shout. When Wes answered the door finally, he had a revolver in his hand, halfway hiding it down behind his leg. Wes grinned quickly but didn't step aside to let Kramer in.

"What's up?" Wes asked, giving Kramer the raised eyebrows and shoulders.

"Talk to you."

"About what?"

"*What* what? You not talking to me now?"

Wes glanced over his shoulder into the trailer's living room and stepped out onto the porch, closing the door behind him.

"Didn't know who it was."

"Who the hell'd you think it was?"

Wes didn't answer, just looked out into the rain in the yard.

"Okay, look, first of all, Barber says if you want your job you better be at work tomorrow and on time. He asked me to come by personally and tell you."

"How come he didn't come himself? You his waterboy now?"

"I also want to talk to you about our new neighbor."

The rain in the yard increased suddenly so that Kramer only heard part of what Wes, turning away from him, said next, only: ". . . mine! . . ."

"You heard about Gowen and our new neighbor?" Kramer persisted. "Fishback or Fishburn or something like that?"

"Yeah. Fisher. Keep your voice down, okay? Yeah, I heard about it."

"Why am I keeping my voice down?"

Wes kept moving away from him and had almost reached the door when Jeanellen came charging down the walkway through the rain bearing a basket of clean laundry. She arrived with a clump on the top porch step, and Wes had to hold the door open for her to avoid getting run over. She went past him and then stuck her head back out and said, "You going to let Kramer stand out in the rain? Come on in, Kramer. Meet your new neighbor."

Wes went in, and Kramer followed. What he took for a young boy in a wet, white shirt arched his back to the heat of the parlor stove and looked back at him, and before Kramer could look away, there was the dark stain of erect nipple beneath the wet cloth and Kramer thought, wait till I tell Gowen.

Wes jerked his head for Kramer to follow and went ahead of him into the kitchen. Jeanellen, puffing over her clothesbasket in the narrow hallway, went away toward the rear bedroom. A coffeepot was perking on the stove, and Wes busied himself.

"Cup, Kramer?"

"No."

Wes went past him back into the living room bearing a steaming mug in two hands. Kramer watched through the doorway as the girl received the mug, her hands on top of Wes's so that the both of them together delivered the first hot sip to her lips. Wes crossed to a shelf and returned with a bottle of whisky, offering to pour a slug of it into her cup. She took the bottle from him and raised it to her lips, her head thrown back and the wet cloth shaping to her arms.

"How'd you get so wet?" Kramer asked from the kitchen, immediately regretting the clumsy sound of his own voice. But neither the girl nor Wes responded.

"Easy, easy!" Wes murmured, pulling the bottle from her mouth so that it made a loud pop.

Kramer came out of the kitchen and went to the front door and said, "Wes?" He waited until Wes started coming along after him, then went onto the porch to the far end where firewood was stacked.

"That right, what Jeanellen said? That the wolf guy's woman?"

Wes's mouth screwed up. "They're not married or anything."

"What's the story on the guy?"

"Fisher is somebody you ought to avoid, Kramer. Something you definitely need to keep your nose out of. Yours and your wacko brother's."

"Weird," Kramer found himself saying, one of Gowen's words that he himself never used. Wes looked at Kramer intently for several seconds and then smiled.

"What's she doing here?" Kramer asked.

"Visiting. Likes a little female company."

"She walk here?"

Jeanellen's voice inside and then Jeanellen at the door, her arms akimbo holding up her big breasts. "Kramer, you give this girl a ride home? She lives down there by you."

Wes turned quickly on his heel. A moment passed between husband and wife.

"Come on out, girl, what'd you say your name was, come on out here. This man's going to take you home. Whyn't you change into those things I give you?" Jeanellen went inside briefly and reemerged with the girl, ushering her with pushy bustle onto the porch.

The Fisher woman made no move to don the flannel workshirt Jeanellen draped across her shoulders. Instead she descended without a word into the rain and started up the slope of the yard on the plank walkway. Wes leaned after her. Jeanellen took a single step forward and said, "Kramer?"

The Fisher woman was waiting for him, staring out the truck's side window into the rain. She didn't turn to him as he got in and started the engine. Lydia was watching from the laundry shack door, arms akimbo like her mother's. Kramer backed and turned the truck around in the narrow driveway. They had started forward and Kramer had put it quickly into second gear for the descent into the standing water when a sudden, dull impact just behind his ear startled him. A mud clot stuck momentarily to the truck's rear window and slid downward, its juice spreading across the expanse of glass. He opened the door and looked back to see Lydia fleeing through the yard. He had thought Lydia liked him. He closed up again and went on.

Momentum was required to make it back up Wes's driveway in the muddy conditions, and Kramer kept his eyes ahead all the way up to the mainline. The percussive racket of the truck's progress over the freshly laid pit-run on the mainline filled the silence in the cab as they wound toward the highway. At the stop sign where the mainline intersected the highway he had an excuse to look over. Her face beneath the cap of black hair was very pale. She looked like no one in particular, no one else he knew, like neither boy nor girl and certainly not like a woman except for the fullness of the lower lip and the steadiness of the smallish black eyes that turned then and studied him in return.

Pretending he had merely been watching for oncoming traffic, Kramer started again and accelerated. They coasted down the long, curving ribbon of asphalt toward the bottom. He kept his eyes on the road as she moved in the seat beside him, drawing the wet shirt over her head, her small yam-shaped breasts jiggling into the light before he could catch himself. She regarded him steadily as she put one arm into the sleeve of Wes Greenly's shirt, drew the body of fresh flannel around behind her bare torso, captured the other sleeve, and, not hurrying the dark tips under cover until he had looked and looked away again, slowly buttoned.

"Here," she said at the juncture of Long Andrew Road. She got out and was turning back toward him as she closed the truck door, a moment in which a person ordinarily would have thanked another person for a ride. But she didn't say it, and so he did: "Thanks."

The crookedness of her teeth surprised him. "For what?" she asked, and laughed. "Letting you look at my tits?" And laughed again, her eyes looking straight into his, and then turned away up Long Andrew, her small haunches alternating. He sat in his truck as she went under the white trunks of the alders growing along the road, following the curve of the river out of sight.

Sunday night the jetstream shrugged, and before dawn a spring snowstorm descended upon the Neslolo Valley. Barber called at five and canceled work. The smell of the snow was overpowering as Kramer lugged firewood from the stack beside the house. About nine A.M. the electricity went out. He called the power company and got a recorded message. Kramer fed the dog, who gyrated and leaped in ecstasy over the snow.

"Yeah, Bucket! You like this stuff, don't you?" His voice sounded louder than normal in the dense air of the near whiteout. It occurred to him that it was possible — no, probable — that the Fisher woman could hear him from across the river. This notion held him in place as if it were novel. Bucket stared eagerly into his eyes as snowflakes accumulated in his hair and on his face. But then, what could he say that would be of interest to her?

He went inside and paced the noisy floor and looked out the window into the cascading white curtain. He built up the stove in the front room and took off his shoes. He prepared an elaborate lunch of instant soup fortified with ground elk. When he realized he had set the table for two, a sudden depression overtook him.

There were places in the cellar where Gowen sometimes hid whisky. Kramer was able to locate only an empty Jim Beam bottle nestled against a plastic zip-lock baggie of pot. This he automatically seized and carried upstairs to be consigned to the woodstove.

He crouched before the cast-iron door of the stove and squeezed the pillow of dried leaves in his fist, inexplicably raising it to his nostrils before throwing it into the fire. He took the extra bowl and spoon from the table to the sink as if they needed washing. He ate his solitary soup and sat over the empty bowl looking out the back window at the snow. The light flattened, and the stove burned down. At dusk the snow ceased. He took down the binoculars from their peg beside the kitchen door and examined one by one the opaque, lit windows of Old Frick's house. The wolves rose occasionally and shook snow from their fur. Gowen's tent was a just barely visible oddity among the stumps and white-draped brush halfway up on the ridge. Darkness fell, and the tent's canvas sides remained unlit. He let the house become dark. When the moon shone briefly through the traveling clouds, his breath became visible. It startled him slightly to see his breath inside the house, and he laughed out loud. He built the stove fire back up and warmed the leftover soup and started the generator so he could watch TV. He was channel surfing when the muffled racket of a pickup truck plowing into the drift at the head of the driveway announced Gowen's return.

Kramer turned the front porch light on and went out. A few snowflakes filtered out of the black sky. Gowen whooped as he came down the yard kicking glittering spray ahead of him.

"You smell like a gin mill."

"Nobody says that anymore, Kramer. People used to say that when there used to be gin mills. There are no gin mills anymore, Kramer. Say something else."

"You get tired of spying on Mr. Fisher?"

"Ah, the lofty Kramer descends . . . very good, bro. What's new? What's going on in the world, such as you know it?"

"You talk first, then I'll decide what I want to say to you."

Kramer followed Gowen inside and watched him disrobe in the heat of the stove. He regarded his brother's bare limbs, remembering when he had been able to pick Gowen up into his arms effortlessly.

"So talk. What's Mr. Wolf-man doing up there? I know you been sneaking around peekin' in his window."

"He's making meth. Just like I told you. A sad tale but true."

"What is that, meth?"

"Methamphetamine. Yes indeed. You take it, fifteen minutes later you want more. Ask your buddy Wes, he knows all about it."

"I just saw Wes yesterday."

"You talked to Wes? My, my, you do get around. And he told you what?"

"Nothing really. He seemed to think your Mr. Fisher was a dangerous individual."

"I worry about you, man. Stuff happens right under your nose. You talk to Jeanellen? What'd she have to say for herself?"

"Nothing. Seemed a little out of sorts."

"Yeah, I'll say. She and Wes are splitting."

"Bull! That's bull!"

"Not according to my source of information."

"One of your little dope customers gossiping with some other little degenerate, one little degenerate to another."

"That's right. One of my little dope customers is real tight with sweet young Lydia, and he says that she says that mommy and daddy are splittin' the sheets. That was this afternoon, so it's as we speak, if you know what I mean."

"Gossip!"

"Eighty-five percent, Krame. Local gossip, it's even higher."

"I was just up there yesterday, and Jeanellen and Lydia were doing laundry."

"Doing laundry, oh . . . well . . ."

"Bull!"

"It was Lydia caught him."

"Him who? Caught what?"

"Caught Wes, in delecto el flagrantee, as they say, doing the nacky with Mr. Wolf-man Fisher's little meth whore. Ah, the neighborhood is going to the dogs, er, wolves, 'scuse me."

"Bull! That's bull!"

"Crazy bitch walks around in the woods in the rain. Looney Tunes. Brain's cooked. You see her while you were up there? Must have just missed her. Too bad. You could have given her a lift. I hear she trades sex for transportation."

Kramer had made no decision not to tell. He had merely hesitated, and hesitation had shaped itself into a small lie of omission, and by the end of *The Late Show* he was schooling himself to think about the Fisher woman only out of Gowen's presence lest his brother pluck the secret from his mind.

In bed for his go-to-sleep dream Kramer constructed his next meeting with the Fisher woman. He came across her in the rain in the woods. He came across her walking down the road in the snow. She was walking down the road in the snow having just come out of the woods. He said . . . , and then she said, I require methamphetamine, I require it every fifteen minutes.

He awoke at his usual time in the predawn and built up the fire. Barber telephoned. A warm rain had started, pushed by a Chinook wind. He and Gowen watched television all day. The brown surface of the river became visible as it filled its ravine. He almost told Gowen about the Fisher woman at supper, but then simply did not. Barber called again during the evening news and said they would try to get something done the next day. "Call your friend, will you?"

"Call him yourself. I ain't your waterboy."

Wes was not there on the landing in the morning. Kramer lost himself in the work of felling second-growth fir into the pulpy snow on Greasy Spoon Ridge.

"I thought he was a friend of yours!" Barber yelled at him over the noise of their saws. Kramer took himself away from the others during lunch break. On the way home he tried and failed to imagine the Fisher woman in the cab of his truck, trading sex for transportation. What was a meth whore? He looked for her along the road and in the trees going past. He pictured Wes holding the steaming mug to her lips.

He came close to telling Gowen about her that night as they orbited around one another in the house before dinner. It was Gowen's turn to cook, and he was ransacking the cupboard for something that did not require complicated preparation.

"You're making a goddamn mess!" Kramer shouted at him.

"The hell's the matter with you?"

Another windstorm came up in the early evening, and again the dogs and coyotes and wolves were quiet all night. Again Wes was not at work. Barber was in a state. Kramer yelled back at him, "He don't belong to me! Go see him yourself!"

Barber let him alone until quitting time. As they were getting into the crummy for the ride down to the landing, Barber asked him to bring two cases of dynamite up with him the next morning. Kramer, of them all the fundamentally sound man and reliable worker, had been Barber's keeper of explosives for years.

"Might as well build road until we can find us a new choker man," Barber said pointedly. "We ain't gonna get any timber moved, seein' as your great friend is so completely goddamn irresponsible. I thought you talked to him. Didn't you say nothing to him?"

"Someone else can set choke," Kramer said back.

"Yeah? Who? You?"

"I don't care."

"Well, I ain't paying you faller's wages for setting choke!"

Everyone was quiet on the way down but wished Kramer goodnight at the landing where their rigs were parked, to show they weren't choosing sides.

Kramer drove fast down the Crown mainline. She was in the cab of the truck with him. She said she wanted to trade sex for transportation, but he said he was willing to give her a ride for nothing.

It was still light when he got to the house. Gowen's truck was not there. He went past the driveway and down the lane that led behind the barn to the old icehouse that had been used for years to store dynamite for Barber Logging. He backed the truck up to the ramp and fished the key to the icehouse from its niche under the steps. Inside he methodically pulled the light chain and took down the clipboard that held a sheaf of papers containing his federal license to handle explosives and the federally mandated log of entries and withdrawals. Automatically he eyeballed the stacks of crates, checking against the balance on his record. He penciled in his intended withdrawal of two crates with the date and his signature and hung the clipboard back on its nail. As he eased the top corner case into his arms, he felt a sharp bite where the heavy box pressed against his belly.

He grunted and put the crate back on top of the stack. He fingered his belly through the front of his shirt, thinking he had pinched a spider and it had bitten him back. A nailhead winked at him in the light. He bent and examined the lid of the crate. All the nails had been started and pushed back into place. The force of his fingertips under the edge of the lid was sufficient to pry up an end; then he yanked the lid the rest of the way off and threw it against the wall, cursing and knowing already what had happened but looking, counting anyway. Four sticks were missing.

"Goddamn you, Gowen!" he shouted.

He retrieved the lid of the crate and hammered it back into place with his fist, cracking the wood and cutting the heel of his hand. He set the box aside — it had been invalidated, and he could no longer be responsible for it — and loaded two others into the back of his pickup. He took the key to the icehouse away with him in his pocket. He and Gowen had already had this discussion. If Gowen wanted to blow stumps in his pot patch, a goddamn dumb idea anyway, he could get his own goddamn dynamite.

He gunned the truck back up the lane and into the driveway. He banged the front door open against the bottle-and-can garbage in the corner and yelled for Gowen. He already knew Gowen was not home, and the foolishness of shouting for him increased his rage. He stomped up the stairs and kicked open the doors to the bathroom and Gowen's bedroom, neither of which he bothered to enter.

As he descended thunderously, he shouted, "Gowen! Gowen!" at the top of his voice. A dull, flat explosion thudded against the south side of the house. Another, louder, followed. Kramer tripped and stumbled heavily as he ran toward the back door, bowling it off its hinges as he went through.

Beyond the back porch railing a great yellow flower was lofting its head against the dark ridge above Old Frick's Spring. The position of the methamphetamine factory was explicitly revealed as a third and very different concussion sent the separated roof and sides of a house trailer skyward like newspapers in a wind. The gleaming tongue of an aluminum storm door wagged back and forth as the front section of the trailer fell noiselessly back into the roiling blob of orange and blue flame. Just as Gowen had said, the location of the meth lab was one that the Kramer brothers knew well, a spot beside Old Frick's Spring where grew a huge big-leaf maple tree that they had played in as children and which now flared in the rebounding blast like a great skeleton holding a hundred candelabra in its arms.

Kramer ran back through the house and the front yard to his pickup and raced to the concrete bridge at Long Andrew Road. He swerved wildly onto the gravel track and ran beneath alder trees standing in the margin of the brown river. Hammering over the cattle guard that marked the entrance to Old Frick's pasture, he looked up at the house on its knoll. The windows were lit with the reflection of the fire on the hill, and the door was standing wide open. The gray forms of the wolves twisted and turned in their cages. Cows were stampeding in wide circles in the pasture. The bull, standing its ground suddenly, charged the oncoming pickup. Kramer swerved off the road as the bull slammed into his fender. The engine screamed as he gunned over wet turf, on across the pasture to the second cattle guard at the edge of the timber.

He could smell the fire now, not the smell of a forest fire but a chemical odor like cat urine or perfume, department store perfume, and then, as he rounded the first switchback, he could hear the crackling and the deep bass hum of the fire above him on the ridge. Flaming brands rained down on the truck's hood. The narrow cut of the roadway was incandescent, and in its center stood a figure. Kramer jammed the brakes as the first muzzle crack sent a slug smashing through the windshield. Another followed, and Kramer tore open his door, his momentum spilling him into the deep ditch beside the road. Pain shot through his leg as he struggled to rise. Above him in the wavering light the muzzle of a gun pointed at his face.

"Mine, Kramer!"

And then nothing but the howling of the fire. Kramer crawled

into the cab of the truck and drove one-legged in reverse down
the switchback into Old Frick's pasture. As he struggled to turn
the truck around in the slippery pasture, he looked up toward the
house and saw her small, still figure watching from a corner of the
chain-link kennels in which the wolves were furiously leaping and
spinning.

Wes Greenly had suckered Gowen, come to the door with a story
that Barber had sent him after dynamite, Kramer busy falling and
it was just a couple of sticks they needed, but right away, so they
had the choker-setter run down the mountain and back real quick.
Sounded plausible. What the hell, how was he supposed to know
Wes wasn't even working for Barber anymore? It wasn't like Kramer
ever communicated anything. Plus, it didn't look like Kramer understood what the hell was going on even though he had gotten his
nose right up in the crack of the whole deal. Goddamn Kramer! Explosives plus any kind of crime equaled federal jurisdiction, and
here he was, he had already had one brush with the Feds, it wasn't
like on TV, he had a record, was looking like an accessory to a capital crime, and Kramer was stuck on the idea this was some kind of
adolescent screw-up where he was going to have to be taught a lesson. Maybe Kramer was in shock. Before he'd even cleaned himself
up after the fire and Wes shooting at him — his clothes still smoking for Christ's sake, never mind the broken foot — he'd sat himself down at the kitchen table with a ballpoint pen and the appropriate government form to make out a report on the four missing
sticks of dynamite. Gowen had come behind him and seen what he
was doing and said to him, "How about driving around in a forest
fire with two cases of dynamite in the back of your pickup truck,
you gonna report that, too?"

"Fine!" Kramer had exploded. He balled up the paper and
slammed it in the stove, and that was when he started with the silent treatment. When Gowen had said to him, "You want to do
something back to him? I'll help you if you want," Kramer had just
looked at him with his eyes bugging out, and about then Gowen figured two things: one, shut up, he's ready to whack you, and two, get
your own story together, because you don't know what the hell he's
going to do.

Gowen spent Friday, the day after the blast, away from the house,
not wanting to be there when the law knocked on the door. He had

gone from the store to the Vildefeld Lunch and then to the tavern, managing to kill the whole day. At first he tried to avoid people, but then, after a few beers, it was business as usual. He kept waiting for it, but no one said to him, Hey, what happened up your way? What was the big noise? It crossed his mind, all that jazz about the local acoustics, Kramer's Bend acoustics in particular that Kramer made such a big deal out of, like the big boom — three of them really, a big one and then boom! boom! two more right after — had been held in place, or maybe deflected somewhere, bounced up into the sky or into some other neighborhood, or maybe somehow actually sucked back into that cul-de-sac where the big big-leaf maple stood beside Old Frick's Spring. No one said anything about the fire either, but then a heavy rain had started up just as Kramer was getting out of there. Like the landscape itself didn't want the news broadcast. He didn't believe this, just liked to play with the idea of it in his mind as he got into a good buzz from the beer and, later out behind the tavern with the guys, the reefer.

Kramer had gone to work that day with his broken foot. When Gowen came home, he was looking out the back window through the binoculars. He still wasn't talking.

"Anybody say anything to you?" Gowen asked him. No answer.

"The Mexicans are gone. Cleared out completely, looks like." Still nothing.

"Jeanellen and Lydia too. Left the goats behind. Can't believe that."

Kramer sighed loudly through his nose.

"I don't get it. Where are the cops?"

Kramer rose and advanced upon him so suddenly he started back. As Kramer rocked past him on the busted foot, he punched the binoculars into Gowen's chest. It was almost friendly, some communication at least. Gowen focused the binoculars on Old Frick's. Wes Greenly was over there, feeding the wolves.

Over the space of the next two weeks Gowen weighed one cover story after another as he waited for the authorities to show up. Between him and Kramer the binoculars were kept on Old Frick's and on the flank of Long Andrew Ridge a good percentage of the daylight hours and into the night. They watched Wes coming and going. No timber cruiser appeared overhead in a helicopter or drove a truck up Long Andrew Road through the blackened patch of timber. They didn't see any firewood poachers, although it was a bad time of year for that anyway with the mud and the snow up high. Hunting season was over, fishing had yet to commence. It could well be that Fisher's meth customers figured he had had to make a quick move, or had been taken by the law. Doubtful Fisher had a dear old mom who called Sundays to see how he was doing, or an ex-wife waiting for a support check.

No one, no deputy sheriff, no state trooper came to the Kramers' door to ask: What happened? What do you know? What did you see? Hear?

Lurking in the back of Gowen's mind when he was sober and let out for a gleeful prance when he was loaded, the wacky idea that had first visited him in the Trail's End Tavern the first day after the blast began to assert itself as belonging to the realm of daylight and reality. Kramer hadn't called the cops, the Mexicans with no green cards wanted none of it, Wes Greenly obviously wasn't about to, nor was Fisher's — now Wes's — little meth whore. That left Jeanellen and Lydia to tell the world. Maybe they hadn't gotten around to it yet. Figured someone else would surely have called it in and they were best out of it. Wes the recipient of a backhanded female absolution: washed that man right out of their hair right away. Or they had told but without picking up a phone to the authorities, their interlocutors maybe disbelieving them, or believing them and wagging their heads still without anybody picking up a telephone.

It was May already. Could it be, was it possible, that such a large event had gone unnoticed by the world? Indeed, it looked as if the only physical testimonials to the murder by dynamite of Mr. Wolfman Fisher and the spectacular wipeout of his enterprise were to be the clunky wad of plaster and cloth applied to Kramer's foot by the alcoholic homeopath in PeeDee, who asked no questions, and, against the deepening pea soup of spring growth on the flank of Long Andrew Ridge the still visible — though at fifty miles per hour only if you happened to look at exactly the right moment between the corner of the Kramer house and the tall stand of trees by the Hinsvaark Bridge — great blackened skeleton of the big-leaf maple.

"It occur to you," he asked Kramer, "that it's just you, me, Wes, and the Fisher woman gonna deal with this crime? Or not, as we choose?"

Kramer just smiled back at him and didn't say anything.

*

May passed, and June. Kramer had gone back to work with the cast still on his foot, his face screwed up with pain, but that had not lasted long. Out of unthinkable carelessness he neglected to face-cut a small alder, and it barber-chaired, smacking him on the crown, luckily a glancing blow but enough to knock him cold. Summarily furloughed until he healed up, Kramer had uncharacteristically given in to his codeine prescription. He slept, and when awake seemed only preparing for more sleep.

Gowen had surreptitiously visited ground zero at Old Frick's Spring not long after the blast. He had gone there again in late spring and several times in the full leaf of summer as irrepressible blackberry, salmonberry, burdock, horsetail, nettles, river grass, and the root suckers of the blasted maple itself progressively obscured and then swallowed completely the metal and glass detritus of Fisher the Wolf-man's meth lab. In mid-July, Gowen spied Wes Greenly hard at work. He hid, watched. By August, daily smoke was rising from a stovepipe jutting from the window of a small pod-shaped trailer that Wes had hauled onto the site. The smell of cat urine came to Gowen on the airs moving up and down the Neslolo River.

Gowen kept his eye out for the Fisher woman. He could pretend to Kramer, who wasn't curious about anything lately, that he had seen the Fisher woman when actually he had not. He climbed up Long Andrew and came down the other side to spy on the house from Old Frick's high pasture. He considered that she might be gone, although the wolves were still there. Getting stoned and peering out from the shade of the timber into the blue-green valley under a high, clean sky — it was actually pretty amusing, in a way. The whole thing could have been made up. Or existed only in their imaginations. Or better, was a thing destined to become an old story, like the old family stories Kramer used to tell him when he was little, a story closed round and kept secret by vast forest.

For the present, the story had become untellable even between themselves. Whenever Gowen attempted to engage Kramer on the subject of the blast, his brother would turn away with that short chopping motion of his hand.

Kramer's taciturnity was a deepening of a trait he already possessed, but other changes in him were more alarming. Even after his foot healed up, Kramer didn't go back to work. He never said he wasn't going back, he just didn't. There wasn't much Gowen could say about any of this, or about Kramer staying abed during the day and roaming around the place at night, packing a pistol everywhere he went. Or about talking aloud to himself out-of-doors. All summer, the most Gowen could get out of his brother was help cutting firewood. For short periods of time, as they worked together, Kramer would seem himself again. But these spells of energy and clarity were followed by even worse bouts of drinking. Most nights Kramer sat with a bottle at the kitchen table looking out the back door, and on nights when the coyotes got the wolves riled up he was apt to charge onto the porch and empty his gun into the sky.

Fall came and the rains and the good logging weather, and still Kramer did not go back to the woods. Gowen met Barber coming off their front porch one day in October and asked him, "He going back?" Barber had looked down and up and back down, as if he were about to make a major pronouncement, but then just said, "I don't know what to tell ya."

A few days before Christmas, Deputy Julius Maksymic pulled Gowen over for a loud muffler as he was cruising down Highway 26 on his way to Seaside. Jule only gave him a warning and didn't even bother to ask him to step out of the truck. He said, "Hey, maybe you can do me a little favor, Gowen. You probably owe me a favor or two, don't you?"

"Yeah, probably so."

"We're looking for a guy maybe you seen or heard about up your way. Meth cook named Lawrence Fisher. Goes by the name of Rex Fisher also. Got a little gal with him. No? Sure?"

"You know I ain't into that, Jule."

"Yeah, yeah. But you would also know, wouldn't you, if he was in the neighborhood."

"Hey, I mind my own business."

"Please don't b.s. me around, Gow."

"No, seriously, listen, Jule, if the dude shows up or I even hear anything, I know who to call."

"The feds got warrants out for both of them. The female is wanted in California and Idaho as a material witness to two murders. Seems she likes the bad boys, goes from one to the other."

Gowen continued on to Seaside so Jule wouldn't get suspicious but finished his shopping in a hurry and returned home. He couldn't wait to tell Kramer. But when he got back to the house, Kramer was not there, and when Kramer finally did come in late that night, he lumbered drunkenly up the stairs and fell into his bed. In the morning when Kramer finally crawled out Gowen still hesitated, unwilling to squander his piece of news on Kramer's morning funk.

"What's the matter with you?" Kramer demanded at supper that night.

"Nothing."

January passed. In February the Neslolo finally did roll up out of her channel and into the pasture. Across her flat, tan surge Gowen watched through the binoculars the wolves in their kennels and Wes Greenly coming and going.

"I don't think she's over there," he said to Kramer.

"She's there," Kramer said.

"I got information on her," he said.

"You shut your goddamn filthy lying mouth!"

One night in March Gowen challenged his brother, attempting to separate him from his bottle, and Kramer beat him brutally. The next day Kramer refused to apologize. Gowen packed and left, removing himself to his framed tent on Long Andrew. It was cold and wet, and he was being stupid not just clearing out and letting Kramer go completely crazy all by himself. But then, even if he couldn't change anything, he had to stay to see how it would end.

Consequently he was in position to spot her in his binoculars, late in the afternoon of a changeable April day, as she crossed the river in an aluminum canoe, tied up at the Kramers' floating dock, and made her way across the wet pasture to the back yard and up onto the back porch to be let in the back door.

He came down then. He circled around behind the barn and ran along the highway to the front of the house. He saw her shadow pass across the windowshade. He crept onto the porch and peered in the window between the edge of the shade and the sash. He saw Kramer holding a cup in front of her, extending it to her with both hands and her hands atop his so that it was together that they delivered the first hot sip to her lips. Then Gowen, who had never in his life knocked on that door, knocked.

BENTLEY DADMUN

Annie's Dream

FROM *Alfred Hitchcock's Mystery Magazine*

THE FARM is seven miles of bad roads from anywhere and has occupied sixty-three acres of scrub pine and rock-laden pasture since Teddy Roosevelt was thrashing around the White House. Now, at the other end of the century, it is home to eighty or ninety senior citizens, several aging cows, a few semiferal chickens, and a handicapped cat.

The majority of the senior citizens ended up at The Farm because they were living their lives on the two-hundred-year plan and handled their money accordingly. The animals, like most domesticated critters, had little choice in the matter.

The animals make do with a large shed, and the barn houses most of the humans. Those who don't live in the barn reside in a motley collection of trailers and RVs that squat like disgruntled sows in the pastures surrounding the barn.

Except for me and the cat. We live in a thirty-six foot mahogany sloop cradled in the middle of a windblown grove of hardwoods in the north pasture.

Annie Kokar, closet misanthrope, Renaissance woman, and retired veterinarian, is the owner of The Farm and keeper of the purse. It is by her efforts that The Farm stays solvent and the residents warm, fed, and relatively free of despair and errant behavior.

I am very attached to the boat. We suit each other, for we are both old drifters, sharing a propensity for solitary wanderings and a desire to keep our distance from others and walk our own path.

Several weeks ago I walked a path.

A path that put Duncan, Annie's son, in prison for more years than he is probably capable of enduring and plunged Annie into a quagmire of despair and anger.

I was told to leave The Farm.

The number of dollars I presently control do not allow for more than a corner room in Teller's Hotel, a dim, crowded slum catering to nearly destitute seniors. Two ancient suitcases and a bulging duffel rested quietly beside several stacks of books, waiting.

I sighed, pulled the last of the Lancers out of the refrigerator, filled a yellow plastic mug, and slumped in the settee.

Cat, always astute, was aware that something profound was happening and, having the feline distaste for disruption and change, was coping by spending most of her time in the cavelike berth under the cockpit. Hearing me fill the mug, she decided to join me, limped out of her nest, and pulled on the cuff of my pants with her good paw. I picked her up, set her on the table, and between sips massaged the scarred tissues of her small, frail body.

I upended the bottle and watched the last drops of wine splash into the mug. I wondered if it would be worth the effort to hike to the barn and snag a bottle from one of the old refrigerators lining the wall in the makeshift kitchen. Thunderstorms were imminent, and Cat, who insists on accompanying me on every journey, does not tolerate thunderstorms well. She clamps herself to my chest, pants like an exhausted puppy, and drools profusely.

I peered out the window to check the weather.

And probably performed a classic double take.

Dressed in bright yellow rain gear a Gloucester lobsterman would envy, gripping a long walking staff, and clutching a plastic bag to her chest, Annie marched across the clearing to the boat. I listened to her climb the stairs, drop into the cockpit, and hammer on the hatch with the staff.

She was undoubtedly here to deliver an ultimatum. I had told her I would be gone by the end of April, and that bitter day was fast approaching. I struggled to my feet and pushed open the hatch.

She lowered an arm, and I grabbed it and helped her down the four steps into the cabin. Annie is somewhere in her seventies, looks it in a handsome way, and stares at the world through hard, flat eyes that calm hurt, frightened animals and make humans squirm. It was Annie who labored over Cat after I appeared at her door with Cat's maimed, blood-soaked body in my arms.

She nodded curtly, handed me the bag, which obviously held a
large bottle, shucked out of her rain gear, and let it drop to the
floor. Then she leaned her staff against the steps and, with a critical
eye, surveyed the stacks of books, the two suitcases, the packed duffel, and muttered, "Going somewhere?"

A number of biting retorts rose, but I pushed them back and
smiled thinly. "I'll be gone by Friday."

With pursed lips she nodded, sat down, and put her hands on
the table. "I'll have a large glass of that wine, please."

So I poured her a glass from the two liter bottle she'd brought,
which must have cost four or five dollars, sat down across from her,
and raised my eyebrows. She ignored the inquiry, hefted Cat to the
table, and ran her long, thin hands over Cat's body. "I'm surprised.
She looks pathetic but is fairly healthy. You've done well by her,
Harry."

"Perhaps, but the five hours you worked on her is what gave her a
future."

Annie smiled briefly and drank. She set the glass down and
sighed.

"I visited Duncan yesterday. He also is doing surprisingly well. I
thought prison would kill him, would reduce him to suicidal pa-
thos. But he seems to be . . . well, if not thriving, certainly coping.
The highly structured life behind bars obviously suits him — he
was almost smiling."

Duncan was going to spend a minimum of fifteen years in that
prison, and Annie's apparent ease with that was disturbing, considering her initial reaction. So I just nodded and kept quiet.

She refilled her glass and studied me with those flat eyes as if
I were an artifact someone had dug out of the south pasture. Then
in a hoarse near whisper she said, "Harry, I've been doing a bit
of thinking. Reasonable, unprejudiced thinking, and I've decided
that, if you want to, you may stay. You've done well by The Farm
and certainly by me, and to evict you over a difference in values is
behavior that is repellent. So, if you want, you may unpack and remain here in the grove."

Casually, and with a surprisingly steady hand considering the
sudden increase in my heart rate, I raised my mug, drank deeply,
and asked, "Where's the string?"

She smiled, the genuine article this time. "No strings, Harry. Stay and do as you please. And if you aren't interested in my little puzzle, that's fine also."

Aha. "Your little puzzle?"

"As I said, you're free to stay. No restrictions. I would not endeavor to coerce you into anything you wouldn't want to do."

Unbidden, a smile crept across my face. "Your little puzzle?" I repeated.

She rummaged in her pants pocket, brought out a ring of keys, and dropped them on the table.

Rain started to hammer the boat, and a hard rumble rolled across the pasture and bowled through the grove. Cat struggled to her feet, teetered on the edge of the table, and with a sorrowful yowl dropped into my arms and laid her scarred head against my chest.

I picked up the key ring and fanned the keys across my palm. Four keys. Two were automotive, with Chrysler's five-pointed star stamped on the end of each one. There was also a smallish key of tarnished brass and a large skeleton key with that characteristic notched piece of flat metal at the working end. I let the keys dangle in my hand, raised my eyebrows, and said, "The keys to the kingdom?"

Annie shook her head and muttered, "Unlikely. A few days ago I noticed that all my kitchenware was on the countertop or stuffed in the dishwasher and my kitchen drawers were filled with crap. It was obvious things had gotten a little out of hand and action was called for."

She paused, took a healthy swig of wine, gave me a thin-lipped smile. "So I set myself to the task, and now my utensils are back in the drawers where they belong and about forty pounds of crap is residing in our illegal landfill."

"A grand blow to the solar plexus of Entropy," I murmured.

"Indeed. In the front of the last drawer, covered by seven hundred and eight pennies, was that key ring. I had forgotten about it. It was Bob's; I found it in his coat pocket two days before he died. He had had two big strokes by then, and it was obvious he was dying. And it was equally obvious that we both wanted to get it the hell over with. At any rate, we were in the process of deciding what to do with things. What child should get what, what to do with The Farm, how badly to lie to the tax people, and all that.

"As I said, I found those keys in a coat of his, an old corduroy thing with a fur collar. He was wearing it the day he had his first stroke." She paused, her eyes on the ceiling, then she mentally shook herself, looked at me, and forced a smile. "I showed him the key ring and asked him what the keys were for and what I should do with them. One of the last coherent things he said to me was, 'My love, you hold the keys to your dream.'"

I picked the keys up and looked at them. "The keys to your dream. Did he explain?"

Annie shook her head. "He was drifting in and out, having good spells, bad spells, but usually not making much sense. Bob and I were married for forty-six and a half years, and he knew I didn't have any dream or dreams worth mentioning. My idea of a dream was a trip to the theater or an art museum, and I rarely mentioned them 'cause I knew Bob had no interest in those things."

I looked away and while pushing the keys around with my finger said, "But . . ."

"Yes, but. As I said, Harry, you're under no requirement to poke around, but if you're curious? Well, you are rather good at ferreting things out. Usually things people would rather keep hidden." She pushed herself up with both hands, struggled into her official Gloucester rain gear, grabbed her staff, and glared at me.

I helped her up the steps, walked her across the rain-slashed deck and down the stairs. She gave me a gimlet smile and, like Diogenes off to search for that mythical honest man, stalked out of the grove.

I put another log in the woodstove, slouched on the settee, and watched the flickering shadows dance around the cabin. Like the ending of an eclipse, the darkness, the deep, dusky fear, slowly seeped out of my soul and allowed me to smile. The grove was mine again. I was, at least for now, spared the dingy hotel room, that fifteen by twenty cell with a sink and the ABSOLUTELY NO PETS sign on the door. I hugged Cat and whispered, "We've been pardoned."

Cat, her claws hooked in my sweatshirt, yowled at the thunder and kept drooling on me.

I woke up early for the first time in days. Hands behind my head, I stared at the ceiling and smiled. Cat, annoyed that the blanket had slipped down her body, lifted her small head off the pillow, put a paw on my arm, and went, "Yeow?"

As I usually did, I gave her a little physical therapy, gently massaging the jagged scars and atrophied muscle. Then we had a quick game of wrestle-the-hand, the first in weeks.

Later, sipping coffee, I watched the squirrels try to get into the birdfeeders. While watching the struggle outside the window I toyed with the key ring I'd left on the table last night. "The keys to your dream?" I muttered. With Cat stretched out and purring in the sling across my chest, I marched through wet, dead hay across the pasture to the barn.

With Annie's connected house, the barn is almost a hundred yards of sagging, much-patched lumber that looms three stories over one's head. The years of renovation into rooms and tiny apartments have turned the interior into a dark maze that only the residents can negotiate without a guide. More than once newcomers have been found sobbing in a narrow dark hallway, lost and wondering what brought them to this groaning, creaking, windblown dump out in the middle of nowhere.

The front half of the second floor of the barn is a multipurpose room. It's a kitchen and dining hall, and the back part of the room is dotted with islands of cast-off furniture. That's the place to linger if your desire is to listen to an unlikely version of who's doing what to whom and why.

I was a little late, but breakfast was still being served and I walked the serving line, gathering eggs, toast, and coffee. As I stood at the end of the line scanning the tables, Mildred Beede, a seamed, white-haired existentialist and sometime drinking acquaintance, gripped my shoulder.

"Harry, if you need help, I can drive you and your things to that hotel."

I gave her a grin that stretched my face. "I've been forgiven and pardoned."

Mildred glanced at Annie, sitting nearby, gripped my shoulder again, and whispered, "That's good, that's very good. But I hope you won't have to jump through too many hoops."

I carried my tray to Annie's table, put Cat on the floor, smiled at Annie, and asked, "What happened to your Chrysler?"

She raised her furry white eyebrows. "Chrysler?"

"Two of the keys belong to a Chrysler Corporation car. What kind and what happened to it?"

"We never owned a Chrysler Corporation car. Bob was devoted to GM, and we owned a long string of Buicks. When they stopped putting those little portholes on the hood, Bob fired off a nasty letter to the Buick people. They wrote back and in a polite way told him to face reality."

"So what was he doing with a set of keys to a Chrysler?"

"I have no idea. I take it you've decided to research my puzzle?"

I shrugged. "Any ideas about the skeleton key?"

"None." She picked up a sausage and bit into it. "The last skeleton key I had was to the attic door of the last house we owned."

"Would you happen to know what Bob was doing the day he wore the jacket?"

"Besides having a massive stroke? He was at the store, taking inventory with Philip."

"The furniture store he owned?"

"Half owned. Philip Kinch was the other half of the business. As I said, they were doing inventory. Philip heard a noise, like someone choking he said, and turned around in time to see Bob fall. Said it was like the left side of his face was melting."

"And he was wearing that coat?"

"Yes, he was. Duncan had given it to him for his birthday two or three years before."

"Who did you and Bob know who owned a Chrysler product?"

She picked up another sausage link and bared her teeth. She chewed, looked at me, and shook her head. "Damned if I can think of anyone."

"Is Philip still around?"

"The last I heard, and this was some years ago — I never did like the man — he was living in town with his daughter. I believe her name is Ogden, Donna Ogden."

I mentally braced myself. "How about Duncan? Did he ever own a Chrysler product?"

Her stare was deadly, but she finally exhaled and whispered, "He always drove Fords."

I found Cat hunkered down in the middle of a rickety card table surrounded by four cooing matrons dressed for a day of spring gardening. A fair-sized chunk of Canadian bacon was firmly grasped in her mouth, and her purr was audible above the baby talk the ladies were emitting as they petted her.

Cat saw me and limped to the edge of the table, and I eased her into the sling. Rose Waterhouse, a thick, white-haired woman with the eyes of an abused Bambi, gave me a lopsided smile. "Rumor has it the Dragon Lady has granted you a stay of execution."

I patted Cat and said, "It's my radiant personality. Tell me, Rose, in your younger days what did you use skeleton keys for?"

She raised her eyebrows, put a finger against her lips, and said, "As I remember, mostly to open doors. My mama's two houses took skeleton keys on the doors as did my first two houses."

"Inside and outside?"

She waved a finger in front of Cat's nose. Cat withdrew into the depths of the sling. "Now that you mention it, mostly inside."

Although cars are handy, they're expensive. So I ride bicycles. My current model is a gray and black marbled mountain bike with twenty-one gears, click shifting, and a suspension system. Instead of panniers I have a yellow and red trailer, which is fortunate, as Cat would object to being stuffed in a pannier.

I put her in the trailer, wrapped her in the patchwork quilt that my ex-wife's grandmother had labored over, and pedaled the seven miles of bad roads to town.

It was a classic spring day, the kind that induces an ardent desire to do nothing of consequence. I wanted to head for the small tree-filled park in the common, plant my aging back against a budding maple, and smile at the world while working my way down a bottle of Lancers. But curiosity prevailed, so I looked up Donna Ogden's address in a graffiti-laden phone booth and headed for Taylor Street.

She lived in a long ranch house with yellow vinyl siding faded nearly white by the sun. On my fifth knock she pulled the door open and gave Cat and me the once-over with smiling brown eyes.

She was dressed in a burlap-colored sweat suit and wore over-sized slippers that looked like bear feet, complete with claws that hung over the threshold like thick white worms. Her brown hair was streaked with kinky strings of gray; she was about thirty pounds overweight, and I doubted she gave a damn. She stepped back, grinned, and said, "A leaned-out man and his mangy cat. This should be interesting."

I smiled and dipped my head. "Mrs. Ogden? My name is Harry Neal. Is your father in?"

"Harry Neal, my father is never out. My father has not been out for something like six goddamn months now."

I nodded again. "Is this voluntary or do you have him chained to the furnace?"

She smirked, pulled a pack of menthol cigarettes out of her pocket, fired one up, and said, "If you leave the cat upstairs with me, you can go see for yourself. Papa is allergic to the things." She turned and walked back into the house.

I followed her into a small living room filled with thirty-year-old furniture. She slumped in a misshapen black recliner, put her cigarette in a glass ashtray filled with smoldering butts, and held out her arms. I slipped Cat out of her sling and with some apprehension handed her over. "Please be gentle, she's rather fragile," I said.

"Rather," she said. "The poor thing looks like she's just been liberated from Dachau. The basement door is in the kitchen, to the right of the dishes."

I paused at a gray door to the right of several stacks of dirty dishes, then pulled it open and descended a staircase made of unfinished two by sixes. Past the furnace, sitting on bare cement, was a new-looking bright red recliner. An old man with a hatchet face and limp, shoulder-length gray hair was slumped in it in front of a huge black television. His left hand, which lay on his thigh, trembled badly. His right hand gripped a stopwatch. The television was off. The man's eyes were open.

I tapped him on the shoulder. "Mr. Kinch? My name is Harry Neal. I wonder if I may talk to you a moment. It concerns your old business partner, Bob Kokar."

He looked at me, looked at the stopwatch, licked his blue lips. "Maury comes on in three minutes and fifteen seconds."

I sighed, avoided looking at that trembling hand, and said, "Mr. Kinch, do you remember your partner, Bob Kokar?"

His manic gray eyes never left the television. "Of course I do. I have Parkinson's, not Alzheimer's."

"Sorry. The day of his stroke, when you and Bob were doing inventory, he had the keys to a Chrysler-made vehicle. Would you happen to know why?"

"Cost you a dollar."

"What?"

"I said, cost you a dollar."

Jesus. I fished a dollar out of my pocket and dropped it in his lap. The spastic hand grabbed it and slowly crushed it into a little ball.

After a long silence I asked again, "Mr. Kinch, what was he doing with keys to a Chrysler car?"

"Because he was driving one that day. Had it parked by the loading dock."

"What kind of car was it?"

"A Chrysler-made vehicle."

"What kind of Chrysler-made vehicle?"

"Cost you a dollar."

I fished another dollar out of my pocket and dropped it in his lap.

"It was a 1976 Plymouth. Station wagon."

"Why was he driving that? Where was his Buick?"

"Cost you a dollar."

I dropped another dollar in his lap. I had three dollars left.

"Buick was at the garage with a flat tire. He was going to make a delivery. The people who ordered the piece let him borrow their car."

I dropped a dollar in his lap. "Who were the people?"

The television came to life. The screen glowed, and an excited voice roared, "And only three flex payments of forty-nine ninety-five, so order now! Order now!"

"Mr. Kinch, who were the people with the Plymouth station wagon?"

He flapped that twitching hand at me. "Get out of here. Maury's on." And on the huge screen appeared a middle-aged man with a stewardess's grin and the eyes of an evangelist. Underneath in black letters I read WOMEN WHO MARRY DWARFS.

I stepped in front of the screen, leaned into his face, and said, "Who were the people with the station wagon?"

Mr. Kinch pushed at me with that spastic hand, leaned way to his left so he could see the screen, and hollered, "I don't know. I never saw them."

I dropped another dollar in his lap, leaned to my right, stared into his eyes, and hollered, "What was the piece? What did they order?"

Mr. Kinch frantically sat upright. "A chest, a big goddamn chest, like a pirate's treasure chest."

Mrs. Ogden was sitting in her recliner, a cigarette hanging out of her mouth and Cat nestled in her arms. She smiled at me. "He give you any trouble? I heard shouting."

"Not much. He was upset that I was causing him to miss the start of something called *The Maury Show.*"

She smiled again. "How much?"

"Five dollars."

She dipped into her sweat suit, pulled out a damp looking fistful of balled-up bills, and counted off five. "Every time I go near the sonofabitch it costs me six or seven dollars, but I get them back when I do the wash."

I smiled sympathetically, eased Cat into her sling, and asked, "Do you remember any of the people who worked for Bob Kokar and your father? Any who are still around?"

Mrs. Ogden lit a fresh cigarette from the butt of her last one. "Cost you a dollar."

I dug in my pocket, found a faded, wrinkled dollar, and dropped it in her smoldering ashtray. She grinned. "You'll find C. C. Dorfman at the health club."

I said, "Thank you," and, as my dollar burst into flames, headed for the door.

There are two health clubs in town. The Muscle Stop, located in the old train station, and Blood Sweat and Black Iron, in the old town garage. I phoned The Muscle Stop, and an angry voice informed me that C. C. Dorfman owned Blood Sweat and Black Iron.

Thanks to a significant raise in taxes, the Public Works Department moved into a new garage four or five years ago, leaving a run-down building of gray cement and red brick. In a line along the front of the garage were four bay doors; stuck on the north end was an awkward looking two story barracks.

I pedaled across a gravel parking lot filled with pickup trucks and sport utility vehicles with tough sounding names and leaned the bike against the first bay door. A confused jumble of noise came

from inside the building, and I thought I heard someone scream. I
put Cat in her sling and walked through a small door built into the
first bay door.

And confronted primordial grunting, cries of exertion, weights
crashing and banging, and rock-and-roll music screaming from
large loudspeakers hanging by clotheslines from steel beams high
above my head. The thick, humid air smelled of dirty socks and
pizza.

Perhaps thirty people were working the weights. Blood Sweat
and Black Iron was just what it said. No treadmills, stairsteppers, or
other modern exercise gizmos, just free weights, I-beams with cables, and crude looking devices with discs of black iron hanging on
them.

I must have appeared lost and confused, which was accurate, for
a short bald man dressed in billowing red pants strutted up to me.
He was muscle on muscle, almost as thick as he was tall, and his
eyes spoke his devotion. He stared a moment at Cat, who was hanging half out of the sling taking everything in, looked at me, and
raised his eyebrows.

I bent down and yelled in his ear, "I'm looking for C. C. Dorfman."

He pointed to the far end of the garage, gave Cat a last look,
shook his head, and strutted back to a barbell with a massive
amount of black iron hung on it.

Clutching Cat, I threaded my way through thousands of pounds
of grunting, sweating, absurdly veined muscle to the other end of
the garage and huddled in a corner, wondering which one of the
mutated creatures might be C. C. Dorfman.

Finally I approached a man who was lying on a bench with a
loaded barbell above his chest and hollered, "Are you C. C. Dorfman?"

He laughed. "Don't very damn well think so," he yelled. "Try the
one with the tits."

I looked to my left and saw a woman standing behind a barbell.
She was my height, looked a young forty, and was dressed in drab
gray spandex shorts and halter. Her brown hair was cut very short,
and like everyone else in the place she was superbly muscled with
veins like rope and her face was a lesson in angles and hollows.

As I watched, she stooped, picked up the bar — which had at
least a hundred pounds hung on it — and pushed it from her chest

to as far above her head as she could reach. She did this fifteen times, then dropped the weight on the floor and did a series of stretches.

I walked over, gave her my friendliest smile, and hollered, "Hello, my name is Harry Neal, could I talk with you for a moment?"

She gazed at me with placid, judging eyes, shrugged, and pointed to a small back door. I followed her out the door into a blissfully silent field of dead weeds and rocks.

Actually I walked, C. C. Dorfman strutted, her highly muscled hips undulating with a primitive sensuality that brought a silly, bemused smile to my face.

As she turned around, I whipped the smile off and said, "I'm a friend of Annie Kokar, and I'm trying to trace Bob's movements on the day he had his stroke. I was talking to Philip Kinch and his daughter, and she said you were working at Kokar and Kinch that day."

She gazed at me, gave Cat a long searching look, and nodded. "Whew, that brings back some memories. You saw Kinch? How is the old bastard? Sometimes when I have five or six dollars to spare I pay him a visit, but I haven't been there in weeks. Frankly, he makes my ass tired."

"I'm not sure how he is. He sits in the basement and seems fixated on something called *The Maury Show*. It cost me five dollars to talk to him. He says he has Parkinson's. Do you remember the day Bob Kokar had his stroke?"

With long callused fingers she slid Cat out of the sling and ran her other hand over Cat's body. "Car get her?"

I nodded. "Yes, it was touch and go for a bit, but Annie pulled her through. She's pretty gimpy but manages."

C. C. Dorfman nodded thoughtfully, squatted down, and laid Cat on her back in the weeds. She held Cat's body with one hand, grasped her bad front leg with the other, and, as she slowly, gently pulled it forward, asked, "So what's the interest in Bob's last normal day?"

"He was carrying some keys with him. Before he died, he hinted to Annie that they might lead to something of value. And he was driving another person's car, a 1976 Plymouth station wagon. Listen, what are you doing to Cat?"

Cat's eyes had suddenly bulged and her purring turned to a drawn-out yowl. C. C. Dorfman now took both front legs and very slowly pulled them forward.

"She's extremely stiff. She needs to be stretched out daily. It'll re duce the scarring of the deep muscle tissue and increase her mobility. With increased mobility she'll be able to build up the atrophied muscle, reduce her discomfort and pain, and lead a better life. So stop screwing around, she's your responsibility, and you're not doing the work. Once a day minimum, stretch her out. If you're too damn lazy, give her to someone who will."

She laced the fingers of both hands in Cat's front and back legs and pulled. Cat yowled and looked at me with what I assumed to be pleading eyes. I put a hand on C. C. Dorfman's extremely muscular back and said, "I want you to stop, you're hurting her."

She stopped, flowed to a standing position, and looked at me with eyes gone fierce. "Listen, turkey, I know what I'm doing. I did three years of vet school at UNH and two summers with a vet in Hanover before I quit. I quit because every time I had to put an animal down, I cried and got drunk. My liver and wallet couldn't take it anymore. So don't give me any crap, all right? I know what I'm doing." And she squatted down and put Cat on her digital rack again.

I pulled a dollar out of my pocket and let it float down to the grass. "Do you remember that '76 Plymouth wagon?"

She stopped torturing Cat, smiled, and tucked the dollar in her halter. Her chest was so muscular that the inside edges of her breasts were striated. "I put a big trunk into that car for Bob. He'd sold it to somebody, and when a tire on his Buick went flat, they lent him the station wagon. I was going to follow him to the person's house and give him a ride back. But then his face melted along with a lot of good stuff in his head, and that was that."

"So what happened to the car?"

She pressed her right thumb deep into Cat's neck muscles. I stood above her, my eyes wandering over her amazing body, and waited. Finally she said, "You know, this is the first time I've thought about it. And I've got a dollar that says Philip never remembered it either, until now I mean. So the answer to your question is, 'I haven't the faintest idea.'"

She put Cat on her left side and dug her fingers into Cat's

scarred right shoulder. Cat was making noises that would break an executioner's heart; to distract her I threw another dollar down. "What does C. C. stand for?"

She rolled Cat over and started torturing her other shoulder. "It's not C. C., it's CeeCee, that's C-e-e, C-e-e, CeeCee." She lifted Cat, placed her in the sling, and gently rubbed the top of her head with a knuckle. "Remember, Neal, once a day minimum. If you don't, I'll find out about it and hunt you down and turn you into a gelding." And she not so gently rubbed the top of my head with several knuckles.

Gretchen's Restaurant is located at the gloomy, litter-strewn end of an alley off Main Street. A bowl of her buck-a-bowl soup weighs about two pounds and keeps financially desperate senior citizens going until the green check comes. I spend a lot of time in Gretchen's, usually sitting alone in a booth that seats six, drinking wine or coffee and on occasion actually buying something to eat.

Gretchen is my age, has never ventured farther than Concord, thirty miles to the south, and could not care less about the human comedy outside the town limits. She does, however, know just about everything about the never-ending comedy outside her door.

I pushed open the heavy, peeling door with the front tire and rolled my bike down the narrow room to the back wall. It was fairly cold out, and the big potbellied stove was spewing out heat and wisps of birch-scented smoke that mixed with the aromas of chicken curry and good coffee.

I leaned the bike against the wall, put Cat in her sling, and, instead of taking the rear booth, walked to the counter and sat down next to the only person who knows more about the townspeople than Gretchen.

Betty Worthen, all hundred and sixty-some-odd pounds of her, is the only policewoman in town. She started out as, and still is, a meter maid; any arrests she makes are on foot and are the result of her own private investigations or an occasional push from a local. Betty and I owe each other some fairly significant favors and generally tolerate each other's numerous flaws.

Cat struggled out of the sling onto the counter and poked her nose in Betty's cup. After a few tentative sniffs she bent her head and lapped up coffee spiked with five or six teaspoons of sugar.

Then she licked her nose and limped down the counter to check out what the other patrons had in front of them.

I stirred Betty's coffee with my finger just to watch her round face break into a grin, ordered my own coffee from one of Gretchen's geriatric waitresses, and said, "Were you around the day Bob Kokar had his stroke?"

Betty stared at her coffee a moment, then drank. "I was fresh out of the police academy, had just kicked my husband and son out of the house, and generally thought I was a hot ticket because I was single again and running around with a revolver on my hip and putting parking tickets on people's windshields. It was Kokar's stroke that brought me back to earth. I was the first official type to get to the store. I heard crying and ran into the back and there's old Philip Kinch and CeeCee Dorfman on the floor holding Kokar. His face had sagged like warm taffy, and he stared up at me with the eyes of a gutshot doe. I was about as helpful as Philip and generally stood around with my thumb up my butt watching him drool."

I pulled out the keys, laid them on the counter, and gave Betty the short version of what I'd been doing.

She moved the keys around with a finger, gave me a side-eyed look, and said, "Glad to hear of your reprieve. I was worried about you living in Teller's Hotel, sitting in one of those musty old rooms drinking yourself to death. I'd feel just a little guilty because I was the one who arrested Duncan, thanks to you.

"As for that station wagon, I can't do anything for you. There'd be no reason for the DMV to keep any records this long, so where would I start? If I were you, I'd ask Philip where the store records are. Maybe you'll get lucky and they're still around. Then you can hunt up the bill of sale for that chest and find out who bought it. Odds are, they're the ones who came down and drove off in that wagon with it."

As I coasted into the barnyard, I noticed that Annie's kitchen window was open. I pulled up to the house, leaned against the window, and said to Annie's back, "Did Bob ever mention a chest he sold that day?"

Annie jerked and dropped a cast-iron skillet on the floor. She stepped over the skillet, which was oozing gray, thick liquid, and said, "Next time knock. A chest? I don't believe so. Is it important?"

"That day, the day of his first stroke, he was going to deliver a chest to someone. Apparently it resembled the classic treasure chest. His Buick had a flat tire, so the someone lent him a car. It was a '76 Plymouth station wagon."

She frowned. "So the Chrysler keys are to the station wagon, and the smaller key could be to the chest. Which means he was babbling when he said they were the keys to my dream. What he might have meant was that he had a key to a chest like a hope chest."

"Possibly," I said. "There are still a couple of things I'm going to check on, but I wouldn't count on going to Key West next winter."

"I won't plan on it." She stared at me a moment, gave me a thin smile, and said, "You've got a bit of a gleam in your eye."

"Your reprieve has swept the acidic fog from my mind and replaced it with mild euphoria."

She nodded and got down on her hands and knees to clean up the mess on the floor. "Well, Harry, as I said, you've been good to The Farm, and after a bit of rational thought I realized it would be ludicrous to punish you for doing what you thought was right."

I watched her a moment. "What I've been wondering is, did you really come to that decision yesterday? Or did you plan on letting me stay weeks ago and allow me to suffer for a while as punishment?"

She slowly raised her head and gave me a heavy-lidded look and a smile that would curdle icewater. We stared at each other for several seconds; then she bent her head to her task, and I left the window and pedaled to the boat.

After supper I spent an hour or so unpacking, then, with Cat snuggled in my lap, sat in the settee with a mug of wine and looked out the window at the grove.

My grove.

After breakfast the next morning I finished unpacking and decided to start Cat on her daily stretches. CeeCee Dorfman was undoubtedly right. I spend twenty or thirty minutes a day stretching, and it made sense that Cat, as handicapped as she was, would also benefit from a daily workout.

I put her on her back in the middle of the cabin, gently took her front legs and pulled them over her head. She yeowled, struggled to her feet, gave me a shocked look and a squeaky little hiss.

I petted her for a bit, massaged her scar tissue, and tried again.
As soon as I started pulling on her legs, she yeowled, lurched to her
feet, and paw raised, claws extended, gave that squeaky little hiss
and limped into her nest under the cockpit

Apparently my technique was just a tad off.

I spent ten minutes on my hands and knees with my head in the
berth staring into Cat's dilated eyes and spewing forth a lot of
pleading nonsense. Finally I reestablished a semblance of trust, got
her bundled up in the trailer, and headed to town. I didn't want to
play Talking for Dollars with Philip Kinch again, so I pedaled to
Blood Sweat and Black Iron.

The parking lot was empty except for a rust-spotted maroon van
with a black iron weight painted on the driver's door. I leaned the
bike against crumbling brick, put Cat in her sling, and pulled on
the small door built into the first bay door.

It was locked. I stood there a moment, looked at the van, then
slapped the door several times with the flat of my hand. I waited a
few moments, then smacked it again.

The door opened suddenly, and CeeCee Dorfman said, "The
door to my apartment is around back, up the stairway."

She was dressed in jeans and a tight yellow T-shirt and was barefoot and braless. She also looked pale, bleary-eyed, and not exactly
delighted to see me. I pasted a smile on my face. "I apologize. Am I
interrupting something or may I come in?"

She gave Cat a quick knuckle rub and stepped back. "Come on
up. I'll spot you a cup of coffee and a glass of CeeCee Dorfman's
Magic Stuff."

I followed her into the garage, through a silent dark forest of
black iron to an open red door marked PRIVATE in white letters.
We climbed narrow stairs, turned right, and entered a large room
that was half kitchen, half living room.

The kitchen part was dominated by a commercial gas stove with
eight burners and a large grill. She pointed at an unpainted picnic
table squatting in front of the stove, and I pulled out a bench and
perched on it. Cat immediately hauled herself out of the sling,
climbed on the table, sat by a restaurant napkin holder, and stared
at CeeCee Dorfman.

CeeCee gave me a mug of steaming coffee and set an empty glass
next to it. From a large blender she poured a thick purple liquid

into the glass. "My Magic Stuff. One quart would keep half a Mongol horde raping and pillaging for a week." She sat next to me, smiled, and said, "So why the visit? You want to join up? Become a bodybuilder? Or do you just want to hang around and stare at my boobs?"

"I'm too old for the former and too reserved for the latter. I came to see you for two reasons. One, I'd like to hire you to stretch and massage Cat. This morning I tried and hurt her, and she got mad at me. If I keep it up, I'll lose her trust. I also want to ask you if you happen to know what happened to Kinch and Kokar's records, especially the bills of sale."

She plucked Cat off the table and scratched her ears. "You're still dogging that car?"

"Not compulsively, not like you dog weights. But I would like to find out who bought the chest. Perhaps they can shed light on Annie's puzzle."

She pursed her lips and nodded. I tried her Magic Stuff. It was thick, smelled like vanilla, and tasted like overripe bananas and malt. I took several gulps and followed it with a few sips of excellent coffee.

"Actually, I do know where K and K's papers might be. After Bob stroked, Philip just barely hung on. Bob was the businessman and kept everything going. Philip was the salesman, liked to gab with the customers and couldn't care less about the rest of it. After Bob had his second stroke and it was obvious he was heading out, we had a going-out-of-business sale and then Philip sold the building to the Catholic Church."

"And the Catholics turned it into a center for senior citizens."

"That they did, but originally, before it was K and K Furniture, it was Osborn's Restaurant. From what Bob said, the place was very popular for several years; then Mrs. Osborn was diagnosed with cervical cancer, fought the good fight, and croaked. Mr. Osborn was devastated, sold the place to Bob and Philip for a song, and the rest you know."

"So where are the records?"

With a small, twisted smile on her face she stared at me. When I didn't say anything, she tapped me lightly in the middle of my forehead and whispered, "Turn on your lights, Neal, or is your battery getting low?"

I finished the Magic Stuff. "The records are still in the building."

"They *may* still be in the building, down in the basement, in the old walk-in cooler. After Bob had his stroke, I did all the bookkeeping, and when the joint was sold, I gave copies of everything to the tax people and the state. But if the nuns didn't hoe the place out, the original paper is still there."

"You don't remember any bill of sale for that chest?"

"It probably crossed the desk, but it wouldn't have rung any bells. As for Cat, I'll do her four times a week. In return I'd like you to join Blood Sweat and Black Iron for a year. I'll only charge you half, three hundred."

"Surely you jest."

"I jest not, and don't call me Shirley."

"I'm sixty-three. Your proposition is ludicrous."

She smiled, shrugged, and said, "You're a very good sixty-three, and after a year doing weights you'd be a fabulous sixty-four, but it's your choice. I don't open the place until two. Bring Cat by any morning. I'll charge you a pound of coffee for four sessions a week."

"Thank you." I reached for Cat. "I'm going to go to the senior center and peek into that walk-in."

"Leave Cat here. As soon as I gulp down some more caffeine, I'll stretch her out. But I gotta do the caffeine first. I was up until three watching a Xena festival on cable."

"A Xena festival?"

"Xena, the kick-butt warrior princess, you dolt. She's my role model."

With Cat gripped in CeeCee Dorfman's thick arms, I left. Cat wasn't happy with the situation, and I could hear plaintive meows as I closed the door and headed down the outside stairway. Halfway down I turned around, went back up, opened the door, and said, "Don't give her any milk or cream; it wreaks havoc with her digestive system."

CeeCee Dorfman looked up from petting Cat and smiled. "Got it. No cream. No milk. See ya later."

Again I started downstairs and again turned around, went back up, and opened the door. But before I could speak, CeeCee pointed a finger at me. "Neal, get a grip and get out."

After stopping briefly at Kreb's Hardware, I pedaled to the se-

nior center. The parishioners were obviously putting their drach-
mas somewhere besides the collection box, for the center needed
paint and more than a few new clapboards. The parking lot looked
like a tank platoon had been using it for maneuvers, and I didn't
see anyplace to lock my bicycle.

I pushed bike and trailer up two wood steps, pulled open one of
the big entrance doors, and managed to get everything inside without damage or mishap. I stood in a wide, short hall and looked into
a room the approximate size of a high school basketball court.

People were milling about or sitting in a strange collection of recliners and easy chairs, reading. A sizable group was seated in a
semicircle around a big television set watching a movie. The movie
was in black and white, and all the men wore suits and hats and all
the women were smiling.

Outside of a nun dressed in traditional garb I was probably the
youngest person in the building. I leaned the bike against the inside wall and strolled into the main room. Trying to look Catholic
and casual, I scanned the place for a likely looking door to the
basement.

To my left was an island of overstuffed chairs and a couch. Most
of the chairs were filled with shapeless, doughy-faced people with
white hair, and most of them were sleeping. And sitting on the
sunken, torn, leather couch, her arm around a sobbing woman
with very thin white hair, was Mildred Beede.

She saw me and gestured, so I walked over to the couch and
raised my eyebrows.

She nodded at the sobbing woman beside her. "I'm a volunteer.
Twice a week I drive in and help Sister Marie run the center. This
place is open to all seniors, and they're short-handed and welcome
any help they can get, even from an old Baptist like me."

Her smile pushed her crinkled face into an overlapping series of
semicircles. "The real surprise is seeing you. What game induces
you to enter this Christian stronghold?"

"I was in the neighborhood and thought I'd drop in. I must have
passed this place a million times and I . . ."

"Harry Neal, a Catholic-run senior center is the last place on
earth you would visit voluntarily, so please don't insult what little intelligence I still possess by feeding me one of your I-just-happened-
to lines."

"Well, I will admit to a certain mercenary bent to my visit."

The sobbing woman patted Mildred's hand, mumbled, "Thank you," gave me a wet, red-eyed glance, and shuffled away. Mildred slumped against the back of the couch, sighed, and said, "Life is truly a harsh mistress, Harry."

"To quote Annie misquoting Thomas Hobbes, 'Life is nasty, brutal, and short.' He wasn't, but he could have been referring to the winter of one's life."

Mildred sighed again. "A certain mercenary bent?"

"In the basement of this building is an old walk-in cooler. It's possible that some records I would like to look at are still in that cooler."

Mildred stared at me a moment, then snorted. "I suspect, Harry, that you will have a lot to answer for when you are dragged before the gods." She dug a clawlike hand into my shoulder for support and stood. "Why don't I show you where the bathrooms are? By coincidence the basement door is just a few steps beyond the men's room."

Side by side, we strolled across the room, weaving through a mixed bag of men and women for whom sixty was young. As I glanced at them, a sharp-edged stone of gloom grew in my consciousness. A few scant years up the road and I might be slumped in one of those recliners drooling on my shirt.

We came to a wood door that appeared to have trench foot. Mildred opened it and motioned me into a dim hall cluttered with stacks of folding chairs, card tables, and two broken couches. She pointed to the end of the hall and whispered, "The key is above the door, the walk-in is near the front, on the north side. But don't get your hopes up. The basement has always been empty 'cause of all the water." She went back into the main room.

I walked down to the end of the hall and stood in front of a peeling, dirt-streaked door. I ran my hand along the sill and found a skeleton key much like the one on Bob Kokar's key ring. I unlocked the door, turned the rusty knob, and fumbled for the light switch.

I went down solid, dirty stairs into a large cement room and walked along the north wall toward the front of the building. Except for a rumbling, foul-smelling furnace and several stagnant pools of black water, the basement was empty. Near the front, embedded in the cement block wall, was a thick, wood-faced door with a large metal handle.

I gripped the handle and yanked. Groaning like a sick animal, the big door opened, and I looked into a musty, foul-smelling blackness that spoke of mold, fungus, and dangerous microbes. I found a light switch, and an encrusted twenty-five watt bulb revealed a small filthy room with wet and corroded metal walls and a damp looking wood floor.

Taking a deep breath, I carefully stepped in and immediately punched through the wood, going ankle deep before hitting cement slab. I took another step and punched through again. With both feet through the wood I squinted and looked around the room.

Except for a row of dirt-covered metal boxes stacked two high, the walk-in was empty.

Breaking through the wood floor with each step, I struggled to the boxes. I put on my Wal-Mart reading glasses and pulled out my brand-new overpriced penlight. Turning it on, I knelt and squinted at the faded labels in metal slots in the middle of each box.

Barely discernible in neat, hand-printed letters was the name Kinch and Kokar, and below the name was a date. Each box seemed to hold a year's worth of paper. Crabbing along, I scrolled through the years until I came to a rusted box that should have contained paper from that fateful day.

Pulling it off the stack, I lugged it out of the walk-in and headed for the dank halo of light created by a lone bulb hanging over the furnace. Halfway across the floor the bottom of the box gave way, and forty pounds of paper fell on my feet.

I sat on the floor next to the mess and held my toes while contemplating the infinite number of things I'd rather be doing. When the pain subsided to a tolerable level, I got on my knees and started pawing through the stuff.

Another year and it would have been too late. The bulk of the papers were black with mold and had a damp, clammy feel. Several thick bundles were stuck together, and when I attempted to peel them apart, they turned to mush in my hands. Kneeling on the wet cement floor I went through what papers I could salvage. It was like working an archaeological dig — ever so carefully teasing apart moldy, moist paper and peering at faded scribbles.

I got lucky.

I threw what remained of the box and the rotting piles of paper back into the walk-in, slammed the door, and made my way back to the big room upstairs.

Surrounded by snoring elders, Mildred was sitting alone on the couch reading last Tuesday's *Boston Globe*. I sat beside her, and she looked at me, smiled, pulled a lace-trimmed handkerchief out of her dress pocket, and wiped my face. "So, Harry, was your trip to the dungeon successful?"

"Would you happen to know an Elinor Obermeyer?"

Her face turned stern, and her voice was suddenly rimmed with flint. "Harry Neal, Elinor Obermeyer is a kind woman who is as innocent now as she was the day she was born. She and Milt are one of the nicest couples I know."

"All I asked was, do you know her."

"And I know you, Harry. You're up to something. You're on the scent. The only thing Elinor and Milt have ever done is be nice, so leave them alone."

I stared at her a moment. "And just what is it that qualifies Elinor and Milt for sainthood?"

"Don't be flip with me, Harry. I didn't say they were saints, I simply stated that they were nice people. They've had their share of troubles over the years and don't need an old ferret like you to come sniffing around their burrow."

"What kind of troubles?"

"Well, quite a few years ago Elinor's brother was killed in a car accident in Connecticut just a week after he moved there. I had attended a going-away party she and Milt held for him. He was a professor at the college and had gotten a nice offer from a Connecticut university. Elinor was devastated.

"And they're in poor health. Sometimes I used to see them around town or having lunch at Gretchen's, and I sometimes see her at church, but not lately, she finds it so hard to move around. They're both quite . . . overweight and frail."

"You, in church? I thought you were a backsliding Baptist."

"I am. And I'm here to tell you the services can be more than a trifle irritating. It's hard to understand how adults can believe that stuff. It's what's after the services that I sometimes enjoy. The coffee and doughnuts in the church basement. I get to talk and mingle with people, and I've made some new friends by my hypocrisy."

"I don't think you could be labeled a hypocrite, Mildred, just a bit devious." I stood, touched her shoulder, and said, "Thanks for your help. Without it I'd still be wandering around looking for the basement door."

"Buy me a drink sometime and tell me what you're up to. Your forays into other people's lives are more interesting than coffee and doughnuts in a church basement. And do leave the Obermeyers alone."

I pounded on CeeCee Dorfman's door, heard her yell, and walked in. She was reclining on a battered futon with Cat stretched out on her stomach, watching television. Cat looked up, opened her mouth, licked her gums, and limped toward me. I took the sling off the picnic table, put it on, and picked her up. She opened her mouth and licked her gums several times, then pawed at my chest and slithered into the sling.

CeeCee Dorfman was watching a tape of a superbly muscled black woman dressed in a white bikini lecturing on nutritional supplements. I watched a moment, then said, "Do you happen to remember Elinor and Milt Obermeyer?"

Without looking up she said, "Sure, nice old couple, both about forty pounds overweight and haven't got a muscle between them. When K and K was open, they bought a bunch of stuff. Spent a ton of money. Actually I think it was Rabart's money."

"They also bought that chest you put in the station wagon the day of Bob Kokar's stroke," I said. Cat kept opening her mouth and licking her chops. I watched her a moment. "Who's Rabart? And what did you do to Cat's mouth?"

"Rabart is — was Elinor's brother. He was killed in a car accident in Connecticut. It's his house that Milt and Elinor live in. It's now their house, of course. They bought a lot of furniture for it."

She stopped talking and focused on the woman, who was flexing her arms and chattering on about proteins. "Cat?" I prompted.

She aimed a remote at the television, which went black.

"I brushed her teeth. It should be done at least three times a week." She flowed off the futon, picked a bag off the picnic table, and waved it at me. "This is her food from now on. Feed her this and only this. No table scraps, no human tuna, no crap."

"You *brushed her teeth*?"

She plucked a toothbrush out of the kitchen sink. "Three times a week. And don't use any fancy toothpaste, just basic stuff. If you don't want to do it, I'll do it when you bring her here. Any morning. But make it before two, that's when I open up."

At the sight of the toothbrush Cat slid out of the sling, hit the floor, and, moving faster than I'd ever seen her move, hobbled over to the stove and crawled under it. I stared at the stove, gave CeeCee my tough look, which made her grin, and said, *"You brushed her teeth?"*

I leaned the bike against the back wall and sat in the last booth. Cat pulled herself out of the sling, perched by the napkin holder, and stared at Gretchen. The place was as quiet as a foggy night, with just the gentle whisper of gray voices mingled with an occasional clink of spoon on bowl.

Gretchen put a chilled mug and a carafe of red wine on the table and slid into the opposite seat. As I poured the wine, she pulled a long pink cigarette out of her pocket and lit it with a hissing lighter. She blew smoke past my right shoulder and pulled a piece of beef out of her other pocket.

CeeCee Dorfman's stinging lecture on why cats should have their teeth brushed and why they should never eat table scraps still hummed in my brain, but I couldn't break up what had become a cherished ritual and told myself that just these times with Gretchen would be okay.

Cat pounced on the beef, shook it, dropped it, and attacked it again before dragging it to the napkin holder, where she put her good front paw on it and looked around the room with narrowed eyes. As she always did, Gretchen smiled and gently pulled Cat's good ear. I drank, set my mug down, and asked, "How well do you know the Obermeyers?"

"Milt and Elinor? Pretty good. They used ta come in here all the time when they were stronger."

"I know a woman who thinks they're candidates for sainthood."

She raised her eyebrows. "Nice is the word for them. Always polite, always inquiring after your health and such, and anyone will tell you what nice damn people they are. But the thing I noticed was, someone else always seemed to pay their way, usually her brother Gordon. When he died down in Connecticut, they got his money and the house, so I guess he's still paying."

"Gordon Rabart," I said.

"Yep. Milt worked for a bit at Kreb's Hardware back when it was Mill's Hardware. And Peter Mill used ta call him Flash Obermeyer 'cause Milt moved about as fast as your average snail. But he didn't last but five or six years. I guess it was easier ta live off of Rabart. As far as I know, Elinor never worked a day in her life."

"So they always lived in Rabart's house."

"Yep. Milt sure didn't make enough working at Mill's to keep a house and all that."

"Rabart paid their way?"

"Yep."

"Then he got killed."

"Yep."

"And then it was Milt and Elinor's house."

"Yep, along with a bunch of dollars. Gordon Rabart was an economics professor and practiced what he preached. Rumor had it he made a fair dollar playing the market."

I pedaled through a cold light rain to The Farm. The wide, knobby tires made a muted hissing sound that lulled me into a trance and the trip seemed short, but when I reached the boat, it was dark and I was cold and irritated.

I got a fire going, fixed myself a plate of stir-fries, and washed them down with a half bottle of Lancers. By the time I finished eating, Cat was giving me meaningful looks and batting her bowl around the floor. So I opened up a box of CeeCee Dorfman's special food, poured some in Cat's bowl, and held my breath.

Cat sniffed at the stuff, which looked like large mouse turds, looked at me, sniffed again, and hunkered down and ate with gusto. Relieved, I poured another mug of Lancers, settled back in the settee, and thought about keys and chests and Gordon Rabart.

Wrapped in a maroon Gore-Tex rain suit, and with the trailer's canvas hood zipped up, I pedaled through a driving rain to town. By the time I reached the common my system was begging for hot caffeine, but discipline prevailed and I locked the bike to a steel railing, put the rain suit in the trailer, and slipped Cat inside my sweat jacket. Head bent into the rain, I trotted across a wide brick walk to the college library.

Fortunately, the front desk was manned by an inattentive coed chatting on the phone. Acting calm and casual I strolled by the desk and ducked into the reference stacks. Slinking from aisle to aisle like a hunted rabbit, I circled around the reference desk, which was manned with manic intensity by one Gloria Somerville, an excellent researcher but hell on illiterate felines.

Safely past Reference, I skulked across two open aisles and, without knocking, burst through a door marked DR. JEREMY HANSON, STUDENT GUIDANCE COUNSELOR.

Before I dropped out of the world, I was a card-carrying member of the college faculty, and Jeremy and I often refought wars, censured world leaders, and reformed the planet while drinking large quantities of cheap wine.

When I burst through his door, his head jerked up from a computer screen. He looked at my dripping face and grinned. "Ah, 'tis Professor Neal seeking refuge from his quixotic ventures, obviously ready to humble himself and slather his mentor with profuse apologies for being such an existential ass."

Jeremy is a year older than me, looks it, and would have achieved greatness if not blocked by numerous dysfunctions, one of which is a fondness for Johnny Walker Red. I sat in the one chair across from his tiny desk, nodded at his computer, and asked, "Can you get the University of Connecticut on that thing?"

Still smiling, he turned back to the screen, tapped on his keyboard for maybe twenty seconds, sat back, and said, "Now what?"

"Seventeen years ago Gordon Rabart, professor of economics, quit his post here for a job at UConn. A week after he arrived, he was killed in an auto accident. I'm curious about what, if anything, they might have on record."

Jeremy's eyebrows rose as his smile faded. He rubbed his face and said softly, "I remember, I went to his going-away party. When I tried to leave with a bottle of champagne, Elinor, his sister, waylaid me and made me return the bottle. The bitch."

He turned to the computer and for the next fifteen minutes either tapped away or watched lines of type scroll up the screen. Finally he went "Aha," leaned back with his hands behind his head, and watched the screen.

Then, his face an empty mask, he turned to me and in a near whisper said, "According to Dr. Franklin Shaw, who has been in the UConn economics department for twenty-two years, Dr. Gordon

Rabart never showed up for faculty indoctrination — his sister called and said he was killed in an auto accident just outside his hometown in central New Hampshire."

"Interesting."

"Yes, very. I must say, Harry, that is one damp and seedy looking cat you have there."

I looked down. Cat had stuck her scarred head out of the jacket and was checking out the office. I stood. "Thank you, Jeremy, I appreciate your time."

"Harry, think back to those golden days of yesteryear and remember the good times we had. And now if we tip the glass once a year I consider it lucky. We're friends, Harry. Just because you turned left at life's fork doesn't mean you have to forfeit your friends."

CeeCee Dorfman, dressed in threadbare jeans and a tight white sweatshirt with large red hands printed over her breasts, opened the door. "Come in out of the rain, Neal, before you get a terminal case of Wet Brain."

I dropped my coat on the floor under the picnic table and sat down, put fifty dollars on the table, and said, "This is for the food and therapy. When you want more, let me know."

She shrugged, put a cup of coffee and an empty glass in front of me, filled the glass with Magic Stuff from the ever-present blender, grabbed Cat, and hauled her out of the sling. With a piece of towel she rubbed her down, then pried open her mouth and smelled her breath. "I'll be damned. You're actually feeding her the food I gave you."

"Of course. Miss Dorfman, would you mind if I left Cat with you for a while? I have a few things I'd like to do, and it would be easier if Cat weren't along."

CeeCee nodded. "No problem. I'll give her her workout and feed her a dish of the Good Stuff, and then we'll lie back and watch a couple of hours of Xena, butt-kicking warrior princess. And if you ever call me Miss Dorfman again, I'll kick you in the cahunas."

"This Xena is on all day?"

"I have a bunch of Xena tapes."

"Why don't you turn off the television and live your own adventures?"

"Why don't you piss up a rope?"

With Miss Dorfman's Magic Stuff gurgling in my stomach I pushed open the door to Gretchen's, walked the creaking floor to the back, and leaned the bike against the wall. As I walked back to the front door, I smiled at Gretchen and said, "I'll pick it up later." She waved a greasy spatula at me and nodded.

Milt and Elinor Obermeyer had inherited a large Victorian house complete with turrets and wraparound porch. The muted shades of brown looked like they had been brushed on yesterday, and the flagstone walk was a study in spatial relations. A blacktop driveway ended at the back of the house, and parked just beyond the porch was a new looking Plymouth Caravan.

I walked across the porch and pushed a gold button to the left of the oak door. After a few moments I pushed the button again, waited a decent interval, then beat the door with the butt of my hand. Finally the door swung inward a few inches, and a white head peeked around the edge just above the knob.

Elinor Obermeyer's face was round and pink and marred by thick horn-rimmed glasses. Her cap of curly white hair looked like it had been carved by a very good artisan, and the rings on the fingers gripping the edge of the door could keep Cat in sushi for all of her mythical nine lives.

I bobbed my head, smiled my best smile, and said, "Mrs. Obermeyer? My name is Harry Neal. I wonder if I may speak to you and your husband for a few moments. It pertains to the 1976 Plymouth station wagon you used to own."

Her eyes widened behind the thick lenses. She stared at me a few moments, then opened the door and straightened up. "Why, that vehicle was wrecked years ago. What possible interest could it have for you, Mr. Neal?"

"Well, it's a rather odd story involving Kinch and Kokar Furniture and the chest you bought from them."

That got me another minute of silent appraisal. Finally she cleared her throat and said softly, "I see. Well, perhaps you'd better come in." She turned and with a shuffling waddle led me into the house. "Would you care for a cup of tea? Or perhaps a glass of sherry?"

"A glass of sherry would be nice," I said.

I slowly followed her through a music room dominated by a grand piano and three loveseats, past a curving staircase, and through an arched portal into a large, opulent living room. To the right, beyond the living room, was a formal dining room. Elinor motioned toward a pale blue wing chair by the fireplace.

She wore a full length dress of subdued red that swished when she walked. I sat, hoping to hell I didn't have any bicycle grease on my pants, and accepted the small glass of sherry she held out to me.

She swished over to a white couch with blue flowers embroidered on it, and sat down. "Milton is taking his bath, and as he is just getting over a bad cold, I don't want to rush him. Now, you say you are here about our old station wagon and a chest we bought?"

I took a minuscule sip of the sherry. "The day you purchased the chest from Kinch and Kokar, Bob Kokar's car was in the garage, and you lent him your station wagon so he could deliver the chest to this residence. Before he could do so, however, he suffered a stroke and was taken to the hospital. Because of the crisis the station wagon was forgotten." I took another sip of my sherry and stared unsmiling at Elinor.

Pulling at the fabric of her dress with hands mottled with brown and purple splotches, she stared wide-eyed at me. Finally, in a low voice she said, "The chest was a present for my late brother Gordon. He was moving to Connecticut the next morning. When Mr. Kokar failed to deliver the chest by late afternoon, I called the store and learned of his accident. I walked to the store and retrieved the car and the chest and drove home. Gordon packed the chest and early the next morning drove down to the University of Connecticut."

"And a week later died in a car accident."

Her eyes glistened behind the glasses. She nodded slowly, "Yes. We — we couldn't believe it. Even now, Mr. Neal, after all these years, I still can't comprehend what happened. It was devastating."

"And he was driving the station wagon when he had the accident?"

She nodded slowly again. "Yes, even at the time it was an old vehicle, but Gordon said it was still very functional and wouldn't trade it in. When the Connecticut police called, they said he went off the road during a heavy rain and hit a tree. They said he probably died instantly. May I inquire why you are asking questions after all these years?"

"Bob Kokar's wife Annie recently discovered the set of car keys you gave him. They were lying in a drawer, forgotten all this time.

She remembered that Bob had mentioned leaving his coat in the car. It was one she had given him on their fortieth anniversary, and she asked me to seek you out and inquire after the car on the very slim chance the coat could be located. Apparently it was a strong symbol of their love." I pasted a smarmy smile on my face, downed the sherry, and wished for more. Lying is thirsty work.

Her pink, flaccid face molded into her version of a sympathetic look. "I don't remember any coat. I think Gordon would have mentioned finding it, and surely he would have found it while packing the car."

I stood and placed my glass on the small table beside her. "I'm sure you're right, Mrs. Obermeyer. Annie undoubtedly has it tucked away somewhere, like the keys to Gordon's station wagon. Someday she'll clean out a closet and there it will be. I'm sorry to have awakened such unpleasant memories."

She struggled to her feet. "Don't fret, Mr. Neal. There is not a day goes by that I don't think of dear Gordon. And I'm sure you're right, someday Mrs. Kokar will find that coat hidden in the back of a closet and she will have fond memories to dwell on."

"Thank you for your time and say hello to your husband for me."

She beamed at me. "It was no trouble at all, Mr. Neal. You may see yourself out, it's getting to be quite a trek to the front door."

I nodded, smiled like an idiot, said, "Thank you," one more time, and headed for the door.

I stopped at the door, took three quick steps backward, and looked toward the living room. Elinor was shuffling through the dining room toward the rear of the house. I opened the front door, closed it hard, and hurried to the stairs. With one hand clamped on the polished oak banister, I watched Elinor disappear through a swinging door, presumably into the kitchen.

Probably looking like a cartoon version of a burglar, I darted through the living room into the dining room and hurried through the dining room to an open doorway into a short hall painted gloss-white. Across from a wall phone was a door. Clenching my teeth, I slowly turned the knob, pulled it open, and stared at shelves of what I assumed to be The Good China. I closed the door, crept to the other end of the hall, and put an ear to a door with at least five coats of high-gloss white paint on it.

Hearing nothing, I eased the door open and entered a pantry crowded with condiments, a toaster, a coffeemaker, two other doors, and silence. I could hear water running and Elinor humming a tuneless ditty on the other side of the left-hand door. With infinite caution I turned the knob of the right-hand door, inch by inch eased it open, and stared down a flight of steep, dirty stairs.

Trembling like a veteran wino, I pulled the key ring out of my pocket and tried to get the skeleton key into the damned keyhole. I finally made it, took a deep breath, and tried the key.

It wouldn't turn.

Jamming the key ring back in my pocket, I retraced my steps as fast as I dared. Quick-walking into the music room, I grabbed the gleaming banister and, taking them three at a time, lurched up the stairs. At the top I stepped onto lush pale gray carpeting and looked down a long hallway with cream-colored wallpaper and numerous doorways. I took a deep breath, and started down the hall. Looking into the first doorway on my left I saw a large bedroom with a huge canopied bed and about ninety square yards of pink.

Across the hall was a smaller bedroom with a single brass bed, a dark bureau, a gray wing chair, and two end tables cluttered with magazines. I turned, heard a coughing, grunting noise, and jumped into the pink bedroom.

Mumbling and snorting like an old bear shuffling through a cornfield, someone came up the hallway, hesitated, then walked into the bedroom across the hall. Blinking sweat out of my eyes, I peeked around the doorjamb and stared at the wide back of an old man with a fat, bulbous neck and a frizzy band of gray hair over his ears. He wore a red and white striped bathrobe and was methodically placing soap dish, razor, and other pieces of bath paraphernalia on top of the bureau.

My eyes nailed to the man's neck, I stepped out of the pink bedroom and, taking giant strides on tiptoe, got the hell down the hall.

I scooted past a bathroom with a black and white checkerboard floor, wafting out moist fumes of aftershave, and crept down three stairs to a closed door. I opened the door and looked into a small, square bedroom in which all the furniture was covered with sheets. I closed the door and started down the hall again, stopped, and went back and entered the room.

I carefully closed the door, crept between two single beds, and faced two doors very close together.

Behind the first door was an empty closet. I opened the second and looked up narrow, dusty stairs. Taking the key ring out of my pocket, I fumbled the skeleton key into the lock and turned it. As I did so, a thick steel bolt slid out of the door and with a soft *snick* locked in place. I almost giggled.

The attic was a dark, musty confusion of still shadows and primitive silence. One small window cast a murky shaft of light down a narrow aisle between stacks of boxes and trunks. In slow motion, every creak of the sagging floorboards sounding like a gunshot, I made my way down the aisle to the dust-caked window and scratched at the encrusted glass with a fingernail.

Well beyond a back yard layered with last fall's leaves, the roof of a shed or garage peeked over the top of a thick nest of spindly maples and high brush that hadn't been trimmed since Hector was a pup.

It would have taken twenty minutes with a putty knife to scrape off the encrusted grime on the window. I gave up on the idea of more sunlight and pulled out my overpriced penlight.

Crawling down the aisle on my hands and knees, I examined the trunks. At the end of the aisle, near the stairs, I found a wall of boxes stacked four high, lifted sheets, and peered at old leather chairs, a desk, and a dried-up leather sofa.

Apparently the Obermeyers didn't care for Gordon's taste in furniture.

I finally found it tucked in a dark corner covered by a gray wool blanket and surrounded by boxes full of plain, functional china and several decades' worth of *The Journal of Applied Economics*.

And it did indeed look like the movie version of a pirate's treasure chest except it was perhaps twice as large and the brass trim looked suspiciously like aluminum. Every move carefully choreographed, I cleared a path through the boxes and, teeth clenched, slowly, ever so slowly, moved the chest away from the corner timbers.

Again I pulled out the key ring, wiped the sweat off my face, and with a fairly steady hand inserted the brass key into the chest.

It turned easily. The penlight between my teeth, I lifted the domed lid until it was fully open and resting on the large hinges.

It was stained and mottled black, probably from fats and fluids and perhaps fungus, and it fell apart at my touch. But there was enough of the original to make out some of the letters. Gordon Rabart had died with his new University of Connecticut sweatshirt on.

I looked down at the jumble of clothes and bones, took a deep breath, and with one finger started poking and pulling at the clothing and pushing at the bones.

And found several ribs with gouges in them. Something had gone through Gordon Rabart, doing terrible, lethal damage in the process.

Slowly, carefully, I closed the lid and, again thinking through every move before I made it, replaced the chest and boxes as I had found them, covered the chest with the dust-heavy blanket, and made my way down those narrow stairs.

I was halfway down the main stairway before I realized Elinor and Milt were having drinks in the music room. I turned around and, with teeth clenched so hard my ears were ringing, crept back up the stairs. Their mumbling, mingled with the occasional clink of bottle on glass, was indistinct. Perhaps I should go down, help myself to some sherry, plant my tired butt on a loveseat, and join the conversation. "I say, Elinor, which one of you did Gordon? And why? Why on earth kill your own brother? The brother who was so kind to you and Milt? The brother who allowed you to live your parasitic life for so many years?"

I sat on the top step, arms on knees, head on arms, for a good twenty minutes before it occurred to me that there must be a back staircase to a house this large. With the caution of a rat in a Park Avenue kitchen, I slunk along those cream-colored walls until I came to the rear of the house and the back stairs.

I tiptoed down and entered a large kitchen teeming with expensive looking gadgets and saturated with the smell of baking ham. In a corner was a wine rack. I grabbed the first bottle that came to hand, eased through the back door, crept across a large screened porch and into the back yard.

The bottle tucked under my arm, I plunged into the heavy growth surrounding the shed and headed for the next street. I thought about having a peek in the shed but didn't want to push my luck.

It was almost five when I made it back to Blood Sweat and Black Iron. I locked the bike to the van with the Black Iron logo painted on it and went into the building.

Wading through the noise, the smells, and the glistening, straining muscles, I found CeeCee talking to a grossly muscled young man with a black ponytail and no neck. She was dressed in yellow spandex and pointing to the muscles on her right inner thigh. Arms folded, his face a blank mask of seriousness, the kid with no neck was staring at her thigh and nodding.

Then the kid, apparently enlightened, walked away. I went up to CeeCee and yelled, "Where's Cat?"

She pointed to a steel-framed apparatus festooned with cables and weights. Hanging from the top of a steel beam was the sling. Cat, her head and left front leg hanging out of it, was fast asleep.

CeeCee plucked the sling off the beam, handed it to me, and yelled, "I stretched her good and brushed her teeth again, just to get her used to it. Where the hell were you? I thought maybe I'd inherited a cat."

"I was catching up on some work," I hollered. "Thank you very much for taking care of Cat. May I drop by tomorrow?"

"You may. Want to stick around and do some iron? I won't charge you." I gave her my famous look of disdain and, with Cat snuggled in the sling, fled Blood Sweat and Black Iron.

Slumped on the settee, one hand gripping a mug of Lancers, the other gently kneading Cat's neck, I listened to the wind whisper in the trees and thought about unfulfilled dreams, self-concern, and murder. Later I refilled my mug, took the cover off my ancient Underwood, and started typing.

I leaned the bike against the wall, then stood by the woodstove and stared at the broad back of Betty Worthen. After a moment she raised her head and looked my way. She picked up her coffee and blue cap, lumbered to the last booth, and slid into the back seat. I sat opposite. "Good morning, Betty."

She took off her cap and carefully placed it dead center on the table. "You're going to screw up my day, aren't you, Harry?"

I pulled the sheet of paper out of my sweat jacket pocket, unfolded it, and slid it across the table. Betty gave me a sour look, fished her glasses out of her blouse pocket, stuck them on the end of her nose, and picked up the paper.

She put the paper down, took off her glasses, and savaged her face with both hands. Then she sipped her coffee, gently set the cup down, and in a near whisper said, "Elinor is what? Sixty-five? Sixty-six? And Milt? He's at least that old. The last time I saw them they appeared to be in the very peak of bad health. They eat more than I do." She shook her big head. "What put you onto them?"

I pulled out the key ring. "Elinor gave Bob Kokar this key ring. It has the keys to that station wagon, which is natural since Bob was going to use it to deliver the chest to their house. It has the chest key, which Bob probably slipped on the ring per Elinor's instructions.

"The skeleton key must have been on the ring with the others when Elinor gave them to Bob. And the question I asked myself was, why have a key to your attic or basement on your car key ring?"

Betty grunted. "Because you are planning to kill your brother, stuff him in his new trunk, and hide his dead ass up in the attic, and you want to make sure everything is handy. It would be frustrating if you wanted to lock the body in the attic and couldn't find the key."

"That's what I assume," I said. "Although locking the attic was somewhat unnecessary, since everybody would think Gordon was buried in Connecticut."

"Sure. But you've just killed your brother. He's *up there*, rotting. Locking the door was probably like sealing a tomb; it finalizes the act, gives it distance, and you don't have to think about it so much. Except the key was in Kokar's pocket . . . but I don't think it bothered those two all that much." She picked up the paper and carefully put her cap on. "Well, I'll go slip this under Chief Morin's nose and tell him we have to arrest that nice old couple, the Obermeyers, for murder. That should get his juices flowing."

I grabbed her wrist. "What are you going to say? Or, to put it another way, how are you going to keep me out of it?"

"I'm not sure, probably tell him I did a little private investigation. Somewhat like I did with Duncan Kokar. What you gotta hope is Elinor doesn't mention your visit. She's a bit dim, but your visit and her and Milt's arrest are going to be very close together. If she mentions you, I'll take a shot at covering it."

"The citizens of this fine community will judge you a wise and diligent policewoman."

"Perhaps, but the gods will judge me a lying hypocrite and no doubt punish me accordingly."

"A woman said much the same about me."

"Harry, when it comes your turn to face the gods, I don't want to be anywhere around."

With Cat mewing nervously, I climbed the stairs to CeeCee Dorf-man's apartment and banged on the door. She answered dressed in a baggy gray sweat suit and wearing a tattered yellow headband with PAIN printed on it in bold black letters. I held out Cat and the bottle of sherry I'd stolen from the Obermeyers. "I'll try to make it back before you open."

She took Cat, who immediately calmed down, and looked at the bottle. "Well, well. This stuff costs around forty bucks. Does this mean you've come acourting?"

"It simply means I'm grateful for your kindness to Cat."

As I reached the bottom of the steps, CeeCee yelled, "Hey, Harry." I looked up at her. "This business of yours, does it have to do with that station wagon?"

"Yes, it does."

She stroked Cat. "You're a sneaky bastard, aren't you, Harry?"

I pedaled back to Gretchen's, left the bike against the back wall, and hurried to Winter Street. Turning the corner, I looked down the street and muttered a few strong words, for I was too late. Three police cars were parked in front of the Obermeyers, and Betty Worthen, Chief Morin, and two other policemen were mounting the front steps. I watched as they knocked, waited, knocked again, and were finally let into the house.

Walking like a tourist, I ambled back to Gretchen's and slumped in the last booth. Gretchen put a chilled mug and a carafe of red wine in front of me, slid into the other seat, and lit a cigarette.

"You look kinda squinty-eyed and restless, like some animal that's been hunted for most of the night and is far from the den." Her eyes widened. "Cat? Where's Cat? She's all right, ain't she?"

I nodded. "Cat's fine. She's at CeeCee Dorfman's getting some physical therapy."

She grinned, and blue smoke drifted from between her yellowed teeth. "CeeCee Dorfman, huh. You giving that gal the benefit of your glittering personality?"

I put a shocked look on my face. "Hardly. She's too young and too tough. You know her?"

"She ain't all that young, and if ya look back far enough, you'd see we're kin. I lent her some money so she could buy the town garage and turn it into a gym. Paid me back within the year. How'd you happen to meet CeeCee? Your lifestyles ain't exactly in sync."

"She used to work at Kinch and Kokar, and I found out she's good with cats." I finished my wine and stood. "I have places to go and things to do. Will you keep an eye on the bike for me?"

"Of course I will. That's one of the perks ya get when ya drink at my restaurant. I watch over *all* the bicycles along the back wall."

As I walked past Winter Street, I looked toward the Obermeyer house. One police car was parked in front, and a lone policeman, fenced in by long ribbons of yellow crime scene tape, was pacing back and forth on the porch. I walked a block, turned up Summer Street, and walked until I was opposite the Obermeyer house.

Trying to look like I did it every day, I ambled through the back parking lot of a small apartment house and traced the path across the vacant lot I'd taken yesterday. As I neared the Obermeyers', I scanned the rear windows, didn't notice any faces staring back, so plunged into the thick island of trees and brush surrounding the shed I'd seen from the attic window.

The shed was a garage, and after seventeen years of neglect, about the only reason it was still standing was its sturdy build and a network of thick vines that gripped it in a tight web.

I forced my way along its side to a set of sliding double doors. The top guide wheels had long since rusted to the tracks, but the bottom guides were gone so I pulled one door out and slipped into a moist blackness that smelled like a zoo and reminded me of the walk-in at the senior center.

Pulling out my handy penlight, I flicked it on and cut a narrow swath through the black space. The left side of the garage held an ancient lump of rust that might have once been a riding lawn-mower, a wheelbarrow with a plastic tub that still glowed a faint red and was filled with some sort of muck, and several lumps that probably had once been bags of fertilizer.

The right side held a rusted, grime-encrusted 1976 Plymouth station wagon. The tires had rotted away, and the car had sunk into the dirt floor to the bottom of its doors. I crept to the driver's door, gripped the handle with both hands, put my right foot against the metal, and with the hinges shrieking in protest, forced the door open.

Time and critters had turned the inside of the station wagon into a primitive landscape. As I gingerly crawled into the remains of the front seats, small furry things scurried in every direction.

Finding nothing in the front, I climbed over the seat into the back. The rear seats were folded flat and piled with rank, decayed clothing infested with tiny, squeaking creatures. I had to put my head into that fetid mess, but I found it under a pile of cloth on the floor behind the front passenger seat.

With effort and some noise I managed to get the door closed and slipped out of that dark world. I plowed through the trees and brush, took several deep breaths, and made my way back to Gretchen's, washed up, and reclaimed my bike.

CeeCee Dorfman opened the door, held out Cat, and smirked. "She didn't scream nearly as much as she did the first couple of times. Not that it bothers me. I just duct-tape her mouth shut and keep going."

I narrowed my eyes and said in a low voice, "Your treatment of Cat has not gone unnoticed. A herd of animal lovers are going to descend on this den of pain any minute now."

"No problem. I'll sign them up for a term of Black Iron. When I'm through with them, *they'll* be animals. Listen, I've got to open up. See you tomorrow?"

I nodded, said, "Thanks," and headed down the stairs.

"How's the thing with the station wagon coming?" CeeCee asked.

"It's almost over."

"Listen, you're going to tell me about it, aren't you?"

I stopped at Gretchen's for a mug of motivation to get me home and saw Betty Worthen sitting alone in the last booth drinking coffee. I bought a carafe of wine and slid into the seat beside her. Cat pulled herself out of the sling, sniffed at Betty's empty cup, sat down by the napkin holder, and stared across the room at Gretchen, Bringer of Beef.

Betty picked up the carafe and filled her cup and my mug. Then she held out her cup. I tapped it with the mug, and we drank.

"Rabart was going to sell the house," she said. "He gave them three months to find another place to live. Apparently his new position in Connecticut was the perfect excuse to sever the cord.

"After all those years of good living at Rabart's expense, spending their golden years in a trailer wasn't in the cards. So at five o'clock the morning after the party they helped him load his trunk into the back of the station wagon. When he turned to Milt to give him a last handshake, Elinor pulled Milt's Knights of Columbus ceremonial sword from under the car and rammed it through his chest.

"Now, if you think about it, even if that thing had severed his aorta, it still would have been a terrible minute or so until he died. Chief Morin asked them if they said anything to him while he lay there with three feet of steel through him, and they looked at Morin like he was some kind of lizard."

Betty drank some of her wine. "They unloaded the chest, folded Rabart into it, and hauled it up to the attic. They called Connecticut and told the university that he was killed in a car accident up here. They waited a week, then spread the word and drove down to Connecticut in a rented car for the 'funeral.' While there, they found a printer who made up a newspaper facsimile describing Gordon's accident and sent it up here to the *Gazette,* which printed the thing. They told everyone that Gordon had always wanted to be buried in Connecticut because that's where his parents were buried, which happens to be true."

She poured more wine in her cup and gave me a sideways look. "They have a good lawyer, and tomorrow everybody meets with the D.A. for a plea-bargain session. Gloria Barbara, our new assistant D.A., thinks they'll get five or six years in the locked ward at the county home."

"Five or six years in a county home?"

"This is rural America, Harry. The courts are backlogged into the next century, and the prisons are jammed. And no one in the D.A.'s office wants to be the one to take those two nice, fat, sick old people before a jury of their peers."

We drank in silence for several minutes. Then Betty tapped me on the hand. "We're going to haul the station wagon out of the garage later this afternoon." She smiled thinly. "About an hour ago Donny Pavia, our new gung-ho apprentice patrolman, radioed in that he thought he'd heard someone prowling around back there and wanted to know if he should check it out. I told him to stay on the porch. Didn't want him to waste some curiosity seeker hiding in the trees."

I nodded slowly. "That was probably a good idea."

*

Annie was in her kitchen, but I decided against any theatrics. I backed away from the window and rapped on the door. When she answered, I said, "Perhaps a glass of wine?"

She nodded, stepped back into the kitchen, and ran her hand through hair that looked like it might have been combed last Christmas.

She pushed a pile of magazines off an ancient wood chair painted three different colors and seated me at the kitchen table, which was a cluttered mishmash of cast-iron pans, three working toasters, about six weeks' worth of newspapers, and a wire cage with a sleek looking gerbil in it.

Cat pulled herself out of the sling onto the table and despite her handicaps threaded her way through the junk without bumping into anything, sat down in front of the gerbil's cage, and clamped her good paw on the wire door.

Annie put a water glass full of white wine in front of me. She raised her own glass, and we toasted and drank.

I pulled the package wrapped in brittle gold foil from under my sweat jacket and handed it to her.

She stared at it for a long time, took a sudden deep breath, and looked at me.

I smiled, gently I hoped, and said nothing. She carefully slipped the stiff, mold-blackened ribbon off the package and tried to unwrap the thick gold foil paper. It was too brittle and fell apart in her hands, so she just pushed it off, revealing a cedarwood box. She studied the box, then pried up the clasp. Reaching in, she plucked several small pieces of yellowed pasteboard out of the box and fanned them out like a hand of cards.

She looked at them a few moments and then whispered, "Two tickets to the Boston Museum of Fine Arts for a special showing of modern Impressionists, two tickets to *The King and I,* and two tickets to the new Boston Aquarium."

She raised her glass and gulped down the wine. Then she pushed herself up with both hands, grabbed the bottle off the counter, and refilled her glass.

We sat in the dim, cluttered kitchen. Annie, the tears flowing down her face, gazed at the tickets in her trembling hand. And I looked out the window at the coming night and listened to the distant rumble of thunder.

Finally Annie came around the table, patted my shoulder twice, and shuffled out of the kitchen.

Cat limped over to the edge of the table, fell into my arms, laid her small head against my chest, and meowed softly as thunder rolled over The Farm.

BARBARA D'AMATO

Motel 66

FROM *Murder on Route 66*

June 11, 1971

ABOUT EIGHT MILES south of Bloomington-Normal, June finally convinced Donald to let her drive. At that point they were a hundred and thirty miles away from Chicago. A hundred and thirty miles from home. Donald had crossed the middle line too often, and she was worried about the amount of champagne he had drunk. The secondhand Packard that was her grandfather's wedding gift held the road through sheer weight, tacking slowly like a working sailboat and not much less hefty than a Packard hearse, but there were giant produce trucks with vertical wooden pickets holding loads of asparagus coming the other way, bound to Chicago probably, and June was terrified about what would happen if Donald steered into one head-on.

Once relieved of driving, David picked a champagne bottle off the floor of the back seat and swigged some of it. Donald's brother had put six of the bottles of champagne that had not been drunk into the car, saying "Celebrate!"

"Do you think you should have all that?" she asked, very cautiously, not wanting to start off their marriage sounding like a nag.

"Why, sure, Juney. If I can't drink champagne today, what day can I ever drink it?"

"Well, that's true."

It was getting late and the sun was low. A noon wedding had been followed by the wedding lunch, then the bouquet-throwing, and finally she had changed into this peach-colored suit and matching little hat, and her new wedding hairstyle. She felt glamorous, but the straight skirt was too tight for comfortable driving. She wondered if she should hike it up, but she would feel brazen to have her thighs exposed. Then she thought, "How silly. We're married." But she still didn't hike it up. Somehow it just didn't seem right.

Her mother had insisted on June and Donald having a good solid snack before they left, and it turned out, much as June hated to admit it, her mother had been right. They would really have been hungry by now otherwise. The woman had also put a package of sandwiches wrapped in wax paper in a bag in the back seat and June had eaten a sandwich while Donald drove. He only seemed to want champagne.

They had passed three or four Motel 66s along Route 66 as they headed south. But they had no connection with each other, Donald said. She said, "Maybe they're a chain, like Howard Johnson's."

But Donald said, "No. Howard Johnson's is restaurants. There aren't any motel chains."

She was sure she'd heard of some, but she didn't want to contradict Donald, because he didn't like being contradicted. And anyway it wasn't important.

Motel 66 Motor Court was nice looking, a dozen separate little cabins painted white with navy blue trim. The cabins were plunked down in a horseshoe shape in the middle of open land. Young trees had been planted between each cabin and the next, but they were saplings and didn't soften the flat, featureless landscape much. June thought that the trees were copper beeches. Donald pulled up to a tiny cabin in the center that had an OFFICE sign in front.

"Do you think we need our marriage license?" June said, as she smoothed her skirt before getting out of the car. She had never checked into a motel before — the idea still made her quite nervous — and she had heard bad things.

"No," Donald said.

"But people say they'll wonder if you're really married, and they check to see if you have luggage —"

By then Donald had entered the door of the office and she followed right away, suddenly feeling alone. As she closed the car door, a little rice blew out. Well, if they don't believe it, she thought, there's the proof.

June heard angry voices, quickly cut off. The office was not more than ten feet by ten feet, with a counter topped with linoleum in the center. The same linoleum covered the floor. The office was spotlessly clean, and in fact a teenage girl with a dustpan and broom was digging dust out of the corner where the two far walls came together.

A cash register sat on a card table against the rear wall. A man sat cranking the handle of an adding machine, holding small sheets of paper in his left hand.

"Welcome to Motel 66," said a pink, plump woman in a pink dress sprigged with blue carnations.

Donald said, "Thanks. We'd like a room."

"How many nights?"

"One."

"That'll be six dollars."

June saw Donald wince, thinking this was more than he had expected to pay. She hoped he wouldn't make a fuss.

The woman seemed to want to gloss over the price too, and talked on breezily. "I'm Bertine, and this is Pete. You're lucky you stopped now. We're full up except for two units."

Pete stood up, saying, "Soon as the sign goes on, people start coming off the highway."

Donald peeled six ones from his roll of wedding money. Pete was very handsome, June noticed, and he smiled at her, then actually winked. Immediately she told herself loyally that Donald was a good-looking man too.

Donald reached out for the key, a big brass key attached to a piece of wood into which the number three had been burned with a wood-burning tool. June patted her hair, unfamiliar and somewhat uncomfortable in its new style. Rice flew out onto the counter.

"Oh, gee!" she said.

Bertine said, "Why you're just married!"

June blushed. "That's right."

"That's so exciting. Isn't that exciting, Pete?"

"Sure is. Congratulations."

"On your wedding trip?" Bertine said.

"Yes. My uncle has a house near Los Angeles he's lending us for two weeks. And we're seeing the country, the Painted Desert and the Petrified Forest and everything, as we go."

"Well, isn't that the best!"

June ducked her head, still embarrassed because these people would know it was her wedding night.

The cleaning girl tipped up her dustpan to hold the dust and headed for the side door of the office. As she passed behind Pete and Bertine, Pete casually reached his left hand back and patted her bottom. Donald noticed, but June did not, and Bertine was standing to Pete's right and could not have seen.

Donald seized the key and headed for the door. June followed him quickly, afraid somebody might embarrass her with wedding night jokes.

As the screen door closed behind them, June heard Bertine say cheerily, "There. There's another car turning in. We're full."

"Oh, yeah. That's swell, isn't it?"

"It is, Pete."

June stopped to listen. She was interested in people.

"It is *now*," Pete said. "How about in a couple of years? Once the interstate is in. Huh?"

"Maybe it won't be so bad. You know the government. It could be years before they even get started. Prob'ly will be. Decades, maybe."

"I heard they started a section near Bloomington."

"Well, that's there. This is here."

"I told you we should never've bought here. Goddamn President Eisenhower anyhow!"

His hand on the car door, Donald said, "Come on, Juney."

As Donald drove the car over to cabin three, June whispered, "They've been arguing."

Donald said, "Obviously. But it's not our problem."

"Oh, no. Of course not."

"We're on our honeymoon," Donald said. He didn't say anything about Pete patting the cleaning girl.

It was past eight-thirty P.M. now, and the sun was setting.

The cabin was as spotless inside as the office had been. The decor was fake rustic, with red and green plaid linoleum, wood-look wallboard, and a white ceiling with wooden beams. June knew the beams were hollow. Her parents had exactly the same thing in their rec room. But she liked it.

The bathroom didn't quite match. All the fixtures were pink.

June said, "This is so exciting. I know I'm just a silly romantic, but here I am getting married in June and my name is June. It's almost like it's *meant*."

"Most people get married in June."

"Yes. That's true." This was not the answer she'd hoped for. She'd rather he'd said something like, "It feels like it was meant for me too." Not wanting to be argumentative, she said, "Well, not everybody's name is June."

Donald picked up a bottle of champagne and went to the bathroom to get a glass. "Pete and Bertine must've got a real deal on pink porcelain," he said, coming out. He poured the glass full.

"Uh — should we go get dinner?" June asked. "There's the Moon Shot Restaurant across the street. Just behind the Phillips 66."

"I'm not hungry. Are you?"

"No, I ate a sandwich."

"Then let's go to bed."

Timidly, June picked up her overnight case — white leather, a gift from her aunt Nella — and went into the bathroom. She showered, then splashed on lilac-scented body lotion. A gift from her niece Peggy.

Embarrassed, thrilled, and a little giddy all at the same time, she took the top item from the overnight case. It was a beautiful lace nightgown, with ruffles at the hem and neckline. The girls from the Kresge five-and-dime where June worked had pooled their money and bought it for her. There were some other gifts at the shower that were embarrassing, but June had pretended to be too sophisticated to notice, and if she hadn't blushed so hard, it would have worked. One of the girls confessed that she had actually "done it" with her boyfriend, and the others glanced at one another, thinking, but not saying, that she was a fallen woman.

The nightgown was a lovely orchid color. There had been much laughing at the shower, when two of the girls insisted it was lilac and would "go" with Peggy's lilac scent. Three of them said the color was orchid, and June herself kept saying lavender, and they all giggled. A satin ribbon in darker orchid was threaded through eyelets around the neckline and tied in a bow in front. June wondered briefly if she would look like a candy box, but then thought, no, it was beautiful, and it went well with her dark hair. She slipped it down over her shoulders, wiggled it over her hips, smoothed everything into place with nervous hands, and stepped out of the bathroom.

Don lay on the bed, on top of the bedspread, asleep in his clothes.

"Donald?" He didn't stir. "Donald? Here I am."

He still didn't stir, so she touched his shoulder. The glass on the night table was empty. Half of the new bottle of champagne was gone.

"Don?"

Mumbly, he said, "Don' bother —"

June sat down in the only chair in the room, a chair with wooden arms and an upholstered plaid seat and back, and watched Don sleep. After forty-five minutes or so, she tried to wake him again, but he didn't even mumble. She stood and gazed out the window; it was long since dark, and there was no moon.

After a few tears had run down her cheeks, June went to the large suitcase and found some cheese crackers her mother had shoved in at the last minute. She spent another half hour munching them slowly, then tried waking Don again. When that didn't work, she got a glass of water, drank it one swallow at a time, then took dungarees and a sweater from her suitcase, changed out of the lovely nightgown, which she draped carefully across the back of the chair — the extra care was intended to contain her anger — and went out for a walk.

An hour and a half later, June came back to the room. She let herself in quietly. Don was not there. Feeling guilty, she went into the bathroom and took a shower. When she got out, she looked at herself in the mirror. It was very mysterious, she thought, that you didn't really know who anybody was, not even yourself. "Serves you right, Don," she whispered. Twenty minutes later he turned up.

His eyes were bloodshot. His hair was stiff and stringy, as if he'd been used upside down as a floor mop. She knew he was hung over, but she didn't want to mention it. Instead she said uneasily, "Where have you been?"

He said, "You weren't here." She didn't respond to that. He said, "I went for a walk."

"Where?"

"Over to the Moon Shot."

"But it closed at ten."

"All I said was I walked over there. I didn't say it was open!"

"Oh."

"And then I walked around a while!"

June and Donald woke up early, even though Donald had a hangover and couldn't open his eyes all the way. They dressed silently, facing away from each other, each not wanting to catch the other's eye. They walked together to the office to return the key.

Finally, Donald said, "Sorry about last night."

Thinking for a few seconds, to try to decide whether she was about to lie or be honest, June finally said, "Me too."

Bertine was alone in the office.

June said, "Well, thanks. It was a — it was a really nice cabin."

"Sure thing," Bertine said, but her eyes were red and puffy and she dragged her feet. It took her several seconds to focus on her job. "Have a happy life," she said. "Come visit again someday."

Donald got behind the wheel of the car. June said soberly, "I guess they've been fighting again."

June 6, 1985

From the back seat, Jennifer, who was seven years old, said, "Why can't we stay at a Holiday Inn? They have a swimming pool."

Donald said, "This is your mother's idea. Not mine. I can think of a lot of better places to be."

June said, "We're having a nostalgia trip."

Don Jr. said, "Well, it's your nostalgia. It's not ours."

They pulled off Interstate 55 onto a deteriorated road that once had been Route 66, running parallel to the interstate. They bumped over potholes so crumbly they must have been unpatched for years. Ahead they saw two concrete islands, four big metal caps over ground pipes, and a shell of the old gas station, two oil bays inside still visible as long narrow depressions with a central hole for the hydraulic lift. There was no sign whatever of the Moon Shot Burgers and Fries. The motel still stood — twelve cabins with beech trees shading them from the summer sun. The cabins were painted white with red trim. The red enamel paint was peeling and the matte white looked chalky and cheap.

June said, "Look, Don, they've changed the name. Now it's the Route 66 Motor Inn."

"This is soooo bogus!" Jennifer said. But she was a nice child, really, and didn't grumble when they stopped the car, even though the place didn't appear to be very prosperous.

Donald said, "A Holiday Inn would be better. Let's go find one."

June said, "No."

Don Jr., usually called Donny, said, "This looks weird."

Donny was thirteen years old. They'd had a fertility problem between Donny and Jennifer, but fortunately nothing permanent. Donny was just starting to make his growth spurt. He hoped by next fall, when he went back to school, he'd discover he'd caught up with the girls in his class, most of whom had put on their growth spurt last year.

He's growing so fast, June thought, studying her gangly child. She could have sworn those pants and the sleeves of the shirt fit when they left Chicago. That was all of six hours ago. Now his wrists stuck out an inch and his ankles an inch and a half. He'd gone up one shoe size a month for the last six months and everybody said feet started to grow first, then the legs. Thank God Donald was a hard-working man.

"Why didn't you go to Florida or something on your honeymoon?" Donny asked.

"Well, partly we had never seen the country. Especially the West. And partly your uncle Mort had a house near Los Angeles that he was going to loan us for two weeks."

"The price was right," Donald said. "Free."

June said, "We had this big old car that your great-grandfather gave us. You'd have laughed at it, Donny."

"Yeah. I wish you'd've kept it."

"Can't keep everything," Donald said.

"You remember your great-grandfather, Donny?"

"Not really. He used to ride me in his wheelbarrow, didn't he?"

Getting out of the car, June said, "We took five days to drive to L.A. We saw the Painted Desert in Arizona, for one thing. And in Amarillo, Texas, we saw a real cattle drive."

Jennifer said, "Big deal."

Donny said, "Why not Las Vegas?"

"We didn't have any money. You kids have been much more fortunate than we were, you know. Thanks to your dad being a good provider." Well, perhaps he was a little possessive, a little rigid too, but maybe being solid meant you had to be rigid.

"We always hear that."

"Well, we didn't have any money, but we saw a lot of the wild West."

Jennifer said, "That's okay, Mom. You're entitled to a life."

"We took Route 66 all the way from Chicago to L.A. Did you know there was even a TV show once about Route 66?"

Looking at the potholed road, Jennifer said, "Route 66 isn't here anymore."

"Neither is George Washington," June said. "But we still study him."

All four of them walked into the central cabin, the one with the OFFICE sign above the door. Donald pulled out his credit card. He had three and was proud of them.

June took one look at the woman behind the cash register. "Why, you're still here!" The woman was older, tougher, plumper, and more frayed.

"Do I know you?"

"You're Betty — no, Bertha —"

"Bertine."

"We were here nearly fifteen years ago. June 11, 1971."

"Oh, my God. The newlyweds!"

Donald said, "Come on, Juney. Let's get a key and go."

June said, "Bertine, do you really remember somebody who was here that long ago? I mean, I remember you and your husband, but it was my wedding trip. Everything was important. You must have a dozen new people here every day."

"Mmm, well, now that I see you, I sort of remember." She hesitated. "Actually it wasn't like every other day."

"Why?"

"I might as well tell you. Pete was killed that night."

"Oh!" June felt shock, even though Pete wasn't anything to her, of course. Not really. She could hardly even picture Pete in her mind's eye anymore, which seemed wrong. She ought to remember him. Handsome, she thought, but she somehow confused him in her mind with Robert Redford. "Was he in an accident?"

"He was beaten to death with a rock. Behind the old Moon Shot Restaurant."

"Oh, my God!"

"He never came home that night. I thought he was — um — was out, you know, somewhere. They found him when the Moon Shot opened for lunch."

"Who did it?"

"I don't know. We never found out. A drifter, I guess. The cops asked about who was here, in the cabins, you know, so I told them all about everybody. But none of you had anything to do with us. We'd never seen any of you before. They talked with the people who worked for us, but nothing came of it. Just nobody a-tall had a motive. I guess it was just one of those things. He was only twenty-eight."

Since each "cabin" had only one room and one big bed, they took two cabins next to each other, number three and number four. Donald and Donny took number four and June and Jennifer took three.

"Jeez, this is truly bogus!" Jennifer said when they unlocked their door and she saw the tiny room. June thought it didn't seem as clean as she remembered it.

From one door away, Donny said to Jennifer, "Hey! I think it's excellent. How many times do you get to visit the scene of a murder?"

"Get inside, Donny," Donald said.

"But, Dad, let's go look at where it happened! She said over by where the restaurant was. Maybe we can find a clue."

"We are *not*," Donald said, veins beginning to stand out on his face, "going to ruin our vacation. And we are not going to say *one more word about murder!*"

June 27, 1999

The sign on Interstate 55 said HISTORIC ROUTE 66! EXIT! HERE!

Just past it, there was a second sign: STAY AT HISTORIC ROUTE 66 MOTEL! ORIGINAL! NOT REBUILT!

And a third sign: SATELLITE BURGERS! JUKEBOXES! MALT SHOP! ONE BLOCK ON RIGHT!

As they came to the exit, a series of six signs in a long row swept past them saying,

!ROUTE 66 AUTO MUSEUM!
SIT IN A REAL 1956 BUICK CENTURY — TWO TONE!
DRIVE AN EDSEL!

Smaller letters under the Edsel offer read: OUR CURATOR MUST ACCOMPANY YOU.

CHEVY BEL AIR — NOT ONE, NOT TWO, THE COMPLETE LINE!
FORD FAIRLANE!

The last sign was shaped like a long hand with a pointing finger and added, ARTIFACTS!NEWSPAPERS! NEIL ARMSTRONG WALKS ON MOON! ORIGINAL FRONT PAGES AND BLOW-UPS! 500 HUBCAPS 500!

It was all so different, with its effort at trying to be the same, June thought. And here we are, back here again, and again the reason is a wedding.

Donny, who was twenty-seven, had dropped out of college after a year, gone to work for a concrete company, then decided building wooden forms and troweling ready-mix was not a lifetime career for him. He had just graduated from the University of Champaign in computer engineering. In his last year he'd met Deborah Henry, who'd been in several classes with him. On June thirtieth they were getting married in St. Louis, where Deborah's family lived.

One more chance, June thought, to drive part of their old, sentimental route.

Jennifer, who was twenty and a junior at Yale, had said, "I'll fly to St. Louis. I did your nostalgia trip once and once was enough."

It wasn't all malt shops and gas-guzzling cars and jukeboxes, June thought. It wasn't romance. It was a lack of options. Her children really believed she was nostalgic. Children were so simpleminded when it came to parents. She was not nostalgic. If she was looking for anything, it was understanding. A search. Who was I then and why?

What a funny, naive little thing I was when we first came here, she thought, uneasily. Brought up with virtually no knowledge

of sex and those unreasonable expectations. All twitterpated at
the idea of my wedding night. It was such a big deal. Not like these
kids.

She remembered Don's anger a couple of years ago when they
found condoms in Jennifer's drawer. Fathers can be so unrealistic.
And when June tried to tell him condoms were a good thing, and
that she had already talked with both children about them, he
yelled, "My mother didn't even know the *word* 'condom' and if she
had, she would never have uttered it in my presence."

"I'm sure, dear," June had said mildly.

They pulled into the Motel 66 driveway.

"Dad, can I take the car over to that museum shop? They might
have moon landing stuff. Memorabilia."

"Absolutely not. If you want the car, I'll go with you."

Donny, who'd been through this before, said indulgently, "Yeah,
Dad. I know. What's yours is yours." To June he said, "Mom, it's
only two blocks. I'll walk fast over there and see what they've got.
Five minutes."

"Just three minutes," Donald said. "We need to find a place
to eat."

Historic Motel 66 was surrounded by recently mowed bright green
grass. Huge beech trees shaded the cabins, except for a gap down
toward the end, where a cabin was missing and half a tree remained
next to the space, a split trunk leaning eastward. Lightning, June
thought.

The bright white and blue paint looked new. The colors struck a
chord in June's memory, but she couldn't quite be sure.

She and Donald entered the office. The old cash register was
back. The walls were covered with black and white blow-ups of Motel 66, each meticulously dated, and a professionally produced sign
above them read, THE HISTORY OF MOTEL 66!

Behind the counter stood a trim white-haired woman in a black
power suit over a sapphire blue silk shirt.

June said, "Oh! Isn't Bertha, uh, Ber — um, isn't she here anymore?"

"I'm Bertine."

"Bertine! I wouldn't have known you!"

Bertine smiled. "I figured if I was gonna spruce up the place I'd spruce up myself too. I kind of remember you, honey, but not quite."

"We're what you called the newlyweds. From 1971. June 11, 1971."

"Oh." Bertine's eyes clouded for a few seconds. "I have to say, I've brought the place along a bit since then. Pete would still recognize it, though."

"It looks great!"

"Well, I'm doing okay. This isn't a way to get rich. But I make decent money. Now. It was hard going for a while."

Donald pulled out his credit cards. "Let me get the keys," he said. "We've gotta go eat."

Bertine said, "See, I have the old cash register, but I hardly know how to take cash anymore. My accountant says never take cash and surely never let any of the help take cash." She laughed. "There's a fragment of Route 66 from Oklahoma City to Vinita, Oklahoma, if you're touring. And a piece of historic 66 in Albuquerque."

June said, "We're not going to L.A. this time. Just St. Louis."

She thought about Uncle Mort, who had loaned them his house. Uncle Mort had run off with a girl he met at his health club, where he was working out because his doctor told him to. The girl was a cardio-fitness trainer, but June's mother would still have called her a flibbertigibbet, if June's mother were still alive.

June walked over to the photo blow-ups. One showed the construction of the cabins and was dated March 27, 1969. One showed a line of late-sixties cars on the curved driveway near the motel office.

Bertine walked over to the photos behind her. June had stopped in front of a big photo of Bertine and Pete, holding hands under a MOTEL 66 sign at the door of the brand-new office.

Donald said, "Come on, Juney. I'm hungry."

"Poor Pete," Bertine said, but June's back was rigid and she didn't turn around.

Donny came bursting in, shouting, "I got a reproduction 1969 *New York Times* moon landing page. Debbie's gonna think it's real fun." When he entered, Bertine caught sight of him and she froze, staring.

Donny came to a stop next to the photo of Pete, age probably twenty-seven.

For a second, Bertine looked back and forth between the photo and Donny.

Bertine tried to ask June something, but the words caught in her throat. It was something like "no motive." June made a small whimpering sound. Then she turned in fear to Donald.

When she saw the expression on his face, she started to scream.

GEARY DANIHY

Jumping with Jim

FROM *Ellery Queen's Mystery Magazine*

I'M LOOKING for a parking spot. I'm also laughing at myself. I feel like a character out of a novel written back when honor was still a believable, even compelling, motivation, and I'm not sure if I want to feel this way, or even if it's safe to, given my line of work.

Yesterday, after I had my last lunch with Nora Davison, I went home, sat down, and just thought. What she had said, especially about the captain on the ship, kept coming back to me. All I could think of was a book I had read back in college called *Lord Jim*. It was mainly about a guy, an officer on a freighter, who tries to live down something he's not even sure he actually did.

He thought the ship he was on was sinking. There were all these pilgrims on board, trying to get to Mecca, and one moment this guy Jim's up on the ship and the next he's down in the lifeboat with the rest of the crew, and he's not sure how he got there. Did he jump? Did he fall over? Was he pushed? He just doesn't know. Bad enough, but then the ship doesn't sink. When the crew finally gets into port there's their ship, already back and safe. Jim gets cashiered or something, and he goes off and tries to atone, to get his honor back. People did that back then.

I finally find a place to park my car. I lock it, then open the trunk and pull out the briefcase. I slam the trunk closed and head for the office complex where Mr. Bradley Davison works. As I walk, swinging the briefcase, I can feel the weight of the gun inside shift back and forth. I start to laugh at myself again.

I normally don't handle maritals. Too messy, often too confusing. Insurance fraud I understand. People running away, not wanting to be found, as natural as the sun rising and setting. Industrial espionage? Hey, it's the American way. But maritals, well, they just take too many zigs and zags; no one's ever sure what's happening or why, least of all me.

However, this one was different. This time the wife didn't want to nail the husband, she wanted to protect him. Different. Enough so that after several moments of listening to some part of my brain scream, "Don't do it. Don't do it!" I agreed to take the case.

The fact that I really liked how Mrs. Bradley Davison looked and spoke, how her eyes seemed to absorb what I was saying, as if she truly believed I had something interesting or important to say, might have had something to do with it. Some women look at a man and calculate the quickest way to make him feel small. Other women make their men feel they can go one-on-one with Michael Jordan, and maybe even win. Later, when I thought about our first meeting, I realized she had stirred something in me that I hadn't felt in a long time. I wasn't sure exactly what that was, but it felt good.

After I agreed to take the case, I let her tell her story. It appeared Bradley Davison was being blackmailed, or at least that's what Nora believed. She had found a briefcase hidden in the garage when she had gone looking for some paint thinner. She had opened the briefcase and discovered a lot of money: hundred-dollar bills, banded, neatly arranged.

"It frightened me at first, like I'd just found a dead rat, or something that had plague virus spread all over it," she said, rubbing her hands against her skirt. "All that money in our garage. It was like I was an actress in this weird movie, standing there with the briefcase open, all that money just pulsating, and meanwhile in the background I can hear Rosie O'Donnell on our TV, making wisecracks. And I can hear the audience laughing. It was surreal."

She didn't ask me if I knew what surreal meant. I was liking her more and more.

She had put the briefcase back where she had found it, then debated the rest of the day whether to question her husband. Undecided, she had let it slide that evening. The following morning, after Bradley had left for work, she had gone back out to the garage. The briefcase was gone.

"I think he's in trouble, Mr. Taylor, and I want you to help him.

He's been a good father, a good provider. I don't want to see him hurt."

She didn't complete the thought. Nothing about him being a good husband, or about her loving him. I had a feeling Nora Davison had learned not to lie about things that were really important to her.

I'm sure Bradley Davison started out a good man. We all do. Where we end up, well, that used to be determined by character. These days, I'm not so sure what it's determined by. Maybe the Fates, maybe the Dow Jones. Who knows.

Bradley Davison was a senior vice president of an international communications company, one of those high-profile, charm-the-investors-with-technology kind of companies that barged into second-, third-, and tenth-world nations and helped them upgrade their internal phone systems from the can-and-string level so drug dealers and arms traders could communicate more efficiently.

He traveled a lot, mostly to Eastern Europe, which meant that his mind had been broadened and that he'd probably also had a lot of opportunities to dip his paw into many of the lucrative polluted streams that flowed over there. Chaos always breeds opportunity, and more chaos.

Given the fact that we're all now global villagers, people in my line of work need to know other people in the same line of work all over the world. We do things for each other, saving on travel expenses and the embarrassment of ordering the wrong dishes in foreign restaurants. I had contacts in South America, the Far East, Australia, and Europe; all very helpful, plus their phone numbers made my personal phone book look very sophisticated.

I placed a call to Frère Jacques (Jacques Chevalier, my very own Continental Op) and gave him the particulars on Mr. Bradley Davison and his company. Jacques was busy, but he said he would look into it as soon as he could. *Merci, mon frère.* Then I started the process of checking up on Mr. Davison back home in the good old U.S. of A., my stomping grounds.

Ah, sweet information. Today it's all available, if you know the right people (most of them nerds you wouldn't have spoken to when you were in high school) and are liberal with your checkbook (in this case, Nora Davison's checkbook). It turned out that Mr.

Davison had made three recent visits to his bank, where he had a safe-deposit box in (significant point) his name only. Each visit had been made (another significant point) on the fifteenth of the month. Today was the thirteenth (a significant possibility immediately arose).

More information. Mr. Davison's phone book (or, most likely, his electronic organizer) was apparently even more sophisticated than mine. His phone records showed that he had a lot of acquaintances in Bulgaria, Albania, Romania, and a couple of the "-stans" that hadn't even existed several years ago. These acquaintances apparently preferred being called in the morning, while they were chomping on goat cheese and dunking their peasant bread in cups of ox-blood tea, or else Bradley suffered from insomnia. He had made most of these calls from his home between two and four in the morning. I faxed the permanent phone numbers to Frère Jacques and then set out to get a better look at Mr. Bradley Davison.

He was a good-looking man, a little over six feet tall, with the kind of prep-school hair that easily slipped down over his forehead, giving him a boyish, pixie kind of look women used to adore. He dressed a little too conservatively for my taste, all tailored grays, power ties, and always correct, if a bit retro, wingtip shoes. But then again, I wasn't pulling down the same bucks he was.

I picked him up several blocks from his house and followed, two cars behind. Traffic was fairly light on the four-lane suburban artery we were traveling on. I knew the address of the executive complex where he had his office, so I wasn't really concerned about losing him. My eye was briefly caught by a gaggle of geese flying in bomber pattern, heading off for winter vacation. I looked back down and Bradley was gone. Damn.

I eased over into the right lane, then into a doughnut shop's parking lot. I got out, scratched my head, and looked in the four cardinal directions. South did the trick. There was Bradley's dark green Ford Expedition parked in a lot two buildings down. Frank Taylor, ace detective, strikes again. I locked my car and walked.

It was a long, two-story building, with stores on the first floor, offices on the second. Kartuchian's Oriental Rugs; above it the Delaware Casualty Company. Scandinavian Accents; above it, PharmPhresh Foods, Inc. (I bet). Shoes 4-U; above it, TMG International Trading. I chose door number three.

I went into Shoes 4-U and immediately became interested in a line of lady's black heels arranged near the window. I've always loved the way heels shape women's calves. I spent five minutes on my inspection and was starting to get worried that the store manager might have me ejected for having a too-obvious shoe fetish when Bradley came out the door that led upstairs to TMG International Trading. He walked to his Expedition and opened the driver's door. Then he placed his hands on the jamb above the door and rested his head on them. He either had a very bad hangover, or very big troubles.

He stayed that way for several seconds, then pushed himself upright and got into his car. He pulled out into traffic and drove off, leaving me holding a stylish, open-toed, sling-back model with a three-inch heel. Lovely. I reluctantly put it down, went outside, and copied down what TMG International Trading particulars there were, then walked back to my car and headed off to Bradley's office complex.

It was time to make my first report, something that could probably have been done over the phone, but that's not why I had taken the case. Phones are so impersonal.

I met Nora Davison at one of my watering holes, The Rusty Bucket. Local, good steaks and burgers, waitresses who knew what I ate and drank and also knew when I was working and left me alone. I took a booth in the back and waited. I was early.

She was on time. I had described her to Frank, the day manager, so as soon as she came in he greeted her and escorted her back to my booth. She slid in opposite me and gave me a tentative smile.

"Drink?" I asked.

"Too early for a martini?"

"It's never too early for a martini," I replied. I ordered, and then considered my client. Short brown hair in a cute cut; large brown eyes in an oval face that seemed made to support a smile; slightly bowed lips and a chin some might consider a bit small but I thought was just fine. She had on a simple white dress with matching white jacket, its sleeves rolled up several times to reveal thin porcelain forearms.

Our drinks arrived. "Cheers," we both said and clinked. She took a decent pull, then set her glass down and looked up at me.

"Gory details?"

"Not yet, just some slightly smudged information."

I quickly told her what I had found out — the withdrawals, the phone calls — and what I was preparing to do. She listened quietly while I spoke, her eyes never once looking down or away. When I finished she sat back and sighed.

"Oh, Bradley, you dumb cluck," she said, sadness rather than anger in her voice. I remained quiet, fingers on the stem of my glass.

"About a year ago," she began, sitting forward and taking possession of her glass, "he started to change. It was like he got on an emotional roller coaster. He'd come back from a trip and he'd be way up there. He was signing deals and making a lot of money. Then, a few days later, he'd start to slide, and by the end of the week he'd be down in the dumps, sitting in his chair in the den, drinking double scotches and staring into the fireplace. Sometimes, he didn't even have a fire on. I tried to talk with him, but he kept on saying he was okay. Working too much, maybe, but he was okay."

She took another sip, then sighed again.

"What about in the last few months?" I asked.

"Worse. There weren't any more highs, just lows. He used to be really involved with the girls, go to their soccer games, go out bike riding with them. He'd even take them out to movies sometimes, said it was going on a date with two of his best girls. That all stopped. Now, he hardly even speaks to them."

I nodded. I was beginning to dislike Mr. Bradley Davison a great deal. Nora brought her hands to her forehead and kneaded the skin, then she dropped her hands and looked at me.

"Mr. Taylor, you'll help him, won't you? He may be a little weak sometimes, but he doesn't deserve what he's going through. He doesn't."

"Mrs. Davison," I said, "I don't know what your husband is involved in yet. Some things I can do, others are out of my control."

She nodded. She understood. There might not be any salvation for her husband. Her eyes got very bright. I had to look away. Some guys just don't know how lucky they are.

When I got back there was a message from Frère Jacques on my machine. I checked the time. Late evening in Paris. I dialed his number and he answered on the third ring.

"*Bonjour, mon frère.* How are things in the city of light?"

"*Bonsoir, mon ami.* They are delightful, as they should be. I assume you received my message." I told him I had. "Well, it seems that your Monsieur Davison is not a very nice man."

"Do tell," I said, not too surprised that I was glad to hear this. "What's he been up to?"

Women. Women down on their luck because the countries they lived in were down on their luck. Women with few talents or skills who needed to eat, or who had families, elderly parents, young children who needed to eat. Women who had only one thing to sell, themselves.

It seemed that, on the side, Bradley Davison was a glorified international assistant pimp, an arranger, the man with the money, the guy who paid the bills and made the arrangements so the girls could fly out of their countries and travel thousands of miles to end up posing for nude pictures to feed the Internet's voracious appetite, or working as crib girls, or even worse, just disappearing. Big business, a lot of money, and a whole hell of a lot of suffering.

I mentioned TMG International Trading to Jacques. He said he hadn't come across the name yet but would check it out. It probably didn't matter. I had a feeling I knew what TMG traded in. I asked him if the police over there were interested in Davison and Jacques replied that as far as he knew, not yet. Jacques had gotten his information from other sources — the competition, in fact. To them, Davison was a small fish in a sea where only sharks mattered.

I thanked Jacques and we wished each other a good evening, but I wasn't sure if I would be able to oblige; I was thinking about Davison: a nice home, a wonderful wife, apparently two great children, and still, he becomes a misery peddler. Go figure.

It was the fifteenth of the month. I followed Bradley when he left his house. He drove straight to his office. I sat in my car, keeping an eye on his Expedition but not really expecting him to go anywhere. The bank he did business with had a branch right in the office complex and that's where he had his private stash. Mr. Davison was a man who liked things convenient.

Around eleven-thirty I got out and walked through the parking lot, taking my time. Inside the complex I stopped at a news kiosk and studied the magazines and papers. I purchased the latest *Time*, then walked over to the shoe-shine stand that faced the elevators as well as the indoor entrance to the bank, sat up on the throne, and gave my shoes a treat.

Eight minutes later, as I was appreciating the rhythmic snapping of the soft cloth as it put a final high shine on my right shoe, the elevator doors opened and Mr. Bradley Davison appeared, briefcase in hand. He went through the bank's glass doors, turned right, and headed for the small room that contained the safe-deposit boxes. Five minutes later he was back out, briefcase still in his hand. He walked to the elevator doors. As if cued, they opened and Bradley disappeared. I paid for the shine, stepped down, and walked over to a bank of phones. I dialed Nora Davison's number. When she answered, I identified myself. She paused. I could hear her take a deep breath, then she asked what she could do for me.

"Did your husband tell you that he'd be late tonight?" I asked.

"Yes," she said, "he called just a little while ago. He said there were a couple of people in from Bulgaria or somewhere and he had been asked to take them out this evening. He said he probably wouldn't be back until after midnight."

"Thanks," I said.

"Is something happening?" she asked. "Is Brad in any danger?"

"I don't know," I answered truthfully. "I think he's going to make another payoff tonight. He's made them before and apparently nothing happened. No reason to think anything will this time."

"No reason to kill the golden goose," she said, her voice fragile.

"Something like that," I said.

"You'll be watching him, won't you?" she said, her voice rising.

"Yes, I'll probably be around somewhere."

"Don't let anything happen to him, Mr. Taylor. Please."

I didn't know what to say. I didn't like Bradley Davison. I didn't like how he made his extra pocket money. In my mind, it was simple poetic justice that someone was blackmailing him. He was getting what he deserved. Maybe he deserved a lot more for all the pain and suffering he had helped to cause.

"Nothing will happen to him," I said before I even knew the words were out of my mouth.

We were in a Ruby Tuesday's about a mile from Davison's offices. He sat at the bar, working on his third scotch. I was at one of the small stand-up counters along the wall, sipping on my Coke, watching him. He was an unhappy man who obviously didn't want to be late for an appointment. He kept on checking his watch every few minutes, and in between he'd cast worried glances up at the large neon clock that hung over the bar's cash register. When he wasn't busy with the time, he kept patting the briefcase that sat on his lap.

Ten minutes later we were out of there. I had a tight tail on him. The evening traffic was still heavy and I didn't think there was any chance he'd catch on that I was behind him. I was just another set of headlights in his rearview mirror. We got on the expressway and headed east. I turned my radio to a jazz station and settled back, following Bradley's lead. We swept through the city on the elevated portion of the expressway and took the service branch that led to only one place: the airport. When the airport's exit came up I followed him down the ramp and into short-term parking. He pulled a ticket from the machine, the gate went up, and he drove through and turned right. I followed and turned left, keeping an eye on his car in my rearview mirror.

I actually got to the terminal before him. I was studying the Arrivals board when he walked through the automatic doors, briefcase in his right hand. Years ago, I would have assumed I was about to see a drop made in one of those public storage bins, the ones you feed quarters, shove your bag into, then lock with a little red key. However, these days, most airports have done away with them. Too easy to stash a bomb and just walk away.

I followed Bradley. He stopped at a Chik-Filet stand to check the time, then proceeded down the hall and stepped inside a bar area called The Flight Line, where everybody took off before they took off.

The bar was crowded. A lot of airports have also banned smoking, fearing, I guess, that people's lungs might explode right there in the lounge and there'd be a nasty lawsuit. Our airport was still this side of smoker civility: it allowed people to light up in the bars. Hence, the crowd. Added to the usual number of people who needed a couple of pops just to get on a plane were the smokers, some stoking up on nicotine prior to boarding, others just having gotten off and reacquainting their lungs with carbon monoxide and other valuable gases.

Bradley looked around. Several tables were open, but there was no room at the bar. This apparently didn't please Bradley. He shifted his weight from one foot to the other, looked at his watch, then glared at the occupied stools. I was less demanding. I went to one of the tables. A woman with tired eyes and varicose veins came up and took my order. I had been good long enough. One beer and some popcorn wouldn't dull my keen detecting skills. As the lady walked away, a man in a leather bomber jacket punched out his cigarette and pushed his stool back from the bar. Bradley was next to the stool before the guy could turn. The guy said something to Bradley, who took a step back, then hopped up onto the stool as soon as the guy cleared.

The waitress brought my beer. I paid, then grabbed a basket, opened the glass doors of a red and yellow popcorn cart, and scooped up a healthy helping. Back at my table, I commenced crunching and sipping as I wondered how Bradley was going to make the drop. Airports don't like storage bins, and they don't like packages, bags, or briefcases left around unattended. Security people are very paranoid these days.

I was enjoying my fourth or fifth handful of popcorn when Bradley stood, a scotch in front of him on the bar, the briefcase at his feet. He said something to the bartender, then turned and started walking in my direction. I almost choked on my popcorn.

He never glanced my way. Instead, he went directly to the popcorn cart, grabbed a basket, and opened the doors. He scooped up some kernels, waited a second, then dropped them back in. Then he scooped up some more, and dropped them in again. Picky eater. I was so fascinated, I almost missed the pickup. Just in time, I realized Bradley was stalling. I jerked my eyes back to the bar and Bradley's briefcase was in the hands of a small man who was moving briskly out of the bar. I stood and passed Bradley, who was still sifting. Out in the corridor I looked for my man. He was halfway down the hall, moving with the flow. I followed.

There was no way I would be able to tail this guy once he got to wherever his car was, but there probably wasn't any need. From the quick look I'd had of him, with his Eddie Bauer windbreaker and his cord trousers, I had a feeling I wasn't dealing with a crime cartel here. If I could get his license plate, I had him.

We were outside. I followed as he walked toward One Hour Parking. A real sport, but then, he had twenty grand in the brief-

case. I took out my car keys and held them in my hand. We were in
the lot; I let him go down a row and followed down the next. He
stopped once, looked around, stared at me, then looked away as I
kept walking, jingling my keys. He stopped at a Lexus, beeped off
the anti-theft, tossed the briefcase inside (what the hell, it was just
another twenty thousand), and got in. He drove by me as I was
leaning over attempting to unlock the door of an '88 Mustang.

ZBE 976. Thank you very much. I straightened up when I saw
him pull up to the exit booth. I was standing at a terminal pay
phone, punching in Nora's number, when I saw Bradley go
through the exit doors and out into the night.

She answered and I said, "He's all right. He's heading home."

"Thank you," she said.

I hung up, then stood there questioning my motive for making
that call. Did I want her to think I was responsible for her husband
getting home safe tonight? That I was some kind of hero? What did
I want from Nora Davison? What did I want from myself?

The following day I had the information I needed. Mr. Franklin
Saunders. 1229 Columbia Boulevard, apartment 2G. One of the
city's newest luxury condos. Mr. Saunders was doing quite well for
himself. Then again, he was being subsidized.

Unauthorized entry into these luxury condos is tough. Again,
with nerds and money on your side, anything's possible, but in this
case neither was necessary. The gods have a funny way of working.

A Ms. Melissa Parker, only daughter of Mr. James Parker, a major
player in the commodities market (very big into pork bellies) had
gotten herself into a little trouble involving some cocaine and a
boyfriend who eventually turned state's evidence. I had assisted the
lovely Ms. Parker in extricating herself from a fling that could have
turned into a nightmare. Her father had been very thankful. As for
the gods? Well, Ms. Parker, bless her soul, just happened also to live
at 1229 Columbia Boulevard, in apartment 3B.

I placed a call to Papa Porkbelly. A half-hour later I received a
call from Ms. Parker, inviting me over for cocktails.

At seven-fifteen I walked through the condo's front entrance carrying a red and green shopping bag from the high-priced specialty
market a block up from the condos. Sticking out was the top of a
wine bottle and an impressive baguette. I gave my name to the

front security guard. He called up to Ms. Parker's luxury apartment and was informed that the lady couldn't wait to see me. He gave me a wink as he indicated where I could find the elevators.

I was quickly deposited on the third floor and greeted by Ms. Parker, resplendent in red hair blown dry by a windstorm, a tight-fitting green cocktail dress, and heels the likes of which I hadn't seen since my foray into Shoes 4-U. She smiled and stepped aside. I went in and set the bag on a table, reached in, and pulled out a Ruger Redhawk .357 with a 7.5-inch barrel.

"Oh, my," Ms. Parker cooed, a smirk on her face.

"Don't even start," I said. "There's some pâté in there, as well as some good-looking Brie. Enjoy." I waved at her as I went out the door, slipping the Ruger into my jacket.

Down to the second floor via the fire stairs: I found apartment 2G, rang the bell, and stepped to the side so the little security camera set discreetly above the door didn't have a good angle on me.

"Who's there?" a voice crackled over the intercom next to the door.

"Really sorry to bother you, Mr. Saunders," I said, trying to get as much contrition into my voice as I could. "Peterson with building security. We're checking all the units. We've got a report about a possible gas leak."

I didn't know if he was going to buy it. Frankly, I wouldn't.

"Only take a minute," I said, not sure whether I was gilding the lily. I heard several locks click, then the door handle turned and there was Mr. Franklin Saunders in the doorway, the original trusting soul.

I personally don't like big handguns. Too unwieldy. Too noisy. Too messy. But everyone's seen *Dirty Harry,* and there's no sense not taking advantage of the Eastwood mystique. I didn't own a .44 Magnum, Dirty Harry's choice, but I didn't think Franklin Saunders would know the difference. He didn't. When I pulled out the Ruger Redhawk he was immediately impressed. When I suggested a conversation, he readily agreed.

I left Mr. Saunders's apartment thirty minutes later. In that time we had become quite intimate. For one thing, I'd learned how he'd stumbled onto Bradley Davison's little sideline: he'd been part of it.

Saunders was a pilot. Before coming into his newfound wealth, he had flown for one of the charter outfits that used to ferry the women out of their homelands. He had twice seen Bradley Davison deliver women to the airport. He had taken pictures. He had made notes. Definitely a man who planned for his future.

I collected the photos he had surreptitiously taken of Bradley and some of the girls, as well as copies of photos of the same girls he had downloaded from several of the Internet smut sites. I also liberated a newspaper article showing photos of a dead Romanian girl who had been found in Marseilles with her throat slit. Saunders had a shot of Bradley standing with the same girl, arm around her shoulder, apparently wishing her bon voyage.

What Franklin Saunders had that I couldn't take away with me was what was inside his head, plus his obvious inclination to use it to better himself. I explained to Mr. Saunders, displaying the Ruger Redhawk for emphasis, that I had been given an option by my employer. I could test how Saunders's head responded to a .357 round, or he could keep the money he'd already received and give me a "Swear to God and hope to die" promise to cease and desist. It was Mr. Saunders's option. Not surprisingly, he chose the latter. I complimented him on choosing wisely, switched the Ruger from my right hand to my left, and drove my fist into his stomach. He doubled over, then dropped to the plush white living-room carpet.

As I kneeled down, the gun barrel resting in front of his eyes, I whispered into his ear: "You go near Bradley Davison again, call him, write him a letter, send him an e-mail or even a singing tele-gram, I'll come back. I'll hit you, Mr. Saunders. I'll hurt you, and then I'll kill you. Do you understand me?"

Curled in a fetal position, he was still able to nod. I patted him on the shoulder, stood, and gathered up my little cache of black-mail goodies. On my way out of the building, I visited Ms. Parker long enough to collect my bag and drop in my gun, then I rode the elevator down and wished the security man a good evening.

We met again at The Rusty Bucket. Our booth. She was wearing a red turtleneck tucked into jeans that favored her immensely. Two martinis stood between us. I watched her pick hers up and sip at it.

"It's all over, Mrs. Davison," I said, my left hand resting on the briefcase that sat next to me on the banquette. Inside was my haul from Franklin Saunders's apartment.

She put the glass down, her brown eyes investigating my face, perhaps trying to read something more than I was willing to show.

"What was it all about?" she asked, her eyes still on me.

I fingered the briefcase lock. She needed to know. What she did with the information was her business, but I couldn't let her walk out without knowing what her husband had gotten himself into, the kind of man he was, what he was willing to do for money. I put pressure on the lock and it clicked open. This was going to hurt her, but in the long run she'd be better off. That's what I told myself.

"You know, it's funny," Nora said, pulling the glass toward her. "When you first get married, you don't realize how important history is, the history you and your husband are going to make."

"What do you mean?" I asked, my hand still on the top of the briefcase.

"You ever been married, Mr. Taylor?"

"For about fifteen minutes."

She shook her head. "Then you never had time for the history to kick in. See, you start out thinking you have everything in common. Then time goes by and you realize you have nothing in common, but you go along with it anyway because the memories start building up. Your first apartment, your first fight, some vacations, some holidays. A mother dying, a father going through cancer."

She played with the base of her martini glass.

"Brad saw both of our children being born, saw them even before I did. We've been through chicken pox and broken bones and even a car accident. It all starts to add up and become something more than just two people, just a marriage; it becomes, I don't know, maybe like a museum, where all these things are on display, things that you expect to have around, maybe even need to have around. They tell you who you are."

She stopped, took a sip of her martini, then just looked at me.

"Your husband's no prize," I said, "but I guess you know that." My stomach was churning.

"I've known it for a long time, Mr. Taylor."

"But there's history, right?"

"Yes, the museum, and I'm one of the caretakers — no, maybe one of the trustees. Whatever. Anyway, there's responsibility there.

The kind you might not really want, but there you are. You've got it. Like the captain of a ship, maybe. Even though you think the ship might start sinking, you stay aboard. You know what I mean?"

My hand fell away from the briefcase. I knew what she meant. I didn't agree, but I understood.

So now I'm walking toward Bradley's office complex, briefcase in hand. Inside is my little treasure trove and the Ruger. I'm about to drop in unannounced on Mr. Bradley Davison and have a little chat. I don't know if he'll listen to me, or if he will even care about what I have to say, but it's the least I can do for Nora.

Franklin Saunders has been neutered. But he was never really the threat. He wasn't what Bradley was worried about when he rested his head against the side of his Expedition after he came out of TMG International Trading. Those boys play a rougher game than Franklin Saunders. They're right up there with Attila the Hun and Vlad the Impaler. You irritate them, like I think Bradley has irritated them, and they'll come after you, your wife, your kids, and your canary. They don't care. There are no rules in their world, except the ones they make up right before they pull out their knives.

Earlier this morning, I went down to my basement and pushed around some old boxes. I found my college copy of *Lord Jim*. I blew the dust off, wiped away some cobwebs, and brought it upstairs. I poured some coffee and sat at the kitchen table thumbing through the book, noting passages I had underlined back when the world was simpler and I didn't have so many scars. I thought about what I would have done in Jim's place. Jump? Who knows. And if I did, would I then seek redemption? Find my lost honor? Did such a thing matter anymore, or even exist?

I'm still thinking about that as I stand in front of the elevators, waiting for a brass door to slide open and whisk me up to where they cut deals, not throats. Will Bradley Davison listen? Does it matter? I don't think he's cut out to handle his playmates with the knives. It's not his type of game. And sooner or later, they'll come after him and his family. They'll come after Nora.

There are only two ways to stop them. One is to make Bradley Davison go away, permanently. The other is to make TMG International Trading go away permanently.

You never know what you'll do when you think the ship's sinking. Some people jump, others stay. The thing about staying is, you never get a chance to do it again. You just go down once. Maybe that's the point. If you're going to stay, going to go down, you might as well do it right, with a little class.

Maybe, after my little talk with Bradley, I'll price out some leather boots, the ones with those killer heels that remind you there's always a little pain mixed in with love. Yeah, as I remember, Shoes 4-U is having a sale. Then maybe I'll go upstairs and show them to the boys at TMG. Find out their opinions on love, and pain.

JEFFERY DEAVER

Triangle

FROM *Ellery Queen's Mystery Magazine*

"MAYBE I'LL GO to Baltimore."

"You mean . . ." She looked at him. "To see . . ."

"Doug," he answered.

"Really?" Mo Anderson asked and looked carefully at her fingernails, which she was painting bright red. He didn't like the color but he didn't say anything about it. She wouldn't listen to him anyway.

"I think it'd be fun," he continued.

"Oh, it would be," she said quickly. "Doug's a fun guy."

"Sure is," Pete Anderson said. He sat across from Mo on the front porch of their split-level house in suburban Westchester County. The month was June and the air was thick with the smell of the jasmine that Mo had planted earlier in the spring. Pete used to like that smell. Now, though, it made him sick to his stomach.

Mo inspected her nails for streaks and pretended to be sort of bored with the idea of him going to see her friend Doug. But she was a lousy actor; Pete could tell she was really excited by the idea and he knew why. But he just watched the lightning bugs and kept quiet. Unlike Mo, he *could* act.

"When would you go?" she asked.

"This weekend, I guess. Saturday."

They were silent and sipped their drinks, the ice clunking dully on the plastic glasses. It was the first day of summer and the sky wasn't completely dark yet even though it was nearly nine o'clock in the evening. There must've been a thousand lightning bugs in their front yard.

"I know I kinda said I'd help you clean up the garage," he said, wincing a little, looking guilty.

"No, I think you should go. I think it'd be a good idea," she said.

I *know* you think it'd be a good idea, Pete thought. But he didn't say this to her. Lately he'd been thinking a lot of things and not saying them.

Pete was sweating — more from excitement than from the heat — and he wiped the sweat off his face and his round buzz-cut blond hair with his napkin.

The phone rang and Mo went to answer it.

She came back and said, "It's your *father*," in that sour voice of hers that Pete hated. She sat down and didn't say anything else, just picked up her drink and examined her nails again.

Pete got up and went into the kitchen. His father lived in Wisconsin, not far from Lake Michigan. He loved the man and wished they lived closer together. Mo, though, didn't like him one bit and always raised a stink when Pete wanted to go visit. She never went with him. Pete was never exactly sure what the problem was between Mo and his dad. But it made him mad that she treated the man so badly and would never talk to Pete about it.

And he was mad too that Mo seemed to put Pete in the middle of things. Sometimes Pete even felt guilty he *had* a father.

He had a nice talk but hung up after only ten minutes because he felt Mo didn't want him to be on the phone.

Pete walked out onto the porch.

"Saturday," Mo said. "I think Saturday'd be fine."

Fine . . .

Then she looked at her watch and said, "It's getting late. Time for bed."

And when Mo said it was time for bed, it was definitely time for bed.

Later that night, when Mo was asleep, Pete walked downstairs into the office. He reached behind a row of books resting on the built-in bookshelves and pulled out a large, sealed envelope.

He carried it down to his workshop in the basement. He opened the envelope and took out a book. It was called *Triangle* and Pete had found it in the true-crime section of a local used-book shop after flipping through nearly twenty books about real-life murders.

Pete had never ripped off anything, but that day he'd looked around the store and slipped the book inside his windbreaker, then strolled casually out the door. He'd *had* to steal it; he was afraid that — if everything went as he'd planned — the clerk might remember him buying the book and the police would use it as evidence.

Triangle was the story of a couple in Colorado Springs. The wife was married to a man named Roy. But she was also seeing another man — Hank — a local carpenter. Roy found out and waited until Hank was out hiking on a mountain path, then he snuck up beside him and pushed him over the cliff. Hank grabbed onto a tree root but he lost his grip — or Roy smashed his hands; it wasn't clear — and Hank fell a hundred feet to his death on the rocks in the valley. Roy went back home and had a drink with his wife just to watch her reaction when the call came that Hank was dead.

Pete didn't know squat about crimes. All he knew was what he'd seen on TV and in the movies. None of the criminals in those shows seemed very smart and they were always getting caught by the good guys, even though *they* didn't really seem much smarter than the bad guys. But that crime in Colorado was a smart crime. Because there were no murder weapons and very few clues. The only reason Roy got caught was that he'd forgotten to look for witnesses.

If the killer had only taken the time to look around him, he would have seen the witnesses: A couple of campers had a perfect view of Hank Gibson plummeting to his bloody death, screaming as he fell, and of Roy standing on the cliff, watching him . . .

Triangle became Pete's bible. He read it cover to cover — to see how Roy had planned the crime and to find out how the police had investigated it.

Tonight, with Mo asleep and his electronic airline ticket to Baltimore bought and paid for, Pete read *Triangle* once again, paying particular attention to the parts he'd underlined. Then he walked back upstairs, packed the book in the bottom of his suitcase, and lay on the couch in the office, looking out the window at the hazy summer stars and thinking about his trip from every angle.

Because he wanted to make sure he got away with the crime. He didn't want to go to jail for life — like Roy.

Oh, sure there were risks. Pete knew that. But nothing was going to stop him.

Doug had to die.

Pete realized he'd been thinking about the idea, in the back of his mind, for months, not long after Mo met Doug.

She worked part-time for a drug company in Westchester — the same company Doug was a salesman for, assigned to the Baltimore office. They met when he came to the headquarters for a sales conference. Mo had told Pete that she was having dinner with "somebody" from the company, but she didn't say who. Pete didn't think anything of it until he overheard her tell one of her girlfriends on the phone about this interesting guy she'd met. But then she realized Pete was standing near enough to hear and she changed the subject.

Over the next few months, Pete realized that Mo was getting more and more distracted, paying less and less attention to him. And he heard her mention Doug more and more.

One night Pete asked her about him.

"Oh, Doug?" she said, sounding irritated. "Why, he's just a friend, that's all. Can't I have friends? Aren't I allowed?"

Pete noticed that Mo was starting to spend a lot of time on the phone and on-line. He tried to check the phone bills to see if she was calling Baltimore but she hid them or threw them out. He also tried to read her e-mails but found she'd changed her password. Pete was an expert with computers and easily broke into her account. But when he went to read her e-mails he found she'd deleted them all.

He was so furious he nearly smashed the computer.

Then, to Pete's dismay, Mo started inviting Doug to dinner at their house when he was in Westchester on company business. He was older than Mo and sort of heavy. But Pete admitted he was handsome and real slick. Those dinners were the worst . . . They'd all three sit at the dinner table and Doug would try to charm Pete and ask him about computers and sports and the things that Mo obviously had told Doug that Pete liked. But it was real awkward and you could tell he didn't give a damn about Pete. He just wanted to be there with Mo, alone.

By then Pete was checking up on Mo all the time. Sometimes he'd pretend to go to a game with Sammy Biltmore or Tony Hale but he'd come home early and find that she was gone too. Then she'd come home at eight or nine and look all flustered, not expecting to find him, and she'd say she'd been working late, even though she was just an office manager and hardly ever worked later than five before she met Doug. Once, when she claimed she was at the office, Pete got Doug's number in Baltimore and the message said he'd be out of town for a couple of days.

Everything was changing. Mo and Pete would have dinner together but it wasn't the same. They didn't have picnics and they didn't take walks in the evenings. And they hardly ever sat together on the porch anymore and looked out at the fireflies and made plans for trips they wanted to take.

"I don't like him," Pete said. "Doug, I mean."

"Oh, quit being so jealous. He's a good friend, that's all. He likes both of us."

"No, he doesn't like me."

"Of course he does. You don't have to worry."

But Pete did worry, and he worried even more when he found a piece of paper in her purse last month. It said: *D.G. — Sunday, motel 2 p.m.*

Doug's last name was Grant.

That Sunday morning Pete tried not to react when Mo said, "I'm going out for a while, honey."

"Where you going?"

"Shopping. I'll be back by five."

He thought about asking her exactly where she was going but he didn't think that was a good idea. It might make her suspicious. So he said cheerfully, "Okay, see you later."

As soon as her car had pulled out of the driveway he'd started calling motels in the area and asking for Douglas Grant.

The clerk at the Westchester Motor Inn said, "One minute, please, I'll connect you."

Pete hung up fast.

He was at the motel in fifteen minutes and, yep, there was Mo's car parked in front of one of the doors. Pete snuck up close to the room. The shade was drawn and the lights were out, but the window was partly open. Pete could hear bits of the conversation.

"I don't like that."

"That . . . ?" she asked.

"That color. I want you to paint your nails red. It's sexy. I don't like that color you're wearing. What is it?"

"Peach."

"I like bright red," Doug said.

"Well, okay."

There was some laughing. Then a long silence. Pete tried to look inside but he couldn't see anything. Finally, Mo said, "We have to talk. About Pete."

"He knows something," Doug was saying. "I know he does."

"He's been like a damn spy lately," she said, with that edge to her voice that Pete hated. "Sometimes I'd like to strangle him."

Pete closed his eyes when he heard Mo say this. Pressed the lids closed so hard he thought he might never open them again.

He heard the sound of a beer can opening.

Doug said, "So what if he finds out?"

"So *what?* I told you what having an affair does to alimony in this state. It *eliminates* it. We have to be careful. I've got a lifestyle I'm accustomed to."

"Then what should we do?" Doug asked.

"I've been thinking about it. I think you should do something with him."

"Do something with him?" Doug had an edge to his voice too. "Get him a one-way ticket . . ."

"Come on."

"Okay, sorry. But what do you mean by 'do something'?"

"Get to know him."

"You're kidding."

"Prove to him you're just a friend."

Doug laughed and said in a soft, low voice, "Does *that* feel like a friend?"

She laughed too. "Stop it. I'm trying to have a serious talk here."

"So, what? We go to a ball game together?"

"No, it's got to be more than that. Ask him to come visit you."

"Oh, that'd be fun." With that same snotty tone that Mo sometimes used.

She continued, "No, I like it. Ask him to come down. Pretend you've got a girlfriend or something."

"He won't believe that."

"Pete's only smart when it comes to computers and baseball. He's stupid about everything else."

Pete wrung his hands together. Nearly sprained a thumb — like the time he jammed his finger on the basketball court.

"That means I have to pretend I like him."

"Yeah, that's *exactly* what it means. It's not going to kill you."

"You come with him."

"No," she said. "I couldn't keep my hands off you."

A pause. Then Doug said, "Oh, hell, all right. I'll do it."

Pete, crouching on a strip of yellow grass beside three discarded soda cans, curled into a ball and shook with fury. It took all his willpower not to scream.

He hurried home, threw himself down on the couch in the office, and turned on the game.

When Mo came home — which wasn't at five at all, like she promised, but at six-thirty — he pretended he'd fallen asleep.

That night he decided what he had to do and the next day he went to the used-book store and stole the copy of *Triangle*.

On Saturday Mo drove him to the airport.

"You two gonna have fun together?" In the car she lit a cigarette. She'd never smoked before she met Doug.

"You bet," Pete said. He sounded cheerful because he was cheerful. "We're gonna have a fine time."

On the day of the murder, while his wife and her lover were sipping wine in a room at the Mountain View Lodge, Roy had lunch with a business associate. The man, who wished to remain anonymous, reported that Roy was in unusually good spirits. It seemed his depression had lifted and he was happy once more.

Fine, fine, fine . . .

At the gate Mo kissed him and then hugged him hard. He didn't kiss her but he hugged her back. But not hard. He didn't want to touch her. Didn't want to be touched by her.

"You're looking forward to going, aren't you?" she asked.

"I sure am," he answered. This was true.

"I love you," she said.

"I love you too," he responded. This was not true. He hated her. He hoped the plane left on time. He didn't want to wait here with her any longer than he had to.

But the flight left as scheduled.

The flight attendant, a pretty blond woman, kept stopping at his seat. This wasn't unusual for Pete. Women liked him. He'd heard a million times that he was cute. Women were always leaning close and telling him that. Touching his arm, squeezing his shoulder. But today he answered her questions with a simple "yes" or "no."

And kept reading *Triangle*. Reading the passages he'd underlined. Memorizing them.

Learning about fingerprints, about interviewing witnesses, about footprints and trace evidence. There was a lot he didn't understand, but he did figure out how smart the cops were and that he'd have to be very careful if he was going to kill Doug.

"We're about to land," the flight attendant said. "Could you put your seat belt on, please?"

She squeezed his shoulder and smiled at him.

He put the seat belt on and went back to his book.

Hank Gibson's body had fallen one hundred and twelve feet. He'd landed on his right side and of the more than two hundred bones in the human body, he'd broken seventy-seven of them. His ribs had pierced all his major internal organs and his skull was flattened on one side.

"Welcome to Baltimore, where the local time is twelve-twenty-five," the flight attendant said. "Please remain in your seat with the seat belt fastened until the plane has come to a complete stop and the pilot has turned off the FASTEN SEAT BELT sign. Thank you."

The medical examiner estimated that Hank was traveling eighty miles an hour when he struck the ground and that death was virtually instantaneous.

Welcome to Baltimore . . .

Doug met him at the airport. Shook his hand.

"How you doing, buddy?" Doug asked.

"Okay."

This was so weird. Spending the weekend with a man that Mo knew so well and that Pete hardly knew at all.

Going hiking with somebody he hardly knew at all.

Going to kill somebody he hardly knew at all . . .

He walked along beside Doug.

"I need a beer and some crabs," Doug said as they got into his car. "You hungry?"

"Sure am."

They stopped at the waterfront and went into an old dive. The place stunk. It smelled like the cleanser Mo used on the floor when Randolf, their Labrador retriever puppy, made a mess on the carpet.

Doug whistled at the waitress before they'd even sat down. "Hey, honey, think you can handle two real men?" He gave her the sort of grin Pete'd seen Doug give Mo a couple of times. Pete looked away, somewhat embarrassed but plenty disgusted.

When they started to eat Doug calmed down, though that was more likely the beers. Like Mo got after her third glass of Gallo in the evenings. Doug had at least three that Pete counted and maybe a couple more after them.

Pete wasn't saying much. Doug tried to be cheerful. He talked and talked but it was just garbage. Pete didn't pay any attention.

"Maybe I'll give my girlfriend a call," Doug said suddenly. "See if she wants to join us."

"You have a girlfriend? What's her name?"

"Uhm, Cathy," he said.

The waitress's nametag said: *Hi. I'm Cathleen.*

"That'd be fun," Pete said.

"She might be going out of town this weekend." He avoided Pete's eyes. "But I'll call her later."

Pete's only smart when it comes to computers and baseball. He's stupid about everything else.

Finally Doug looked at his watch and said, "So what do you feel like doing now?"

Pete pretended to think for a minute and asked, "Anyplace we can go hiking around here?"

"Hiking?"

"Like any mountain trails?"

Doug finished his beer, shook his head. "Naw, nothing like that I know of."

Pete felt rage again — his hands were shaking, the blood roaring in his ears — but he covered it up pretty well and tried to think. Now, what was he going to do? He'd counted on Doug agreeing to whatever he wanted. He'd counted on a nice high cliff.

But then Doug continued. "But if you want to be outside, one thing we could do, maybe, is go hunting."

"Hunting?"

"Nothing good's in season now," Doug said. "But there's always rabbits and squirrels."

"Well —"

"I've got a couple of guns we can use."

Guns?

Pete said, "Okay. Let's go hunting."

*

"You shoot much?" Doug asked him.

"Some."

In fact, Pete was a good shot. His father had taught him how to load and clean guns and how to handle them. ("Never point it at anything unless you're prepared to shoot it.")

But Pete didn't want Doug to know he knew anything about guns so he let the man show him how to load the little .22 and how to pull the slide to cock it and where the safety was.

I'm a *much* better actor than Mo.

They were in Doug's house, which was pretty nice. It was in the woods and it was a big house, all full of stone walls and glass. The furniture wasn't like the cheap things Mo and Pete had. It was mostly antiques.

Which depressed Pete even more, made him angrier, because he knew that Mo liked money and she liked *people* who had money even if they were idiots, like Doug. When Pete looked at Doug's beautiful house he knew that if Mo ever saw it then she'd want Doug even more. Then he wondered if she *had* seen it. Pete had gone to Wisconsin a few months ago. Maybe Mo had come down here to spend the night with Doug.

"So," Doug said. "Ready?"

"Where're we going?" Pete asked.

"There's a good field about a mile from here. It's not posted. Anything we can hit we can take."

"Sounds good to me," Pete said.

They got into the car and Doug pulled onto the road.

"Better put that seat belt on," Doug warned. "I drive like a crazy man."

The field looked familiar to Pete.

As Doug laced up his boots, Pete realized why it was familiar. It was almost identical to a field in White Plains — the one across the highway from the elementary school. The only difference was that this one was completely quiet; the New York field was noisy. You heard a continual stream of traffic.

Pete was looking around.

Not a soul.

"What?" Doug asked, and Pete realized that the man was staring at him.

"Pretty quiet."

And deserted. No witnesses.

"Nobody knows about this place. I found it by my little old lonesome." Doug said this real proud, as if he'd discovered a cure for cancer. "Lessee." He lifted his rifle and squeezed off a round.

Crack . . .

He missed a can sitting about thirty feet away.

"Little rusty," he said. "But, hey, aren't we having fun?"

"Sure are," Pete answered.

Doug fired again, three times, and hit the can on the last shot. It leapt into the air. "There we go!"

Doug reloaded and they started through the tall grass and brush. They walked for five minutes.

"There," Doug said. "Can you hit that rock over there?"

He was pointing at a white rock about twenty feet from them. Pete thought he could have hit it but he missed on purpose. He emptied the clip.

"Not bad," Doug said. "Came close the last few shots." Pete knew he was being sarcastic.

"So, what? We go to a ball game together?"

"No, it's got to be more than that. Ask him to come visit you."

"Oh, that'd be fun."

Pete reloaded and they continued through the grass.

"So," Doug said. "How's she doing?"

"Fine. She's fine."

Whenever Mo was upset and Pete'd ask her how she was she'd say, "Fine. I'm fine."

Which didn't mean fine at all. It meant, I don't feel like telling you anything. I'm keeping secrets from you.

They stepped over a few fallen logs and started down a hill.

The grass was mixed with blue flowers and daisies. Mo liked to garden and was always driving up to the nursery to buy plants. Sometimes she'd come back without any and Pete began to wonder if on those trips she was really seeing Doug instead. He got angry again. Hands sweaty, teeth grinding together.

"She get her car fixed?" Doug asked. "She was saying that there was something wrong with the transmission."

How'd he know that? The car broke down only four days ago. Had Doug been there and Pete didn't know it?

Doug glanced at Pete and repeated the question.

Pete blinked. "Oh, her car? Yeah, it's okay. She took it in and they fixed it."

But then he felt better because that meant they *hadn't* talked yesterday or she would have told him about getting the car fixed.

On the other hand, maybe Doug was lying to him now. Making it *look* as if she hadn't told him about the car when they really had talked.

Pete looked at Doug's pudgy face and couldn't decide whether to believe him or not. He looked sort of innocent but Pete had learned that people who seemed innocent were sometimes the most guilty. Roy, the husband in the *Triangle* book, had been a church choir director. From the smiling picture in the book, you'd never guess he'd kill a soul.

Thinking about the book, thinking about murder.

Pete was scanning the field. Yes, there . . . about fifty feet away. A fence. Five feet high. It would work just fine.

Fine.

As fine as Mo.

Who wanted Doug more than she wanted Pete.

"What're you looking for?" Doug asked.

"Something to shoot."

And he thought: Just witnesses. That's all I'm looking for.

"Let's go that way," Pete said and walked toward the fence.

Doug shrugged. "Sure. Why not?"

Pete studied it as they approached. Wood posts about eight feet apart, five strands of rusting wire.

Not too easy to climb over, but it wasn't barbed wire like some of the fences they'd passed. Besides, Pete didn't want it *too* easy to climb. He'd been thinking. He had a plan.

Roy had thought about the murder for weeks. It had obsessed his every waking moment. He'd drawn charts and diagrams and planned every detail down to the n'th degree. In his mind, at least, it was the perfect crime.

Pete now asked, "So what's your girlfriend do?"

"Uhm, my girlfriend? She works in Baltimore."

"Oh. Doing what?"

"In an office."

"Oh."

They got closer to the fence. Pete asked, "You're divorced? Mo was saying you're divorced."

"Right. Betty and I split up two years ago."

"You still see her?"

"Who? Betty? Naw. We went our separate ways."

"You have any kids?"

"Nope."

Of course not. When you had kids you had to think about some-body else. You couldn't think about yourself all the time. Like Doug did. Like Mo. Pete was looking around again. For squir-rels, for rabbits, for witnesses. Then Doug stopped and he looked around too. Pete wondered why, but then Doug took a bottle of beer from his knapsack and drank the whole bottle down and tossed it on the ground. "You want something to drink?" Doug asked.

"No," Pete answered. It was good that Doug'd be slightly drunk when they found him. They'd check his blood. They did that. That's how they knew Hank'd been drinking when they got the body to the Colorado Springs hospital — they checked the alcohol in the blood.

The fence was only twenty feet away.

"Oh, hey," Pete said. "Over there. Look."

He pointed to the grass on the other side of the fence.

"What?" Doug asked.

"I saw a couple of rabbits."

"You did? Where?"

"I'll show you. Come on."

"Okay. Let's do it," Doug said.

They walked to the fence. Suddenly, Doug reached out and took Pete's rifle. "I'll hold it while you climb over. Safer that way."

Jesus . . . Pete froze with terror. Doug was going to do exactly what Pete had thought of. He'd been planning on holding Doug's gun for him. And then when Doug was at the top of the fence he was going to shoot him. Making it look like Doug had tried to carry his gun as he climbed the fence but he'd dropped it and it went off.

Roy bet on the old law enforcement rule that what looks like an accident probably is an accident.

Pete didn't move. He thought he saw something funny in Doug's eyes, something mean and sarcastic. It reminded him of Mo's ex-pression. Pete took one look at those eyes and he could see how much Doug hated him and how much he loved Mo.

"You want me to go first?" Pete asked. Not moving, wondering if he should just run.

"Sure," Doug said. "You go first. Then I'll hand the guns over to you." His eyes said: You're not afraid of climbing over the fence, are you? You're not afraid to turn your back on me, are you?

Then Doug was looking around too.

Looking for witnesses.

"Go on," Doug encouraged.

Pete — his hands shaking from fear now, not anger — started to climb. Thinking: This is it. He's going to shoot me. I left the motel too early! Doug and Mo must have kept talking and planned out how he was going to ask me down here and pretend to be all nice and then he'd shoot me.

Remembering it was Doug who suggested hunting.

But if I run, Pete thought, he'll chase me down and shoot me. Even if he shoots me in the back he'll just claim it's an accident.

Roy's lawyer argued to the jury that, yes, the men had met on the path and struggled, but Hank had fallen accidentally. He urged the jury that, at worst, Roy was guilty of negligent homicide.

He put his foot on the first rung of wire. Started up.

Second rung of wire . . .

Pete's heart was beating a million times a minute. He had to pause to wipe his palms.

He thought he heard a whisper, as if Doug were talking to himself.

He swung his leg over the top wire.

Then he heard the sound of a gun cocking.

And Doug said in a hoarse whisper, "You're dead."

Pete gasped.

Crack!

The short, snappy sound of the .22 filled the field.

Pete choked a cry and looked around, nearly falling off the fence.

"Damn," Doug muttered. He was aiming away from the fence, nodding toward a tree line. "Squirrel. Missed him by two inches."

"Squirrel," Pete repeated manically. "And you missed him."

"Two goddamn inches."

Hands shaking. Pete continued over the fence and climbed to the ground.

"You okay?" Doug asked. "You look a little funny."

"I'm fine," he said.

Fine, fine, fine . . .

Doug handed Pete the guns and started over the fence. Pete debated. Then he put his rifle on the ground and gripped Doug's gun tight. He walked to the fence so that he was right below Doug.

"Look," Doug said as he got to the top. He was straddling it, his right leg on one side of the fence, his left on the other. "Over there." He pointed nearby.

There was a big gray lop-eared rabbit on his haunches only twenty feet away.

"There you go!" Doug whispered. "You've got a great shot."

Pete shouldered the gun. It was pointing at the ground, halfway between the rabbit and Doug.

"Go ahead. What're you waiting for?"

Roy was convicted of premeditated murder in the first degree and sentenced to life in prison. Yet he came very close to committing the perfect murder. If not for a simple twist of fate, he would have gotten away with it.

Pete looked at the rabbit, looked at Doug.

"Aren't you going to shoot?"

Uhm, okay, he thought.

Pete raised the gun and pulled the trigger once.

Doug gasped, pressed at the tiny bullet hole in his chest. "But . . . But . . . No!"

He fell backwards off the fence and lay on a patch of dried mud, completely still. The rabbit bounded through the grass, panicked by the sound of the shot, and disappeared in a tangle of bushes that Pete recognized as blackberries. Mo had planted tons of them in their backyard.

The plane descended from cruising altitude and slowly floated toward the airport.

Pete watched the billowy clouds, tried to figure out what they looked like. He was bored. He didn't have anything to read. Before he'd talked to the Maryland state troopers about Doug's death, he'd thrown the true-crime book about the Triangle murder into a trash bin.

One of the reasons the jury convicted Roy was that, upon examining his house, the police found several books about disposing of evidence. Roy had no satisfactory explanation for them.

The small plane glided out of the skies and landed at White Plains airport. Pete pulled his knapsack out from underneath the seat in front of him and climbed out of the plane. He walked down the ramp, beside the flight attendant, a tall black woman. They'd talked together for most of the flight.

Pete saw Mo at the gate. She looked numb. She wore sunglasses and Pete supposed she'd been crying. She was clutching a Kleenex in her fingers.

Her nails weren't bright red anymore, he noticed.

They weren't peach either.

They were just plain fingernail color.

The flight attendant came up to Mo. "You're Mrs. Jill Anderson?"

Mo nodded.

The woman held up a sheet of paper. "Here. Could you sign this, please?"

Numbly Mo took the pen the woman offered and signed the paper.

It was an unaccompanied-minor form, which adults had to sign to allow their children to get on planes by themselves. The parent picking up the child also had to sign it. After his parents were divorced Pete flew back and forth between Wisconsin and White Plains so often he knew all about airlines' procedures for kids who flew alone.

"I have to say," she said to Mo, smiling down at Pete, "he's the best-behaved youngster I've ever had on one of my flights. How old are you, Pete?"

"I'm ten," he answered. "But I'm going to be eleven next week."

She squeezed his shoulder, then looked at Mo. "I'm so sorry about what happened," she said in a soft voice. "The trooper who put Pete on the plane told me. Your boyfriend was killed in a hunting accident?"

"No," Mo said, struggling to say the words, "he wasn't my boyfriend."

Though Pete was thinking: Of course he was your boyfriend. Except you didn't want the court to find that out because then Dad wouldn't have to pay you alimony anymore. Which is why she and Doug had been working so hard to convince Pete that Doug was "just a friend."

Can't I have friends? Aren't I allowed?

No, you're not, Pete thought. You're not going to get away with dumping me the way you dumped Dad.

"Can we go home, Mo?" he asked, looking as sad as he could. "I feel real funny about what happened."

"Sure, honey."

"Mo?" the flight attendant asked.

Mo, staring out the window, said, "When he was five Pete tried to write 'Mother' on my birthday card. He just wrote M-O and didn't know how to spell the rest. It became my nickname."

"What a sweet story," the woman said and looked like *she* was going to cry. "Pete, you come back and fly with us real soon."

"Okay."

"Hey, what're you going to do for your birthday?"

"I don't know," he said. Then he looked up at his mother. "I was thinking about maybe going hiking. In Colorado. Just the two of us."

EDWARD FALCO

The Instruments of Peace

FROM *Playboy*

THE KID drove up in a chartreuse sports car. Convertible. He arrived with the top down, his dark hair windblown, a small gold ring in his right ear. When he stepped out of that car in my driveway, wearing blue jeans and a red T-shirt, my sixteen-year-old daughter went ghost pale and leaned back against the wall by the living room window. I was in the kitchen making breakfast, scrambling eggs in a pink bowl with a wire whisk. I could see my daughter's back, and beyond her, through the window, Chad Barnnett, the youngest son of a well-known criminal. He was tall — six-one, maybe six-two — broad-chested and muscular. I had agreed to give him a job for the summer. We lived in the boondocks on a small farm where we stabled standardbreds from the racetrack ten miles away toward town. It was just me and my daughter. Her mother had left me before Amy had turned three.

"Oh my God," Amy said when she could finally speak. "Is that him?"

"Seems likely." I put the eggs down on the stove and joined her at the window. Chad appeared to have decided he was at the right place. He pulled a lightweight jacket out from behind the front seat, slipped it on, and started up the walk to the front door.

Amy bolted for her room. It was a little after nine and she'd been out of bed for an hour, though she hadn't showered and cleaned up yet. She stopped at the stairs and pointed to me emphatically. "Do not tell him I'm up," she stage-whispered. "Tell him I was out late last night and I'm sleeping in." She charged up the stairs two at a time, like a little kid, her pale-blue, wrinkled sleepshirt billowing out behind her.

I went out to meet him, and whatever anxieties I had about hous-ing the son of a gangster dissipated quickly. He had a sweet smile and the kind of good looks that charmed even an old guy like me, who had essentially been ordered to give him summer work, as well as a place to stay. Not that I was actually given an order. Ollie Lundsford, the trainer who accounted for virtually all of my farm's business, had asked me to do him a favor. Every Friday night, I played poker with Ollie and a bunch of characters from the track, and I saw him just about every day. When he asked me to hire Chad, I didn't think twice. I hired someone every summer anyway. Still, there was something in the tone of his voice that suggested an urgency to the request that couldn't really be refused. "I need you to do me a favor," he had said — and the word "need" had carried a ton of weight. Chad offered me his hand. "Mr. Deegan?"

I nodded, we shook hands, and I invited him in for coffee. In the kitchen he sat at the table and commented on the huge copy of Shakespeare's collected plays that was propped up and open on the counter next to the stove so I could read while I was cooking. He asked me if I was reading Shakespeare; I told him I was, and he told me he had read him for the first time in his English classes. He was twenty-two and had just finished his first year of college after working odd jobs out of high school. He liked sports, especially bas-ketball and football, both of which he played on intramural teams. By the time I called up the stairs for Amy to join us, I wasn't worried anymore about this kid being the son of Jimmy Smoke, which is what the papers called his dad.

"Amy," I yelled from the foot of the stairs, holding the skillet in my hand and scrambling her eggs. "Come on down here and meet our guest."

A moment later Amy came into the kitchen wearing apple-green velvet-trimmed pajamas that looked more like elegant evening at-tire than something you might sleep in. Her shoulders were bare and her breasts were prominently outlined under a flimsy camisole before she covered herself — to my great relief — by buttoning a matching cardigan. Her hair was brushed, and she had make-up on.

Chad stood up when she entered the room, and they shook hands politely. "Pleasure to meet you, Amy," he said in a tone of voice downright avuncular, which pleased me.

"Uh-oh," Amy said, gesturing toward Chad's eggs, toast, and or-

ange juice. "I see my father's started taking care of you already."
She sat next to Chad at the table. "You got to watch out for him,"
she whispered, as if I couldn't hear her. "If you let him, he'll be
tucking you into bed at night."

"Amy thinks I'm overprotective." I put her eggs and toast on the
table in front of her, and buttered her toast and dipped it in egg before she figured out the joke and slapped my hand away.

Chad laughed. He said, "You guys are pretty funny."

"We're a team," I said. "Me and Amy."

"Oh, please," Amy rolled her eyes. "I can't wait to get out of here
and go to college. This is like hell, living in the middle of Nowhere,
USA. You know how far you have to drive to get to a decent music
store? Two hours. You know —"

"Amy," I said. "I'm sure Chad wants to hear about how miserable
your life is." I picked up Chad's plate and gestured for him to join
me. "Time to see the farm."

Outside, the early summer weather had turned the land into an
expanse of mud and grass. Everything that wasn't green was brown
and muddy — and a lot of what was green was muddy too. Things
would remain that way until July, when the heat finally baked the
ground dry. In the anteroom, two pairs of galoshes stood upright
and waiting. I picked up my pair and directed Chad to a closet,
where old galoshes and boots were piled in a corner. "I hope you
don't mind mud," I said. "You'll be living with it for the next
month." On the brick walk, I looked up and drew in a deep breath
of fresh air and let the sun warm my face. "So," I said, when he
came up beside me, "you have a girlfriend?"

"Several," he answered, grinning in a way that was supposed to
be a between-men thing, as if he expected me to pat him on the
back for being such a hotshot.

"I'll show you the barns first," I said.

Chad followed along quietly while I gave him the tour. He
seemed troubled by the mud, which he sank into up to his calves at
one point, muddying his clean denims. There were a handful of
fractious racehorses on the farm, and I pointed them out to him
first. At the stud barn, we stopped in front of His Majesty's stall. HM
was the worst of the lot. "This one," I said, pointing to HM, who
had come to the front of the stall to check out Chad, "stay away
from him. I'd put him down if it was up to me, but Ollie insists on
keeping him."

Chad moved to the stall. "He doesn't look mean," he said. "He doesn't look any different from the others."

"Take my word for it," I said. I moved him along.

Just out of the barn, he stopped suddenly and looked around, as if he were actually seeing the place for the first time. He looked up toward the mountain ridges, which were already lush and green, and his eyes followed the satiny folds of hollows and rises down to the green pastureland of the farm, which was divided and enclosed by white fences. Inside the farm's corrals, horses grazed lazily.

"Not a bad place to spend your summer," I said. "As long as you don't mind working some."

"I don't mind," he said.

At his cabin, he leaned against the door frame to pull off his boots.

I opened the door for him. "It's hardly luxury," I said. "But it's cozy enough."

He looked through the doorway at the single bed with its brass headboard, at the oval, cord rug in the center of the wood floor, and at the red-and-white-checked curtains over the windows on the back and side walls. "It's nice," he said. "It looks good."

I opened an old ball-foot armoire I had dragged over from the storage barn and cleaned up a few days earlier. "This is your closet," I said, and then I pointed to the bathroom, which was directly across from the bed. "I thought about putting a door on the bathroom for you, but then I figured, it's only you in here, so —"

Chad nodded. "Be fine."

"Okay, then. I'll send Amy to get you for lunch." I started for the door.

"Mr. Deegan," he said, stopping me. "I didn't mean, before, what I said about having girlfriends . . . I didn't mean to sound like some sort of loverboy or something. It's not like that."

"That's good," I said, "because —" I was standing in the doorway and moved back inside the cabin and closed the door. "Because Amy's at that age now where she's still a kid but doesn't want to be one anymore. It's a dangerous age for a young girl."

"I understand," Chad said. "You don't have to worry about me." He brushed his hand through his hair. "I'll tell her I have a serious girlfriend."

"Good," I said. "Because, don't tell her I told you this, but —" I hesitated a moment, not certain I should continue. I said, "She hasn't even had a first boyfriend yet. She'd be mortified if she knew I told you that, but it's something you should know. It's because we live out here in, as Amy says, Nowheresville. Still, she thinks she knows things, but she doesn't know anything yet."

"Like I said," Chad touched his heart, as if swearing an oath. "You have nothing to worry about from me."

I put my hand on his arm, as if to say thanks, and then turned to leave.

"Long as we're talking," he continued. "You know about my family, right?"

"I know what I read about your father in the newspapers."

Chad closed his eyes for an instant, as if gathering the resolve to explain and pushing down frustration, like a celebrity who's just been asked the same dumb question for the millionth time. "He's not my father," he said. "He's my mother's husband. We have a simple relationship. I hate him and he hates me."

I looked at him in a way that I thought might prompt him to explain, but his eyes had gone steely, as if he had just said all he had to say on the subject. I pushed a little. "Doesn't that worry you?" I asked. "Having someone like that hate you?"

"My mother would never let him do anything. I'm not worried."

"Well," I said, meaning to dismiss the subject, "maybe time will make you closer."

"I doubt it," he said. "He had my father killed."

"He had —" I started to echo him stupidly, the amazement in my voice momentarily turning me into the boy.

"You can see the problem."

"I guess so," I said. "Like Hamlet." I had no idea how to continue.

"I have nothing to do with Jimmy and he has nothing to do with me. So you don't have anything to worry about on that score either. I just want to be a college student with a summer job, you know what I mean?"

"Yes," I said. "I do," and I touched his arm. I said, "I'll send Amy for you for lunch," hoping my tone let him know that the subject of his family was done with as far as I was concerned. On the way back to the house, I turned it over in my mind. I was curious, of course, but I wasn't about to ask. In a way, it made me feel protective. Amy never understood that about me, my protectiveness. Linda, her mother, hadn't either. There's a reason for it. I was raised poor, in a bad part of Brooklyn. My father was a mean drunk, my sister was raped when she was sixteen, and when I was not much older I was robbed and beaten half to death by two guys wearing sweatshirts with hoods pulled to tiny openings around their eyes. They beat me just because they wanted to — no special reason.

After the attack, I spent months in the hospital, my heart full of murder. Nights, I'd have dreams in which beatings my father delivered merged with the street beating. Days, I'd fall into long, bloody reveries of violence so awful it frightened me — half daydreams, half trances in which I'd inflict every manner of nightmare on the men who beat me. For a while I thought I was losing my mind. I came back slowly. I didn't lose my mind and I didn't withdraw from the world. I just moved to a more secluded part of it. My father's boss owned a horse farm up in the mountains, and I went to work for him when I got out of the hospital. I've worked around horses and on farms ever since. I became careful, protective.

Amy couldn't appreciate these things, but I thought maybe Chad could, having been through some himself — and after working with him only a few weeks, it was clear that I was right. He rapidly turned into a combination ally and mediator in my frequent, though usually minor, conflicts with Amy. Whatever he told Amy, she seemed to hear clearly. I suspected his working without a shirt, sweat glistening over the muscles of his chest and stomach, had something to do with the explanations always being so convincing.

In any event, things ran a lot more smoothly with Chad on the farm. Amy seemed happier with him around, even if he did — as he had told her — have a serious girlfriend. She took to going to bed early most nights and sleeping late in the mornings, and in general appeared to be more relaxed and comfortable than she had been in years. She was looking forward to the fall, when she'd start her senior year in high school. Chad turned out to be excellent help, working all day, finishing up the jobs I'd given him, and often going on to other things that needed doing. Evenings he spent in his cabin, hardly ever going into town. The only problem I had with him involved the phone bill, which was exorbitant. When I took it to him, he explained he was calling a girlfriend and buddies from home and college and agreed to pay the extra charges. When I pointed out that if he didn't cut back on the calls, he'd wind up sending a good portion of his summer earnings to Ma

Bell, he nodded, but not resentfully, the way Amy would have nodded. By midsummer, I was already worrying about his leaving and thinking of ways I might entice him back next year.

Ollie stopped by the farm more frequently with Chad here, which I also considered a benefit. Ollie was probably less than ten years older than me, but he always treated me in a fatherly way. He was a stocky, blond-haired, blue-eyed Swede with a fondness for poker and his stout, churchgoing wife. He supposedly had some dubious connections at the track — I had heard this implied by other trainers and farmers — but I never heard a word about it from him, and I never saw him do anything the least bit unseemly. Asking me to hire Jimmy Smoke's son for a summer job was the only thing in twelve years that had given me the least cause for worry — and that was going fine. Then, on a morning in the first week of August, when I was at his stables picking up hay, he invited Amy and me to his house for dinner.

I backed my truck into the stable and lowered the tailgate, while he opened the stall door and dragged out four bales of special high-grade hay he had been holding for me. He tossed a bale onto the truck. "Hey, Paul," he said. "The wife's making something special tonight. Why don't you and Amy come out and join us?"

I didn't answer right away. I pulled a bale of hay from the stack, threw it onto the truck, and went back for another, which I slid onto the tailgate. Ollie had never invited me to dinner before. Ollie never invited anyone to dinner. I said, as if he didn't know it, "We've never been to your house for dinner. Actually, we've never been to your house at all."

"This will be the first time then, won't it?" he said, tossing a bale of hay at me, playfully too hard.

I was knocked back a couple of steps before regaining my balance. "Okay," I said. I didn't see how we could refuse. "What should we wear?"

"Dress nice," he said. "My wife'll bring out the good china. We'll do the whole deal for you." He winked at me and closed the stall door. "Be there by seven. Don't be late." He turned and hurried to the other end of the stable, where he had an office.

At my truck, I pulled a ball of twine from under the front seat and took my time tying down the hay, which didn't need to be tied down at all. The pit of my stomach stirred the way it does when something doesn't seem right. I was tempted to follow Ollie into his office and ask him what was going on, why all of a sudden the invitation to dinner. By the time the hay was tied down, I had decided to let things play out as they would. I got back into the cab of the truck and instead of heading out the front entrance I did a three-point turn and started down the dirt road that crossed the stables and went through the farm and wound around to a back entrance, which was closer to town, where I planned on stopping at the supermarket. In the rearview mirror I saw Ollie come out of his office. He watched me drive away, looking annoyed. I usually asked him if it was all right to drive across the farm — but he had walked away and I couldn't imagine why it wouldn't be Okay. I couldn't imagine — until I passed the bunkhouse where he sometimes put up extra help.

At the back of the house, taking overnight bags out of the trunk of a deep-blue Lincoln Continental, were two guys who might as well have had the word "gangster" emblazoned in neon on their backs. They wore dark suits with dark shirts and matching dark ties. Their hair was cut short and slicked back. At the sound of my truck, one of them turned around quickly, and I saw the straps of a shoulder holster before he could adjust and button his jacket. Then the other turned around and our eyes met as I drove past. They didn't look happy. In my rearview, I saw one of them slam the trunk shut, and then they both went into the bunkhouse. I drove only a little farther up the road before pulling onto the grass and spinning back around toward the stables.

Ollie was still standing outside with his hands on his hips, and I pulled the truck right up to his toes before cutting the engine and jumping out and slamming the door. "Ollie," I said. "Guess who I just saw."

Ollie set his jaw and crossed his arms over his chest.

"Two of the king's men. Back at the bunkhouse."

He looked perplexed. "You saw who?"

"I saw the two guys Jimmy Smoke sent. That's why we're having dinner together tonight, isn't it? So it's just the kid on the farm when they get there?"

Ollie looked at me with disgust and shook his head slowly. He went back into his office and stood by the open door, waiting for me to join him.

I hesitated a moment, then went into the office and took a seat at the side of his desk, as if I were about to be interviewed for a job. I stared at his empty leather chair.

Ollie closed the door. "You saw two guests of mine. They're staying at the bunkhouse."

"No . . ." I said, slowly, as if I had considered and then rejected his assertion. "I saw two killers. Sent to do something to a boy I've been working with all summer. A kid I like."

"Really," Ollie said. "You like him?" He walked around me and took his seat behind the desk.

"Yes," I said. "I like him."

Ollie leaned forward. "Why would you think —"

"Will you stop it?" I said. "I know about the kid's relationship to his stepfather. I know who his stepfather is. I know they hate each other. Now all of a sudden you arrange for me and Amy to be off the farm, and two thugs show up wearing guns under their thug uniforms. Have I led you to believe I'm a stupid man, Ollie?"

"Never thought it for a second."

"Then stop bullshitting me."

Ollie folded his hands in his lap and looked at me patiently. "Those phone calls you mentioned, the ones the kid was making all over the country? What if they weren't to his college buddies and his girlfriend? What if the little asshole was trying to have Jimmy killed? What if the clown had it stuck in his head that Jimmy killed his father and nothing but revenge would do? What about that, Paul? Would that make things a little more understandable to you?"

I hesitated before answering. Half of me was ready to argue with Ollie. The other half was in shock to hear him tacitly confirm a killing. After a long moment, I said, "The details are supposed to make a difference to me? Not that I'm sure I believe them. But what is it you think — that if I understand why, then it'll be okay? I'm not going to have a problem with two killers coming out to my farm after a kid who's working for me?"

Ollie put his elbows on the desk and covered his face with his hands. He spoke into his palms. "All that I said is what if."

"Well, what if nothing. It makes no difference."

"None at all?"

"None," I said, still amazed he'd think it might.

He crossed his arms on the desk and moved closer to me. "What if I happened to know for a fact that Jimmy's raised this kid like his own son? That he did everything a father could do, but the kid's been screwing up since puberty, between girls and drugs and money? What if Jimmy's spent a small fortune between abortions and lawyers and rehab with this kid, and now the little asshole is hell-bent to do away with him, hell-bent trying to pull together every old enemy Jimmy's got? What if, Paul? What if it's either one way or the other, Jimmy or Chad — and this is all Chad's doing? This is the way Chad wants it? Then what? Still make no difference?"

"I don't believe it about this kid," I said. "He's —"

"He's slick, is what he is," Ollie said, raising his voice a little.

"That's not the way he comes across to me."

Ollie stared at me. "I thought you were smarter than this," he said. "I thought you knew more about the way things were than this."

"How's that?" I said. "What have I ever done to make you think you could arrange a murder on my farm and I'd look the other way?"

"What I just said," he answered. "I thought you knew the way things were."

"Look. I'm going back to the farm; I'm warning Chad."

Ollie stood up behind the desk. "And what good will that do, Paul? Except to complicate your life."

"Is that a threat?" I said. "To complicate my life?"

"Not from me," Ollie said. "I can't tell you what Jimmy's going to do."

I said, "I thought that you were my friend."

"I am your friend," he said. "Come to my house for dinner tonight. What's going on between Jimmy and Chad — you can't do anything about it. Only a fool would get in the way of a thing like this. It's an act of God. The only thing you should be looking for is how to keep you and yours safe. *That*," he said, "is what I thought you'd understand."

"Like I said," I started for the door. "I'm going back to the farm. I'm finding the kid."

"Think about what you're doing," Ollie said. When I was already out the door, he called after me. "I'll be expecting you for dinner!"

I didn't answer. I got in my truck and went out the front gate and started for the farm. My foot fell heavily on the gas as I sped along the two-lane roads, worrying over Ollie's threat. I didn't believe he'd do anything to harm Amy or me. I didn't think it was possible I had so misjudged the man. Nor did I think he'd let Jimmy Smoke do anything to us — as long as it was in his power to prevent it. That, of course, was the problem. What if he couldn't keep Jimmy Smoke from, say, burning down the farm, which is where his name came from, as I understood it — his connection to mysterious fires. While I was worrying about all this, I recalled Ollie stopping by the farm a few days earlier to check on His Majesty — he had looked the horse over, gone through his stall, even asked me if he was as mean as always — and I realized with absolute certainty that he kept HM for Jimmy Smoke. I was sure of it. When the time came that Jimmy needed a believable accidental death, HM would be waiting. Sometimes I'm good at reading things, and I read this with certainty: Chad was going to wind up in the stall with HM, crushed and beaten to death. He'd get Chad out of the way in an accident no one would question — an accident on a farm where the kid was working a summer job hundreds of miles away from Jimmy and his associates. Jimmy got rid of his kid, and he kept his wife. When I realized these things, I started worrying that maybe I had misjudged Ollie all these years. Maybe I'd be in trouble once I warned Chad.

None of this, though, had any bearing on what I was about to do. I wouldn't let it. When I considered Ollie's arguments and they began to gather weight — what if this was really a skirmish in a war between killers? I reminded myself that Chad was a kid, a boy, and that to go eat a pleasant dinner while he was getting beaten to death would make me a murderer. That pushed me hard, that thought. On the farm, dust flew up in clouds behind the truck as I drove the dirt road out to Chad's cabin. The horses looked up from their grazing to watch the truck speed by, as if they were my audience. Otherwise, the farm was so quiet, you'd think no one worked it. Amy was in the house probably, enjoying the air-conditioning. Chad was either working or eating lunch. I pulled up to the cabin and hit the brakes, and when I skidded into the concrete foundation, the rubberized front of my bumper thumping into the cabin wall, I realized how fast I had been going.

I got out of the truck carefully, not wanting to look panicked. At the cabin, I knocked twice and when Chad didn't answer, I opened the door and stepped inside. I was shocked for a moment by the mess. The bed was unmade and the sheets were rumpled and soiled. The floor was littered with garbage: grocery store bags, pizza boxes, clothes, even farm tools. I noticed, sticking out from under the bed, the wooden handle of a twitch I had been looking for just that morning. I knelt to retrieve the twitch and then jumped back at the sight of someone moving in the bathroom. It only took me an instant to realize it was my own reflection in the mirror. When I straightened up, my heart was pounding. The mess in the cabin made me angry. It seemed like a small matter compared to the larger situation at hand — but it angered me. I couldn't help it. Even the walls, which I had painted at the beginning of the summer, appeared soiled. At the top of the bed, a large discolored area darkened the white paint. I couldn't imagine what had made the stain. Sweat? Did he stand on his bed and lean against the wall naked and sweaty? The stain had roughly the proportions of someone's back.

I muttered a curse at the condition of the cabin and looked around one more time for damage. In the bathroom I noticed a grapefruit-sized hole in the plasterboard by the sink, and my mouth fell open. When I examined it, it looked like he might have simply put his fist through the wall. "Son of a bitch," I said aloud, and I touched my hand to my forehead and looked down, gathering my thoughts. At my feet, the bathroom's wastebasket overflowed. Under a crumpled, stained sheet of toilet paper, something glittery caught the light, and when I moved the paper away with my toe, I saw it was an empty condom wrapper. I kicked the basket over and scores of wrappers spilled onto the floor, along with a good number of used condoms, some of them still soggy, others stiff and brittle. I leaned back against the sink and heard myself moan, as if I had just been told someone I love had died. In the bedroom, a brief search turned up Amy's pajamas, the apple-green ones she had worn on his first day at the farm. They were folded neatly in one of the armoire's drawers, along with several other items of her clothing — and something about how her few things were neatly folded and stacked, surrounded by the squalor of his things, made it all more painful. I picked up the pajamas and held them to my chest, and when I turned around, Chad was standing in the doorway.

At first he looked like the same Chad, same boyish, sweet expression. Then he saw that I was holding Amy's pajamas, and he noticed the overturned wastebasket, and the pleasant expression on his face melted away. It was as if a mask came off, revealing someone I didn't know, someone different: cold where Chad was warm, impenetrable where Chad was vulnerable. He stood in the doorway, his legs spread as if for solid balance, his arms crossed on his chest. He said, "She wasn't going to stay a virgin forever, Deegan. She's nearly seventeen."

I dropped her pajamas back into the dresser drawer. I wanted to ask him when it had happened. I wanted to ask how long it had been going on. I knew, though, that it had to be at night, after I was asleep. Probably every night. The whole damn summer. That was why she had taken to going to bed early and sleeping late. It explained her mood too — which I realized now was happiness. Hard to believe, how I didn't see it all summer. She was in love with him.

Chad remained in the doorway, solid as a statue. I wanted to get past him, into the sunlight and out of the squalor of the room. He met my eyes, his stare hard and powerful, as if he were the stronger man and he knew it. "Chad," I said, "just get out of my way."

He didn't move. "Deegan," he said, "you can't protect her from the world. I'm telling you as a favor. She's not dumb. She sees the way you've kept boys away from her, the way you've kept her hidden out here."

"You're giving me a lesson on raising kids, Chad? After taking advantage of my sixteen-year-old daughter. After —"

"I didn't take advantage of her, Deegan. I'm the best thing that ever happened to her. Those are her words. Ask her. She'll tell you."

"I'm sure," I said. "I'm sure she will." I looked down at the floor a moment and then back up at Chad. I took a step toward him. "Get out of my way, Chad."

He moved aside. "It's insulting," he said, "trying to keep her from growing up. Not letting her make her own choices, whatever the consequences."

I stepped past him. From outside, I said, "You make a good argument, Chad. You make your point well." I closed the door on him and walked away.

At the house, I found Amy sitting on the porch rocker, writing in her journal. She was wearing a white summer dress with bright-red flowers, and she had her legs crossed under her, the light cotton fabric draped over her knees and the chair. She appeared sullen and barely looked up until I spoke to her, telling her we were going to the Lundsfords' for dinner. She gave in without a serious struggle. She went up to her room and a minute later, I heard music come on. In the living room, I sat and held my head in my hands. I wasn't thinking much about anything. Somewhere outside a colt whinnied, and the sound slid through the house, high, along the ceiling and out the windows, while the low pulse of bass notes from Amy's room traveled through the floorboards.

I spent the rest of the afternoon in a strange, spacey state of mind. It seemed impossible that I would just go to Ollie's for dinner while I knew Chad was being beaten to death. I would tell him. I had to. Yet the afternoon went by and I never left the house. At six, I went up to my bedroom and showered and dressed for dinner. I knocked on Amy's door to tell her we would be leaving soon. She didn't answer right away, but opened the door instead and offered me a bright smile and a kiss on the cheek. She said she'd be ready in half an hour, and I said fine and then went downstairs, thinking that gave me plenty of time to go tell Chad. But I never left the kitchen. I stood by the sink looking out the window, until I heard Amy coming down the stairs. I was looking at the mountains, at their velvety coat of trees in the evening light and the way the darkness of the hollows was accented by the bright sun on the rises, turning the lush green woods into a garment fit for a king, thick and luxurious, draped over the body of the mountains.

"Well?" Amy said.

I turned away from the window and found Amy dressed neatly in a long, dark, drawstring skirt and a modest white blouse. "You look lovely," I said.

Amy smiled and did a pretend curtsy.

In our car, in the driveway, with Amy in the passenger's seat alongside me, I took the keys from the glove compartment. I put them in the ignition but hesitated then, as if I were trying to remember something.

Amy said, "Is anything wrong?"

I turned to look at her but didn't respond.

"You're sweating," she said, and handed me some napkins from the glove compartment.

"Must be hot flashes." I mopped the sweat from my forehead and understood in that moment that I was planning on going to dinner and leaving Chad to his fate; that someplace, on some level, I had decided that Ollie was right, that what was going on between Chad and Jimmy was one act in an endless bloody drama and that my responsibility was to Amy, to keep her safe, to take care of my family. I also understood in that moment before I started the car that I couldn't do it. I said, "Would you mind waiting one minute, Amy? I need to tell Chad something before we leave."

"What?" she asked, obviously annoyed at my timing.

"It won't take a minute," I said, and I hurried from the car to the pickup, which was parked alongside us in the drive. I winked at Amy as I drove away. She looked back at me as if I had grown another head.

At the cabin I flung the door open without knocking and found Chad standing by the armoire. "Chad," I said, approaching him. "How well did you do in that English class?" I hit him hard across the chest with a forearm and knocked him down on the bed. "Remember Rosencrantz and Guildenstern? Remember what Claudius tries to do to Hamlet?"

For a moment he looked like he was going to jump at me. Then he seemed to change his mind. He said, "What the fuck are you talking about, Deegan?" He pulled himself along the mattress and sat up with his back against the headboard.

"I saw two guys at Ollie's farm. They were driving a blue Lincoln Continental and wearing shoulder holsters. I saw them right after Amy and I were invited to dinner by a guy associated with your stepfather, a guy who's never invited anybody to dinner before in his life."

Chad didn't say anything, but his face started to go pale at the mention of the blue Lincoln.

"You recognize the car?"

"It's mine," he said. He stopped abruptly, as if he suddenly remembered who he was talking to. "What did they look like?"

"Turns out your stepfather owns HM, Chad. Why do you think he would own a horse like that? That's a dangerous animal."

Chad seemed to think a moment. "Sure," he said, talking more to himself than to me. "Of course."

"Be gone when I get back, Chad. You can leave Amy some sort of note — but don't see her again. Is that fair?"

He didn't answer. He was still pale and looking away from me, at the far wall, as if he were looking through it to the mountains beyond.

I closed the door firmly and drove back to Amy, who was waiting for me with a puzzled, exasperated expression. "All done," I said, and started for Ollie's.

It didn't take long to figure out why Ollie never invited anyone to his home. We weren't in the house two minutes before Margaret asked us if we were saved. In the years since I'd last seen her, she'd gone from stout to massive, and the glittering intensity in her eyes struck me as half mad. She brought out the Bibles, three of them, one for Amy, one for me, and her own. Ollie watched all this with a sad, impotent expression, letting us know he was sorry for her behavior but unable to do anything about it. Until dinner was ready, Amy and I sat trapped on two uncomfortable, straight-back chairs, answering questions posed by Margaret about our interior, spiritual lives. She asked questions, we answered politely, and then she lectured us, beginning every little speech the same way: *When you know Jesus,* she'd start, and then she'd tell us how much fuller our lives would be once we were saved.

Ollie and I never got a chance for a private word, though I'm not sure I would have told him anything. From time to time, while Margaret went on and on, I worried over the consequences of what I had done. I imagined a blue Lincoln Continental arriving at our door and delivering a pair of thugs who'd execute us, gangland style, a bullet apiece in the back of the head. At one point, I had a vision of the farm in flames, while a dark-suited young man held a gun to the back of Amy's head. The image was so disturbing, I think I must have made a noise of some kind, grunted or moaned, because Ollie and Amy both turned to look at me, though Margaret went on, deaf to anything but the import of her message.

Eventually there was dinner, a dried-up, barely edible meat loaf. Margaret had indeed brought out the good china for us, but she had apparently neglected to wash it before setting the table. The plates and glasses, even the pewter candleholder at the center of a wrinkled, white tablecloth, were coated with a thin, greasy substance, the kind of grime that might accumulate after years of disuse on a pantry shelf. It was a strange experience, that meal. It began with a standing grace, during which we all held hands while Margaret intoned St. Francis' Prayer, the one that begins *Lord, make us the instruments of thy peace.* No one ate more than a bite or two of meat loaf, which Margaret seemed not to notice. By the time we were back in our car, heading for the farm, Amy had gone from discomfort to distress to amusement. "She's crazy," she laughed, grasping her seat belt with both hands, as if she needed to steady herself. "The woman's out of her mind!" She leaned close and gave me a deadpan look. "Did you see that meat loaf?" She screamed.

I laughed along with Amy, but my thoughts raced ahead to the farm. There was a stretch of driveway right before we reached the garage from which Chad's cabin was visible, and the spot alongside the cabin where he parked his car. It was late but the moon was almost full and Amy would be able to see the cabin clearly if she was looking — and I suspected she would be looking. I started up the drive speedily, hoping to hurry past the clear view of the dark cabin, and then almost hit the brake when I saw Chad's chartreuse convertible. Alongside me, Amy stretched and yawned, though I had seen her head turn toward the cabin as soon as it came into view. "I'm sleepy," she said.

I nodded, my throat suddenly so dry I wasn't sure I could speak. I got out of the car at the house and stood silently while Amy started for the door. I listened hard but heard only the sounds of the farm: a breeze rustling leaves, a horse rattling a bucket in one of the barns.

"Are you coming?" Amy held the door.

I looked down at the front tires, as if I had been concerned about the car, and then followed Amy into the house. I went to the kitchen and opened the fridge. I cleared my throat. "I think I need something to eat."

"No kidding," Amy said. She put her arm around my shoulder and looked into the fridge with me a moment. "I'm tired, though." She kissed me on the cheek and said, "I'll see you in the morning," and went up to her room.

I closed the refrigerator, and when I heard the door to her room shut, I turned off the lights and looked out the back window. Chad's car was exactly where it had been when Amy and I left. I hesitated a minute at the sink, looking out at the farm's shadows, at the fence and the posts and the dark planks of the barns, the only sounds those coming from Amy's bedroom and the dull knocking of my own heart. I went out the back door and cut through a corral, walking at first but then jogging until I reached the steps of Chad's cabin. The lights were out, but the door was half open. "Chad," I said, and it came out sounding like a question I was asking myself. I pushed the door open and called his name again, though it was obvious, even in the dark, that the cabin was empty. In the bathroom I heard a steady trickle of water falling from the shower nozzle. I turned on the lights and the only things I saw clearly before bolting out the door and hurrying to the stud barn were the bloody handprints on the shower stall.

"I told him," I said aloud. I almost shouted it. When I reached the barn, I was running, and when I saw the light on in HM's stall, I knew what I was going to find. I stopped running before I got to the stall. HM stood looking out, facing me. He threw his head back twice, cocky and full of himself. "You bastard," I said to him, and then I said, again, "I told him." I knew what I was going to find in the stall and I didn't want to see it, and then when I did finally step up to the door and take hold of the bars and look in, it was as if I had stepped into a dream. I felt the numb paralysis of a nightmare, and I was unable for an instant to understand what I was seeing. When I did finally understand, I couldn't think about it. I backed away from the stall empty-headed. I backed away from both of them, with their dark suits and dark ties, their heads bashed in, their faces bloody and slack over the crushed bones of their skulls. I backed away from the sight of them and walked out of the barn dazed.

I made my way toward the house, through the open gates of the empty corral, in the moonlight. I was stunned and dizzy. I wasn't thinking at all. I was listening — to the small sounds coming from the grass at my feet, to horses moving in the pastures, like there was a peaceful song being composed around me in the dark somewhere and I had to strain to hear it. I was looking — at the mountains, which seemed to undulate in the moonlight, powerfully, like ocean swells. I made my way toward my house, as if moving to a place of safety, a place where I could rest and figure things out. As I neared the back door, a light came on in Amy's bedroom window, and I stopped a moment and watched her lean close to her dresser mirror, carefully examining her face, and then lean back and begin lazily brushing her hair. I touched my face and felt that both my hands were slick with still-wet blood — and for a moment then I must have lost my mind, because I stood there thinking I had murdered them, those two kids in HM's stall, those boys who were only Chad's age if not younger. It lasted a second or two, that belief, that *knowledge* that I was the murderer, before I solved the equation and understood that the bars of the stall must have been bloody and I got blood on my hands when I gripped them. But still, it lingered, that sense that I was the murderer. I was shaken. I struggled toward the house, surrounded by the peace of dark mountains and fields, knowing only that I needed to get cleaned up before Amy saw me. I didn't want to frighten her. I didn't want her to see me with blood all over my face and hands. I didn't want her to wonder who I was.

TOM FRANKLIN

Grit

FROM *Poachers and Other Stories*

For Uncle D, Robert, Steve, Jim, Simon, and Bryan

CHUGGING AND CLANGING among the dark pine trees north of
Mobile, Alabama, the Black Beauty Minerals plant was a rickety
green hull of storage tanks, chutes, and conveyor belts. Glen, the
manager, felt like the captain of a ragtag spaceship that had crash-
landed, a prison barge full of poachers and thieves, smugglers and
assassins.

The owners, Ernie and Dwight, lived far away, in Detroit, and
when the Black Beauty lost its biggest client — Ingalls Shipbuilding
— to government budget cuts, they ordered Glen to lay off his two-
man night shift. One of the workers was a long-haired turd Glen
enjoyed letting go, a punk who would've likely failed his next drug
test. But the other man, Roy Jones, did some bookmaking on the
side, and Glen had been in a betting slump lately. So when Roy,
who'd had a great year as a bookie, crunched over the gritty black
yard to the office, Glen owed him over four thousand dollars.

Roy, a fat black man, strode in without knocking and wedged
himself into the chair across from Glen's desk, probably expecting
more stalling of the debt.

Glen cleared his throat. "I've got some bad news, Roy —"

"Chill, baby," Roy said. He removed his hard hat, which left its
imprint in his hair. "I know I'm fixing to get laid off, and I got
a counteroffer for you." He slid a cigar from his hat lining and
smelled it.

Glen was surprised. The Ingalls announcement hadn't come until a few hours ago. Ernie and Dwight had just released him from

their third conference call of the afternoon, the kind where they both yelled at him at the same time.

"How'd you find that out, Roy?" he asked.

Roy lit his cigar. "One thing you ain't learned yet is how to get the system doggie-style. Two of my associates work over at Ingalls, and one of 'em been fucking the bigwig's secretary."

"Well —"

"Hang on, Glen. I expect E and D done called you and told you to lay my big fat ass off. But that's cool, baby." He tipped his ashes into his hard hat. "'Cause I got other irons in the fire."

He said he had an "independent buyer" for some Black Beauty sandblasting grit. Said he had, in fact, a few lined up. What he wanted was to run an off-the-books night shift for a few hours a night, three nights a week. He said he had an associate who'd deliver the stuff. The day-shifters could be bought off. Glen could doctor the paperwork so the little production wouldn't be noticed by Ernie and Dwight.

"But don't answer now," Roy said, replacing his hard hat. "Sleep on it tonight, baby. Mull it over."

Glen — a forty-two-year-old, ulcer-ridden, insomniac, half-alcoholic chronic gambler — mulled Roy's idea over in his tiny apartment that evening by drinking three six-packs of Bud Light. He picked up the phone and placed a large bet with Roy on the upcoming Braves-Giants game, taking San Francisco because Barry Bonds was on fire. Then he dialed the number of the Pizza Hut managed by his most recent ex-wife's new boyfriend, placed an order for five extra-large thick-crust pies with pineapple and double anchovies, and had it delivered to another of his ex-wives' houses for her and her boyfriend. Glen had four ex-wives in all, and he was still in love with each of them. Every night as he got drunk it felt like somebody had shot him in the chest with buckshot and left four big airy holes in his heart, holes that grew with each beer, as if — there was no other way he could think of it — his heart were being sandblasted.

The Braves rallied in the eighth and Bonds's sixteen-game hitting streak was snapped, so when Roy came by the next day, Glen owed him another eight hundred dollars and change.

Roy sat down. "You made up your mind yet?"

"Impossible," Glen said. "Even if I wanted to, I couldn't go along. Ernie and Dwight'd pop in out of nowhere and we'd all be up the creek."

Today Roy wore tan slacks and a brown silk shirt. Shiny brown shoes and, when he crossed his legs, thin argyle socks. A brown fedora in his lap. The first time Glen had seen him in anything but work clothes.

Roy shook a cigar from its box and lit it. "Glen, you the most gullible motherfucker ever wore a hard hat. Don't you reckon I know when them tight-asses is coming down here?"

"How? Got somebody fucking their wives?"

Roy hesitated. "My cousin's daughter work in the Detroit airport."

Glen's mind flashed a quick slideshow of Ernie and Dwight's past disastrous visits. "You might've mentioned that four years ago."

"Baby," Roy said, "I'll cut you in for ten percent of every load we sell."

"There's a recession, Roy. I can't unload this grit to save my life, and if I can't, you sure as hell can't."

Roy chuckled. "Got-damn, boy." He pulled out a wad of hundred-dollar bills. "This is what I done presold. I got friends all up and down the coast. They got some rusty-ass shit needs sandblasting. You ain't no salesman, Glen. You couldn't sell a whore on a battleship."

"Roy, it's illegal."

"Go look out yonder." Roy pointed to the window overlooking the black-grit parking lot.

Glen obeyed. A big white guy with a little head was leaning against Roy's cream-colored El Dorado, carving at his fingernails with a long knife.

"That's my associate, Snakebite," Roy said. "He'll be delivering the stuff. He also collect for me, if you know what I mean."

Glen knew.

"Up till now," Roy said, "you been getting off easy 'cause you was the boss. Now that that's changed . . ."

Glen looked at him. "You threatening me, Roy?"

"Naw, baby. I'm a businessman." Roy took out his pocket ledger. "As of now, I'm forgetting every got-damn cent you owe me." Glen watched Roy write *paid* by the frighteningly high red figure he would've been having nightmares about, had he been able to sleep.

Roy started running his phantom night shift Monday through Wednesday nights. To keep the four day-shifters quiet, he gave them a slight payoff — a "taste" — each week. So they clocked in in the mornings and pretended the machinery wasn't hot, that the plant hadn't run all night. And Glen, hung over, took his clipboard and measuring tape out and stared at the dwindling stockpiles of raw grit where Roy had taken material. Then he went back across the yard into his office, locked the door, rubbed his eyes, doctored his paperwork, and — some days — threw up.

Staring out the window, he worried that the day shift would rat to Ernie and Dwight. He'd never been close to the workers — in his first week as manager, four years before, he'd confiscated the radio they kept in the control room. Instead of spending afternoons in his office making sales calls the way the previous manager had, Glen had stayed out in the heat with the men, cracking the whip, having the plant operator retake grit samples, watching the mill-wright repair leaks, making sure the payloader's fittings were well-greased. He timed the guys' breaks, stomped into the break room if they stayed a minute past their half hour. If someone got a personal phone call, Glen would go to another extension and pick up and say, "Excuse me," in an icy tone and wait for them to hang up.

In the plant, they were supposed to wear hard hats, safety glasses, steel-toe boots, leather gloves, earplugs, and, depending on where they worked, a dust mask or respirator. Glen struck here too, because his predecessor had let the guys grow lax. In those first months, Glen had stepped on their toes to check for steel and yelled in their ears to check for plugs. He'd written them up for the tiniest safety violation and put it in their permanent files.

So they hated him. They took orders sullenly and drew a finger across their throats as a warning signal when he approached. They never invited him to participate in their betting pools or asked him to get a beer after work.

Now Glen swore to give up gambling. He locked himself in the office during the day and made halfhearted sales calls: "The unique thing about our sandblasting grit," he'd say wearily, "is that no piece, no matter how small, has a round edge." At night, he

stayed home and watched sitcoms and nature shows instead of
baseball. When cabin fever struck, he went to the movies instead of
the dog track or the casino boats in Biloxi. He even managed to
curb his drinking on weeknights.

Until early July. There was an Independence Day weekend series
between Atlanta and the Cards in St. Louis and the plant had
a four-day weekend. A drunk Glen, who when lonely sometimes
called 1-900 handicapping lines, got a great tip from Lucky Dave
Rizetti — "A sure by-God thing," Lucky Dave promised. "Take the
Bravos, take 'em for big money." And Glen took them, betting almost two grand over the four games. But the series was filled with
freaky incidents, relief pitchers hitting home runs, Golden-Glovers
making stupid two-base throwing errors, etc.

So on Tuesday, the holiday over, Glen was back in debt. Then
add the fact that the lawyers of exes two and three had been sending letters threatening lawsuits if Glen didn't pay his alimony. The
lawyers said they'd get a court order and garnish his wages. Christ,
if Ernie and Dwight got wind of that, they'd fly down and can him
for sure.

They came twice a year or so, the old bastards, for spot inspec-
tions, speaking in their Yankee accents and wearing polished hard
hats on their prim gray crew cuts. They would fly in from Detroit, first class, and rent a Caddy and get suites at the top of the
Riverview downtown. They'd bring rolled-up plans to the plant and
walk around frowning and making notes. Glen always felt ill when
they were on-site — they constantly grumbled about lack of production or low sales figures or how an elevator wasn't up to spec.
They'd peer into his red eyes and sniff his breath. He would follow
them around the plant's perimeter, his chin nicked from shaving,
and he'd nod and hold his stomach.

On Tuesday, after Independence Day, Glen sat in his office staring
at the electric bill — he would have to account for the extra power
the phantom night shift was using — when Roy stuck his head in
the door. He smiled, smoking a cigar, and sat down across from
Glen's desk.

"Just come by to tell you we fixing to start running four nights a
week," Roy said.

Glen started to object, but there was a shrill noise.

"Hang on." Roy brought a slim cellular phone out of his pocket.

Glen shrugged and doodled (man dangling by noose) on his desk calendar while Roy took another order for grit.

When Roy snapped the phone shut, Glen said, "No. You can't go to four nights. Who the hell was that? They want *two* loads? Never mind. Your night shift's gotta stop altogether, end of story."

"Impossible," Roy said.

"Impossible?"

"Look out the window."

Glen obeyed, saw a cute young woman in Roy's car. She was frowning.

"You see that pretty little thing?" Roy asked. "You know how old she is? Nineteen, Glen. *Nineteen.* She the freshest thing in the world, too. She go jogging every morning, and when she come back she don't even smell bad. Her breath don't stink in the morning." Roy coughed. "I wake up my breath smell like burnt tar."

"Roy —"

"You think a fresh little girl like that's with me 'cause she love me? Hell no. She with me 'cause I'm getting rich. So no, baby, we can't stop. Business just too damn good. Which remind me —" He opened his ledger. "You back up in four figures again."

"Roy, just stick to the subject at hand. I'm not asking you to stop. I'm ordering you to stop."

"Baby," Roy said quietly, "you ain't exactly in a strong bargaining position. Who's E and D gonna hold responsible if they hear about our little operation? You the manager. You the one been falsifying records. Naw, baby. The 'subject' ain't whether or not old Roy's gonna stop making grit. The 'subject' is what to do about all that money you owe me."

What they did was compromise. Roy said he'd been too busy to make grit and look after his bookmaking business. So Glen would go to work for him, at night. Roy would forget about the two grand and pay Glen ten bucks an hour to work nine hours a night, four nights a week.

"I bet you can use the extra bread," Roy said. "That alimony can eat a man up."

Then Roy said he needed Glen's office; the phones were better. It was quieter, he said. He could think. So that night Glen worked in the plant and Roy used the air-conditioned office. Sweating under the tanks, Glen saw Roy's fat silhouette behind the curtains, and he uncapped his flask and toasted the irony. He spent the night in the hot, claustrophobic control room, watching gauges, adjusting dials, and taking samples; climbing into the front-end loader once an hour and filling the hopper with raw material; on top of the tanks measuring the amount of grit they'd made; and standing by the loading chute, filling Snakebite's big purple Peterbilt.

At six that morning, with the plant shut down and Roy gone, Glen slogged to the office before the day-shifters clocked in. The room smelled like cigars, and Glen made a mental note to start smoking them in case Ernie and Dwight popped in. He locked the door behind him and pulled off his shoes and poured out little piles of grit. He lay back on his desk, exhausted, put his hands over his face, shut his eyes, and got his first good sleep in months.

Snakebite, six foot five, also slept during the day, in his Peterbilt, in the cab behind the seat, the truck parked among the pines near the plant. He showered every other day in the break room and ate canned pork and beans and Vienna sausages that he speared with his pocketknife. He had a tattoo on his left biceps, a big diamondback rattler with its mouth open, tongue and fangs extended. He wore pointed snakeskin cowboy boots but no cowboy hat because adult hat sizes swallowed his tiny head. To Glen, he looked like a football player wearing shoulder pads but no helmet. He said he "hailed" from El Paso, Texas, but he'd "vamoosed" because his wife, a "mean little filly" who'd once stabbed him, had discovered that he was "stepping out" with a waitress in Amarillo.

Glen knew this and much more because Snakebite never stopped talking. One night, as the truck loaded, Snakebite showed Glen a rare World War I trench knife, a heavy steel blade with brass knuckles for a handle.

"I collect knives," Snakebite said. "Looky here." He bent and pulled up a tight jeans leg over his boot, revealing a white-handled stiletto.

"My Mississippi Gambler," Snakebite said. "It's a throwing knife. See this quick unhitching gadget on the holster?" He flipped a snap and the knife came right out of his boot into his hand. "This is the one my wife stabbed me with," he said. He showed Glen the scar, a white line on his left forearm. Glen didn't have any scars from his ex-wives that he could show, so he uncapped his flask and knocked back a swig. He offered the flask to Snakebite, who took it.

"Don't mind if I do, Slick," he said, winking.

"Where's this load going?" Glen asked, nodding toward the black stream of grit falling into the truck. He'd been curious about Roy's clients, thinking he might try to steal the business.

Snakebite grinned and punched him in the shoulder. "Shit, boy. You oughta know that's classified. You find out old Roy's secrets and he's outta business. Then I'm outta business."

"So." Glen swallowed. "I hear you do a little, um, collecting for Roy."

Snakebite drained the flask. "Don't worry about that, Slick. Old Roy ain't never sicced me on anybody I liked. And even if he did, hell, it ain't ever as bad as you see in the movies."

Working nights for Roy Jones Grit, Inc., Glen wore a ratty T-shirt, old sneakers, a Braves cap, and short pants. He turned off every breaker and light he could spare to keep the electric bill low, so the place was dark and dangerous. He began carrying a flashlight hooked to his belt. He tried to cut power during the day, too. He adjusted all the electrical and mechanical equipment to their most efficient settings. He even turned the temperature dial in the break-room refrigerator to "warmer" and stole the microwave (supposedly a great wattage-drainer) from its shelf and pawned it, then called the day-shifters in for a meeting where he gave the "thief" a chance to confess. No one did, and the meeting became a lecture where Glen urged the men to "conserve energy, not just for the good of the plant, but for the sake of the whole fucking environment." To set an example, he told them, he would stop using the air conditioner in the office.

But not Roy: Roy ran the AC full-blast all night so that the office was ice-cold. Not that Glen had a lot of time to notice. Typically it took one man to operate the plant and another the loader. Doing both, as well as loading Snakebite's truck, Glen found himself run ragged by morning, so covered with sweat, grit, and dust that the lines in his face and the corners of his eyes and the insides of his ears were black, and his snot, when he blew his nose, even that was black.

*

One evening in mid-July Glen trudged to the office to complain. He opened the door and came face-to-face with the young woman from Roy's car. She had lovely black skin and round brown eyes. Rich dark hair in cornrow braids that would've hung down except for her headband. She wore bright green spandex pants and a sports bra.

"Hello," Glen said.

"Right." She flounced into the bathroom.

Glen hurried to Roy's desk. "What the hell's she doing here?"

Roy had his feet and a portable television on the desk. He was watching the Yankees. "Your new assistant," he said. "You just keep your got-damn hands off her."

"She can't work here." Glen glanced at the TV. "What's the score? What if she gets hurt? She's just a girl."

"Woman," she said from the door.

"Tied up," Roy said.

"Sorry," Glen said. "Miss . . . ?"

"Ms."

Roy cranked the volume without looking at them. "You been whining about having too much work every night," he told Glen, "so Jalalieh gonna start driving the loader for you."

Jalalieh.

Ja-LA-lee-ay.

As Glen instructed her in the operation of the Caterpillar 950 front-end loader, she stayed quiet. It was crowded in the cab and he had to hang on the stepladder to allow her room to work the levers that raised, lowered, and swiveled the bucket. She smelled good, even over the diesel odor of the payloader, and he soon found himself staring at her thighs and biceps.

"You work out a lot?" he asked.

"Careful big bad Roy don't see you making small talk," she said.

"Pull back on the bucket easy," he said. "You'll spill less."

"That's better, little man. Keep it professional."

So with great patience and fear he instructed her on how to gain speed when heading in to scoop raw material, how to drop the bucket along the ground and dig from the bottom of a pile, locking the raise lever and working the swivel lever back and forth as it rose to get the fullest bucket. He showed her how to hold a loaded bucket high and peer beneath it to see, how to roll smoothly over the rough black ground and up the ramp behind the plant to the hopper. How to dump the bucket while shifting into reverse so the material fell evenly onto the hopper grate, and how to back down the ramp while lowering the bucket. She caught on quickly and within a few nights was a much better loader operator than most of the day-shift guys. Glen watched from the ground with pride as she tore giant bulging bucketfuls from the piles and carried them safely over the yard. And as he noticed the way her breasts bounced when she passed, he felt the hot, gritty wind swirling and whistling through the caves of his heart.

A few nights later, while Glen and Snakebite watched the truck load, Snakebite explained about his tiny head.

"Everybody on my daddy's side's got little bitty heads," he said. "It's kinda like our trademark. We ain't got no butts, either. Look." He turned and, sure enough, there was all this spare material in the seat of his blue jeans. Snakebite laughed. "But me, I make up for it with my dick."

"Pardon?" Glen said.

"Well, I ain't fixing to whip it out, but I got the biggest durn cock-a-doodle-doo you liable to see on a white man. Yes sir," he said, low-ering his voice so it was hard to hear over the roar of the plant, "when I get a hard-on, I ain't got enough loose skin left to close my eyes."

Glen, whose penis was average, took out his flask. He was un-screwing the lid when Jalalieh thundered past in the loader. When Glen glanced at Snakebite, the truck driver was looking after her with his eyes wide open.

The next night, as the truck loaded, something clattered behind them. Glen unclipped his flashlight and Snakebite followed him around a dark corner to the garbage cans. An armadillo had gotten into the trash, one of its feet in an aluminum pie plate.

"Well, hello there, you old armored dildo," Snakebite said. When it tried to dart away, he cornered it. "Tell you what, Slick" — he winked at Glen — "you keep a eye on our friend and I'll be right back."

He trotted toward his truck and Glen kept the flashlight aimed at the armadillo — gray, the size of a football, just squatting there, white icing on its snout. Soon Snakebite reappeared with a brief-case. He set it on a garbage can and opened it and rummaged around, finally coming out with something bundled in a towel. He unwrapped it and Glen saw several different-colored knives.

Snakebite grinned. "I bought 'em off a circus Indian chief used to chuck 'em at a squaw that spun on a big old wagon wheel."

He took a knife by its wide blade and flicked it. The armadillo jumped straight up and landed running, the handle poking out of its side. Snakebite fired another knife, which ricocheted off the armadillo's back. Another stuck in its shoulder. A fourth knife bounced off the concrete. Glen glanced away, ashamed for not stopping Snakebite. When he looked again the armadillo lay on its side, inflating and deflating with loud rasps.

"I hate them sum-bitches," Snakebite said. He stepped forward and drew back his foot to punt the armadillo.

Suddenly a light flared, catching the two men like the headlights of night hunters: Jalalieh, in the loader, bore down on them, the bucket scraping the ground, igniting sparks. Glen dove one way and Snakebite the other as she plowed in like a freight train, sweeping up the armadillo, the garbage cans, the knives. In a second she was gone, disappearing around the plant, leaving them flat on their bellies with their heads covered like survivors of an explosion.

"That's a hot little honey," Snakebite said once he was back on his feet. He dusted off his jeans. "You reckon old Roy'd sell me a piece of that? Add it to my bill?"

It wasn't Glen's jealousy that surprised him. "You owe Roy money?"

"Yep. Borrowed it to get my truck painted."

"Roy's a loan shark too?"

"You ever see *Jaws?*" Snakebite asked.

Glen said he had.

"How 'bout *The Godfather?*"

"Yeah."

"Well, if Michael Corleone waded out in the ocean and fucked that shark, then you'd have old Roy."

Later, as Jalalieh climbed out of the loader, Glen stood waiting in the shadows.

"A what?"

"Tour," he repeated. "See the Black Beauty, it's a state-of-the-art facility."

"This dump?"

"With cutting-edge technology." He grinned. "Get it?"

She folded her arms.

"Okay," Glen said. "The unique thing about our grit is that no piece —"

"Has a round edge. So what?"

Nevertheless, she allowed Glen to lead her around the plant, explaining how the raw material from the loader fell onto a conveyor belt, then into a machine similar to a grain elevator. From there it rode up into the dryer, a tall cylindrical oven which used natural gas to burn the moisture out. Next, the dry grit flowed into the crusher, a wide centrifuge that spun the grit at high speeds and smashed the grains against iron walls, pulverizing any outsized rock into smaller pieces. Finally, atop the plant, Glen showed her the shaker, a jingling, vibrating box the size of a coffin. Raising his voice to be heard, he explained how the shaker housed several screens and sifted the grit down through them, distributing it by size into the storage tanks under their feet.

Staring at the shaker, Jalalieh said, "It's like one of those motel beds you put a quarter in."

Every night and day the dryer dried and the crusher crushed and the shaker shook, sifting grit down through the screens into their proper tanks. To keep pieces from clogging the screens, rubber balls were placed between the layers when the screens were built. Little by little, the grit eroded the balls, so they'd gradually be whittled from the size of handballs down to marbles, then BBs, and finally they'd just disappear so that, every two weeks or so, Glen's day-shift guys would have to build new screens, add new balls. Since Glen had begun sleeping during the day, the workers had gotten lax again. While the grit clogged the shaker and gnawed holes in chutes and pipes and elevators and accumulated in piles that grew each hour, the day shift played poker in the control room, sunbathed on top of the tanks, had king-of-the-mountain contests on the stockpiles.

One morning, Glen was snoring on his desk when he heard something thump against the side of the office.

He rolled over, rubbing his eyes, squinting in the bright light, and he looked out the window at the plant shimmering against the hot white sky. Then he saw his entire four-man day crew and some

tall guy playing baseball with an old shovel handle. There was a
pitcher on a mound of grit with a box of the rubber screen balls
open beside him. There were two fielders trying to shag the flies.
There was a catcher wearing a respirator, hard hat, and welding
sleeves for protection. The batter was Snakebite, and he was whack-
ing the pitched balls clear over the mountains of grit, nearly to the
interstate.

Glen closed his eyes and went back to sleep.

Every night Glen scaled that ladder up between the storage tanks
— quite a climb in the dark, over a hundred feet with no protection against gravity but the metal cage around the ladder. At the
top, catwalks joined the tanks. Out past the handrails, darkness
stretched all around, and in the distance blinked the lights of radio
towers and chemical-plant smokestacks. The Black Beauty had its
own blinking yellow beacon on a pole high above, a warning to low-
flying aircraft, the one light Glen feared shutting off — certainly
that would be illegal. It blinked every few seconds, illuminating the
dusty air, and Glen followed his flashlight beam from tank to tank,
prying open the heavy metal lids and unspooling over each an ancient measuring tape with a big iron bolt on its end.

A few nights after Jalalieh's tour, Glen climbed the ladder to take
measurements. It was nearly dawn, and he'd just finished when he
saw her. Hugging her knees, Jalalieh sat overhead, atop the tallest
elevator platform, appearing and vanishing in the light. Glen crept
over and scaled the short ladder beside her, the first faint smear of
sunrise spreading below them.

"Pretty," he said.

She shrugged. "Don't tell that asshole you saw me here."

"Snakebite?"

"Roy."

Glen gripped the ladder hopefully. "You love Roy?"

She shook her head.

"So you're with him because he . . . buys you things?"

"What things? My little brother owes him money. Roy and I came
up with this arrangement."

Glen felt a rush of horror and glee. Her affection suddenly
seemed plausible. He hung there, trying to say the right thing. He
wanted to explain why he hadn't stood up for the armadillo — be-

cause pissing Snakebite off might be dangerous — but that made him sound cowardly. Instead he said, "What would Roy do to your brother if you didn't honor your arrangement?"

Jalalieh glanced at him. "He's already done it."

"Done what?"

"He had that truck driver cut the toes off his foot with wire cutters."

Glen was about to change the subject, but she'd already swung to the tank below. By the time he descended, she was gone. He thought of the armadillo again, the knives, how Jalalieh had barreled in and taken control. It reminded him of the first time he'd accompanied his second ex-wife's father to a cockfight, which was illegal in Alabama. What had unsettled Glen wasn't the violence of the roosters pecking and spurring each other — he actually enjoyed betting on the bloody matches — but that several hippie-looking spectators had been smoking joints, right out in the open. Later he attributed his discomfort to that being his first and only experience outside the law.

Until now. Now the Black Beauty was a place with power up for grabs, a world where you fought for what you wanted, where you plotted, used force.

It was just getting light, time to shut down the plant, but Glen stood under the tanks, watching the dark office across the yard, where no doubt Roy slept like a king.

"Got-damn it, Glen," Roy said. "Ain't I told you to get some damn cable in here?"

Glen stood in his sneakers and baseball cap, Jalalieh behind him in the office door. "This is a business, not a residence," Glen said. "There's problems getting it installed."

"Then you better nigger-rig something by tomorrow night." Roy rose from his chair behind the desk, which had two portable TVs on it. "What?" he said to Jalalieh. "The little girl don't like that word? 'Nigger'?"

"Try 'African American,'" she said stiffly.

"Fuck that," he said. "I ain't no got-damn African American. I'm *American* American!"

She turned in a clatter of braids and vanished.

"And you," Roy said, "you got to clean this pigsty up."

Glen went cold. "Oh, Christ," he said. "When?"

"They flying in Wednesday night. Be here first thing Thursday." Ernie and Dwight.

So in addition to his other work, Glen spent the night cleaning his plant. He patched holes and leaks with silicone. He welded, shoveled, sandblasted. Replaced filters and built new shaker screens and greased bone-dry fittings and paid Jalalieh fifty bucks to straighten the stockpiled material with the loader. By daybreak the place was in sterling shape and a solid black, grimy Glen trudged over to the office. He hid Roy's TVs in the closet. Sprayed Pledge and vacuumed the carpet and Windexed the windows and emptied an entire can of Lysol into the air. He flipped the calendar to — what month was it? — August.

No time to go home, so Glen showered in the break room, using Snakebite's motel bar of Ivory soap and his sample-sized Head & Shoulders. When he stepped out, cinching his tie, it was seven, nearly time for the day shift to begin. He hurried to the plant to see things in the light. Perfect. Not a stray speck of grit. Gorgeous. In the office, he took out the ledgers and began to fudge. An hour later he looked up, his hand numb from erasing. Eight o'clock. They'd be here any second.

By ten they still hadn't arrived. The day-shifters had clocked in and, seeing the plant clean, understood there was an inspection and were working like they used to. For a moment, staring out the window at the humming plant and the legitimately loading trucks and the men doing constructive things in their safety equipment, Glen felt nostalgic and sad. He grabbed the phone.

"I said don't be calling this early," Roy growled.

"Where the hell are they?"

"Chill, baby. I had 'em met at the airport."

Images of Ernie and Dwight fingerless, mangled, swam before Glen's eyes. "My God." He sat down.

"Naw, baby." Roy chuckled. "I told a couple of my bitches to meet 'em. Them two old white mens ain't been treated this good they whole life."

"Hookers?" Glen switched ears. "So Ernie and Dwight aren't coming?"

"I expect they'll drop by for a few minutes," Roy said. "But Glen, if I was you, I wouldn't sweat E and D. If I was you, baby, I'd be

scared of old Roy. I'd be coming up with some got-damn money
and I'd be doing it fast."

True to Roy's word, Ernie and Dwight showed up in the afternoon,
unshaven, red-eyed, smelling of gin and smiling, their ties loose,
wedding rings missing. They stayed at the plant for half an hour,
complimenting Glen on his appearance and on how spic-and-span
his operation was. Keep up the good work, they said, falling back
into their Caddy, and standing in the parking lot as they drove
away, Glen saw a pink garter hanging from the rearview mirror.

Glen spent the rest of the day and most of his checking account
bribing one of his ex-wives' old boyfriends, a cable installer, to run
a line to the office. Then he went to apply for a home-improvement
loan. Sitting across from the banker, who looked ten years younger,
Glen stopped listening as soon as the guy said, "*Four* alimonies?"
    Back at the plant, he hoped the new cable (including HBO and
Cinemax) would ease Roy's temper. He filled the hopper and fired
the plant up early. From behind the crusher he saw Roy drive up,
saw him and Jalalieh get out. They didn't speak: Roy went into the
office, carrying another TV, and Jalalieh stalked across the yard to
the loader. She climbed in and started the engine, raced it to build
air pressure. She goosed the levers, wiggling the bucket the way
some people jingle keys. Catching Glen's eye, she drew a finger
across her throat.
    Just after dusk Snakebite's Peterbilt rumbled into the yard. It
paused on the scales, then pulled next to the plant and stopped
beneath the loading chute. Glen had the grit flowing before Snakebite's boots touched the ground. He stuffed his trembling hands
into his pockets as the trucker shambled toward him.
    "I'm real sorry, Slick," Snakebite mumbled, his eyes down. "It's
nothing personal. Have you got the money? Any of it?"
    Glen shook his head in disbelief, which also answered the ques-
tion.
    "I'll give you a few minutes," Snakebite said, "if you wanna get
drunk. That helps a little."
    Glen glanced at the dark office window — Roy would be there,
watching.
    "It won't be too bad," Snakebite said. "Roy needs you. He only
wants me to take one of your little fingers, at the first knuckle. You

even get to pick which one." He jerked a thumb behind him. "I keep some rubbing alcohol in the truck, and some Band-Aids. We can get you fixed up real quick. You better go on take you a swig, though." Snakebite had moved so close that Glen could smell Head & Shoulders shampoo.

He pointed toward the control room, and when Snakebite looked, Glen bolted for the ladder, and shot up through the roaring darkness.

It was breezy at the top, warm fumes in the air from nearby insecticide plants. Backing away from the edge, Glen slipped and fell to one knee. He felt warm blood running down his bare leg.

"Jalalieh?" he whispered. *"You up here?"* Searching for a weapon, he found the measuring tape with the bolt on the end. He scrambled to his feet and watched the side of the tank as it lit and faded, lit and faded.

In one flash of light a hand appeared, then another, then Snakebite's tiny head. His wide shoulders surfaced next, rubbing the ladder cage. On the tank, he wobbled uncertainly in his boots. He looked behind him, a hundred feet down, where his truck purred, still loading.

Glen let out a few feet of the measuring tape. Began swinging the bolt over his head like a mace.

"Slick!" Snakebite called. "Let's just get it over with. It won't even hurt till a few seconds after I do it. Just keep your hand elevated above your heart, and that'll help the throbbing."

He took a tentative step as a gust of hot, acrid wind swirled. He bent to roll up his pants leg, then disappeared as the light faded. When he appeared again, he held the Mississippi Gambler. "It's real sharp, Slick. Ain't no sawing involved. Just a quick cut and it's all over."

Glen moved back, swinging his mace, the shaker rattling beside him, the tank humming beneath his sneakers. He stepped onto the metal gridwork of a catwalk and the ground appeared for a moment, far below, then vanished. When the light came again Snakebite loomed in front of him. Glen yelled and the mace flew wildly to the right.

Snakebite struck him in the chest with a giant forearm that sent Glen skidding across the catwalk, his cap fluttering away. He tried to rise, but the truck driver pinned him flat on his belly, his right arm twisted behind him.

"Hold your breath, Slick," Snakebite grunted.

Glen fisted his left hand and felt hot grit. With his teeth clenched, he slung it over his shoulder.

Snakebite yelled, let him go. Glen rolled and saw the big man staggering backward, clawing at his eyes.

There was only the one ladder down, and Snakebite had it blocked, so Glen began to circle the shaker. A glint of something white bounced off the rail by his hand — the Mississippi Gambler — and Snakebite charged, the trench knife gleaming.

Glen dodged and, running for the ladder, got pegged in the shoulder by the shaker. He spun, grabbing his arm, and fell, kicking at Snakebite, who swiped halfheartedly with the trench knife. Glen scrabbled to his feet and feinted, but the truck driver moved with him, and Glen was cornered. Snakebite, pulsing in and out of the darkness, lifted his giant hand as if someone had just introduced them.

Glen slowly raised his right hand, balled in a fist. "How could you cut off her brother's toes?" he yelled.

"Whose brother?" Snakebite grabbed Glen's hand and forced the pinky out. "Don't watch," he said.

Glen closed his eyes, expecting the cut to be ice-cold at first.

But the howl in the air was not, he thought, coming from him. He opened one eye and put his fist (pinky intact) down. The truck driver, clutching his tiny head with both hands, still had the trench knife hooked to his fingers. Behind him, Jalalieh was backing away with an iron pipe in her fist. Snakebite dropped the trench knife and fell to his knees. He rolled on his side and curled into a ball.

Glen picked up the knife.

"Come on," Jalalieh hissed. "Roy's on his way!"

They hurried across the tanks and the spotlights flared, as if the Black Beauty were about to lift off into the night. Glen knew Roy had flipped the master breaker below. Jalalieh took his arm and they crept to the rail. Roy was pulling himself up, sweaty, scowling, a snub-nosed pistol in one hand. Glen began to kick grit off the edge to slow him.

"Got-damn it!" Roy yelled, and a bullet sang straight up into the night, a foot from Glen's chin.

"Jesus!" He pushed Jalalieh behind him and they stumbled back.

Glen remembered a proposal he'd sent Ernie and Dwight a year ago — one that called for another access way to the top, stairs or a caged elevator.

A long minute passed before Roy finally hoisted himself onto the tanks, grit glittering on his cheeks and forehead. Breathing hard, he transferred the pistol to the hand holding the rail and with the other removed his fedora and dusted himself off. He took a cigar from his shirt pocket and chomped on it but didn't try lighting it.

"Girl," he said to Jalalieh. "Get over here."

She left Glen, careful of the shaker, more careful of Roy.

"Get your ass down there and fill up that got-damn hopper," he ordered. "It's fixing to run out."

She shot Glen a look he couldn't identify, then disappeared down the ladder.

"Snakebite!" Roy yelled.

The big driver stirred, grit pouring off him. He rubbed the back of his head with one hand and his eyes with the other. There was blood on his collar and fingers. He blinked at Roy.

"Shit, baby," Roy laughed, "we wear hard hats in the plant for a reason, right, Glen?"

Snakebite, his eyes lowered, limped across the catwalk and stuffed himself into the ladder cage.

Holding the pistol loosely at his side, Roy watched Glen. "You want something done right," he muttered, "don't send no stupid-ass Texas redneck." He slipped the gun into his pants pocket and turned, walked toward the ladder. "I'm gonna garnish your salary," he called over his shoulder, "till your debt's paid off."

Glen followed him, his heart rattling in his chest. When he lifted his hand to cover his eyes, he saw the trench knife.

Roy was crossing the catwalk, holding the rails on either side, when Glen lunged and hit him in the back of the neck with the brass knuckles. The cigar shot from his mouth and Roy was surprisingly easy — a hand on his belt, one on his collar — to offset and shove over the rail. Falling, Roy opened his mouth but no sound came out. With eyes that looked incredibly hurt, he dropped, arms wheeling, legs running. He was screaming now, shrinking, turning an awkward somersault. Glen looked away before he hit the concrete.

*

On the ground, Glen could feel the tanks vibrating in his legs. He took deep breaths, hugging himself, and felt better. His heart was still there, hanging on, antique maybe, shot full of holes and eroded nearly to nothing, but still, by God, pumping. He went to a line of breakers and flipped one. The spotlights died.

He heard footsteps, and Jalalieh ran past him in the dark. Glen reached for her but she was gone. He followed. They found Snakebite standing by Roy's body. He'd thrown a tarp over him.

"He slipped," Glen said.

"Right." Jalalieh ran her brown eyes over Glen, then looked up into the darkness. "He must've."

"God almighty," Snakebite said. He rubbed his nose. For a moment Glen thought the truck driver was crying, but it was just grit in his eyes.

Jalalieh knelt and pulled back the tarp. There was blood. Without flinching, she went through Roy's pockets and found his gun, the keys to his car, his roll of money, and his ledger. She stood, and Glen and Snakebite followed her into the control room. Inside, she studied the ledger. Looking over her shoulder, Glen saw an almost illegible list that must have been Roy's grit clients. He strained to read them but Jalalieh flipped to a list of names and numbers. Glen's own debt, he noticed, was tiny in comparison to Snakebite's, and to Jalalieh's.

Jalalieh's?

Glen frowned. "What about your little brother?"

"What brother?" She licked her thumb and began counting the money. Behind her, Snakebite sat heavily in a chair.

"So, wait," Glen said, "you were paying Roy by, by —"

"By fucking, Glen." She glanced at him. "You want it spelled out, little man? He was fucking you one way and me another way. And the truth is, you were getting the better deal."

"What now?" Snakebite asked, his voice like gravel.

"You deliver, same as always," Jalalieh said. "And keep quiet. Nothing's changed."

With the truck driver gone, Glen grew suddenly nauseated. He crossed the room and took a hard hat from the rack and filled it with a colorless liquid. He closed his eyes and breathed through his nose.

At the control panel, Jalalieh tapped the dryer's temperature gauge. "How hot does this thing get?"

Glen had cold sweats. "Thousand degrees Fahrenheit," he said, which didn't seem nearly enough to warm him.

She smiled. "Shut the plant down."

Half an hour later things were very quiet, only the fiddling of crickets from nearby trees. Jalalieh came in the loader. Glen looked away while she scooped Roy, tarp and all, off the ground.

He walked through the plant, pausing to kick open a cutoff valve that released a hissing cloud of steam. At the dryer, Jalalieh lowered the bucket and dumped Roy's body. One of his shoes had come off. In heavy gloves, Glen turned the wheel that opened the furnace door. It took them both to lift the fat man and, squinting against the heat, to cram him into the chamber. Jalalieh pitched his fedora in, then sent Glen after the shoe. By the time they'd closed the door and locked the wheel, they could see through the thick yellowed porthole that Roy's clothes and hair had caught fire.

Jalalieh followed Glen into the control room and watched him press buttons and adjust dials, the plant puffing and groaning as it stirred to life. She said she wanted to ignite the dryer, and when it came time to set the temperature she cranked the knob into the red. For an hour they sat quietly, passing Glen's flask back and forth, while Roy burned in the dryer, while his charred bones were pounded to dust in the crusher and dumped into the shaker, which clattered madly, sifting the remains of Roy Jones through the screens and sending him through various chutes and depositing the tiny flecks, according to size, into the storage tanks.

Two weeks later Jalalieh called the plant, collect. She told Glen that Ernie and Dwight were slated for another surprise inspection on September fifth. She gave him the phone numbers of two reliable hookers. Then she read him her account number in the bank where Glen was to deposit her cut. She wouldn't give her location, but said she lived alone, in a cabin, and there was snow. That she jogged every day up mountains, through tall trees. That she'd taken a part-time job at a logging plant, for the fun of it, driving a front-end loader. "Only here they call it a skidder," she told him.

"Ja —" he said, but she'd hung up.

He replaced the phone and leaned back in his chair. Propped his feet on his desk. It was time to throw himself head, body, and heart into work. He speed-dialed Snakebite on the cellular phone and told him to be at the plant by eight. Tonight would be busy. You'd think, from all the sandblasting grit they were selling, that the entire hull of the world was caked and corroded with rust, barnacles, and scum, and that somebody, somewhere, was finally cleaning things up.

DAVID EDGERLEY GATES

Compass Rose

FROM *Alfred Hitchcock's Mystery Magazine*

"AND A MAN shall be as the shadow of a great rock in a weary land, as rivers of water in a dry place," the preacher read from his text. He glanced across at the two mourners and shrugged his coat closer. The day was overcast, and there was a sharp wind. The other two men were better dressed for the weather. The preacher closed his prayer book and stepped back from the grave. "May the Lord bless you, and keep you, and make His face to shine upon you, both in this life and the life to come, now and forevermore." He heard them murmur an amen.

There was no sexton for the little churchyard, and the preacher himself rode circuit, serving a number of small communities, none of them able to afford him a settled living. The two mourners had dug the grave that morning, although they were older men, not accustomed to stoop labor, and one of them had a game leg. The brief service over, they filled in the hole, stones and sandy soil rattling on the lid of the makeshift coffin. It had been carpentered from undressed planks, for want of better, and the corners buckled under the weight of the earth. Then it was covered from view.

"Did he have family, do you know?" the preacher asked.

"Back in Ohio or some such place as I recollect, but I misdoubt they were close," the stout, shorter man said. He was leaning on the shovel, holding it much like a staff, but his efforts didn't seem to have tired him particularly. "I'd imagine we made better provision."

The preacher looked at the wind-scoured landscape around them and nodded. This corner of West Texas was a refuge to the kind of men who'd left family feeling behind them, for the most part, to stay one jump ahead of the law. The railroads and the automobile had worked mighty changes, but it was still a desolate spot, no more inviting than a penitent's iron bed. The preacher sometimes questioned his calling.

The second man pressed a heavy coin into his hand. It was a twenty-dollar gold piece, the preacher realized with a start. Better than a week's wages to some. He felt slightly embarrassed by the transaction.

The shorter man read his doubts. "You can't set a price on the Lord's work," he said, not unkindly.

The preacher thanked them both and took his leave. He was grateful, and puzzled. The two sturdy old men struck him as out of place. Not strangers to the country, exactly, but long absent from it, like a pair of returning prodigals. A part of him wondered if it were simple Christian charity that had brought them such a distance to bury a pauper.

She'd grown accustomed to the treachery of men. Treated with indifference, or casual cruelty, she'd learned over time not to trust their confidences or the occasional kindness. She traded on her looks until her looks were gone and her stock fell. She'd worked the cowtowns and the railheads, saloons and fancy hotels, but she wasn't canny or skillful enough to rise above her station, and her luck deserted her along with her youth. Now she was a two-dollar whore, past fifty, with no prospects but a lonely end from consumption or venereal disease, another tarnished jade cast aside by Fate. She had none to call friend and took little comfort in religion.

Her given name was Sarah Bledsoe, but she was known as Fat Sally. She had a crib behind the stables for which the farrier collected a garnish on her earnings. Most of her custom came from soldiers at the army post four miles distant, but the troopers were paid but once a month and spent their money first on whisky. Nor was she the first in men's hearts. There were other women to service their needs, prettier, younger, clever and coquettish. Fat Sally was left with drunken doughboys too out of pocket to afford the better class of whore. She took the rougher trade and sometimes suffered for it. There was often vomit on her bed linen, and her body was seldom without bruises, or worse.

Somewhere she had a daughter, at least twenty by now but given up for adoption years before. Perhaps the girl had followed her into a life of degradation or been bound over to indenture or discovered escape in marriage only to find her husband brutish and weak. There was no way of knowing, but it was odds on that the girl's life was an improvement on her own.

Sally Bledsoe figured she'd played out her string. This sorry place would see the death of her.

The war in Europe was now a year old, but the United States had yet to be drawn in. Wilson's reelection platform in 1916 was neutrality, avoiding an open breach with any of the belligerents, though anti-German sentiment ran high.

The president may have chosen not to take sides in the European war, but the revolt in Mexico was closer to home. All along the border country there were skirmishes between *federalistas* and undermanned army garrisons, and Texas Rangers had taken the field against guerrillas raiding on American soil, some of them no better than bandits. In the Big Bend patience was wearing thin. Vigilante reprisals were common. Ugly incidents had reached the papers back East.

Placido Geist knew the country was a tinderbox. He'd traveled to Olvidados with an apprehension of the risks, but he felt an obligation. After they buried the Dutchman in the windswept graveyard, he showed Spengler the letter. It had been franked a month and a half earlier and had taken more than half that time to reach him. By then the man who signed the letter was already dead.

"I didn't know the Dutchman could write so much as his own name," Spengler said, putting on his spectacles as he unfolded the crumpled sheet of foolscap.

Placido Geist didn't comment. His face had a secret, Indio cast. A lifetime of hunting dangerous men on both sides of the border had left its mark, or more particularly an absence, as if his flexibility of expression had been put aside in favor of a less demanding protocol, a formal gravity that reflected his severe and deliberate temper.

Spengler sat back on the deal bench, straightening his leg. He'd been buckshot in the right knee years ago, an old wound that troubled him more with age. He was a former El Paso city marshal, prudent and shrewd but not entirely without delicacy. Placido Geist considered him a friend.

The cantina was a crude affair, low adobe walls and raw logs for rafters. Spengler drew the candle closer across the scarred table and examined the letter, taking his time. It wasn't the fist of an educated man, the coarse block printing a chore to parse. There was no salutation.

I NEVER AST NO MAN A SERVICE (the letter read). THERE WAS A PRICE TO BE PAID FOR WHAT I DONE, AND I PAID IT. I MAKE NO APOLOGY, BUT I LEFT A CHILD BEHIND. SARAH BLEDSOE IS THE MOTHER. THE LAST I KNEW, SHE WAS IN LUBBOCK OR AMARILLO, BUT SHE MOVED SOME SINCE, AND I DONE LOST TRACK OF HER. I ATTACH NO BLAME TO SARAH. SHE MADE HER OWN WAY IN A HARD WORLD, WITH LITTLE ENOUGH TO SHOW FOR IT, AND MAY WELL HAVE ALREADY DEPARTED THIS LIFE. I FIGURE MY DAUGHTER IS A WOMAN GROWN HERSELF BY NOW, AND WOULD GO BY ANOTHER NAME, HAVING BEEN RAISED APART. I MADE SMALL PROVISION FOR HER IN THE PAST, BUT I HAVE LAID SOME MONEY BY, WHICH WAS HONEST GOT. I LOOK TO YOU TO SEE SHE GETS IT.

Spengler put the letter down and took off his glasses, rubbing the bridge of his nose between his thumb and forefinger. "Well, son of a bitch," he sighed.

"Not game I much care to flush," Placido Geist said.

"That girl could be anywhere, blown to the four quarters of the wind," Spengler said.

"A foundling, passed from hand to hand."

Their excuses were halfhearted, the ritual grumbling of men who knew better than to shirk an incumbency. Otto Maas, a.k.a. the Dutchman, had gone to prison for manslaughter half a lifetime previous, and Spengler and Placido Geist had put him there. There was never any doubt he'd killed the man, a low sort who'd needed killing, but there were extenuating circumstances, as there so often are. Placido Geist had always been of the opinion that an injustice was done and that he owed the Dutchman a reckoning. Now the debt had come due, the Devil to pay and no pitch hot.

"You never had children, I take it?" Spengler asked him.

Placido Geist was abashed by the question, his future wife having died at an early age and the baby she was carrying dead with her, but Spengler had no way of knowing that and certainly intended no malice. "He must have labored some over that letter," Placido Geist said, changing the subject.

Spengler nodded. "If he knew he was dying," he said.

"How not? He wouldn't have written it otherwise."

"Did he try to find her himself, do you know?"

Placido Geist shrugged. "He would have lacked the temperament, the skills, and the wherewithal," he said. "But he knew enough to leave it with us, more's the pity."

She'd been named Rose at birth, a pretty choice for a pretty infant, plump and baby-fragrant, with no foreknowledge of her thorny future.

A whore's child, she was treated as such, taunted early and often with the stigma of having been born on the wrong side of the blanket. Later she would be struck by the hypocrisy, but at the time she was wounded, nursing her isolation and her grievance. The orphanage in Veronica was run, efficiently and without religiosity, by a grass widow from the North Platte whose common-law husband had been a hardware drummer lured by the promise of quick riches in the Klondike goldfields nearly twenty years before, of whom nothing had been heard since. Mrs. Abercrombie no longer anticipated riches or rescue, and she taught her young charges likewise, not to rely on false promises but to depend on their own diligence alone. It was a well-established recipe, plain and reliable as short crust, spoiled only in being overhandled.

Rose grew to detest the Abercrombie recipe, no pie in the sky, and found it no proof against disappointments. She was a moody girl, cheerful and sullen by turns, but she did her assigned chores on schedule and learned her letters, and when at the age of nine she was farmed out to a childless Hutterite couple who owned a tannery in Muleshoe, near the New Mexico line, she knew better than to complain. The work was smelly and arduous, the acids discolored her skin and blistered her hands, her foster parents were free with the strap but otherwise ungenerous, and she was altogether miserable.

Even a short time can seem very long to an unhappy child. Rose felt herself bound on the wheel. She ran away from the Hutterite couple after two months but was returned, fortuitously, to the care of Mrs. Abercrombie. Rose didn't consider it a stroke of luck, but then she was ignorant of other, worse possibilities. Placed in a series of foster homes over the next few years, Rose fit in with none of them. She wanted desperately to please, of course, to be taken in by someone kind, but the cards were stacked against her, and perhaps her need was too obvious, her desires too raw. She was labeled an incorrigible, thankless and spiteful. Her ungovernable nature simply testified to her tainted origins.

"The fruit doesn't fall far from the tree," the records clerk said with a wink of complicity.

Placido Geist was not a man to find wickedness in a child or look for blame in an accident of birth. He himself would have fathered a bastard had Amarita lived to bear his baby. He made no reply.

The clerk scanned the dog-eared ledger, running his finger down the columns. The crabbed penmanship was awkward, with common words misspelled, but someone had at least taken pains to note the particulars of people's lives, their coming into this world and their taking leave of it. The ink had faded to a rusty tracing, so faint in places as to be almost illegible.

The clerk shook his head. There was nothing in the old book for the dates Placido Geist had given him. "Things weren't as efficient back then, you understand," he said to the aging bounty hunter somewhat condescendingly. "Nowadays we order our vital statistics with better utility."

Placido Geist was inclined to agree, after a fashion. He'd noticed one of the new noiseless typewriters on the desk behind the counter. But there was still something human and plaintive about the faded entries written years before with a steel-nibbed pen in that uncertain but earnest hand.

He thanked the clerk and left. Spengler was waiting for him across the square from the courthouse. The stairs would have given him trouble, and he'd found a spot on a bench in the shade of an elm, taken his place with the other old men who showed up regularly to share tobacco and swap lies. It was just above noon, the day making up cloudless and hot. The empty Texas sky was as blue as glazed china, so bright it hurt the eyes.

Placido Geist crossed the square into the shade of the tree. Spengler broke off the conversation he was having with one of the men on the bench and got heavily to his feet.

"This is beginning to look like a fool's errand," Placido Geist told him.

They had little enough to go on, in truth, and it was a cold scent. They'd started in Lubbock and then taken the train north to Amarillo. In both places there was no record of a child born to Sarah Bledsoe, nor did they cut sign of a woman of Sarah's description after all this time. They turned south again, the two of them canvassing the country in between, asking at courthouses and county seats, looking up baptismal records, talking to retired lawmen, interviewing doctors and midwives, although they took for granted that many a woods colt had slipped through the cracks and the likelihood of attaching a name or a history to an unbranded stray was scant.

Spengler, however, looked pleased with himself. "I've got a line on Sarah," he said. "She was here in town not more than eight years ago, according to the courthouse gossips. They used to call her Fat Sally, but she owned to the name Bledsoe when she appeared before the local magistrate and admitted to maintaining a disorderly house. Not your better class of place, I don't suppose, but she was never the highest class of whore, either."

Placido Geist nodded thoughtfully. It was the first daylight they'd seen. "What was the disposition?" he asked.

"They assessed a stiff enough fine to get a lien against the property and put her out of business."

"I take it she moved on," Placido Geist said.

Spengler shrugged. "She didn't have a pot to piss in or a window to throw it out of, and none to go surety for her," he said. "The sanctimonious bastards might just as well have turned her out naked."

"What's the nearest town of any size, somewhere she'd be able to pitch her tent for a quick return?"

"Buffalo Lake's a water station on the railway spur to Clovis," Spengler said. "She'd likely pick up some trade there, drovers and day labor, section hands. Not a rich vein to mine, but enough for a grubstake and her train passage."

"If that's the best we've got, we'd best get to it."

"I'm thinking that's exactly what Fat Sally Bledsoe told herself at the time," Spengler commented dryly.

"Beggars can't be choosers," Placido Geist said.

He was a cut above her usual line of custom, she could see that from his dress and manner, and a stranger to town, but a curiously faceless man without what a Wanted poster or a bench warrant would have described as distinguishing characteristics. Sally was a shrewd enough judge of men to sniff out the faint odor of menace about him, a shadow behind his quite ordinary features, something that hinted at the pursuit of a secret vice. In this, however, she was all too ready to accommodate him, since it raised her price to humor a favored peculiarity. Avarice stilled her caution. She took him behind the stables to her room.

He seemed almost apologetic when he killed her, as if it were a necessary but distasteful exercise and he took no pleasure in it. He did it with dispatch, breaking her neck cleanly so as to cause her the least suffering, and Sally had not even time to wonder at the injustice of it. He'd given her no alarm, which he counted a blessing or she would have stiffened at his touch and struggled, making the business more difficult, but there had been no unseemly thrashing or disturbance. He took pride in the details, after all, an oddly clinical vanity that provided for his own safety as well. No one had seen them go off together, and when he left her in the soiled bedclothes, no one saw him walk away. If they had, he didn't have a face people remembered. It was an asset in his line of endeavor.

They had some rough country to cover, but Spengler found sitting a horse uncomfortable so they'd hired a trap. It was no luxury, all the same. The day's travel over poorly graded roads obviously did his bad knee no good, although Spengler made small complaint. It wasn't his way. He shared a litany of stubborn virtues with the old bounty hunter, neither of them given to bellyache or boast. Like other men of their generation, they were used to solitude and the silence of their own company, and doing for themselves. Spengler still rolled his own smokes, not having accustomed himself to buy tailor-mades. Granted, there was much to be said for the conveniences of the modern world, but not for the erosion of homely skills that attached to that convenience. To a man like Spengler or Placido Geist, born well before the turn of the century, the novelties of the new age seemed confining, less a melioration than a shrinking horizon line, or perhaps the years had made them rigid and unforgiving. The qualities that had shaped them were no longer in demand, were in fact something of an embarrassment. They were both hopelessly out of fashion.

The more immediate difficulty was the physical distance they

had to cover, retracing the steps of somebody several times removed from them in the past, a woman who'd left little enough impression on the ground she'd walked across — "No more footprint
than a fly," as Spengler observed — and whose comings and goings
went unremarked for the most part by the various other pilgrims
she met in her passage.

They picked up her trail in Buffalo Lake, a slim trace it was
agreed, without telling particulars but sufficient to lead them south
to Nazareth and from there to Spade. A chance encounter sent
them up Blackwater Draw to Ochiltree, once a cattle camp serving
the Goodnight-Loving Trail, but now a ghost town abandoned to
the elements. They doubled back, bearing east toward the Salt Fork
of the Brazos. The settlements were fewer, desolate and mean, each
less prepossessing than the last, and the cribs more verminous as
Sally slipped down the rungs of her profession. They ran an aging
madam to earth who recalled mention of a daughter in the few
confidences Sally shared with her, but the old bawd had no idea
where or in what circumstances the girl had been left.

On their way north again, they passed through Veronica, where
it seemed convenient to stay the night before pushing on, and
when they stabled the horse at the livery they were told of the late
Mrs. Abercrombie. Had the sad event not still been fresh in people's minds, they wouldn't have heard about it at all, nor attached
any significance to the story.

A wood-frame house, it had burned to the ground, the old
woman inside it. She was retired, of course, long past the age when
she could handle the demands of children. A lucky thing that she
lived alone, if unlucky for her. Such mishaps were all too common.
The flue in the coal oil stove was faulty, most like, so the heat built
up inside the walls before the fire kindled, and when it took light,
the place went all at once, in a sudden burst like phosphor.

"An orphanage at one time, you say?" Placido Geist asked the liv-
eryman, glancing sidelong at Spengler.

But whatever record of her charges Mrs. Abercrombie had kept
were lost in the fire, they learned, and although they'd only just
happened on her name and hadn't known to interview her, it was
still an opportunity missed. They'd already left too many stones un-
turned.

*

Deliverance comes in unexpected guises, Rose discovered. She was fifteen when her pregnancy damned her for good and all. An arrangement was concluded, her keeper being nothing if not resourceful, and the unwanted child disposed of. Rose was discarded as well, her disgrace complete, to make her own way in the world.

Fortune favors the bold, it's been said, and Rose was enterprising enough to seize the occasion. Cast off, she was easy prey, she realized, but knew her own strengths, and she determined immediately not to be taken advantage of. She hitched up with a confidence artist named Trotter, a fixture on the medicine show circuit, giving him to understand she would reward him with her favors in exchange for his protection. Trotter was satisfied with the bargain and all the more easily led, like most men, believing himself her master. He passed Rose off as his ward, given her age, so as not to outrage convention. She participated in the fiction while it suited her, and when it no longer did, some months later, she allowed a minister's wife in Bent Grass to force the secret from her gently, her glee masked by the pretense of shame. Trotter, not a complete fool, took to his heels and escaped a severe hiding or worse at the hands of the local vigilance committee, but he made his escape without money or means, Rose having expediently looted his cash box and possibles. She already had her eye on the next prize.

Bent Grass, the county seat, had been incorporated only nine years before with the coming of the railroad. The springs, which fed a branch of the upper Colorado, had been known to the Comanche and to buffalo hunters, and later to ranchers, before attracting farmers who planted cotton and grain. Chief among the stockmen was Ansel Pym, who had settled the country in the early days, fighting Indians and rustlers and making good his claim on enormous holdings. Old Ansel was now well into his eighties, the tenacious relic of a notoriously bloodier time. His son Desmond had died of the cholera, but Des had left a son of his own, and Young Ansel was his grandfather's heir. The boy wasn't cut from the same cloth as the old man, being generally regarded as a spoiled brat, an indiscriminate womanizer with a vicious streak, but this estimation of his character was seldom voiced, Old Ansel not being a man to answer discourtesy with soft speech.

Rose had suffered herself to be taken under the wing of the minister and his wife. She knew of the younger Pym's prospects, as who in that windswept country didn't, and she arranged an introduction, seemingly in passing. They met at a church bazaar, Young Ansel forehandedly corralled into an appearance, grudging the need. The obverse of exercising his proprietary *droit du seigneur* was to live up to other, more boring feudal obligations. He enjoyed playing the mikado and dispensing favor but resented having to pretend to a common interest with dirt farmers. He usually oiled himself up as thoroughly as possible in anticipation of such dreary events, exhibiting a glazed and belligerent drunkenness as proof of his indifference. He was unprepared to be smitten by the lively young girl presented by the minister's wife and lost for a moment his natural arrogance.

Rose, just shy of sixteen, had flowered. She was both coltish and sly, with a lopsided smile that suggested doubtful innocence. Young Ansel felt the promise of heat and warmed to the task. For her part, Rose recognized the predator in him at first blush and was undeceived by his attentions. But she yielded to them, enough to keep her fish on the line and set the hook. She read him clearly enough to see that he was as wayward and unscrupulous as she was. He needed a touch of the spur, she thought to herself. With luck and the judicious exercise of cruelty, he could be brought to heel. It would take careful management, and she mustn't lose patience, but in the end she would be his wife, a fact as certain to her as that of her clouded birth. When her husband came into possession of his inheritance, she would assume her rightful mantle and become undisputed mistress of Pitchfork, richest *estancia* in the far reaches of West Texas, without the penalty of the past to haunt her.

It was three weeks now since they'd buried the Dutchman, and they felt no closer to finding his daughter than they had the day they filled in the grave.

"I'm inclined to think we've discharged any indemnity," Spengler said, easing his bulk wearily in the seat. "No fair man would reproach us for putting paid to this."

"No fair man," Placido Geist agreed. The dead don't play fair, he might have remarked. They saddle us with undertakings not easily requited. He gathered in the reins and clucked at the spent horse, coaxing her to pick up her feet. They could make out the town across the dusty flats, some few miles distant in the dusk. It didn't look like much.

"Sorry excuse for a town," Spengler said, by way of conversation.

They'd made inquiries at the army post. Soldiers were on familiar terms with whores as a rule, but for some reason the troopers were surly and reticent, unwilling to say much.

"You get the feeling they weren't telling us something?" Spengler asked.

We have left undone those things which we ought to have done, and we have done those things which we ought not to have done, Placido Geist thought, rehearsing the General Confession. There is no health in us.

"You're mighty pensive," Spengler said, rather put out.

"I was considering sin," Placido Geist said.

"You had much occasion for weaknesses of the flesh lately?" Spengler asked him.

Placido Geist smiled ruefully. "Gluttony, perhaps," he said.

Spengler straightened his leg. "You opine those soldier boys are ashamed of their carnal appetites?" he asked.

"Most men can be shamed," Placido Geist said.

Spengler was irritated with the bounty hunter's gnomic replies, which were more opaque than no answer at all. "Spit it out, damn you," he said. "Don't talk in riddles."

Placido Geist glanced over at him, Spengler's vehemence taking him by surprise. He'd always thought the man taciturn and slow to rile, never sudden.

"Excuse me," Spengler said, ill at ease with his own unfocused anger and abashed at his sharp words.

"No injury meant," Placido Geist said.

Spengler sighed and massaged his sore knee. He'd taken to wearing lace-up brogues in recent years instead of the boots with underslung heels he'd always favored in the past. The flat soles were easier on his feet than something made to fit a stirrup, now that he no longer rode with any facility or eagerness. "Few sins gall a man's pride more than his own presumption," he said, speaking as if to himself.

"Sometimes a man bites off more than he can chew," Placido Geist admitted. "We took on the Dutchman's endeavor because it suited us to think we had honest pretext."

Spengler nodded morosely. "And so far we've got nothing to show for our pains," he said. "Two old fools on a fool's errand as you called it. We figured to do our best, but our best hasn't been near good enough."

Placido Geist studied him unblinking. "Oh, for Christ's sake," Spengler muttered. "I never counted on becoming a garrulous bore, not if I lived past four score year and ten. I don't imagine you'd discourage me from keeping my thoughts private."

Placido Geist had left his own doubts unvoiced for the most part, but they were still distracting.

"There's nothing to be gained by denying the obvious," he observed.

"Or in anticipating setbacks," Spengler said.

"Let's see what we turn up," Placido Geist told him.

They paid a courtesy call at the jail. They found the constable on duty to be affable, but not, as Spengler put it afterward, the sharpest knife in the drawer. There had been a recent murder, and the man was well beyond his depth. The victim was of no consequence, he was quick to relate, a woman of easy virtue, but the crime was disturbing in itself. The usual offenses were no more serious than disturbing the peace or creating a public nuisance, this last a euphemism for relieving one's bladder in plain view. Spengler and Placido Geist were sympathetic and asked the details, less from any real interest than out of a politic show of manners, and so learned of Sally Bledsoe's death. They were a day late and a dollar short.

She'd been buried in Boot Hill, without ceremony, and there was only a scuffed wooden marker sinking into the ground as the loose earth settled. Her name had been burned into the board with a shank of hot iron. It was misspelled BLEDSO. Below that was the present year. Some wit had added a crude caricature in bright yellow crayon underneath, a female stick figure with her legs spread, like the letter M. It was the only bit of color decorating the grave. Spengler knelt down awkwardly and scrubbed it out with the sleeve of his coat. Placido Geist helped him slowly to his feet again. Neither man met the other's eyes.

They walked back from the graveyard and stopped at the stables, thinking to examine the room out back that Sally had died in, but they didn't have much stomach for it. Nobody had taken notice of her absence, and she'd been dead two days in the heat before the stableman thought to look in on her. The smell still clung despite efforts to bleach it out, and the place was altogether cheap and forlorn in any case. They regarded it sadly from just beyond the open doorway, not stepping inside. Sally had lived a joyless and brutish life and died in like fashion. There was no remedy for it.

"This is a hard piece of luck," Spengler remarked.

"We seem to be getting more than our due," Placido Geist said to him, his cast of mind inward and speculative.

"We're not the only ones," Spengler said.

They looked at each other. They both knew the road they were going down, and they'd reached a fork.

"You're thinking about the woman who ran that orphanage, back in Veronica," Placido Geist said. "Burned to death."

"And now Sally," Spengler said. "Her neck broken. It's somewhat previous, considering we got a late start."

Placido Geist nodded. "Somebody's been over this ground before us," he said. "Covering the tracks."

The curiously faceless man had a name, which was Messenger. To others in the trade he was known as Handsome Andy, but it was something of a joke, so few people being acquainted with his features. There was no likeness of him to circulate, and descriptions of his appearance never tallied. He arranged his commissions through an intermediary, a lawyer in San Antonio who limited his practice to the repair of indiscretions large and small and sold his services dear. Messenger had been well paid for executing this assignment, the job requiring considerable legwork.

Now he sat on the verandah of a small transient hotel in Odessa, putting his thoughts in order. He was recently arrived from the town of Muleshoe, where he'd found nobody with any memory of the Hutterite couple who once owned a tannery there, using otherwise unwanted children as labor, bound over for the work of curing hides until they reached majority in exchange for coarse provender, an iron bedstead, hand-me-down clothes, and rudimentary schooling. Messenger admired the efficacy of the enterprise on the whole, but he was somewhat affronted by its complete shamelessness.

He was certainly no sentimentalist, however, and his sympathies, such as they were, lay in the present. He was giving careful reflection to the wording of a telegram, not a report to the attorney but a direct communication with the client. It was a breach of professional etiquette Messenger regretted, although it seemed the only sure way. He couldn't trust a third party.

BREEDING STOCK SECURED. ALL OTHER BIDDERS OUT OF THE RUNNING. WILL FORWARD NECESSARY DOCUMENTS FOR YOUR APPROVAL AND PROVIDE AUTHENTICATION.

He was amused by that last touch, a glancing blow, the silken whisper of threat suggesting there were damaging materials as yet to be delivered.

His attention wandered. The hotel was built pueblo-style out of stuccoed adobe brick, the cut ends of the heavy *vigas* projecting through the outer walls at parapet height. He noticed a line of tiny ants climbing the stucco, and looking closer he saw there were hundreds of them, an army in miniature marching up and down the wall. He couldn't imagine the generalship of such a campaign, the effort, the immeasurable distances, no end in sight. It put him in mind of Aztec pyramid builders, steadfast in their exalted mystery. GO TO THE ANT, THOU SLUGGARD! No, he didn't like that. It wouldn't do to quote Scripture anyway, not under the circumstances. Keep it simple. Plain speaking, brisk and businesslike, the syntax uncluttered, four-square and serviceable as a handshake. SELLER READY TO DEAL. SUGGEST YOU MAKE SERIOUS OFFER. This was the tricky part, what price to name. Blackmail called for a delicate touch.

"What did the Dutchman die of?" Spengler asked. "I don't recall your saying."

"Pleurisy, I was told," Placido Geist said. "Prison did his lungs no benefit."

Spengler nodded. "Bad diet, penitentiary food."

"Rancid meat, no decent vegetables or fresh fruit. It's surprising he lasted as long as he did."

It was unlikely any suspicion would attach to the Dutchman's death, but it couldn't be altogether discounted. If there were a pattern to the other deaths, the Dutchman's came to look equally fortuitous.

"Do we have reason to believe Sally ever told anybody the name of the girl's father?" Placido Geist asked, thinking out loud.

"She told the Dutchman," Spengler said.

"It might have been a misguided kindness," Placido Geist remarked.

"How so?"

"A man serving a twenty-year sentence for manslaughter would likely take comfort in knowing there was something left behind to remember him by," Placido Geist said.

"You presuppose this act of kindness to be Sally's."

Placido Geist looked at him in surprise. "A whore is no less Christian in her actions for being a whore," he said.

Spengler turned and gazed out the window of the railway coach, his thoughts intemperate. He didn't want them read on his face. "I meant no disparagement," he said gruffly.

Placido Geist let it pass. He had little wish to trespass on another man's privacy. His own thoughts were at odds with themselves, adrift on opposing currents.

"Would she have written him in prison, do you think?"

Placido Geist wondered about that himself. "Prison mail is read and censored before being passed on," he said.

"There was no such letter in the Dutchman's effects."

"Unless someone took it, as convincing evidence."

Spengler was silent again. The scrub of the Llano Estacado rolled by beside the tracks, stunted piñon and juniper flattened into ungainly shapes by the scouring wind. Dust devils spun across the cracked earth, and sand hissed against the carriage windows, sifting in past the rattling transoms.

Who profits? Placido Geist asked himself.

The problem lay in assigning a motive. The one common thread was the orphan girl, passed from hand to hand with no surviving chronicle of her bumpy itinerary. The only person who knew the stages of her journey with any certainty was Sally's daughter herself if she were still alive, and that spurred his mind in a direction he jibed away from like a horse refusing the bit. He felt the Dutchman's charge, meant to redress an unredeemed wrong, had less auspiciously opened a can of worms. He realized it was a mistake to hold himself responsible for events he couldn't control — it was self-serving, in fact, an old man's immodesty — but he couldn't shake the notion that he and Spengler were somehow being used in the office of bellwether, a plough turning the soil, with the husbandman of death treading the furrows behind them. He tried to shrug off this fantastical presentiment, reminding himself that the Devil hath power to assume a pleasing shape, playing to our most favored conceits, but it unsettled him nonetheless. If they were the instrument of another, all unwitting, and yet managed to discover the girl's whereabouts through some coincidence or stroke of chance, they'd have led the assassin right to her.

"Pitchfork," Spengler said, breaking into his reverie.

They were traveling south from Lubbock to the junction at Big Spring, where they could board the through train to El Paso. The right-of-way cut across the northeast corner of the Pym spread, Old Ansel having granted an easement to the Rio Grande railroad and their assigns in return for a freight stop on his own land for shipping cattle. Feedlots flanked the sidings, platforms, and loading chutes built up next to the tracks. The famous boxed brand was burned into the fence posts at regular intervals, as if there were any need to advertise ownership, the fortunes of the family being so widely known.

"They say the old man still rode out to check his stock, winter and summer," Spengler remarked.

Placido Geist nodded. "Died in a fall from his horse, I believe, a year or so back," he said.

"You knew him?"

"Knew of him," Placido Geist said. "How not?"

"I've heard the boy hasn't proved the old man's get, the blood thinner, two generations removed," Spengler said.

"A truant disposition by most reports."

"He married a girl of no family, it's said. Chaste but undowered. His grandfather can't have been pleased."

Placido Geist shook his head, smiling. "Ansel Pym had dynastic ambitions to be sure," he said. "Nor was he a man in any wise to be crossed. But in like manner he put little store by the good opinion of lesser mortals."

Spengler sighed. "You take too practical a view," he said. "And overly scrupulous. Why spoil a story for lack of the facts?"

"A fabrication can't be at odds with the facts," Placido Geist said. "Old Ansel judged a man by his worth, much the same way you look first at a horse's teeth, and he was no fool about horses, either. He wouldn't refuse his consent to such a marriage if the girl were of good character."

"And if she weren't?"

Placido Geist shrugged.

"The proof is in the pudding," he said. "The old man could have forbidden the match, but he didn't. It speaks for itself."

Spengler subsided. He would've gone on, volunteering instructive examples of many an honest rustic led to grief by some adventuress, like a calf to the gelding, but Placido Geist seemed to have lost interest. In this Spengler misread his man, as his speculations opened up the very train of argument the bounty hunter had avoided.

Who profits? he'd wondered. One possibility was all too plain. Sally's daughter might have risen in the world and left her past behind her, perhaps marrying a man of property and reputation. But if that past were exposed, she risked losing all her gains. It was simple enough. Erase the evidence and the past became a blank book. She could write her own history, could make it eventful or unremarkable, whatever she desired, with no one to correct or accuse her, none to bear witness. If that meant murder, to burn yesterday's soiled pages to ashes and secure the present against mischief or reversal, then murder would be readily done. No longer a victim of circumstance but still hostage to fortune, she was only protecting her investment.

Rose Pym had never lacked for invention. She'd invented herself, after all. Marriage, she soon discovered, needed a steady diet of sham, or hers did anyway, so it didn't matter practically whether others had made a better bargain. She contrived a pregnancy early, which strengthened her position, but even before the boy Desmond was born, she found an ally in Old Ansel, who was by no means blind to his grandson's faults. The old man respected ambition, and recognizing it in Rose, he encouraged her to take on more of his own burden, reposing in her both his confidence and his authority. She was saddened by his death, as it meant she had to exercise that authority over both the ranch and her husband. While he was alive, the old man had kept Young Ansel's excesses in check, but with his grandfather dead, the new *patrón* demanded a submission from his retainers that the old man had earned and he had not. Like most weaklings Ansel was a bully, and Rose knew the hands spoke of her husband behind his back with contempt. They called him *borracho* — drunkard — and made fun of his pretensions. Rose understood ridicule was dangerous. It made for bad discipline. She saw the men grow insolent and mutinous and knew their disdain for Ansel could rub off on her. She determined to win them over, realizing she'd set herself no easy task.

Leaving the infant Desmond in the care of his wet nurse, she embarked on her new enterprise. It meant rising early, wearing men's clothing, riding out in all seasons and in all weather, just as Old Ansel had done, making it her business to learn the men and equipment, the terrain, and the animals.

The great herds of beef no longer grazed on open range, but the fenced pasturage was enormous. She often slept in the saddle or on the ground and went days without a bath. She drank thick, scalding coffee at line camps, swallowed dust on the trail, went wet in sudden storms, and never complained for herself, always taking time to listen to complaints from the working cowboys. They humored her at first, thinking she only amused herself, and then came grudgingly to admire her interest and stamina.

Rose was careful not to undermine her husband, but inside six months it was common knowledge who held the reins. Ansel was tolerated, his habitual drunkenness blunting any interference with actual ranching, and the outfit recovered its self-respect. Rose signed the contracts and managed the accounts, and she was regarded privately as Old Ansel's real legatee.

She had good reason to be proud, but she knew better than to court complacency. And despite her precautions, when true hazard presented itself, it came on her blind side.

"Well, the worm turns," a voice said familiarly.

She'd just stepped off the raised sidewalk and was about to mount the buckboard. He spoke from a little behind her and to the left. She glanced over her shoulder into the street. He had his back to the sun, and it took her a moment to recognize him. It was Trotter.

He lifted his hat and smiled at her politely, showing off his manners, but she didn't doubt the courtesy was ironic.

"I heard you'd done well for yourself," he said, moving slightly closer so as to speak quietly but not close enough to give offense. "I see I heard right." She could smell his mail-order cologne, thick and sweet, and the faint odor of naphtha on his woolen suit.

"Cat got your tongue?" he inquired provokingly.

Rose looked up at him with a steady and alert gaze, neither fearful nor shy. If anything, she was disappointed in him. This was no chance encounter.

Trotter dropped his eyes, at a loss. He'd obviously rehearsed himself, but he seemed to have forgotten his lines. She waited for him to gather his faculties. "The thought of tar and feathers doesn't improve a man's disposition," he told her.

"It might work wonders for your appearance," she said.

"You did me an injury," he said, with a flash of temper.

"You seem none the worse for wear."

Trotter stifled his anger. "I've a proposition I'd like to put to you," he said.

"I can well imagine," Rose said, her amusement bitter.

"Is there a place we could discuss it?"

"I have no wish to be seen with you," she said.

"You're making this disagreeable."

"How would it be otherwise?" she asked him. "Fine words butter no parsnips. Name your price and be done with it."

Her directness took him by surprise. He wanted to twist the knife a little. Rose wasn't having any. "I'm not going to stand out in the street, damn you," she said, fiercely. "Speak up or give way."

Trotter had been of two minds whether to approach her at all, but her intransigence decided him. He was not to be discarded like a failed suitor, he insisted, nor would he be satisfied with a token payment. He demanded a stipend, a set reward on a fixed schedule, mortgaging his silence.

Rose heard him out and agreed.

They came to an understanding that the money would be delivered by hand and in secret. Trotter was pleased with himself. He thought it a handsome accommodation, of mutual benefit. He said so.

Rose refused his pleasantries. This was no occasion for social graces. She felt an urge to throw up.

Trotter looked up the street. With the railroad bringing in trade and disposable goods, Bent Grass was no longer a sleepy prairie cowtown but a place of opportunity, keeping pace with the changing times. Soon the rutted roadway would give way to pavement, the wooden storefronts to brick, the gas fixtures to electric. "This is a likely spot to stake a claim," Trotter remarked to Rose. "We could have both chosen less happily." He smiled like a conspirator.

She swallowed her rising gorge.

"Don't be a nuisance," she said. "You're unwelcome here, make no mistake. Whatever our commerce, we'll conclude it at a distance."

"I wouldn't leave it too long," he advised her.

"No," Rose told him. "I'll send someone."

And send someone she did.

"How many killings?" the judge asked.

"Who can say? Two that we know of, or anyway suspect. There might be a half dozen more." Placido Geist studied his whisky morosely, turning the glass between his hands. "Not that it matters much. There's little chance we can bring the murderer to book."

On his infrequent trips to Austin, Placido Geist always took the time to visit with Judge Lamar. They enjoyed each other's company and yarned together over a whisky or a game of chess. Placido Geist had told the story, and twice the judge had gone to the sideboard to refill their glasses. Now that the meat of the tale was told, Lamar was chewing on the bones. Versed in the rules of evidence, he found the other man's argument unpersuasive legally, but experience told him the bounty hunter wouldn't chase a false scent.

"It's mostly smoke," Placido Geist said. "Everything at secondhand, gossip or hearsay, none of it solid."

"I take your point," the judge said, "although we're not in front of a jury."

"Even in Texas juries are loath to hang a woman."

Lamar shrugged. "The injustice was done that girl by her birth and no fault of her own," he said. "How do we know what other wrongs were done her, each following from the first? She's led a gypsy life."

Placido Geist smiled without humor. "Is this your line of defense?" he asked.

"Oh, it's wholly inadequate for a capital crime," Lamar said. "Then again, which of us is pure in heart?"

Placido Geist sketched the air with his hand, a gesture of acquiescence. "I admit my reasons are selfish," he told the judge. "I don't know the name she was born with or what name she goes by now. I doubt whether I could find her if I tried any harder. Nor am I dead certain that I'm right about this. It's too slippery to grasp."

"You'd like to be sure, one way or another."

"Every act has consequences, but not necessarily those we foresee," Placido Geist said. "I took the Dutchman's shilling in the hope I could lay his ghost to rest, but I succeeded only in disturbing other ghosts out of the unquiet past. It does me no distinction."

"This is churlishness," Lamar said shortly.

Placido Geist was stung by the reproach, but he realized the judge hadn't intended a gratuitous insult.

"We all look for resolutions," Lamar said. "Something neat, a means of satisfaction, or even redemption. But that instinct runs counter to the rule of entropy, the natural reign of chaos. We try to impose order, discipline, a sense of fitness, because it suits our vanity to think we are the measure of destiny, that man is made in the image of God, with mastery over the brute forms of the earth and over our own narrative, as if history weren't messy, accidental, and arbitrary. You can't blame yourself for failing in a responsibility when there's no reckoning."

"Does that absolve us?" Placido Geist asked him.

Lamar snorted. "The mark of a criminal is not that he breaks the law but that he feels it doesn't apply to him and other men are fools not to simply take what they require or deserve," the judge said. "The criminal doesn't consider what's lost in the transaction. An outlaw, in the original sense, isn't just someone trying to escape penalty but a man who's placed himself beyond legal protection. There's your choice. An honest man owns up to his responsibilities not from fear of censure but because he understands the limits of the social compact. We accept this construct, this common fiction, as a convenience."

"You contradict yourself," Placido Geist told him. "You say on the one hand that man's endeavors are no more than a tissue of futility and on the other that we owe ourselves an accounting. Which do you believe?"

"Where's the contradiction?" Lamar asked. "I say only that this evident artifice keeps misrule at bay. Most of us have very little patience with ambiguity or mixed results. We like our answers straight, our oracles unclouded. We ask for a simple table of elements — earth, air, fire, water — or an easy calculus to explain the Furies that drive us."

"You make it too abstract," Placido Geist said.

"Very well," the judge said. "In plain English, that whore's child has slipped through your fingers. You have lost very few bounties over the years, a point of some pride, and this shabby business is left at loose ends."

"She'll cheat the noose," Placido Geist pointed out.

Lamar sighed. "She won't be the first, nor will she be the last," he said. "Any more than some innocent might stand in for her on the scaffold, and without prejudice."

The bounty hunter thought this rather a startling admission for a man retired from the bench, but he chose not to pursue it. In his time Lockjaw Lamar had sent more than a few men to the hangman, and if he'd doubted their guilt, this was the first Placido Geist had heard of it.

They set out the chess pieces, and their talk turned to other things. Politics, of course, a staple of Judge Lamar's discourse and the reason he kept his residence in the state capital. Men they'd known, both good and bad, most of them dead now and the few still living a reminder of their own obstinate durability. The passing of time and the nature of memory. The changes that had overtaken both themselves and the country in a single lifetime.

It wasn't all old man's talk about the past by any means. The judge kept his ear to the ground and enjoyed a bit of current scandal.

There was a recent case in West Texas, a woman found in a hotel room with a man not her husband. Adultery was not at issue, as she'd shot him stone dead when he presumed on her virtue. She was handsomely acquitted of manslaughter at her trial, having a skillful lawyer and the sympathy of the jury on her side, and the fact that she was married to a man of considerable property did her no harm. The few questions that lingered after the verdict were put to rest by her obvious composure, startling in one so young.

"Mrs. Ansel Pym," Lamar told him in answer to his question. "Child chatelaine of Pitchfork."

"Ah," Placido Geist said. He remembered Spengler's comment about the girl. "Chaste but undowered."

"I beg your pardon?"

"Nothing. Who was the man in her hotel room?"

"The dead man was identified as one Messenger, a villain of some reputation," Lamar said.

Placido Geist nodded. "He was known as Handsome Andy," he said. "A jack of all trades, they say, but a proper brigand. I'd always heard nobody knew what hc looked like."

"Curiously enough, her lawyer did," the judge said. "He defended him years ago on a forgery charge."

"Did he get him off?" Placido Geist asked, smiling.

"Yes, he did. We're talking about Johnny Beauchamp out of San Antonio, a man who never takes the losing side."

"Speaking of villains of some reputation," Placido Geist remarked, without malice.

"The fellow's a scoundrel, no question," Lamar said. "I wonder he didn't employ Messenger himself in some capacity."

"If he had, the Pym woman did him a service," Placido Geist said. "Handsome Andy might have embarrassed any number of people had he ever been put in the witness box."

Lamar chuckled. "Dead men tell no tales," he said.

"I wonder what brought them together."

"Ranch business, or that was his pretext for meeting with her," the judge said. "Apparently she keeps the pursestrings and wears the pants as well. Her husband is a hopeless drunk, not to put too fine a point on it."

"And she holds the prize," Placido Geist said.

Lamar put the chessmen back in position on the board. They'd won a game apiece. Lamar picked up a white pawn and a black one and put his hands behind his back.

Handsome Andy would have been there to sell, not buy, Placido Geist thought. He wasn't in the cattle business, and surely rape wasn't on his mind.

The judge held his clenched hands out, a pawn in each. The white pawn moved first.

The richest spread in West Texas, and now it was hers. He reached out and tapped Lamar's left hand. Lamar opened it and showed him the black pawn. Placido Geist sat forward. He'd be a move behind for the rest of the game, and he couldn't afford a mistake, not if he wanted to win.

Then again, he reasoned, neither could she.

ROBERT GIRARDI

The Defenestration of Aba Sid

FROM *A Vaudeville of Devils*

MARTIN WEXLER woke up one morning last September with a
slight hangover and the vague certainty that something was wrong.
Dull blue light slatted through the venetian blinds over the windows fronting Massachusetts Avenue. He heard the thump and
gurgle of water running from upstairs apartments, toilets flushing,
keys scraping in locks down the hall, all the normal sounds of
life stirring for another day in the world. The digital clock on the
microwave in the kitchenette on the other side of his efficiency
glowed 7:32 A.M. in square amber numbers. He was due in court in
just under two hours.

Martin sat up, reached for his glasses on the night table, cluttered with pennies, crumpled scraps of paper, broken mechanical
pencils, unread briefs, bits of food, and other junk. He got out of
bed, showered, put in his contacts, shaved. He put on a pale blue
button-down, somewhat wrinkled from its third wearing since the
dry cleaners; a red and yellow striped tie with faint soup stains on
the third band of color; and his second-best navy blue suit, just now
going a little sheeny on the seat of the pants. He checked himself in
the mirror; he looked presentable enough. He felt healthy. Everything was fine. But the something wrong would not let him go; it
had its teeth in him and was biting down hard.

Not until he was halfway through his breakfast of stale Cocoa
Puffs did he remember what was bothering him: as of today, he was
the most incompetent attorney in the Public Defender's Service of
the District of Columbia. The former most incompetent attorney, a
scattered woman named Genevieve Claibourne, had been fired the

previous afternoon. Martin thought about Genevieve as he walked down Massachusetts to the Metrobus stop. He had always liked her. She was a petite, loud redhead from Dallas with a wry sense of humor, not unaware of her own limitations. A diehard Cowboys fan, which is a tough thing to be in any Washington office. Like everyone, like Martin himself, she had started out with vague ideals about defending the poor and innocent and ended up bewildered by the utter brutality of modern urban life.

He was a little late getting to the bus stop this morning and so waited alone in the heavy stillness directly following the end of rush hour. The wind off the river stank of a chemical he couldn't identify. He bought the *Washington Post* from the usual blue machine but suddenly didn't feel like reading. He folded the bulky paper under his arm and watched the G2 making its laborious ascension from the tunnel under Scott Circle in a cloud of dark exhaust.

You had to be a drunk or insane or you had to do many stupid things in a row to get fired from the PDS, or you had to — as in Genevieve's case — do one stupid thing that gets picked up by the news media. That was plain bad luck, Martin thought. In any organization incompetence, even of the most blatant variety, was often tolerated for years. He wasn't a good lawyer, everyone knew that. He didn't have a mind for details, or he didn't apply himself; he couldn't decide which. Without Genevieve around, his own errors would stand out that much more glaringly. He could already feel the heat, like an ant squirming beneath a magnifying glass.

Martin's second case of the morning involved a young black man who called himself Ibn Btu Abdullah but whose real name was Tarnell Edwards. He was accused of stealing dogs from the yards of million-dollar homes in the Cleveland Park neighborhood of Upper Northwest and had been apprehended on elegant Newark Street in the act of stuffing a toy poodle into an old knapsack that also contained two marijuana blunts in a cut-down Pringles can — which accounted for an additional possession charge. Tarnell was a likable, dark-complected, dreadlocked youth just two weeks past his eighteenth birthday. He seemed surprised when Martin told him he would be tried as an adult in criminal court.

"I thought that was twenty-one or something," Tarnell said.

"People take dognapping very seriously in this town," Martin said. "I'll be straight with you, Tarnell. You could be facing time in Lorton."

Tarnell folded his hands like the Catholic school boy he had once been, looked out the narrow gun slit window of the holding cell, saw nothing there but wire mesh and empty sky, and looked back again. He tried to speak; emotion choked his voice. He slumped back in his chair and rubbed his eyes with his fingers.

"Fucking shit!" he managed finally. "They're going to fuck me up for one mothafucking dog?"

"Thirty-five dogs have disappeared in Upper Northwest over the last few months," Martin said, trying to sound reasonable. "The police want to blame them all on you. If you were acting with accomplices, if anyone else was involved, I need to know now. I'm your lawyer, remember?"

Tarnell was silent for a whole minute, thinking. Martin could almost see the wheels working, the improbabilities flashing up one by one, only to be shot down, exploding like skeet in midair. Finally Tarnell sighed.

"OK," he said. "A couple of these brothers I know, they've got pit bulls, right? They fight them on Saturday night in this place in Anacostia, and people come from all over and a lot of money goes down. So, it's like, the brothers they don't want their fighters going soft during the week, so they like to keep them sharp on other dogs, like training, like a boxer or something. So they give one hundred dollars or two hundred dollars a dog depending on how big he is and fifty dollars for cats. I never done it before, but I needed the money, so I get on the Metro —" He stopped talking when he saw the expression on Martin's face.

"What happens to the dogs?" Martin said.

Tarnell gave him a blank look.

"If we could arrange to have some of those dogs returned to their owners, it might help our case."

"They messed up, man," Tarnell said at last. "Nothing left. Meat."

Martin shuddered. He remembered seeing a piece on the news about an old woman whose bichon frise had been stolen from her front porch one afternoon. The dog was her only companion, had been with her seventeen years, ever since before her husband died. Martin remembered the woman crying and holding up a little red collar studded with rhinestones. It was all she had left of both her husband and the dog.

"This does not look good," he said, shaking his head. "You were caught with a dog in your bag; they're going to get a conviction on the basis of that evidence. I might be able to work a deal, but you're going to have to give the cops everything. The names of the buyers. The men with the pit bulls."

"They'll kill me," Tarnell said, and his eyes got big and scared. "I give you their names, I'm dead. These are some rough boys, you dig?"

"I'm really sorry," Martin said, and he stood up and got his papers together and stuffed them into his briefcase. "You think it over, but I don't see any other way."

"It's only dogs," Tarnell said. "Not like they killing people."

Martin turned to the door. "It's other people's dogs, Tarnell," he said.

"That's not what this is about," Tarnell said, and there was bitterness in his voice. "It's white people's dogs! White people, they love their dogs more than they love their kids. Up there in Cleveland Park, they got those big beautiful houses, huge stretch of green out front with all them flowers and you know what? Where are the kids? No kids playing in the streets in the yards, nothing. I say that's bullshit! I say fuck 'em and fuck their dogs too!"

Martin pressed the security buzzer for the guard to open the door. He shifted his briefcase from one hand to the other and turned back for a moment.

"Remember not to say that to the judge, Tarnell," he said. Then the door opened, and he stepped out into the long corridor full of cages.

Later that afternoon Genevieve Claibourne came up to the PDS offices in the Moultrie Center to clean out her desk. Tayloe, the department head, carrying a large cardboard box with the solemnity of someone bearing a funerary urn, escorted her through the labyrinth of cubicles. His dark face was impassive; his eyes set straight ahead. He spoke to Genevieve for a while in a low, serious voice, then left her alone in her cubicle, which was next to Martin's. Martin heard her slamming drawers and sniffling a little, and he poked his head around the dusty burlap-covered divider to see how she was doing.

"How are you doing?" he said.

Genevieve looked up from where she was sitting on the floor surrounded by stacks of legal documents and other papers.

"Terrible," she said. "What the hell do you think?" She was wearing grass-stained tennis shoes and old jeans and a white turtleneck, today's uniform for the unemployed. Tears had smudged the mascara around her eyes.

Martin didn't know what to say. He felt embarrassed for her but also thankful that he wasn't the one cleaning out his desk. "I know how you feel," he said finally. Then he thought of something. "You going to be around for a while?"

Genevieve made a helpless gesture at the surrounding piles of papers.

"I could use a drink after work," Martin said. "How about it?"

Genevieve smiled through her tears, and Martin got up and tried to enlist some of the other attorneys for a happy hour to soften her departure. It wasn't easy. Most people don't like to associate themselves with failure. In the end he managed to convince only Jacobs and Burn, two attorneys on the low end of the pecking order without much seniority and with nothing to lose.

At six they went over to the D.C. Bar, a dingy basement establishment on 4th Street popular with the attorneys and investigators of Judiciary Square only because of its proximity. It was the sort of place where the Christmas decorations never came down and they had Bud and Bud Light on tap and Michelob and Michelob Light in the bottle. From the shoulder-high window, the terra-cotta frieze of the Grand Army of the Republic — soldiers, sailors, generals on horseback, mules, cannon, caissons, wagons — could be seen winding its way around the old Pension Building across the street toward a glorious victory just beyond the next cornice.

After two rounds of Bud, Burn insisted on a round of shots. He was not yet thirty, blond, big-shouldered and muscular. He had been an avid surfer during his years at the Loyola Marymount Law School in Los Angeles. Four shot glasses of cheap Pepe López tequila were poured before anyone could protest. The bartender handed over a plate of brown lime wedges and a saltshaker. Burn took a lime wedge between the thumb and forefinger of his left hand, salted his skin just above the wrist, and held up the shot glass in a toast with the other.

"Here's to getting fired," he said.

Genevieve frowned, but she followed Burn's lead and downed her shot just the same. A few minutes later she and Burn did another, and then she sighed and laid her head against Burn's shoulder.

"Why don't we all go over to Arribé after this and dance with the Eurotrash?" she said to everyone, though she was really just talking to Burn.

Martin barely sipped his tequila. He would be thirty-five next month; the hard stuff sat uneasily in his stomach these days. Jacobs pushed his shot aside untouched. He was in his late forties, with a wife and two kids neatly ensconced in a split-level with a well-trimmed lawn out in Gaithersburg. Being a lawyer was a second career for him. He had been a salesman of heating and air-conditioning systems for twenty years before finally deciding to go to law school.

"Getting too old for tequila," Jacobs said.

Martin nodded. "Me too." But both of them had already drunk just enough beer to loosen their inhibitions.

"Failing to file a continuance can happen to anyone," Jacobs said in a voice he thought only Martin could hear. "It could happen to me or you. But the newspaper thing was bad. Those bastards in the press! That poor little kid's face all over the front page."

"I was thinking exactly the same thing earlier," Martin said.

Genevieve lifted her head from Burn's shoulder and spun toward them on her barstool. "How do you think I feel?" she almost shouted, her bottom lip trembling. For a moment it looked as if she were going to break into tears.

"Just try to forget about it," Burn said, and patted her consolingly on the arm. "It's not you, honey; it's just the way things are."

She put her elbows on the bar and put her head in her hands. She was more than a little drunk now. "Everything is so goddamned serious these days," she said to her empty glass. "One little mistake."

"You want my opinion," Burn said. "You were overextended, spread thin."

"No different from everyone else," Genevieve said in a glum voice. "Some can deal; others can't. I guess I couldn't deal without messing up." Then she looked up and spun the barstool again in

Martin's direction. "You're next," she said in a voice that held the grim resonance of prophecy. "You better be careful, Wexler! I've seen some of your filings. They're a mess."

No one could think of anything to say after that. Genevieve went off to Arribé with Burn, Jacobs caught the Red Line to Shady Grove, and Martin walked over to the Metrobus stop on C Street with unfinished work under his arm as always. Perhaps, as Burn said, Genevieve had spread herself too thin. Maybe the answer was as simple as that. She had been dividing her time between her PDS work and the half dozen cases left over from a defunct private practice in which she had specialized — rather ineptly — in representing the interests of children in custody matters. The facts of Genevieve's last case were now well known to everyone in the service:

The child involved in the custody dispute, five-year-old Lashandra Shawntell Williams, had been living with her father, twenty-year-old Dontel Alonso Williams, in a dilapidated row house at T and Todd Streets, Northeast, on a block presided over by a gang of murderous African-American youths known as the Todd Street Posse. Dontel did no work, collected no unemployment checks, yet always seemed to have plenty of cash on hand. Lashandra's mother, Elisa-Marie Cunningham, had disappeared under questionable circumstances in 1997; the child's maternal grandmother, Mrs. Bernice Cunningham of Oxon Hills, Maryland, had been trying to gain custody ever since her daughter's disappearance.

At the hearing before Judge Marcus Cooper in June, Bernice Cunningham's request for custody had been denied, mostly because Dontel had showed up exactly on time, wearing a nice silver-gray Hugo Boss suit and six-hundred-dollar lizardskin loafers. Mrs. Cunningham got one look at the suit and the fancy shoes and that afternoon filed a motion for reconsideration, suggesting in her statement that Mr. Williams lived off the profits of a criminal enterprise. A second hearing date was set, and investigators were assigned to the case. An investigation like that takes time. It had been up to Genevieve to file a continuance to provide this time and to coordinate with investigators. Juggling seventeen other cases of varying degrees of complexity, she had forgotten about the case entirely.

Then, in August, members of the Todd Street Posse pulled up at the curb in front of Dontel Williams's house in a purple Humvee decorated with gold trim and blue neon belly lights like the Goodyear blimp. Dontel Williams sat on the couch in the living room, oblivious, watching *Space Ghost Coast-to-Coast* on the cartoon network, comfortably high from a mixture of marijuana and Martell as his daughter played with a broken electronic toy on the floor at his feet. In the next few seconds seventy-five rounds of ammunition from various pieces of military ordnance poured through the living-room window. A single bullet shattered the little girl's skull; she was pronounced dead by paramedics arriving at the scene. Possessed of the kind of luck available only to the irresponsible bastards of the world, Dontel survived the attack without a scratch.

At twilight every evening the branches of a large magnolia just outside the window adjacent to Martin's cubicle filled up with thousands of dark birds. They squawked and chattered noisily for an hour before swirling off again in a great fluttering cloud as the light drained from the sky in the west. They were not as small as sparrows or as large as crows. Grackles perhaps or rooks; he had always meant to look them up in a bird book at the library. But it didn't matter what they were called. He was amused by the thought that they seemed to be gossiping about each other, like idlers in a Parisian café. It gave him pleasure to pause from his work and watch them there, black feathery shadows hopping about in the green shadows of the thick leaves.

Now Martin leaned back in his chair, hands behind his head, and stared out the window in the last moments before the birds swept off to the horizon. He didn't hear the portentous knocking on the metal edge of the burlap divider, didn't realize that Tayloe stood at the threshold of his cubicle, waiting.

"You with us, Wex?" Tayloe said at last.

Martin started and almost fell out of his swivel chair. "Hey, Winston, I didn't see you there!"

Tayloe advanced into the cubicle, frowning. He was a light-skinned black man originally from Trinidad, and the lilt of the islands lingered around his voice like fading perfume. He carried under his arm a large Pendaflex file, which he deposited with a heavy thump on Martin's desk. As if in response to this, the birds in the magnolia tree took wing in a single instant and flew off into the descending night.

"There they go," Martin said.

Tayloe raised an eyebrow, unimpressed. "Clear your desk," he said. "I've reassigned all your other cases. This is what you're working on next."

Martin stared down at the Pendaflex file, which was long and black and thick and reminded him vaguely of a coffin. His heart sank. He'd been feeling tired lately, discouraged. His energies weren't up to a challenge just now.

"You ever hear of Alexei Smerdnakov?" Tayloe said.

Martin shook his head.

"What about Aba Sid?"

"No."

"What do you know about the Russian Mafia?"

Martin shrugged. "Not much."

Tayloe tapped the file with his knuckle. "Then you've got some reading to do. And you better read carefully. This one's a homicide."

Martin blinked once. "You're kidding." He'd never done a homicide before, Tayloe had never let him. He'd only done small-time stuff: dognappings, prostitution, domestic battery. He didn't blame anyone for these paltry assignments; his record in court was abysmal. He'd lost nearly 80 percent of the cases that made it to trial. He was on a particularly bad streak right now: the last six verdicts had gone to the prosecution. Anxiety rose to Martin's throat, and he could hardly swallow.

Tayloe allowed himself a humorless smile. "It's time you earn your keep, my friend." He gave Martin a hard squeeze on the shoulder and disappeared around the burlap divider.

For long minutes afterward, Martin stared down at the bulging Pendaflex, loath to turn the brown cover and lay bare the sad and terrible history concealed within.

In the Soviet Union during the bad old days of the Communist regime, the most common method of birth control for women was abortion. Condoms, diaphragms, the pill, sponges, IUDs, spermicidal cream, and the rest all were products of the decadent West and available only on the black market. Anya Sobakevich, the woman who gave birth to Alexei Smerdnakov, underwent thirty abortions over a twenty-year period. Alexei, her third pregnancy (by a Captain Smerdnakov of the uniformed division of the KGB), was the only one she allowed to come to term, perhaps because she was under some illusion that the captain planned to marry her. When it became apparent that he had no such plans, she abandoned the child without a qualm on the doorstep of the Chermashyna People's Orphanage in Moscow.

Captain Smerdnakov was purged from the ranks for ideological reasons shortly after this incident and finished his days on a gulag in Siberia; Anya Sobakevich died of alcohol poisoning many years later, a month after undergoing her final abortion. The fate that awaited little Alexei, though just as dire as either of these, was far more subtle:

In the nursery of the Chermashyna Orphanage, he was hardly ever touched by the nurses and only held for a minute or two at feeding time. Many less hardy infants died from this fundamental neglect, but not Alexei. He was tough from the beginning, a large baby with big hands and big feet and a thick head of black hair. As soon as his teeth came in, he began to bite. When he learned to walk, he also learned to kick and punch. At five years old he strangled a litter of kittens the headmistress was raising for the younger children to play with. When he was eight, for no reason at all, he pummeled an eight-year-old classmate senseless and hung him by the neck with a bit of rope from a pipe in the basement. The classmate was cut down just in time by the boiler engineer.

Alexei was then transferred to a juvenile correction facility in the Ukraine, where at ten he stabbed a teacher in the leg with a compass point. Finally, as a teenager, for the brutal assault and robbery of a party member in good standing, he was sentenced to the same work camp in Siberia where his father had died years before. There his true education began. There his skin was gradually covered with a series of crude tattoos: a penis with wings; two women going down on each other; alligators; heroin poppies; detailed portraits of Lenin and Marx, one on each buttock respectively. There he learned to cheat at cards and use the weak for personal gain. There he killed his first man, with a shovel blow to the back of the head. This hapless victim was a fellow inmate whom Alexei rather liked. Their argument had flared up over nothing, the last two cigarettes in a stale pack of Sputniks.

In those days the Siberian gulags bore the same relationship to Russian organized crime syndicates that farm team baseball bears to the major leagues in the United States. At the age of twenty-one,

Alexei was released and made his way to Vladivostok on the Pacific coast, where a place already awaited him in the Grushnensky Syndicate. Vladivostok was a wide-open city then, a haven for the various corruptions of both East and West. Alexei started out as a bodyguard and common thug and quickly became known in the criminal underworld for his ability to kill a man with his bare hands. His favorite method was to seize the victim's hair from behind, jam a knee in the small of the back, and jerk down with great force, snapping the spine as easily as popping the head off a shrimp.

Alexei was by now a large man, six feet three, 285 pounds. At twenty-five his black hair hung long and glossy to his shoulders; his eyes showed an utterly dark black, devoid of any light. He was not bad-looking in a thick-necked, brutal sort of way. And as it turned out, he possessed another valuable talent besides bare-handed spine snapping: he was a natural at running whores.

Alexei's bosses at the Grushnensky Syndicate recognized his potential and quickly put him in charge of a small stable of three young Korean whores. His character encompassed just the right combination of sensuality and utter cruelty needed for such work. The whores feared him for his sudden rages but loved him with equal fierceness in the way that such women love the men who exploit them. They did not cheat him, they were loyal, and with whores loyalty is the highest virtue. Four years later Alexei was the syndicate's chief pimp in Vladivostok, controlling hundreds, mostly Korean girls under the age of seventeen. It was from one of his favorites that Alexei Smerdnakov acquired the nickname Aba Sid, though the reference — probably Russian sexual slang — is obscure.

A single Polaroid snapshot exists of him from this period. Alexei is standing naked and grinning like the devil in the big room of his apartment on Sudokhodny Street. His pale skin makes a stark contrast with the dark black scrawl of his tattoos; his penis, semierect, nuzzles his thigh like a grazing animal. On the wall behind him is a large velvet painting of a woman making love to a black panther. The beast's claws are dug into the flesh of the woman's breasts, but the expression on her face is sheer ecstasy. The whore who took the snapshot, a sixteen-year-old Korean girl named Kim Sung Kim, was found with her throat cut by police two weeks later in a pile of restaurant rubbish.

Directly following this grisly discovery, for reasons unknown,

Alexei Smerdnakov left everything behind in Vladivostok and emigrated illegally to the Brighton Beach section of Brooklyn. There he eventually claimed political asylum and became a citizen of the United States.

The central cell block had its own peculiar smell, which Martin hated — a stale, vaguely urinous odor, but urine mixed with booze and unwashed flesh and antiseptic fumes and laced with other less palpable odors: fear, cruelty, ignorance, despair. At one time or another over 50 percent of the black male residents of the District age seventeen to thirty-five passed through its scarred metal doors, sat on the plastic benches in the limbo of the holding cells, cigaretteless, pants drooping, no laces in their shoes, waiting for lawyers or bail bondsmen or a friend with cash, or waiting for no one at all.

At 7:30 A.M. on Tuesday Martin showed his badge and driver's license to the guard at the front entrance, passed through the metal detector, signed in, and turned left into the long corridor that led to the consultation rooms. Halfway down, he passed a burly Hispanic man coming in the opposite direction. Martin was always oblivious at that hour of the morning, his higher brain functions still muzzy with sleep, and he brushed against the man's shoulder without noticing. The man instantly spun around and caught him from behind with an arm around the throat. Martin squawked, helpless; it was a choke hold, illegal in many jurisdictions across the country. He couldn't cry out because he couldn't take a breath. For a moment panic blurred his vision.

"Federal marshal!" the man shouted in his ear. "You under arrest!" Then, just as Martin realized who it was, the arm fell away and the hallway filled with booming laughter.

"God damn it, Caesar!" Martin turned around, rubbing his throat. "That's not funny!"

But it was funny, and Caesar Martinez couldn't stop laughing. "You should see your face, you poor SOB." He doubled over and slapped his thigh, and at last Martin joined him for a reluctant chuckle.

A few years ago, when Caesar was an investigator with PDS, the two men had worked together on a scandalous case involving a prostitution outcall service staffed with Georgetown University coeds. Martin's client at the time had been a pretty young senior from a solid middle-class Boston Irish family, who in her spare time specialized in bondage and rough sex for three hundred dollars an hour. A powerful member of the United States Senate had been one of her regular clients. Caesar uncovered this tasty bit of information during a series of exhaustive interrogations of the other young call girl/coeds — all of whom at one time or another had tied the senator spread-eagled to a bed frame in the rumpus room of his Capitol Hill town house and penetrated him anally with a black dildo he kept in a velvet box for that purpose. In light of this information, the case against Martin's coed was quickly plea-bargained down to a misdemeanor, and she was able to graduate on time and with honors.

Caesar finally stopped laughing and squeezed Martin's hand in a firm grip.

"How the fuck you doing, Wex?" he said.

"Busy," Martin said. "How are the feds treating you?"

"Got a health plan, good benefits," Caesar said. "I get my teeth fixed for free plus I get Columbus Day off. Better than that old freelance shit with the PDS."

The two of them talked for a few minutes about their lives. Caesar had come over from Cuba in the Mariel boatlift of '81 with nothing, unable to speak a word of English. Now he had eight years on his pension, a town house in Alexandria, a modest cabin cruiser docked on the Anacostia, and an attractive twenty-four-year-old wife expecting their first child. He was doing better than Martin these days.

"What about you?" Caesar said. "You still seeing that Dahlia chick?"

Martin shrugged. "Off and on," he said. "No commitments, nothing like that."

"Hey, man, keep it up!" Caesar said. "Once you walk up that aisle, they got you by the *cojones!*" The two men laughed. Martin shifted his briefcase from one hand to the other; he was on his way to see a client in the lockup, he said.

"Anything interesting?" Caesar asked.

Martin hesitated. "Yeah," he said, lowering his voice. "It's a homicide."

Caesar whistled. "That's not your thing at all," he said.

Martin nodded. "You're right about that," he said, and he leaned close. "Tell me something. Who do you recommend in the office now? I have a feeling I'm going to need a really good investigator."

Caesar thought for a moment. "Gotta be McGuin," he said. "He's great, the best. Don't matter how strange he looks. The man's always busy, booked up months in advance, but for you I'll put in a good word."

"Thanks a lot," Martin said, and the two shook hands again and parted.

Martin took his place on the hard plastic chair in the soundproof booth and opened his briefcase on the counter. The door was ajar in the corresponding booth on the other side of the thick Plexiglas, and he saw wavy shapes moving around in the big room over there like fish in a fishbowl. Finally a darkness blotted out the light. A huge man wearing the rough overalls of the D.C. Department of Corrections squeezed into the booth and with difficulty reached behind himself to close the door. Childishly drawn tattoos scrawled down the man's arms to his wrists and up his neck to his chin.

For half a second Martin stared. The man filled the booth almost completely. He could have been a professional athlete except for his disturbing black eyes, which looked at once too intelligent and completely devoid of human sentiment, and his hands, which looked clumsy, pig-knuckled. His black hair, streaked with white, was cut close to his head; his thick sideburns were neatly trimmed into sharp points.

Martin heard the big man's chair creak. He crossed his arms and sat back, waiting for Martin to say something. This behavior was surprising. Usually prisoners couldn't wait to talk, to rush out with their story before he'd even introduced himself. Martin tapped his pencil nervously on the counter and glanced down at his yellow pad, the first page half covered with doodles. He never wrote anything important on the thing; it was a prop, an aide-mémoire. Doodling was something like a vocation to him, one of his few genuine talents.

"You Alexei Sergeyevich Smerdnakov?" Martin asked finally.

The man nodded, expressionless.

"I don't know if you realize it, but you've been charged with first-degree murder in the death of" — he checked his page of doodles — "Katerina Volovnaya. Since it has been determined that you are unable to provide representation, the District of Columbia has —"

"You going to get me out of here, asshole?" Smerdnakov smashed his fist down on his half of the counter, and Martin felt the vibration through the glass. "This place stinks like horse-shit!" Smerdnakov spoke English with a Russian accent tinged with Brooklyn. His eyebrows moved dramatically when he spoke.

"I'm afraid bail is going to be out of the question, considering the charges," Martin said. "Also, your Russian background makes you a risk for flight."

Smerdnakov poked a thick finger against the glass. "I'm an American citizen," he said angrily. "I demand right to liberty!"

"Being a citizen is not the point here," Martin said. "You proba-bly still have family in Russia. From the District's point of view, you could decide to pay them a visit tomorrow. Then they'd never get you back for trial."

Smerdnakov flashed an ugly smile. His teeth were white and square, with narrow gaps between them, the teeth of a giant, teeth made for crushing bones. When he breathed, the prison overalls stretched taut across his chest.

"I have no family in Russia," he said. "I got no friends neither. I got friends in Brooklyn. I want to go back."

"Why don't you tell me what happened in your own words?" Mar-tin said. "We'll start there."

The Russian sighed. "Somebody killed my girlfriend, that's what happened," he said. "Now they try to blame it on me because of some things I did in Russia a long time ago."

Martin nodded, waited for more. When Smerdnakov didn't say anything else, Martin said, "I'm on your side here, Mr. Smerd-nakov. I'm your defense attorney. I'm going to need details. Every-thing you can remember."

Smerdnakov brought his face close to the Plexiglas screen. Mar-tin could almost feel his hot breath steaming through the small holes, clouding the booth.

"Nobody's on my side but me," the Russian said. "Defense, of-fense, you're all fucking lawyers as far as I can see. Who'd you suck off this morning, the DA?"

Martin was offended by this language. He looked down at his pad, doodled a stick figure clown holding a balloon, looked up, and tried again.

"I can't help if you don't let me," he said wearily. "Try to calm down, and tell me what happened."

Smerdnakov leaned back again and crossed his arms. "Okay, ass-hole," he said. "I tell you once. Me and my girlfriend come down here from Brooklyn for a little fun, you know. We meet some Russian guys at this bar — and the cops already ask me, I don't fucking remember their names — and these guys say, 'Hey, let's go dancing, I know a fun place.' So we go with them and we dance and we're down in the VIP room of this fucking club and we're dancing and having a good time. So I have a couple of beers, and I need to take a piss. I leave my Katinka with these guys, and when I come back from the bathroom, there she is lying on the floor, my necktie is twisted around her neck, and she's completely dead. Then the cops come and they put the cuffs on me and they say I did it, that everyone saw me. That's all I know. You want more, fuck you, you go find out yourself."

Smerdnakov stood up abruptly and squeezed out of the booth. Martin sat there for a long minute. Then he gathered his things and went back to the Moultrie Center, his mind working on trying to find a way out from under this case. He caught Tayloe in the hall-way, brown bag in hand, on his way to lunch.

"Can I talk to you?"

Tayloe rolled his eyes. "How about after lunch, Wex?"

"I'm having trouble with the Smerdnakov case," he said. "The defendant is completely hostile."

"I'll give you five minutes," he said, frowning.

They went across Indiana Avenue to the unkempt little park in the shadow of the Superior Court building. Tayloe was famous for his frugal ways. He packed his own lunch and ate it on the bench out here every day, weather permitting. The two of them settled down, and Martin waited as Tayloe carefully laid his napkin across his lap and unwrapped his sandwiches, always the same: one mayo, cheese, and cucumber on potato bread; one mustard, cheese, and tomato on rye. Today there was also a bottle of Evian water, a pear, and a small Ziploc of trail mix.

"I see no reason to pay seven or eight dollars for lunch every day for a sandwich I can make just as easily at home," Tayloe said a bit defiantly. Then he took a bite of his cheese and cucumber sand-wich, chewed carefully, and swallowed. "You'd be surprised how much that adds up to every year."

"About the Smerdnakov case . . ." Martin began.

Tayloe held up his hand. "Just let me finish my first sandwich before we get to it."

"Yes, of course."

Tayloe ate with maddening slowness. He took small bites and chewed thirty-two times, each time. Martin looked around, feeling uncomfortable and tired. This little park was depressing. The bushes were ragged, the grass patchy and yellow-looking. A drunk slept unmoving on the bench on the other side of a bronze art deco nymph feeding a bronze doe. Gilding hung in peeling strips off the nymph's bronze flanks, her arms covered with creeping green corrosion. Rickety-looking scaffolding rose up the brick side of the Superior Court building next door. Built in the neoclassical revival style popular at the turn of the century, this structure was apparently of some historical interest. They were doing a complete renovation. Many of the windows of the upper stories gaped open, covered only with thin plastic sheeting.

Tayloe swallowed the last bite of his sandwich, folded up his napkin, brushed crumbs from his lap.

"All right," he said. "What is it?"

Martin explained the situation. Smerdnakov was completely hostile, uncooperative, he said. Maybe it was a personality thing, but it wasn't working between them, and he didn't feel comfortable handling his first homicide with an uncooperative defendant.

". . . and so I'd like to withdraw from the case," he concluded. "Maybe you could get somebody else. Reeve loves to do homicides."

Tayloe nodded and took a bite of his pear. He chewed and swallowed, then dabbed at his mouth thoughtfully with half a napkin.

"Let me put it this way," he said. "Do you think you're a very good lawyer?"

Martin was taken aback by the question. He didn't know what to say.

Tayloe nodded and squinted up at the sky. "I'll answer that question for you," he said. "Personally I like you, I think you're a nice guy, but let's be honest, you're a terrible lawyer. You've lost your last six cases. In fact, you're the worst lawyer in the department. Worse in your own way than Genevieve was. If you want to keep your job — and believe me, there's enough evidence to fire you easily tomorrow — you will not withdraw from this case."

Martin was stunned by the bluntness of these words. He didn't
know how to respond. Half of him wanted to punch Tayloe in the
face; the other half wanted to get up, run away, find something else
to do with the rest of his life.

"W-what, w-why do you —" he stuttered. Then he stopped himself and caught his breath. "Okay," he said. "You think I'm a bad
lawyer. That's your prerogative. Why the hell would you want to
keep a bad lawyer on a homicide case?" But as soon as he'd asked
this question, he had the answer. He looked over at Tayloe, who was
smiling at him in a curious way. The man had just finished eating
his pear; all that was left was the gnawed stump in his hand.

Tarragon was a chic little restaurant in a strange neighborhood,
a sort of no-man's-land bordered by the warehouses and abandoned industrial buildings of New York Avenue on one side and
the Whitworth Terrace housing project on the other. Limousines
stood double-parked at the curb out front; the drivers smoked and
chatted idly with each other, their backs to the darkness. Valets in
red jackets scurried out into traffic to take car keys from men in
good-looking dark suits and women in spangled dresses with stiff,
sculptural hair. The chef, René Balogh, had been named chef of
the year by a noted California culinary organization. Reservations
had to be made far in advance, and Dahlia Spears was always very
thorough. She had called in July for dinner in September.

Things being the way they were with the Smerdnakov case, Martin would have preferred to stay home tonight, but it was hard to
say no to Dahlia. Now he sat glumly across from her at the prominently placed table she had specified, on a raised area at the back
of the room overlooking the other diners. The furnishings, mostly
big, faux-Gothic pieces, looked as if they had come out of the
House of Usher. The floors of the restaurant were done in a highly
polished black tile; Martin kept waiting for one of the waiters to
slip, food flying. The only good thing about tonight was that Dahlia
would pay. They had attended law school together at American,
but she had graduated near the top of her class, gone the corporate route, and was now a junior partner with Abel, Nichols &
Feinstein, a firm that specialized in patent law.

". . . at that party after the Gold Cup last spring?" Dahlia was saying. "You remember? That's where you met Camilla and Tony. Anyway, last week, Camilla picked up and went off to Okracoke with

Tim Lane, even though supposedly they weren't going to see each other again. Not after . . ."

Martin hardly knew what she was talking about. He was preoccupied, not in the mood for light conversation. Despite her intelligence, in conversation Dahlia often lapsed into mindless chatter. All she needed was an occasional "unh-hunh" or a nod of the head, and she could go on for hours. But now she reached over and rapped Martin on the knuckles with the handle of her butter knife. "Hey, you're not listening!"

"Sorry," Martin mumbled. "Just tired, I guess."

Dahlia narrowed her eyes. "Jesus Christ, someone might think you work for a living," she said. "That was one of the reasons you didn't want to go into corporate, remember? So you wouldn't have to pull eighty-hour weeks."

"This new case," Martin heard himself say. "It's a real tough one."

"You want to tell me about it?" Dahlia put down the butter knife. "Maybe I can help."

Suddenly there was concern in her voice. Martin looked up surprised and studied her face. Dahlia was an attractive, confident woman in her mid-thirties with the blunt, practical haircut so popular with lady lawyers. She always seemed busy, happy, wrapped up in her life. But now he saw something in her eyes, an uncertainty he hadn't seen there before. Maybe she was not as happy as she pretended. She had recently gained about ten pounds, which showed as a softening of the chin. She was getting older, and she lived in a beautiful apartment in a beautiful neighborhood — but completely alone, without love or even a cat. She had been married briefly in the late eighties to a Virginia hunt country heir who turned out to be a drunken idiot. There had been other relationships since then, a few serious, but she always drifted back to Martin in the end. They had dated off and on during law school, then drifted apart; these days they were old friends who still shared a certain intimacy. Sometimes they slept together, sometimes not, depending on her moods and whether Martin was dating anyone else, which was rare.

Now Martin almost told her everything, but he fought the impulse. "It's nothing," he said. "The usual bullshit. I'll tell you some other time."

Dahlia shrugged. "Suit yourself," she said, and turned away to scrutinize the wine list, and there followed a bit of an awkward silence until the appetizers came. After that they were occupied by the food, and Dahlia's talent for chatter returned. She talked about a couple they both knew who were getting divorced — they had seemed so much in love; they'd had a baby; then the wife started sleeping around — she talked about the weather; she talked about a movie she had just seen, about her job, which was boring, about her mother, a well-known eccentric, who had decided to marry an Arab met while shooting craps at an Atlantic City casino.

"That'll be husband number six or seven for Mom," Dahlia said. "I forget which. I stopped going three marriages ago." She ordered another bottle of wine, and Martin drank and found himself actually being diverted by her chatter, and for a few minutes he forgot all about Smerdnakov.

"See, that wasn't so bad," she said as they stood outside at the curb, dinner over, waiting for the valet to bring around her Saab. Then without warning, she reached her arm around his waist and leaned up and kissed him on the lips. Much to Martin's surprise, they ended up going back to her apartment in the Broadmoor and making love. It had been about eight or nine months since their last encounter. He'd almost forgotten what to do, what she liked. Her breasts were improbably large for her narrow frame; he busied himself with them while he remembered the rest. Afterward they lay together in her big bed in the dark and watched the reflection of the headlights of the cars going up Connecticut Avenue toward the Maryland line.

"You want to tell me about it now?" Dahlia said softly, just when he thought she was asleep.

"That would be a breach of ethics," he said. "Not supposed to discuss cases pending in a lady's bedroom."

"Don't think of me as a lady, think of me as a lawyer," she said, and Martin put his fingers over her lips and could feel her smile. He understood now, without knowing how he knew, that he stood on a kind of threshold with her.

"Okay," he said at last. "It's not a pretty story . . ." And he told her about Genevieve's getting fired and about the Smerdnakov case and his conversation with Tayloe of the week before.

"Maybe Tayloe has a point," he said. "Maybe I am a lousy lawyer. Maybe I've been lazy or stupid or both. But there's one thing I believe in, and that's, well —" He stopped abruptly. Suddenly he felt embarrassed.

Dahlia squirmed with impatience. "Come on, Martin. Don't stop there. What is it?"

Martin cleared his throat. "Justice," he said. "Don't laugh. I believe in justice. I believe that people are innocent until proven guilty and all that crap. So Tayloe gives me a homicide case, my first homicide case, despite my record, despite everything. Why?"

Dahlia didn't say anything.

"Because he wants me to lose," Martin said quietly. "Because someone, maybe even the FBI, called Tayloe and said, 'Listen, we know you're the public defender and all that, but we think it would be great if you could help us lock up this Smerdnakov guy and throw away the key.' And Tayloe said, 'No problem, I'll put my worst man on the case.' And that would be me."

They were silent awhile. A loud siren started up from the fire station next to the Uptown Theater; bare seconds later the ladder truck howled off into the night. From somewhere in the great building came a heavy thump and the faint echo of laughter. Dahlia pressed herself close. Martin felt her breasts pillowing out against his arm. Her lips were a half inch from his ear.

"You want to get them?" she whispered. "You want to really get them?" Martin gasped as she reached down and took hold of him between the legs. "Then here's my advice, one word — win."

Staring down at his shoes, unusual two-tone wingtips in an extremely high state of polish, McGuin shuffled his way through the labyrinth of the PDS and presented himself at Martin's cubicle about noon. He sat with some difficulty on a stack of document boxes across from Martin's desk and, without lifting his head, raised a hand in greeting.

"I really appreciate this," Martin said.

"I'm only helping out as a favor to Caesar," McGuin said to his shoes. "If the chief hears about me taking a case out of turn, he'll have my ass."

"Of course," Martin said. "I'll do whatever I can to expedite the process. I've got everything you need right here . . ." He fumbled with the mess of papers on his desk and knocked the Smerdnakov file onto the floor. Documents went sliding across the brown carpeting, worn slick by years of lawyers' leather soles. "Shit. Excuse me." He knelt and tried to put the documents back in order. McGuin snorted impatiently, his head bobbing like an apple.

Martin glanced over at him with a sheepish smile. Just having the man around was disconcerting: McGuin suffered from a rare physical disability in which the vertebrae of his spine immediately below the skull were fused together, causing his head to face directly downward. In conversation he compensated by leaning back as far as possible and rolling his eyeballs toward the bridge of his nose; talking to him was like talking to a turtle. Ordinary movements were difficult, and he was always bumping into things. Still, McGuin was one of the best investigators who had ever worked with the department. Maybe because he was always looking at the floor, he caught little clues — faint scuff marks, bits of hair, tiny bloodstains on a stair landing — that other people missed.

Martin finally got the file together and tried to hand it off to the investigator. McGuin shook his head, a curious side-to-side movement that seemed to involve his whole torso.

"I don't have time to read the whole damned file," he said. "I want to know what *you* know."

Disappointed, Martin carefully put the file back on his desk and summarized the police report as best he could.

On the night of September 5 the defendant, Alexei Sergeyevich Smerdnakov, was seen entering Club Naked Party at 9th and F Streets downtown in the company of the victim, Katerina Volovnaya, and a group of unidentified foreign men, probably Russians. Once inside, the entire party proceeded downstairs to the club's VIP room, where they danced and drank vodka and beer for approximately an hour and a half. According to witnesses in the club, Katerina danced with Smerdnakov. Then for some reason a loud argument ensued, and he left her on the dance floor and went by himself over to the bar. She proceeded to dance with several of the men in their party in a very provocative manner, finally pulling the front of her dress down to expose her breasts.

At this point, witnesses said, Smerdnakov became enraged. Allegedly he dragged Katerina by the hair to a dark corner of the VIP room, removed his necktie, twisted it around her neck, and pulled it tight. This happened quickly; so much force was used that her esophagus was crushed in a matter of seconds. Smerdnakov let the body drop where it was and went upstairs to continue his dancing. He was arrested in the crowd on the main dance floor when police arrived thirty minutes later. The Russians who had come in with the couple left hurriedly by a fire door immediately following the incident and had not yet been located. The actual strangulation was witnessed by patrons and employees of the club. Police had taken statements from several of these witnesses.

McGuin didn't say anything for a few minutes after Martin had finished his account. With his head bent he appeared to be meditating. He was an Irishman and like most Irishmen, a drinker. Martin had heard that he drank Guinness through a straw. Finally McGuin reared back and rolled his eyes.

"Are you aware the grand jury has handed down a murder one indictment on this?"

"That means nothing," Martin smiled weakly. "You know how it is: the grand jury could indict a ham sandwich if it wanted to."

"Manslaughter might be a possible plea," McGuin said, ignoring the stale joke. "But most likely you're looking at murder two. The guy dancing afterward is going to look bad to a jury. Maybe you can say he was so drunk he didn't know. Something like that. How drunk was he?"

"Not very," Martin said. "Apparently he only had two drinks the whole time and appeared sober. That's according to the bartender. Of course he had been drinking before. He may have been a little drunk, yes. But he wasn't incoherent."

McGuin wagged his head up and down, and Martin couldn't shake the idea that here was a turtle wearing nicely polished shoes. "How about an insanity plea?" McGuin said. "Any history of psychiatric treatment?"

Martin plucked a bit of lint off the cuff of his shirt. He was getting a little annoyed with this approach. "I didn't ask you up here for legal advice," he said. "I'm a lawyer, you know. My client insists he's innocent — as in not guilty. He says he was in the bathroom taking a piss at the time of the murder."

McGuin let out a short laugh like an exclamation. "Huh! That's a good one!"

"Nevertheless, that is our position," Martin said coldly. "We've got to find witnesses who saw him go into that bathroom. We've got to question the witnesses who say they saw him strangle Ms.

Volovnaya. Mr. Smerdnakov thinks it was one of the men they came in with. He hardly knew them. They had met just a few hours before at a bar in Adams Morgan."

McGuin shrugged, and his shoulders folded up like an accordion. "So you actually believe the man's innocent?"

"I do," Martin said.

"Let me tell you something." McGuin shifted uncomfortably on the boxes. "Do you know anything about your client?"

"I know what's in the police report," Martin said quietly. "I know what he told me himself."

"Well, let me fill you in. This Alexei Smerdnakov's a well-known son of a bitch, member in good standing of the Russian mob. Everyone, the FBI, the DEA, they've been after him for years."

"That's none of my business," Martin said. "I'm his defense attorney, not his conscience. I don't care what Mr. Smerdnakov did last year or the year before that. I care only what happened on the night of September fifth. And that's what I want you to find out."

When McGuin was gone, following his shoes into the corridor, Martin leaned back in his chair and stared out at the thick-leaved magnolia tree stirring in the wind. The happy congregation of birds was hours away, at dusk. It was quite hot for early October, in the low eighties. The air-conditioning in the building produced only a faint, cool rattle; the windows did not open. Just now crowds of interested parties — criminals, cops, lawyers — moved up and down the sidewalk past the hot dog stands in front of the Moultrie Center all ready to tell their own version of the truth about some terrible incident to a half-attentive judge. Suddenly Martin felt overwhelmed. Across Indiana Avenue, the scaffolding of the Superior Court, empty of construction workers for the lunch hour, stood idle in the sun.

On January 10, 1984, two Grushnensky Syndicate soldiers met Alexei Smerdnakov at Kennedy Airport. He carried an overnight bag with a single change of clothes and twenty thousand dollars in cash in a money belt around his waist. Two Cuban cigars were wrapped in tissue paper in the inside breast pocket of his thin coat. He had come from Vladivostok just forty-eight hours before; he couldn't speak a word of English. The soldiers introduced themselves by their gang aliases — Borodin and Kutuzov — put him into the passenger seat of a battered 1972 Ford LTD, and drove out to Brighton Beach, breaking every speed limit on the way as a matter of principle.

There, in the small back room of a Russian restaurant called the Kiev, they gave him a MAC-10 semiautomatic machine pistol with two banana clips of ammunition. Then they brought out three bottles of vodka and a carton of Marlboros and drank and smoked and waited for darkness. It was four in the afternoon. At ten-thirty that night, vodka bottles empty, carton half gone, sky over the Atlantic showing a frozen black, Borodin led Alexei out the back door of the Kiev into a blind alley that cut down the center of the block. Rats scuttled about in the garbage here, foraging for restaurant scraps. Halfway down, a rectangle of faint red glowed from a small window in a steel door. An extinguished Chinese lantern hung over the blackened lintel.

Borodin motioned for Alexei to wait in the shadows, then stepped up to the door and pressed a buzzer. A full minute later a red curtain inside drew back, and white light fell across his face. Borodin smiled into the light and nodded. The red curtain closed sharply, followed by the sound of dead bolts unlocking. In the moment before the door opened, Borodin said to Alexei, "It's very simple. Kill them all," and moved out of the way.

Alexei made no sign that he understood these instructions, but when the door swung out on its heavy hinges, he stepped forward, lowered his MAC-10, and began to shoot. The doorman, a fat Mongolian, let out a sharp grunt and fell back in a splatter of blood. Alexei stepped calmly over his body into the shallow entrance hall.

At the other end stood a door padded in red leather and decorated with Chinese characters painted in gold. He kicked it open to reveal an ornate red and gold room in which about fifteen Chinese men sat around felt-covered tables, gambling at mah-jongg. No one had heard the quick burst of gunfire; loud Chinese rock music blared from huge speakers chained to the ceiling. Smoke hung in a thick cloud beneath red-shaded lamps. In the hands of the gamblers the ivory mah-jongg tiles gleamed like fish scales in dirty water. Hundred-dollar bills, dull green against the vivid green felt of the tables, were stacked in neat piles at the gamblers' elbows. Two bored young women, naked except for garter belts, stockings, and spike-heeled pumps, sat on stools against the far wall. One smoked a cigarette and read a women's magazine; the other, head tilted to one side, mouth open, appeared to be dozing.

Poised on the threshold for a long beat, Alexei carefully chose his first targets. The gun felt heavy and warm in his hands. The muzzle velocity of a MAC-10 is such that a man standing in the middle of a crowd of people can begin firing and all of them will hit the ground dead or wounded before they can stop him. The woman reading the magazine saw Alexei first and began to scream. As her scream reached its highest octave, he squeezed the trigger. The gamblers scattered instantly. They were unarmed; according to club rules, weapons were always checked at the door. Some tried to dive beneath the tables; others ran for another exit at the far end of the room, which had been locked from the other side.

Alexei spent the first clip, knocked it out, loaded another. Blood showed as a dark stain against the red walls, soaked into the green and blue pattern of the Chinese carpet. Soon the room was a mess of splintered wood and gore. Most of the gamblers were dead after the first clip, but a few were still alive, moaning in the general heap of bodies. The woman with the magazine remained on her stool against the wall. She sobbed without making a sound. Alexei walked around the room, casually putting a single well-placed round into each victim's skull. The woman with the magazine was last. When he reached her, he smiled and brought the muzzle against her forehead. She closed her eyes.

Just then Borodin rushed in from outside. He gasped and choked back a mouthful of vomit. He hadn't been prepared for the extent of the carnage.

"Come on, let's get out of here," he shouted. "Now!"

Alexei looked up. The emptiness in his blue eyes made Borodin shudder.

"No," Alexei said. "Get out if you want. To do the job right, you've got to kill the head." He squeezed the trigger and there was a small explosion and the girl with the magazine jerked back and fell over sideways. Then Alexei turned quickly and let loose a spray of bullets that nearly tore Borodin in half; he walked over just to be sure and put another round behind the man's ear. When he was satisfied that everyone was dead, he collected all the bills from the floor that were not bloody or bullet-torn and stuffed them into the pockets of his coat, and he went out into the alley and down to the back room of the Kiev, where Kutuzov was waiting nervously, glass of vodka in hand.

"Where's Borodin?" Kutuzov said.
Alexei leveled the gun at his side and began to fire.

Copper vats of fermenting beer blew steam and bubbled behind a
floor-to-ceiling wall of tinted glass opposite the bar. Young men in
surgical green medical scrubs, bandannas tied over their long hair,
worked purposefully behind the glass. They measured hops and
barley into capacious bins, checked the aspirators and temperature
gauges, scribbled their observations on tearaway pads of blank
newsprint. A chalkboard announced the work in progress in large
letters: NOW BREWING MARAUDER BOCK.

The assistant United States attorney for the District of Columbia
watched the brewers at work, increasingly annoyed. He stood waiting for Martin Wexler at the long mahogany bar at the National
Star Brewing Company Bar & Grill at 12th and New York Avenue.
Martin was already a half hour late. The AUSA was a tall, dis-
tinguished-looking black man named Malcolm Rossiter. Today he
wore a dark blue Continental-cut suit; his shirt collar shone star-
tlingly white in the pleasant dimness of the big room. His tie of pale
blue silk with yellow squares probably cost a week of Martin's salary.
A well-trimmed mustache presided over his upper lip. He was a
busy man; he didn't have the time to be kept waiting. But he smiled
and nodded a genial greeting as Martin stepped up to the bar out
of breath, nearly forty-five minutes late.

"Sorry I'm so late," Martin panted. "My bus broke down, and
I couldn't get a cab to stop. I had to jog all the way from Dupont
Circle."

"Don't worry about it," Rossiter said, and he sounded sincere. "I
haven't been here ten minutes. What can I get you?"

Martin glanced at the beer menu and picked an India pale ale,
which came served in a tall, delicate glass that looked like a dessert
flute. When he tasted it, he grimaced. It had the green, bitter taste
of most microbrews.

"Something wrong?" Rossiter asked. A flute of bock sat flat and
nearly untouched on the bar in front of him.

Martin shrugged. "These brew pubs are going up all over the
place," he said. "I just wish they'd learn how to make beer first.
Think of the people who make Pilsner Urquell, or the Belgians.
These are people who have been making beer for hundreds of

years." Beer was one of the few things that Martin had strong opinions about.

Rossiter nodded blandly. He hadn't asked Martin to meet him at the National Star to discuss the quality of the beer. He checked his watch and pushed his flute of bock aside.

"I've got to catch a train," he said, "so I'll cut right to the chase. We need to talk about the Russian."

Martin set his ale on the counter and wiped his mouth with his knuckles. "I think you should know something, sir," he said quietly. "I am not prepared to compromise my position on this case."

Suddenly Rossiter was very angry. "I'm here talking man to man with you," he said, and he was almost shouting. "I'm not talking legal ethics. You got that?"

Surprised, Martin didn't say anything.

"This Alexei Smerdnakov, he's an animal, a public menace. He's a murderer, a rapist, a pimp, a pornographer, a drug smuggler, and whatever else. He's got an FBI file like a brick. You should know that; it's sitting on your desk. You've read the damned thing!"

"No, I haven't," Martin said.

Rossiter's mouth dropped. "Why the hell not?"

Martin took a long draft of his bitter ale. The stuff was too carbonated; it burned going down. "Somehow an FBI file appeared anonymously in my box two days ago, like magic," Martin said. "I don't need to tell you how irregular that is. Frankly I was shocked. The FBI doesn't release files unless the person in question is dead. Well, my client is not dead, and I'm not going to read the damned thing. I don't have the time. I'm too busy preparing my defense. Mr. Smerdnakov's past has no bearing on this case."

Rossiter shook his head. "You know something, man? You're weird."

Martin smiled. "Probably," he said. "I'm a public defender."

Rossiter frowned and picked up his flute of bock and drank off a half inch. "You're right," he said absently. "This stuff is nasty. I'll take Budweiser any day." Then he turned to Martin. "Do you know why this man is availing himself of the resources of the Public Defender's Service in this matter?"

"For the usual reason, I suppose," Martin said. "He needs representation and doesn't have enough money to provide an attorney of his own."

Rossiter laughed. "Wrong again, my friend! Smerdnakov is the head of the third-largest criminal syndicate in New York City, neck and neck with the Galliani family. He's got a corporate headquarters in Brooklyn, another headquarters in Vladivostok, according to Interpol, and no one knows exactly how much he pulls in a year. The FBI estimates his profits run into the hundreds of millions. But the guy is one smart bastard. He's got it rigged so on paper he makes nothing, he's in debt. He's using the PDS because he wants us to know he can shit on the law whenever he feels like it! Get what I'm saying now?"

Martin thought for a long second. "Not really," he said.

Rossiter sighed. "How many witnesses testified to the grand jury that they saw this man strangle his girlfriend?"

"I don't have access to that information," Martin said quietly.

"Well, I'll tell you, my friend! Nine witnesses saw him do it, and you know how many witnesses are going to come forward with their story when it comes time to testify in open court? None. Exactly zero. We won't be able to find them! They'll be dead or on permanent vacation in Mexico."

"That's bullshit," Martin said. "You believe that, take them into protective custody."

Rossiter threw a twenty-dollar bill on the bar. "Protective custody costs a lot of money, and it's hard to arrange. There's a cheaper way."

"What's that?" Martin said.

Rossiter straightened his tie and picked up his briefcase. "You're a well-known bungler," he said under his breath. "Do everyone a favor. Bungle this one."

Martin watched him go. Rossiter walked quickly out through the etched glass door and had barely raised his hand when a cab was there as if it had been waiting just around the corner all the time. Martin turned back to his ale, which he drank down quickly. The aftertaste was very similar to cigarette ash. To kill it, he ordered himself a double shot of Irish whisky and sipped slowly as the bar filled up with the after-work crowd, bright, young self-assured men and women in expensive clothes. How did they do it, go through the world with such certainty? He recognized a few faces from Judiciary Square but turned away before he caught their eye. A defense lawyer has got to believe in the innocence of his client, he wanted to say to them. No matter what.

*

Police cars sat double-parked down the center line along Indiana Avenue. A TV news crew was interviewing someone on the front steps. The satellite dish of its communications van reached sixty feet toward the sky, swaying in the wind at the end of its telescoping antenna like the nest of a large bird in a tall tree.

Alexei Smerdnakov slumped at the bare table in one of the consultation rooms at the Moultrie Center, hands in the pockets of his prison overalls, thinking about cunts. There were all kinds out there, cunts like flowers, cunts like a closed fist, cunts like a bunch of oily rags, cunts dry as dust. The plastic folding chair sagged under his weight. A buzzer sounded, the security door opened, and Martin stepped in, briefcase in hand. The Russian looked up, neither interested nor uninterested.

"Alexei, how are you doing?" Martin said cheerily. He put his briefcase on the table, withdrew his legal pad and two cheap plastic pens, and sat down. This was the first time he'd been in the same room with the man without a sheet of Plexiglas between them, and the experience wasn't entirely comfortable. Smerdnakov's physical presence was that much more intimidating up close. The muscles in his forearms bulged like Popeye's; the tattoos looked deeply incised, black scars against bleached skin.

The Russian grinned, showing his giant's teeth. "You ask if I am enjoying prison?" he said.

"Yes, something like that." Martin swallowed nervously. He had the feeling he was in the presence of a wild bull. Show the wrong color and the bull would charge.

"In Siberia they put me in the hole for two weeks," Smerdnakov said. "You ever been in the hole?"

Martin shook his head.

"It was freezing cold, and I was naked. Also, there were many" — he paused, searching for the word — "lice. You fall asleep, and they are covering you, sucking your blood. That was hard time. This is like a holiday."

"Glad to hear you're taking it so well," Martin said.

"But there is one thing I'd like you to do for me." The Russian leaned forward, plastic creaking. He brought his huge face close and whispered the word gravely: "Cigarettes."

"I'm sorry, my friend," Martin said. "It's against the law to smoke in public buildings in the District of Columbia. Plus, if the marshals catch me giving you a cigarette, my career is toast. You're going to have to wait till you get out of here to light up."

The Russian slammed his fist down on the table. Martin noticed there were Cyrillic letters tattooed on his knuckles. In an instant his face had become an evil mask.

"Get me a smoke, you crawling little bastard!"

Martin flinched, but he managed to hold the Russian's eye. "Are you finished?" he said, his voice wavering a little. "Can we discuss your case now?"

Smerdnakov muttered something in his own language and sat back and crossed his arms. "Lawyers, they are the same assholes wherever you go," he said, and he spit on the floor a half inch from Martin's shoe.

Martin took a breath and composed himself. "Let me explain something to you, Alexei," he said. "I've already taken a load of crap on your behalf. There are people who really want to see you go down. I'm the only thing that stands between you and a murder rap."

Smerdnakov appeared not to be paying attention. He studied the sliver of sky beyond the thick glass of the gun slit window.

"Alexei?"

The Russian looked back lazily.

"I want a confirmation one last time. I just want to make sure you're still committed to pleading not guilty. Because it's going to be a real fight, I want to warn you. And it's risky. Right now we might be able to do a deal, go for murder two, even manslaughter —"

"I am an innocent man!" Smerdnakov roared. "No deals!"

"All right, fine . . ." Martin patted the air between them with his hand in a calming gesture. "I'm going to need some answers on a couple of important aspects of your story we haven't covered yet. This is not going to be pleasant, but I think it's necessary, okay?"

Smerdnakov studied his well-manicured fingernails and did not answer. The nail of the pinkie finger of his right hand was about an inch long. Martin wondered briefly how he managed to keep his nails so clean and unbroken; then he pushed the thought out of his mind. He took a deep breath.

"Before the murder you and Ms. Volovnaya were arguing. What was that about?"

"When she drinks vodka, my Katinka she acts like a whore," Smerdnakov said. "So we are dancing together, and she is dancing like a whore for everyone to see her body. I tell her to stop, she says no . . ." He shrugged, and his voice trailed off.

Martin nodded and added a locomotive and a big-eyed fish to the doodles on his yellow pad. "Okay," he said without looking up. "I want you to think about when you found her on the floor. Tell me exactly what happened."

Smerdnakov thought for a minute. "I come out of the bathroom from taking a piss," he said, "and it's a long piss like a horse because I was drinking beer, not vodka, and I see quick enough that everyone is gone. Katinka and the men we came with, they are gone. I am very angry at first, and I think, *The bitch! She has gone away with them!* And then I look around and I see a body lying on the floor across the room and I know somehow it is her. I run over and take her in my arms, and she is stone dead. Someone has killed my Katinka while I was pissing!"

"What about the witnesses?" Martin said. "The bartender and the DJ and the busboy and the rest, who have told the police they saw you strangle Ms. Volovnaya? What do you say to them?"

Smerdnakov hit the table again, hard, this time with the flat of his hand. "I say they are fucking wrong!" he shouted. "They got the wrong guy!"

"Okay, calm down," Martin said. "Think about it from the jury's point of view. How could they get the wrong guy, all those people?"

Frowning, Smerdnakov leaned back and folded his arms across his chest. "Down in this club it is dark, and there is much cigarette smoke," he said at last. "Maybe these people, they saw me when I was picking her up and holding her in my arms, I don't know. But I did not kill her! Someone else did!"

"So here's the big question," Martin said, forcing himself to meet the Russian's eyes again. "Who did it? Got any ideas?"

Smerdnakov scratched his cheekbone with one beautiful fingernail. "Must be one of the men we came in with," he said. "I think then they were new friends, but maybe they were old enemies. In my work I have many enemies."

Martin let this comment pass. He studied his page of doodles again, adding a very carefully drawn spoon.

"Okay, so you find your girlfriend dead," he said in a voice as completely without inflection as he could make it. "You don't call the police; you don't call the hospital. You go back upstairs and you dance for another half hour until the police come because somebody else called them. How do you explain that?"

"I tell you," Smerdnakov said, "if you give me a cigarette."

Martin sighed. "First of all, I don't smoke," he said, "so I don't have any cigarettes. Second, as I've told you before, it's illegal to smoke in public buildings in the District of Columbia. We're talking a five-hundred-dollar fine. Now if you'll —"

"You Americans are a bunch of cocksuckers!" Smerdnakov interrupted. "In this country any kid can pick up a gun and shoot another kid and get a couple of years on probation. But smoking is illegal, a big crime!"

"Alexei," Martin said patiently, "we were talking about the dancing."

Smerdnakov threw up his hands. "It is the way we are in Russia," he said. "Only a Russian would understand this. Many terrible things happen to us: wars, famine, communism. We are used to such terrible things. We can't cry every time somebody dies, or we would never be able to breathe for the tears. Stalin he killed forty millions! So we must remain tough, hard. My sweet Katinka is dead. So what do I do, cry? Maybe inside, but not outside, no! In Russia, in the gulag, I see many people die, men, women, children. I know I can do nothing to bring my Katinka back, she is dead. So I go upstairs to dance and drink and forget. The police, everything else, they come soon enough, no matter what I will do."

Smerdnakov withdrew into himself when he had finished this speech. He crossed his arms over his chest, and his eyes went slightly out of focus. But Martin was excited. He felt Alexei had just handed him the key to unlock this case. He jumped out of his chair and paced the small room twice. On his second pass he paused before the narrow window that gave out on the Superior Court building across the street. A bit of sun had pierced the low clouds, and the peeling bronze nymph in the garden over there seemed to glow in a pool of her own mysterious light.

Behind him now, Alexei stirred, cleared his throat. "Come on, asshole," he said, but this time his voice was wheedling, cajoling. "Can't you get me a cigarette?"

*

The next afternoon, perched on a concrete planter in Judiciary Square eating a banana, Martin saw a man coming through the lunchtime crowds with his head down, staring at the ground as if searching for something precious he had lost. It wasn't until the man got closer that he realized it was McGuin. Somehow, without seeming to look ahead at all, McGuin was making straight for him. Martin wondered how McGuin managed such feats of navigation until he saw something glittering in the man's right hand. A small square of mirror. But that didn't make the skill involved in just getting from point A to point B any less impressive; it must be hard seeing the world as an upside-down reflection.

"Tried calling you all day," McGuin said gruffly. "Where the hell have you been?"

"Out of the office mostly," Martin said, taken aback. "What's up?"

"Next time, check your messages," McGuin said. "We've got a meeting in a half hour."

Martin looked at his banana, slightly confused. "You mean, right now?"

The FBI Headquarters building is an ugly yellowish concrete pile that takes up the entire block bordered by 9th and 10th and D and E. With its rows of honeycomb windows, it always reminded Martin of an enormous hive in which the bees make no honey and are better left undisturbed.

"What's this all about, McGuin?" Martin said, pausing on the sidewalk in front of the entrance on 10th.

"You'll find out in a minute," McGuin said, and pushed him through the automatic doors and into the narrow arch of the metal detector. This device went off and before he was allowed to pass, Martin was forced to remove his watch, his keys, and loose change and then undergo a frisking from a stern-faced guard with a device resembling an electronic fraternity paddle.

Inside, the long, bland corridors were suffused with a hush and a stale, waxy smell that Martin associated with church. He had been here twice before on other cases, and each time, for reasons he could not articulate, the place made his skin crawl. Perhaps it was because in a certain sense, everyone was a potential criminal to the FBI. Somewhere, locked away in a vault below street level, there still existed top secret surveillance files on thousands of innocent

American citizens, including such people as Hemingway, Greta Garbo, John Updike, the creators of *Howdy Doody*, Jimi Hendrix, Vanna White.

Martin followed McGuin into the big steel elevator, heavy and slow as an armored car, and up to a conference room on the seventh floor. Chairs upholstered in beige vinyl stood empty around a long metal table topped with plastic wood. On the wall a framed picture of J. Edgar Hoover and another of the president. In one corner, beside the American flag, a coffeemaker steamed quietly.

"Help yourself to coffee," McGuin said, settling himself at the table. "It was fresh this morning."

"You seem just a little too comfortable around here," Martin said, and he sat down in a chair at the far end of the table from McGuin.

The investigator's lip curled. "What do you mean by that, Wexler?" he said.

"I mean an FBI file on Smerdnakov appeared on my desk last week. Any idea how it got there?"

"No," McGuin said, and he didn't say anything more.

The two of them sat in strained silence for ten minutes. The sound of traffic heading up Constitution toward the vanilla ice-cream-scoop dome of the Capitol did not penetrate the fortress-thick walls. Martin couldn't shake the feeling that he was being watched by surveillance cameras, and he began to sweat imperceptibly. Finally the door opened and a man in a rumpled gray suit entered the room, carrying two thick files bound with large rubber bands. He was tall and gangly, of an indeterminate age between forty and sixty. His brown hair was parted over the bald spot on top of his head.

The man put the files on the table and came around to Martin's chair. "Mr. Wexler?"

Martin stood up and they shook hands. The man introduced himself as Agent Walters and said he was acting deputy assistant chief of the Organized Crime and Racketeering Division.

"That must be an interesting job," Martin said, "but I don't get why you wanted me to come in today."

Agent Walters exchanged glances with the top of McGuin's head.

"Please, sit down," he said to Martin.

Martin sat down again as Agent Walters settled himself in the chair directly across the conference table. He removed the large rubber bands from the first file, opened the cardboard cover, shuffled through some papers.

"I'll just take a case at random," he said, and picked out a Xeroxed page covered with typescript. He glanced at it, then fixed his eyes on the acoustic tile of the ceiling. "Several years ago New Jersey police found the torso of a young woman in a storm drain in Secaucus, New Jersey. Her legs were later discovered in Westchester, New York, in some bushes beside a tennis court, and her head turned up in Connecticut in the men's bathroom at a rest stop on 95 North. There it was, face up, staring out of the steel toilet bowl. Pretty public place to leave a head, don't you think? A troop of Cub Scouts from Pennsylvania pulled in that morning in a bus. The kid who found —"

"Excuse me!" Martin interrupted. "Do you mind telling me what all that has to do with me?"

Agent Walters removed his gaze from the ceiling and fixed it on the vicinity of Martin's chin. His eyes were red-rimmed and mistrustful, a dull, muddy brown. The eyes of a man who had seen far too much of the world.

"They found parts of the woman's body in three different states," he said. "So we were called in. We put her back together, did a little detective work, and dug up her rap sheet. Tatiana Ostronsky, former prostitute, originally from Minsk, in those days Soviet Union, now Belarus. Busted for solicitation and possession a few times in the eighties. Busted in '91 in a NYPD raid on a Grushnensky Syndicate brothel in Brighton Beach and" — he paused for effect — "former mistress of our friend Alexei Sergeyevich Smerdnakov."

Martin pushed his chair back and stood up. "I thought we were heading in that direction," he said. "Not interested." He looked over at McGuin, who appeared to be studying the reflection of his face in the glossy finish of the table. "And thanks for all your help with the case, McGuin."

McGuin didn't respond to this sarcasm.

Agent Walters followed Martin to the door and out into the corridor. "Try to understand who you're dealing with, please," he said. "The man's probably the most bloodthirsty Russian national since Ivan the Terrible."

They arrived at the steel elevator, and Martin pressed the button marked DOWN. The elevator came; the steel doors parted. Agent Walters was still at his side.

"We've made a copy of the complete file for you," he said, sounding a little desperate. "It took my assistant a whole day. That stuff we sent over last week was just a fraction of what we've got. I'll messenger the new stuff this afternoon."

Martin stepped into the elevator and pressed the button for the lobby. "Don't bother," he said. "I'm not going to read it."

Agent Walters put his hand against the rubber bumper and opened his mouth to say something more, but Martin shook his head.

"Even the devil himself has got the right to a fair trial," he said.

Agent Walters stepped back and the steel doors of the elevator closed and Martin began the slow descent alone.

Immediately following what became known as the Mah-Jongg Massacre, Alexei Smerdnakov decided to disappear. They had brought him over as a hired gun; hired guns are used once and thrown away. But he had hit them before they hit him, and now no one in America knew his face. There are worlds within worlds in New York City; Alexei chose one nearby. He left the Kiev by the back door, walked a mile down Brooklyn Avenue through the drizzling cold, and turned left on 227th Street. There, two blocks from the sea, he found a run-down motel called the Surf Side, done up in fading fifties turquoise and dirty sea-foam white stucco. A hand-lettered sign in the window in Cyrillic characters announced RUSSIAN SPOKEN HERE — MONTHLY RATES.

Behind the front desk a twelve-year-old Estonian girl with a missing tooth took his money. He paid in advance for the whole month, and she pretended not to notice the spattering of blood on his clothes. She had dirty blond hair and knowing eyes and was rather pretty in a prepubescent slut sort of way. *One false tooth and one more year, and she'll be ready to work for me,* Alexei thought. He signed his name as Aba Sid, gave a fictitious address in Vladivostok, and went up to a room on the third floor. He took off his shoes and coat and lay on the bed and fell asleep.

The Surf Side was not the sort of establishment to bother a sleeping man who had paid for the month, and when Alexei awoke, it was nearly midnight three days later. He showered, put on clean clothes, and set about counting his money. He had gathered an additional fifteen thousand dollars from the wreckage of the mahjongg parlor, bringing his fortunes in America up to thirty-five thousand. An unambitious man will squander such a sum all at once on expensive booze, gambling, cheap women, and cocaine or, worse, gradually on the necessities of living. Alexei was not one of these. His ambition was boundless. He was also very lucky, which in criminal matters is more important than skill or foresight.

As it turned out, a drunken Bulgarian pimp known as Mitya, loosely connected with the Grushnensky Syndicate, ran a string of whores out of the second floor of the SurfSide. The whores were more or less evenly divided among Chinese, Russian, and Dominican women between the ages of sixteen and thirty-eight. The Dominicans worked the side streets down by the promenade at 187th; the Chinese received customers in six rooms set aside for their use on the second floor; the Russians acted as high-priced call girls with beepers and knockoff designer clothes and rented out for fifteen hundred dollars for the evening, just like escorts in Manhattan.

Alexei only gradually discovered these details. The first six months of his residence at the SurfSide he spent quietly learning English in evening classes offered at the Brighton Beach YMCA. When he could speak well enough to be understood, he applied for his citizenship as a political refugee, which in that era of the Reagan presidency was swiftly granted. Meanwhile, he also became intimate with one of the Russian whores working for Mitya, a twenty-five-year-old former beautician who called herself Lomi. Alexei knew how to manipulate prostitutes the way other men know engineering or investment banking. Soon Lomi was spending all her spare hours on her back in his room, working his cock for nothing.

But Alexei had another agenda besides getting laid. Together one dark evening Lomi and Alexei planned Mitya's murder. It was a simple enough matter. Lomi enticed the unsuspecting procurer to an empty room at the motel with some Colombian pink flake she said had been given her by a grateful client. They snorted the blow, and Lomi undid Mitya's trousers and was performing fellatio on him as Alexei entered the room and drew the blade of a sharpened kitchen knife across the man's jugular. Afterward they had to clean up the blood, using mops and buckets of hot water, and the indoor-outdoor carpeting was completely ruined. The Bulgarian's death didn't make any more of an impact than this. The operation at the SurfSide continued uninterrupted, now with Alexei and Lomi in charge. Lomi managed the girls gently and with tact, as only a woman can, and Alexei handled the muscle and the money. Business prospered.

At last, a year later, Alexei received a summons to the Grush-nensky Syndicate headquarters, on the thirty-seventh floor of the Taft Building on Court Street in downtown Brooklyn, two blocks from the neoclassical edifice of Borough Hall. The Russian Mafia in Brooklyn was not run as a family like the Italian Mafia — with all the arcane loyalties and heated betrayals of family life — but as a cold corporate entity. The three men at the top, known as the Directors of the Central Committee, based all decisions on sound business principles: on statistics and market share and profit and loss. These men were not gangsters but businessmen in sober three-piece suits with M.B.A.'s, wives, children, summer homes in the Hamptons.

Alexei presented himself at the appointed time and was ushered into a plush conference room by a polite middle-aged woman with a stenographer's pad. She sat in a chair in the corner and prepared to take notes. The Directors of the Central Committee were seated at the far end of the conference table, going through sales figures from the previous quarter over a quick lunch of roast beef sandwiches and borscht, ordered from a nearby Russian deli. The floor-to-ceiling window behind them showed the tall buildings of downtown; behind these, in the distance, the graceful brownstones of Brooklyn Heights and the buttresses and black cables of the great bridge.

The directors were surprised. They had expected the Bulgarian, and they studied Alexei with some suspicion. For his part he recognized their weakness immediately: these were men who had never gotten blood on their hands. They had never shot someone point-blank between the eyes before breakfast, never bludgeoned a woman to death and gone happily into the next room and raped her thirteen-year-old daughter.

The first director cleared his throat. "Where's the Bulgarian?" he said.

"The Bulgarian is dead," Alexei said.

"What happened to him?" the second director said.

"I killed him." Alexei drew a hand across his throat to indicate how.

The third director said nothing.

"Syndicate associates can only be terminated under direct orders from the Central Committee," the second director said. "You had no such orders. Since —"

"And just who the hell are you anyway?" the first director interrupted angrily. "We've never even seen you before!"

"They call me Aba Sid," Alexei said. "I came over from Vladivostok last year."

The first director leaned both elbows on the table. "We can have you sent back there in a box, you know. Just like that," and he snapped his fingers.

"Give us one reason we shouldn't put a bullet in your brain right now," the second director said.

Alexei shrugged. "Take a look at the books. I've doubled your profit in six months. You're making twice as much with me as with the Bulgarian."

There followed some fumbling with papers; then the appropriate sale charts were produced. The directors put their heads together and muttered to one another in low tones. Alexei heard the faint tap of the calculator, the scratch of pencil on paper. At last the first director raised his head.

"You've done quite well, it's true," he said. "But what guarantees do we have that you will continue to produce?"

"Trust me," Alexei said, and he grinned ferociously, showing his square, healthy teeth.

The directors decided to trust him, and Alexei went back to the SurfSide with their blessing. This was a fatal mistake. They had forgotten that the first business of crime is crime, not business. And the weapon of crime is violence, not bottom-line economics. Within two months all three of the directors were dead, along with their wives and children, and the Grushnensky Syndicate was left with a vacuum at the top.

In the yearlong gang war that followed, nearly two hundred people were shot, burned, stabbed, or garroted, a quiet massacre barely reported in the media. Only one grisly case made the cover of the *New York Post,* when parts of a young woman's dismembered body turned up in three states. The woman was later identified as a Russian prostitute named Tatiana Ostronsky, also known as Lomi. She had been the mistress of the man who eventually emerged victorious in the struggle for control of the Grushnensky Syndicate, Alexei Sergeyevich Smerdnakov.

Martin fired McGuin the day after their unscheduled visit to the FBI and hired an independent investigator out of the department's discretionary fund. The new investigator, a hip, articulate young man, no older than thirty, worked part-time for Hilbrandt and Harding out of Bethesda, Maryland. With the other part of his time, he was finishing up a Ph.D. dissertation in philosophy and religion of the ancient world at Catholic University.

He showed up for the preliminary interview at Martin's cubicle on Thursday morning, wearing a black wool suit with narrow lapels, a black turtleneck, and round, green-lensed sunglasses. A shock of white hair stood straight up from his scalp. He looked more like a rock star from the New Wave era than either an investigator or a philosopher. He introduced himself as André Drelincourt and offered a damp handshake as pale as his skin.

"Is that French?" Martin asked.

Drelincourt smiled. "French Canadian," he said. "My father was from Quebec."

Martin had his doubts at first, but Drelincourt proved a quick study. He reviewed the PD case file and the police report overnight and called Martin in the morning with a plan.

"The first thing we do," he said, "is go down to that club and talk to some witnesses. I want you to come with me. Is that all right with you?"

"Sure," Martin said, relieved that the investigation seemed to be moving forward at last.

"I'll tell you why I want you along," Drelincourt said. "Are these witnesses credible? I can tell you from experience that club people rarely are. Since their grand jury testimony, they've had a chance to mull over their statements to the police. Talk to them now, and you'll get a good idea of what's going to happen on the witness stand."

Drelincourt picked Martin up in front of the Moultrie Center in a vintage black Mercedes 280 SE convertible with the top down. It was a bit battered, but the red leather of the seats and the walnut dash gleamed with a rich patina only the years can give.

"Nice ride," Martin said.

Drelincourt brushed his finger against the ivory knobs of the Blaupunkt shortwave.

"Fifty percent of investigation work is image," he said. "You've got to make an impression, intimidate people a little bit. I can't tell you the confessions I've heard from people sitting right there, where you're sitting, in the front seat. Get them in the car, close the door, drive around the block, and boom, they start spilling their guts."

Club Naked Party occupied a Victorian building on a decrepit block slated for demolition sometime in the early 2000s. Once it had been the national headquarters of the Young Christian Woman's Temperance League. A granite crane gripping a cross in one claw and an oak leaf in the other, the ancient symbols of the movement, still decorated the facade, but this teetotaling bird was grimed over with the dirt of a century and half obscured by a marquee that announced two words, *NAKED PARTY,* in giant neon script.

Martin and Drelincourt went up the front steps and passed beneath both the marquee and the motto of the YCWTL, carved into the keystone — *Sobriety, Chastity, Honor* — and entered a place where these virtues had no meaning. Aziz and Munzi Jehassi, the Lebanese brothers who owned the club, had gutted the period interior to expose the beams and brick and ductwork. The dance floor was tiled in patterned vagina-pink rubber blocks; over the bar hung huge Technicolor paintings of naked men and women fingering their genitals. Now empty, the place smelled of spilled beer and last night's cigarettes. A young woman in a torn white T-shirt cleaned up behind the bar.

Aziz Jehassi, a thickset man with a beard worthy of the Prophet himself, sat at a table in the corner, going over the receipts. His shiny suit reflected faint light from the high windows. He sprang up, receipts flying, as Martin and Drelincourt came across the dance floor. When they were close enough, he grabbed Martin's hand and shook it vigorously. He was always ready to help the police, he said. Drelincourt stopped a few steps behind and crossed his arms, impassive as Joe Friday interrogating a hippie.

"There's been a misunderstanding," Martin said. "I'm not the police. I'm with the Public Defender's Service."

Jehassi looked confused for a moment; then he nodded. "We are happy to help any representative of the District government," he said. "Please, what may I get you?" He waved at the bar, and the three of them went over and sat down. After some discussion, two Cokes and a ginger ale were brought by the young woman in the torn T-shirt.

Jehassi's dark eyes glittered nervously; a few beads of sweat appeared on his upper lip.

"We are most anxious to clear up this matter," he said. "For such a thing to happen at my club . . ." He wagged his head sorrowfully and pulled at his long whiskers.

"It must have been quite a shock," Martin said sympathetically. "We'd just like to talk to some of the witnesses, if you don't mind."

Jehassi turned to the young woman behind the bar. "Daisy, go get them from downstairs!" he ordered in a voice used to command.

Martin opened his briefcase and prepared to interview the witnesses at Jehassi's table in the corner, hastily cleared of paperwork. There were now only four: the VIP room bouncer, who was an ex–Howard University football player named Jason Thompson; Arturo, the Guatemalan busboy; the DJ, a young black kid known as Funk Master Swank, whose real name was Charles Emerson; and Daisy, the barmaid. Three other witnesses had disappeared the week before; they had simply failed to show up for work, and now their phones were disconnected. And the two patrons who had witnessed the crime were also gone. According to Drelincourt's sources at District police headquarters, they had left town without forwarding addresses.

The interviews went better than Martin could have hoped:

"It was dark as shit down there, and with the strobe lights going, I couldn't see a damned thing," Funk Master Swank said.

Arturo pretended that he spoke no English and showed Martin his green card.

"I work legal," he said. "I pay the tax."

"Why did you tell the police you saw Mr. Smerdnakov strangle Ms. Volovnaya if you now say you didn't see what you said you saw?" Martin asked Thompson.

The ex–football player thought for a few minutes, something

like panic blooming behind his dull eyes. "I made a mistake," he said finally. "It must have been somebody else."

Daisy, the barmaid, was the last to be interviewed. She was an anorexic-looking young woman, about twenty-six, her blond hair cut short and pulled back with a battered rhinestone barrette. Six earrings hung from one ear, five from the other, a ruby stud glittered in her nose, but she had excellent bone structure. She looked to Martin like a concentration camp survivor who had been accessorized by Gypsies. Still, he tried to avoid staring at her breasts, reduced by starvation but undeniably pert, pointing up at him from beneath her torn T-shirt. She would be quite beautiful if she gained a little weight and fixed herself up, Martin found himself thinking.

"Like, I didn't see anything, man!" she said before Martin could speak. "Nothing at all!" She swiped her thin hand through the air for emphasis.

Martin nodded and consulted his usual padful of doodles. This was getting a bit ridiculous. He added a butterfly with one wing crushed.

"That's not true," he said when he looked up. He noticed now that her eyes were beautiful. "You saw something. It doesn't have to go any further than this table. But I need to know."

Daisy shot a sideways glance at Drelincourt who sat on the banquette at Martin's right hand, observing discreetly from behind his green sunglasses.

Martin turned to the investigator. "Just a couple of minutes, André," he said.

Drelincourt nodded and withdrew to the bar. Now the young woman leaned forward.

"I don't appreciate lying," she said. "I'm an honest person, that's me, I'm a straightedger, okay? But I'm scared. I'll tell you what I saw that night. I saw that Russian guy strangle a woman. First he hit her, and like, everyone was horrified. Then he dragged her by her hair, by her hair, man, over to the corner, and he's like, shaking her and no one does anything. But this is the VIP room, okay? The customer's always right because he's paying a fortune to be down there, and he's got to know somebody cool to get through the door in the first place. And you know, all sorts of weird things go on; it's what puts the naked in Naked Party. I mean I've even seen two men fucking a girl, you know, at the same time on one of the couches, like, right in front of everybody."

Martin was shocked. "You mean, rape?"

Daisy shook her head. "No, I mean the girl was really getting off. Like orgasming."

"Oh." Martin felt his face go red.

"So here's the deal. The Russian bastard hits her again, and then he takes his tie out of his pocket and puts it around her neck, and this girl, she's so terrified, she's not even moving, she's like hypnotized. Then he starts to twist. I can see her eyes pop out, her tongue. I scream for Thompson to do something, but by the time he gets there, the Russian bastard has moved off, and the girl is dead. Lying on the floor dead."

Martin held up a police mug shot of Smerdnakov. "This is the man, you're sure?"

Daisy nodded. "That's the motherfucker," she said. "He came in with a bunch of real hard-looking guys. Russian Mafia, if you ask me. We get them in here sometimes; they road-trip down from New York in rented limos to party, and they drink vodka all night until they're stinking drunk. Big tippers, though, I've got to give them that."

"What about these other Russians?" Martin said. "What did they look like?"

Daisy hesitated. "They were all big guys, tattooed," she said. "Which makes me think they were mob types. But what are you really asking me, could I have made a mistake? Got the wrong guy?"

"It's a consideration," Martin said.

"No," she said, tapping Smerdnakov's photograph. "That's him. I'll tell you now, but I'm not going to say it in court, understand? I'll look right at the motherfucker and I'll say, 'Never seen that guy before in my whole fucking life.'"

Martin was surprised by this frank admission. He slipped Smerdnakov's picture back into his file, tucked the file into his briefcase. "Let me ask you something," he said, looking away, a little spooked by the fear showing in her face. "Why are you so willing to perjure yourself?"

Daisy leaned across the table, hugging her elbows. "Because someone called me one night last week at like, three A.M. It was a foreign-sounding voice, a guy. If I didn't keep my mouth shut, he said, I'd be raped repeatedly, then hacked to pieces and my pieces would be left in different states up and down the East Coast. That's what the bastard said, they've done it before, he said. And the next day you know what I found?"

Martin was afraid to ask.

"Half of a rat stuffed into my mailbox in my building. The other half I found in my locker right downstairs here when I got to work." Daisy stood up abruptly. "Anything else?"

"No, thanks," Martin said, and he tried to smile. "You've been a big help."

She was a tough girl, Martin saw now, but not nearly as tough as she pretended. Tears were shining in her eyes. She turned and walked away from him with a nice swaying hip motion that wasn't practiced or false but as natural as an island girl. He watched her sway across the dance floor, pick up a dirty rag, and resume her work behind the bar.

In traffic, in Drelincourt's Mercedes a half-hour later, Martin couldn't think with the top down. There was something about this case he wasn't getting; he still couldn't quite figure the right line to take for the defense.

"Do you think you could put the top up for a bit?" Martin said. "It's the glare."

"You're the boss," Drelincourt said, and he pulled over to the curb, hopped out, and released the top. When it came up to the pegs, both of them took one of the chrome latch handles and pulled it closed. They sat there for a while, the Mercedes ticking over quietly, waiting for a break in the rush-hour traffic.

"I told you they were slippery characters," Drelincourt said. "Club people. I should know, I used to play in a band called Solon. Ever hear of us?"

"No," Martin said.

"We were among the best of the second rank. No recording contract but almost a couple of times, and a pretty good following at the colleges. We worked the circuit from Austin to Athens for a few years, and we worked the beaches. If I had a dollar for every time some club screwed us over . . ."

He pulled into traffic now and pointed the star on the grill up

13th toward Logan Circle. "That girl, Daisy, told me she's being threatened," Martin said. "I'm sure the others would tell me the same thing if . . ." He didn't finish.

Drelincourt offered a shrug that impressed Martin as particularly Gallic. "This Smerdnakov, everyone's heard of him, right?" he said.

"I hadn't," Martin said. "Until a couple of weeks ago."

"Oh, yeah, one of the biggest operators in New York," Drelincourt said. "Russian Mafia. Nasty character. You know that by now, I hope."

"Whatever the man's done in the past is none of my concern," Martin said. "I just want to get to the bottom of what happened that night. Daisy said the other Russians were big guys with tattoos. Well, Smerdnakov is a big guy with a tattoo. Also, she said he took his tie out of his pocket when he strangled her. Why was his tie in his pocket?"

"He was dancing, right?" Drelincourt said. "Probably got sweaty and took it off."

"Exactly," Martin said, excited. "And it could be the tie fell out of his pocket — I mean, they dance pretty vigorously at those places, don't they? — and then someone else got their hands on it. I think we could be looking at a criminal conspiracy here."

Drelincourt smiled into the faint blue striations of the windshield glass. "I've got to hand it to you, you're really trying to believe. You really think he's innocent? I mean, look where he comes from."

"Like I said, you can't try the man's whole life," Martin said wearily. "You've got to take one crime at a time."

Drelincourt was silent as they swung into the mess of cars going pell-mell around the circle.

"The courts are in sad shape these days," Drelincourt said when he had picked up 13th Street again. "Overheated, flooded, bursting at the seams. Larceny, rape, homicide, fraud, drugs, grief, misery. You know what I think? I think we need the Inquisition back."

"You mean, like in Spain?"

"That's right," Drelincourt said. "Catch crime at the root, where it starts. Here . . ." He tapped his black jacket over a spot closely approximating the heart.

*

Martin's apartment seemed empty tonight. He paced the single messy room, stood rocking on his heels in the alcove that formed part of the turret, surrounded by windows overlooking the traffic on Massachusetts. There was plenty of work to do, but he couldn't concentrate tonight. He kept thinking about the way Daisy the barmaid swung her hips away from him across the dance floor, and he thought of her small, sharp breasts, her thin, hungry look. Suddenly, he got a flash of her on her back, legs open, abandoning herself to pleasure. What was the word she had used. Orgasming.

Martin went straight to the phone and called Dahlia. She picked it up on the second ring, but her voice sounded hollow on the other end.

"What are you, on speakerphone?"

Dahlia laughed. "No, silly, I'm taking a bath."

"In the tub?" Martin felt a pleasant swelling between his legs.

"That's right, I'm soaping my luscious curves as we speak."

"How would you like me to come over right now and scrub your back?" Martin said, and it surprised the both of them. Usually she was the one to make the first move.

Dahlia hesitated; then she laughed again. "Honey," she said, her voice an octave lower, "you're turning into a little wild thing lately. Must be the moon."

"Something like that," Martin said. "How about it?"

"All right then," Dahlia said. "Get your butt over here before the water gets cold."

They made love once in the tub — a painful process, during which Martin hit his forehead on the faucet — and in the bed afterward. Then Dahlia got hungry, and Martin crawled out from between the sheets and went into the kitchen to make popcorn. He stood stark naked in her perfect kitchen, waiting for the kernels to pop. His feet were cold against the floor of painted Mexican tiles. The whole place was spotless, done in a trendy southwestern motif that he found vaguely irksome. A maid came twice a week; it was impossible to sit on any of the furniture in the living room without messing the slipcovers and sending Dahlia on a tirade. Usually he found it extremely uncomfortable here and couldn't wait to leave, but not tonight. Tonight it seemed like home.

He took the bowl of popcorn, buttered and salted and sprinkled with Parmesan cheese, back to bed. They sat there eating, absently watching an old movie on AMC with the sound turned off. It was a World War II drama, set in Italy with William Holden playing a war-weary soldier and some woman Martin couldn't identify playing a war-weary WAC. These characters seemed to lose each other, find each other, and lose each other again. It was hard to tell much more without sound.

"Better this way," Dahlia said. "Then we can make up the plot ourselves."

"Right," Martin said. "It's about two lawyers falling in love during World War Three."

Dahlia frowned. "How's the case going?" she said.

Martin told her. "The guy's a gangster," he concluded. "Involved in some pretty bad shit. But I still think he's innocent of this murder. I think he really loved the woman who was killed; he just doesn't show it like everyone else. If you ask me, he was set up by one or more of the other Russians there that night. They were probably gangsters too."

"Russian gangsters," Dahlia said, shaking her head. "That's what gets me. They come over here to our country, we let them in, and they proceed to make life worse for everybody. It's not just the Russian gangsters, it's all the other gangsters from all over the world who just have to come to the good old U.S.A. to commit their crimes. You want my opinion?"

Martin sighed. "Everyone's a social critic," he said.

"It's our Anglo-Saxon legal system. English common law. It only works for Anglo-Saxons. Everyone else abuses the fuck out of it. Who the hell came up with this innocent until proven guilty crap? Thomas Jefferson? They don't do it that way in France, you know."

"Wait till you're arrested for something you didn't do," Martin said. "Then call me. I think you'll change your mind."

She ignored him. "Every nationality gets the legal system it deserves. The Russians lived under totalitarian regimes for centuries. You know what they did to gangsters in the old days under communism? Hell, they just took them out back and shot them."

Martin filled his mouth with popcorn so as not to say anything to spoil the mood.

"It's a good thing you're a patent attorney," he said when he had chewed and swallowed. "Dahlia Spears, hanging judge."

She laughed. She didn't understand the seriousness of his commitment to justice, despite everything, despite the sad state of the world, despite even his own incompetence. He hardly understood himself. He could not express it clearly with words. It was a quiet feeling of rightness, that was like light hitting water, that was like those summer afternoons spent with his great-aunt Hatch on the porch of her old place at Oxford on the Eastern Shore when he was a kid, and a strange bird — Aunt Hatch always said it was a parrot, blown by storms somehow from the jungles of South America — squawking in the quiet gloom of the box hedge.

Selecting a jury for the Alexei Smerdnakov trial, Martin was more careful than he'd been with any other case in his ten-year career with the Public Defender's Service. The voir dire continued eight hours a day for three solid days, with many bench conferences and hasty lunches, broke for the weekend, and resumed again on Monday.

There is a science to composing the most sympathetic jury, many competing theories, experts, demographics, prejudices. Martin had only one criterion in mind, and it was this: neither the juror nor members of that juror's immediate family could have been the victim of a violent crime, ever. In the District of Columbia, a city with the nation's second-highest murder rate per capita (exceeded only by New Orleans), this criterion proved impossible to meet. The potential jurors, mostly black and poor, reported one after another that they had experienced shootings, stabbings, violent assaults, sometimes more than once, that they had been witness to fratricide, parricide, rape. Day after day Martin was confronted with the absurd and numbing toll of violence in urban America.

Finally, on Friday, the fourth day of jury selection, Martin accepted twelve jurors and two alternates, only five of whom had managed to escape the urban holocaust. These were the core, these were the ones on which he'd concentrate: three aging black church ladies, a twenty-one-year-old white college girl, and a Pakistani man who managed a service garage for taxicabs in Mount Pleasant. One of the church ladies, a recently retired missionary for the African Methodist Episcopal Church, had been stationed in Ghana for the last twenty-five years; the other two lived alone and were unmarried. Since statistically most violent crime occurs at home, perpetrated by one family member against another, these ladies had managed to avoid any life-threatening incidents by re-maining single. The college girl was a Mormon from Scipio, Utah, a little town in the middle of that distant state where children played barefoot in the dirt streets on Saturday night and no one locked his door. The Pakistani, a naturalized citizen, barely spoke English. It was possible that he hadn't entirely understood Martin's questions during the examination period.

The other seven jurors — two unemployed black males; a His-panic female who ran a housecleaning service; two senior citizens, both ex-career civil servants, both white; a Korean-American wait-ress; a young white male, marginally employed in office temporary work who described himself as "Writer" on his questionnaire — all had been brutalized at some time or another in the past, but not seriously and not in the last five years. This was the best Martin could do.

At the end of the day Martin felt drained. He had that dry taste at the back of his throat that can only be remedied by a cold beer. He took the elevator up to the fourth floor of the Moultrie Center and convinced Jacobs and Burn to join him for happy hour at the D.C. Bar. Because of the high-profile nature of the Smerdnakov case, Martin's status had improved somewhat around the office. His face had not yet appeared on the evening news or in the papers, but there was a feeling that it would. Even if he lost — the certain out-come, it was generally agreed — the case would probably help his career. Also, Martin was known to be working hard on this one, pursuing every angle to prove his client's innocence.

"Wex is wasting his time if you ask me," Burn said to Jacobs when Wexler left them together at the bar to use the bathroom. It was just after six-thirty, and the place was crowded with attorneys and paralegals from Judiciary Square. "I feel sorry for the bastard. The spotlight's right on him now, and he's going to melt like an ice cube."

Jacobs grunted. "There's no such thing as bad publicity," he said.

"You're shitting me," Burn said. "Think what happened to Genevieve. Wex is going to be defending a monster, a public men-ace. If he weren't such a fuckup, Tayloe wouldn't have given the case to him in the first place. He's going to lose big, and that's just going to confirm his status as a legal idiot. Good for the commu-nity, I suppose. Bad for old Wex."

"You could be right about that." Jacobs nodded.

Always a quick urinator, Martin got back in time to catch the last part of these comments.

"Thanks for the confidence, guys," he said as he stepped up to the bar.

Jacobs stared down into his mug of Bud Lite, embarrassed. Burn didn't say anything.

"Sorry, Wex," Burn said at last. "But you're the first to admit what a crappy attorney you are."

Wex straddled his stool again. He was silent for a moment, then he cleared his throat.

"Yes," he said. "I was a crappy attorney, but not anymore. There's something about this case. I feel I'm doing the best work of my life. What the hell can you say about a dognapper caught with a poodle in his knapsack or a prostitute caught fucking an underage kid in the back of a van in the school parking lot? That's the usual fare for me. This is totally different."

Jacobs looked up. "How so?"

Martin smiled. "You heard it here first. My client's innocent."

Jacobs and Burn exchanged uneasy glances.

"You don't mean you really believe that?" Jacobs said.

"I do," Martin said. "Or I'd withdraw from the case."

"Like I was saying to Jake here," Burn said, "the pressure's driven you crazy. Go to Tayloe before it's too late! Get on your knees and beg for your old cases back!" This was meant as a joke, but it came out wrong.

Martin put down a ten-dollar bill, more than enough to pay for his Budweiser, made his excuses, and left them sitting at the bar. Outside, the light was fading in the sky over the old Pension Building. The terra-cotta army, frozen in rank, changeless, resolute, marched lockstep along the pediment into the shadow of coming night.

A swollen red gash taped together with three paper stitches zigzagged up Smerdnakov's forehead, making him look a little like Boris Karloff as Frankenstein's monster. A deep purple bruise extended across his left cheek. Martin's first thought when he came into the consultation room was: *That's not going to look good in court,* then he felt ashamed of himself.

"How did it happen?" he said as he sat down at the table.

"Got a cigarette, asshole?" Smerdnakov said, ignoring the question. It was his standard greeting.

Martin shook his head, "Not till this trial's over," he said. "When you get out of here, I'll buy you a whole carton of Marlboros."

"Prick," the Russian said. "Fucking asshole! One day I'm going to rip your head off."

"Great," Martin said, unimpressed. "Better wait till after the trial. Why don't you tell me about those?" He gestured toward the Russian's battered face.

Smerdnakov shrugged. "Some niggers tried to fuck me up the ass," he said. "In the shower. It's not about love, you know; it's about power." He began to cackle like a madman.

"Do you need a doctor?" Martin said, concerned.

"Don't worry, prick," Smerdnakov said. "I'm not the one in the hospital. Two poor niggers got their heads smashed in."

"We'll have you put in isolation," Martin said. "That way you'll be safe until the trial."

"No way," the Russian said. "If they try to fuck me again, I'll kill them. Want to know something about me?"

Martin looked at him blankly.

"I'm fucking crazy. I'm completely insane." He began to cackle again, and the cackling rose to a maniacal sort of laugh.

Martin cringed inwardly. All at once he could imagine Smerdnakov murdering innocent children, tearing the heart out of someone and eating it, but he pushed these unproductive thoughts out of his mind. Better to think of the emotional vacancy and sociological conditions that produced the cruelty, the violence. Suddenly he saw a stark room, filth on the floor, so cold that breath steamed in the air. A young boy, naked, is tied to a metal chair. A man in the green and red uniform of the old Soviet police enters, takes off his coat, rolls up his sleeves, removes his thick leather belt, all without uttering a single word. The boy begins to wail before the first blow hits the flesh of his back. The cold of course makes it worse . . .

Martin passed a hand across his brow as if to banish such cruelties from his imagination. He knew one thing for certain: injustice in the past could only be expiated by justice now.

"Listen to me, Alexei," he said, his voice serious. "We've only got three days till the trial. I don't want anything to happen to you in the meantime, okay? So stay out of fights; don't do anything stupid. I think we've got a decent case here if you'll just work with me."

The Russian was surprised for the briefest instant. He glanced out the narrow window, glanced back.

"Why the hell do you care what happens to me?" he said at last.

"It's very simple," Martin said patiently. "I'm your lawyer."

They spent the next two hours going over last details for the trial. Smerdnakov's attitude puzzled Martin. For someone who might be facing life in prison, or worse, he seemed utterly detached from the consequences.

Martin tried to describe this detachment to Dahlia later, as they lay together in bed. The case had brought them closer, though Martin couldn't exactly say why. He had hardly spent a night in his own apartment in the last three weeks.

"I keep getting the feeling that the man's playing a game," Martin said, "and that I'm a fool for going along with it."

"You're only a fool if you're putting in all this work to save his ass and you believe him to be guilty," Dahlia said. "If you think he's innocent, then it's worth it."

Martin rolled over and put a hand against the tender skin at the side of her neck. "My career has been a joke until now," he said quietly. "Everyone knows that, especially the guys at the office. I'm staking everything on Alexei's innocence. Whatever else he may have done, I know he did not commit this crime."

Dahlia was moved by the emotion in Martin's words. For once she didn't come back with a wisecrack or an ironic comment. She took him in her arms and they made love very tenderly and it lasted a long time. Afterward Martin lay awake in the dark as Dahlia slept. He couldn't sleep, but not from anxiety or fear. He wanted to savor the moment: he felt exalted; he felt loved.

The morning of the trial was clear and cold for late October. In forty-eight hours the temperature had dropped nearly fifty degrees from the low eighties to the mid-thirties. Such drastic changes are common in the capital, where the seasons can pass one to the other over the course of a single night. Martin awoke shivering at 5:25 A.M. of the digital clock and couldn't get back to sleep. He dragged his overcoat out of the closet, threw it over his shoulders, and walked the apartment until dawn. He could feel the lid lowering, the pressure increasing. He sat on the couch to go over some last notes; then he fell asleep and woke up with just forty-five minutes to shower, shave, and make it to the courtroom.

He performed his ablutions in a dead panic, shaved, dressed without wounding himself too badly, and, as luck would have it, caught a cab for Judiciary Square right at his front door. But he was stopped on the steps of the D.C. Superior Court by a reporter and a camera crew from News Channel 8. The reporter, a fresh-faced young Chinese woman, successfully blocked his passage. The camera operators were burly, squat, hairy men wearing battery-pack bandoliers around their thick chests like Mexican revolutionaries. Out of breath, Martin could barely speak.

"Please," he gasped. "I'm really late."

The video camera was whirring. He could see the reflection of his head, bigger than life on the face of the assistant peering into the monitor.

"Kate Chu, Channel Eight news," the reporter said, jabbing the microphone at his nose. "What's your assessment of Mr. Smerdnakov's chances for acquittal?"

"No comment," Martin said because he had heard other people say this on TV, and he lunged past her up the steps beneath the scaffolding and into the building.

The D.C. Superior Court, circa 1902, had been declared a historic landmark and was still undergoing a slow, painstaking renovation after two years of costly work. Space restrictions at the Moultrie Center forced its use now before completion, and the ornate interior presented a confusion of workers and plastic sheeting. The upper floors were as yet incomplete, their windows open to the elements; yellow police tape closed off the great staircase. Historic courtroom number one, however, had been finished just days before; the Smerdnakov case would be the first to use it since the trial of University of Maryland basketball star Bhijaz Dalkin for possession of crack cocaine. The interior of this room was beautiful, all polished wood and brass fixtures, and smelled of new paint and industrial glues. The carpet, done in a design that repeated the great seal of the District of Columbia against a green background, felt incongruously lush beneath Martin's feet as he stepped through the heavy bronze-faced doors.

He hurried up the long central aisle toward the bench just as

Judge Yvonne Deal was taking her seat. At seventy-two she was a prominent and respected member of the District's black aristocracy. A former friend of Martin Luther King's, she had marched on the Freedom Trail, been attacked by dogs and fire hoses in Birmingham, teargassed in Selma. Martin knew her tough-as-nails reputation, her history of severity in sentencing violent criminals. Today her enveloping dark robes were set off by an outrageous curly silver wig. A pair of Emmanuelle Khanh eyeglasses with huge gold frames made her look like a wizened, intelligent insect.

"Glad you could make it, counselor," she said, when Martin took his place at the defense table. "If you keep us waiting again, I'll find you in contempt, understand?"

Not a good way to start any trial. Martin apologized, muttered something about being stuck in traffic, and fumbled to open his briefcase. The first thing he saw was the top sheet of his legal pad, now completely covered in doodles of all description. He glanced over at Smerdnakov. The Russian was wearing the same mauve Armani suit he had been wearing the night of the murder, matched rather ridiculously with one of Martin's own conservative lawyer-stripe ties. Smerdnakov's own tie, a gaudy hand-painted number, had been confiscated as People's Exhibit Number One.

"Courage," Martin whispered.

The Russian glared as if he had just been insulted. "You are an asshole," he said, loud enough to be heard by spectators in the front row of the gallery. Then he turned his impassive gaze toward the newly cleaned stained glass window behind the judge's bench, a brilliant green, yellow, and red rosette portraying George Washington dressed in a toga ascending into heaven.

Martin took another moment to get his papers together and managed a glance at the prosecution table: representing the District of Columbia, Assistant United States Attorney Malcolm Rossiter, flanked by two bright-eyed young lawyers. The first, an attractive young blond woman wearing an impeccable blue suit; the second a thin young man with skin white as a sheet of Xerox paper. New faces to Martin; probably fresh out of Georgetown Law.

Judge Deal called the courtroom to order. The court reporter touched her fingertips to the keys of her machine, which made a quick ratcheting sound. The court clerk rose from his chair beside the judge's bench. He was a paunchy, pink-faced man with black hair and sideburns and bore a striking resemblance to Elvis Presley in his fat period.

"Case number F-four-zero-four-five dash nine-nine, the United States versus Alexei Sergeyevich Smerdnakov, will come to order," he intoned. "The charge is murder in the first degree."

"Are the principals ready to proceed in this matter?" Judge Deal asked.

"The government is ready, Your Honor," Rossiter said, rising from behind the prosecution table with a dignity Martin knew he would never be able to muster.

Martin stood and took a deep breath. "The defense is ready," he said.

Judge Deal studied him critically for a beat through her bug glasses; then she looked down at the papers on her bench. "Does the plea of not guilty stand?"

"It does, Your Honor," Martin said.

At this a faint gasp went up from the gallery, now nearly full of journalists and other lawyers who had dropped by to hear the opening arguments.

"Order!" Judge Deal called out sharply; then she turned to the court clerk. "You may proceed with the swearing in of the jury."

Martin watched carefully as the members of the jury stood in a body, raised their right hands, and repeated the oath. As they mumbled the familiar words, he studied their contrasting faces — black, white, tan, young, old, male, female, American, foreign — and he felt an emptiness in his gut where certainty should be. This wasn't a jury; it was the Tower of Babel! How could such a disparate group reach a consensus on the innocence of his client? Why had he chosen them in the first place? He couldn't remember now.

Then the jurors sat down again, and Judge Deal instructed the prosecution to proceed with opening statements. Rossiter proved to be a deliberate and repetitive speaker. He made his points forcefully and then made them again, almost exactly as he had made them the first time. The defendant, Alexei Sergeyevich Smerdnakov, was a notorious gangster, a violent man whose activities were well known to the FBI and other law enforcement agencies, he told the court. Alexei Sergeyevich Smerdnakov, the defendant, alias Aba Sid, was an infamous racketeer, well known to law enforcement officials.

Martin should have objected strenuously both times to this statement, but he did not. He was too busy watching his core jurors.
One of the church ladies was already asleep. The other two seemed
to be studying the ends of their noses. The Pakistani garage manager looked confused. Only the college girl — Martin checked his
jury sheet — Denise Wheeler, seemed to be paying attention. She
sat forward, elbows on the railing, eyes fixed on the prosecutor. Every now and then, as Rossiter plodded along, she would look over
at Smerdnakov, impassive and solid as the Rock of Gibraltar, sitting
in his low-backed chair at Martin's side.

The prosecution's statement proceeded exactly as Martin had
expected. Rossiter followed with a brief overview of the case. The
United States would produce witnesses, he said, who had seen the
defendant strangle Ms. Volovnaya at Club Naked Party. The United
States was also in possession of the murder weapon, a necktie that
witnesses would identify as belonging to the defendant, upon
which had been found bits of skin and hair. DNA analysis proved
the skin and hair had come from both the defendant and victim.

". . . the United States intends to show much more than this!"
Rossiter said, his voice ascending to a dull but forceful mono-
tone. "We will show that not only did the defendant murder Ms.
Volovnaya, but he felt absolutely no remorse after he had committed this heinous crime. For as she lay dead, murdered, on the floor,
the defendant proceeded upstairs to continue his dancing. That's
right, he danced with joy, with abandon, until police arrived to
place him under arrest for murder."

When Rossiter sat down, an appreciative silence filled the courtroom. The gallery was now quite crowded. The only free seats were
at the very back of the room. In position on an end seat directly behind the defense table, the sketch artist from the *Washington Post*
had just brought out her pad and box of colored chalks.

"Mr. Wexler?" Judge Deal said. "Is the defense ready for opening
statements?"

Martin nodded, stood, and approached the jury. He buttoned
his jacket, unbuttoned it. He scratched the back of his head,
crossed his arms, and appeared lost in thought. He'd practiced every gesture beforehand, first in his bathroom mirror, then with
Dahlia as a coach.

"If I seem a little preoccupied this morning," he said, "it's because I am. I am preoccupied by this case! Never in all my years as a public defender have I seen a man who looks so guilty, who so readily fits the image we have of a guilty man, who —" He interrupted himself and swung toward Smerdnakov. "Look, what do you see? A thug, a bruiser, right? Look at his face! A known criminal, the prosecution says! But ladies and gentlemen of the jury, this man is innocent of the crime he is accused of today! Indeed, here is a man devastated by the loss of a woman he dearly loved, a victim of circumstances beyond his control, a man set up by dastardly companions to take the fall for a crime he did not commit . . ."

Martin went on in this vein for some time. Two hours later, during the lunch recess, he couldn't remember exactly what he had said, but he was certain of its effectiveness. He had watched his core jurors watching him. The church ladies had woken up; Denise Wheeler's lips had parted in eagerness to hear every word; even the Pakistani had looked less dazed, all of them gripped by a tentative belief in the inherent goodness of mankind — and hence the innocence of the defendant — that at some point grips all jurors hearing a successful defense, that is as catching one to the other as the flu.

Over the course of the next three days the prosecution did its best to punch holes in the presumed innocence of Alexei Sergeyevich Smerdnakov.

First, it brought out material witnesses — Aziz Jehassi among them — to establish the Russian's presence at the club. Martin cross-examined Jehassi, who was extremely nervous on the stand. The club owner stuttered over his replies, his face flushed; great stains slowly appeared under the arms of his silk jacket.

"When my client and Ms. Volovnaya entered your club, were they alone or in the company of others?" Martin asked.

"No, no," Jehassi said. "They were not alone. They were with a large party."

"I see," Martin said. "The members of this party, how would you describe them?"

Jehassi thought for a minute. "They were males," he said. "Well dressed, big, strong-looking."

"Russians?"

"Yes," Jehassi said. "I think so."

"Objection!" The blond woman who was Rossiter's assistant rose out of her seat, a mechanical pencil in her right hand. "Calls for speculation."

"Sustained," Judge Deal said. "Rephrase, Mr. Wexler."

Martin thought for a moment. "How would you describe the behavior of these men?"

Jehassi licked his lips. "They were very loud, rowdy. They drank a lot of vodka."

"Were they speaking English?"

"No, not English." Jehassi shook his head. "It sounded to me like Russian."

The day after the Jehassi cross-examination, the prosecution trotted out its expert witnesses. Dr. Gopi Annan, pathologist, testified on the cause of death. Dr. Albert Weisel, a specialist in DNA analysis, testified that skin and hair samples on the tie matched skin and hair samples taken from both the defendant and the victim.

"The preponderance of epidermal and hair follicle samples is identical to similar samples scraped from the skin of the defendant," Dr. Weisel said. "This would be consistent with the prosecution's contention that the item of neckwear in possession of investigators had been worn by the defendant several times before the evening in question. Also, epidermal samples matching the victim's DNA showed stresses consistent with extreme lateral pressure, or, if you will, blunt-force trauma to the esophageal region. In the layman's term, strangulation."

The jurors looked on blankly as Dr. Weisel concluded his testimony. Martin chose not to cross-examine. From experience, he knew that juries have a limited tolerance for aggressive cross-examinations. Attorneys who constantly question witnesses' testimony are seen as bullies or worse. He had decided to save his aggressive behavior for the most damaging aspect of the trial, the presentation of the eyewitnesses.

On day three of the prosecution's case, Martin girded himself for the onslaught of upstanding and credible men and women who would solemnly swear they had seen Alexei Smerdnakov strangle Katerina Volovnaya at Club Naked Party. To his great surprise, the first witness — usually the strongest for the prosecution — was a hard young woman named Bunny Celeste Williams, whom he im-

mediately recognized as a former prostitute unsuccessfully defended by Jacobs on a corruption of minors charge a few years
before. She had gone under another name in that case, but the
change had not altered her dubious character. At best Bunny
Celeste Williams was a barely credible witness for the other side; at
worst she was a disaster. Martin couldn't believe his good fortune.
Their star witness was a convicted criminal, a woman who had once
acted as a recruiter of underage girls for the sex trade and — if
memory served him correctly — a recovering heroin addict.

Martin squirmed through Rossiter's examination of this witness,
trying to conceal his glee. He listened as Bunny described how she
was sitting at the bar in the VIP room that night, waiting for a
friend. How she had seen the defendant assault the victim, then
drag her to a darkened corner of the club, where he then strangled
her to death. Smerdnakov appeared nervous during this testimony,
in marked contrast with his cool demeanor up to this point. Martin
thought his lapse in composure odd but didn't have time to consider the matter. When Bunny stepped down from the witness box,
it was 11:45 A.M. Martin rose and asked Judge Deal for an early recess for lunch. He needed time to prepare his cross-examination,
he said.

Judge Deal wagged her silver wig in Martin's direction. "Are you
sure it's not because you're itching to get your hands on a Big Mac
and fries, Mr. Wexler?" she said, and there was a titter of laughter
from the gallery.

Martin took this ribbing with good humor. "If I have time for an
apple over the next hour and a half, Your Honor, I'll be lucky," he
said. Judge Deal granted the recess, and Martin ran across the
street to Jacobs's cubicle. One arm in the sleeve of his suit jacket,
Jacobs was preparing to head out for lunch.

"Gotta run," he said, fitting his arm through the other sleeve.
"Love to chat but —"

"Just two minutes of your time," Martin said. "I need the case
files for Bunny Celeste Williams. You remember her?"

"No," Jacobs said.

"Sorry," Martin said. "Her name wasn't Bunny Celeste Williams
in those days. She was the one they caught out at Marshall High —"

"Oh, yeah," Jacobs interrupted, "that slut. What do you want
with her?"

Martin smiled. "I'm looking for a hot date tonight."

He read the files at Jacobs's desk, the sordid details coming back to him.

Six years ago Ms. Williams had been arrested on the premises of John C. Marshall High School in Falls Church while attempting to recruit underage girls for what she said was a talent agency. The scheme was ancient, old as the hills. The girls were promised lucrative careers as fashion models and actresses and lured across the District line, where they were offered drugs and taken to wild parties. This highlife did not last long. Eventually hooked on powder or pills, grades foundering, misunderstood by their parents, these naive innocents ran away from home and embarked with gusto upon the long slide down to the gutter. They began by dancing naked at one of several seedy strip joints off Florida Avenue and ended up, scantily clad in the coldest weather, walking the streets near 12th and Mass for the profit of men with names like Johnny C. or Big Red.

Bunny Williams had been charged with a first-degree felony, which was then plea-bargained down by Jacobs to a misdemeanor. At the time Bunny had been addicted to heroin, a substance she blamed for her criminal behavior. The judge agreed. She was sentenced to an abbreviated term of imprisonment of eight months, consenting to enter an addiction treatment program in prison and to continue treatment after her release.

When the trial reconvened at one-thirty, Martin was ready. Bunny took the stand, looking confident. She wore a demure blue dress with white polka dots and a pair of spectator pumps. Her hair, dyed flaming red, was pinned up on the back of her head in a French twist. Her face, heavily lined beneath layers of thick makeup, was prematurely aged by drugs and late nights and a life ruled by a single maxim: just do whatever feels good right now and to hell with the consequences.

"Ms. Williams," Martin said, approaching the stand, "do you know me?"

Bunny searched his face. "I don't think so," she said in a firm voice, but Martin thought he saw her lower lip tremble.

"Because I think I know you," he said. "Or at least I know *about* you."

Bunny nodded stupidly.

"Why don't you tell the court about your felony conviction in 1993?" he said as casually as possible, and turned away to face the jury. Rossiter's blond assistant frowned, tightening the grip on her mechanical pencil. Rossiter himself showed no expression beyond professional interest.

"I don't know what you want me to tell," Bunny said, her voice tremulous.

"What was the charge?" Martin said. "Let's start with that."

Bunny was silent. The thick makeup around her eyes was beginning to crack a little.

"Ms. Williams?" Martin said.

"Which charge?" she said in a voice he had to lean forward to hear. "There was more than one."

"The one you were convicted for," Martin said. "The charge that landed you in prison."

"Solicitation of minors for the purposes of prostitution," she said in one breath, and there was an audible exclamation of surprise from the jury. The church ladies shook their heads. Denise Wheeler removed her elbows from the railing and leaned back with a frown. The Pakistani appeared confused.

"But I don't do them things no more," Bunny Williams protested. "That was a long time ago."

"Of course," Martin said. "But let me ask you something else: are you still involved in the methadone treatment program for recovering heroin addicts?"

Bunny nodded, cheeks flushed beneath her makeup. She was beginning to get angry. "Once you're involved in methadone treatment, you're in for life," she said tartly. "Addiction is a disease. Methadone is no different from kidney dialysis."

"Please restrict your answers to yes or no unless I ask you to elaborate," Martin said.

Bunny opened her mouth to speak; then she closed it again and pressed her lips together in a hard line.

Martin paced up and down before the witness box, hands behind his back, studying the carpeting, forehead furrowed in concentration, a pose that Dahlia had called "junior Clarence Darrow." At last he stopped and looked Bunny Williams right in the eye.

"When you take methadone, does it produce a feeling of wellbeing?"

"You mean, a buzz?" she said.

"If you want, a buzz, a high," Martin said.

Bunny thought for a moment. "Maybe a little," she said. "It's what I need just to keep me going, keep me normal, like everyone else."

"And had you taken methadone on the day of the murder?"

Bunny nodded. "I went to the Farragut Clinic that afternoon," she said. "I'm not ashamed of it."

Martin felt his ears tingle. "And that night, in the VIP room of Naked Party, did you have anything to drink?"

Bunny hesitated. "I'm not sure," she said.

"Yes or no," Martin said.

"I had a gin and tonic," Bunny said. "One lousy gin and tonic. And it cost enough, seven bucks!"

Martin stopped pacing and positioned himself so he faced both the woman in the witness box and the jury. "So the night in question, when you witnessed my client strangle Ms. Volovnaya in a dark corner of a dark room, you were taking methadone, which produces a high, and drinking, which, as I'm sure many of us here are aware, also produces a high, a disorientation of the senses. Is that correct?"

"Not like you mean it," she said.

"Yes or no, Ms. Williams," Martin said in a voice that held all the authority of legal procedure.

Bunny Williams hung her head. Angry tears rolled down her cheeks.

"Yes," she said.

Later that evening, after the trial had adjourned for the day, Martin took the Red Line from Judiciary Square to Cleveland Park and walked up the long block from the Metro station to the Broadmoor. He was exhausted; his feet hurt; his briefcase felt like a lead weight in his hand. He let himself into the front door with the key Dahlia had given him, took the elevator to the eighth floor, and let himself into her apartment. The place was dark; Dahlia wasn't home from work yet. Martin poured himself a glass of milk in the kitchen, then collapsed on the couch with the local news on the television.

When Dahlia came home an hour later, she found him asleep

there, snoring gently, one of the couch pillows balanced over his face. She managed to get him up, get the clothes off him, and get him into the tub in the pink bathroom. Then she disrobed and joined him in the warm water. It was the last moment of twilight. Traffic hummed along up Connecticut; a pleasant darkness lit by the yellow windows of the mansions descended over the neighborhood. Dahlia opened a jar of pink bath salts and dropped a handful in the water beneath the running tap. In less than a minute the suds threatened to engulf them both.

The water felt smooth as oil against Martin's skin. This was the first bubble bath he'd had since he was a kid. He leaned back against the rim of the tub. Every muscle ached. For him, being in court was a physically exhausting process, like running the marathon or digging a trench. Dahlia faced him from the other end of the tub, the faucet perched like a parrot over her right shoulder. Her breasts seemed to float in the water, half hidden by the bubbles. He didn't think he'd be able to make love to her tonight. He could barely summon the energy to wiggle his toes.

Dahlia had turned the lights out in the bathroom and put candles on saucers on the sink and the floor. A bottle of white wine and two glasses lay on ice in a Styrofoam cooler within arm's reach. This wasn't a celebration of anything, she said, just the halftime event.

"You've got the wine and woman right here," she said, reaching down to pour a glass. "All you've got to do now is sing."

"Please," Martin croaked. "I can't even whisper."

"You just lie there, honey," Dahlia said. "Soak it all out."

Martin dozed off for a moment and woke himself up talking about the case: ". . . why they didn't have any solid witness . . ."

"What's that, honey?" Dahlia put her glass of wine on the floor.

Martin rubbed his face with a damp washcloth and sat up. "There were supposed to be a dozen witnesses that saw Smerdnakov do the deed," he said. "But this ex-hooker was all the prosecution could come up with. One single eyewitness, with a criminal record to boot. Something's not right here."

"Maybe you're just too good for them," Dahlia said. "Maybe Rossiter knew you'd chew them to pieces in the cross."

"That can't be true," Martin said.

"Don't be so hard on yourself," she said. "You're a good lawyer and getting better every day." She slid toward him through the bubbles. When she had wedged herself against him, Martin felt his energy returning.

"Still, it's strange," he murmured. "I really thought they had a tight case."

"Who knows, maybe God's talking to you right now," Dahlia said. "Because you're defending an innocent man."

Martin smiled. "God doesn't talk to lawyers," he said.

"But whatever you do tomorrow, don't give them what they think they're going to get." Her voice was serious now; her eyes showed deep concern. "Hit them with something new, something they haven't seen. Astonish them."

Martin thought about what he'd have to do to astonish Malcolm Rossiter, and he almost laughed. The man had seen every trick in the book in his fifteen years with the U.S. attorney's office. Then, suddenly, he remembered a piece of advice out of first-year law: for half a semester he'd had a professor named Alden Clarke, a broken-down old southern drunk, who in the 1930s and 1940s had been one of the most famous trial lawyers in America. Clarke, at least eighty then, used to wear white Colonel Sanders suits gone yellow with age and black string ties more like a scribble on his shirtfront than a real tie. He was a relic from another era, a vanished South of dusty white courtrooms, fans pulling slowly overhead, last veterans of the Civil War, ancient as mummies, dozing in the sun on benches on the other side of the square.

Martin could remember the exact class session. Clarke had entered the auditorium twenty minutes late, his battered leather portefeuille under his arm, smelling faintly of bourbon. Upon attaining the podium, he'd fixed the class with one watery, jaundiced eye. "The law is complex," he had said. "But juries are simple. Therefore, the best way with a jury is always the simplest."

Martin hadn't thought much of this plain advice at the time, but now it came back to him with the clarity of a revelation. What could be simpler than an innocent man protesting his innocence?

The prosecution rested. A cold winter light filtered through the stained glass rosette behind Judge Deal's head. She was framed in the glow like a haloed saint in an icon, as stern and unyielding.

"Mr. Wexler, are you ready to present the case for the defense?" she said.

Martin rose to his feet unsteadily. His mouth felt dry; he seemed incapable of uttering a single word. Inexplicably his knees ached. Nonetheless, his voice came out clear and strong.

"I am ready, Your Honor," he said.

Judge Deal blinked, wise as an owl. "Proceed," she said.

Martin cleared his throat for theatrical effect and advanced to the center of the courtroom, halfway to the jury box, but no farther. It was as if he intended to present his case to a wider audience, to the world itself.

"I call to the stand" — he indicated the defense table with a dramatic sweeping gesture — "Alexei Sergeyevich Smerdnakov!" For a long moment the Russian stared. He hadn't expected this; no one had expected this. At the prosecution table Rossiter and his cohorts looked startled, then utterly relieved. This was the blunder they had been waiting for.

"Mr. Smerdnakov, you have been directed to testify," Judge Deal said sternly.

The Russian heaved himself up and lumbered around the table toward the witness box. The courtroom was silent; his shoes creaked as he walked. The court clerk swore him in. Smerdnakov settled down with difficulty; his massive torso seemed to fill the entire box. Martin looked up at him and saw disdain and anger in the Russian's eyes.

"Alexei, did you kill Katerina Volovnaya?" he said.

"No," the Russian said in a thick voice.

Martin nodded and clasped his hands behind his back. Shoulders hunched, he appeared lost in thought, troubled by the fate of nations, like Nixon on the eve of resignation.

"Why don't you tell the court exactly what really happened that night?" he said, and he unclasped his hands and moved to a spot where he would be able to make eye contact with the jury.

"OK," the Russian said. "You heard it from me before, but I tell again . . ." and he proceeded with his story, now so familiar to Martin: Smerdnakov had gone to the bathroom. When he had come back, his new friends had scattered, and his woman was dead. "I wanted to cry," he said. "But I don't know how to cry. My life has been very hard in old days of the Soviet Union. I look at her lying there on the floor and I think maybe she has drunk too much vodka, and I'm going to give her a piece of my mind when we get back to the hotel. Then I reach down to pick her up and I think to myself: *My God, she's dead! The woman I love is dead!*"

Martin nodded, sympathetic. "And what did you do then?"

Smerdnakov stared at the floor. "Nothing," he said. "I couldn't do nothing. I knew she was dead. I figured the police would come soon enough, and I was very angry and very sad, and so I danced."

"Wasn't that behavior" — Martin chose his words carefully — "this dancing, a little unusual, given the circumstances?"

The Russian shook his head. "You must know what it is like where I am from. When somebody dies who you love, when there is no food to eat, when KGB is coming to get you and there's no place to hide, we dance. Life is so hard we must dance to forget."

Martin glanced over at the jury. He thought one of the church ladies might have a tear glittering in her eye.

"So this dancing, it's a cultural thing?"

Smerdnakov looked puzzled; then he nodded. "Yes, it is my culture."

Martin kept Smerdnakov on the stand for the next hour and a half. Through a carefully planned series of questions, he was able to touch on nearly every aspect of the case, concluding with the identity of the mysterious Russians who had accompanied Smerdnakov and Katerina to the club.

"So you didn't know any of these men?"

"Never met them before in my life," Smerdnakov said. "We were having a few drinks at the Rio Bar and we run into these other Russians. You know, this doesn't happen too often and one of them is from Vladivostok, where I used to live, so we're talking and I buy him a drink and he buys me a drink and then his friend says, 'Hey, I know a place to dance.' So we go to dance. It is only later I think that the one from Vladivostok is looking at my Katinka out of the corner of his eye, you know, like he really wants to sleep with her or something. I think what happens is I go away to the bathroom and he grabs her and tries to force her, you know, and she doesn't want any of it, and then he gets pissed off like a real psychopath, and he kills her, just like that. When the police come, I give them this man's description, but they say no, they have already caught the murderer and it is me."

Martin carefully omitted questions regarding one very important point from his examination. When he released the witness to the prosecution for the cross, he sensed that Rossiter and his team could barely contain their excitement. They conferred for a quick moment before approaching the stand; the sound of their lowered voices was like the busy hum of a hive of bees, ready to swarm.

"Does the prosecution wish to examine this witness?" Judge Deal said.

"We do, Your Honor," Rossiter said, and his blond assistant came forward, smoothing out her blue suit with her hands. Her name was Emily Blake, Martin had learned; she had graduated from Harvard Law the previous spring. Now she motioned to her young colleague, who brought a flat plastic tub marked *evidence* from under the table. She removed from the tub a large plastic bag containing a hand-painted psychedelic necktie and, holding it out like a piece of filthy laundry, approached the witness box.

"Mr. Smerdnakov, is this your tie?" she said.

Smerdnakov looked at it and nodded. "Yes," he said.

"Were you wearing this tie the night of the murder?"

"Yes," he said again.

"Are you aware that this tie has been identified by expert witnesses as the same one used to strangle Katerina Volovnaya?"

Smerdnakov's expression darkened; then he nodded.

"I can't hear you, Mr. Smerdnakov!" Emily Blake's voice rose to an unpleasant shriek on the last word. Martin saw the Pakistani garage manager wince.

"Yes," Smerdnakov said.

She replaced the bag in the evidence tub and turned to confront the Russian, hands on her hips like a shrewish wife.

"Tell me something else, Mr. Smerdnakov," she said. "How did your tie come to find its way from around your neck to Ms. Volovnaya's? Did it fly there on its own?"

The Russian sighed. "I have no idea," he said. "I took it off earlier and put it down with my jacket."

"I see," Emily Blake said. "And why do you suppose a man would wear a tie out for the evening and then take it off?"

Martin tried to hide his smile behind the doodles of his legal pad. She had just broken one of the prime rules of trial law. Never ask a witness a question if you don't already know the answer.

"I take off my coat and my tie because I was dancing and it was very hot in the club," Smerdnakov said. "Ask anyone who saw me. I do not wear a coat and tie when I am dancing."

Emily Blake looked abashed. It was obvious she didn't know what to say next.

Judge Deal stared down at the young attorney through her big glasses. Behind her silver head in the stained glass rosette Washington seemed to have paused on his way to heaven.

"Ms. Blake?" Judge Deal said. "Do you wish to proceed with this witness?"

Rossiter stood up hastily. "I'll take it from here, if Your Honor pleases," he said.

"Mr. Wexler?" Judge Deal said.

"I have no objection." Martin shrugged, but he was surprised. Switching lawyers in the middle of a cross was bad form, almost never done, and made his own case look that much better.

Rossiter exchanged places with Emily Blake, who, somewhat red in the face, resumed her seat at the prosecution table. He now continued the cross-examination of Smerdnakov with vigor, but to no avail. He could not succeed in unnerving the Russian enough to discredit his version of events the night of the murder, and when Smerdnakov stepped down, Martin was sure the jury was solidly on the side of the defense. Martin then proceeded to call the remaining witnesses from the club. One by one, they were sworn in by the court clerk and testified that Smerdnakov was not the man they had seen strangling Ms. Volovnaya in the smoky darkness of the VIP room at Naked Party.

The most memorable testimony came from Daisy, the barmaid. For the occasion she wore a white thrift store beaded sweater, a pretty Betsey Johnson minidress, and her Sunday black Doc Martens boots, newly shined. A single pair of rhinestone teardrop earrings dangled from her ears. She sat straight-backed in the witness box, hands in her lap, and spoke in a clear voice when she answered Martin's questions.

"Was there dancing in the VIP room?" He rested his hand comfortably on the railing. He appeared relaxed; he could have been in his own living room.

"There's always dancing," Daisy said.

"How many people were dancing, do you suppose?"

Daisy cocked her head, one earring bumping gently against the side of her throat. "About a hundred, I guess."

"Did you observe the defendant dancing?" Martin's voice took on a commanding pitch.

"Yes, I did," Daisy said.

"And while he was dancing, was he wearing a necktie and suit jacket?"

Daisy shook her head. "No," she said.

"Since there were a hundred people dancing that night," Martin said, "how is it you can remember my client so clearly?"

"I remember because his shirt was hanging open down to his belly button," Daisy said. "He looked like some seventies disco king. And his chest was really hairy. It was pretty gross."

Somehow this was just the right detail. As Daisy stepped down, she flashed Martin a veiled look whose meaning was not readily apparent. But it didn't matter now; he felt it in his bones. The case was over, and he had beaten one of the top prosecutors in the city. A single glance at his opponents confirmed everything: Rossiter and his assistants sat there, slumped in gloom, surrounded by the useless mess of their papers, defeated. The light out the stained glass window had grown dim with afternoon. Martin checked his watch; it was nearly five. Judge Deal rubbed her hands together as if she were trying to warm them.

"Given the lateness of the hour," she said. "We will adjourn until tomorrow morning." Then she flashed Martin an unexpected smile. "Bright-eyed and bushy-tailed, counselor."

Martin took her advice, went home, threw himself in bed following the evening news, and fell asleep within five minutes. That night he slept soundly, and if he dreamed at all, dreamed only of darkness and silence.

The summation for the prosecution was made first thing the next morning by the young pale-faced lawyer, who as yet had not uttered a single word during the course of the trial. Rossiter, it appeared, had washed his hands of the case. Now that everything was lost, the second string would get a chance to play. But the pale lawyer proved to be the best of the three. He spoke in a courtly central Virginia accent directly to the jury, and he did his best to simplify. He was not patronizing them; he was merely explaining things in the clearest way he knew how. This case was open and shut, he said. Anyone could see that. The defendant, Alexei Sergeyevich Smerdnakov, was a man with a history of violence, a fact that the defense had not even bothered to refute.

"I am aware that they have provided several witnesses to testify

Alexei Sergeyevich Smerdnakov was not the man seen murdering Ms. Volovnaya." He stood very still before the jury box, his skin shining like marble. "But I ask you to consider his behavior directly following the murder. Think, use your common sense, people! I don't care what country you're from, if your girlfriend is murdered while you're in the bathroom, your response is not going to be to go upstairs and dance some more until the police show up to arrest you! That's crazy! That is the action of a sociopath who knows the system all too well and knows for whatever reason that he has a good chance of getting away with his crime. Why ruin a perfectly good evening of drinking and dancing just on account of one little old murder?"

This young lawyer was smart, capable, and polite. He concluded his comments with a rousing call for a guilty verdict, then thanked the judge and the jury for their patience and retreated to his seat at the prosecution table with all the gracious dignity of Robert E. Lee at Appomattox.

At last the defense was free to make its summation. Martin ostentatiously filled a glass of water, drank it down. He cracked his knuckles, jammed his hands in his pockets, and shambled over to the jury box. He felt like Henry Fonda playing the young Lincoln in *Young Mr. Lincoln*. In that film Abraham Lincoln, still a bumpkinly country lawyer, uses a detail gleaned from the *Farmer's Almanac* to defend a man wrongfully accused of murder. Martin remembered this scene in some compartment of his mind as he began to speak.

"Ladies and gentlemen of the jury," he said, "I'm sure you're all worn out by the events of the last two weeks. No doubt you'd like to finish up with this case, get home, and not have to worry about any of this ever again." He saw the church ladies nod their heads at this. "So I will try to wrap up my remarks as quickly as possible . . ."

Martin reiterated the highlights of the defense: the prosecution's version of the truth was built on questionable circumstantial evidence and the testimony of a single, dubious eyewitness, an ex-prostitute who had admitted to being high on drugs and alcohol at the time of the murder. According to witnesses, the murder weapon was not on the defendant's person minutes before the murder . . . etc. Halfway through his presentation, he interrupted himself suddenly, took a deep breath, and passed a hand across his brow. Then he made eye contact with each member of the jury in turn.

"We have been talking about cold facts here so far," he said. "But I'm going to forget the facts now, and I'm going to talk about feelings." His voice softened. He was no longer a lawyer arguing a complicated legal case but just an average guy, worried about simple justice. "My client is a man numbed by grief, a man suffering from emotional shock. A man who has lost the woman he loved in a terrible crime, only to see himself accused of that same crime. We are all decent, God-fearing people here. We are fair people, but we are not miracle workers. We cannot restore to my client the life of the woman he loved. But we can give him back his own life; we can ransom it back from a prosecution too eager to find a criminal for every crime, whether the person they find is guilty or not. Ladies and gentlemen, Mr. Smerdnakov is innocent! Give his life back to him, let him go free!"

Martin turned away abruptly and walked back to the defense table. When he sat down, he realized he felt a little giddy. He tried to focus on the doodles on his pad and found he was suffering from a sort of tunnel vision brought about by his own eloquence. The doodles now seemed larger than life to him, giant, childish renderings of locomotives, sports cars, puppies, clowns, balloons, and odd, exaggerated mazelike patterns and geometric shapes. He hardly heard a word of Judge Deal's instructions to the jury, barely saw them leave their box and exit through the door to the deliberation room. His own thoughts were jumbled, disorganized. He wanted to grab the hulking Russian beside him by the shoulders and shout, "I think we beat them!" But instead, he remained in his seat unmoving, dumb as a stone, staring into the haze of colored light from the stained glass window. Presently he realized Judge Deal herself was gone, where, he couldn't exactly say.

"We got to take him now, sir."

Martin looked up, startled. It was the court clerk accompanied by a U.S. marshal whom Martin recognized immediately, Caesar Martinez.

"Caesar," Martin said, "you on this detail?"

Caesar nodded. "Asked for it special," he said. "Heard you were burning up the courtroom. Had to get down here to see for myself."

The court clerk held a pair of leg irons; a pair of handcuffs hung clipped to his belt. He stepped up and indicated that Smerdnakov should stand out of his chair.

"Is that strictly necessary?" Martin said.

"We got to put them on him, Wex," Caesar said. "It's the rules, you know that."

Martin moved aside as the court clerk affixed the leg irons to Smerdnakov's ankles and snapped the handcuffs around his wrists.

"We're taking him upstairs to the holding cell," Caesar said. "He's going to be up there till the jury decides what they want to do with him or till closing time, whichever comes first. You coming?"

"Of course," Martin said.

They went through the door at the left of the judge's bench. The renovation of the building had not yet extended to the back-stage portion of the courtroom; five-gallon tubs of paint and folded stepladders leaned against the wall in the room that would one day serve as the judge's chambers. A scarred metal fire door was propped open on a hallway at the end of which a new elevator waited, its doors open. They went into the elevator, and the court clerk pressed four. It felt close inside, stifling. The faint reek of the Russian's body odor mixed uneasily with the strong, sweet aroma of Caesar's cologne.

"I got to tell you, Wex," Caesar said now, "I heard that summation. Fucking great!"

"Thanks," Martin said.

"I knew you could do it, man," he said. "There's a pool going at Moultrie, you hear about that? I mean everyone threw in some cash. Your pals from PDS, the investigators, everyone. I got to say, most of the money went against you. But I put fifty on your ass to win."

Martin smiled. "How much did McGuin put up for the prosecution?"

"Guess I fucked up there," Caesar shook his head. "Maybe that son of a bitch's a little too tight with some people."

"Yeah," Martin said. "I found out the hard way."

The elevator opened on a long corridor without carpeting or electrical fixtures, lined with offices in various states of complete-ness. The temporary holding cell was a bare room with a steel door and thick wire mesh over the window.

"Sorry there ain't no chairs in here," the court clerk said. "We don't want nothing the prisoners can use as a weapon. The new cells downstairs got nice benches bolted to the floor. That'll be up and running next month."

"I'll be right out here if you need me, champ," Caesar said, and he went into the corridor with the court clerk, and the door was bolted, leaving Martin and Smerdnakov inside. It was the first time they'd been alone together since the beginning of the trial.

"Hey, asshole," the Russian said. "Got a cigarette?"

Martin shook his head. "Just a couple more hours, Alexei," he said. "Then you can smoke all you want on the outside."

Smerdnakov crouched down against the rough cement of the wall. "This is fucking cruel and unusual punishment!" he said, and for the first time Martin thought he heard real distress in his voice. "I've got to wait here to find out whether I go to jail for the rest of my fucking life and I can't even smoke a fucking cigarette?"

Martin looked down at Smerdnakov crouching there like a trapped animal and felt sorry for the man. He had endured so much in the last few months — the vicious murder of his girlfriend, his own arrest, humiliation, assault — and borne it all with absolute impassivity.

"You know, you're right!" Martin said. "You should be able to smoke a cigarette if you want. This is ridiculous!" He turned and knocked on the door. The dead bolt shot back immediately, and the door opened. Caesar stuck his head in.

"What can I do for you, counselor?"

Martin stepped out into the corridor. He looked around; the court clerk had gone. "Listen, Caesar," he said in a low voice. "My man here needs a cigarette something fierce. You know what I'm saying?"

"Can't do it," Caesar said. "If they find out I let someone smoke up here, they'll have my ass. One whiff of smoke, I get written up for disciplinary action, the whole nine yards."

Martin put his hand on Caesar's shoulder. "As a favor to me," he said. "The poor bastard's been through hell. You can't let him have just one cigarette? Look at it this way, it's your big chance to make up for McGuin."

Caesar stood back and scratched the side of his nose, thinking. He glanced down the empty corridor and nodded. "All right,

Wex," he said. "I'll tell you what . . ." He pushed the door open and gestured to the Russian. "Come on, man, cigarette break!"

Smerdnakov stood up, a dumb peasant smile on his face. Caesar led the way down the corridor, opening doors until he found an unfinished office with no glass in the windows. The thin torn sheet of plastic stapled over the empty frame billowed out in the wind. Through one of the larger tears, Martin caught a glimpse of the peeling nymph, shivering in the garden four stories below.

Caesar reached into the inside pocket of his jacket and removed a pack of Marlboro Reds and tossed them to the Russian. A book of matches was tucked into the cellophane. "I'll give you two ciga-rettes' worth," he said. "You blow the smoke out the window, and if anyone asks you where you got the cigarette, I'm going to deny ev-erything." He grinned and closed the door behind them.

Smerdnakov sat down on the window ledge, his fingers trem-bling. He managed to get a cigarette out of the pack, lit it, and drew the smoke deep into his lungs. He held the smoke in for as long as he could, then let it out with a deep, contented sigh. His disposi-tion seemed to improve almost instantly. He held out the pack to Martin.

"Hey, asshole, want a cigarette?"

"I don't smoke," Martin said. "Stuff'll kill you." He still felt dazed from the trial. He couldn't think of anything to say and scuffed the toe of his shoe along the rough cement floor. For once the Russian filled the silence.

"Listen," he said. "You're not a bad lawyer. You ever come to Brighton Beach, I might be able to fix you up with a job."

"Oh?" Martin said idly. "What kind of job?"

"My organization needs good lawyers," Smerdnakov said. "Good smart lawyers who know the score. With a little bit of muscle and a couple of good smart lawyers, you rule the world."

"I'm not that smart," Martin said. "You want the truth, my record stinks. It's just that this time I had the luxury of defending an inno-cent man."

The Russian gave him a blank look. Then he tipped his head back and began to laugh, and he laughed until tears came to his eyes. "You really think I'm innocent?" he said when he could speak. "I take it all back. You are a fucking idiot!"

Martin felt his heart drop into his stomach. "What are you telling me?" he said; then he stopped himself. "No, I don't want to hear it, not a word!" He turned around twice, quick, spasmodic jerks, like a dog chasing its tail. Then he turned back to the Russian, unable to stop himself. "Are you telling me you killed your Katinka? You strangled her?"

Smerdnakov took another deep drag from his cigarette. Suddenly he was very serious. "Sure," he said quietly. "What the fuck did you think?"

Martin was stunned. For ten full seconds he forgot to take the next breath. "Why?" he managed finally, and it came out halfway between a choke and a whimper.

Smerdnakov shrugged. "She pissed me off," he said. "She was a stinking drunken whore. I told her not to drink no more. But she went up to the bar and got another vodka; then she started taking her clothes off in front of everyone."

"Wait a minute." Martin still couldn't believe what he was hearing. "You strangled her because she bought another drink?"

"You know the old Russian song 'Volga Boatman'?" Smerdnakov said. "Very old song. Here, listen . . ." and he hummed a few bars.

Martin couldn't speak. He wanted to run, scream.

"Like I tell you, things have always been very tough in Russia. They're tough now, but in the old days they were really tough. The Volga boatmen, they were always fighting. Fighting the Tatars, the Poles, everybody, and they had to be really, really tough. So this one boatman, he is the toughest of them all; then he falls in love with a beautiful girl. Then one day he strangles her and throws her body in the river. You know why? Because she was making him too soft with her love. If you want to be tough, you can't have a woman around for very long. So, if you want the truth, I started to like her a lot, my Katinka. She was same as me, from nothing and damned clever. So . . ." He took another drag of his cigarette.

"So you killed her," Martin said in a whisper. Almost imperceptibly he moved a couple of steps forward.

The Russian nodded. "You did a real good job in there," he said. "Especially with that fucking slut, that Bunny woman. For a few seconds I almost shit my pants. *Who's this bitch?* I thought. My guys tell me they already took care of the witnesses. All of them. But that fucking nigger prosecutor was holding out. He found one stupid little slut to tell the truth."

Martin watched Smerdnakov's face. An expression of unconscious ferocity flickered across it like a shadow. He realized now that this man was irredeemably bad, that everything he had held as true about him — and about many other things as well — was a lie.

"They think they can protect her," Smerdnakov was saying now. "The fucking idiots. When I get out of here, I'll find that little slut and personally cut her throat. Then I'll fuck her while she's bleeding to death. I swear it."

Martin didn't think about what he did next. He lunged at Smerdnakov and hit him with both hands in the center of the chest and shoved with all his might. For a terrible moment the Russian teetered on the brink, his eyes rolling wildly. He fought, but cuffed and shackled, cigarette still smoking between his lips, he couldn't maintain his balance. With a loud ripping sound, the thin plastic sheeting gave way under his bulk, and he fell over backward and plummeted headfirst to the hard concrete five stories below. Only in the last few feet of his descent did he let out a short, terrified cry. Martin heard the sound of his head splitting on the pavement and turned away. At that moment the door flung open, and Caesar sprang into the room.

"What's going on here? Where's the —" He stopped short when he saw Martin's ashen face.

Martin's lips felt cold. "He jumped. My client jumped." It was the only thing he could think of to say.

Caesar let out an exclamation and ran to the window and looked down. A puddle of blood was spreading over the sidewalk. Two police officers were already sprinting across the park toward the body from the direction of Indiana Avenue.

"What do you mean, the motherfucker jumped?" Caesar shouted. "Why the fuck did he do that?"

For a second Martin couldn't think. Then his mind began to work, creaking like a machine that hadn't been used in years. "He confessed," he said. "He confessed that he strangled that woman, and he said he couldn't take the guilt anymore. He was out the window before I could stop him."

Caesar stepped back, bewildered, rubbing his hands together. "Shit, man. Shit . . ." He didn't know what to believe.

Downstairs, in the deliberation room, the church ladies knelt on the floor, joined hands, bowed their heads, and loudly called on

Jesus. Denise Wheeler knelt beside them and folded her arms over her bosom to address the odd deity of the Mormon Church. The Pakistani garage manager spread his jacket across the new linoleum, lowered himself onto his hands and knees, consulted a pocket compass for the direction of Mecca, and whispered in Urdu a prayer to Allah, the Just and the Merciful. The other jurors bowed their heads out of respect or offered silent prayers of their own devising. One of the old men took out a rosary, rested his elbows on his knees, clasped his hands, and began murmuring the paternoster.

Twenty minutes passed this way. Then everyone was done praying, and Denise stood and smiled at the others. She had been selected foreman.

"We've done God's work here today," she said in a sweet voice. "We can all be proud of ourselves."

"Amen," the church ladies said in unison. The Pakistani frowned and said nothing.

Then Denise went out into the hallway to inform the court clerk that the jury had reached its verdict.

CHAD HOLLEY

The Island in the River

FROM *Greensboro Review*

> They had been strong, as those are strong who know neither doubts
> nor hopes.
> — Joseph Conrad

WE SLEPT in the car that night somewhere in Louisiana, and it got bad cold on us. My buddy Louis kept squirming and cussing up in the front seat, and in the back I curled tight and hunted heat down in my coat. I dozed enough to dream I was freezing all the way to death, and it wasn't like they say it is. It was the hardest way I've ever gone in my dreams.

We were back on the interstate hours before daylight. Louis's heater wouldn't come on, and in the glow of the dash lights we rode hunched forward, gritting our teeth, and not a word between us. At one point I did reach over and bang the heater knobs with the heel of my hand. When nothing happened, I slid my hand back under my thigh and hunkered down again.

"I keep hoping that heater'll decide to come on," I said. Talking made the road noise seem louder inside the car.

"Well, you know what they say, Raymond," Louis said. "Hope in one hand and shit in the other, you'll see which hand gets warm."

I didn't answer him.

We finally went over the river into Vicksburg, and with it now getting morning enough that we could see our breath inside the car, we started up into the Delta. We had been gone almost six months. All we planned to do was drive up through the Delta and go through Silas, just to see if things would look different to us now, I guess, and keep going. I was the one said we ought to do it. I don't know. Neither of us could really think straight anymore.

A small, weak sun came up, and I rode looking out my window. There was the Delta, a vast sheet of mud under the white sky, still as a picture all the way to the horizon. Black trees standing out there in the mud and sometimes a solitary metal farm building far out in the distance made the Delta seem even bigger and emptier. I don't know why I expected any different. I have never seen that emptiness blink. I let my forehead fall against the cold glass.

"I've seen enough," I said. "This can all just go to hell."

Louis didn't answer. We were about an hour out of Vicksburg and another one yet from Silas.

"You can drop me off or I don't care what we do," I said, "but I ain't going through Silas."

I looked over at Louis. He was squinting his eyes like he was thinking. He was cold and haggard as I was, and he looked especially skinny with his leather streetcoat buttoned up and his Dodgers cap pulled down hard on his head. Finally he gave me that ever-game little shrug of his and that nonchalant tone.

"You want to see if they still got that branch bank up here in Shardale?"

We didn't have all that much cash on us, but we weren't broke enough to need to stop in Shardale either.

I turned my face to the window again. Alongside us, row ends bent past at the speed of thought.

"I don't care what we do," I said.

Outside of Shardale we stopped at an old store to top off our gas. There was frost on the pumps. In the trunk of the car I dug through my bag until I found the .45 automatic I had picked up in L.A. It hurt to hold that chunk of ice.

Along the highway as we came into Shardale there was a John Deere place that had apparently gone out of business and next to it a little run-down feed store. Louis watched them go by. "Damn," he said, and he kind of winced and smiled at the same time. "We drove two thousand miles to hit a bank in Shardale." He shook his head, apparently as amused with us as ever. It had been weeks since I myself had been all that amused. But it used to be we both laughed at us all the time. And I think we both knew that's all we were ever really about. It wasn't like we had some solemn friendship or something. We were just running buddies from high school who hadn't yet figured out what to do next and both thought that was real funny. When we left Silas I know I laughed my head off. I couldn't believe us. It was on a weekday afternoon near the end of August, and Louis and I were standing around in the gravel lot of Mitch's store out near the elevator. One of those days I just didn't have what it took for working all day at a grain elevator in Silas, Mississippi. So I had left the elevator at lunch, told them I had the stomachache. Louis was supposed to be helping some guy out that way with his catfish ponds, even though Louis had just gotten out of county lockup under suspicion of stealing some of that same guy's equipment, which come to find out he had in fact done. So that afternoon we were talking about that and drinking beer out of a cooler I kept on my back seat. Eventually, we stood against my car without talking, and after a while we started humming rocks at Mitch's sign out by the road. Not thinking much about it, I sung out this one line my daddy used to sing over and over from some song I never heard.

"We got to get outta this place . . ."

Louis stopped throwing rocks.

"We should," he said. "No plan, no goodbyes, just scot-free asshaulin'." He dusted his hands and started grinning. "That'd be hilarious."

"Where should we go?" I said.

I threw another rock.

"You name it, baby," Louis said, and when I didn't answer him right away he said, "Seriously."

I was serious. I had another rock in my hand, and I turned to the knee-deep field of soybeans that began at the edge of Mitch's parking lot and threw the rock far as I could through the dead space out over the field. The rock pattered on the leaves not far away.

"L.A.," I said.

Louis's lean, sunburnt face had broken into a big smile. He nodded toward his car and started across the gravel. Louis was not one to be outdone for spontaneous.

"We can take the Buick," he said, and for a second I thought he was wanting to leave right then. I got nervous. The loud whine of the locusts went suddenly electric in my head.

But when Louis got his door open and one leg inside he looked back at me and said, "Dark-thirty, baby. Have your shit packed."

That's all he said, and he was smiling the whole time. But that evening he pulled up in the road out front of my aunt's house. And my shit was packed. We laughed and laughed.

When we hit a liquor store in New Mexico I didn't even have a gun. Like Louis said once, all you need is one gun and it doesn't even have to work. We probably hit six or eight places in those months out west, and I found out, it ain't that big a deal really. Cashiers and tellers are trained to come off the money with no fuss. Anybody can take it. Long as you don't monkey with the ones behind glass. And then the other tricky thing is when some of these places have a cop inside. That had happened to us once, at this quickie store out in California. But, you know, when you get to the door and see there's a damn cop standing in there, there's no law says you got to go on in and make a mess. So that night when I got up to the glass doors and saw this woman cop inside, I said, "Oh shit," and tried to turn around. But Louis was behind me and he plowed us both on in. The woman cop was sipping coffee at the end of the counter. Louis walked right at her. He had an expression I'd never seen on his face before, all flushed and serious. In one smooth move he whipped his snubnose .38 out of his streetcoat and put that joker right in her face, and he backed the hammer. Then he just stood there with his arm leveled at her eyes. It was not a pleasant thing to be around, with the hammer on that .38 ready to drop and having no idea what was going on in Louis's head, but I went on and did the talking and everything went fine. Later we laughed at his new theory: If you let them study you from a distance they could identify you again no problem, but if you stuck your face right up in theirs they wouldn't remember shit. Which is funny, but like I said, by the time we were riding back into Shardale, laughing at this kind of thing had long since gotten old for me.

When we got into Shardale that morning, we pulled into the bank's customer parking lot, and there were no other cars there. We parked up near the glass doors and sat with the car idling. We were in no hurry and weren't worried about folks seeing us, because best we knew nobody out west had started looking for us by name. Louis checked the cylinder on his .38 one last time and snapped it shut. I'd checked my piece several times coming into town and I wasn't checking it again.

"Well," Louis said, and he sighed like he was tired, "game time."

We left the car idling and stepped up onto the sidewalk. My spine was starting to jump from the cold and from being geared up. I had my empty duffel bag in my hand. We entered the bank, Louis in front.

The bank was small, just one large room, and inside it was warm and soft and quiet, with carpet and lots of plants. In the middle of the room there was an expensive-looking sofa and a nice coffee table. It was just a bank, but I couldn't get over how cozy and civilized it felt, and paused there inside the glass doors beside Louis, I was suddenly embarrassed to be doing this.

There were no customers in the room and no teller at the counter, but across the lobby there was a cop. He was a big old boy, standing with his butt against the wall and his hands in his pockets.

Louis started across the lobby toward him.

I looked at the cop just enough to see that he was watching us. I let Louis get a little closer to him and I went up to the counter.

The only girl working was standing back near the drive-through window and had not noticed me yet. She was talking softly on the telephone. Beyond her, out the teller window, there were the two drive-through lanes and then a bare, black pecan tree at the edge of an empty field. The tint in the window made the sky over the field look darker, like it might rain. I took a deep breath of the dry, warm lobby air.

That's when I heard a cheerful voice say, "Louis Day," and I turned to see the cop smiling at Louis.

My first thought was that the guy might have played baseball for Shardale — we used to play them all the time. But then his red hair and his big ears registered, and I knew who it was. The cop was damn Yancy Purvis, this guy from Silas that went to school with me and Louis.

Louis's face had turned dark red. He did not answer Yancy. He just walked up in front of him.

Yancy had stopped smiling. "Louis," he said.

Louis raised his pistol into Yancy's face. He thumbed the hammer back.

"My God," said the girl. She had come to the counter. We looked each other in the face, and I unzipped my coat to show the grip of my pistol. I laid the duffel bag up on the counter.

As I watched the girl stack money over into the bag, it was hard for me to concentrate. Louis's leather coat kept creaking, but the one time I looked back, neither Louis nor Yancy had moved. Yancy's butt was still against the wall, his hands still in his pockets.

Yancy had graduated a year ahead of us, and sometime afterward we all started seeing him around Silas in his police outfit. Everybody used to joke about it. But I never did think it was that funny. I mean, nobody could deny that Yancy Purvis was a retard, and here they were letting him walk around Silas, and then Shardale too I guess, with a loaded gun and the right to arrest people. They must let anybody do it. Though I'll confess, I couldn't do it. Because when you think about it, if a guy's going to step up and claim a spot as the law, he better know down deep that the good of society and what-have-you is an absolutely worthwhile thing. Or at least better be pretty damn hopeful about it.

When we walked out of the bank, the cold met us immediately. We had Yancy with us. Louis had handcuffed him. Nobody talked, but Louis handled Yancy and that pistol like a man who's decided something way inside his head, a man I wasn't crazy about getting in that car with.

Louis drove us out of Shardale. We stayed close to the speed limit, sat for a red light. It was very quiet in the car. It reminded me of riding in the car when my daddy was around and all of us would stare off in a different direction, scared to say anything.

We left Shardale's few houses and stores and churches, and the Delta opened up again, big and winter-wet and empty. It was getting to where I couldn't watch out the window anymore. I was wishing to God that we had driven east into the hill country. But we were heading west, farther out into the Delta, to find this cousin of Louis's who lived inside the Mississippi levee. Louis said the guy was a certified nut and wouldn't care if we laid over with him a couple of days. That had sounded fine to me, mostly because I wanted to go over inside the Mississippi levee. I had never been, though I had lived my whole life not two hours from it and always heard about it from folks who hunted over there. I was curious to finally see it for myself. But I didn't know whether we'd even get there now.

I zipped my coat up and turned my back to my door.

Louis was stone-faced. His left hand was up on the wheel, and his right hand still held his pistol flat on the seat beside him.

Somebody finally said something. It was Yancy.

"Ray," he said. His voice was small, but calm. "Why are y'all pulling this crap?"

I set my eyes on the highway out front of us. I didn't answer him.

"Ray."

I never looked back there at him.

Yancy then said, "Louis?"

I watched what happened out the corner of my eye. Louis jerked the pistol up off the seat. He started glancing over in the back, and Yancy said, "Come on, man . . . now . . . wait," and Louis kept his hold on the steering wheel and got the pistol over in the back seat and Yancy was yelling, "Don't, come on . . ." when Louis looked back there again. I stared hard as I could at the windshield.

It sounded like the world fell on the car. Then a ringing silence.

It took me a second to hear Yancy laboring down in the seat.

Louis still had his arm hung over the seatback, and he started looking back there again. I put my fingers in my ears.

There were two more severe thumps.

When I took my fingers out of my ears, there was a faraway hum in the car, but no noise in the back seat. The car stunk with pistol smoke.

Louis brought his arm back over the seat and rested the gun beside him. But I saw how he kept holding it, kept his finger curled on the trigger, and it made me glance around for my gun. It was down in the floor, on my duffel bag at my feet. But Louis finally left his pistol where it was and rolled down his window.

I had gotten almost no sleep the night before and then been keyed up all morning, and now I started feeling hollow and sleepy. For a while I tried to think through what we could do with Yancy Purvis's body but I couldn't stay with it for remembering different things about him from school and from seeing him out nights in his uniform in Silas, and then I couldn't think about anything but how cold I was getting again. I let my head fall back against the headrest and just sat there watching the road with Louis.

There was no mistaking the levee when it appeared. Out there in front of us was a high mound sown with the brightest green winter grass. It ran out of sight in both directions. I sat up to look at it, at how long it was and green it was, and I couldn't take my eyes off of it.

The road we were on turned in front of the levee and ran along-side the foot of it for a little ways, but in the turn there was a gravel ramp that ran up on top of the levee. Louis slowed down and took the ramp, and we turned south on the gravel road that ran along the top. The dull, gray Delta shadowed us on our left. But out my window on our right was that land inside the Mississippi levee that I had never seen before. For some reason I had come to hope like hell that it was as different as they said it was, and I tell you, it didn't let me down.

Rising up here and there out of the tall yellow grass inside the levee were trailers up on stilts, regular trailers, but held fifteen or twenty feet up in the air on bowed iron girders. Beyond them the hardwood ran so thick you couldn't see the sky through their tops, all those black branches wild and matted like a huge nest of water moccasins. When there were breaks in the trees you could see oxbow water, wide and choppy, and birds that looked like sea-gulls floated and fell and gusted low over the water, and above them small dark birds rode the wind in circles like bits of ash in the thermals of a fire, and the wind came up on the levee and whipped against Louis's car. Out in one lake we passed I saw a heavily wooded island.

When I looked over at Louis he didn't seem to have even glanced over inside the levee, and it occurred to me that he had probably seen this before. Though I wondered if he had ever been much impressed by it, even the first time he saw it, and I thought probably not.

We rode south on the levee for a good while, but I can't say how long because I lay my head back again finally and closed my eyes and gave my mind over to the lake wind that whistled and brushed against the car. I did not sleep, but I found myself walking a river is-land, with blue mud and wet roots and flood-twisted trees and loud birds and old, heavy-headed deer, and from deep under the firm earth where I stood I felt the giant slide of more dark water than I could imagine. I tried to go to that island in sleep, but could not slip away from the freeze inside the car, from thoughts of Yancy, from what remained on my left.

The next thing I remember was hearing Louis say, "Shit. Shit." When I opened my eyes, he was watching the rearview mirror. We had sped up considerably. I looked back to see blue lights flashing up on the levee.

Louis banged the steering wheel with his fist. His eyes began searching out in front of us.

I sat up and turned in my seat to watch back, steadying myself with a hand up on the dash. I saw Yancy's dark sleeve, but I didn't look down in the seat. The car behind us looked like a deputy sheriff's. I couldn't tell whether it was gaining on us.

All I could think to say was, "We got to get off of here."

Louis did not say anything.

There was nowhere to get off the levee. On our left lay a mud field. On our right the hardwood had come up near the levee and was flooded with still, khaki water. There were no roads or ramps or trailers in sight. We went on like this for several minutes. Louis kept surging the gas and whenever he did the car skittered side to side beneath us.

When the roadblock appeared way down the levee, my first thought was that a bunch of deer were standing in the road. But we got closer and the blue lights came on and my head went really hot and started tingling and Louis was muttering something. I picked my pistol up off the duffel bag and it felt light as air in my hand. I could barely tell I was holding it. Something about this made my gut sick. We did not slow down and we got close enough to see it was two brown patrol cars parked across the levee and behind them a red pickup with a flashing light up on the dash, and we left the levee, down the Delta side. It might have made no difference, but I would've tried the other side.

I felt the body of the car leave the ground completely for a heartbeat before we hit the foot of the levee and started across a soggy bean field. We didn't go twenty-five yards before Louis's car sank to the chassis.

When the Buick quit on him, Louis snatched up his pistol from where it had fallen into the floorboard and he opened his door and slogged out into the bean field, trying to get up enough momentum to run.

I still held my pistol in my hand. I opened my door and stood up into the field. The air was raw and wet and I could smell the mud I was standing in. That field ran all the way back to a dim treeline on the horizon. I looked into that long, empty distance, and then I looked at Louis, huffing and grunting but not really going anywhere, not even started on crossing all that field. I sat down in the mud beside the car.

The police cars were peeling down off the levee. They stopped at the edge of the field, their lights still flashing. I watched the officers jump out, all zipped up in their brown coats, and one of them hollered to us. I reared back and threw my gun into the air toward them. It didn't go very far.

They wanted me to get up and walk toward them with my hands on my head, but I sat where I was. I did get scared they might shoot me, so I lay back flat on the mud.

I quit listening to them and just lay looking up at the low, white sky. There was nothing in it. The sky did not look like something that was deep. I thought something inside me was going to die, and I laid my arm across my eyes. Out on that river island, I went down on a bed of crackling summer vine.

When they got to me they were still yelling at Louis, who was somewhere out there on the other side of the car. They got me over on my stomach and I saw the old white-haired man in the bunch, who I'm guessing was the sheriff, look over in Louis's back seat. "Oh man," he said and ran the back of his hand across his mouth. He opened the door and kneeled in.

Two of the deputies stripped my coat off me and got me handcuffed and started hustling me through the mud toward the patrol cars at the levee. I was shivering. Behind us they were still yelling at Louis.

The deputies shut me in a patrol car, where it was dry and warm. The radio was hissing softly. Out the window I could see Louis, a little ways out in the field beyond his car. He wasn't trying to run anymore. He was standing, facing the men who watched him from behind his car. They all had their guns drawn. One of them had a rifle laid across Louis's hood and was looking at Louis through the scope. While I was watching, Louis made like he was going to raise his pistol and when he did, puffs of smoke went up from the car and there was a cluster of pops. Louis sat down in the field, then jammed his shoulder into the mud. His neck was twisted so that his faced turned up to the sky. But I think he just fell that way.

The radio squawked clean and crisp, and I laid my cheek against the window glass. A deputy was approaching the patrol car. More than anything right then, I wanted to thank him for keeping that car warm.

EDWARD LEE

ICU

FROM *999*

IT CHASED HIM; it was *huge*. But what was it? He sensed its im-
mensity gaining on him, pursuing him through unlit warrens,
around cornerways of smothered flesh, and down alleys of ichor
and blood . . .

Holy Mother of God.

When Paone fully woke, his mind felt wiped out. Dull pain and
confinement crushed him, or was it paralysis? Warped images,
voices, smears of light and color all massed in his head. Francis
"Frankie" Paone shuddered in the terror of the nameless thing that
chased him through the rabbets and fissures of his own subcon-
scious mind.

Yes, he was awake now, but the chase led on:

Storming figures. Concussion. Blood squirting onto dirty white
walls.

And like a slow dissolve, Paone finally realized what it was that
chased him. Not hitters. Not cops or feds.

It was *memory* that chased him.

But the memory of *what?*

The thoughts surged. *Where am I? What the hell happened to me?*
This latter query, at least, shone clear. Something *had* happened.
Something devastating . . .

The room was a blur. Paone squinted through grit teeth; without
his glasses he couldn't see three feet past his face.

But he could see enough to know.

Padded leather belts girded his chest, hips, and ankles, restraining him to a bed which seemed hard as slate. He couldn't move. To

his right stood several metal poles topped by blurred blobs. A long line descended . . . to his arm. *IV bags,* he realized. The line came to an end at the inside of his right elbow. And all about him swarmed unmistakable scents: antiseptics, salves, isopropyl alcohol.

I'm in a fucking hospital, he acknowledged.

Someone must've dropped a dime on him. But . . . He simply couldn't remember. The memories hovered in fragments, still chasing his spirit without mercy. Gunshots. Blood. Muzzleflash.

His myopia offered even less mercy. Beyond the bed he could detect only a vague white perimeter, shadows, and depthless bulk. A drone reached his ears, like a distant air conditioner, and there was a slow, aggravating beep: the drip monitor for his IV. Overhead, something swayed. *Hanging flowerpot?* he ventured. No, it reminded him more of one of those retractable arms you'd find in a doctor's office, like an X-ray nozzle. And the fuzzed ranks of shapes along the walls could only be cabinets, *pharmaceutical* cabinets.

Yeah, I'm in a hospital, all right, he realized. An ICU ward. It had to be. And he was buckled down good. Not just his ankles, but his knees too, and his shoulders. More straps immobilized his right arm to the IV board, where white tape secured the needle sunk into the crook of his elbow.

Then Paone looked at his left arm. That's all it was — an arm. There was no hand at the end of it. And when he raised his right leg . . .

Just a stump several inches below the knee.

Nightmare, he wished. But the chasing memories seemed too real for a dream, and so did the pain. There was *plenty* of pain. It hurt to breathe, to swallow, even to blink. Pain oozed through his bowels like warm acid.

Somebody fucked me up royal, he conceded. The jail ward, no doubt. *And there's probably a cop standing right outside the door.* He knew where he was now, but it terrified him not knowing exactly what had brought him here.

The memories raged, chasing, chasing . . .

Heavy slumps. Shouts. A booming, distorted voice . . . like a megaphone.

Jesus. He wanted to remember, yet again, he didn't. The memories *stalked* him: pistol shots, full-auto rifle fire, the feel of his own piece jumping in his hand.

"Hey!" he shouted. "How about some help in here!"

A click resounded to the left; a door opened and closed. Soft footsteps approached, then suddenly a bright, unfocused figure blurred toward him.

"How long have you been awake?" came a toneless female voice.

"Couple of minutes," Paone said. Pain throbbed in his throat. "Could you come closer? I can barely see you."

The figure obliged. Its features sharpened.

It wasn't a cop at all, it was a nurse. Tall, brunet, with fluid-blue eyes and a face of hard, eloquent lines. Her white blouse and skirt blurred like bright light. White nylons shone over sleek, coltish legs.

"Do you know where my glasses are?" Paone asked. "I'm near-sighted as hell."

"Your glasses fell off at the crime scene," she flatly replied.

Crime scene, came the bumbling thought.

"We've sent someone to recover them," she added. "It shouldn't be too long." Her vacant eyes appraised him. She leaned over to take his vitals. "How do you feel?"

"Terrible. My gut hurts like a son of a bitch, and my hand . . ." Paone, squinting, raised the bandaged left stump. "Shit," he muttered. He didn't even want to ask.

Now the nurse turned to finick with the IV monitor; Paone continued to struggle against the freight of chasing memory. More images churned in some mental recess. Fragments of wood and ceiling tile raining on his shoulders. The mad cacophony of what could only be machine gun fire. A head exploding to pulp.

Blank-faced, then, the nurse returned her gaze. "What do you remember, Mr. Paone?"

"I —" was all he said. He stared up. Paone never carried real ID on a run, and whatever he drove was either hot or chopped, with phony plates. The question ground out of his throat. "How do you know my name?"

"We know all about you," she said, unfolding a slip of paper. "The police showed us this teletype from Washington. Francis K. 'Frankie' Paone. You have seven aliases. You're thirty-seven years old, never been married, and you have no known place of legal residence. In 1985 you were convicted of interstate flight to avoid prosecution, interstate transportation of obscene material depicting minors, and multiple violations of Section 18 of the United States Code. Two years ago you were released from Alderton Federal Penitentiary after serving sixty-two months of concurrent eleven- and five-year jail terms. You are a known associate of the Vinchetti crime family. You're a child pornographer, Mr. Paone."

Christ, a fuckin' burn, Paone realized. *Somebody set me up.* By now it wasn't hard to figure: lying in some ICU ward strapped to a bed, shot up like a hinged duck in a shooting gallery, one hand gone, one leg gone, and now this stolid bitch reading him his own rap sheet off an FBI fax. He sure as shit hadn't gotten busted taking down some candy store.

"You don't know what you're talking about," he said.

Her eyes blazed down. Her face could've been carved from stone. *Yeah.* Paone thought. *I'll bet she's got a couple kids herself flunking out of school and smoking pot. Bet her car just broke down and her insurance just went up and her hubby's late for dinner every night because he's too busy balling his secretary and snorting rails of coke off her tits, and all of a sudden it's my fault that the world's a shithouse full of perverts and pedophiles. It's my fault that a lot of people out there pay righteous cash for kiddie flicks, right, baby? Go ahead, blame me. Why not? Oh, hey, and how about the drug problem? And the recession and the Middle East and the ozone layer? That's all my fault too, right?*

Her voice sounded like she had gravel in her throat when again she asked: "What do you remember?"

The query haunted him. The bits of memory blurred along with the room in his myopic eyes — bullets popping into flesh, the megaphone grating, spent cartridges spewing out of wafts of smoke — and chased him further, stalking him as relentlessly as a wild cat running down a fawn, while Paone fled on, desperate to know yet never daring to look back . . .

"Shit, nothing," he finally said. "I can't remember anything except bits and pieces."

The nurse seemed to talk more to herself than to him. "A transient-global amnesic effect, retrograde and generally nonaphasic, induced by acute traumatic shock. Don't worry, it's a short-term symptom and quite commonplace." The big blue eyes bore back into him. "So I think I'll refresh your memory. Several hours ago, you murdered two state police officers and a federal agent."

Paone's jaw dropped.

At once the chase ended, the wild cat of memory finally falling down on its prey — Paone's mind. He remembered it all, the pieces falling into place as quickly as pavement to a ledge-jumper.

The master run. Rodz. The loops.

And all the blood.

Another day, another ten K, Paone thought, mounting the three flights of stairs to Rodz's apartment. He wore jersey gloves — no way he was rockhead enough to leave his prints anywhere near Rodz's crib. He knocked six times on the door, whistling "Love Me Tender" by the King.

"Who is it?" came the craggy voice.

"Santa Claus," Paone said. "You really should think about getting a chimney."

Rodz let him in, then quickly relocked the door. "Anyone tailing you?"

"No, just a busload of DJ agents and a camera crew from *60 Minutes.*"

Rodz glowered.

Fuck you if you can't take a joke, Paone thought. He didn't much like Rodz — Newark slime, a whack. Nathan Rodz looked like an anorectic Tiny Tim after a bad facelift: long, frizzy black hair on the head of a pudgy medical cadaver, speedlines down his cheeks. Rodz was what parlance dubbed a "snatch-cam" — a subcontractor, so to speak. He abducted the kids, or got them on loan from freelance movers, then shot the tapes himself. "The Circuit" was what the Justice Department called the business: underground pornography. It was a $1.5-billion-per-year industry that almost no one knew about, a far cry from the *Debbie Does Dallas* bunk you rented down at Metro Video. Paone muled all kinds of underground: rape loops, "wet" S&M, animal flicks, scat, snuff, and (their biggest number) "kp" and "prepubes." Paone picked up the masters from guys like Rodz, then muled them to Vinchetti's mobile "dupe" lab. Vinchetti's network controlled almost all of the underground porn in the East; Paone was the middleman, part of the family. It all worked through mail drops and coded distro points. Vinchetti paid two grand for a twenty-minute master if the resolution was good; from there each master was duped hundreds of times and sold to clients with a taste for the perverse. "Logboys," the guys who did the actual rodwork, were hired freelance on the side; that way, nobody could spin on Vinchetti himself. Paone had seen some shit in his time — part of his job was to sample each master for quality: biker chicks on PCP blowing horses and dogs, addicts excreting on each other and often consuming the produce of their bowels. "Nek" flicks. "Bag" flicks. Logboys getting down on pregnant girls, retarded girls, amputees and deformees. And snuff. It amazed Paone, in spite of its grotesquery: people *paid* to see this stuff. They *got off* on it. *What a fucked-up world,* he thought a million times over, but, hey, supply and demand — that was the American Way, wasn't it? If Vinchetti didn't supply the clients, someone else would, and as long as the money was there . . .

I'll take my cut, Paone stonily thought.

The biggest orders were always for kp. According to federal stats, 10,000 kids disappeared each year and were never seen again; most of them wound up in the Circuit. The younger the kids, the more the tapes cost. Once kids got old (fourteen or fifteen) they were deemed as "beat," and they were either sold overseas or put out on the street to turn tricks for Vinchetti's pross net. One thing feeding the other. Yeah, it was a fucked-up world, all right, but that wasn't Paone's problem.

The competition was squat. Only one other East Coast family ran underground porn, the Bontes, and they had a beef with Vinchetti going way back. Both families fought for pieces of the hard market, but the Bontes only owned a trickle of the action, and Paone could've laughed at the reason. Dario Bonte, the don, thought it was unethical to victimize children. *Ain't that a laugh,* Paone had thought. *The son of a bitch'll string women out on junk and put them in scat films till they starve to death, but he won't do any kiddie.* What a chump. Most of the money was in kp anyway. No wonder Bonte was losing his ass. And every now and then some foreign outfit would try to move on Vinchetti's turf with kp from Europe.

But they never lasted very long.

All in all, Paone's job was simple: he bought the masters, muled them to the lab, and kept the snatch-cams in line — guys like this muck-for-brains short-eyed scumbag Rodz.

"I got five for ya," said Rodz, "the usual." Rodz's voice was more annoying than nails across slate, a nasally, wet rasp. "But I been thinking, you know?"

"Oh, you think?" Paone asked. He'd never seen such a pit for an apartment. Little living room full of put-it-together-yourself furniture, smudged walls, tacky green-and-brown carpet tile; an odiferous kitchen. *Buckingham Fucking Palace this ain't.*

"Like two K a pop is getting pretty skimpy these days," Rodz went on. "Come on, man, for a fucking master that Vinchetti's crew'll dupe hundreds of times? That's serious green for him. But what about me? Every time I make a master for your man, I'm sticking my neck out a mile."

"That's because you were *born* with a mile-long neck, Ichabod."

"I think two-point-five at least is fair. I mean, I heard that the Bonte family's paying three."

"The Bontes don't do kiddie porn, grapehead," Paone informed him. "And anybody in the biz knows that."

"Yeah, but they do snuff and nek and all the other hard stuff. I'm the one busting my ass making the masters. I should be able to go to the highest bidder."

Paone stared him down. "Watch that, Rodz. No jive. You master for Vinchetti and Vinchetti only. Period. You want some advice? Don't even *think* about peddling your shit to some other family. The last guy who pulled a stunt like that, you know what happened to him? Jersey cops found him hanging upside-down in some apartment laundry room. Blowtorched. And they cut off his cock and Express Mailed it to his grandmother in San Bernardino."

Rodz's face did a twitch. "Yeah, well, like I was saying, two K a pop sounds pretty square."

I thought so, Paone regarded.

"So where's that green?"

Paone headed toward the back bedroom, where Rodz did his thing. "You don't touch doggie-doo till I see the fruits of your labor."

He sat down on a couch that had no doubt served as a prop in dozens of Rodz's viddies. High-end cameras and lights sat on tripods, not the kind of gear they sold down at Radio Shack. The masters had to be shot on large-format inch-and-a-quarter high-speed tape so the dupes retained good contrast. The five boxed tapes sat before a thirty-five-inch Sony Trinitron and a studio double-player by Thompson Electronics. "Good kids this time too," Rodz complimented himself. "All level." Sometimes a kid would freak on camera, or space out; lots of them were screwed up from the get-go: Fetal Cocaine babies, Fetal Alcohol Syndrome, Battered Child Syndrome. There were times when Paone actually felt sad about the way things worked.

Now came the sadder part: Paone had to sit back and watch each master; lighting, resolution, and clarity all had to be good. He plugged in the first tape . . .

Jesus, he thought. Pale movement flickered on the screen. They were always the same in a way. What bothered Paone most were the faces — the forlorn, tiny faces on the kids, the *look* while Rodz's stunt cocks got busy. *What do they think?* Paone wondered. *What goes on in their heads?* Every so often the kid would look into the camera and offer a stare that defied description . . .

"At least let me UV the cash while you're watching," Rodz said.

"Yeah, yeah." Paone threw him the stuffed envelope. His face felt molded of clay as he watched on. Rodz always fronted his flicks with cutesy titles, like *Vaseline Alley, The Young and the Hairless, Stomper Room.* Meanwhile, Rodz himself donned nylon gloves and took out the band of century notes. Ten grand didn't look like much. He scanned each bill front and back with a Sirchie ultraviolet lamp. Technicians from Treasury worked liaison with DJ and the Bureau all the time. Their favorite game was to turn someone out and dust buy-money with invisible uranyl phosphate dyes. Dead solid perfect in court.

"Clean enough for ya?" Paone asked. "I mean, a clean guy like yourself?"

"Yeah, looks good." Rodz's face looked lit up as he inspected the bills. "Unsequenced numbers too. That's great."

Paone winced when he glanced back to the screen. In the last tape, here was Rodz himself, with his hair pulled back and a phony beard, doing the rodwork himself. Paone frowned.

"Sweet, huh?" Rodz grinned at himself on the screen. "Always wanted to be in pictures."

"You should get an Oscar. Best Supporting Pervert."

"It's some fringe bennie. And look who's talking about pervert. I just make the tapes. It's your people who distribute them."

Rodz had a point. *I'm just a player in the big game,* Paone reminded himself. When the money's good you do what you gotta do.

"I'm outa here," Paone said when the last master flicked off. He packed up the tapes and followed Rodz out to the living room. "I wish I could say it's been a pleasure."

Rodz chuckled. "You should be nicer to me. One day I might let you be in one of my flicks. You'd never be the same."

"Yeah? And you'll never be the same when I twist your head off and shove it up your ass."

By the apartment door, Rodz held the speedlined grin. "See you next time . . . I'd offer to shake hands except I wouldn't want to get any slime on you."

"Thanks for the thought." Paone polished his glasses with a handkerchief, reached for the door, and —

Ka-CRACK!

"Holy shit!" Rodz yelled.

— the door blew out of its frame. Not kicked open, *knocked down,* and it was no wonder when Paone, in a moment of static shock, noted the size of the TSD cop stepping back with the steel-head door ram. An even bigger cop three-pointed into the room with a cocked revolver.

"Freeze! Police!"

Paone moved faster than he'd ever moved in his life, got an arm around Rodz, and began to jerk back. Rodz gasped, pissing his pants, as Paone used him as a human shield. Two shots rang out, both of which socked into Rodz's upper sternum.

"Give it up, Paone!" the cop advised. "There's no way out!"

Bullshit, Paone thought. Rodz twitched, gargling blood down his front, then suddenly turned to dead weight. But the move gave Paone time to duck behind the kitchen counter and shuck his SIG 220 chock-full of 9mm hardball. *Move fast!* he directed himself, then sprang up, squeezed off two rounds, and popped back down. Both slugs slammed into the cop's throat. All Paone heard was the slump.

Shadows stiffened in the doorway. A megaphone boomed: "Francis Frankie Paone, you're surrounded by Justice Department agents and the state police. Throw down your weapon and surrender. Throw down your weapon and surrender, throw down your —" and on and on.

Paone shucked his backup piece — an ice-cold Colt snub — and tossed it over the counter. Another state cop and a guy in a suit blundered in. *Dumb fucks,* Paone thought. He sprang up again, squeezed off two sets of doubletaps. The cop twirled, taking both bullets in the chin. And the suit, a DJ agent, took his pair between the eyes. In the frantic glimpse, Paone had time to see the guy's head explode. A goulash of brains slapped the wall.

No way I'm going down. Paone felt surprisingly calm. *Back room. Window. Three-story drop into the bushes.* It was his only chance . . .

But a chance he'd never get.

Before he could move out, the room began to . . . vibrate. Three state SWAT men in Kevlar charged almost balletically into the room, and after that the world turned to chaos. Bullets swept toward Paone in waves. M-16s on full-auto spewed hot brass and rattled away like lawn mowers, rip-stitching holes along the walls, tearing the kitchen apart. "I give up!" Paone shouted, but the volley of gunfire only increased. He curled up into a ball as everything around him began to disintegrate into flying bits. Clip after clip, the bullets came, bursting cabinets, chewing up the counter and the floor, and when there was little left of the kitchen, there wasn't much left of Paone. His left hand hung by a single sinew, his right leg looked gnawed off. Hot slivers of steel cooked in his guts.

Then: silence.

His stomach burned like swallowed napalm. His consciousness began to drift away with wafts of cordite. He sidled over; blood dotted his glasses. EMTs carried off the dead police as a man in blue utilities poked forward with a smoking rifle barrel. Radio squawk eddied foglike in the hot air, and next Paone was being stretchered out over what seemed a lake of blood.

Dreamy moments later, red and white lights beat in his eyes. The doors of the ambulance slammed shut.

"Great God Almighty," he whispered.

"I told you you'd remember," the nurse said.

"How bad am I shot?"

"Not bad enough to kill you. IV antibiotics held off the peritoneal infection, and the EMTs got tourniquets on your arm and leg before you lost too much blood." Her eyes narrowed. "Lucky for you there's no death penalty in this state."

That's right, Paone slowly thought. And the fed statutes only allowed capital punishment if an agent was killed during a narcotics offense. They'd send him up for life with no parole, sure, but that

beat fertilizing the cemetery. The fed slams were easier than a lot of
the state cuts; plus, Paone was a cop-killer, and cop-killers got instant status in stir. No bulls would be trying to bust his cherry.
Things could be worse, he recognized now. He remembered what
he'd told that punk Rodz about taking things for granted; Paone
stuck to his guns. He was busted, shot up like Swiss cheese, and had
left a hand and a leg on Rodz's kitchen floor, but at least he was
alive.

Yeah, he thought. *Hope springs eternal.*

"What are you smiling about?" the nurse asked.

"I don't know. Just happy to be alive, I guess . . . Yeah, that's it." It
was true. Despite these rather irrefutable circumstances, Paone was
indeed very happy.

"Happy to be alive?" The nurse looked coldly disgusted. "What
about the men you murdered? They had wives, families. They had
children. Those children are fatherless now. Those men are dead
because of you."

Paone shrugged as best he could. "Life's a gamble. They lost and
I won. They're the ones who wanted to play hardball, not me. If
they hadn't fucked with me, their kids would still have daddies. I'm
not gonna feel guilty for wasting a bunch of guys who tried to take
me down."

It was ironic. The pain in his gut sharpened yet Paone couldn't
help his exuberance. He wished he had his glasses so he could see
the nurse better. Hell, he wished he had a cold beer too, and a
smoke. He wished he wasn't in these damn hospital restraints. A little celebration of life seemed in order, like maybe he wouldn't
mind putting the blocks on this ice-bitch nurse. Yeah, like maybe
roll her over onto the bed and give that cold pussy of hers a good
working over. *Bet that'd take some of the starch out of her sails.*

Paone, next, began to actually laugh. What a weird turn of the
cards the world was. God worked in strange ways, all right. *At least
He's got a sense of humor.* It was funny. *Those three cops bite the dust and
I'm lying here all snug and cozy, gandering the Ice Bitch.* Paone's low and
choppy laughter did not abate.

The nurse turned on the radio to drown out her patient's unseemly jubilation. Light news filled the air as she checked Paone's
pulse and marked his IV bags. The newscaster droned the day's
paramount events: A heat wave in Texas had killed a hundred peo-

ple. Zero-fat butter to hit the market next week. The surgeon general was imploring manufacturers to suspend production of silicone testicular implants, and a U.S. embassy in Africa somewhere just got bombed. It made things even funnier: the world and all its silliness suddenly meant nothing to Paone. He was going to the slam. What difference did anything, good or bad, make to him now?

He squinted up when another figure came in. Through the room's blurred features, a face leaned over: a sixtyish guy, snow-white hair and a great bushy mustache. "Good evening, Mr. Paone," came the greeting. "My name's Dr. Willet. I wanted to stop by and see how you're doing. Is there anything I can get for you?"

"Since you asked, Doc, I wouldn't mind having my glasses back, and to tell you the truth I wouldn't mind having another nurse. This one here's about as friendly as a mad dog."

Willet only smiled in response. "You were shot up pretty bad but you needn't worry now about infection or blood loss. Those are always our chief concerns with multiple gunshot wounds. I'm happy to inform you that you're in surprisingly good shape considering what happened."

Jolly good, Paone thought.

"And I must say," Willet went on, "I've been anxious to meet you. You're the first child pornographer I've ever had the opportunity to speak with. In a bizarre sense, you're famous. The renegade outlaw."

"Well, I'd offer to give you an autograph," Paone joked, "but there's a problem. I'm left-handed."

"Good, good, that's the spirit. It's a man of character who can maintain a sense of levity after going through what you've —"

"Shhh!" the nurse hissed. She seemed jittery now, a pent-up blur. "This is it . . . I think this is it."

Paone made a face. From the radio, the newscaster droned on: ". . . in a year-long federal sting operation. One suspect, Nathan Rodz, was killed on-site in a frantic shootout with police. Two state police officers and one special agent from a Justice Department task force were also killed, according to authorities, by the second suspect, an alleged mob middleman by the name of Francis 'Frankie' Paone. Paone himself was under investigation for similar allegations, and thought to have direct ties with the Vinchetti crime family, which is said to control over fifty percent of all child pornography marketed in the U.S. Police spokesmen later announced that Paone, during the shootout, managed to escape the scene, and is currently the subject of a statewide manhunt . . ."

Paone's thoughts seemed to slowly flatten. "What's this . . . Escaped?"

The nurse was smiling now. She opened a pair of black-framed glasses and put them on Paone's face . . .

The blurred room, at last, came into focus.

What the fuck is this?

A tracked curtain surrounded him, as he would expect on an ICU ward, but then he noticed something else. It wasn't an X-ray nozzle that hung overhead; it was a retractable boom, complete with microphone. And one of the IV stands wasn't an IV stand at all; it was a stand for a directional halogen light.

"What the hell kind of hospital is this!" Paone demanded.

"Oh, it's not a hospital," Willet said. "It's a safe house."

"One of Don Dario Bonte's safe houses," the nurse was delighted to add.

Willet again. "And we're his private medical staff. Generally our duties are rather uninvolved. When one of the don's men gets shot or hurt, we take care of him, since the local hospital wouldn't be safe."

Bonte, Paone thought in slow dread. *Dario Bonte — Vinchetti's only rival . . .*

"And the police were all too happy to hand you over to our goodly employer," Willet continued. "Half of the state police are on Don Bonte's payroll . . . and this way, the suffering taxpayers are spared the cost of a trial."

Paone felt like he was about to throw up his heart.

The nurse's breasts shook when she giggled. "But we're not just going to kill you —"

"We've got some interesting games to play before we do that," Willet said. "See, our job was to make sure you survived until Junior could get here —"

A door clicked open, and then the nurse reeled back the curtain to reveal a typical basement. But that was not all Paone saw. Standing in the doorway before some steps was a frightfully muscular young man with short dark hair, chiseled features and —

Aw sweet Jesus holy shit —

— and a crotch so packed it looked like he had a couple of pota-
toes in his pants.

"Three guesses why they call him Junior," the nurse giggled on.

"And three more guesses as to what happens next," Willet said.
Now he had shouldered a high-end Sony Betacam. "You see, Mr.
Paone, *your* boss may own the market share for child pornography,
but *our* boss owns a share of the rest. You know, the *really* demented
stuff. And as a gut-shot amputee, you'll be able to provide us with a
very special feature, don't you think?"

Paone vomited on himself when Junior began to lower his jeans.
The nurse jammed a needle into Paone's arm, not enough sodium
amytal to knock him out, but just enough to keep him from putting
up much of a fight. Then the nurse took off his restraints and
flipped him over.

"Don Bonte doesn't like child pornographers," she said.

The stitches across Paone's abdomen began to pop, and he
could hear Junior's footsteps approach the bed.

"As they say," Willet enthused, "lights, camera, action!"

DENNIS LEHANE

Running Out of Dog

FROM *Murder and Obsession*

THIS THING with Blue and the dogs and Elgin Bern happened a while *back, a few years after some of our boys — like Elgin Bern and Cal Sears — came back from Vietnam, and a lot of others — like Eddie Vorey and Carl Joe Carol, the Stewart cousins — didn't. We don't know how it worked in other towns, but that war put something secret in our boys who returned. Something quiet and untouchable. You sensed they knew things they'd never say, did things on the sly you'd never discover. Great card players, those boys, able to bluff with the best, let no joy show in their face no matter what they were holding.*

A small town is a hard place to keep a secret, and a small Southern town with all that heat and all those open windows is an even harder place than most. But those boys who came back from overseas, they seemed to have mastered the trick of privacy. And the way it's always been in this town, you get a sizable crop of young, hard men coming up at the same time, they sort of set the tone.

So, not long after the war, we were a quieter town, a less trusting one (or so some of us seemed to think), and that's right when tobacco money and textile money reached a sort of critical mass and created construction money and pretty soon there was talk that our small town should maybe get a little bigger, maybe build something that would bring in more tourist dollars than we'd been getting from fireworks and pecans.

That's when some folks came up with this Eden Falls idea — a big carnival-type park with roller coasters and water slides and such. Why should all those Yankees spend all their money in Florida? South Carolina had sun too. Had golf courses and grapefruit and no end of KOA campgrounds.

So now a little town called Eden was going to have Eden Falls. We were

going to be on the map, people said. We were going to be in all the brochures.
We were small now, people said, but just you wait. Just you wait.

And that's how things stood back then, the year Perkin and Jewel Lut's
marriage hit a few bumps and Elgin Bern took up with Shelley Briggs and
no one seemed able to hold on to their dogs.

The problem with dogs in Eden, South Carolina, was that the owners who bred them bred a lot of them. Or they allowed them to run
free where they met up with other dogs of opposite gender and
achieved the same result. This wouldn't have been so bad if Eden
weren't so close to I-95, and if the dogs weren't in the habit of bolting into traffic and fucking up the bumpers of potential tourists.

The mayor, Big Bobby Vargas, went to a mayoral conference up
in Beaufort, where the governor made a surprise appearance to tell
everyone how pissed off he was about this dog thing. Lot of money
being poured into Eden these days, the governor said, lot of steps
being taken to change her image, and he for one would be goddamned if a bunch of misbehaving canines was going to mess all
that up.

"Boys," he'd said, looking Big Bobby Vargas dead in the eye,
"they're starting to call this state the Devil's Kennel 'cause of all
them pooch corpses along the interstate. And I don't know about
you all, but I don't think that's a real pretty name."

Big Bobby told Elgin and Blue he'd never heard anyone call it
the Devil's Kennel in his life. Heard a lot worse, sure, but never
that. Big Bobby said the governor was full of shit. But, being the
governor and all, he was sort of entitled.

The dogs in Eden had been a problem going back to the twenties and a part-time breeder named J. Mallon Ellenburg who, if his
arms weren't up to their elbows in the guts of the tractors and com-
bines he repaired for a living, was usually lashing out at something
— his family when they weren't quick enough, his dogs when the
family was. J. Mallon Ellenburg's dogs were mixed breeds and mon-
grels and they ran in packs, as did their offspring, and several generations later, those packs still moved through the Eden night like
wolves, their bodies stripped to muscle and gristle, tense and angry,
growling in the dark at J. Mallon Ellenburg's ghost.

Big Bobby went to the trouble of measuring exactly how much
of 95 crossed through Eden, and he came up with 2.8 miles. Not

much really, but still an average of .74 dog a day or 4.9 dogs a week. Big Bobby wanted the rest of the state funds the governor was going to be doling out at year's end, and if that meant getting rid of five dogs a week, give or take, then that's what was going to get done.

"On the QT," he said to Elgin and Blue, "on the QT, what we going to do, boys, is set up in some trees and shoot every canine who gets within barking distance of that interstate."

Elgin didn't much like this "we" stuff. First place, Big Bobby'd said "we" that time in Double O's four years ago. This was before he'd become mayor, when he was nothing more than a county tax assessor who shot pool at Double O's every other night, same as Elgin and Blue. But one night, after Harlan and Chub Uke had roughed him up over a matter of some pocket change, and knowing that neither Elgin nor Blue was too fond of the Uke family either, Big Bobby'd said, "We going to settle those boys' asses tonight," and started running his mouth the minute the brothers entered the bar.

Time the smoke cleared, Blue had a broken hand, Harlan and Chub were curled up on the floor, and Elgin's lip was busted. Big Bobby, meanwhile, was hiding under the pool table, and Cal Sears was asking who was going to pay for the pool stick Elgin had snapped across the back of Chub's head.

So Elgin heard Mayor Big Bobby saying "we" and remembered the ten dollars it had cost him for that pool stick, and he said, "No, sir, you can count me out this particular enterprise."

Big Bobby looked disappointed. Elgin was a veteran of a foreign war, former Marine, a marksman. "Shit," Big Bobby said, "what good are you, you don't use the skills Uncle Sam spent good money teaching you?"

Elgin shrugged. "Damn, Bobby. I guess not much."

But Blue kept his hand in, as both Big Bobby and Elgin knew he would. All the job required was a guy didn't mind sitting in a tree who liked to shoot things. Hell, Blue was home.

Elgin didn't have the time to be sitting up in a tree anyway. The past few months, he'd been working like crazy after they'd broke ground at Eden Falls — mixing cement, digging postholes, draining swamp water to shore up the foundation — with the real work

still to come. There'd be several more months of drilling and bilg-
ing, spreading cement like cake icing, and erecting scaffolding to
erect walls to erect facades. There'd be the hump-and-grind of rolling along in the dump trucks and drill trucks, the forklifts and
cranes and industrial diggers, until the constant heave and jerk of
them drove up his spine or into his kidneys like a corkscrew.

Time to sit up in a tree shooting dogs? Shit. Elgin didn't have
time to take a piss some days.

And then on top of all the work, he'd been seeing Drew Briggs's
ex-wife, Shelley, lately. Shelley was the receptionist at Perkin Lut's
Auto Emporium, and one day Elgin had brought his Impala in for
a tire rotation and they'd got to talking. She'd been divorced from
Drew over a year, and they waited a couple of months to show respect, but after a while they began showing up at Double O's and
down at the IHOP together.

Once they drove clear to Myrtle Beach together for the weekend. People asked them what it was like, and they said, "Just like
the postcards." Since the postcards never mentioned the price of
a room at the Hilton, Elgin and Shelley didn't mention that all
they'd done was drive up and down the beach twice before settling
in a motel a bit west in Conway. Nice, though; had a color TV and
one of those switches turned the bathroom into a sauna if you
let the shower run. They'd started making love in the sauna, finished up on the bed with the steam coiling out from the bathroom
and brushing their heels. Afterward, he pushed her hair back off
her forehead and looked in her eyes and told her he could get used
to this.

She said, "But wouldn't it cost a lot to install a sauna in your
trailer?" then waited a full thirty seconds before she smiled.

Elgin liked that about her, the way she let him know he was still
just a man after all, always would take himself too seriously, part of
his nature. Letting him know she might be around to keep him ap-
prised of that fact every time he did. Keep him from pushing a bullet into the breech of a thirty-aught-six, slamming the bolt home,
firing into the flank of some wild dog.

Sometimes, when they'd shut down the site early for the day — if
it had rained real heavy and the soil loosened near a foundation, or
if supplies were running late — he'd drop by Lut's to see her.
She'd smile as if he'd brought her flowers, say, "Caught boozing on
the job again?" or some other smartass thing, but it made him feel

good, as if something in his chest suddenly realized it was free to breathe.

Before Shelley, Elgin had spent a long time without a woman he could publicly acknowledge as his. He'd gone with Mae Shiller from fifteen to nineteen, but she'd gotten lonely while he was overseas, and he'd returned to find her gone from Eden, married to a boy up in South of the Border, the two of them working a corn-dog concession stand, making a tidy profit, folks said. Elgin dated some, but it took him a while to get over Mae, to get over the loss of something he'd always expected to have, the sound of her laugh and an image of her stepping naked from Cooper's Lake, her pale flesh beaded with water, having been the things that got Elgin through the jungle, through the heat, through the ticking of his own death he'd heard in his ears every night he'd been over there.

About a year after he'd come home, Jewel Lut had come to visit her mother, who still lived in the trailer park where Jewel had grown up with Elgin and Blue, where Elgin still lived. On her way out, she'd dropped by Elgin's and they'd sat out front of his trailer in some folding chairs, had a few drinks, talked about old times. He told her a bit about Vietnam, and she told him a bit about marriage. How it wasn't what you expected, how Perkin Lut might know a lot of things but he didn't know a damn sight about having fun.

There was something about Jewel Lut that sank into men's flesh the way heat did. It wasn't just that she was pretty, had a beautiful body, moved in a loose, languid way that made you picture her naked no matter what she was wearing. No, there was more to it. Jewel, never the brightest girl in town and not even the most charming, had something in her eyes that none of the women Elgin had ever met had; it was a capacity for living, for taking moments — no matter how small or inconsequential — and squeezing every last thing you could out of them. Jewel gobbled up life, dove into it like it was a cool pond cut in the shade of a mountain on the hottest day of the year.

That look in her eyes — the one that never left — said, Let's have fun, goddammit. Let's eat. Now.

She and Elgin hadn't been stupid enough to do anything that night, not even after Elgin caught that look in her eyes, saw it was directed at him, saw she wanted to eat.

Elgin knew how small Eden was, how its people loved to insinuate and pry and talk. So he and Jewel worked it out, a once-a-week thing mostly that happened down in Carlyle, at a small cabin had been in Elgin's family since before the War Between the States. There, Elgin and Jewel were free to partake of each other, squeeze and bite and swallow and inhale each other, to make love in the lake, on the porch, in the tiny kitchen.

They hardly ever talked, and when they did it was about nothing at all, really — the decline in quality of the meat at Billy's Butcher Shop, rumors that parking meters were going to be installed in front of the courthouse, if McGarrett and the rest of Five-O would ever put the cuffs on Wo Fat.

There was an unspoken understanding that he was free to date any woman he chose and that she'd never leave Perkin Lut. And that was just fine. This wasn't about love; it was about appetite.

Sometimes, Elgin would see her in town or hear Blue speak about her in that puppy-dog-love way he'd been speaking about her since high school, and he'd find himself surprised by the realization that he slept with this woman. That no one knew. That it could go on forever, if both of them remained careful, vigilant against the wrong look, the wrong tone in their voices when they spoke in public.

He couldn't entirely put his finger on what need she satisfied, only that he needed her in that lakefront cabin once a week, that it had something to do with walking out of the jungle alive, with the ticking of his own death he'd heard for a full year. Jewel was somehow reward for that, a fringe benefit. To be naked and spent with her lying atop him and seeing that look in her eyes that said she was ready to go again, ready to gobble him up like oxygen. He'd earned that by shooting at shapes in the night, pressed against those damp foxhole walls that never stayed shored up for long, only to come home to a woman who couldn't wait, who'd discarded him as easily as she would a once-favored doll she'd grown beyond, looked back upon with a wistful mix of nostalgia and disdain.

He'd always told himself that when he found the right woman, his passion for Jewel, his need for those nights at the lake, would disappear. And, truth was, since he'd been with Shelley Briggs, he and Jewel had cooled it. Shelley wasn't Perkin, he told Jewel; she'd figure it out soon enough if he left town once a week, came back with bite marks on his abdomen.

Jewel said, "Fine. We'll get back to it whenever you're ready."

Knowing there'd be a next time, even if Elgin wouldn't admit it to himself.

So Elgin, who'd been so lonely in the year after his discharge, now had two women. Sometimes, he didn't know what to think of that. When you were alone, the happiness of others boiled your insides. Beauty seemed ugly. Laughter seemed evil. The casual grazing of one lover's hand into another was enough to make you want to cut them off at the wrist. *I will never be loved,* you said. *I will never know joy.*

He wondered sometimes how Blue made it through. Blue, who'd never had a girlfriend he hadn't rented by the half hour. Who was too ugly and small and just plain weird to evoke anything in women but fear or pity. Blue, who'd been carrying a torch for Jewel Lut since long before she married Perkin and kept carrying it with a quiet fever Elgin could only occasionally identify with. Blue, he knew, saw Jewel Lut as a queen, as the only woman who existed for him in Eden, South Carolina. All because she'd been nice to him, pals with him and Elgin, back about a thousand years ago, before sex, before breasts, before Elgin or Blue had even the smallest clue what that thing between their legs was for, before Perkin Lut had come along with his daddy's money and his nice smile and his bullshit stories about how many men he'd have killed in the war if only the draft board had seen fit to let him go.

Blue figured if he was nice enough, kind enough, waited long enough — then one day Jewel would see his decency, need to cling to it.

Elgin never bothered telling Blue that some women didn't want decency. Some women didn't want a nice guy. Some women, and some men too, wanted to get into a bed, turn out the lights, and feast on each other like animals until it hurt to move.

Blue would never guess that Jewel was that kind of woman, because she was always so sweet to him, treated him like a child really, and with every friendly hello she gave him, every pat on the shoulder, every "What you been up to, old bud?" Blue pushed her further and further up the pedestal he'd built in his mind.

"I seen him at the Emporium one time," Shelley told Elgin. "He just come in for no reason anyone understood and sat reading magazines until Jewel came in to see Perkin about something. And

Blue, he just stared at her. Just stared at her talking to Perkin in the showroom. When she finally looked back, he stood up and left."

Elgin hated hearing about, talking about, or thinking about Jewel when he was with Shelley. It made him feel unclean and unworthy.

"Crazy love," he said to end the subject.

"Crazy something, babe."

Nights sometimes, Elgin would sit with Shelley in front of his trailer, listen to the cicadas hum through the scrawny pine, smell the night and the rock salt mixed with gravel; the piña colada shampoo Shelley used made him think of Hawaii though he'd never been, and he'd think how their love wasn't crazy love, wasn't burning so fast and furious it'd burn itself out they weren't careful. And that was fine with him. If he could just get his head around this Jewel Lut thing, stop seeing her naked and waiting and looking back over her shoulder at him in the cabin, then he could make something with Shelley. She was worth it. She might not be able to fuck like Jewel, and, truth be told, he didn't laugh as much with her, but Shelley was what you aspired to. A good woman, who'd be a good mother, who'd stick by you when times got tough. Sometimes he'd take her hand in his and hold it for no other reason but the doing of it. She caught him one night, some look in his eyes, maybe the way he tilted his head to look at her small white hand in his big brown one.

She said, "Damn, Elgin, if you ain't simple sometimes." Then she came out of her chair in a rush and straddled him, kissed him as if she were trying to take a piece of him back with her. She said, "Baby, we ain't getting any younger. You know?"

And he knew, somehow, at that moment why some men build families and others shoot dogs. He just wasn't sure where he fit in the equation.

He said, "We ain't, are we?"

Blue had been Elgin's best buddy since either of them could remember, but Elgin had been wondering about it lately. Blue'd always been a little different, something Elgin liked, sure, but there was more to it now. Blue was the kind of guy you never knew if he was quiet because he didn't have anything to say or, because what he had to say was so horrible, he knew enough not to send it out into the atmosphere.

When they'd been kids, growing up in the trailer park, Blue used to be out at all hours because his mother was either entertaining a man or had gone out and forgotten to leave him the key. Back then, Blue had this thing for cockroaches. He'd collect them in a jar, then drop bricks on them to test their resiliency. He told Elgin once, "That's what they are — resilient. Every generation, we have to come up with new ways to kill 'em because they get immune to the poisons we had before." After a while, Blue took to dousing them in gasoline, lighting them up, seeing how resilient they were then.

Elgin's folks told him to stay away from the strange, dirty kid with the white-trash mother, but Elgin felt sorry for Blue. He was half Elgin's size even though they were the same age; you could place your thumb and forefinger around Blue's biceps and meet them on the other side. Elgin hated how Blue seemed to have only two pairs of clothes, both usually dirty, and how sometimes they'd pass his trailer together and hear the animal sounds coming from inside, the grunts and moans, the slapping of flesh. Half the time you couldn't tell if Blue's old lady was in there fucking or fighting. And always the sound of country music mingled in with all that animal noise, Blue's mother and her man of the moment listening to it on the transistor radio she'd given Blue one Christmas.

"*My* fucking radio," Blue said once and shook his small head, the only time Elgin ever saw him react to what went on in that trailer.

Blue was a reader — knew more about science and ecology, about anatomy and blue whales and conversion tables than anyone Elgin knew. Most everyone figured the kid for a mute — hell, he'd been held back twice in fourth grade — but with Elgin he'd sometimes chat up a storm while they puffed smokes together down at the drainage ditch behind the park. He'd talk about whales, how they bore only one child, who they were fiercely protective of, but how if another child was orphaned, a mother whale would take it as her own, protect it as fiercely as she did the one she gave birth to. He told Elgin how sharks never slept, how electrical currents worked, what a depth charge was. Elgin, never much of a talker, just sat and listened, ate it up, and waited for more.

The older they got, the more Elgin became Blue's protector, till finally, the year Blue's face exploded with acne, Elgin got in about two fights a day until there was no one left to fight. Everyone knew — they were brothers. And if Elgin didn't get you from the front,

Blue was sure to take care of you from behind, like that time a can
of acid fell on Roy Hubrist's arm in shop, or the time someone hit
Carnell Lewis from behind with a brick, then cut his Achilles tendon with a razor while he lay out cold. Everyone knew it was Blue,
even if no one actually saw him do it.

Elgin figured with Roy and Carnell, they'd had it coming. No
great loss. It was since Elgin'd come back from Vietnam, though,
that he'd noticed some things and kept them to himself, wondered
what he was going to do the day he'd know he had to do something.

There was the owl someone had set afire and hung upside down
from a telephone wire, the cats who turned up missing in the
blocks that surrounded Blue's shack off Route 11. There were the
small pink panties Elgin had seen sticking out from under Blue's
bed one morning when he'd come to get him for some cleanup
work at a site. He'd checked the missing-persons reports for days,
but it hadn't come to anything, so he'd just decided Blue had
picked them up himself, fed a fantasy or two. He didn't forget,
though, couldn't shake the way those panties had curled upward
out of the brown dust under Blue's bed, seemed to be pleading for
something.

He'd never bothered asking Blue about any of this. That never
worked. Blue just shut down at times like that, stared off somewhere as if something you couldn't hear was drowning out your
words, something you couldn't see was taking up his line of vision.
Blue, floating away on you, until you stopped cluttering up his
mind with useless talk.

One Saturday, Elgin went into town with Shelley so she could get
her hair done at Martha's Unisex on Main. In Martha's, as Dottie
Leeds gave Shelley a shampoo and rinse, Elgin felt like he'd stumbled into a chapel of womanhood. There was Jim Hayder's teenage
daughter, Sonny, getting one of those feathered cuts was growing
popular these days and several older women who still wore bee-
hives, getting them reset or plastered or whatever they did to keep
them up like that. There was Joylene Covens and Lila Sims having
their nails done while their husbands golfed and the black maids
watched their kids, and Martha and Dottie and Esther and Ger-
trude and Hayley dancing and flitting, laughing and chattering

among the chairs, calling everyone "Honey," and all of them — the
young, the old, the rich, and Shelley — kicking back like they did
this every day, knew each other more intimately than they did their
husbands or children or boyfriends.

When Dottie Leeds looked up from Shelley's head and said,
"Elgin, honey, can we get you a sports page or something?" the
whole place burst out laughing, Shelley included. Elgin smiled
though he didn't feel like it and gave them all a sheepish wave that
got a bigger laugh, and he told Shelley he'd be back in a bit and
left.

He headed up Main toward the town square, wondering what it
was those women seemed to know so effortlessly that completely escaped him, and saw Perkin Lut walking in a circle outside Dexter
Isley's Five & Dime. It was one of those days when the wet, white
heat was so overpowering that unless you were in Martha's, the one
place in town with central air-conditioning, most people stayed inside with their shades down and tried not to move much.

And there was Perkin Lut walking the soles of his shoes into the
ground, turning in circles like a little kid trying to make himself
dizzy.

Perkin and Elgin had known each other since kindergarten, but
Elgin could never remember liking the man much. Perkin's old
man, Mance Lut, had pretty much built Eden, and he'd spent a lot
of money keeping Perkin out of the war, hid his son up in Chapel
Hill, North Carolina, for so many semesters even Perkin couldn't
remember what he'd majored in. A lot of men who'd gone overseas
and come back hated Perkin for that, as did the families of most of
the men who hadn't come back, but that wasn't Elgin's problem
with Perkin. Hell, if Elgin'd had the money, he'd have stayed out of
that shitty war too.

What Elgin couldn't abide was that there was something in
Perkin that protected him from consequence. Something that
made him look down on people who paid for their sins, who fell
without a safety net to catch them.

It had happened more than once that Elgin had found himself thrusting in and out of Perkin's wife and thinking, Take that,
Perkin. Take that.

But this afternoon, Perkin didn't have his salesman's smile or
aloof glance. When Elgin stopped by him and said, "Hey, Perkin,

how you?" Perkin looked up at him with eyes so wild they seemed about to jump out of their sockets.

"I'm not good, Elgin. Not good."

"What's the matter?"

Perkin nodded to himself several times, looked over Elgin's shoulder. "I'm fixing to do something about that."

"About what?"

"About that." Perkin's jaw gestured over Elgin's shoulder.

Elgin turned around, looked across Main and through the windows of Miller's Laundromat, saw Jewel Lut pulling her clothes from the dryer, saw Blue standing beside her, taking a pair of jeans from the pile and starting to fold. If either of them had looked up and over, they'd have seen Elgin and Perkin Lut easily enough, but Elgin knew they wouldn't. There was an air to the two of them that seemed to block out the rest of the world in that bright Laundromat as easily as it would in a dark bedroom. Blue's lips moved and Jewel laughed, flipped a T-shirt on his head.

"I'm fixing to do something right now," Perkin said.

Elgin looked at him, could see that was a lie, something Perkin was repeating to himself in hopes it would come true. Perkin was successful in business, and for more reasons than just his daddy's money, but he wasn't the kind of man who did things; he was the kind of man who had things done.

Elgin looked across the street again. Blue still had the T-shirt sitting atop his head. He said something else and Jewel covered her mouth with her hand when she laughed.

"Don't you have a washer and dryer at your house, Perkin?"

Perkin rocked back on his heels. "Washer broke. Jewel decides to come in town." He looked at Elgin. "We ain't getting along so well these days. She keeps reading those magazines, Elgin. You know the ones? Talking about liberation, leaving your bra at home, shit like that." He pointed across the street. "Your friend's a problem."

Your friend.

Elgin looked at Perkin, felt a sudden anger he couldn't completely understand, and with it a desire to say, That's my friend and he's talking to my fuck-buddy. Get it, Perkin?

Instead, he just shook his head and left Perkin there, walked across the street to the Laundromat.

Blue took the T-shirt off his head when he saw Elgin enter. A smile, half frozen on his pitted face, died as he blinked into the sunlight blaring through the windows.

Jewel said, "Hey, we got another helper!" She tossed a pair of men's briefs over Blue's head, hit Elgin in the chest with them.

"Hey, Jewel."

"Hey, Elgin. Long time." Her eyes dropped from his, settled on a towel.

Didn't seem like it at the moment to Elgin. Seemed almost as if he'd been out at the lake with her as recently as last night. He could taste her in his mouth, smell her skin damp with a light sweat.

And standing there with Blue, it also seemed like they were all three back in that trailer park, and Jewel hadn't aged a bit. Still wore her red hair long and messy, still dressed in clothes seemed to have been picked up, wrinkled, off her closet floor and nothing fancy about them in the first place, but draped over her body, they were sexier than clothes other rich women bought in New York once a year.

This afternoon, she wore a crinkly, paisley dress that might have been on the pink side once but had faded to a pasty newspaper color after years of washing. Nothing special about it, not too high up her thigh or down her chest, and loose — but something about her body made it appear like she might just ripen right out of it any second.

Elgin handed the briefs to Blue as he joined them at the folding table. For a while, none of them said anything. They picked clothes from the large pile and folded, and the only sound was Jewel whistling.

Then Jewel laughed.

"What?" Blue said.

"Aw, nothing." She shook her head. "Seems like we're just one happy family here, though, don't it?"

Blue looked stunned. He looked at Elgin. He looked at Jewel. He looked at the pair of small, light-blue socks he held in his hands, the monogram *JL* stitched in the cotton. He looked at Jewel again.

"Yeah," he said eventually, and Elgin heard a tremor in his voice he'd never heard before. "Yeah, it does."

Elgin looked up at one of the upper dryer doors. It had been swung out at eye level when the dryer had been emptied. The center of the door was a circle of glass, and Elgin could see Main Street reflected in it, the white posts that supported the wood awning over the Five & Dime, Perkin Lut walking in circles, his head down, heat shimmering in waves up and down Main.

The dog was green.

Blue had used some of the money Big Bobby'd paid him over the past few weeks to upgrade his target scope. The new scope was huge, twice the width of the rifle barrel, and because the days were getting shorter, it was outfitted with a light-amplification device. Elgin had used similar scopes in the jungle, and he'd never liked them, even when they'd saved his life and those of his platoon, picked up Charlie coming through the dense flora like icy gray ghosts. Night scopes — or LADs as they'd called them over there — were just plain unnatural, and Elgin always felt like he was looking through a telescope from the bottom of a lake. He had no idea where Blue would have gotten one, but hunters in Eden had been showing up with all sorts of weird Marine or army surplus shit these last few years; Elgin had even heard of a hunting party using grenades to scare up fish — blowing 'em up into the boat already half cooked, all you had to do was scale 'em.

The dog was green, the highway was beige, the top of the tree line was yellow, and the trunks were the color of army fatigues.

Blue said, "What you think?"

They were up in the tree house Blue'd built. Nice wood, two lawn chairs, a tarp hanging from the branch overhead, a cooler filled with Coors. Blue'd built a railing across the front, perfect for resting your elbows when you took aim. Along the tree trunk, he'd mounted a huge klieg light plugged to a portable generator, because while it was illegal to "shine" deer, nobody'd ever said anything about shining wild dogs. Blue was definitely home.

Elgin shrugged. Just like in the jungle, he wasn't sure he was meant to see the world this way — faded to the shades and textures of old photographs. The dog, too, seemed to sense that it had stepped out of time somehow, into this seaweed circle punched through the landscape. It sniffed the air with a misshapen snout, but the rest of its body was tensed into one tight muscle, leaning forward as if it smelled prey.

Blue said, "You wanna do it?"

The stock felt hard against Elgin's shoulder. The trigger, curled

under his index finger, was cold and thick, something about it that
itched his finger and the back of his head simultaneously, a voice
back there with the itch in his head saying, "Fire."

What you could never talk about down at the bar to people who
hadn't been there, to people who wanted to know, was what it had
been like firing on human beings, on those icy gray ghosts in the
dark jungle. Elgin had been in fourteen battles over the course of
his twelve-month tour, and he couldn't say with certainty that he'd
ever killed anyone. He'd shot some of those shapes, seen them go
down, but never the blood, never their eyes when the bullets hit. It
had all been a cluster-fuck of swift and sudden noise and color, an
explosion of white lights and tracers, green bush, red fire, screams
in the night. And afterward, if it was clear, you walked into the jungle and saw the corpses, wondered if you'd hit this body or that one
or any at all.

And the only thing you were sure of was that you were too
fucking hot and still — this was the terrible thing, but oddly exhila-
rating too — deeply afraid.

Elgin lowered Blue's rifle, stared across the interstate, now the
color of seashell, at the dark mint tree line. The dog was barely no-
ticeable, a soft dark shape amid other soft dark shapes.

He said, "No, Blue, thanks," and handed him the rifle.

Blue said, "Suit yourself, buddy." He reached behind them and
pulled the beaded string on the klieg light. As the white light
erupted across the highway and the dog froze, blinking in the
brightness, Elgin found himself wondering what the fucking point
of a LAD scope was when you were just going to shine the animal
anyway.

Blue swung the rifle around, leaned into the railing, and put a
round in the center of the animal, right by its rib cage. The dog
jerked inward, as if someone had whacked it with a bat, and as it
teetered on wobbly legs, Blue pulled back on the bolt, drove it
home again, and shot the dog in the head. The dog flipped over on
its side, most of its skull gone, back leg kicking at the road like it
was trying to ride a bicycle.

"You think Jewel Lut might, I dunno, like me?" Blue said.

Elgin cleared his throat. "Sure. She's always liked you."

"But I mean . . ." Blue shrugged, seemed embarrassed suddenly,
"How about this: You think a girl like that could take to Australia?"

"Australia?"

Blue smiled at Elgin. "Australia."

"Australia?" he said again.

Blue reached back and shut off the light. "Australia. They got some wild dingoes there, buddy. Could make some real money. Jewel told me the other day how they got real nice beaches. But dingoes too. Big Bobby said people're starting to bitch about what's happening here, asking where Rover is and such, and anyway, ain't too many dogs left dumb enough to come this way anymore. Australia," he said, "they never run out of dog. Sooner or later, here, I'm gonna run out of dog."

Elgin nodded. Sooner or later, Blue would run out of dog. He wondered if Big Bobby'd thought that one through, if he had a contingency plan, if he had access to the National Guard.

"The boy's just, what you call it, zealous," Big Bobby told Elgin.

They were sitting in Phil's Barbershop on Main. Phil had gone to lunch, and Big Bobby'd drawn the shades so people'd think he was making some important decision of state.

Elgin said, "He ain't zealous, Big Bobby. He's losing it. Thinks he's in love with Jewel Lut."

"He's always thought that."

"Yeah, but now maybe he's thinking she might like him a bit too."

Big Bobby said, "How come you never call me Mayor?"

Elgin sighed.

"All right, all right. Look," Big Bobby said, picking up one of the hair-tonic bottles on Phil's counter and sniffing it, "so Blue likes his job a little bit."

Elgin said, "There's more to it and you know it."

Playing with combs now. "I do?"

"Bobby, he's got a taste for shooting things now."

"Wait." He held up a pair of fat, stubby hands. "Blue always liked to shoot things. Everyone knows that. Shit, if he wasn't so short and didn't have six or seven million little health problems, he'd a been the first guy in this town to go to The 'Nam. 'Stead, he had to sit back here while you boys had all the fun."

Calling it The 'Nam. Like Big Bobby had any idea. Calling it fun. Shit.

"Dingoes," Elgin said.

"Dingoes?"

"Dingoes. He's saying he's going to Australia to shoot dingoes."

"Do him a world of good too." Big Bobby sat back down in the barber's chair beside Elgin. "He can see the sights, that sort of thing."

"Bobby, he ain't going to Australia and you know it. Hell, Blue ain't never stepped over the county line in his life."

Big Bobby polished his belt buckle with the cuff of his sleeve. "Well, what you want me to do about it?"

"I don't know. I'm just telling you. Next time you see him, Bobby, you look in his fucking eyes."

"Yeah. What'll I see?"

Elgin turned his head, looked at him. "Nothing."

Bobby said, "He's your buddy."

Elgin thought of the small panties curling out of the dust under Blue's bed. "Yeah, but he's your problem."

Big Bobby put his hands behind his head, stretched in the chair. "Well, people getting suspicious about all the dogs disappearing, so I'm going to have to shut this operation down immediately anyway."

He wasn't getting it. "Bobby, you shut this operation down, someone's gonna get a world's worth of that nothing in Blue's eyes."

Big Bobby shrugged, a man who'd made a career out of knowing what was beyond him.

The first time Perkin Lut struck Jewel in public was at Chuck's Diner.

Elgin and Shelley were sitting just three booths away when they heard a racket of falling glasses and plates, and by the time they came out of their booth, Jewel was lying on the tile floor with shattered glass and chunks of bone china by her elbows and Perkin standing over her, his arms shaking, a look in his eyes that said he'd surprised himself as much as anyone else.

Elgin looked at Jewel, on her knees, the hem of her dress getting stained by the spilled food, and he looked away before she caught his eye, because if that happened he just might do something stupid, fuck Perkin up a couple-three ways.

"Aw, Perkin," Chuck Blade said, coming from behind the counter to help Jewel up, wiping gravy off his hands against his apron.

"We don't respect that kind of behavior 'round here, Mr. Lut," Clara Blade said. "Won't have it neither."

Chuck Blade helped Jewel to her feet, his eyes cast down at his broken plates, the half a steak lying in a soup of beans by his shoe. Jewel had a welt growing on her right cheek, turning a bright red as she placed her hand on the table for support.

"I didn't mean it," Perkin said.

Clara Blade snorted and pulled the pen from behind her ear, began itemizing the damage on a cocktail napkin.

"I didn't." Perkin noticed Elgin and Shelley. He locked eyes with Elgin, held out his hands. "I swear."

Elgin turned away and that's when he saw Blue coming through the door. He had no idea where he'd come from, though it ran through his head that Blue could have just been standing outside looking in, could have been standing there for an hour.

Like a lot of small guys, Blue had speed, and he never seemed to walk in a straight line. He moved as if he were constantly sidestepping tackles or land mines — with sudden, unpredictable pivots that left you watching the space where he'd been, instead of the place he'd ended up.

Blue didn't say anything, but Elgin could see the determination for homicide in his eyes and Perkin saw it too, backed up, and slipped on the mess on the floor and stumbled back, trying to regain his balance as Blue came past Shelley and tried to lunge past Elgin.

Elgin caught him at the waist, lifted him off the ground, and held on tight because he knew how slippery Blue could be in these situations. You'd think you had him and he'd just squirm away from you, hit somebody with a glass.

Elgin tucked his head down and headed for the door, Blue flopped over his shoulder like a bag of cement mix, Blue screaming, "You see me, Perkin? You see me? I'm a last face you see, Perkin! Real soon."

Elgin hit the open doorway, felt the night heat on his face as Blue screamed, "Jewel! You all right? Jewel?"

Blue didn't say much back at Elgin's trailer.

He tried to explain to Shelley how pure Jewel was, how hitting something that innocent was like spitting on the Bible.

Shelley didn't say anything, and after a while Blue shut up too.

Elgin just kept plying him with Beam, knowing Blue's lack of tolerance for it, and pretty soon Blue passed out on the couch, his pitted face still red with rage.

"He's never been exactly right in the head, has he?" Shelley said.

Elgin ran his hand down her bare arm, pulled her shoulder in tighter against his chest, heard Blue snoring from the front of the trailer. "No, ma'am."

She rose above him, her dark hair falling to his face, tickling the corners of his eyes. "But you've been his friend."

Elgin nodded.

She touched his cheek with her hand. "Why?"

Elgin thought about it a bit, started talking to her about the little, dirty kid and his cockroach flambés, of the animal sounds that came from his mother's trailer. The way Blue used to sit by the drainage ditch, all pulled into himself, his body tight. Elgin thought of all those roaches and cats and rabbits and dogs, and he told Shelley that he'd always thought Blue was dying, ever since he'd met him, leaking away in front of his eyes.

"Everyone dies," she said.

"Yeah." He rose up on his elbow, rested his free hand on her warm hip. "Yeah, but with most of us it's like we're growing toward something and then we die. But with Blue, it's like he ain't never grown toward nothing. He's just been dying real slowly since he was born."

She shook her head. "I'm not getting you."

He thought of the mildew that used to soak the walls in Blue's mother's trailer, of the mold and dust in Blue's shack off Route 11, of the rotting smell that had grown out of the drainage ditch when they were kids. The way Blue looked at it all — seemed to be at one with it — as if he felt a bond.

Shelley said, "Babe, what do you think about getting out of here?"

"Where?"

"I dunno. Florida. Georgia. Someplace else."

"I got a job. You too."

"You can always get construction jobs other places. Receptionist jobs too."

"We grew up here."

She nodded. "But maybe it's time to start our life somewhere else."

He said, "Let me think about it."

She tilted his chin so she was looking in his eyes. "You've *been* thinking about it."

He nodded. "Maybe I want to think about it some more."

In the morning, when they woke up, Blue was gone.

Shelley looked at the rumpled couch, over at Elgin. For a good minute they just stood there, looking from the couch to each other, the couch to each other.

An hour later, Shelley called from work, told Elgin that Perkin Lut was in his office as always, no signs of physical damage.

Elgin said, "If you see Blue . . ."

"Yeah?"

Elgin thought about it. "I dunno. Call the cops. Tell Perkin to bail out a back door. That sound right?"

"Sure."

Big Bobby came to the site later that morning, said, "I go over to Blue's place to tell him we got to end this dog thing and —"

"Did you tell him it was over?" Elgin asked.

"Let me finish. Let me explain."

"Did you tell him?"

"Let me finish." Bobby wiped his face with a handkerchief. "I was gonna tell him, but —"

"You didn't tell him."

"But Jewel Lut was there."

"What?"

Big Bobby put his hand on Elgin's elbow, led him away from the other workers. "I said Jewel was there. The two of them sitting at the kitchen table, having breakfast."

"In Blue's place?"

Big Bobby nodded. "Biggest dump I ever seen. Smells like something I-don't-know-what. But bad. And there's Jewel, pretty as can be in her summer dress and soft skin and makeup, eating Eggos and grits with Blue, big brown shiner under her eye. She smiles at me, says, 'Hey, Big Bobby,' and goes back to eating."

"And that was it?"

"How come no one ever calls me Mayor?"

"And that was it?" Elgin repeated.

"Yeah. Blue asks me to take a seat, I say I got business. He says him too."

"What's that mean?" Elgin heard his own voice, hard and sharp.

Big Bobby took a step back from it. "Hell do I know? Could mean he's going out to shoot more dog."

"So you never told him you were shutting down the operation."

Big Bobby's eyes were wide and confused. "You hear what I told you? He was in there with Jewel. Her all doll-pretty and him looking, well, ugly as usual. Whole situation was too weird. I got out."

"Blue said he had business too."

"He said he had business too," Bobby said, and walked away.

The next week, they showed up in town together a couple of times, buying some groceries, toiletries for Jewel, boxes of shells for Blue.

They never held hands or kissed or did anything romantic, but they were together, and people talked. Said, Well, of all things. And I never thought I'd see the day. How do you like that? I guess this is the day the cows actually come home.

Blue called and invited Shelley and Elgin to join them one Sunday afternoon for a late breakfast at the IHOP. Shelley begged off, said something about coming down with the flu, but Elgin went. He was curious to see where this was going, what Jewel was thinking, how she thought her hanging around Blue was going to come to anything but bad.

He could feel the eyes of the whole place on them as they ate.

"See where he hit me?" Jewel tilted her head, tucked her beautiful red hair back behind her ear. The mark on her cheekbone, in the shape of a small rain puddle, was faded yellow now, its edges roped by a sallow beige.

Elgin nodded.

"Still can't believe the son of a bitch hit me," she said, but there was no rage in her voice anymore, just a mild sense of drama, as if she'd pushed the words out of her mouth the way she believed she should say them. But the emotion she must have felt when Perkin's hand hit her face, when she fell to the floor in front of people she'd known all her life — that seemed to have faded with the mark on her cheekbone.

"Perkin Lut," she said with a snort, then laughed.

Elgin looked at Blue. He'd never seemed so . . . fluid in all the time Elgin had known him. The way he cut into his pancakes, swept them off his plate with a smooth dip of the fork tines; the swift dab of the napkin against his lips after every bite; the attentive swivel of his head whenever Jewel spoke, usually in tandem with the lifting of his coffee mug to his mouth.

This was not a Blue Elgin recognized. Except when he was handling weapons, Blue moved in jerks and spasms. Tremors rippled through his limbs and caused his fingers to drop things, his elbows and knees to move too fast, crack against solid objects. Blue's blood seemed to move too quickly through his veins, made his muscles obey his brain after a quarter-second delay and then too rapidly, as if to catch up on lost time.

But now he moved in concert, like an athlete or a jungle cat.

That's what you do to men, Jewel: you give them a confidence so total it finds their limbs.

"Perkin," Blue said, and rolled his eyes at Jewel and they both laughed.

She not as hard as he did, though.

Elgin could see the root of doubt in her eyes, could feel her loneliness in the way she fiddled with the menu, touched her cheekbone, spoke too loudly, as if she wasn't just telling Elgin and Blue how Perkin had mistreated her, but the whole IHOP as well, so people could get it straight that she wasn't the villain, and if after she returned to Perkin she had to leave him again, they'd know why.

Of course she was going back to Perkin.

Elgin could tell by the glances she gave Blue — unsure, slightly embarrassed, maybe a bit repulsed. What had begun as a nighttime ride into the unknown had turned cold and stale during the hard yellow lurch into morning.

Blue wiped his mouth, said, "Be right back," and walked to the bathroom with surer strides than Elgin had ever seen on the man.

Elgin looked at Jewel.

She gripped the handle of her coffee cup between the tips of her thumb and index finger and turned the cup in slow revolutions around the saucer, made a soft scraping noise that climbed up Elgin's spine like a termite trapped under the skin.

"You ain't sleeping with him, are you?" Elgin said quietly.

Jewel's head jerked up and she looked over her shoulder, then back at Elgin. "What? God, no. We're just . . . He's my pal. That's all. Like when we were kids."

"We ain't kids."

"I know. Don't you know I know?" She fingered the coffee cup again. "I miss you," she said softly. "I miss you. When you coming back?"

Elgin kept his voice low. "Me and Shelley, we're getting pretty serious."

She gave him a small smile that he instantly hated. It seemed to know him; it seemed like everything he was and everything he wasn't was caught in the curl of her lips. "You miss the lake, Elgin. Don't lie."

He shrugged.

"You ain't ever going to marry Shelley Briggs, have babies, be an upstanding citizen."

"Yeah? Why's that?"

"Because you got too many demons in you, boy. And they need me. They need the lake. They need to cry out every now and then."

Elgin looked down at his own coffee cup. "You going back to Perkin?"

She shook her head hard. "No way. Uh-uh. No way."

Elgin nodded, even though he knew she was lying. If Elgin's demons needed the lake, needed to be unbridled, Jewel's needed Perkin. They needed security. They needed to know the money'd never run out, that she'd never go two full days without a solid meal, like she had so many times as a child in the trailer park.

Perkin was what she saw when she looked down at her empty coffee cup, when she touched her cheek. Perkin was at their nice home with his feet up, watching a game, petting the dog, and she was in the IHOP in the middle of a Sunday when the food was at its oldest and coldest, with one guy who loved her and one who fucked her, wondering how she got there.

Blue came back to the table, moving with that new sure stride, a broad smile in the wide swing of his arms.

"How we doing?" Blue said. "Huh? How we doing?" And his lips burst into a grin so huge Elgin expected it to keep going right off the sides of his face.

*

Jewel left Blue's place two days later, walked into Perkin Lut's Auto Emporium and into Perkin's office, and by the time anyone went to check, they'd left through the back door, gone home for the day.

Elgin tried to get a hold of Blue for three days — called constantly, went by his shack and knocked on the door, even staked out the tree house along I-95 where he fired on the dogs.

He'd decided to break into Blue's place, was fixing to do just that, when he tried one last call from his trailer that third night and Blue answered with a strangled "Hello."

"It's me. How you doing?"

"Can't talk now."

"Come on, Blue. It's me. You okay?"

"All alone," Blue said.

"I know. I'll come by."

"You do, I'll leave."

"Blue."

"Leave me alone for a spell, Elgin. Okay?"

That night Elgin sat alone in his trailer, smoking cigarettes, staring at the walls.

Blue'd never had much of anything his whole life — not a job he enjoyed, not a woman he could consider his — and then between the dogs and Jewel Lut he'd probably thought he'd got it all at once. Hit pay dirt.

Elgin remembered the dirty little kid sitting down by the drainage ditch, hugging himself. Six, maybe seven years old, waiting to die.

You had to wonder sometimes why some people were even born. You had to wonder what kind of creature threw bodies into the world, expected them to get along when they'd been given no tools, no capacity to get any either.

In Vietnam, this fat boy, name of Woodson from South Dakota, had been the least popular guy in the platoon. He wasn't smart, he wasn't athletic, he wasn't funny, he wasn't even personable. He just was. Elgin had been running beside him one day through a sea of rice paddies, their boots making sucking sounds every step they took, and someone fired a hell of a round from the other side of the paddies, ripped Woodson's head in half so completely all Elgin

saw running beside him for a few seconds was the lower half of
Woodson's face. No hair, no forehead, no eyes. Just half the nose, a
mouth, a chin.

Thing was, Woodson kept running, kept plunging his feet in and
out of the water, making those sucking sounds, M-15 hugged to
his chest, for a good eight or ten steps. Kid was dead, he's still running. Kid had no reason to hold on, but he don't know it, he keeps
running.

What spark of memory, hope, or dream had kept him going?

You had to wonder.

In Elgin's dream that night, a platoon of ice-gray Vietcong rose in a
straight line from the center of Cooper's Lake while Elgin was inside the cabin with Shelley and Jewel. He penetrated them both
somehow, their separate torsos branching out from the same pair
of hips, their four legs clamping at the small of his back, this Shelley-Jewel creature crying out for more, more, more.

And Elgin could see the VC platoon drifting in formation toward
the shore, their guns pointed, their faces hidden behind thin wisps
of green fog.

The Shelley-Jewel creature arched her backs on the bed below
him, and Woodson and Blue stood in the corner of the room
watching as their dogs padded across the floor, letting out low
growls and drooling.

Shelley dissolved into Jewel as the VC platoon reached the porch
steps and released their safeties all at once, the sound like the
ratcheting of a thousand shotguns. Sweat exploded in Elgin's hair,
poured down his body like warm rain, and the VC fired in concert,
the bullets shearing the walls of the cabin, lifting the roof off into
the night. Elgin looked above him at the naked night sky, the stars
zipping by like tracers, the yellow moon full and mean, the shivering branches of birch trees. Jewel rose and straddled him, bit his
lip, and dug her nails into his back, and the bullets danced through
his hair, and then Jewel was gone, her writhing flesh having dissolved into his own.

Elgin sat naked on the bed, his arms stretched wide, waiting for
the bullets to find his back, to shear his head from his body the
way they'd sheared the roof from the cabin, and the yellow moon
burned above him as the dogs howled and Blue and Woodson held

each other in the corner of the room and wept like children as the
bullets drilled holes in their faces.

Big Bobby came by the trailer late the next morning, a Sunday, and
said, "Blue's a bit put out about losing his job."

"What?" Elgin sat on the edge of his bed, pulled on his socks.
"You picked now — now, Bobby — to fire him?"

"It's in his eyes," Big Bobby said. "Like you said. You can see it."

Elgin had seen Big Bobby scared before, plenty of times, but now
the man was trembling.

Elgin said, "Where is he?"

Blue's front door was open, hanging half down the steps from a
busted hinge. Elgin said, "Blue."

"Kitchen."

He sat in his Jockeys at the table, cleaning his rifle, each shiny
black piece spread in front of him on the table. Elgin's eyes wa-
tered a bit because there was a stench coming from the back of the
house that he felt might strip his nostrils bare. He realized then
that he'd never asked Big Bobby or Blue what they'd done with all
those dead dogs.

Blue said, "Have a seat, bud. Beer in the fridge if you're thirsty."

Elgin wasn't looking in that fridge. "Lost your job, huh?"

Blue wiped the bolt with a shammy cloth. "Happens." He looked
at Elgin. "Where you been lately?"

"I called you last night."

"I mean in general."

"Working."

"No, I mean at night."

"Blue, you been" — he almost said "playing house with Jewel
Lut" but caught himself — "up in a fucking tree, how do you know
where I been at night?"

"I don't," Blue said. "Why I'm asking."

Elgin said, "I've been at my trailer or down at Doubles, same as
usual."

"With Shelley Briggs, right?"

Slowly, Elgin said, "Yeah."

"I'm just asking, buddy. I mean, when we all going to go out?
You, me, your new girl."

The pits that covered Blue's face like a layer of bad meat had faded some from all those nights in the tree.

Elgin said, "Anytime you want."

Blue put down the bolt. "How 'bout right now?" He stood and walked into the bedroom just off the kitchen. "Let me just throw on some duds."

"She's working now, Blue."

"At Perkin Lut's? Hell, it's almost noon. I'll talk to Perkin about that Dodge he sold me last year, and when she's ready we'll take her out someplace nice." He came back into the kitchen wearing a soiled brown T-shirt and jeans.

"Hell," Elgin said, "I don't want the girl thinking I've got some serious love for her or something. We come by for lunch, next thing she'll expect me to drop her off in the mornings, pick her up at night."

Blue was reassembling the rifle, snapping all those shiny pieces together so fast, Elgin figured he could do it blind. He said, "Elgin, you got to show them some affection sometimes. I mean, Jesus." He pulled a thin brass bullet from his T-shirt pocket and slipped it in the breech, followed it with four more, then slid the bolt home.

"Yeah, but you know what I'm saying, bud?" Elgin watched Blue nestle the stock in the space between his left hip and ribs, let the barrel point out into the kitchen.

"I know what you're saying," Blue said. "I know. But I got to talk to Perkin about my Dodge."

"What's wrong with it?"

"What's wrong with it?" Blue turned to look at him, and the barrel swung level with Elgin's belt buckle. "What's wrong with it, it's a piece of shit, what's wrong with it, Elgin. Hell, you know that. Perkin sold me a lemon. This is the situation." He blinked. "Beer for the ride?"

Elgin had a pistol in his glove compartment. A .32. He considered it.

"Elgin?"

"Yeah?"

"Why you looking at me funny?"

"You got a rifle pointed at me, Blue. You realize that?"

Blue looked at the rifle, and its presence seemed to surprise him. He dipped it toward the floor. "Shit, man, I'm sorry. I wasn't even

thinking. It feels like my arm sometimes. I forget. Man, I am sorry."
He held his arms out wide, the rifle rising with them.

"Lotta things deserve to die, don't they?"

Blue smiled. "Well, I wasn't quite thinking along those lines, but
now you bring it up . . ."

Elgin said, "Who deserves to die, buddy?"

Blue laughed. "You got something on your mind, don't you?" He
hoisted himself up on the table, cradled the rifle in his lap. "Hell,
boy, who you got? Let's start with people who take two parking
spaces."

"Okay." Elgin moved the chair by the table to a position slightly
behind Blue, sat in it. "Let's."

"Then there's DJs talk through the first minute of a song.
Fucking Guatos coming down here these days to pick tobacco,
showing no respect. Women wearing all those tight clothes, look at
you like you're a pervert when you stare at what they're advertising." He wiped his forehead with his arm. "Shit."

"Who else?" Elgin said quietly.

"Okay. Okay. You got people like the ones let their dogs run wild
into the highway, get themselves killed. And you got dishonest people, people who lie and sell insurance and cars and bad food. You
got a lot of things. Jane Fonda."

"Sure." Elgin nodded.

Blue's face was drawn, gray. He crossed his legs over each other
like he used to down at the drainage ditch. "It's all out there." He
nodded and his eyelids drooped.

"Perkin Lut?" Elgin said. "He deserve to die?"

"Not just Perkin," Blue said. "Not just. Lots of people. I mean,
how many you kill over in the war?"

Elgin shrugged. "I don't know."

"But some. Some. Right? Had to. I mean, that's war — someone
gets on your bad side, you kill them and all their friends till they
stop bothering you." His eyelids drooped again, and he yawned so
deeply he shuddered when he finished.

"Maybe you should get some sleep."

Blue looked over his shoulder at him. "You think? It's been a
while."

A breeze rattled the thin walls at the back of the house, pushed
that thick dank smell into the kitchen again, a rotting stench that

found the back of Elgin's throat and stuck there. He said, "When's
the last time?"

"I slept? Hell, a while. Days maybe." Blue twisted his body so he
was facing Elgin. "You ever feel like you spend your whole life waiting for it to get going?"

Elgin nodded, not positive what Blue was saying, but knowing he
should agree with him. "Sure."

"It's hard," Blue said. "Hard." He leaned back on the table,
stared at the brown water marks in his ceiling.

Elgin took in a long stream of that stench through his nostrils.
He kept his eyes open, felt that air entering his nostrils creep past
into his corneas, tear at them. The urge to close his eyes and wish it
all away was as strong an urge as he'd ever felt, but he knew now was
that time he'd always known was coming.

He leaned in toward Blue, reached across him, and pulled the
rifle off his lap.

Blue turned his head, looked at him.

"Go to sleep," Elgin said. "I'll take care of this a while. We'll go
see Shelley tomorrow. Perkin Lut too."

Blue blinked. "What if I can't sleep? Huh? I've been having that
problem, you know. I put my head on the pillow and I try to sleep
and it won't come and soon I'm just bawling like a fucking child till
I got to get up and do something."

Elgin looked at the tears that had just then sprung into Blue's
eyes, the red veins split across the whites, the desperate, savage
need in his face that had always been there if anyone had looked
close enough, and would never, Elgin knew, be satisfied.

"I'll stick right here, buddy. I'll sit here in the kitchen and you go
in and sleep."

Blue turned his head and stared up at the ceiling again. Then he
slid off the table, peeled off his T-shirt, and tossed it on top of the
fridge. "All right. All right. I'm gonna try." He stopped at the bedroom doorway. "'Member — there's beer in the fridge. You be
here when I wake up?"

Elgin looked at him. He was still so small, probably so thin you
could still wrap your hand around his biceps, meet the fingers on
the other side. He was still ugly and stupid-looking, still dying right
in front of Elgin's eyes.

"I'll be here, Blue. Don't you worry."

"Good enough. Yes, sir."

Blue shut the door and Elgin heard the bedsprings grind, the rustle of pillows being arranged. He sat in the chair, with the smell of whatever decayed in the back of the house swirling around his head. The sun had hit the cheap tin roof now, heating the small house, and after a while he realized the buzzing he'd thought was in his head came from somewhere back in the house too.

He wondered if he had the strength to open the fridge. He wondered if he should call Perkin Lut's and tell Perkin to get the hell out of Eden for a bit. Maybe he'd just ask for Shelley, tell her to meet him tonight with her suitcases. They'd drive down 95 where the dogs wouldn't disturb them, drive clear to Jacksonville, Florida, before the sun came up again. See if they could outrun Blue and his tiny, dangerous wants, his dog corpses, and his smell; outrun people who took two parking spaces and telephone solicitors and Jane Fonda.

Jewel flashed through his mind then, an image of her sitting atop him, arching her back and shaking that long red hair, a look in her green eyes that said this was it, this was why we live.

He could stand up right now with this rifle in his hands, scratch the itch in the back of his head, and fire straight through the door, end what should never have been started.

He sat there staring at the door for quite a while, until he knew the exact number of places the paint had peeled in teardrop spots, and eventually he stood, went to the phone on the wall by the fridge, and dialed Perkin Lut's.

"Auto Emporium," Shelley said, and Elgin thanked God that in his present mood he hadn't gotten Glynnis Verdon, who snapped her gum and always placed him on hold, left him listening to Muzak versions of The Shirelles.

"Shelley?"

"People gonna talk, you keep calling me at work, boy."

He smiled, cradled the rifle like a baby, leaned against the wall. "How you doing?"

"Just fine, handsome. How 'bout yourself?"

Elgin turned his head, looked at the bedroom door. "I'm okay."

"Still like me?"

Elgin heard the springs creak in the bedroom, heard weight drop on the old floorboards. "Still like you."

"Well, then, it's all fine then, isn't it?"

Blue's footfalls crossed toward the bedroom door, and Elgin used his hip to push himself off the wall.

"It's all fine," he said. "I gotta go. I'll talk to you soon."

He hung up and stepped away from the wall.

"Elgin," Blue said from the other side of the door.

"Yeah, Blue?"

"I can't sleep. I just can't."

Elgin saw Woodson sloshing through the paddy, the top of his head gone. He saw the pink panties curling up from underneath Blue's bed and a shaft of sunlight hitting Shelley's face as she looked up from behind her desk at Perkin Lut's and smiled. He saw Jewel Lut dancing in the night rain by the lake and that dog lying dead on the shoulder of the interstate, kicking its leg like it was trying to ride a bicycle.

"Elgin," Blue said. "I just can't sleep. I got to do something."

"Try," Elgin said and cleared his throat.

"I just can't. I got to . . . do something. I got to go . . ." His voice cracked, and he cleared his throat. "I can't sleep."

The doorknob turned and Elgin raised the rifle, stared down the barrel.

"Sure, you can, Blue." He curled his finger around the trigger as the door opened. "Sure you can," he repeated and took a breath, held it in.

The skeleton of Eden Falls still sits on twenty-two acres of land just east of Brimmer's Point, covered in rust thick as flesh. Some say it was the levels of iodine an environmental inspector found in the groundwater that scared off the original investors. Others said it was the downswing of the state economy or the governor's failed reelection bid. Some say Eden Falls was just plain a dumb name, too biblical. And then, of course, there were plenty who claimed it was Jewel Lut's ghost scared off all the workers.

They found her body hanging from the scaffolding they'd erected by the shell of the roller coaster. She was naked and hung upside down from a rope tied around her ankles. Her throat had been cut so deep the coroner said it was a miracle her head was still attached when they found her. The coroner's assistant, man by the name of Chris Gleason, would claim when he was in his cups that the head had fallen off in the hearse as they drove down Main toward the morgue. Said he heard it cry out.

This was the same day Elgin Bern called the sheriff's office, told them he'd shot his buddy Blue, fired two rounds into him at close range, the little guy dead before he hit his kitchen floor. Elgin told the deputy he was still sitting in the kitchen, right where he'd done it a few hours before. Said to send the hearse.

Due to the fact that Perkin Lut had no real alibi for his whereabouts when Jewel passed on and owing even more to the fact there'd been some very recent and very public discord in their marriage, Perkin was arrested and brought before a grand jury, but that jury decided not to indict. Perkin and Jewel had been patching things up, after all; he'd bought her a car (at cost, but still . . .).

Besides, we all knew it was Blue had killed Jewel. Hell, the Simmons boy, a retard ate paint and tree bark, could have told you that. Once all that stuff came out about what Blue and Big Bobby'd been doing with the dogs around here, well, that just sealed it. And everyone remembered how that week she'd been separated from Perkin, you could see the dream come alive in Blue's eyes, see him allow hope into his heart for the first time in his sorry life.

And when hope comes late to a man, it's quite a dangerous thing. Hope is for the young, the children. Hope in a full-grown man — particularly one with as little acquaintanceship with it or prospect for it as Blue — well, that kind of hope burns as it dies, boils blood white, and leaves something mean behind when it's done.

Blue killed Jewel Lut.

And Elgin Bern killed Blue. And ended up doing time. Not much, due to his war record and the circumstances of who Blue was, but time just the same. Everyone knew Blue probably had it coming, was probably on his way back into town to do to Perkin or some other poor soul what he'd done to Jewel. Once a man gets that look in his eyes — that boiled look, like a dog searching out a bone who's not going to stop until he finds it — well, sometimes he has to be put down like a dog. Don't he?

And it was sad how Elgin came out of prison to find Shelley Briggs gone, moved up North with Perkin Lut of all people, who'd lost his heart for the car business after Jewel died, took to selling home electronics imported from Japan and Germany, made himself a fortune. Not long after he got out of prison, Elgin left too, no one knows where, just gone, drifting.

See, the thing is — no one wanted to convict Elgin. We all understood. We did. Blue had to go. But he'd had no weapon in his hand when Elgin, standing just nine feet away, pulled that trigger. Twice. Once we might been

able to overlook, but twice, that's something else again. Elgin offered no de-
fense, even refused a fancy lawyer's attempt to get him to claim he'd suffered
something called Post Traumatic Stress Disorder, which we're hearing a lot
more about these days.

"I don't have that," Elgin said. "I shot a defenseless man. That's the long
and the short of it, and that's a sin."

And he was right:

In the world, case you haven't noticed, you usually pay for your sins.

And in the South, always.

THOMAS H. MCNEELY

Sheep

FROM *The Atlantic Monthly*

BEFORE THE SHERIFF came to get him, Lloyd found the sheep out by the pond. He'd counted head that morning and come up one short. He did the count over, because he was still hazy from the night before. And he'd waked with a foul smell in his nose. So he had gone into Mr. Mac's house — it was early morning: the old man would be dead to the world — and filled his canteen with white lightning. He felt shaky and bad, and the spring morning was cold. He shouldn't have gone to town the night before.

The sheep lay on its side in some rushes. A flow of yellowish mucus was coming from its nose, and its eyes were sickly thin slits that made it look afraid. Lloyd thought the sheep honorable — it had gone off to die so that it wouldn't infect the rest of the flock. Lloyd knew that the sheep's sickness was his fault and that he couldn't do anything about it, but he squatted down next to the animal and rubbed its underside. In this hour before sunrise, when the night dew was still wet, the warmth and animal smell felt good. Lloyd moved his hand in circles over the sheep's lightly furred pink skin and lines of blue veins, its hard cage of ribs, its slack, soft belly. Across the pond the sun peeked through the Panhandle dust over a low line of slate-gray clouds. With his free hand Lloyd took his canteen from a pocket in his jacket, clamped it between his knees, opened it, and drank. For a moment the liquor stung the sides of his tongue; then it dissolved in him like warm water. The sheep's lungs lifted up and down; its heart churned blood like a slowly pounding fist. Soon the sun broke free and the pond, rippled by a slight breeze, ignited in countless tiny candle flames. When Lloyd was a child, Mr. Mac used to tell him that at the Last Judgment the

pond would become the Lake of Fire, into which all sinners would
be cast. Lloyd could still picture them falling in a dark stream, God
pouring them out like a bag of nails. The sheep closed its eyes
against the light.

When Sheriff Lynch walked up behind him, Lloyd started. He
still caressed the sheep, but it was dead and beginning to stiffen.
His canteen felt almost empty; it fell from his fingers. By the sun
Lloyd saw it was almost noon. Big black vultures wheeled so high
above that they looked the size of mockingbirds. Uneasiness creeping on him, Lloyd waited for the sheriff to speak.

Finally the sheriff said, "Son, looks like that sheep's dead."

"Yessir," Lloyd said, and tried to stand, but his legs were stiff and
the liquor had taken his balance.

"You look about half dead yourself." The sheriff picked up
Lloyd's canteen from the dry grass, sniffed it, and shook his head.
"You want to turn out like Mr. Mac? A pervert?"

Lloyd waggled his head no. He thought how he must look: his
long blond hair clumped in uncombed cowlicks, the dark reddish-
gray circles around his eyes, his father's dirty herding jacket hanging off his broad, slumped shoulders. Sheriff Lynch stood there,
his figure tall and straight. He wore a star-shaped golden badge
hitched to a belt finely tooled with wildflowers. His face was burnt
the rust color of Dumas County soil, the lines on it deep, like the
sudden ravines into which cattle there sometimes fell. His eyes
were an odd steely blue, which seemed not to be that color itself
but to reflect it. He studied Lloyd.

"That probably doesn't make much of a difference now," he
said, lowering his eyes as if embarrassed.

"What?" Lloyd said, though he'd heard him.

"Nothing. We just need to ask you some questions."

Lloyd wondered if Mr. Mac had found out about the sheep somehow. "But I ain't stole nothin'," he said.

"I'm fairly sure of that," the sheriff said. A grin flickered at one
corner of his mouth, but it was sad and not meant to mock Lloyd.
"Come on. You know the drill. Hand over your knife and shears
and anything else you got."

After Lloyd put his tools in a paper bag, the sheriff squatted next
to the sheep and ran his hand over its belly. His hand was large and
strong and clean, though etched with red-brown creases.

*

When they got up to the house, Lloyd saw three or four police cars parked at odd angles, as if they'd stopped in a hurry. Their lights whirled around, and dispatch radios crackled voices that no one answered. Some policemen busied themselves throwing clothes, bottles, and other junk out of Lloyd's shack, which was separated from the house by a tool shed. Others were carrying out cardboard boxes. Lloyd recognized one of the men, name of Gonzales, who'd picked him up for stealing a ten-speed when he was a kid. Lloyd waved at him and called out, but Gonzales just set his dark eyes on him for a moment and then went back to his business. Mr. Mac stood on the dirt patch in front of the house, his big sloppy body looking like it was about to fall over, talking to a man in a suit.

"If you're gonna drag that pond," he said, his eyes slits in the harsh, clear sunlight, "you're gonna have to pay me for the lost fish. I'm a poor old man. I ain't got nothin' to do with thisayre mess."

The man started to say something to him, but Mr. Mac caught sight of Lloyd. His face spread wide with a fear that Lloyd had never seen in him; then his eyes narrowed in disgust. He looked like he did when he saw ewes lamb, or when he punished Lloyd as a child.

"Mr. Mac," Lloyd said, and took a step toward him, but the old man held up his hands as if to shield his face.

"Mr. Mac." Lloyd came closer. "I 'pologize 'bout that 'er sheep. I'll work off the cost to you someway."

Mr. Mac stumbled backward and pointed at Lloyd; his face was wild and frightened again. He shouted to the man in the suit, "Look at 'im! Look at 'im! A seed of pure evil!"

Lloyd could feel his chest move ahead of his body toward Mr. Mac. He wanted to explain about the sheep, but the old man kept carrying on. The sheriff's hand, firm but kind, gripped his arm and guided him toward a police car.

The sheriff sat bolt upright on the passenger side and looked straight ahead as the rust-colored hills passed by outside. A fingerprint-smudged Plexiglas barrier ran across the top of the front seat and separated him from Lloyd. As always, the hair on the nape of the sheriff's neck looked freshly cut. Lloyd had expected them to take his shears and bowie knife, but why were they tearing up his shack? And what was Mr. Mac going on about? Still drunk, probably. He would ask the sheriff when they got to the jail. His thoughts turned to the sheep. He should've put it out of its misery — slit its throat and then cut its belly for the vultures. Not like at slaughter, when he would've had to root around with his knife and bare hands and clean out its innards. What a godawful stink sheep's insides had! But this would've been easy. It wouldn't have taken a minute.

In the jail two guards Lloyd didn't know sat him down inside a small white room he'd never seen before. The man in a suit who had been talking to Mr. Mac came in, with Sheriff Lynch following. Lloyd hadn't gotten to ask the sheriff what was going on. The man put what looked like a little transistor radio on the table and pressed a button and began to talk.

"Is it okay if we tape-record this interview?" he asked Lloyd.

Lloyd shrugged and smiled a who's-this-guy? smile at the sheriff. The sheriff gave him a stern, behave-yourself look.

"Sure," Lloyd said. "I ain't never been recorded before."

"Okay," the man said. He said all their names, where they were, what date and time it was. Then he opened a file folder. Lloyd didn't like his looks: he had a smile that hid itself, that laughed at you in secret. Mr. Mac could get one of those. And the man talked in one of those citified accents, maybe from Dallas.

"Okay," the man said. "My name is Thomas Blanchard. I am a special agent with the Federal Bureau of Investigation. I work in the serial-homicide division." He shot his eyes up at Lloyd, as if to catch him at something. "Do you understand what that means?"

"Which part?" Lloyd said.

"Serial homicide — serial murder."

"Nope."

"It means to kill more than once — sometimes many people in a row."

"Okay," Lloyd said.

The man gave him another once-over and said, "You are being held as a material witness in seventeen murders that have occurred in and around this area. You have not been charged in any of them. Should you be charged, you will have the right to counsel, but at this time you have no such right per se. However, as a witness, should you wish to retain counsel, that is also your right. Do you wish to do so?"

Lloyd tried to put the man's words together. Blanchard bunched up his shoulders, like a squirrel ready to pounce. The sheriff leaned back his chair and studied the ceiling.

After he had drawn out the silence, Lloyd said, "I don't know. I'm still pretty drunk to think about suchlike. Would I have to pay for him?"

Blanchard's hand snaked out to the tape recorder, but the sheriff looked at Lloyd and said, "Lloyd, you think you're too drunk to know what you're sayin'? I mean, to the point of makin' things up or disrememberin'?"

"Oh, no," Lloyd said. The sheriff asked him if he was sure, and he said yes. Then the sheriff told him that to retain a lawyer he would have to pay for one. In that case, Lloyd said, he didn't want one.

"Sheriff," he said. "What's thisayre all about?"

The sheriff told him he would find out.

But he didn't, not really. Blanchard asked Lloyd about the night before. He'd gone to Genie's Too, where the old Genie's used to be. He'd brought a canteen of Mr. Mac's stuff with him for setups, because they'd lost their license. He saw all the usual people there: Candy, Huff, Wishbone, Firefly. Dwight, Genie's old man, did the colored-baby dance, flopping around this brown rag doll and flashing up its skirt. Everybody seemed to be having a real good time. Big plastic bottles were on nearly every table; people were talking — men arguing, women listening. People leaned on each other like scarecrows, some dancing slow and close, others just close, doing a little bump-and-grind.

Blanchard asked him if he had met anyone, danced with anyone. Lloyd grinned and blushed and sought out the sheriff, who smiled this time. Lloyd said, "I always been shy. I guess it's my rearing, out on that old ranch. And they got their own group there at Genie's, everybody always foolin' with everyone else's."

By the end of his answer the sheriff's smile had gone.

Blanchard asked Lloyd the same thing about ten different ways — had he seen anyone new there? The questions got on his nerves. He said, "Sheriff, now what's this about?"

The sheriff told him to have some patience.

Blanchard asked about places in Amarillo, Lubbock, Muleshoe, Longview, Lamesa, Reno, Abilene — bars Lloyd had sneaked away to when he wanted to be alone. The ones he could remember were all about the same as Genie's, each with its own little crowd. Blanchard mentioned places from so long ago that Lloyd began to feel as if he were asking about a different person. He drifted off into thinking about Mr. Mac.

Mr. Mac, when Lloyd would ask him where they were, used to say that all he needed to know was that they were in the United States of America. He used to tell Lloyd that where they were was just like Scotland, and then he'd start laughing to himself until his laughs trailed off into coughs. The sheriff had never, ever laughed at him like that. He didn't have those kinds of jokes inside him.

Blanchard began asking personal questions: Did he have a girl-friend? Had he ever? No. How long had he been out at the ranch? All his life — about thirty years, according to Mr. Mac. Was he a virgin?

"Now, Sheriff, have I got to answer that?" In truth he didn't know what he was, because, as he often reflected, he didn't know whether what Mr. Mac had done made him not a virgin.

Perhaps sensing this, the sheriff told him no, he didn't have to answer any more questions. In fact, it might be better to quit for the day. "I'm afraid, though, son, we're gonna have to hold you as a suspect."

"Suspect of what?" Lloyd said, a sweat creeping on him like the cold rain when he herded in winter.

Lloyd woke to the stink of his own sweat, and he seemed wholly that sweat and that stench — the stench was him, his soul. The overhead light had been switched on. It was a bare bulb caged by heavy wire. He glanced at the steel place he was in: steel walls, floor, ceiling, toilet, stool, table. Everything was bolted down. The steel door had a small square high window made of meshed security glass, and a slot near its bottom, with a sliding cover, for passing food. Lloyd hid his face in the crook of his arm and shook and wished he could go to Mr. Mac's for some white lightning.

The door clanked open. Lloyd could tell it was the sheriff even though he kept his face hidden and his eyes shut tight. The sheriff put a plastic plate on the table and said, "I was afraid of this." Then he left.

Maybe the food would help. Lloyd stood up, but his legs felt wob-bly and his eyes couldn't focus right. He lurched to the stool, planted himself on it, and held the edge of the table. When he picked up the plastic fork, it vibrated in his fingers. His touch sent a jangling electrical charge through his arm and down his back. The harder he gripped, the more he felt as though he were trying to etch stone with a pencil, yet only this concentration made any steadiness possible. Keeping his face close to the plate, he scooped the watery scrambled eggs into his mouth. He fell to his knees and threw up in the toilet. Curled facedown on the floor, Lloyd felt a prickly, nauseous chill seep into his muscles and begin to paralyze him.

Someone not Sheriff Lynch, who seemed by his step to be burly and ill-tempered, grabbed Lloyd's shoulder and twisted his body so that he faced the ceiling. The floor felt cold and hard against the back of his head. The man spread Lloyd's eyelids, opened his shirt, and put a cold metal disc on his chest. Lloyd had not noticed until now, but his heart was racing — much faster than the sheep's. That seemed so long ago. Mr. Mac was angry with him. The man started to yank down Lloyd's pants. Lloyd moved his lips to say no! No! But his limbs and muscles had turned to cement. His mouth gaped open, but he couldn't catch any air. The chill sweat returned. He was a boy again. Mr. Mac's heaviness pressed the air from his lungs, pinned him from behind, faceless, pushing the dull, tearing pain into him; he choked Lloyd's thin gasps with old-man smells of sweat and smoke and liquor and his ragged, grunting breath. The man rubbed something on Lloyd's right buttock and then pricked it with a needle. He left without pulling up Lloyd's pants.

Lloyd's body softened, and the cement dissolved; a cushiony feeling spread through him, as though his limbs were swaddled in plush, warm blankets. He could breathe. He could not smell himself anymore. "Son," he heard the sheriff say. "Put your pants on."

The two of them sat in the little white room, this time without Blanchard.

"Sheriff." Lloyd's words seemed to float out of his mouth. "Sheriff, what's all thisayre 'bout?"

Sheriff Lynch sat across the table. His face changed faintly as animals and unknown faces, and then the spirits of Mr. Mac and Blanchard, passed through it. He popped a peppermint Life Saver, sucked on it hard, and pulled back into focus.

"Let me ask you a question first, son, and then I'll answer yours."

He reached down next to his chair and put two Ziploc bags with Lloyd's shears and bowie knife in them on the table. Both the shears and the knife were tagged, as if they were in hock. The sheriff pressed them a few times with the tips of his long rust-colored fingers, lightly, as though to make sure they were there, or to remind them to stay still. "Now," he said. "I think I already know the answer to this question, but I need to know from you." He pressed them again. "Are these your knife and shears?"

How should he answer? The sheriff leaned back, waiting, with a look on his face that said he didn't want to hear the answer.

"Maybe," Lloyd said.

"Maybe." The sheriff joined his hands behind his head and pointed his eyes up and away, as though he were considering this as a possible truth.

"Maybe," Lloyd said.

"Lloyd Wayne Dogget," the sheriff said, turning his not-blue eyes on him. "How long have I known you? I knew your daddy and your grandpappy when they were alive. I know more about you than you know about you. And you ain't never been able to lie to me and get clear with it. So I'll ask you again — are these your knife and shears?"

Mr. Mac had given Lloyd the shears when he was sixteen. They were long and silvery. At the end of each day of shearing, after cutting the sheep's coarse, billowy hair, Lloyd would sharpen them on a strop and oil them with a can of S'OK to keep off the rust. The merry old man on the green can, a pipe in his mouth, always reminded him of Mr. Mac.

"What if I say yes?" Lloyd said.

Sheriff Lynch sucked on the Life Saver and blew out a breath. He leaned close to Lloyd and put his elbows on the table. "To tell you the truth," he said, "it doesn't make a whit's difference." He pressed the plastic bags again. "There's blood on these tools matches the type of a young lady people saw you leave Genie's with, a young lady who turned up murdered. And I confiscated these two things from you. So it doesn't make a whit's difference what you say, whether you lie or not. I'm just trying to give you a chance to get right with yourself, to be a man." He sank back and ran his hands through his stubbly iron-gray hair as he bowed his head and looked at the bags. He massaged his clean-cut neck. "Maybe to get right with the Lord too. I don't know. I don't believe in that kind of thing, but sometimes it helps people."

To Lloyd, the sheriff seemed embarrassed about something. Lloyd wanted to help him. But he was also afraid; he could not remember any young lady, only smiling dark-red lips, the curve of a bare upper arm, honky-tonk music, Dwight flinging the colored baby doll around.

"Okay, Sheriff," he said. "Since it don't make any difference, you know they're mine."

The sheriff escorted him to the showers, where he took Lloyd's clothes and gave him an inmate's orange jumpsuit and a pair of regulation flip-flops. After Lloyd had showered and changed, the sheriff told him he was under arrest for capital murder, read him his rights, and handcuffed him. They got in his car, Lloyd riding in the front seat, and drove the two blocks to the courthouse. The judge asked him if he had any money or expected any help, and he said no, which was the truth.

Every morning Sheriff Lynch came to Lloyd's cell and walked with him down to the little white room, where Lloyd talked with his lawyer. When the sheriff opened the door to the room, Lloyd watched his lawyer and the sheriff volley looks under their pleasantries. He remembered a cartoon he'd seen: Bluto and Popeye had each grabbed one of Olive Oyl's rubbery arms. They were stretching her like taffy. He couldn't remember how it ended.

Raoul Schwartz, the lawyer Lloyd had been assigned, said the judge had granted Lloyd a competency hearing, but not much money to do it with. He, Schwartz, would have to conduct the tests himself and then send them to a psychiatrist for evaluation. In two months the psychiatrist would testify and the judge would decide whether Lloyd was competent to stand trial. Schwartz said they had a lot of work to do. Schwartz said he was there to help.

Schwartz was everything the sheriff was not. He had short, pale, womanish fingers that fluttered through papers, fiddled with pencils, took off his wire-rimmed granny glasses, and rubbed the bridge of his nose. When he got impatient, which was often, his fingers scratched at a bald spot on the top of his forehead. Lloyd thought he might have rubbed his hair off this way.

Schwartz wouldn't let him wriggle out of questions, sometimes asking the same ones many times, like Blanchard. He asked about Lloyd's whole life. Sometimes the glare of the white room and Schwartz's drone were like being in school again, and Lloyd would lay his head down on the slick-topped table between them and put his cheek to its cool surface. "Come on, Lloyd," Schwartz would say. "We've got work to do."

Also unlike the sheriff, Schwartz cussed, which was something Lloyd could never abide, and the little man's Yankee accent raked the words across Lloyd's nerves even worse than usual. When Lloyd told him that Sheriff Lynch had been out to talk to Mr. Mac after a teacher had spotted cigarette burns on his arms, Schwartz murmured, "Excellent, excellent. Fucking bastard."

"Who's the effing bastard?"

"Mr. Mac." Schwartz's head popped up just as Blanchard's had when he'd wanted to catch Lloyd at something, only this time it was Lloyd who had caught Schwartz in a lie.

Schwartz began giving Lloyd tests. Lloyd was worried that he might fail them, but he didn't say anything; he had already gotten the impression that this man thought he was stupid. But it was the tests that were stupid. First Schwartz asked him about a million yes-or-no questions. Everything from "Do you think your life isn't worth living?" (no) to "Do you ever see things that aren't there?" (sometimes, in the woods). Then came the pictures. One showed a man and a boy standing in opposite corners of a room. At first Lloyd just said what he saw. But this wasn't good enough. Schwartz said he had to interpret it. "Tell me what you think is going to happen next," he said. When Lloyd looked at it closely, he figured the boy had done something wrong and was about to get a good belt-whipping. Schwartz seemed pleased by this. Finally, and strangest of all, Schwartz showed him some blobs of ink and asked him to make something out of them. If Schwartz hadn't been so serious, Lloyd would have thought it was a joke. But when he studied them (Schwartz had used that word — "interpret" — again), Lloyd could see all different kinds of faces and animals, as he had when he'd talked to Sheriff Lynch about his knife and shears.

It took only one little thing to tell him what the sheriff thought about this testing.

One morning the sheriff walked Lloyd down the hallway without a word, and when he unlocked the door to the white room, he stepped back, held it open, and swooped his hand in front of Lloyd like a colored doorman.

"Mr. Dogget," he said, for the first time making fun of Lloyd in some secret way.

The sheriff turned and let the door close without so much as a glance at Schwartz. Lloyd wanted to apologize to the sheriff. He was beginning to understand that it came down to this: the worse the sheriff looked, the better he, Lloyd, looked. He felt he was betraying the sheriff, with the help of this strange, foul-mouthed little man. Schwartz seemed to see everything upside down. When Lloyd had told him about Mr. Mac, even though Schwartz said it must have been awful, Lloyd could tell that in some way he was pleased. When he told Schwartz about times when a lot of hours passed without his knowing it, like when he'd sat with that sheep, or about drinking at least a canteen of Mr. Mac's white lightning every day for the past few years, Schwartz began scribbling and shooting questions at him. Same thing with the pills and reefer and acid and speed he'd done in his twenties. Even the gas huffing when he was just a kid. Lloyd felt dirty remembering all of it. Schwartz wanted details. Lloyd could almost see Schwartz making designs out of what he told him, rearranging things to make him look pitiful.

"I don't want to do no testin' today," Lloyd said as soon as the door had shut. He sat and leaned back in his chair, arms dangling, chest out.

"Okay," Schwartz said. "What do you want to do?"

"I been thinkin'," Lloyd said. "It don't make no difference if I was drunk or not. That don't excuse what I did."

"But you don't know what you did."

"That don't make no difference. They got the proof."

"They have evidence, Lloyd, not proof."

Another bunch of upside-down words. "But if I can't remember it, then ain't what they got better than what I can say?"

"Lloyd," Schwartz said, his head in his hands, massaging his bald spot. "We've been over this about every time we've talked. I know that it doesn't make common sense at first. But our criminal-justice system — that misnomer — is predicated upon the idea of volition. It means you have to commit a crime with at least an inkling of intention. You can't be punished in the same way when you don't have any idea what you're doing."

This kind of talk made Lloyd's head ache. "All I know," he said, "is I don't want to go foolin' around with truth. It's like the sheriff says — I got to get right with myself and be a man."

"The sheriff says this?" Schwartz's head popped up.

Lloyd nodded.

"Do you talk to the sheriff often?"

"I been knowing Sheriff Lynch since forever. He's like my daddy."

"But do you talk to him? How often do you talk to him?"

"Every chance I get." Lloyd felt queasy. He knew he'd said something he shouldn't have. But his pride in his friendship with the sheriff, perhaps because it was imperiled, drove him to exaggerate. "When we come from my cell, mostly. But any time I want, really. I can call on him any time."

"I don't think it's a good idea for you to be talking to him about your case," Schwartz said.

"And why not?"

"Because anything — *anything* — you say to him becomes evidence. As a matter of fact, I don't think it's a good idea for you to talk to him at all."

"So who'm I gonna talk to? Myself? You?"

For the next couple of days the sheriff didn't speak to Lloyd unless Lloyd spoke to him first. Schwartz must have done something. But the sheriff never looked at him hard or seemed angry. He mainly kept his words short and his eyes on the floor, as if he was sad and used to his sadness. Lloyd wanted to tell him how he was trying to get right but it was hard. Eventually Lloyd realized that even if he said this, the sheriff probably wouldn't believe him. If he were trying to get right, then he wouldn't be letting this Schwartz character make him look pitiful. Each morning Lloyd rose early, dressed, and rubbed his palms to dry them as he sat on the edge of his bunk, waiting. When he walked in front of the sheriff down the hallway to the white room, Lloyd could feel the sheriff's eyes taking him in. He tried to stand up straight and walk with manly strides, but the harder he tried, the smaller and more bent over he felt. He was careful not to wrinkle his prison outfit, pressing it at night between his mattress and a piece of plywood the sheriff had given him for his back. He combed his hair as best he could without a mirror.

At night Lloyd lay on his bunk and thought about Schwartz. Of course, Schwartz had tricked him into more tests. Next they were going to take pictures of his brain. Lloyd studied Schwartz's words: "volition," "interpret," "diminished responsibility." They all meant you couldn't be punished for your mistakes. This didn't square with Lloyd; he had been punished for plenty of mistakes. That was what Mr. Mac had punished him for; that was what the sheep died of. When you missed one on a head count and it got lost and fell into a ravine; when you forgot to give one a vaccination and it got sick, like the one that had died before Lloyd was taken away, you were punished. But how could he expect Schwartz, a womanish city boy, to understand this?

On one side were Schwartz and the law, and on the other were the sheep and God and the earth and Sheriff Lynch and Mr. Mac and everything else Lloyd had ever known. Who was he to go against all that — to hide from that terrible, swift sword the Almighty would wield on the Final Day? His fear was weak and mortal; it drove him out of his cell to plot with this fellow sinner to deceive God. Some nights Lloyd moaned in agony at the deceit of his life. For in his pride he had latched onto the notion that since he could not remember his gravest sins (and he believed they were all true, they must be true), he should not have to pay for them in this life. Oh, he would pay for them in eternity, but he flinched at paying here. What upside-down thinking! What cowardice in the face of sins that were probably darker, cloaked as they were in his drunken forgetting, than any he could have committed when he had "volition," as Schwartz called it. Because Lloyd did not know his sins, he could not accept his punishment; but for the same reason they seemed to him unspeakably heinous.

Lloyd lay on his bunk in the darkness and thought about the pictures he had seen of his brain. Two officers he didn't know had driven him to a hospital in Lubbock to get them taken. The hearing was in a week. Schwartz had pointed out patches in the pictures' rainbow colors, scratching his bald spot and pacing. He'd said that although parts of Lloyd's brain were damaged so that alcohol could cause longer and more severe blackouts in him than in normal people, such damage might not be enough for the court to recognize him as incompetent. And the rest of the tests had proved that he had a dissociative condition but not multiple-personality disorder. Lloyd had wanted to ask if Schwartz thought he was incompetent, but he figured he wouldn't get a straight answer.

In the darkness of the steel room Lloyd touched his head, trying to feel the colored patches of heat and coolness that the pictures showed in his brain. He imagined he could sense some here and there. He had come a long way — not many people knew what their brains looked like. But the thought that he might be incompetent frightened him. What if someday one of those big machines they put over his head was put over his chest and a picture was taken of his soul? What would it look like? He saw a dark-winged creature with tearing claws, cloaked in a gray mist.

The knock came to Lloyd in a half dream, and at first he thought he had imagined the sheriff's voice. The whole jail was quiet; all the inmates were covered in the same darkness.

"Lloyd? Lloyd? You awake, son?" The voice didn't sound exactly like the sheriff's, but Lloyd knew that's who it was. He rose and went to the door, too sleepy to be nervous. He peered out the square window. The glare of the hallway made him squint. The sheriff stood in silhouette, but his steely eyes glinted. Looking at him through the crosshatches of wire in the security glass, Lloyd thought that he, too, looked caged.

"I'm awake, Sheriff."

The door opened, and the sheriff said, "Come on." Lloyd could smell whiskey. He followed the sheriff out past the booking area. Everything was still and deserted in the bare fluorescent light. Gonzales dozed in a chair at the front desk with a porno magazine in his lap. The sheriff opened the door to his office, making the same mocking gesture as before, though this time he seemed to be trying to share his joke with Lloyd. He snapped the door's lock and sat down behind his desk. A single shaded lamp glowed in a corner, casting shadows from the piles of paper on the desk and reflecting golden patches from plaques on the walls.

The sheriff pointed at a low-backed leather chair and told Lloyd to have a seat. "Excuse me gettin' you out of bed, son. I figured this was the only time we could talk."

"It's no trouble."

"You can prob'ly tell I been drinkin'," the sheriff said. "I don't do it as a habit, but I apologize for that too. I been doin' it more lately.

I do it when I'm sick at heart. At least that's my excuse to myself, which is a goddamned poor one, unbefitting a man, if you ask me. But I am. Sick at heart."

He took a long pull from a coffee mug. Lloyd followed it with his eyes, and the sheriff caught him.

"And no," he said, "you can't have any. One of us got to stay sober, and I want you to remember what I'm gonna tell you." He leaned across the desk. "You know what a vacuum is, son? I mean in a pure sense, not the one you clean with."

Lloyd shook his head.

"Well. A vacuum is a place where there ain't anything, not even air. Every light bulb" — the sheriff nodded at the lamp behind him — "is a vacuum. Space is mostly vacuum. Vacuum tubes used to be in radios. And so on. A place where there ain't nothin'. Is that signifyin' for you?"

Lloyd nodded.

"Good. So we, because we're on this earth with air to breathe, we are in a place that's not a vacuum that's in the middle of a vacuum, which is space. Think of a bubble floating out in the air." The sheriff made a big circle above the desk with his fingertips. "That's what the earth is like, floating in space. Are you followin' me?"

"I think so."

"Well, are you or aren't you?" the sheriff said with sudden violence. Not waiting for an answer, he yanked open his desk drawer and took out a large folding map of the world. He tumbled it down the front of his desk, weighted its top corners with a tape dispenser and a stapler, and came around the desk to stand next to Lloyd. He told Lloyd what it was and said, "I study this all the time. Do you know where we are right now?"

To Lloyd, the shapes on the map looked like those inkblots. By reading, he found the United States and then Texas, and then he gave up. He shrugged his shoulders. "I don't know, Sheriff."

"That's okay," the sheriff said gently. He pointed to a dot in the Panhandle which someone had drawn with a ballpoint pen. Cursive letters next to it said "Dumas." "This is where we are. Two specks within that dot, on the dark side of the earth, floating in space. Over here" — he pointed to Hong Kong — "it's lunchtime. Japs eatin' their noodles or whatever. Here" — he pointed to London — "people just risin', eatin' their sausages and egg sandwiches."

He stepped back, behind Lloyd, and put his hands on the chair. The heat of his body and the smell of his breath washed over Lloyd.

"But look, son," the sheriff said, "how many places there are. It's some time everywhere, and everybody is doin' something."

The sheriff stood there for a few moments. Lloyd felt as he had when he was a child watching TV — he couldn't imagine how all those people got inside that little box. Now he couldn't fathom people inside the little dots. The world was vast and stranger than he had ever imagined.

"We are all here doin' things," the sheriff said, "inside this bubble that is not a vacuum. We all breathe the same air, and everything we do nudges everything else." He stepped over and propped himself on the edge of his desk, next to the map, and crossed his legs. The lamp's soft light cast him in half shadow.

"And this is why I'm sick at heart. Because I thought I knew you. Separation is the most terrible thing there is, especially for a man like me." The sheriff gestured to take in the whole room. "This is what I got. It ain't much. You and I aren't that far apart, son. Both of us solitary. But what you done, son, and I do believe you did all that, that separates a man from the whole world. And that's why I said you need to get right with yourself."

Lloyd bowed his head.

"You don't need to tell me you ain't done that." The sheriff's voice rose and quickened, began to quiver. "You and I both know you ain't. But that itself — a negativity, a vacuum — ain't nothin' to breathe in. Things die without air. So what I'm askin' you is, I want to do my own competency exam, for my own self. This is between Lloyd Wayne Dogget and Archibald Alexander Lynch. I need to know what's inside you to know what's inside myself. So you tell that lawyer of yours I'll stipulate to whatever he wants. Remember that word — 'stipulate.' Now get outta here." He turned from Lloyd and began folding the map with shaking hands. The corner weighted by the tape dispenser tore. Lloyd could not move.

"Shit," the sheriff muttered. He wheeled unsteadily on Lloyd, his eyes wide with panic and surprise at what he'd said. Lloyd could tell he was afraid, but not of him, as Mr. Mac had been. The sheriff was afraid that he might show his own soul to Lloyd and so break out of the bubble in which he lived. "Git!" he yelled. "Go tell Gonzales to take you back! Get outta here before I say somethin' foolish!"

*

"He wants you to do *what?*" Schwartz paced in the little white room, looking at the floor.

Lloyd was sitting at the table, turning his head to follow Schwartz. Was Schwartz right with himself? He repeated what the sheriff had told him.

"What does that son of a bitch want?" Schwartz said to himself.

"I wish you'd stop cussing around me."

Schwartz made a distracted noise.

"I mean it," Lloyd said. "It's offensive."

Schwartz made another noise. He had gathered his lips together into a pucker with his fingers, and he looked at the floor as he paced.

"Especially cussing on the sheriff." When Schwartz didn't answer, Lloyd said, "Are you hearing me? Don't cuss on the sheriff."

"I don't know what kind of game he's trying to play." Schwartz did not stop or raise his eyes from the floor. "But I would guess he's trying to trick some kind of confession out of you."

"Sheriff don't play no games with me," Lloyd said. "He don't have no tricks. You're the one with all the tricks."

"I'll take that as a compliment."

"Sheriff's the one tryin' to help me get right."

"Sheriff's the one tryin' to help you get dead," Schwartz said, mimicking Lloyd.

"Okay, man." Lloyd stood up and pushed his chair away. It squealed on the floor, and Schwartz stopped. Lloyd saw that his own fists were clenched. He hesitated.

"What are you gonna do, Lloyd? Beat me up? Go ahead. I've been expecting this."

"You think I'm stupid," Lloyd said. "And all them tests is to make me look pitiful and incompetent. What do you think that's done to my trying to get right?"

"What do you think that means, Lloyd — 'getting right'?" Schwartz moved close to him. He stared straight at Lloyd as he spoke. "It means giving up."

That night, and for the days and nights to come, Lloyd turned over in his mind all he had seen and heard. What he had known before was like some foreign language that now he couldn't understand. The worlds of Schwartz and the sheriff, of man and God, of what was in the law and what was in the fields, began to blur, and yet between them grew a chasm in which he hung suspended. He tried to remember what had happened in the places Blanchard had said he'd been, but he couldn't. He could not make them connect the way the sheriff had said all the people in all those dots on the map did. An indifference grew around him, a thin glass glazing that separated him from the rest of humankind.

The sheriff led him down the hallway to the white room without a word or a look, and left him with Schwartz. The hearing was the next day. Lloyd felt as though he were about to take another test. He had fought with Schwartz tooth and nail over the sheriff's proposal, and in the end had gotten his way by threatening to fire him. After Lloyd sat down across the table from him, Schwartz explained that he and the sheriff had struck a deal: the sheriff had agreed that he would not testify about his "competency exam," as he called it, on the condition that he not have to reveal to Schwartz beforehand what it was going to be about.

"I don't like this," Schwartz said, pacing, clicking the top of a ballpoint pen so that it made a *tick-tick* sound, like a clock. He sat down again, his elbows on the table and his hands joined as though in prayer, and brought his face close to Lloyd's.

"I want to tell you the truest thing I've ever seen, Lloyd. I've seen a man executed. When you are executed in Texas, you are taken to a powder-blue room. This is the death chamber, where the warden, a physician, and a minister will stand around the gurney. Since executions can take place in Texas only between midnight and dawn, it will have that eerie feeling of a room brightly lit in the middle of the night. Before this, in an anteroom, a guard will tell you to drop your pants. Then he will insert one rubber stopper in your penis and another in your anus, to prevent you from urinating and defecating when your muscles relax after you have died. When you are lying on the gurney, the guard will secure your arms, legs, and chest to it with leather straps. The guard will insert a needle, which is attached to an IV bag, into your left arm. Above you will be fluorescent lighting, and a microphone will hang suspended from the ceiling. The warden — I think it's still Warden Pearson — will ask whether you have any last words. When you're finished, three chemicals will be released into your blood: sodium thiopental, a sedative that is supposed to render you unconscious; pancuronium bromide, a muscle relaxant, to collapse your diaphragm and lungs; potassium chloride, a poison that will stop your heart.

"I could tell that my client could feel the poison entering his veins. I had known him for the last three of his fifteen years on death row; he was old enough to be my father. At his execution I was separated from him by a piece of meshed security glass. There was nothing I could do when he began writhing and gasping for breath. The poison — later I found out it was the potassium chloride, to stop his heart — had been injected before the thiopental. Imagine a dream in which your body has turned to lead, in which you can't move and are sinking in water. You have the sensations given you by your nerves and understood in your brain, but you can't do anything about them. You struggle against your own body. But really, it is unimaginable — what it is like to try to rouse your own heart.

"What if everything goes as planned? A nice, sleepy feeling — the sedative tricking your nerves — will dissolve your fear. The question is, will you want it taken away, fear being the only thing that binds you to life? Will you want to hold on to that, like the survivor of a shipwreck clinging to a barnacled plank? Will you struggle, in the end, to be afraid?"

Schwartz slumped back in his chair and began again to *tick-tick* the top of his pen so that it made a sound like a clock. The whiteness and silence of the room seemed to annihilate time, as though the two men could sit there waiting forever. They fell on Lloyd like a thin silting of powdered glass.

"You spend a lot of time thinkin' about that, don't you?" Lloyd said.

"Yes."

"You told me that to scare me, didn't you?"

"Yes."

Lloyd thought that Schwartz might have gotten right with himself, in his own way, by seeing what he had seen and thinking on it. But something still didn't add up.

"How do you know I'd be afraid?" Lloyd said. "How do you know that would be the last thing I'd feel?"

"I don't know that." Schwartz *tick-ticked* the pen. "You can never know. That's what's terrible about death."

"Lots of things you don't know when you're alive. So what's the difference?"

Schwartz's fingers stopped, and he stared at Lloyd as though he had seen him purely and for the first time. A knock at the door broke the brief, still moment, and Sheriff Lynch entered. He carried under his arm a stack of manila folders, which he put down on the table. Schwartz rose, studying Lloyd. He shook the sheriff's hand when it was offered. His eyes, though, were fixed on Lloyd. The sheriff caught this, but smiled pleasantly and told Schwartz it was good to see him again.

"Lloyd," he said, and nodded at him. He lifted a chair from the corner, put it at the head of the table, and sat.

"I think I need a little more time to consult with my client," Schwartz said.

The sheriff pressed his fingers a few times on top of the folders. "Okay. How much time do you think you'll need?"

"We don't need no more time," Lloyd said, rocking back and forth in his chair. "I'm ready."

"I'd like to look at what you've got there first."

"But that wasn't the agreement, Mr. Schwartz."

"Come on," Lloyd said. "I'm ready."

"Why don't you listen to your client?"

Looking from Lloyd to the sheriff, Schwartz paled. He seemed pinned in place for a moment; then he took off his glasses and rubbed them on his shirt. He put them on again. Sheriff Lynch stared at the stack of folders, his fingertips resting on them like a pianist's, his expression one of patient indulgence toward a child who was finishing a noisy tantrum. Lloyd clenched his hands between his thighs, wondering what would be revealed to him.

"Do you mind if I stand?" Schwartz said.

"Go right ahead." Sheriff Lynch pressed his fingers again to the top folder, as if for luck or in valediction, took it from the stack, and opened it in front of Lloyd. Lloyd did not see at first what was there, because Schwartz had made a sudden movement toward the table, but Sheriff Lynch, with the slightest warning lift of his hand, checked him. He faced Schwartz a moment and then turned to Lloyd.

"Go ahead, son," he said. "Tell me what you see."

When Lloyd looked down, he was disappointed. It was another

one of those crazy tests. He saw shapes of red and pink and green and black. It was the inkblot test, only in color. He studied more closely to try and make sense of it. He realized it was a picture of something. He realized what it was.

"I think I got it," he said to the sheriff. The sheriff nodded to help him along. "It's a sheep," Lloyd said.

"Look at it a little more closely, son." Lloyd saw Schwartz again move and the sheriff again check him while keeping his neutral blue eyes on Lloyd. Lloyd went back to the picture. He had missed some details.

"It's a sheep gutted after slaughter," he said.

"Turn the picture over, son," the sheriff said. This time Schwartz did not move and the sheriff did not hold up his hand. Paper-clipped to the back of the picture Lloyd found a smaller photo of a young woman. She had straight brown hair, wore blue jeans and a red-and-white-checkered blouse, and sat in a lawn chair, smiling to please the person who held the camera.

"Now turn the picture over again," the sheriff said, in his calm, steady voice. "What do you see?"

Lloyd tried to puzzle it out, but he couldn't. There must be something he wasn't seeing. He studied the picture. As he followed the shapes and colors of the sheep's emptied body, a trickle of pity formed in him for all three of them — the woman, the sheep, and himself — and dropped somewhere inside him. The glaze over him tightened. He could only tell the sheriff that he saw a sheep.

After the sheriff left, gathering the folders under his arm, the room went back to its silence.

"If I'd known," Schwartz said. "I would've had him testify."

"What?" Lloyd said. "If you'd known what?"

"Never mind." Shielding his face with his pale fingers, Schwartz laid his other hand on Lloyd's shoulder. "Never mind, Lloyd. You're perfect the way you are."

They had sat there a long time, the sheriff opening a folder in front of him, asking him the same questions, and then putting it aside. And in each folder Lloyd had seen the same things: a gutted sheep and a pretty young woman. He knew that the sheriff was try-ing to do something to help him get right, but as the glaze thick-ened, that chance seemed ever more remote. Before he left, the sheriff had nodded to Lloyd, to acknowledge that he had found his answer, but his gesture was as distant as that of a receding figure waving a ship out to sea. With each drop of pity Lloyd felt himself borne away yet drowning, so that he knew the heart of the man in the execution chamber, suffocating and unable to move, and he wondered how he would survive in this new and airless world.

MARTHA MOFFETT

Dead Rock Singer

FROM *The Chattahoochee Review*

I DIDN'T BELIEVE IT when someone pointed her out to me
and told me she had once been married to Screwbosky. I was always
surprised to learn something about him I didn't already know. Like
everybody who's made it through the last ten years, I felt proprietary about the facts of his life. I could recite all the milestones,
chapter and verse — and footnotes. The first concert at the Spectrum in Philadelphia, and right after it the all-night concert in
Pittsburgh. The first gold record. The succession of brand names
as he switched guitars, the motorcycle accident, the first time he
snorted coke, the last time. Between what Screwbosky said to us
and what he'd sung to us — and taking into consideration the
books, the reviews, the interviews, and the newspaper stories — I
thought I was in possession of pretty well everything about him that
was public knowledge. At any rate, it was rare that anybody ever
told me anything new. I also felt proprietary about his music. I lived
it before he wrote it, surely I had a special right to feel that it was in
some way mine, more meaningful to me than just any listener.
Then this guy reaches over for a deviled egg and jerks his shoulder
toward a woman at the end of the room. One wife I knew about,
that was documented. So who was he talking about?

My disbelief must have registered on my face. "When she was
younger, man," my informant hissed as he pushed me along the table that was serving as a bar and pointed me in the direction of the
far end of the split-level living room. Through the French windows
at the other end of the room, Long Island Sound was a bright gray
and the sky darker, as if the water was the source of light. The man

beside me said something more, but the house was pounding with the worst kind of disco music and I couldn't hear him. Some stored information was filtering into my conscious mind.

Yes. There had been an early marriage. Before Chicago, before the first album. A Sarah Lawrence type. There was something — a name, a label — that defined her. What had it been? A paragraph in one of those personality-cult magazines was coming back, something about her family or her background. What was it? I knew I'd get it in a minute. I remember stuff like that.

The people at the cocktail party Douglas had dragged me to formed such a classic suburban group that I had not bothered to make distinctions among the ones I had met so far. Doug's new house was two streets over, one of some two dozen houses on a six-acre spit of land jutting away from the Connecticut shore. Local inhabitants like to think they live on an island, and in fact call the place Perth Island, although you won't find it in an atlas. At one end of this piece of prime real estate, it's true, the approach is over a bridge that lets the tide into a shallow bay. At that end, you could very well imagine you were on an island. But the other end is solid marshland, with a tidal creek trickling through. Perth Island could hardly be called a peninsula, much less an island. It's a comma-shaped piece of land, firmly anchored at the head to the mainland, and attached at the other end by the bridge. I'd call it an aneurysm, in honor of the local death rate. Douglas says he waited for the overstressed executive who previously owned his house to drop dead, and finally he did.

Doug's new house was not a new house, it was an old house newly purchased and now in the process of being modernized. "Nick, come and look it over," he said to me after he'd signed the mortgage papers. I had come out to take a look. On the last day of the weekend, he insisted that we drop in at the party for a couple of drinks. It would give him an opportunity to meet some of his new neighbors. Knowing Douglas, I could bet he'd soon be on the board of the Perth Island Improvement Association, the group that made the rules on where people could park, what hours the two tiny scraps of communal beach could be used, how early one could put out the garbage, and other vital matters. WELCOME TO PERTH ISLAND. There was a sign at the little stone bridge that marked the causeway leading to the mainland. "Parking Rules

Strictly Enforced P.I.I.A." That was so that no strangers could come and use the beaches that the Perth Islanders raked and dredged and patrolled so possessively.

My weekend invitation was partly a working arrangement. I was supposed to advise Douglas on the basic renovations for the house and rehearse him on what he was to say to the contractor. Doug had vague but stubborn ideas of what he wanted, and he trusted me to read his mind and tell him how to express his wants. It was a fair exchange. Food and drink, a weekend in the country, a morning swim when the tide was high, in return for strolling around Doug's property and talking about wood and glass and square footage. And then if he liked my designs for the kitchen, I was going to try to make a deal with him to do it myself. I've done similar projects for other friends. The art gallery near the corner of West Broadway and Prince — all my ideas, though I don't get the credit.

All in all, an OK weekend. Even this party was not what I'd expected it to be. I'd forgotten the kinds of tasty things they serve at parties, and I was munching out on pâté and deviled eggs with caviar and all those things that I never have because I eat pretty simply when I eat at my place and I never go to parties because they're a waste of time.

"Which one is she?" I asked, looking at the group of people at the other end of the room. The women all looked alike to me. They were wearing the style that comes after preppy. Simple dresses, real pearls. Or skirts with shirts like their husbands', with a cable knit sweater over their shoulders. Very League of Women Voters. Only this was a party, so they were all knocking it back — and it wasn't white wine spritzers, it was vodka with maybe an ice cube. As I got closer I could see they were all mostly a little zonked.

"That's her," my informant said, and I peeled away from him as I suddenly remembered.

Storey Stanton, that was her name. Elizabeth Storey Stanton. That's what I was trying to remember earlier — that she was called by her middle name. I was in college before I met anyone whose first name was actually a surname. Stuart, Tyler, Grantland, Brookes, and Phelps are from my freshman yearbook. Good old Phelps.

She was looking into her drink as if there was something floating in it. I was close enough to crane over her and look into her glass. There was nothing in it but the light reflecting off the surface of the drink, mooning back into her eyes. Elizabeth Storey Stanton. Radcliffe. That was it.

She looked up at me suddenly, shocked that anyone was standing there, so close to her. "I'm sorry," I said. "I didn't mean to make you jump. Is there something wrong with your drink? Can I get you another?"

"No. No, please don't get me another. As a matter of fact, you could take this one away."

I didn't know what she wanted, but her voice was so humorless that I decided to do exactly as she said.

She wasn't bad-looking. Fine light hair, cut off in a straight line at her shoulder. Eyes with those deep heavy lids that make it look like it takes an effort to hold them up. She reminded me a little of Eva Marie Saint, when she got to be too old for ingenue roles and they stuck her in comedies that didn't suit her. I see her on TV late at night, gamely playing them through with the tension-etched smile, the weary gesture, the palpable civility. This woman even had the same kind of stance, elbows close to the body, one hand waving the glass in the air. "Give it to me," I said, taking the drink out of her hand. "You don't need that. Come and talk to me instead."

I put our drinks down and took her hand and she followed me quietly enough. I didn't know where I was going, of course, but I looked through an open door and found a small breakfast room, with a small glass table set for the morning meal. "Sit here," I told her, and put her at one end of the table while I went to sit at the other. She smiled at me over the top of the table and I felt for a moment that we were actually sitting down to breakfast together.

She picked up an empty water glass and twirled it in her hands. "I'm afraid I've deprived you of your drink," she apologized. "We don't both have to go on the wagon at the same time."

"It's OK," I told her. I almost said then, Look, I know who you are, Elizabeth Storey Stanton Screwbosky. You're Lizzy in "Hard Midnight." And "Bedtime Storey" is your song. And I guess you're the one "Right of Way" was written for. You're in all those early songs, the harsh ballads, the forty-fives I had to go back and find after that first time I saw him opening a concert for Led Zeppelin in Boston, the songs of loss that preceded the moving, speeding songs he was singing by the time of the Chicago concert. I walked out after his opening in Boston. I was afraid the heavy metal sound of Zeppelin would drive his songs out of my head.

But something stopped me from using her name — something told me to talk to her as if I didn't know who she was, as if nobody had come up and hissed in my ear, "See that skinny washed-out blonde on the other side of the room? Swear to God, she was married to Screwbosky." I might have talked to her anyway. She's that kind of woman. The kind I pick up outside the Third Avenue exit of Bloomingdale's, looking for a cab to take them to the Plaza. I thought then that I could have her. If I wanted to go to the trouble.

"Are you a friend of Karen's?" she asked, naming our hostess's daughter, one of the handful of people I had met coming in.

"No."

"No? A business friend of Oscar's?"

"No."

"An uninvited guest?" She smiled.

"Almost. I came with Douglas Miller. He just bought a house on Dolphin Circle."

"I know," she nodded. "The old Chatwin place."

I shrugged.

"I don't know why we call it the old Chatwin place. The Chatwins were in it only ten years. That doesn't seem very long, does it?" She had been smiling but it faded away. I wondered if she had remembered that it was just about ten years ago that Screw had died. Of course they must have been separated a long time before that. She was already out of his life before I ever heard of him. I would have remembered.

Her face was still, and I had a chance to look at her again. I thought she was about thirty-four or thirty-five. Her face looked softer up close, and younger. She glanced at me, to see if I was thinking what she was thinking, and I made my face say something else. But behind it, I was still thinking about Screw's death. At that time I had thought, and had said to anybody who would listen, presidents are replaceable, the pope is replaceable, Screwbosky is not replaceable. And still nobody knows what happened. Somebody said an international terrorist got him. The dude caused me some terror, all right. The first I knew about it was six o'clock in the morning when my clock radio clicked on and they were playing his songs, on and on, all day and all night, for weeks.

"You don't live around here, do you?" she was saying.

"In the city," I said. "West Sixty-eighth Street. I come to the suburbs when I'm invited."

"I haven't been into town in such a long time, months and months. I'm going in next week, though. Thursday. It's our anniversary, and my husband is taking me to lunch at the Russian Tea Room."

They always mention their husbands pretty early in the conversation. It's like flipping open a wallet to show an I.D. They all travel on their husbands' passports, these thirty-five-year-old women.

I wonder if they ever think about how they can't be found unless you *do* know their husbands' names. "We're in the book," they say, but she isn't; she's hidden behind her husband's name.

She was smiling across the table, relaxed now, pretty and sort of earnest, trying to draw me out. I felt then that the way she looked was the way she was, and I never had any reason to change my first impression. Now she entered into the game of the breakfast table. "Crumpets?" she asked. "Shall I pour your tea?"

"Yes, Elizabeth."

She shot me a startled glance.

"Elizabeth Barrett. And I'll read your sonnets and smuggle you out of this house and onto the next Alitalia flight."

She looked over the gleaming crystal and china on the table and shook her head. "No . . . you be D. H. Lawrence and I'll be Mrs. Weekley, the wife of your history professor, kindly having you in for a glass of sherry."

I smiled at her, but I wondered if that was supposed to remind me that she was married. "How about Napoleon and Josephine?" I asked.

"Oh, OK. Let me change my costume." She pulled her belt up under her breasts into an Empire line, and twisted two strands of hair in front of her ears, to lie against her cheeks. How could she have known that such pretense would please me?

I love these games. "There's a terrific letter from Napoleon, in Verona, to Josephine, in Milan," I told her. "First he scolds her for not writing to him and for flirting. Then he asks, 'What do you do all day, Madame? What robs you of the time to write? Who can this wonderful new lover be who rules your days and prevents you from attending to me? Beware, Josephine; one fine night the doors will be broken down and there I shall be.'"

I said the last words in a voice that was a surprise even to me. She looked at me, startled. I remember stuff like that, I can't help it.

The music from the other room reached us here, but it was just background sound. The room we were in was quiet. It was domestic, in a funny way, with her sitting at one end of the table and me at the other. "I can see that life outside the city can be quite comfortable."

She opened her mouth to answer, but then she stopped. I couldn't figure out why for a moment, because I was obviously attentive. Then I realized that "Happy Hour" was playing, one of Screwbosky's sweetest songs, an old one. *I swear to you, if you buy me a drink, I'll give you a happy . . . happy hour.*

Things like this must happen to her all the time. "I always liked that song," I said, to remind her that I was still there, and to see whether the music was something we could talk about. She looked at me blankly.

"I was saying, suburban life looks quite comfortable from here."

"Comfortable?" she asked, as if comfort had never had any place on her list of requirements.

"Why don't you come into the city sometime," I said, which she could read like an invitation if she wanted to. "There's nothing like the city. It'll turn you on."

"Oh, I know," she said. "I'm looking forward to Thursday."

That wasn't what I meant, but before I could say anything more someone blocked the small amount of light coming in at the door. I looked around. A suburban type. He was wearing his hair about half an inch too long for the cut, and his clothes were a size too large. "I want you to call home and check on that sitter," he said. He didn't say it unpleasantly. Just stating that that was what he wanted. She sighed.

"You know everything is all right. We'd be the first to hear if anything was wrong. But of course I'll call and make sure." She turned and looked into space somewhere between the man and me. "This is my husband, George Talbot. George, this is a friend of Karen's."

Did you catch it?

"I'm Nick," I told her.

"Nicholas?" her husband asked, to make sure.

"No. Actually, Nicholai," I said.

"Glad to meet you." She had cooled his interest in me by labeling me with Karen's name. I wondered why. He looked back at her. "Would you go and call the sitter? Easier from here than during dinner."

"Excuse me."

She left the room and he called after her, "One more drink and we'll have to move on." He turned to me. "We are expected for dinner a couple of houses down," he explained. Her introduction left me still not knowing her name, as far as she was concerned. It left me with nothing to call her but Mrs. Talbot, which of all her names suited her least. The important thing was that I knew where she would be on Thursday. Ah, nothing is accidental, says Sigmund.

I couldn't decide whether to remain neutral with her husband or ingratiate myself with him. I began to talk to him about the ideas I had for designing and building a kitchen for Doug. It would be stark — white Italian tile and natural wood, the wood sanded finer and finer and then rubbed with linseed oil. I found myself saying things to him like, "Carpentry is applied physics — a skill for dealing with the material world." Pretty soon he was talking about all the projects he was going to get started on, as soon as he found the time. I was bored until Doug came along to fetch me, saying it was time to leave if I wanted to make my train back to the city. I was wearing faded jeans and my old Irish knit sweater, but when I put on the leather trench coat that Douglas had given me, I was better dressed than any of these suburban middle-level executives. Doug had given me the coat when he decided to abandon the city for the country, to show he wasn't abandoning friends. It was the color of cinnamon and so fine you could wring it like a towel. Such gifts mean nothing to Douglas. He gets everything wholesale. Such gifts mean nothing to me, either.

I did not see her again as we made our way out of the house, but I thought about her going in on the train. Doug had kindly allowed me to take the sections of the Sunday *New York Times* he had finished with to keep me occupied on the ride in. But I mostly thought about Screw, and how long he'd been dead, and how he had died.

However it was he had died. No one ever believed the official statements. His family came and recovered the body and took it away for private ceremonies, or perhaps just to hide it, get him buried and forgotten as soon as possible. His father, the insurance salesman, had taken charge. The way Screw hated his father had helped me immensely in hating mine. His old man told reporters that it was natural causes and that they might as well leave him alone in the future, as he would never have anything more to say on his son's death or life. And he never did.

It was late when I got home, but I put on the early albums, *The Arm of the Needle* and *Hard Midnight,* but not going any farther than the year Screw switched from acoustic to electric guitar. I couldn't sleep, but I was peaceful. I had not had a project for a long time. I love it when I'm absorbed in a project — it's the only time I do like. And I haven't had a project since my father died. My last best project was his funeral.

I checked the answering device on the phone for messages. Nothing. I felt good. I still had three-quarters of a joint to smoke, something one of my passengers had passed me in lieu of a tip. The only thing that spoiled the serenity and hope of that evening was that the damn phone started ringing. I use the telephone a lot, but very few people have my number — only Douglas, my mother, a couple of others. So when it rang the first time I answered it without thinking, expecting it to be one of them. But I knew immediately that the voice belonged to no one I knew.

"Hey, man, can you do me a favor?"

"You've got the wrong number," I told him.

"Chuck, this is Jim. You know, Jim."

"You've got the wrong number. Dial again."

"Can . . . you . . . hear . . . me?" the voice came.

"Fuck off," I said, and hung up.

The record came to an end and in the silence before the next record dropped, the telephone rang again. It was the same voice.

"Hey, Chuck, we got trouble on this line. Can you hear me now? This is important. You've got to give Hal a message for me. Will you do that for me?"

"Man, for the last time, you have got the wrong number," I said. "What number are you dialing?" Evidently he couldn't hear me, or I was unable to interrupt him. He babbled on. I hung up again.

I was asleep the next time the phone rang. The tuner, still on, glowed like a banked campfire in the corner.

"Chuck, it's important. You know I wouldn't bother you if it wasn't important. Tell Hal I can't come tomorrow, will you? I can't keep the appointment, tell him. Something's come up, I can't get there. Will you do that for me?"

"Sure."

"You gonna tell him? It's important. I can't get there. Got it?"

"Sure," I said.

"Thanks. Don't forget. Thanks, pal."

What a bummer. I thought I'd never get back to sleep. Finally, I got up and put on The Last Album. Screw had called it *Days Too Long*, but everybody calls it The Last Album. It had everything in it of Screwbosky's attitude toward death — and, as he said, he'd thought about it a long time. One part of him thought that life was too short. The other part thought that it was long enough.

I came down through the park on my bike with the wind blowing in my face. The sun was sitting high on top of the big horse chestnuts on the east side of the park. On the other side, a three-quarter moon was still in the sky, hanging white in the west. The two balls faced each other across the park, with me coming down between them. I cycled down the West Side traverse and shot out of the park at Columbus Circle, changing lanes twice and circling the statue to cut on down to Fifty-seventh Street. I turned east and passed Carnegie Hall, passed the restaurant, passed the spot where I once picked up Mick Jagger and two of his friends, and spun on down to Fifth. It was too early, I knew. But I'm like that. Always on time. Once I figure out what I'm going to do, doing anything else is a waste of time.

Anyway, I'd had it with the apartment. I had to get out. I'd been cleaning since I woke up that morning, and hardly made a dent. I just closed off the kitchen, figuring I would clean only the areas that would be visible. First, the bathroom. Change the cat's box. Put up some new towels. I have this trick of scraping down the sink and tub with a single-edged razor blade. That gets the crud off. Then I pour bleach over everything, and what's left turns white.

Then the bedroom. God, what a mess. I'd got out of the habit of making the waterbed. I couldn't sleep on it anymore, I'd been sleeping on a sleeping bag on the living-room floor. One of the cats had caught a claw in the plastic and started a slow leak. Then she pissed in the gutter of water that rimmed the bed. I had to mend the leak, bail out the stinking water, and wipe the bed down. And find some clean sheets. I didn't want to have to do a laundry. Luckily, there were some clean sheets, so I just stuffed everything that was dirty into one of the closets and closed the door.

The bathroom looked good. The bedroom was OK with the lights off and the curtains drawn. The living room would have to stay as it was, there was not much I could do about it. It was clean enough — there is not much furniture, besides my desk and work-table. The room is full of projects, scale models, theater designs, and so forth. Mostly unfinished. My friends like to think of me as an artist. They're always introducing me as an artist or an architect or a designer. But I'm too self-critical to really get anywhere. None of the things I've started ever get finished. Nothing I do matches the idea as it first comes to me. And yet these half-done things suggest the whole things, so what's the use of further fooling around? I'd just as soon be introduced as a cabby. Sometimes I correct people, after they've introduced me. "No, I'm not an artist. I drive a cab."

I drove this week, three days in a row, to make a little money. I have this arrangement with Mike at the garage; he lets me take a cab out anytime I want to. I don't make a lot. You have to hustle to make money driving, and I won't hustle. But it suits me OK, driving. Gets me out of my apartment. I'd go crazy if I didn't make myself get out from time to time.

Somewhere in the living room, in one of the big portfolios, I was sure I had a poster of the 1986 tour, the one that never happened. That poster is probably worth a lot of money now. A collector's item. Screwbosky was dead before the first concert of the tour. After the sixties and the seventies were over and nobody much was dying anymore, he had to die. I had tickets for that tour. Madison Square Garden. I hadn't seen him in a long time, just bought the records. I had never been physically closer to him than sitting down front, next to the stage, or standing by the corridor when the band passed through the auditorium to the platform. It never occurred to me then to try to get close to him. I just liked his music. He was part of a good time. It was a good time because I didn't know yet that it was almost over. And now I have this second chance. Storey Stanton, now Mrs. Talbot, once Storey Screwbosky, was going to give me that chance. To get close to him.

What had I done with that poster? Just going through all my old stuff was slowing me down, wasting time, and I didn't want to look at the past that much. I spotted the poster just as the phone rang. I didn't want to talk to anybody at the moment, but I heard the telephone butler activate, so I flipped the switch so that I could hear the caller.

Yeah, it was Mom. Sophia. Hello, you little dumpling. She had already called twice that morning, but as usual she was intimidated by the recorded greeting and couldn't bring herself to speak. I currently had the machine set up so that it started with the cavalry charge played at top volume by the best bugle you'd ever want to hear. It galvanizes most of my callers into saying whatever it is that's on their minds. Not Sophia. She leaves her little silent moment of waiting on the machine, and hangs up.

But this time she is going to speak up. Brave little woman, Sophia. She talks fast, to get in as much as she can to her allotted half-minute.

"Peter? Peter, why don't you answer your telephone? Your mother needs to speak to you. Why did you come into the shop on Monday? The clerks, they don't know what to say to you. You took money from the cash register, they don't know how to say no to you. I am not there on Mondays, you know that. On Mondays I go to see Father Stephanotis. Father wants to see you. He has not seen you since the funeral. He says, Peter is such a fine-looking young man. And such a brain. Why does he do the things he does? I don't know, I have no answer, I am only a mother —"

She ran out of time. Not that there was any more to say. I ran the tape back, and then played it again, transferring it to the big tape recorder. It would be worth playing around with, maybe. Now that she's left a message, I'll have to call her back in the next day or two. Have to keep those rent checks coming. Sophia pays my rent in an arrangement by which the checks are debited against whatever my share of the estate will be. You have no idea how much time I have to spend on her to keep this arrangement going.

I tacked up the poster. Screw is wearing leather pants and an open leather jacket, no shirt. He's holding a mike in his left hand, high and close to his face, like a light. His Gibson J-200 is hanging from his neck. His right hand cups his ear. His eyes are half closed, his head turned a little so that his two trademarks, the beaky nose and the wild hair, are outlined against the spotlights. National Tour, June 17–July 23, 1986, it says. I was still enrolled at Columbia that year. I was still going to be a college graduate, a professional.

*

I almost coasted into a yellow cab that was making the light late. "Watch it, you stinkin' coprolite," he said. Or that's what I think he said. "Get outta my way, shitstabber," I replied. He shouted something more as he accelerated down Fifty-ninth Street, and I gave him the finger. Of course, I belong to that confederacy of cab drivers. I had been driving all week, but now I was on the other side — one of them — the vast army of bodies whose aim in life is to keep cab drivers from reaching their destinations swiftly and efficiently.

I crossed over to the park side and cycled back to the west end of the park, where there's a broad paved entrance. I circled around there, just inside the park, killing time, doing figure eights and slow U-turns, testing the slow-speed stability of the bike. I've rebuilt this bike about three times. I went slower and slower, until the bike was motionless, balanced in a perfect track stand. I held it for a minute or two, then pushed off into another series of U-turns, dodging pedestrians. There was a hot-dog vendor standing there watching me. He's got the good ones, with the onion sauce, the sauerkraut, and the pickle relish, but I don't eat crap like that anymore. When the kitchen is cleaned up, I prepare my own food — brown rice, vegetables, tofu, yogurt. I didn't get around to cleaning the kitchen today, just closed the door, but I'm going to do it next. It's good that I'm beginning to get the place cleaned up. I haven't brought anybody home for a long time, because it was such a mess. Since the last one, I just haven't bothered. The last one was this woman I met on the 104 bus. I sat down beside her and she just came home with me. The one before that was when I was making a long-distance call and needed some help from the operator. The operator turned out to be this woman with a great voice. I got to talking to her and I talked her into coming to my apartment on her lunch break. Can you believe that? I just wanted to see if she would really come. I can't remember now which was which, they both left the same way. Just gathering themselves up, rolling over to the side of the bed, feeling around for their clothes. They looked like they forgot already. I really resent that, when they just get up and go. After all, I give full measure in bed. Oh, yeah, it's more than just performance with me.

I headed back downtown and wasted some time leaning against the iron gate at the subway. I was across the avenue when I saw them come out of the restaurant. They walked a few steps on the sidewalk and then turned to face each other. I couldn't tell if they were talking or not, it didn't look as if they were. Damn it, what were they going to do next? Logically, he should go back to his office and she should go shopping or to a movie. Isn't that what suburban ladies do on their day in town?

What's-his-name, George, turned and started for the near corner, and she watched him walk away. I started crossing the avenue, knowing that neither one of them would notice me at this point. She crossed her wrists in front of her, pulling her jacket tight. Then she turned and started for the far end of the block, heading toward Fifth.

I came up behind her, passing her the first time, just glancing around, keeping close to the sidewalk. It was then that I saw that her eyes were full of tears and she probably couldn't have seen me anyway. I circled back and came by her again, this time calling out.

"Hey. Hey, Mrs. Talbot. Mrs. Talbot?"

She brushed the tears away quickly, almost as if she was just brushing her hair back. I had passed her again by now. I turned around and cycled down the sidewalk, stopping beside her. "Hello, Mrs. Talbot. I thought that was you." I smiled at her. "What are you doing in town?"

"Oh, it's —"

"It's Nick. Remember me?"

"Of course I do. How are you?"

"Fine. Wait a minute." I got off the bike and turned it to face the direction she was walking in and fell into step beside her. "Where are you heading?"

She flung up her hands, with her elbows pressed in to her waist, in that funny angular movement I had noticed before.

"I don't know."

"Come home with me," I said.

She looked at me, dry-eyed now and alert.

"Let me make you a cup of tea, I've got some Celestial Tea at home. We can walk up through the park. I live just up the avenue, between Lincoln Center and Central Park West. It's really nice in the park today. Come on."

She came.

*

She was all right in bed. She really was. I was surprised. I mean, I had thought about fucking her, but I hadn't thought about her, how she would be. She really was there for me, holding on to me, patting and stroking. I loved the way she touched me. I asked her later about that, how it was that she was so good with her hands. She said she thought she had learned how to touch people from holding her children, that she had not known before.

You're probably wondering what we talked about, coming up through the park. Nothing much. I pointed out the moon and the sun to her, they were still there. I sang a Provençal song about the moon. I told her I liked her hair. I told her I was an orphan. I told her that story I always tell, that I remember when I was four or five years old my father used to tie me up in a blanket and throw me over his shoulder and go for a walk. I'd peer out at the world . . . people would say, "What have you got in that sack?" And my father would answer, "My fortune." Women always like that story.

When she got too excited, she tried to hold us both back, literally dragging me back by my hair, my shoulders, finger by finger, to slow us down. Also, she had a way of suddenly opening her eyes and looking right at me when something good was happening. I noticed all the things about her that made her different, and I began to find out how to make them happen. And I knew that Screwbosky must have noticed, too, and worked at it, too.

It is a point of pride with me to do this well. Anybody who does something really well tends never to do it less than well. That's one reason I finish so little. If it's not going well, I won't do it.

She kept her eyes closed a lot of the time. I guess to concentrate on what she was feeling. I began to stroke inside, moving easily and deep. Her legs flew apart then, and she flew apart inside, too, opening in front of me and I followed, moving past bands of flesh and rings like chine into a snug space beyond. I can do this . . . oh, about five or six minutes before I have to shift to something else.

With my hands, I stroked her thighs along the outside, and directed her by touch to press her legs together under me, so that she would grasp me as tightly as possible. Her flesh moved with me as I moved, the outer membrane sliding with me, the deeper flesh less yielding, and then meeting the blank warmth of that far wall. I took her head between my hands and turned her face up to mine. I kissed her until she fought for breath, and finally we both moaned, open-mouthed, and I felt a thrill of pleasure shake my ass, as rare a thing for me as completing one of my designs. Rarer.

And yet, when it was over, she sat on the frame of the waterbed and dressed herself, pantyhose and pleated skirt, and a shirt with a ribbon at the neck. I wanted her to lie down and talk for a while. I wanted to question her about Screwbosky. She had glanced at the poster, passing through the living room, but had made no comment. I wanted to ask her if she had ever suggested any words to Screwbosky for a song, and if so which ones they were. I wanted to ask if he was as tall as I am. If he was as good in bed.

But she was combing her hair, and already thinking ahead, of the trip across town, of the train, of dinner; as far as I was concerned, she was already taking the roast from the oven. I pulled her back over onto the bed. I didn't care whether she went or stayed, but why couldn't she stay for a few minutes? She stretched out next to me. I jiggled the waterbed. I once saw someone put a baby on its back on a hard surface, and it lost its equilibrium in the same way. She adjusted her body with little jerks. "Come back on Monday," I said.

"Monday . . ." She really had not thought ahead to another meeting.

I could see that she had thought this was just a lucky fuck — no consequences, no guilt, no connection at all to her life. But now that she did think of going to bed with me again, her eyes narrowed on her calendar, probably stamped with the name of a suburban bank and hanging with the train schedule beside the wall telephone in her kitchen.

"Monday," I said.

"Ohhh, Monday's too hard. Getting the girls off to swimming lessons, getting the week started . . ."

"It has to be Monday. You want it to be Monday too."

She drew up in bed and sat with her arms wrapped around herself, her face partly hidden by her hair.

I pulled at the strand of hair until she bent her head. Then I kissed her and caught her lip between my teeth. "Come on Monday," I said. She struggled away, making a great wave in the waterbed that rocked us to and fro.

*

The apartment looked so good that after she left I decided to stay in. I did a little more cleaning and then I started fooling around with both tape recorders. I played Sophie's message again, pushing the Pause button and running the tape backward and forward as I fit my side of the conversation onto the new tape.

"Peter?"

"Sophie, you old douche bag, how are you?"

"Peter, why don't you answer your telephone?"

"I'm too busy jerking off, Ma."

"On Mondays I go to see Father Stephanotis."

"That faggot! He'll never lift his cassock for you, Ma. You're wasting your time."

"He says, Peter is such a fine-looking young man."

"I bet he does. But I'm saving it for the women, Ma."

"They don't know how to say no to you."

"You're right, Ma. They don't. Such a cock."

"And such a brain."

"I agree."

"I am only a mother —"

"That's right, Sophie, you little dumpling. Only a mother. And don't you forget it."

"That first Christmas, I actually tried to send Christmas cards, Tiffany Christmas cards embossed with our names. Our formal names, Mr. and Mrs., then I signed them, Storey and Screw. It sounds silly now. I was trying to have a marriage, you know. Be married. I kept after Screw to give me his list. I finally discovered that he didn't know most of his friends' last names, and had no idea where they lived. They mostly got together when it was time to go on the road, or they ran into each other at coffee houses and clubs, or at the studio. The only people whose addresses and phone numbers he knew were his agent, his manager, his lawyer, and his producer.

"Everybody always knew where to find Screw," she added. We were camping on the living room floor. The waterbed was leaking again. I had my sleeping bag unfolded and spread out, so there was plenty of room. I was stretched out on my back, Storey was sitting up with her arms around her knees, a favorite position of hers. I had both pillows, and an ashtray on my chest with a joint. We kept lighting it and taking a hit and putting it out again.

Along the edge of the sleeping bag were the remains of break-fast. Storey had gone around by Murray's for bagels and cream cheese and smoked fish, and somewhere along the way she had picked up orange juice and champagne. That was all right. That was sweet of her, although I don't really like people giving me things unless it's something I specifically want.

While she talked about Screwbosky, I looked up at the poster. I kept putting his records on, playing a cut here and a cut there, sometimes a whole album. I was trying to make it seem that he was there with us, that there were three of us, but it wasn't working. Somehow the things she was telling me were not what I expected. She seemed to remember the most inconsequential things. And not to remember big things at all. She didn't remember the first time she heard "Right of Way." Imagine not remembering the first time you heard it. I remember the first time I heard it.

"We were living on the third floor of a brownstone in the West Village," she was saying. "It was nice. Small. But it had a lot of charm. There was a garden below, at the back, with a brick wall around it. Our apartment looked down into the garden. Screw's fans used to hang around in the alley, on the other side of the wall. They used to jump up and catch the top of the wall and try to look over. They'd hang there until their arms got tired, then they'd drop back to the sidewalk. Sometimes I'd look down and see just their fingers showing on the top of the wall."

"How did you meet him?"

"It was between semesters at Radcliffe. I was doing an internship at a theater in the city. I was getting credit, no pay. It was one of those improvisational theaters, where the audience takes part, so the performance is different every night. Screw came in several times. He thought that he was doing something similar at his concerts. There were times when he wanted to control his audience, and times when he wanted to turn it loose. He was studying the actors' techniques, and talking with the director. I met him there."

"And you started going out with him?"

"Um-hmmm."

"And?"

"And we got married."

"How long?"

"Two years . . . two and a half."

"How come you broke up?"

"He didn't want to be married anymore. I wanted to be married, but not to him. I wanted to be married to a businessman, a lawyer, a doctor, anybody but a rock musician. I wanted a house in the suburbs. I wanted children. I thought I was wasting my time in that life, and not having any of the things I wanted."

"Maybe you just weren't his type," I suggested.

She looked at me for a moment. "But I was. Every woman he had after me was just like me. The girl he was married to when he died — she was a Sarah Lawrence film student, and her father's a vice president at IBM."

I wondered if she had been much different fifteen years ago. Of course she had. Her hair had been paler and longer probably. She'd probably been thinner, or thin in a different way. She must have been narrower across the shoulders too. Now she had that band of muscle across her back that comes from carrying a couple of kids around. I wondered if she'd been more talkative then, more fun. She seemed to me to be always preoccupied, always thinking of all the things she had to do. She came in once, twice a week; but she always seemed to be thinking about making it home before school was out or phoning Connecticut to see if the man was going to fix the clothes dryer. All those details drove me crazy — she could never just forget about them and listen to me. Only when we were making love would she concentrate on me. Then I would realize — this is what she came for. I tried to play some of my own tapes for her, but she just waited politely through them until it was time to crawl into the sack. I even played part of my father's funeral eulogy for her, not the part Sophia doesn't like, but the part where Father Stephanotis says he was a pillar of the Greek community in New York. All she said was, "I thought your father was a Russian émigré."

That brought me up short. Reminded me, once again, to decide what I'm going to do with these tapes. At one time, I thought I'd use them, turn them into an art form of some kind. One idea was to build a gigantic 1930s kind of radio cabinet, the kind that looks like it has an art deco face, with all the cabinetry and wood veneers done just right, and play the tapes through it, in a big empty gallery, in a big white room like a squash court, with a dim orange light coming from the radio dial. Now, I don't know. If I ever have to leave this apartment, I might just dump all the tapes in the trash cans up and down Columbus Avenue. I might mail them to some-

body. They could be evidence. Of what? I don't know. I've taped
and retaped and messed around with them so much, nobody could
reconstruct the originals.

"Tell me about the concerts," I said. I wanted to hear something. I mean, he was somebody. He had talent, he had money.
He was a big star. She must remember all that. "What were the concerts like?"

"I didn't see a lot. I never liked going on the road. There was
nothing for me to do, and the hotels and motels . . . I never liked
that part. Screw didn't like to take me on a tour, either; being married didn't go with touring. I think Screw wanted me to stay at
home and keep things organized, and take care of him when he
was there."

"Sounds great," I said.

"Well, he did want a home, and in some ways I succeeded in giving him the things he wanted."

"Like . . . ?"

"I think I introduced him to a lot of things, taught him something about food, although he still wanted the kitchen stocked with
the kinds of junk food he always wanted when he was high."

I guess it doesn't work to hear ordinary things about him while
his songs are playing on the stereo. I wasn't sorry I had decided not
to try to tape what she was saying that day. I could have set up the
big tape recorder behind the speakers and she would not have seen
that it was running. But then I couldn't have played the albums,
and I wanted to listen to them while she was there.

The week before, I did get her to tell me one interesting thing
about Screw, and I was taping at the time. I asked her if she had
ever inspired any of his songs. Here, I'll play that section into this
tape. I'll probably get rid of the original with the rest of the junk,
but this bit is worth saving. Listen.

"He used to make me tell him my dreams, in case there was
something he could use. He said people were only truly original in
dreams."

There. For those three digits I ran two hours of tape.

I crawled over the sleeping bag and put on another album. I kept
hoping maybe some of the songs would remind her of something,
bring back some kind of painful scene that she would suddenly begin to tell me about.

"Ironed sheets."

"What?"

"Not the no-iron synthetic sheets, but real sheets that had to be ironed. He loved them. He would snap one over us and then smooth it around us. I can still remember . . ."

"Were you with him in Chicago? March of 1983?"

"No. I was back in school by then, at Barnard, trying to finish my last year. But I went with him to London that summer."

"Oh, God, you were at the Wembley Stadium concert." I started looking for my tape of *Live at Wembley*.

"Yes. We had a lovely time in London. We went to Harrods. We bought absolutely everything. Everything we saw that we wanted, everything that was perishable or eatable or wearable, we had it all sent to the hotel. But in one whole year that was the only thing we really did together."

"And now he's dead."

"Yes."

"It could happen to any of us. Any moment."

She smiled, and I thought she wasn't listening to me, but she explained why she was smiling. She didn't think it could happen to her.

"Last week after I met you at the museum — wasn't it Tuesday? I was crossing Park Avenue, on my way to Grand Central to get the three-thirty-five, and I got caught by the light and barely made it across the street, and I was thinking how awful if I were struck down on my way home from meeting you. And then I thought I couldn't possibly die like that since I had to get home to pick up the kids at the orthodontist's."

"Like insurance? As long as you're covered, nothing's going to happen."

"Right. As long as I have to get their breakfasts, patch their jeans, and show up at tennis camp on parents' day, nothing very terrible can happen to me."

"You really believe that," I told her.

She shrugged. "I don't know. I appreciate what I've got. I wouldn't like to lose it. The mornings seem awfully nice to me, all of a sudden. This past week . . . calling the kids for breakfast, watching them pick the raisins out of their sticky buns . . . then that panic at eight-thirty when it's time to leave for school, the search for ponytail holders and schoolbooks, and the odd sums of money they need at the last minute for field trips and library fines. I do like all that."

"Then why are you here with me?"

"Well, because. I'm afraid of getting old and then wishing I'd done more, lived more. Don't you find that you never regret the things you've done, only the things you've failed to do? When I get old, sitting in my rocking chair, I don't want to be sorry. And I'm here because I've always wanted to know something about myself. I just wanted to know. Now I do. I owe you for that. I've never lived the way I've lived in the past few weeks. It's very good, as you must know." As she talked, her hands were moving over me, eating at me with wonderful scoops. I pulled her over me, and we went at it again.

I crawled off the sleeping bag again and put on *Blown*. A studio album. Lots of craftsmanship, lots of painstaking construction. The title, like the best of Screw's work, illustrated his gift for ambiguity. I don't know how many ways that title can be read. Blown away, dead. Blown by a blowjob. Driven by the wind. Out of breath. Blossomed-blown. Blowing-it blown. I never knew that I was attracted to ambiguity — Christ, that I loved ambiguity — until Screw. And the vocal.

"Listen to this," I said to Storey, as if she hadn't heard it before. Against the technical perfections, he pitched a vocal sound with an energy that came from rage.

It's much better to listen to this album high. You can listen harder. "You want some hash?" I asked Storey. I had some on my desk somewhere in a twist of aluminum foil. A customer had laid it on my dash instead of a tip.

She nodded and I got up and foraged around until I found a cardboard cylinder from a roll of toilet paper and a straight pin. I took it back to the sleeping bag. Storey watched me cut a penny-size hole on the side of the cardboard roll, shape a little piece of foil over it, stick some pinprick holes in it, and set a lump of hash into the little depression over the hole. I showed her how to put her palm on the end of the roll and wait until the cylinder filled with smoke, then inhale the whole cool tube of smoke from the other end.

"You know what I like about us?" she asked.

I stirred uneasily. Who was she talking about? Us? There was no us. "What?" I asked.

"We do such simple things. We do simple things for pleasure. We never talk about money. We never exchange all those money signals, key words, brand names. Everybody else talks about money. We never spend money, either, have you noticed? We don't even buy a token, we walk everywhere."

"Yeah, you're a cheap date," I laughed.

"My house is so full of possessions, and I spend so much time cleaning and sorting and maintaining them, sometimes I feel like some sort of suburban shopping bag lady."

"That's what you wanted, Mrs. Talbot," I reminded her.

"Yes," she said. She lay still for a while, gazing up at the ceiling, her hands pillowing her head. "Listen . . . I can't come in next week."

"Why not?"

"I'm sorry, I can't. The girls are going off to tennis camp. There's a lot to do to get ready. Then on the weekend we're going to drive them up to Maine. Stay overnight. It's a big deal. You know."

"No, I don't."

"Well, it is."

"If you can't make it into town, maybe I'll come out to Connecticut."

She turned her head and looked at me. There was such a look of surprise in her eyes. The idea had never occurred to her.

"Let George drive the kids to camp. You stay home. I'll come out for the weekend."

"Nooo . . ." she breathed.

"Why not? Why not, why not?"

"It just wouldn't work."

"It wouldn't do to intrude on your real life, is that it?"

"Nick, don't do it. Please don't come to Connecticut."

"There's no reason why I shouldn't. It has nothing to do with you, as a matter of fact. I have connections there. I have to see Doug about some materials for the kitchen. I know where he can get some slate, but I have to do some measuring to get an estimate." She was quiet for a while. "I won't be there," she said finally.

"That's OK, lady. I have a real life too."

She looked at me. She took one hand from behind her head and reached over to me, stroking my shoulder. "Don't do this," she said.

"Don't you do this," I replied. She was the one who started it. I realized now that she had come today to say this — that she wouldn't be here next week. I rolled over and wrapped myself around her, she was lying straight and still, with me curling around her — something like the photo of John Lennon with Yoko on *Rolling Stone*, if you remember that cover. She began to put her fingers through my hair, in a soothing kind of way, but I twisted my head away, I didn't want it. I kissed her eyes and her neck. Then I lowered my head and fastened onto her breast. I felt her settle patiently, as she must have for her children, waiting for the tension in the jaw to slacken with a small shudder and the greedy mouth to let go. Gradually she began to realize that I would not let go; nothing would make me let go. I felt her stomach contract, her nipple cautiously trying to remove itself, trying to slide through my teeth. "Nicholai!" she whispered. "Let me go." I lay like a deadweight. I was covering her everywhere, I could feel the tension everywhere, if she were on her feet she would be running. But her breast didn't move. The muscles in her shoulders bunched, but the breast held still. Was she thinking about me now at last? Me, Nicholai, son of aristocratic Russian émigrés? Me, Peter, spoiled son of a Greek shopkeeper? Or the me that Douglas Miller picked up at a SoHo party and who can't find quite the right bribe . . . "Nick, please," she said. "Let me go. I'll see. About the weekend. I'll see what I can do. Let me go." And then, of course, I did. I put my hands on her hips and turned her so that she lay facing me. I pressed my thumbs into the hollows in front of the hipbone. Then I pulled myself over her and began to fuck. A bed adds a lot of resiliency to fucking. A bed sinks, bounces. Goes along with the flesh. On the floor, everything is harder. Everything resists more. Sometimes the floor is exactly hard enough. It is exactly what you want.

I thought about the way Screwbosky defused sex by letting people call him by his nickname. When you'd hear the crowd yelling it, cheering it, it became more a name than a word. "Screw! You!" people would shout at concerts. I'd think about that sometimes when I was in bed with someone. Think about him, or think his name, Screw! Screw! in the rhythm of what I was doing.

I relaxed my grip and she got to her knees and then to her feet and took a couple of steps across the room. She just made it to the wall, where she leaned against it, her forehead and palms and one hip resting against it as if it was softer than the floor; I really loved her then, looking at her back, but I realized it was a kind of pity. I had to feel pity for her before I could feel the love. Against the wall, she was full of grace and desperation; I could have watched her forever. She ground against the wall, turning slowly to look at me, and her fingers caught the edge of the poster. She tore a long strip from the lower half. Actually it improved the poster, improved its relationship to the wall. It looked better now.

I jerked my hips in her direction. "You don't like it?" I asked.

"Not like that."

"Look, if you only like the things about me that give you pleasure, you're in trouble."

Later I realized that I was taking a chance, saying something like that to her, something that was absolutely true. But I find it works out OK to tell the absolute truth some of the time. It adds something to the whole project. For both people. I thought I'd explain that to Storey when I went out to Connecticut to talk to her about our relationship.

The relationship I had with Douglas Miller was based on his assumption that he was under obligation to me. He wasn't actually. What happened was that the first time we met was at a big loft party downtown on a Friday night, where there were a lot of fantastic people and even a few who were famous. Doug was out of his element, not having a very good time, but content to be there staring at everybody.

He had seated himself in a chair of regal proportions in the middle of the room, which was not helping him any. I watched him for a while, then went over and sat on the floor, my back straight against one carved leg of the chair as if I was chained there, the back of my head almost touching his hand, which rested on the chair's ornate arm. Now he looked interesting. All through the evening, people came over and talked to us and then walked away. It was like holding court. People approached, exchanged a few words, and gave place to the next courtier. It was a little trick that just happened to work, but Doug went on thinking I could do that anytime I wanted to. He thought that anytime I chose, I could turn anything into an occasion. That if I didn't, it was because I was mad or bored or stubborn.

So when I turned up at Perth Island, in the middle of his renovations, with piles of sand and gravel spoiling his lawn, he was not inhospitable. He was more discomfited by the fact that I had driven out in the cab. Nobody ever saw a taxi on Perth Island, except for the occasional Darien town taxi that ferried guests over from the train station. But mine was yellow, a real taxi. I obligingly stashed it in his garage, out of sight.

I would have to make up the mileage to Mike out of my own pocket. He was going to be mad when I didn't bring it back to the barn tonight. I'll be surprised if he ever lets me take it out again. He's tired of putting himself out for me, I can tell.

After I parked the cab, I looked around the main floor of Doug's house and told him it was coming along fine. It was. Most of the older houses there were bungalows and fishing camps built along the shore around the turn of the century. They are still unassuming to look at, with their odd shapes and shingled upper stories, but on the inside many of them have been elaborately remodeled. Doug was putting in a glass wall on the west, facing over the marsh and catching a sail's worth of the Sound to the south. I told Douglas that he'd be getting a great view.

"I'm going to go for a walk on the beach," I said. "Just needed to get out of town, unwind for a couple of hours."

"Suit yourself, Nick. Come back up for a beer later."

"Sure," I said.

I walked over to East Beach and took off my shoes and rolled up my jeans and walked back and forth at the waterline for a while, looking for shells or whatever the tide had brought in. Then I went over to the sea wall and sat there, leaning against a stone pillar, perfectly content to watch the small boats offshore, swinging on their anchors like weather vanes.

It wasn't long before I saw them. I figured she and the little girls — she had two — would walk along the beach one more time before the kids went away to camp. Sure enough, I heard a door bang along the edge of the low cliff that rose from the beach, and two skinny little girls, blond and suntanned, came scuffing along in their flip-flops, with Storey right behind them. When they reached the beach, they turned down the other way, where there's a long walk before the beach ends at Rocky Point. I jumped off the sea wall and walked in their footsteps, but faster.

When I came up behind her, I said hello, in the warmest way I could. I didn't want to alarm her, or announce my presence in some awkward way. She cut her eyes around at me and they almost rolled in her head — for a moment I could see only the whites of her eyes.

She took a few fast steps and her hands shot out and grabbed her kids' necks, not hard, but one hand on each. I could see the strength in her hands, and I knew how they felt on the backs of those little flower-stalk necks.

"Hi," I said to the kids. "I hear today's the big day. You're taking off for camp." They looked a little confused, wondering who I was and how I knew about them. But polite. They said yes, and that they couldn't wait; the younger one, the anxious one, said to Storey, "Mommy, did you pack my box of stationery? And Mille Bournes? And two bathing suits, *two?*"

"You're all packed," Storey assured her. "Now, let's get down to the Point and back. Pick up a stone along the way to leave at Rocky Point." They took off, walking down the beach like storks, their long skinny legs joined at bony knees so articulated they looked as if they'd bend either way. Maybe they were at an awkward age. "How old are they?" I asked.

"Pick a stone!" she called behind them. "It's part of our beach-clearing project," she explained to me. See how she's always thinking about something else? Women like that are responsible for gravity. If they ever let up, we'll all go streaming off the earth, like dandelion seeds. "Seven and nine," she said. "Lizzie's nine. The other one is Cora."

We walked along silently, in the same direction as the children, watching them grow smaller ahead of us. "We're leaving right after lunch," she said. "We're planning to drive to Bangor and spend the night, and then take the girls over to the camp tomorrow morning. We'll be back home sometime tomorrow evening."

"I have to talk to you."

"It will have to wait."

"It won't wait. We have to talk."

"It's not fair to pressure me like this. This is not the way to do it."

I felt like pointing out that it was going to work, but I decided to wait and let her see for herself. She sighed. "I'll come in to New York on Tuesday. Monday, even. Day after tomorrow. Can't it wait until then?"

I was silent, matching my pace to hers exactly. The sand was wet and took our footprints in deep impressions.

"Please, Nick!"

"Tell him you have a headache and can't go. It's too late to change all the plans now. He'll drive the kids up to camp. I'll come over later. We'll have a drink. We'll sit down and talk. We'll have plenty of time, no pressure."

She sighed again.

"You want them to get off to camp, don't you?"

She nodded. I could almost see her thinking of the packed foot-lockers. They were all ready to go.

"Or I could come over now —"

"No," she said. "No. I'll try to stay. We'll talk." She was silent for a moment. "I want to talk to you," she said. Ahead of us, the girls came to a halt and pinged their rocks onto the Point, where they rattled over the boulders and sent the gulls cawing into the air.

"Nick, could you go before they get back?"

I hated her for saying that. The kids had accepted me as a friend of hers. She didn't like that. She hated it. She would like it if no one but Storey knew of my existence.

"I'll see you later," I said, and touched her shoulder. She froze. You'd think I'd never touched her before, never done the things she had so willingly let me do. "Later," I repeated, loudly, and she managed to nod. Then she walked forward to meet the children, not looking back.

I was over at the bridge when they left. It was late in the afternoon. I guess they didn't get away as early as they had expected to. Maybe they waited to see if Storey's headache would go away.

I was watching about a dozen people, mostly kids, fish for shiners from the rocks below the bridge. It was high tide, and the little bay was so full that the grasses along the edge were drowning. The Land Rover was packed to the roof, and two bright faces in the front seat pressed against the window to watch the fishing while George slowed for the bump on the arch of the bridge. I stayed there for a while, leaning on the parapet and watching the activity. Then I walked over to Storey's house.

When you enter the house from the lane, you find yourself on the middle level, entering through the kitchen. On this side, it was a two-story house, with an old-fashioned gabled roof. On the opposite side, where the cliff drops down to the beach, it was three stories high. Each level had a deck — a wooden porch, really — with a railing around it and a wooden staircase going down. Storey let me look around while she was making coffee.

I really looked around, even going down to the basement, which was partly a garage and partly a workroom and storage area. George had stored the storm windows on the rafters up near the ceiling. Metal shelving along the walls held neatly labeled boxes, and a large sheet of pegboard displayed an assortment of tools. I had to admire George. Over near the doors that opened onto a paved area, there was a small Sunfish with its sail leaning against the wall and various beach chairs, floats, water toys, and life preservers.

Upstairs, I prowled around the dining room, reconstructing lunch from the remains on the table. One of the kids, probably Cora, had left nearly a whole plateful of food, partly hidden under a piece of toast. There was cold coffee in two yellow cups.

Storey was clinking away in the kitchen. She put a whole pot of coffee on a silver tray. The cups had saucers, and the milk was in a little crystal pitcher. She couldn't help making it attractive, I suppose. She couldn't help making domesticity seem worth the effort. She called out, asking me to come and take the tray into the living room. "Do you want something to eat?"

"No, just coffee," I said. "Come on, I'm pouring yours."

She came in and sat at a little writing desk, leaning on an elbow, stirring her cup.

"Nick," she said, and I waited. "Nick?" she asked. "Have I been unfair to you?" And then I knew she was about to be.

"We went out to dinner the other night," she went on. "Not really out, just here on the island. A dinner party. I was sitting next to a man, I think he's a stockbroker. Something on Wall Street. He talked to me at the dinner table, not about anything in particular, and then he suddenly said, 'You look like you're about to bolt. Are you a bolter?'"

"And I said No. No, no, no, you've got me all wrong. I'm not a bolter. And I'm not, Nick. I'm going to stay here, I'm going to stick with what I've got, and I'm not going to see you again."

"We're just going into another phase," I told her. "I feel it too. At first I just wanted to hear about Screwbosky, learn all I could about him. Now I want . . ."

"I know what you want," she said, looking around the room, which was beginning to grow dark. "But there's no place for you. There's no way you can come into my life. I never wanted that." She rubbed her head, as if she really had a headache.

"I thought about what you said, the last time I saw you in town. That I like only the things about you that gave me pleasure. When I got home that night, when I was getting ready to have my bath and go to bed, I took off my clothes and your smell rose up around me on the air. I thought to myself, it's true, I do like only the things about him that give me pleasure. Why else would I lie in bed with a neurotic boy?"

She looked at me apologetically and I stared back at her.

"I know you think that I was just taking, not giving. I'm sorry for that. But there's nothing more I can do."

"This is good," I said. "This is very good. We're communicating. Go on. Go on talking. We're talking about us now, I think it's an improvement."

She frowned at me, beginning to be a little angry. "You're not listening to what I'm saying."

"Don't talk to me like that."

"Listen to what I'm saying, Nick."

"I'm not your child."

"Can you just listen to me quietly for a minute, and then —"

"I'm not your child."

She met my eyes finally. "I know," she said.

I laughed when I saw the beds. I didn't know anybody who had twin beds. I pulled the covers off her bed and put us both in. The bedroom was dim, and the moon was just coming up over the water. I jumped up and opened the doors that led out onto the upper deck and let the evening air flow in. Every now and then I looked over at George's bed, as if he might be there quietly asleep, unnoticed.

"Isn't this nice?" I asked her. "Isn't it good? Isn't it worth it?"

She did not reply, but her hands slid over me, carving me up, pulling me together.

*

When it was over, and after her tears had dried, she said, "That's the last time."

"No," I said.

"But it was good. I want to be honest with you. It was good. I loved it."

"Don't be silly," I said. "It doesn't have to stop. I won't let it." I didn't say that as a threat, but she took it as one.

"Please don't cause trouble," she begged.

I grinned at her. If only she knew what a talent I have for causing trouble. It was a gift, almost. "Be reasonable and I won't," I said.

She was thoughtful. "I calculated the price I might have to pay for this . . . this adventure. It's high, but I can do it. If things are going to be unpleasant, awkward, I'm ready for it. Even if things become painful, I've figured that in too. But there's a point beyond which I won't go. You might as well know that now. That's why I stayed behind, to talk to you. The best thing is to end it now, while we can still be civil. While we can still be friends."

"We're not friends," I told her. "We're lovers. None of my friends are frustrated housewives."

She threw off the covers, exasperated. She walked to a closet and reached in blindly. She must have recognized what she was looking for by touch alone; she pulled out a dressing gown and put it on, knotting the sash tightly. "I'm going to make some more coffee," she said briskly, "and then we'll see about getting you to the train station. Come down when you're dressed."

She walked out, and I listened to her steps fading down the stairs. Bitch, I thought. I didn't get up immediately. I arranged the pillows under my head and watched the moon. I decided I liked it here. I wondered if I could drive George out of his wee little neat bed. I looked across at it. There was a night table between, with a lamp and a telephone extension on it. There was a lambskin rug between the beds, curling like waves in a channel. I wondered how often George crossed that moat.

The phone rang then. I could hear its echo downstairs. Without waiting for a second ring, I picked up the receiver. "Hello!" I said. "Hello?"

If only I had it on tape. By now Storey had picked up the downstairs phone, and we were all on the line.

"Is this George?" I interrupted him. "Did you get there all right? No trouble on the road? Did you —"

I was drowned out by a babble in my ear, Storey and George both talking at once. I replaced the receiver gently and left them to it.

Minutes later I heard her step on the stairs again. Her dressing gown made loud slithers of sound as she whirled through the door. I couldn't see her face, but I imagined that she had gone white with rage; as she talked, I could hear her teeth striking as her jaws snapped on her words.

"Get out of my house."

I lay still. It is always easy for me to stay calm when other people are angry.

"You have gone beyond any limits I recognize. Get out. Now, this minute. I have never been more serious in my life."

When she saw that I was not listening to her, she began to fling herself around the room, jerking open drawers and throwing things around in the closet.

"You haven't even told me how Screw died," I told her.

"He just died. That's all, he just died!"

"Nobody just dies. He was thirty-one years old, for God's sake. How did he die?"

"If I tell you, will you get out?"

I lay back with my arms behind my head, waiting.

"He got meningitis. He went to Europe, and he got meningitis. His fever was a hundred and five. He just got sick and died."

I lay still.

"I've told you. Now get out of here."

"I don't believe you," I said.

"If you won't leave, I will," she said, and left the room with her clothes under her arm.

I hoped she wasn't going to call in the cops. I reached over and took the telephone off the hook and laid it down on the night table.

The house was quiet. Reluctantly, I climbed out of bed and got dressed. I had wanted to stay the night. I opened the bedroom door and walked down the hall, passing the rooms that belonged to the children. It was quiet as a tomb, but I could imagine them there — Lizzie, the one Storey says never sleeps, with her transistor radio to her ear, and Cora, in the next room, grinding her teeth in her sleep.

Downstairs I heard a door open and close. Was it someone going out or coming in?

I retreated to the bedroom and let myself out onto the deck. From here I could simply descend to the beach and walk away. But I waited to see who was in the house.

I stood in the cool night air and peered in through the glass pane. The bedroom door opened slowly and spilled some light from the hall across the carpet. Douglas came creeping into the room like a blind mole. Doug! Of all people for Storey to summon to her rescue, Doug was about the most ineffectual soul she could have picked. I whistled at him, and he jumped as if he'd been prodded.

He came over to the door and looked out. "Nick?" he whispered.

"What do you want, Doug? Why don't you go home and send Storey back over here? Stay out of it."

"Nick, what in God's name are you up to? You're spoiling things for me, I can tell you that. You're going to ruin me."

"What will the neighbors say?" I asked mockingly.

"Now, come along," he said, reaching for me. He grabbed for my shoulder and got a piece of shirt, which he began to twist. I never liked him touching me.

I hit him on the jaw first and then buried my fist in his belly. He wasn't in shape, so that was enough. He staggered over to the railing and caught himself on it, retching to recover the breath I had driven out. "Take it easy, Doug," I advised him. I went down the outside staircase, to avoid going through the lighted house.

As I was starting down the second flight of stairs, Doug passed me. If I had blinked I would not have seen him. He fell like a diver. He must have leaned too heavily on the railing, lost his balance, and flowed over. He made no sound as he fell, but he did make a sound when he landed on the terrace below. I was passing the living room level. I peered into the room, where one lamp was lit, but it was empty. I went on down to the bottom. Doug lay in a dark heap. I went over to him and felt around. I couldn't feel any movement in his chest. I lifted his head and touched the back of it. My fingers went through his hair and seemed to keep going. I thought his hair was damp and his head was soft. I didn't think a head should feel that way. I reached up to feel my own scalp for comparison, and my fingers were tacky with wet. I'd stayed long enough, I decided. Things were getting messy. I wasn't in control anymore. I didn't even want to be. Enough is enough.

I walked along the side of the house to the alley, and then through the narrow lanes to Doug's house.

Storey sat in a straight chair, her hands clenched on the table in front of her. She was staring sightlessly at one of Doug's awful oil paintings. I could see her through the unfinished window that would have given Doug one of the best views on the island. In a few minutes, I thought, she'll realize how long Doug's been gone. She'll walk over to her house to see what is going on. How in the hell is she going to explain the events of the night? Jesus, George may think it was Doug who answered the phone! It was a mess, all right. And the ironic thing was that I would probably never even know how it all turned out.

I opened the garage doors quietly. I opened the door to the cab, but I didn't get in. I released the brakes and put the gears in neutral and pushed the car out of the garage and was a few yards down the street before I jumped in and started the motor. Fifteen minutes later I was on the New England Thruway, heading for Manhattan.

There was not much traffic, and the drive calmed me down. I was still angry, of course. I should never have let Storey get under my skin like that. I should never have wanted anything from her. All I wanted, really, was some information. I am thinking of getting into music myself, the production end of it. And old Doug. Doug had always been dispensable. Now another suburban type would move in and start yet another remodeling job on Doug's new house.

A little past Stamford, I drew even with a Chevrolet in the lane on my right. There was enough illumination from the dashboard to see the occupant. It was a woman. Pretty, as far as I could see, and completely absorbed in the road ahead. She was driving with one hand. The other hand was out of sight, buried in the V of her shirt. I watched her for a while, turning my head from the highway to the other car, keeping a steady speed. I suddenly figured out what she was doing. Examining the right quadrant, the left quadrant, checking the crinkly flesh around the aureole. She was doing a routine breast check, just like she'd been taught or read in a manual or saw on TV. I laughed when I'd figured it out. I tried to catch her eye, to give her the old thumbs-up signal, encouraging, but traffic was picking up and I couldn't stay even with her car. I've always liked women like her — softening up a little, allowing themselves a sag here and there, of the flesh, of the spirit. They're more touching then. If I could have caught her eye, I bet I could have got her to pull over, after we got off the highway, and go with me for a drink. But it's probably a good thing I didn't make contact, because I had to get home and get my stuff cleared out.

As soon as I got to my apartment, I listened to my machine for messages. There was nothing important. If Sophie had called, she had not left a message. I retaped my recorded greeting.

"Hello. This is the telephone butler at 736-9780. Is this by any chance Peter's mother? He has left a message for you. He may want to sleep at home tonight. Could you move those boxes out of his old room for him? Thank you."

I rewound the tape. I'll leave it set up while I pack, then I'll take the machine with me. I paid good money for that.

I'm going to dump all the tapes into a plastic garbage bag. All these tapes have to go. I've got one tape of Storey; that's going too. The tape that's on now — well, I can do several things with it, can't I? I can erase it — just run it through the machine with the Record button on. I can mail it to Storey, she could probably use it to clear her fair name. Or I can leave it here for the police to find, after she tells them where to look for me. It's like a confession, after all, isn't it? Although I don't know whether it could be used in court. Wouldn't it be like self-incrimination? A violation of my civil rights?

Or I can dump it in the trash tonight, along with everything else that has my real name on it, and everything connecting me with Nicholai. Son of Russian émigrés. Artist and lover.

JOSH PRYOR

Wrong Numbers

FROM *Zoetrope*

DORA SPARKS was alone in her office when her ten-thirty walked in looking every bit as unemployable as she'd expected. He was tall, bald by choice — she could see the razed roots of his hair lurking just beneath the shiny dome of his scalp — and had the sinewy tattooed arms of a carnival-ride operator. She made sure the electroplated gold letter opener Pac Bell had given her was in easy reach. IN RECOGNITION OF A JOB WELL DONE was engraved on the blade.

"So, Mr. Karloff," said Dora. "What brings you to Pac Bell?"

"A man's gotta eat," said Karloff.

"Karloff . . . That's an interesting name. Wasn't he a vampire or something?"

"No relation." Karloff smiled. His teeth were big and yellow.

Dora pretended to study his résumé. When she looked up he was holding the letter opener, familiarizing himself with its heft the way a surgeon might with a new scalpel. There were flies tattooed on his knuckles.

"This is nice," he said. "What do I have to do to get one?"

Dora had been friends with Marcy since she'd been hired by Human Resources. Marcy was one of the last of the innocents. True, she was only half Dora's age, but the distance separating them may as well have been light-years. Dora had taken it upon herself to make sure her friend didn't go through life with blinders on. Today Marcy had wanted to know why she wasn't going to hire Karloff.

"Just because he didn't gouge my eyes out doesn't mean I should give him a job."

"But all his references checked out," said Marcy. "His last boss said he was a super-nice guy and a real whiz with phones."

"Are we talking about the same Karloff? Bald, scary looking, teeth like a horse . . ."

Marcy pinched the crust from her egg-salad sandwich and tossed it to the pigeons. "He looked a little rough."

"The guy was a ghoul! He probably drinks blood with dinner."

"I heard George Johanson's going to hire him anyway," said Marcy. "I guess he ran into him leaving your office this morning. Apparently they know each other from AA."

"Good for George Johanson. Let *him* shoot himself in the foot. I'm not going to send that creep into a complete stranger's house to install phone lines. Once he gets inside, who knows what he might do."

That night when Dora got home her husband, Frank, had already set the table. There were three place settings instead of the usual two. She sure wasn't in the mood for company. Marcy had been right. George Johanson had gone ahead and hired Karloff despite Dora's recommendation. Couple of drunks, she thought. I hope you both fall off the wagon. "Sweetheart," she called. "I'm home."

Dora could hear Frank's voice above the hiss of running water. "I'm in the kitchen."

A thick layer of steam obscured the ceiling. She could hardly see the light fixtures. A pot of water boiled furiously on the stove. Dora blazed a trail through the steam and reduced the burner setting to simmer. Frank was hunched over the sink stripping the wilted leaves from a head of lettuce. The garbage disposal sputtered and growled.

"Oh, there you are."

"I thought I'd give you a hand with dinner," said Frank.

Dora flicked off the disposal and kissed him on the cheek. "We'd better open a window before the wallpaper starts to peel."

Frank continued to pull apart the head of lettuce. He was drawing dangerously close to the pale yellow leaves at its core that almost no one likes to eat. "Eileen called me at work today. She wants to stay with us for a couple of weeks."

"I thought she was serving a life sentence."

"*Six months.*"

"Well, I don't want her staying in my house."

"Your house?" He began building a salad using the jaundiced leaves.

"She just got out of jail for crying out loud," said Dora. "She's an ex-con!"

"She's my sister. You make her sound like such a shady character. She's not a necrophiliac for Christ's sake! She was in for mail fraud."

"She's a drug addict, Frank. What do you think she was spending the money on?"

"I already told her yes."

Dora didn't try to hide the anger in her voice. "What if she steals something?"

"Like what?"

"Our wedding silver. She could sell it to buy crack or whatever it is she does."

"Dexatrim," said Frank. "Eileen was addicted to diet pills."

The nerve! Showing up at our front door fresh out of jail and expecting me to pay for the taxi. Dora would've rather reached into the garbage disposal when it was running than give big fat Eileen money out of her own purse. It was bad enough that they were going to be providing her with room and board. "More salad, sweetie?" Dora asked.

Eileen studied the anemic-looking greens in front of her. "What about you?"

"Don't worry about me," said Dora. "You're our guest." Avoiding Frank's eyes, she scraped the oil-soaked remnants onto Eileen's plate.

"You'll have to pardon the condition of the lettuce," said Frank. "I didn't have time to run to the store."

"Don't be silly," said Eileen. "The center leaves are the most tender."

Dora cleared her throat. "So . . . Eileen. How's it feel to be on the outside?"

"Dora!" Frank looked annoyed.

Eileen stared at the tomato wedge on the end of her fork. "Beats the hell out of sharing a sweaty little cell with a bunch of sex-crazed dykes."

Frank rolled his eyes. "Dora, she's pulling your leg. It was minimum security. I was there. She could've busted out with a banana
and bus fare."

"Frank!" said Dora. "Don't interrupt."

"Put it this way," said Eileen. "The guards don't leave chocolates
on your pillow at bedtime."

When Dora got home from work the following night, Eileen was
stretched out on the living-room sofa watching TV.

"Did anyone call today?" Dora asked. The cordless phone was sitting on the coffee table next to an empty box of Ritz crackers.

"The phone's been ringing off the . . ." Before Eileen could finish, the phone rang.

Dora answered. The voice on the other end sounded Chinese.
"I'm sorry," said Dora. "You must have the wrong number."

"Videophone?" asked Eileen.

"How'd you know?"

"Apparently your number's listed in the Korean newspaper under an advertisement for some kind of videophone. Must be a heck
of a deal. They've been calling all day."

Dora suggested they turn off the ringer, but Eileen said she was
expecting an important call from her probation officer.

By the time Frank got home the phone was quiet. When Dora told
him about the misprint he suggested she call the Korean newspaper and clear things up.

"Maybe if Eileen's busy answering the phone all day it'll keep her
out of trouble," said Dora.

"I'm sure she's got more important things to do."

"She was watching TV and stuffing her face when I got home."

"Give her time to adjust," said Frank.

"She should be looking for work."

"Oh, Dora," Frank sighed, "leave her alone."

Dora lay in bed that night thinking about the possibilities of a
phone that allowed you to see the person you were talking to. If
everyone had videophones, she wouldn't need to conduct job interviews in person anymore. She could simply dial a prospective
employee and give him a quick once-over. She wouldn't need the
letter opener.

*

Marcy wasn't at work the following morning. When Dora asked Judy the receptionist if Marcy was sick, she was told that Marcy had been fired for having sex with George Johanson on company time. The two of them were supposed to be working after hours on the new database when Jerry the janitor had caught them "going at it like a couple of rabbits" in the middle of the conference table.

"Who around here didn't see that coming a million miles away?" whispered Judy. "Those two couldn't keep their hands off each other."

Dora had to swallow her gum to keep from choking on it.

When Dora got home that night the house was empty. She laid her hand on top of the TV. It wasn't even warm. She half expected to find Eileen hiding out in the pantry, inhaling her nonstick cooking spray from a paper bag. It was the kind of thing drug addicts with no money did to get high. The average suburban home was like a drugstore to these people. But the pantry was empty.

Dora checked the answering machine. The message display flashed "20." One of the calls was from Marcy. Her voice sounded different somehow — not like the Marcy who'd been shocked to hear that certain men and women preferred sex with animals. The nineteen other messages were people calling about the videophone.

Seven-thirty rolled around and still no Frank or Eileen. Dora was inventorying her jewelry when the phone rang. "Hello." She could hear a woman's shrill laughter in the background but there was no reply. "Eileen, is that you?" Nothing. "If you're calling about the videophone you have the wrong number." Dora was about to hang up when a man replied. His voice had the rehearsed, overfriendly tone of a salesman.

"Hi. My name's Bill Pratt and I'm calling on behalf of Alcoholics Anonymous. We're sponsoring a raffle to benefit alcohol-awareness programs in neighborhood high schools."

"Sorry, but I'm really busy right now." Dora wanted to check the wedding silver before Eileen showed up.

"Everyone who donates receives two tickets to the Splendini Brothers Carnival."

"I'm sure it's wonderful," said Dora, "but I told you I'm busy." She hung up.

Dora was halfway to the dining room when the phone rang again. This time she grabbed the cordless. "Hello."

"Yes, I'm calling about the videophone." It was the same over-friendly voice.

"Look," said Dora, "I don't think you're very funny."

"You're right. It's just that it's such a worthy cause I feel like I should give you a chance to redeem yourself."

"Please don't call here again," said Dora. She beeped the line dead.

Dora had hardly taken a step when the cordless went off in her hand. She jumped. "I know someone who's in AA," she warned. "Don't make me report you to the head drunk."

"Look, lady . . . I used to have a drinking problem. If you'd talked to me this way a couple of years ago, I would've found the nearest bar and drunk myself into a rage thinking about you tucked away all safe and sound behind your goddamn telephone! You have AA to thank that I don't come over there right now and bash your fucking brains out!"

Dora was on her third glass of wine (or was it her fourth?) when Frank and Eileen walked in the front door. They were laughing and carrying on like old college buddies.

"Guess what," said Frank. "Eileen found a job."

"I'll be back on my feet in no time," said Eileen.

"Congrats," said Dora. When she tried to stand, her legs gave out and she slumped back into the cushions.

"What's wrong, sweetie?" Frank asked. "You don't look so hot."

"A man threatened me over the phone."

Frank's smile lost its robust curve. *"What man?"*

"I don't know. He said he was calling for donations for AA and wanted to bash my brains in because I wouldn't give him any money."

"That's one way of going about it," said Eileen.

"Oh shut up, you stupid cow!"

"Dora!" said Frank. "Don't talk to Eileen that way."

Eileen put her hand on Frank's shoulder. "It's okay. I'd be a little edgy too." Eileen acknowledged Dora with a frown. "I'm gonna call my probation officer and tell her the good news."

As soon as Eileen was out of the room Dora buried her face in Frank's chest and cried until her tear ducts ached. That night she lay in bed alongside her snoring husband wondering what Bill Pratt — if that was really his name — looked like. Probably no worse than some of the creeps she interviewed. Besides, as long as they were separated by who-knows-how-many miles of phone line there was nothing he could do to her.

When Dora called Marcy from work the next day a man answered the phone. "I'm sorry," said Dora. "I must have the wrong number."

"Dora?"

"Who's this?"

"I thought I recognized your voice. It's George . . . George Johanson. Hold on. Marcy's right here."

Dora could hear the rustle of bed linens and her friend's little-girl giggle.

"Howdy, stranger," said Marcy. "Long time, no see."

Dora wanted to hang up. "If you're busy, I can call back."

"George and I are eloping!"

"Excuse me?"

"We leave for Bora Bora mañana." Marcy squealed and dropped the phone. *"George!* Stop that." She retrieved the phone. "I would've told you sooner . . ."

"Marse — *Please!* Everyone in the office saw it coming."

"You sounded so surprised," said Marcy.

Dora changed the subject. "Ask George if he knows someone from AA named Bill Pratt."

Marcy held the receiver away from her face and asked. "Nope," she said. "Should he?"

"Guess not."

"Well, sweetie . . ." said Marcy. "We still got a lotta packin' to do. Wish us luck."

Dora could hear George in the background. "Bye, Dora!" he shouted. She was glad she didn't have a videophone. She could picture him lying in bed, his spent penis drooping between his slack thighs, a gin-and-tonic smile warping his shapeless lips as not-so-innocent Marcy attempted to straddle him for the third or fourth time since sunrise.

If anyone could cheer Dora up it was Frank. She dialed him at work and was greeted by a young man she didn't recognize. "Good afternoon," he said in a professional-sounding voice. "FPI."

"Excuse me," said Dora. "I must've dialed incorrectly."

"What number are you trying to reach?"

Dora recited the number of Frank's direct line.

"I see what happened," said the young man. "We're four three *five* three. You must have reversed the last two numbers."

"I'm sorry . . ."

"No need to apologize. Perhaps I can be of assistance."

"Well," said Dora, "now that I've got you . . ."

She gave a detailed account of the disturbing call she had received from Bill Pratt, and how at the very least she thought they could run a background check and make sure he wasn't another Jeffrey Dahmer. The young man listened attentively, his *hmms* and *hunhs* intimating a familiarity and understanding that Dora was sure came from long-term exposure to the criminal mind. He hadn't said a word and already she was feeling better.

"I don't know how to say this, ma'am," he said at last, "but I think you misunderstood me. This is the F *Pee* I, not the F *Bee* I. I work for the Film Preservation Institute."

"I feel like such an idiot."

"Don't. Happens all the time."

"I'm sure you've got better things to do than listen to other people's sob stories."

"The guy you told me about sounds like a real nutcase."

Dora liked this person. "If you don't mind my asking . . ."

"I was hoping you would. Mainly we document and preserve non-mainstream endeavors in cinema. Obscure stuff."

"I don't mean to sound dumb . . ."

"Film noir," he said. "The wonderful world of demise. We currently house the world's largest collection of snuff."

"Snuff?"

"You know . . . Boy meets girl. Girl invites boy back to her place. Boy dismembers girl with a bone saw while the camera rolls. That kind of shit."

"That's awful!" said Dora.

"Think of it as a magic kingdom for psychopaths."

Dora was overcome by a sudden chill. "Bill . . ." she asked. "Is that you?"

"God, Dora. I wish I could see your expression. I bet Meryl fucking Streep couldn't capture the look in your eyes."

Dora's mouth fell open like a garage-sale nutcracker. *He knows my name!*

When Dora came to, Jerry the janitor was giving her mouth-to-mouth. She nearly gagged on his tongue. Everyone in the office was huddled over her as though she were dead. The top of her blouse was unbuttoned. It had been Jerry's idea to massage her heart until the ambulance arrived.

When Frank tucked Dora into bed that afternoon she asked him to check the answering machine.

"Already did," he said. "It's empty. Eileen called the newspaper yesterday and told them about the misprint."

"Oh," said Dora. The little blue pills the doctor had given her made her face feel rubbery. "I thaw she's whirring."

"She starts Saturday."

"I tho hap fo'er."

Frank kissed her on the forehead. "We'll be downstairs if you need us."

"Frine?"

"Yes, sweetheart?"

"He cah meeth by my name." Dora tried to sit up but the room was spinning.

"He probably got it out of the phone book."

"Frine," said Dora. "Ina wunnoo die."

When Dora awoke, the house was quiet. "Frank," she called. "Frank!" But there was no answer. He was probably in the kitchen with the door closed. She remembered Jerry the janitor sticking his tongue in her mouth and stopped in the bathroom to gargle with Listerine. She swished the bitter solution around until the roof of her mouth tingled and burned. The minty vapors made her light-headed.

She descended the stairs and tottered into the living room, still slightly off balance from the drugs. Eileen was lying on her back in the middle of the floor with the cordless pressed to her ear.

"I didn't know you were still up," said Dora.

Eileen looked surprised and cupped her hand over the receiver. "It's only eight-thirty," she said. "How do you feel?" She sat up and crossed her legs Indian-style.

"I feel great." Dora staggered to her left and almost knocked over the lamp Frank's aunt had given them for their twentieth wedding anniversary. "Where's your brother?"

"He went out to get you some wonton soup," said Eileen. "He should be back any minute."

"Who you talkin' to?"

"Some guy," said Eileen. "I think it's a wrong number."

"Then hang up."

"It wouldn't be polite."

"Hang up! It might be him!" Dora could feel her legs start to give. She staggered into the entry, knocking over the coatrack, and unplugged the cordless at the base.

"That wasn't very nice," Eileen called from the living room.

At that moment Frank's key bit into the dead bolt and the door swung open. Dora collapsed to her knees and sobbed until her eyes were nearly swollen shut. Frank helped her to bed and fed her another one of the little blue pills.

Despite Frank's suggestion that she take a few days off to regain her strength, Dora wanted to get on with her life. There was no reason why everything shouldn't be business as usual. The first day back at work she hired everyone she interviewed. Men without references, men with little or no experience, men whose faces twitched when asked if they had ever committed a felony, men with bad BO. She kept the letter opener close by, often clutching it in her hand beneath her desk. She had even started carrying it home with her in her purse. Go for the eyes, she would repeat to herself in the dimly lit bowels of the parking garage. Go for the eyes.

Toward the end of the week, she was interviewing a volunteer from the Center for Eating Disorders — *a vomit jockey!* — when it dawned on her that whoever was stalking her phone lines was probably someone she had turned down for a job. Someone with a motive and an intimate understanding of telecommunications. She was sure of it! Only who?

The detective Dora spoke with epitomized the too-little-too-late stories she'd heard about on the news. She told him about the misprinted ad for the videophone in the Korean newspaper and the menacing stranger who had been harassing her ever since.

"I'm sorry, Mrs. Sparks," said the detective, "but you yourself admit to having initiated contact with this person."

"I don't know how he did that," explained Dora. "I was trying to call my husband."

"Be that as it may . . ." he said. "We need more to go on than a few wrong numbers. Nine times out of ten nothing bad comes of something like this."

In spite of the detective's reassurance, she was unable to escape the feeling that the odds were somehow stacked against her.

Dora could no longer sleep without the aid of the little blue pills. Overcome by exhaustion, she was forced to take a leave of absence. Mostly she lay in bed writing letters to people she would have usually telephoned. Although Frank was dead set against her using drugs, he agreed to allow her to finish out the prescription. By then they would have an unlisted number and everything would be back to normal.

Eileen's first day on the job was a Saturday, the same day, coincidentally, that Dora finished her pills. It had been days since she had heard from the voice. Maybe he had tired of her. She looked in the bathroom mirror and saw that her eyes were underscored with dark circles. A little sunlight would do her good. She sheathed the letter opener in her bathrobe pocket and ventured outside to collect the mail. Among the catalogs and coupon books was a postcard from Marcy. In less than thirty words her friend detailed how well George filled out a Speedo, and then asked if Dora would pick up her mail. Buoyed with a sense of purpose, Dora showered, shaved her armpits, and slipped into her favorite sundress. Once on the road she rolled down the windows and put on a tape that she and Frank liked to listen to when they were feeling romantic. She turned the volume up so loud she could hardly hear herself think.

She was lip-synching the words to "Stand by Me" when her cell phone started ringing. At first she thought it was part of the song, a secondary instrument orbiting the periphery of the main melody — a tambourine maybe. However, when the song ended the phone was still ringing. Without thinking, Dora ejected the tape and took the call on the speaker.

"You naughty girl." The voice seemed to come from everywhere at once. It was invasive, godlike. "Driving under the influence."

"Leave me alone!" cried Dora. She tried to hang up but the phone would not disconnect.

"Dora, sweetie, I'm worried about you. You sound out of sorts. Are you sure those pills you've been popping aren't affecting your judgment?"

"What do you want from me?"

"I'm calling on behalf of the annual Red Cross blood drive. Of course, you'd have to sober up before we could accept a donation."

"I don't . . . under . . . stand."

"Blood, Dora," said the voice. "Vampire's burden. You never know when someone you love might need it."

Unable to endure another second of the sadistic baritone, she ripped the phone out of the center console and threw the up-rooted unit out the window. She swung a U-turn into the oncoming lane, setting off a chorus of angry horns, and floored the accelerator for home.

Dora ran over the mailbox pulling into the driveway, and staggered to the front door like a wounded game animal. Once inside, she engaged the dead bolt and peeked through a slat in the shutters, expecting the oxidized flanks of a van or a long, low-slung sedan to creep by the front of the house. She was certain she had been followed, but the street was empty. Trembling in fear, she realized she'd left the letter opener on the passenger seat. Who was she kidding? If the voice wanted her dead, she was dead. He knew her every move. She had even considered the possibility that it was her own husband. But that was crazy. This was real life, not a talk show. Frank loved her.

Half crazed, Dora filled a coffee cup with gin, ran a cold bath, and went from room to room yanking the phones, wires and all, out of the wall. One by one she committed them to the bathtub, silencing each one. By the time she went after the cordless, water had overflowed the coral-pink fiberglass tub and was spreading across the bathroom floor. Not finding the receiver in its cradle, she ransacked the guest room, scattering Eileen's meager possessions with the force of a tornado. Frank's convict sister had spent nearly every night for the past week mumbling into the AWOL cordless.

By the time Frank got home, the overflow water from the bathtub had transformed the carpet in their bedroom and the entire upstairs hall into a stain-resistant marshland. Dora could hear her husband swearing as he slogged up the last few steps and peered into the guest room where she lay in a quivering heap among the unfolded clothes and thumb-worn *People* magazines, bawling her eyes out.

"Jesus, Dora!" Frank shouted. "The house is sinking. Call a plumber . . . *Do something!*"

Dora looked into his eyes. "It's you, isn't it, Frank?"

Frank shook his head as if to say, *You poor creature.* And like that he was gone.

Dora crawled after him. The carpet squished under her hands and knees. As she reached the bathroom door the sound of running water halted abruptly and she could hear Frank cursing under his breath. When she peeked inside, he was staring at the bathtub. With a flick of his hand he sent a tube of dandruff shampoo gliding across the silvery surface like a toy battleship. He must have sensed her presence because he spoke without turning his head. "For Christ's sake, Dora!" he said, submerging his arm to the elbow in an attempt to retrieve the drowned telephones. "Have you lost your mind?"

Dora was looking at the TV in the living room when Eileen walked in wearing her uniform from Hot Dog on a Stick. She smelled of corn-dog batter and deep-fryer grease. Frank was upstairs shouting into the cordless. Dora didn't dare ask where he had found it.

"What's going on?" Eileen wanted to know.

Even as Dora explained what had happened she was not convinced any of it was real. The last two weeks had been like living in a nightmare.

For half an hour, Frank had called every carpet cleaner in the yellow pages hoping to find someone to vacuum up the water before the floorboards started to rot. Apparently everyone had gone home for the night. Frank had ordered Dora to stay on the couch and not to move. Eileen patted her on the head and went upstairs to help clean up the mess with bath towels, bedsheets, and anything else absorbent they could find.

That night Dora lay awake well past midnight, haunted by the cold godlike voice that had possessed her car. She craved the dreamless oblivion of the little blue pills but the prescription bottle was empty. She'd checked it twice. She had even read the warn-

ing labels on every product in the medicine cabinet looking for
something that "may cause drowsiness," but the strongest thing she
could find was a crinkled tube of fungicide that had made her lips
go numb.

Dora could hear Eileen's laughter warbling in the thin-walled
confines of the guest room. She slipped out of bed and tiptoed
down the hall. The damp carpet was cold beneath her bare feet.
Despite Frank's efforts it still squished when she walked. Soon she
was standing outside the guest-room door, her need for the little
blue pills as deeply felt as the nerve endings prickling beneath the
surface of her skin. The door was slightly ajar. Eileen was lying on
the bed, the cordless pressed to one ear. "I already told you who it
was," she said. "Don't even joke like that. It's not funny." She buried her face in the pillow and cackled like a witch.

Eileen jumped when Dora pushed open the door. "I've gotta
go," she said into the phone. "You can tell me all about it tomorrow
night."

"Hot date?" Dora asked.

"We'll see." Eileen drew her knees in close to her chest and
pulled her T-shirt down over her legs. A glittery decal on the front
read A SMILE IS LIKE A BUTTERFLY . . . IT GOES WHEREVER
IT PLEASES AND IT PLEASES WHEREVER IT GOES. Little yel-
low-and-blue butterflies fluttered around the stylized letters. "So,
what brings you to this neck of the woods?"

Dora could picture the phones lying on the bottom of the bathtub. They reminded her of the personal effects left behind by the
victims of a shipwreck. "I couldn't sleep," she said.

"Insomnia's the pits."

"I was hoping you might know a secret remedy."

"I could warm you some milk in the microwave."

"I was thinking of something a little stronger," said Dora.

"What about the pills the doctor gave you?"

"The jerk only gave me enough for four days."

"Did you try taking a hot bath?"

Dora didn't want to go anywhere near a bath. It would be like returning to the scene of a crime. *"Hel-lo!"* Dora knocked on her own
head. *"Is anyone home?"*

Eileen frowned.

"I'm not asking for heroin!" said Dora. "All I want is something
that'll knock me out for a few hours."

"I don't have anything."

"Don't act so fucking pure." Dora leveled her index finger at Eileen. "I know all about your seedy little life."

Eileen's lower lip trembled. Tears wet her eyes. She looked small sitting on the bed, childlike. "Why are you doing this?" she pleaded.

"There must be someone you can call."

"I'm on probation. If I get caught doing anything illegal, they'll put me back in jail."

"Be a bitch then," said Dora. "But if you're hiding anything from me, I swear I'll find it." With that she yanked out the dresser drawers one by one and dumped their contents on the floor: maraschino-cherry nail polish, a black-and-white photo of Frank and Dora at their wedding, a Fleet's enema, tampons, men's XL T-shirts, a half-eaten Snickers, black control-top panties, a children's illustrated Bible, a rubber-banded stack of legal documents . . .

Dora was tearing through the pile on her hands and knees when she noticed Eileen reaching out to her. "Don't you dare touch me!" hissed Dora. "Or I swear to God I'll wrap that stupid T-shirt around your neck and hang you out the window so all the neighbors can see what a little tramp you are!"

Eileen recoiled as if snakebitten. "Please, Dora," she sobbed. "You're scaring me."

When Eileen's date arrived, Dora was propped up on the sofa, the episode in the guest room as distant now as the dull thud of his knock on the front door. Despite Frank's earlier objections, he now agreed medication was the way to go. At least until their lives were back in order. He did not want a repeat of last night. The new pills were pink and football shaped. They suffused her with a warm sense of well-being that tickled the base of her skull. Carbonation for the mind. Millions and millions of tiny bubbles . . . She could hear them whispering her name. *"Dora . . . Dora . . ."*

The fog cleared and she could see Eileen hovering over her, her smiling face virtually indistinguishable from the wilted get-well balloon bouquet Frank had brought home — what was it? — two, maybe three days ago.

"I want you to meet someone," said Eileen.

Dora could see Frank standing in front of the TV, his arms and legs and face much longer than she remembered.

"No," said Eileen. "Over here."

Before Dora's brain could transmit the necessary impulses to her neck muscles, she was descended upon by another face. Teeth bared, it seemed as though the grinning well-wisher would not stop until his canines were firmly planted in her throat.

"Dora," said Eileen. "This is Max." A dark-haired man in khaki slacks and a powder-blue oxford shirt stood over her.

"I know Dora," said Max. "We work together." He smiled and gave a little wave.

Dora thought she would swallow her tongue.

"I'll be darned," said Frank. "How'd you and my sister meet?"

"Wrong number," said Eileen. "Max called about the videophone and we just started talking."

"Best mistake I ever made," said Max.

For the first time in a week Dora's mind was besieged by a horrible clarity: the man from AA who wanted to bash her brains in, the snuff films, the godlike voice in her car just yesterday. It was Karloff! Immobilized by fear, she desperately tried to locate her husband, his face drawn in a wicked fun-house grin all the way across the room. "It's him, Frank!" she croaked. "He's the one who's been calling me!"

"Oh, for Christ's sake, Dora . . ." Frank turned to Karloff. "My wife's been under a terrible strain lately. You'll have to forgive her."

Karloff looked at Dora, then at Frank, and nodded gravely.

"But it is, Frank!" cried Dora. "I swear!"

"I don't have to take this shit!" Eileen shouted.

"Eileen — *please*," said Frank. He knelt in front of Dora. "Sweetheart . . . Look at yourself. Yesterday you thought it was me. We'll get through this but you have to make an effort. Now apologize to Max."

Dora turned her attention to Karloff. "Show them your tattoos!" she said. "I bet you didn't know he was wearing a wig!"

Karloff looked embarrassed. "Chemo," he said. "A few months ago I had this thing with my prostate. I'm still not comfortable with my new look."

"We're outta here!" said Eileen. She grabbed Karloff by the arm and stormed out of the house.

Dora dragged herself from the sofa and went after them. "You can't let her leave with him!" she begged. "He's crazy!" Frank strait-jacketed her with his arms and kicked the door closed.

Dora watched through the window as Karloff and Eileen pulled away from the curb in his red-and-white Pac Bell van. She could see the felled mailbox lying on the front lawn.

"It's okay," Frank whispered in her ear, "Everything is going to be just fine."

When Frank called Dora down to dinner Friday night, she thought it would be just the two of them. Eileen had been spending most of her free time with Karloff. With each passing day the pink football-shaped pills plunged Dora more deeply into a wonderful walking trance. As she descended the stairs, she could see the eager faces awaiting her arrival.

Frank. Eileen. Karloff.

All week Frank had been going on about what a nice guy Max was and how good he was for Eileen. "Dora, honey," he said. "The three of us chipped in and got you a get-well present. It was Max's idea."

Karloff smiled timidly and nodded. He was wearing a blond wig that made him look like a young Robert Redford.

Eileen threw her arms around Dora and said, "I'm sorry for being so insensitive. I know how rough the last couple of weeks have been on you."

Dora wondered if she was dreaming, an extension of the same prolonged nightmare. The voice, Karloff's wig, the green-and-yellow polka-dotted box in the center of the coffee table.

"Well," said Frank. "Aren't you going to open it?"

Eileen bounced on her toes like a little girl. "Open it," she chimed.

Dora plopped down on the sofa and began stripping away the wrapping. She hadn't realized how strong the pink football-shaped pills were until the last of the paper had been removed. She stared at the package in utter bewilderment, the odd markings on its surface no more familiar to her than if she had been attempting to decipher Egyptian hieroglyphs.

"Don't try to read it, silly," said Eileen. "It's Korean."

"It's a videophone," said Frank.

"Max thought of it," Eileen said proudly. "He heard about our phone shortage."

"It's the best on the market," said Karloff. "I have the same one at home."

"This way you'll always know who you're talking to," said Frank.
Dora didn't know what to say.

Eileen beamed. "Max said he'd come over Sunday and set it up."

"No, no . . ." said Dora. "I'm sure Pac Bell wouldn't mind sending
someone over during the week."

"Sunday'll be just fine, Max," said Frank. "I've got a golf date but
Dora will be here." Frank put his arm around her. "Won't you,
honey?"

Frank hadn't been gone five minutes when Karloff showed up
bright and early Sunday morning. Although Dora hadn't seen
Eileen since the night they had given her the videophone, she assumed she was at work dipping skewered hot dogs in corn batter.
Drawing on two pills' worth of courage Dora released the dead bolt
and opened the door. If she was going to die, at least she wouldn't
feel it.

"Good morning," said Karloff.

Dora was surprised at how respectable he looked in his freshly
pressed uniform and blond wig. If anything, he now looked too
good for the job she'd denied him. "Well, aren't you the cat's
meow," she said.

Karloff made as if to adjust an invisible bow tie.

For a moment they just smiled at each other. At last Dora said,
"Come in."

Although it hadn't rained in weeks, Dora was impressed that
Karloff wiped his feet on the doormat before entering. "Where do
you want it?" he asked.

Dora noticed an array of potentially lethal instruments dangling
from Karloff's tool belt. So this is it, she thought. Why hadn't she
just given him the job — let someone else take a screwdriver in the
heart?

"The videophone . . ." he said. "What room do you want it in?"

"I'm sorry," said Dora. "I'm still waking up. How about the
kitchen."

Dora was amazed at how quickly and efficiently Karloff worked.
Watching him install the videophone, she forgot how frightened
she was. Maybe she had been wrong. Maybe he wasn't such a bad
guy. "You know, Max," said Dora. "I have a confession to make."

"You don't like the phone here."

"No, no. You're doing a beautiful job. It's just that . . . Remember when I interviewed you?"

Karloff secured the base to the wall and looked at her.

"Well," Dora said, "I wasn't going to hire you."

"I know. Marcy told me."

"You just . . ."

"I know I'm not the most clean-cut-looking guy."

"I'm so ashamed of myself."

Karloff smiled. "Don't give it a second thought. If I were you, I wouldn't have wanted to send me into a complete stranger's house looking like I did."

"I'm so relieved you understand." Dora touched him on the shoulder. "Frank and I both think you're really good for Eileen."

"That's nice of you to say but apparently Eileen doesn't think so."

"Why? I think she really likes you."

Karloff frowned. "Eileen called me and broke up the night after we gave you the videophone. I guess she met someone else."

"*No?* That's terrible!"

"I just wish she'd had the decency to dump me in person. I hate it when people hide behind their telephones. They make brave people out of cowards."

"Well, don't you worry. I'm sure there are plenty of nice women who'd be interested in you." Dora pinched his cheek. "Just between you and me, I never thought much of her anyway."

"You're sweet," said Karloff, "but I'd better be going. I'll call you when I get home to make sure the phone works."

For the first time in weeks Dora was anxious for the phone to ring. She thought about what Karloff had said about telephones making brave people out of cowards. It comforted her to think that the man who had been threatening her didn't even have the courage to show his face. When the videophone rang, she snatched the receiver from its cradle.

"Dora, it's Max. Can you hear me?"

"Yes, but I can't see you."

"Press the green button on the base."

Dora located the button and pressed it. The screen flickered on. "I feel so high tech." She couldn't help giggling.

"How's that?" Karloff asked.

Dora could make out a shadowy figure in the center of the six-inch screen that could have easily passed for a tabloid snapshot of Bigfoot. "You're still a little blurry," she said.

"See the dials on the side of the screen? That's your brightness, contrast, and focus. Fiddle with those and see what happens. I'll be right back."

Dora got everything adjusted so that a wide-angle image of Karloff's kitchen came into view. It was like looking through a peephole. A set of carving knifes and a white Formica countertop occupied the lower part of the screen. In the background she could see a smoking ashtray resting atop a small dining table. The room was wallpapered with a pattern of yellow ears of corn and dancing scarecrows. When Karloff returned he was no longer wearing his wig. He was breathing heavily and mopping his bald brow with a paper towel. "Can you see me now?" he asked. His face took up the entire screen.

"Clear as crystal," said Dora.

"What do you think? It's a good way to unmask who you're talking to."

"Oh, Max. Thank you so much."

"Hold on. Someone here wants to say hi to you." The screen went black.

"Max," Dora called. "I can't see you." She could hear his voice in the next room. It was muffled, far-off.

"Be right there."

Dora was startled by the sound of glass breaking and was about to call his name again when the screen blinked back on. It was Eileen. One eye was nearly swollen shut, the other ringed in yellow and purple. Her mouth was covered by a strip of silver tape, and her arms appeared to be bound behind her back. Her cheeks were adorned with the letters *H* and *I,* as if tiny red lightbulbs had been screwed directly into her skin. Karloff clutched her by the hair like a bunch of carrots. "Oops," he said. "I forgot to dot the *i.*" He plucked a burning cigarette from the ashtray, took a slow drag, and applied the glowing tip to Eileen's cheek.

Dora gaped in horror. "Max!" she howled. "What are you doing?"

"Making sure your new phone is working."

Eileen was wearing the butterfly T-shirt. It was tattered and bloody, a tear in the front exposing one of her breasts. "Oh God, Max!" Dora pleaded. "Let her go!"

"You told me you didn't care much for Eileen."

Eileen's eyes locked on Dora, tears streaming down her cigarette-scarred cheeks, wetting the marquee-style letters like rain. Mucus bubbled from her nostrils. Bloody stalactites drooled from her chin. Her fear was more real than anything Dora could have imagined. She desperately wanted to hang up, to disconnect from the image in front of her. But she couldn't — not face-to-face like this.

Karloff's hand passed in front of the screen. Dora could see the flies tattooed on his knuckles, the way they seemed to crawl from the gaps between his fingers as though hatched from the poison yolk of his fist. Then slowly, with a theatrical flair, he laid the slender blade of a filet knife to Eileen's throat.

Dora screamed, "Oh God, Max . . . *No!*"

"You know what they say," said Karloff, holding the knife steady. "One picture . . ."

With that he pressed Eileen's face to the screen, and with a fluid stroke opened a line of communication that would define state-of-the-art well into the millennium.

SHEL SILVERSTEIN

The Guilty Party

FROM *Murder and Obsession*

JUDGE *Vernon Hobbs had been known for some unusual and unorthodox rulings.*

There was the occasion when Leon Poole and Maurice Stebner came before him for a judgment on a 1938 De Soto.

It seems they had bought the vehicle together from Orville Clayton's lot with Leon's three hundred dollars, eighty-seven of which was owed by Orville to Maurice to settle a wager on the World Series. Maurice then did what was disputed to be six hundred and forty-two dollars' worth of repair and restoration, for which he demanded full payment or the De Soto.

Judge Hobbs suggested joint ownership or selling the damn thing and splitting the profits — but by then there was so much bad blood between the boys, as to who said what, and who promised which, and who indeed was the De Soto's rightful owner.

"Well, then," said Judge Hobbs, "I am gonna render a decision based upon the wisdom of Solomon. Is either one of you boys versed in or acquainted with the biblical tale of Solomon and the two mothers?"

The boys had to admit that Scripture was not their long suit.

"Good," said Judge Hobbs, "I wouldn't want either of you anticipating my ruling, which is — that the aforementioned De Soto be cut in half, and one half awarded to each of the claimants. Leon, is that all right with you?"

"Fine with me," said Leon.

"And Maurice, do you find this acceptable?"

"I'll go for that," said Maurice, "but who gets the front half and who gets the back half?"

"I'll take the front half," said Leon.

"The hell you will," shouted Maurice, "the front half's got the engine, the radio, the hood ornament, and the —"

"Order," called Judge Hobbs, banging down the claw hammer he used as a gavel. "I'm amending my decision — the De Soto will be split lengthwise — thereby giving each of you an equal —"

"Well, who gets the driver's side?" demanded Leon. "That's got the mahogany wheel, the transmission, gearshift, the —"

"And who's supposed to saw that damn engine in half?" Leon whined. "You try cuttin' through a windshield and an engine, with a chain saw, and you're sure as hell gonna mess up a —"

Judge Hobbs banged his hammer.

"Well," sighed Judge Hobbs, "I can see from the incredible willingness of both claimants to gladly destroy this unique and classic example of automotive art that neither one of them is the rightful owner. And the court hereby impounds said vehicle as property of the court to be used at the court's discretion on various court business on weekends and holidays, and if there is any question as to the right of the court to impound said De Soto, I'm sure that something can and will be found in the trunk or glove compartment to justify my decision. These proceedings are concluded — everybody go home."

"And that," said Judge Hobbs later, as he and Clarence Sawyer, his bailiff, sat sipping some good apricot brandy, "is the last time I try to render a verdict based upon anybody's wisdom but my own."

It was too damn hot.

Judge Hobbs leaned back in his swivel chair and turned up the fan as high as it would go. He didn't want to lean too far back. They might see that he was wearing short pants underneath his robe. That might be interpreted as being unjudicial or, at best, undignified.

Carefully, Judge Hobbs rolled up the brief that lay upon his desk. The fly was on the rim of the coffee cup. One swat — *justice* — swift and sure. But *was* it just? What was the fly doing but exercising its nature? What was young Billy Ray doing but exercising his? But if that were the case, who deserved to be punished for anything?

Judge Hobbs closed his eyes and tapped the rolled papers against his palm. He hoped that this would look contemplative. The fly was moving down the inside of the cup now. As long as it stayed there it was safe. Did the sonofabitch know that?

"All right," said Judge Hobbs, unrolling the brief and flattening it out, "all right, let's proceed with these — *Clarence,* will you turn that damn thing off."

"I got the sound down, Judge," said the bailiff.

"Well, I can still hear it," said Judge Hobbs. "What's the score, anyway?"

"Eight to two, Bluebirds, top of the fifth — they just brought in that Binky Lewis. He's as wild as a —"

"Well, I think that Lewis boy might be able to hold a six-run lead," said Judge Hobbs, wiping his neck with his handkerchief.

"Judge, they got two men on and —"

"Damn it, Clarence, at least turn the *sound* off — and announce these proceedings — in a proper and official manner."

Clarence snapped off the sound and stood up, pouting.

"Hear ye, hear ye, first district court, Menasha County, now in session, *Honorable* Vernon Hobbs presiding — all rise."

He had hit the *Honorable* a little too hard.

"Too hot to rise," said Judge Hobbs, throwing Clarence his stern look. "Stay sittin'."

"The state versus William Raymond Brockley," continued Clarence. "The charge, sexual battery, assault with a deadly weapon, kidnapping, resisting arrest —"

"All right," said Judge Hobbs, "I'm tired of list'nin'."

The fly had taken off.

Judge Hobbs turned toward Billy Ray. Damn, the boy was too good-looking to have to force anyone into anything.

"Billy Ray, you've decided to forgo and dispense with a trial by a jury of your peers."

"Yes, sir," said Billy Ray.

"Well," said Judge Hobbs, "that may be a wise decision, since most of your peers around here would like to see you strung up slow and sliced down a piece at a time. A few of 'em might even be blood-related to Eunice Tillman."

"The young lady is in critical condition at Baptist Hospital," said Lew Porter, district attorney and proprietor of Porter Brothers General Contracting, Roofing, and Aluminum Siding, "and is at this time physically and emotionally unfit to attend this hearing. Therefore, Your Honor, the state requests a one-week postponement until the young lady —"

"The young *lady's* condition has been upgraded to stable," interjected Buddy Linz, defense attorney and co-owner of Buddy's Four Alarm Chili And Pit Bar-B-Cue.

"Well, I think we can proceed ahead," said Judge Hobbs. "I want to get this over and done with as soon as possible."

Lew Porter stood up. How did he manage to look so dry and unwrinkled in a three-piece suit on a day like this?

"Your Honor," said Lew Porter, "the state will prove that on the night of —"

"*Attempt* to prove," snapped Judge Hobbs. Lew Porter sighed.

"*Attempt* to prove that on the night of April seventeenth, the accused, Billy Ray Brockley, did willfully and forcibly —"

"Come to think of it, Lew, you don't even have to attempt to prove anything," said Judge Hobbs. "Sit back down — I have all the pertinent facts right here." He tapped the rumpled brief. "This don't look like that big of a deal."

"We know you'll render a fair and impartial judgment, Your Honor," said Buddy Linz.

Lew Porter groaned and sat back down.

Judge Hobbs had the reputation of being one of the goodest and oldest of the county's good old boys, two of his favorite expressions being "Boys will be boys" and "Let he who has never been young cast the first stone." Also Judge Hobbs had been heard to remark on more than one occasion that it didn't serve much purpose slappin' young people in jail.

"In the spring the sap will rise," he would sigh, his eyes looking back a long time ago. "The fruit turns ripe and the pickers come. That's nature — you can't stop it or slow it down."

"All right," said Judge Hobbs, tossing the brief aside and turning to Billy Ray Brockley, "Billy Ray, you've been advised by counsel that my decision will be binding?"

"Yes, sir," said Billy Ray.

"'Cause I sure as hell don't want to hear no bitchin' or moanin' later that I been too severe — or too lenient — and I sure as hell don't want to hear the word *appeal* interjected anywhere into these proceedings. I mean I don't want to even sniff the word *appeal,* and anybody — defense attorney or prosecutor — who even breathes or whispers that word is gonna find me somewhat prejudicial in my rulings on his future cases — is that understood? All right, you wanted my decision on this case and you'll get it — and abide by it. Billy Ray — how do you plead to these charges?"

"I didn't do it."

"You didn't meet Eunice Tillman at the VFW Blue Moon Dance on the night of . . . April seventeenth?"

"I met her."

"You didn't dance with her?"

"We danced . . . awhile."

"You didn't get her drunk?"

"You don't have to get Eunice drunk," said Billy Ray. "She's always —"

"You didn't drive her to the Larkspur Underpass?"

"Yes, sir — But I didn't do it."

"Didn't do . . . what?"

"The rest of it. I'm not guilty."

"You sayin' she led you on? 'Cause if she led you on —"

"I'm sayin' I didn't do it."

"You didn't do it."

"Not . . . really."

"Not really?"

"I . . . witnessed it."

"You witnessed it."

"Bein' done — yes, sir."

"Bein' done — by who?"

"I don't like to name names, Judge. I just —"

"Bein' done by *who*, damn it?"

Billy Ray closed his eyes.

"By . . . Sam."

"Sam?"

"Sam Johnson, Your Honor."

"Sam Johnson?" Judge Hobbs picked up the brief. "I don't see any Sam Johnson listed in this —"

"Sam Johnson," said Billy Ray. "My . . . thing."

"Your . . . thing?"

Buddy Linz stood up.

"My client is referring to his . . . member, Your Honor, his . . . sexual member, his —"

"I can see what he's referring to," said Judge Hobbs. "He's clutchin' the damn thing."

Judge Hobbs leaned forward.

"Billy Ray — you're sayin' that *that* is Sam Johnson?"

"Yes, sir."

"You've given him a . . . name?"

"That's his name, Judge. *Sam.*"

"A first name too."

"Well, sir, there's a lot of Johnsons out there."

"Hopefully not related to this case," said Judge Hobbs, picking up his pen and beginning to write. "Mister Johnson? *J-O-H-N-S-O-N?* He's the guilty party?"

"I call him Sam," said Billy Ray. "It's not so formal."

"Well, I want to keep things formal as possible," said Judge Hobbs. "Samuel Johnson. No middle initial?"

"No, sir."

"Just first and last name — you didn't make a little checkered coat for the sonofabitch, did you? With a little straw hat and a cane?"

"No, sir."

"And you say that this 'Samuel Johnson' on the night of April seventeenth, and against the person of Eunice Tillman, did willfully and forcibly, without your aid, cooperation, or collaboration —"

"He's got a mind of his own, Judge," said Billy Ray. "There's no reasoning with him — he just gets a notion and does . . . anything that comes into his head."

"I know, son," sighed Judge Hobbs, "but as an innocent observer and witness to the alleged attack, did you do anything to restrain the aforementioned Samuel Johnson from —"

"There's no holding him, Your Honor," said Billy Ray. "He's . . . unrestrainable — I tried — he just . . . shook me off."

Lew Porter was on his feet.

"And what the hell were *you* doing, while Sam Johnson was forcing Eunice Tillman into the back seat? What were you doing when your buddy Sam was forcing Eunice Tillman to perform a —"

"I couldn't have gone against him," Billy Ray pleaded. "I was afraid."

"Afraid?" asked Judge Hobbs. "Afraid of what?"

"Of what he might . . . do . . . to me."

"To *you?*" Judge Hobbs was wide awake now. "What could he have done to you?"

"You don't know him, Your Honor. The bastard's got no conscience — he might do . . . anything. He's got a . . . power, Judge. He just . . . takes over. You don't know Sam Johnson."

Lew Porter was up and screaming now — the veins in his neck about to bust. His face was right in Billy Ray's.

"And I imagine it was the same Sam Johnson who drove your Thunderbird to the Larkspur Underpass. I wanna see it, Your Honor, I want a demonstration of Sam Johnson drivin' a stick shift, I wanna see Sam Johnson holdin' a knife to somebody's throat — this knife, Your Honor — I'm introducin' this Barlow as Exhibit A. And I wanna see —"

"You don't have to introduce that knife to me," said Judge Hobbs, picking up the Barlow and turning it over slowly. "This was your daddy's fishin' knife, wasn't it, Billy? I believe if he knew you were leavin' it layin' around within easy reach of such unsavory characters as this Sam Johnson, he'd be spinnin' in his grave." He turned to Buddy Linz.

"Buddy, this defense that you've cooked up is highly unique and creative, I must say. You realize if I allow it and it becomes a precedent, any forger can claim that it was his hands that did it, and not him. Anybody can kick somebody to death and claim it was his feet."

"Next thing you know," chimed in Lew Porter, picking up the line of reasoning, "next thing you know the arsonist is blaming the match, the sniper is blamin' the bullet, the ax murderer —"

"That's our defense," said Buddy Linz, "and I've got a trunkload of psychiatric books and psychological studies and psychiatrists' opinions that'll back me up."

"Sam Johnson did it," said Billy Ray. "I'll swear to it."

Lew Porter was sweating now. That three-piece suit was beginning to look like wet cardboard.

"Your Honor," he said, "this . . . this incredible 'my-pee-pee-did-it-not-me plea' is so outrageous — so desperate — so without any legal foundation, that no one can possibly —"

"I'm going to allow it," said Judge Hobbs, "and if it brings down upon my head a torrent of legal criticism and controversy, well, then, they'll just have to put me on the same bench with boys like John Marshall, Louis Brandeis, and Oliver Wendell Holmes — in presenting a ruling that will forever influence future jurisprudence.

"Because, gentlemen, I find this theory of a . . . member . . . having a will of its own to be reasonable and within the scope of human experience.

"Have we all not at some time or other been led down pathways dark and devious? By something stronger than our hearts or heads? And is justice not to be tempered with mercy? And who indeed can stop the sap from rising in the young sapling?"

Lew Porter groaned and held his head in his hands.

"Billy Ray, I find you innocent of all charges specified here. I do find you guilty of witnessing a felony and not immediately reporting it, but in light of your coming forth now and identifying the guilty party, I'm suspending sentence. I don't suppose Sam Johnson has any money."

"Not a cent, Your Honor," said a cheerful Billy Ray.

"Well, then, seein' as how he's a friend of yours —"

"Former friend," said Billy Ray.

"Whatever — I'm ordering you to pay whatever medical costs Eunice Tillman may run up due to the actions of your former friend Sam Johnson. And I hope this serves as a lesson to you to refrain from any associations with violent, abusive members."

"Thank you, Judge," said Billy Ray, getting up with a grin. "And I'm sure gonna be more selective in the future about hangin' out with bad company."

Judge Hobbs sat there. Billy Ray was hugging Buddy Linz. Lew Porter was putting his papers together. Clarence was fiddling with the horizontal. Billy Ray started toward the door. Judge Hobbs picked up his gavel.

"Where you goin', son?" asked Judge Hobbs.

"Home . . . to dinner . . . like you said. I think my momma is makin' a meat loaf."

"Well, good," said Judge Hobbs, "but who you takin' with you?"

"Buddy . . . if he wants to come — hell, all of you, if you like meat loaf. There'll be plenty."

"Well, you ain't takin' no convicted felon home to your momma's table, are you?" asked Judge Hobbs.

Billy Ray looked confused.

"I mean, son, you're innocent and free to go — free as a bird."

Billy Ray sighed.

"But that heartless cold-blooded sex fiend, Sam Johnson, I'm findin' him *guilty*" — Judge Hobbs banged his gavel — "of aggravated sexual assault and kidnapping. I'm sentencing the ruthless sonofabitch to twelve years' confinement in the state correctional facility at Joliet."

"Judge —" said Billy Ray.

"Son," said Judge Hobbs, raising a restraining finger, "I know how hard it is to take leave of a loved one for an extended period of time, so as a special consideration, I'm gonna give you the opportunity to accompany your friend, your former friend, to Joliet, or you can stay behind and let him go on alone . . . You look pale, son . . . Mr. Linz, why don't you escort your client to the men's room. I think he needs a glass of water . . . Oh, and Clarence — give Billy Ray his daddy's Barlow — he's innocent and it's his property. Take all the time you need, son," he said softly to Billy Ray, "but when you come out of there, Sam Johnson *is* goin' to prison . . . Next case —"

"There ain't no next case, Judge," said Clarence.

"Well, then, turn up the sound," said Judge Hobbs, "and let's find out whether or not that Lewis kid can hold a six-run lead for five damn innings."

PETER MOORE SMITH

Forgetting the Girl

FROM *The MacGuffin*

I HOPE this video camera works. Anyway, this (*click*) is a blowup of a model's eye, the bluest I've ever seen. The only other time I remember seeing that exact color of blue was the day my sister Nicole drowned. It was everywhere: in the water, in the sky, Nicole's skin. Blue, I remember, and coughing. And gold, the gold of the light off the surface of the water, like an empty frame. I was eight. No, seven. I almost drowned trying to rescue little Nicole. She was five. I look back and see myself coughing, coughing, and coughing. Nicole. She's the one girl I've been trying to remember.

(*click*)

Here's one I forgot — Marcie — with the usual drowning in gin. Before Marcie I forgot (*click*) Alexis, a blonde, in marijuana's blue-gray haze. I had attempted to forget Alexis once before by going on an outdoor camping adventure (*click*) with some friends, that's Jamie and Derek, but I forgot to bring those things you nail your tent down with, and I ended up forgetting her in some cheesy motel, I forget what it was called.

Let me explain.

My name is Kevin Wolfe. I am a studio photographer. I do headshots, two hundred a package. Developing is extra. You've probably seen my flyers on lampposts all over the city. Almost every girl who comes into this studio, every actress (*click*), every model (*click*) (*click*), at least the ones I find pretty, I ask out. It's simply a matter of policy. They almost always say, "No." So I do this forgetting thing, this ritual. I know it's weird. Like this one: (*click*) name was Colleen Something, all willowy, green eyes, chestnut hair. I don't remember anything about her, really, just how she kept extending her neck into the shot (*click*), there it is, muscles all tense, like she was on the prow of a sailboat and leaning into the wind. "Relax," I told her.

"Sorry," she kept giggling. "I'll relax, I'm so sorry."

(*click*) Look at her face. Have you ever seen eyes that green? This is a perfect photograph, I have to say. The way the shadow of her nose falls across her cheekbone. The way her hair reflects the light. Colleen hardly needed any makeup, I remember, skin like ivory. She never came to pick up her pictures, though, either. I left messages on her answering machine, but the beep just kept getting longer and longer and longer, and then one day all I got was ringing. I guess I scared her. That's what my assistant Jamie said, anyway. Apparently I do that sometimes.

Colleen's memory played on in my psyche like an extended remix. So how'd I forget her? Trying to clear my mind, and failing. Jamie gave me this tape, "Relaxation Through Meditation." She said it would help me rest, gain focus, whatever. I'd close my eyes and let the TV screen inside my head go static, but then I'd see Colleen's bright face fade up, her eyes green and cool as Central Park in September, and I'd zoom in on her red lips moving, saying, "No, Kevin, but thank you, anyway."

It's like I have to perform this ritual, some conscious act of forgetting, and then it's okay. You know when you're in a museum, and you're looking at a painting, and it's freaking you out, like that blue-period Picasso of the woman crying, all jagged tears and awfulness, and it gets inside you? Well, all you have to do is turn your head and walk through the door into the next room of the museum where there's another painting, a Mondrian or a Rothko or whatever, a calculation of colors, abstract and meaningless, just waiting for you. Just walk through those doors.

In the end, I did forget green-eyed Colleen. It's not that I *forgot* her, understand, it's that I made it so I didn't care anymore. I don't care. (*click*) This is a picture of me not caring. Jesus, I look like a serial killer. I am the original, mean-looking white man. Now do you see why I stay behind the camera? Oh yeah, sometimes this projector sticks, so I apologize in advance.

Sometimes, all I do is close my eyes, and when I've opened them up again, I've forgotten her, whoever she was.

(*click*) (*click*)

Sheila, for instance. She *almost* went out with me. She's not as pretty as she looks in this shot. I mean, she's all done up here. And not to brag or anything, but I'm an amazingly great photographer. "You single?" I remember asking. Jamie had hustled in to apply more makeup, adjust Sheila's hair, or whatever, always taking extra care with the heavier ones.

Sheila rolled her eyes. "I'm only nineteen," she said.

"I meant, do you have a boyfriend."

Jamie painted hollows of blush onto Sheila's cheeks.

I was awarded a smile. "No-oo," Sheila sang.

"Maybe we could go to a movie," I said.

Jamie froze.

"Sure, okay," Sheila said finally. She was trembling, I could tell. A lot of girls have a hard time saying no, especially the younger ones, and especially if they're not from New York. They're trying to be polite all the time, like their mothers told them to be. But in the end, you end up — I mean, *I* end up — on the receiving end of a can-we-please-just-be-friends speech, when the truth is they really have no intention of being your friend at all. And the last thing I need is a *friend*. (*click*) (*click*) (*click*) And look at these shots. Sheila wouldn't even glance at the camera after that. The muscles of her face got all tight. See along the jaw? That's fear. I remember her foot twitching on the rim of the stool, of this stool I'm sitting on now, twitching just like this. Sheila called the day I was supposed to meet her, saying she'd forgotten about other plans, a relative was in from out of town, blah blah blah. Bitch was chubby, anyway. I forgot her at the newsstand, looking through all the fashion magazines at the skinny supermodels, the emaciated and beautiful, the rich and famished.

Perhaps you'd like the grand tour. I'll simply detach the videocam from its tripod and point it around for you. As you can see, this is a photography studio. These are my lights. This is my camera. It's getting old, I suppose. But these things are expensive. This is my backdrop. It doubles as a projection screen. Turn around again, and this is my projector. I always take at least a few slides of the girls who come in here. That's my kitchenette over there, and behind that partition I've got a mattress. I used to have an apartment across town, but what with rent and everything and since I was always here, you know how it goes . . . I've got some chairs there in the waiting area. This is Jamie's makeup table. And this is the body.

This (*click*) is Beth Dalewell, a petite model who, surprise of surprises, wanted to act. Check her out: shiny dark hair in a bob, those big, brown, watery eyes, her mouth permanently curved into a half smile. Cute, isn't she? Do you see the way her skin is? Finely knit, like cream-colored silk. And her clothes, sort of preppy, but extremely tasteful. That skirt's pretty short too, if you know what I'm saying. I'll never forget the way she looked me dead in the eye, and said, "Yes," flat out.

"You will?" I practically knocked my camera over.

"What do you want to see?" Beth asked.

Jamie was hunching over her makeup desk. Her back, broad as a billboard, was turned to us. She always wore big, droopy pink or yellow sweatshirts and these pleated skirts that she made herself out of all kinds of cheap fabric, weird tartans, paisleys, stripes, and checks. Colorful clothes were supposed to hide her hugeness, I guess.

I had no idea what Jamie was thinking at that moment. I mean, I knew she got uncomfortable when I asked a girl out, but I just thought it was a feminist thing. All I could think of now was, what did I want to see? My mind went blank. I couldn't conjure up a single movie that was playing anywhere. I get so stupid when a pretty girl's around. A comedy? A mystery? "I don't know," I shrugged at Beth. "Anything, anything you want. You pick." Beth was looking at me, so I adjusted the lights to blind her. It makes me nervous when people look at me.

"I'll call you," Beth said, squinting, "later this afternoon. I'll look in the paper and then I'll call you up."

I was starting to get giddy inside. I felt kind of trembly. My hands shook. I knew what would happen now. At least I thought I did. I'd send Jamie home and cancel the rest of my appointments for the day. I'd go out and buy flowers for the place. I'd do the dishes. I'd spray air freshener around, empty out the ashtrays, throw out the garbage. I'd change the sheets on my bed. I was feeling that agitation already. Beth would call. She'd have picked out one of those English movies set a hundred years ago. We'd meet in front of the theater. After the movie we'd find a nice Italian place, have a bottle of wine, maybe two, a little stimulating conversation. On the way home I'd invite her in for a drink. And so on. And so forth. It was going to be awesome, I was thinking. Truly incredible.

Jamie waddled over to Beth with the powder brush. "Let me even out your skin," she said acidly. "You're all blotchy."

"What are you talking about?" I said to Jamie. "Get away from her with that thing." It was too late, though. Jamie dusted Beth with the brush. "And maybe after we can get a bite to eat?" I asked, ignoring Jamie.

Beth smiled through the powdery makeup, motes of dust floating in the air in front of her face. "Absolutely," she said. "Why not?" (*click*) Beautiful Beth. Here's another picture of her. As you can see, I started shooting wildly after that. (*click*) (*click*) I already had *the* shot, anyway. And, I figured, now that Beth was going to be my girlfriend and everything, I'd have plenty of time to take more photos of her. Especially headshots for her acting career, plus others of a more personal, private nature, if you know what I mean. (*click*) Here's a blowup. I guess her skin was a little blotchy after all. But what a face.

(*click*) Here's a face, Nicole's face, a little girl's face, a nothing face. I blew this up from an old picture I found in Grandma's bottom bureau drawer. I was trying to remember exactly what Nicole looked like, her expression, what beamed out. See those wide cheekbones, slits for eyes? This isn't her, though. I mean, it's *her*. But not her. Nicole had a softness, a prissiness, that this doesn't capture. This is just a face. She used to sing. Stupid stuff. Tra-la-la, skipping around Grandma's back yard, around and around that pool.

She would not have been pretty, my sister. When she grew up, if she had grown up, she would not have been a beauty. The truth is, she would have looked like me.

I don't have many good pictures of Jamie, because I never really took a photo of her directly. Sometimes she'd inadvertently walk into the shot, though. (*click*) Okay, here's one. Ignore the other girl there. Jamie had mousy-brown hair which, look, already had streaks of gray in it, even though she was only twenty-eight or something, a circular face, a narrow, needle nose. Her cheeks always seemed a little reddish — not from makeup, she never wore any, just from running around out of breath all the time, wheezing like

an asthmatic. Her best friend was this guy Derek, a homosexual.
You saw a picture of him from our ill-fated camping attempt. I always thought Jamie was in love with him. What can I tell you about
her? Jamie was from somewhere in Ohio, Columbus or Cincinnati.
Her father was a vacuum cleaner salesman or hardware store manager or something pathetic. Her mother was dead or in Canada, I
think. She always had a piece of her hair twisted around in her
mouth. Her smile indicated nervousness, and her teeth were all
filmy. She had small, dark eyes that flew around the four corners of
the room when you looked directly at her. She talked a million
miles a minute until the one minute a girl showed up in the studio
for pictures, then she'd go all silent and shy, and let me do the talking. I paid Jamie almost nothing, just over minimum wage, but she
never complained about money. She never complained, period.
She liked the Artist Formerly Known As Prince, Ursula K. Leguin
novels, and Mike and Ike candies.

(*click*)

So, you're saying, what about this body?

Well, let's start with a hand. Because in the dark, all through the
movie, I kept looking at Beth's. I was like that guy in the Edgar
Allan Poe story, right? I was fixated on it. It was sitting there on top
of her thigh, on that denim skirt she wore, fingers curling geomet-
rically inward, curving like a nautilus, the whole hand a resting animal, alive but waiting. Beth's hand. I just wanted to hold that hand.
Finally, I got up the courage to reach over and touch it with my
middle finger, just lightly, like it was a mouse I might scare off. Beth
was firm, though, sudden, and took my wrist — for a split second I
thought, *Yes!* — placing it solidly, lonesomely, on the maroon, velvet arm of the chair. Now it was my hand that was the animal, a
dead mole the cat dragged in, rotting there. I didn't look at Beth's
face, but I knew she was rolling her eyes and sneering, the bitch. I'd
seen it before, that look. I was so humiliated, though, that I was
deaf, that I couldn't hear anything, not even the Dolby Surround
Sound in the movie theater, just the rushing of blood in my ears.
You know that sound, like you're under water? I would have to forget Beth with some severity, I realized. This would not be easy. Forgetting Beth would not be easy at all. I started planning rituals of
drunkenness. I had been feeling my sexual appetite looming, so I
thought I might go down to the porno shops on Eighth Avenue.

There's a place you can go where you step inside a booth and a girl takes her clothes off for you. It's disgusting, really. But sometimes nothing can help you forget a girl better than another one, naked, offering her breasts.

I just sat next to Beth for the next fifteen minutes or so, until I realized that she was far, far away, that she would *hate* me, that if I were truthful, if I really told her who I was, if she really *knew* me, she'd hate me forever. I leaned next to her, and I could tell she was disgusted, I could feel her shrinking away from my closeness. Why the hell did she go out with me in the first place? What's wrong with her, I thought. "I'm going to the bathroom," I whispered. I got up, and then I walked out of the movie theater and onto Twenty-third Street. It's strange to do that, you know. You're used to leaving the movies with a huge crowd of people. But it was just me, all alone, walking out. I walked a few blocks as if on automatic pilot to a public phone I remembered on the corner of Twenty-sixth and Seventh, don't ask me why, but I thought of *bowling*, and I popped my quarter in.

"Hello?"

"Jamie, it's me," I said. "What are you doing?"

"Watching TV. What happened to your date?"

"What date?"

"Oh."

"Are you hungry?" I asked.

"No," Jamie said.

"Will you meet me?"

I had this picture in my head. I wanted to go bowling. At the Port Authority Bus Terminal, they have this bowling center. You'd never know it was there, but there it is. And you just can't go bowling alone. Who could go bowling alone? So that's why I called Jamie. I wanted to forget Beth by bowling my sorrows away. Why did I do that? What made me make that choice? Why bowling? And why Jamie? I mean, I hold no malice in my heart. Do I?

(*click*)

The truth is, women *are* objects. I mean, the feminists can say what they want, but when it comes right down to it, girls are made of bone and muscle and blood. They have eyes and chins and cheekbones and lips, arms and breasts, hair . . . You're behind the camera over there looking at them, you're creating a moment, an object in space, you're saying, "Smile, look this way, smooth your hair, that's it, *perfect*."

They're saying, "How do you want me? Here? Like this?"

(*click*)

We were standing in the flickering lights of the pinball machines at the Port Authority Bus Terminal. There was the smell of urine and antiseptic, cigarettes and cleaning supplies. Jamie had said she wanted to play the *Star Trek: The Next Generation* pinball game with multiple levels. I wanted to bowl and was still trying to convince her. "I don't know how to bowl," she kept saying. Her eyes were everywhere but on me. "And," she almost whispered, "I don't want to wear someone else's shoes." She pressed the button for one player.

"You agreed to bowl," I said. "You met me here on the pretense of bowling." We'd been out socially before, but never in such degenerate surroundings. It amused me to see her here.

I slouched against the blinking machine and watched Jamie inexpertly paddle the silver ball into the starships of the Klingon Empire. The game was over quickly. Jamie's shoulders slumped downward as she turned toward me, defeated, with something to say, I could tell, her eyes moving everywhere. "Is this . . . helping you?" she said finally. As usual, she was sucking on a piece of her hair. It was all pointy and wet, like she was going to thread it through the hole of a needle. I wondered when was the last time she washed it.

"What do you mean," I said, "the pinball?"

"I mean with that girl, with Beth. Is this helping you, you know . . . with your . . . forgetting thing?"

(*click*)

Angie. Forgotten with a pint of Deep Chocolate.

(*click*)

Darlene. I forgot her by watching the Gulf War on CNN.

(*click*)

Vanessa. I forgot how I forgot her.

(*click*)

Jamie had never mentioned that she knew about this before about forgetting. I said, "Um." That is exactly what I said in response, "Um," and a nod. It was all I could think of. I must admit I was freaked out. I felt like someone had just lifted the trunk and found me there, where the spare tire and gas can should be.

"Because I don't mind," Jamie said, and now she looked directly at me. "I mean, I like helping you, helping you do whatever, whatever it is, you know what I mean?"

(*click*)

Have you ever been taken over by an alien?

(*click*)

Sometimes I remember things about my sister Nicole for no discernible reason. These pictures are just there in my head. For instance, Nicole used to have this pillowcase. You know, some kids have blankets or teddy bears, things that comfort them. For her it was this pillowcase. All ratty and filled with holes, it had a floral motif, but it was designed, I think, by the same people who did the graphics for *Laugh-In*. The flowers were all loopy and cartoony, like they'd exploded across it. Nicole used to get inside that pillowcase and curl up, completely covered, she was so little.

Let me show you something else. I just have to turn on the Super Eight projector. Do you know how hard it is to find these things nowadays? This footage of Nicole I found last time I was home. My uncle Arnie shot it when he was a teenager. Okay, here it is. See? That's the back yard at my grandmother's. There's the pool she drowned in. That's me in the water. I used to like to sit in the shallow end with my nose just above the water's surface like that. I wouldn't move, just let the water go all still and quiet. In the sun, the surface of the water would become reflective, and I'd get lost in the blue and the gold. It was beautiful. I guess I was always visual, a born photographer. Under the water I'd let my body relax and sort of float. I'd cross my legs. It was its own kind of meditation, I suppose. I remember the sounds too. The water lapping at my ears very gently, very slowly. That echoing sound under water. The light glinting blue and gold, white and gold, white and blue.

"Hey," I asked Jamie, "do you want to get drunk?" The truth was, I didn't want to play pinball. But it suddenly occurred to me, there in the middle of the Port Authority Bus Terminal, surrounded by all the alcoholics and junkies, prostitutes and petty thieves, that I would much, much rather get smashed, completely and totally blotto, than play pinball or bowl or anything else. It had been, after all, the original idea. I was picturing Beth, her cute shoulders in the flickering movie-light. I kept seeing her hand resting there in the dark of her lap, that creamy skin. That fucking bitch.

Jamie started, "I don't really —"

"Oh, come on, Jamie," I cut her off, "a couple of belts won't hurt you."

She hesitated, then she said, all resignedly, "All right."

I gave her a smile. Nervously, she smiled back, her teeth pointy and green. "This way," I said. I led her over to the Port Authority Bowling Center Snack Bar and ordered a couple of beers. When they came, I toasted Jamie, downed my whole cup, and asked the derelict behind the counter for another round. He served them in big waxy-paper cups, and it was cold, straight from the tap, deliciously numbing. "A couple more of these," I said, "and then I know a fabulous place on Tenth."

Jamie belched. And throughout the evening, amazingly, she kept up beer for beer. After a while, it became shot for shot. It was pretty funny seeing her drink that way. Big, fat girl there knocking them back with me — little skinny guy at some terrible bar in New York's most depraved part of town. There was something about the drinking and that, you know, that it was Jamie, my assistant, that made me relax, let me rest it a bit. I did forget Beth. And not just in the usual way I forget a girl, like I said, not just that I made myself not care anymore. I honestly and truly wasn't thinking about Beth at all. I was looking at Jamie and I was seeing into her squinty eyes and her puffy cheeks, and it came to me in the midst of this drunken stupor that nothing mattered anymore, she *knew,* I could tell her anything, that I could offer my body to her, eyes closed, palms out, I could explain. I told her about Nicole. We slid into the wooden bench of a booth in the back of that seedy place, and I relayed the story of how I sat in the pool watching the light and how my grandmother pulled Nicole out of the water, her body limp and blue. It came out of me like a wound gushing. Jamie opened up too, telling me her life story, that there was this guy in her high school, she was so incredibly in love with him, but he was gay, blah blah blah. And it's like, it's like something amazing happened. It's like I was watching. I mean, I was doing it, I was there, with Jamie, in the bar, on the hard wooden bench with all the names scratched onto it, but I was also very far away. My true self was up around the ceiling, far up, just watching. And I could see myself sitting there. And I could see huge Jamie, and she was just a tiny, little, infinitesimal speck.

(*click*)

This is a picture I took of a pile of garbage. I use it to illustrate what Jamie's apartment was like. Hell, it was practically a closet. It was decorated like a teenage girl's bedroom, too, with pop music and movie posters lining the walls, audiotapes and compact discs piled so high they practically reached the ceiling. As far as furniture goes, this place had just enough room for one double mattress. I watched as we fumbled together onto it. It smelled sour. These huge sweatshirts and skirts she wore were heaped all over. She pushed a pile off her bed so we could sit on it, and she turned off the light. As if from that far-off vantage point, I saw the two of us kissing sloppily. I looked through the darkness and held witness as we rolled around on her unwashed bedclothes. I soared away to an even greater distance when I saw myself unbuttoning my shirt. And when I saw her peel off her clothes, unbundling that sweatshirt, twisting off that skirt, I retreated even farther in the recesses of the ceiling. I saw her folds of flesh from two places, from my eyes which were stupid and drunken, and from somewhere else, up above, far off, sickened. "I love you, Kevin," Jamie was saying. "I've always loved you." She was sort of crying.

"Yes," I heard myself say, my hands caressing her immense breasts, "Yes, I know. It's okay. I know everything."

Then she started calling me "Kev-ee."

(*click*)

This is Jean. Forgotten after a long, hot bath.

(*click*)

This is Fiona. I forgot her by going to a nightclub.

(*click*)

I forgot Brenda at the Museum of Modern Art.

(*click*) (*click*) (*click*)

I forgot, I forgot, I forgot.

(*click*)

It's like there were two parts of me, the one doing it, and the other one watching. I slipped out of the bed, with Jamie snoring there, her mouth open, her teeth pointing ceilingward. I had the plan. This was something I had to forget. I had made a mistake. I knew I had the drop cloth. I like to keep the studio freshly painted, so I always have plenty of supplies. I left her apartment surreptitiously. Did anyone see me? No. I'm sure of it. I came back here and got everything ready. I unrolled these huge plastic sheets of drop cloth onto the floor, right by the door. I pulled this stool over to that wall, and then I waited. I just sat there. I knew she'd be in at nine. She was always punctual. I kept the lights off, and I listened to her footfalls all the way up the stairs, and when she got to the door she did something strange — she knocked. She never knocked. But today, maybe because of last night, because she thought I might still be sleeping it off, who knows why, today she knocked. "Come in," I said, and my voice cracked. I watched the knob turn, and as soon as she was inside I was behind her with the hammer. I'd thought one hit would do it, but I was wrong. She turned around to look at me. Here's an example of how wrong I was: it wasn't even Jamie.

It was Beth.

(*click*)

This is New York. People scream all the time.

People are also made of stronger stuff than you'd think. Girls are especially. It took several whacks. You know that sound? Like from the movies? Big, squishy thuds? Beth went down and started twitching, trying to get away, I guess on sheer instinct. She couldn't have known what the fuck I was doing this for. She turned around and faced me as she fell, and she put her hands up in the air. She saw me too. I caught that look of recognition, that spark of understanding. And now, it's like I'm still the one watching, but I'm even further away. I'm watching myself through a telescope turned the wrong way around. Or maybe I'm the one watching through this videocam. Maybe I'm you.

Hello there.

Come on, I had to forget all this somehow.

(*click*)

I just wish I could remember more about Nicole. I mean, what the hell was she doing in the water? She wasn't allowed. She was too little to swim. I barely knew how to swim myself. I was only, what, eight or nine or something.

(*click*)

I guess Beth was coming to yell at me. Or maybe she wanted the film. Whatever. I didn't mean to . . . you know. It was Jamie I wanted. And it was Jamie who showed up, like, five minutes later. Talk about a surprise. There I was, covered with blood, pieces of

Beth's head everywhere. But Jamie got it, I have to say. She sussed
out the situation right off.

"What are you going to do with her?" she said.

I was still kind of numb from the whole thing. I looked up.

"Why don't you hop in the shower," she said gravely, "and I'll
wrap her up." So I did. And when I was in there, I started thinking.
It's kind of my thinking place, you know, standing there under the
hot water, watching the steam rise and stick to the tiles. I started
thinking about my mistake. I started thinking about Jamie out
there wrapping Beth up in the plastic sheets. And I wondered if I'd
ever be able to forget now, if I'd ever be able to forget last night
with Jamie, or this morning with Beth. And then something hit me
that was even more important. Would Jamie? Would Jamie be able
to forget?

(*click*)

Beth wasn't very big. So after we wrapped her in the plastic we
shoved her into a huge bag with lots of other trash and garbage.
Then she went out onto the street. The garbage guys come around
pretty often, and I've watched them heave those trash bags up into
the truck. They don't know what's in there, and I'm willing to bet
they don't want to. I wonder how many other people are out there
in the landfills, rotting away.

Anyway, it was a nervous day. I even had a couple of appointments, which I kept because I didn't want to arouse suspicion. See?
(*click*) This is Jilah, a girl from Thailand. Pretty. And this (*click*) is
Meredith. Skin's not so good. Not so pretty. And this — well, this
next one didn't have an appointment or anything, but since I'd
never really gotten a decent shot before — this is Jamie. Her eyes
were always like that, looking away. I couldn't get her to look at the
camera. She just wouldn't do it. "Why don't you sit up there on the
stool?" I had asked her.

"Me?"

"Sure," I said. "Just for one shot."

"But I don't have any makeup or anything."

"It's not a glamour shot," I said. "Come on."

She made that clicking sound girls make with their tongues, then
slid up onto the seat and looked at her hands.

I adjusted the camera. I futzed with the lights. "You know," I told
her, "I've got a problem."

"I won't tell anyone," she said.

"Oh, I know that," I said. "I know you wouldn't do that. But you have to understand, Jamie, that I can't go around remembering all this. I have to forget. I have to forget all this, or I'll go crazy."

"Oh."

And that's when I took this photo.

"Do you know what I mean?" I asked her.

"I think so," she said. Then she cried, very softly, for quite a while. Then she told me in a voice all trembly and sorrowful that she'd been thinking about it for a long time, anyway, and that she had a whole bottle of blue Valiums in her backpack. And we calmly talked about how it would all happen. We'd wait until it was really late. Then we'd lay out the sheets of plastic. She'd write a note — I'd help her — about how she didn't have anything or anyone, and that nothing made any difference. I could drop it in the mailbox in the morning. And I'd pour her a big glass of water, and she'd take those little blue pills, two at a time, until they were all gone. She'd lie down, then, and go to sleep. It would be beautiful, I thought. I said so, too. I told her that.

And that's just how it was. Beautiful.

Here's a blowup of Nicole's eyes. (*click*) Here's one of her mouth. (*click*) Her hand. (*click*) I floated there in the water, watching, my eyes and nose just above the surface, my mouth and ears beneath the water. You know that sound? That underwater sound? And the next thing I remember is coughing. I couldn't get the water out of my lungs. And then my grandmother was there, and she leaned down and waded in. Nicole must've still been in the water then. Why did she jump in the water? I was out, though, coughing. Why was I coughing? And she was still in the water, in the pool, in the blue. A blue just like this. (*click*) Now the projector's stuck again. Shit. (*click*) (*click*) (*click*) That's what it looked like, though, flashes of white. I saw the whole thing through flashes of white, empty slides. The sun flashing off the water. (*click*) (*click*) Like this. (*click*) (*click*) (*click*) Oh Jesus, I watched her. I watched the whole thing happen through the blue and the gold and the white flashes. The white flashes. I saw Nicole. I saw her pointing, running, I saw her jumping. Did she think I was drowning? Was she trying to save me? I watched. I knew what was happening but like with Jamie I was far,

far away. I was watching through the light. And then my grand-mother came out and yelled at me. *"Kevin!"* And I was startled. I in-haled some water, that's why I was coughing. Nicole was floating facedown, among the flashes (*click*) (*click*) when my grandmother came out and yelled. She pulled Nicole out, and then I got out, coughing. And my parents came out and I was still coughing and someone said Kevin tried to save her, he tried to pull Nicole out, my grandmother, I think, saying, but he couldn't, oh the poor dear. But I knew what happened. I knew Nicole wasn't supposed to be in the water, and I watched it. I was looking through the light, into the heart of the light. I knew my sister was drowning and I watched it, I let it happen, because it was beautiful to see.

(*click*)

Under the water, she called my name.

(*click*)

What I saw was a flash of light, like these empty slides. (*click*) (*click*) (*click*). And what I heard? What did I hear?

Put your hands over your ears.

Press down.

BRAD   WATSON

Water Dog God

FROM   *Oxford American*

BACK IN LATE MAY a tornado dropped screaming into the canyon, snapped limbs and whole treetops off, flung squirrels and birds into the black sky. And in the wet and quiet shambles after, several new stray dogs crept into the yard, and upon their heels little Maeve. You've seen pictures of those children starving on TV, living in filthy huts and wearing rags and their legs and arms just knobby sticks, huge brown eyes looking up at you. That's what she looked like.

These strays, I sometimes think there is something their bones are tuned to that draws them here, like the whistle only they can hear, or words of some language ordinary humans have never known — the language that came from Moses' burning bush, which only Moses could hear. I think sometimes I've heard it at dawn, something in the green, smoky air. Who knows what Maeve heard, maybe nothing but a big rip-roaring on the roof: the black sky opens up, she walks out. She follows an old coon dog along the path of forest wreckage through the hollow and into my yard, her belly huge beneath a sleeveless bit of cloth you might call a nightslip.

I knew her as my Uncle Sebastian's youngest child, who wouldn't ever go out of her room, and here she was wandering in the woods. They lived up beyond the first dam, some three miles up the creek. She says to me, standing there holding a little stick she's picked up along the way, "I don't know where I'm at." She gives it an absent whack at the hound. He's a bluetick with teats so saggy I thought him a bitch till I saw his old jalapeño.

I said, "Lift up that skirt and let me see you." I looked at her white stomach, big as a camel's hump and bald as my head, stretched veins like a map of the pale blue rivers of the world, rivers to nowhere. I saw her little patch of frazzly hair and sex like a busted lip wanting nothing but to drop the one she carried. Probably no one could bear to see it but God, after what all must have climbed onto her, old Uncle Sebastian and those younger boys of his, the ones still willing to haul pulpwood so he hadn't kicked them out on their own, akin to these stray dogs lying about the yard, no speech, no intelligent look in their eyes.

This creature in Maeve would be something vile and subhuman.

I said, "The likes of those which have made your child, Maeve, should not be making babies, at least not with you. It was an evil thing that led to it."

She said, "Well, when the roof lifted off the house and blew away I climbed on out. They was all gone, out hiding or gone to town."

She took to wearing the little blue earphones radio I got in the mail with my Amoco card. I had no idea what she was listening to. She wandered around looking at nothing, one hand pressing a speaker to an ear, the other aimless, signing. She scarcely ever took them off, not even when she slept. She was quiet before, but now with her head shot through with radio waves she was hardly more than a ghost.

She would never even change out of her nightslip, though when I'd washed it for her it nearly fell apart. She was pale as a grub, hair a wet black rag all pressed to her head. Not even seventeen and small, but she looked old somehow. She'd seen so very little of the world and what she'd seen was scarcely human. She would forget, or just not bother to use, the toilet paper. Climb into the dry bathtub and fall into naps where she twitched like a dreaming dog. She heaved herself somehow up the ladder and through the little hole in the hallway ceiling to sit in the attic listening to her headset until she came down bathed in her own sweat and wheezing from the insulation dust. Maybe the little fibers got into her brain and improved her reception.

I made her put on a raincoat over the nightslip and took her to the grocery store, since I didn't want to leave her alone. I thought if I took her there she wouldn't think herself so strange compared with some of the women who lurk those aisles. Town is only three miles away but you would not think it to stand here and look at the steep green walls of the canyon. And what does it matter? The whole world, and maybe others, is in the satellite dish at the edge of the yard, and I have sat with Maeve until three in the morning watching movies, industrial videos, German game shows, Mexican soap operas. It's what Greta would do sometimes while she was dying, her body sifting little by little into the air. When I started to get the disability and was home all the time I could see this happening, so I wasn't surprised when one morning I woke and she didn't. I grieved but I wasn't surprised. She was all hollowed out. We'd never had a child as she was unable, and near the end I think she believed her life had been for nothing.

I felt the same way about myself after some twenty-odd years at ChemGlo. Sometimes it seems I wasn't even there in that job, I'd only dreamed up a vision of hell, a world of rusty green and leaky pipes and tanks and noxious fumes. But as I was not there anymore and was not dead, I began to believe or hope my life might have some purpose, though nothing had happened to confirm that until Maeve appeared.

At the grocery store I couldn't get her away from the produce section. She wouldn't put on any shoes, and she was standing there in her grimy, flat, skinny bare feet, the gray raincoat buttoned up to her chin, running her dirty little fingers all over the cabbages and carrot bunches, and when the nozzles shot a fine spray over the lettuce she stuck her head in there and turned her face up into the mist. I got her down to the meat and seafood area, where she stood and looked at the lobsters in their tank until I had everything else loaded into the cart, and I lured her to the cashier with a Snickers bar. She stood behind me in the line eating it while I loaded the groceries onto the conveyor belt, chocolate all over her mouth and her fingers, and she sucked on her fingers when she was done. And then she reached over to the candy shelf in the cashier chute and got herself another one, opened it up and bit into it, as if this was a place you came to when you wanted to eat, just walked around in there seeing what you wanted and eating it.

I looked at her a second, then just picked up the whole box of Snickers and put it on the conveyor belt.

"For the little girl," I said.

The cashier, a dumpy little blond woman with a cute face who'd been looking at Maeve, and then at me, broke into a big smile that was more awkward than fake.

"Well," she said to Maeve, "I wish my daddy was as sweet as yours."

Maeve stopped chewing the Snickers and stared at me as if she'd never seen me before in her life.

Understand, we are in a wooded ravine, a green, jungly gash in the earth, surrounded by natural walls. This land between the old mines and town, it's wooded canyons cut by creeks that wind around and feed a chain of quiet little lakes on down to ours, where the water deepens, darkens, and pours over the spillway onto the slated shoals. From there it rounds a bend down toward the swamps, seeps back into the underground river. The cicadas spool up so loud you think there's a torn seam in the air through which their shrieking slipped from another world.

One evening I was out on the porch in the late light after supper and saw Maeve sneak off into the woods. The coon dog got up and followed her, and then a couple of other strays followed him. When she didn't come right back I stood up and listened. The light was leaking fast into dusk. Crickets and tree frogs sang their high-pitched songs. Then from the woods in the direction she'd headed came a sudden jumble of high vicious mauling. It froze me to hear it. Then it all died down.

I went inside for the shotgun and the flashlight but when I came back out Maeve had made her way back through the thicket and into the ghostly yard, all color gone to shadowy gray, the nightslip wadded into a diaper she held to herself with both hands. I suppose it wasn't this child's first. She walked through the yard. What dogs hadn't gone with her stood around with heads held low, she something terrible and holy, lumpy stomach smeared with blood. She went to the lake's edge to wash herself and the slip, soaking and wringing it till she fell out and I had to go save her and take her into the house and bathe her myself and put her to bed. Her swollen little-girl's bosoms were smooth and white as the moon, the leaky nipples big as berries. I fed her some antibiotics left over from when I'd had the flu, and in a short time she recovered. She was young. Her old coonhound never came back, nor the others that went out with him, and I had a vision of them all devouring one another like snakes, until they disappeared.

I couldn't sleep and went out into the yard, slipped out of my jeans and into the lake. I thought a swim might calm me. I was floating on my back in the shallows looking up at the moon so big and clear you could imagine how the dust would feel between your fingers. My blood was up. I thought I heard something through the water, and stood. It was coming from across the lake, in the thick bramble up on the steep ridge, where a strange woman had moved into an empty cabin some months back. I heard a man one night up there, howling and saying her name, I couldn't tell what it was.

I'd seen her in town. She carried herself like a man, with strong wiry arms, a sun-scored neck, and a face hard and strange as the wood knots the carvers call tree spirits. I heard she's an installer for the phone company.

When I stood up in the water I could hear a steady rattling of branches and a skidding racket, something coming down the steep ridge wall. I waded back toward the bank, stopped and looked, and she crashed out of the bushes overhanging the water, dangling naked from a moonlit branch. She dropped into the lake with a quiet little splash, and when she entered the water it was like she'd taken hold of me. I didn't do that to myself anymore, though maybe I should've because I was sometimes all over Maeve in my sleep until she began to shout and scratch, for she was too afraid to sleep alone but must not be touched even by accident. But now here I was spilling myself into the shallows where the water tickled my ankles.

I saw her arms rise from the water and wheel slowly over her round, wet head and dip again beneath. She made no noise. She swam around the curve up into the shallows, stood up, and walked toward me and never took her eyes off my own.

She took my hand, and looked into the palm. She had a lean rangy skinned-cat body, and a deep little muttering voice.

"Small slim hands," she said, "a sad and lonely man. You see the big picture, but you have no real life." She grumbled a minute. "Short thin fingers, tapered ends. A stiff and waisted thumb, hmmm. Better off alone, I suppose." She pressed into the flesh below my thumb. "Ummhmm," she said, tracing all the little cracks and stars and broken lines in the middle of the palm with a light fingernail. She looked at it close for a second, then dropped it. She turned and sighed and looked back across the lake. I turned my eyes from her saggy little fanny and skinny legs.

"My name's Callie. I'm your neighbor," she said.

"I know it," I said.

She said, "Who's that little girl you taking care of?"

"My niece," I said. She was my younger cousin, but I had told her to call me uncle because it sounded more natural. I said, "She's had a hard life."

"Mmm," she said, and we were quiet for a while. "Well, the world ain't no place for an innocent soul, now is it?"

"It is not," I agreed.

"Must be hard on a man," she said.

"I don't know what you mean."

"I mean being alone out here with a pretty little girl."

"She's my niece, I'm not that way."

She turned and looked at me and then at the house for a minute.

"Why don't you come on up to the ridge sometime and pay me a visit?" Her thin lips crooked up and parted in a grin. She raised a hand and walked back into the water and swam around the curve into the cove and out of sight. I sat down on the bank. There was a sound and I turned my head to see Maeve up from bed and standing unsteady on the porch, fiddling with the little blue headphones radio, which she didn't at the moment seem to understand how to use. Then in a minute she had them on again, and just stood there.

Now that she wasn't carrying, she roamed the canyon with the strays. She ate raw peanuts from a sack I had on the kitchen counter, and drank her water from the lake down on her hands and muddy knees. She smelled like a dog that's been wallowing in the lake mud, that sour dank stink of rotten roots and scum. I finally held her in the bathtub one day, took the headphones off her head, and plunged her in, her scratching and screaming. I scrubbed her down and lathered up her head and dunked her till she was squeaky, and plucked a fat tick out of her scalp. But when I tried to dress her in some of Greta's old clothes, shut up in plastic and mothballs all these years, she slashed my cheek with her raggedy nails and ran through the house naked and making a high, thin, and breathless sound until she sniffed out the old rag she wore and flew out through the yard and into the woods buck naked with that rag in her hand and didn't come back till that evening, wearing it, smelling of the lake water again, and curled up asleep on the bare porchboards.

When I went to the screen door she didn't look up but said from where she lay hugging herself, "Don't you handle me that way no more."

"I had to clean you, child."

"I can't be touched," she said.

"All right."

"That woman at the big store said you was my daddy."

"But you know I'm not, I'm your uncle."

"I don't want no daddy," she said. "I just come out of the woods that day I come here, and I didn't come from nowhere before that."

"All right," I said, though my heart sank when she said it, for I wanted her to care about me in some way, but I don't think that was something she knew how to do. I fixed her a makeshift bed on the sofa in the den where I finally convinced her to sleep. As long as I kept my distance and made no sudden moves toward her and did not ever raise my voice above the gentle words you would use with a baby, we were all right. But it was not a way any man could live for long and I wondered what I could do — send her back to Sebastian's place, where she was but chattel? I feared one day she would wander into the woods and go wild. I might have called the county, said, Look, this child, who has wandered here from my uncle's house, is in need of attention and there is nothing more I can do.

Who would take in such a child but the mental hospital up in Tuscaloosa?

I figured Sebastian thought she'd been sucked up into the twister and scattered into blood and dust, until the afternoon I heard his pickup muttering and coughing along the dam and then his springs sighing as he idled down the steep drive to the house, and then the creaking door and I was out on the porch waiting on him. He stopped at the steps and nodded and looked off across the lake as if we were lost together in thought. Uncle Sebastian was old and small and thin and hard as iron and he had the impish and shrewd face of all his siblings. His face was narrow and his eyes slanted down and in and his chin jutted up so that if you viewed him in profile his head was the blade of a scythe and his body the handle. He blinked in the sun and said, "We been most of the summer fixing up the house after that tornado back in the spring."

I said, "Anybody hurt?"

"Well, we thought we'd lost little Maeve." And he turns to me. "Then I hear tell she's showed up over here, staying with you."

"Where would you hear that?" I said, and he said nothing but I saw his eyes shift just a fraction up toward the ridge where the crazy woman's house is perched.

The strays had shown little interest in Sebastian's arrival and kept mainly to their little scooped-out cool spots under the bushes, a flea-drowsing shade. Hardly moved all August; through the long hot days all you'd hear was the occasional creaking yawn, wet gnashing of grooming teeth, isolated flappity racket of a wet dog shaking out his coat. Hardly any barking at all. We heard a rustling and Maeve stood at the edge of the yard in her headphones, a scruffy little longhaired stray at her heels.

"She *was* with child," Sebastian said.

"She lost it."

"That late?" he said and looked at me a long moment, then back at Maeve. "You keeping her outdoors and living with dogs?"

"If it was true, it would not be so different from what she came from," I said.

"Go to hell," Sebastian said. "Living out here by yourself, you going to tell me you ain't been trying some of that?"

"That's right."

"Them boys of mine done all wandered off now she's gone. I ain't got no help."

He walked slowly toward Maeve, who was standing there with two fingers of one hand pressed to the speaker over her right ear, head cocked, eyes cut left looking out at the lake. The little stray slinked back into the brush. Only when Sebastian laid his hand on Maeve's arm did she lean away, her bare feet planted the way an animal that does not want to be moved will do. He began to drag her and she struggled, making not a sound, still just listening.

I walked up behind Sebastian and said his name, and when he turned I hit him between the eyes with the point of my knuckle. Small and old as he was, he crumpled. Maeve did not run then but walked over to the porch, up the steps, and into the house.

I dragged the old man by his armpits to the water, and waded out with him trailing. Maeve came out again and followed in her nightslip to the bank, and stood there eating a cherry popsicle. She took the popsicle out of her mouth and held it like a little beacon beside her head. Her lips were red and swollen-looking. She took the blue headphones off her ears and let them rest around her neck. I could hear the tinny sound of something in there, now it wasn't inside of her head.

"What you doing with that man?" she said.

"Nothing," I said.

"Are you drownden him?"

I said the first thing that came to mind.

"I am baptizing," I said. "I am cleansing his heart."

It was late afternoon then. I looked back over my shoulder at Maeve. She was half lit by sunlight sifting through the leaves, half in shadow. A mostly naked child in rotten garment.

Underwater, Uncle Sebastian jerked and his eyes came open. I held him harder and waded out to where it was up to my shoulders and the current strong toward the spillway, my heart heavy in the water, the pressure there pressing on it. Behind me, Maeve waded into the shallows.

"I want it too, Uncle," she called.

Sebastian's arms ceased thrashing, and after a minute I let him go. I saw him turning away in the water. Palms of his hands, a glimpse of an eye, the ragged toe of a boot dimpling the surface, all in a slow drifting toward the spillway, and then gone in the murk. Maeve lifted the gauzy nightslip up over her head as she waded in, her pale middle soft and mapped with squiggly brown stretch marks. I pushed against the current trying to reach her before she got in too deep. There was such unspeakable love in me. I was as vile as my uncle, as vile as he claimed.

"Hold still, wait there," I said at the very moment her head went under as if she'd been yanked from below.

The bottom is slippery, there are uncounted little sinkholes. Out of her surprised little hand, the nightslip floated a ways and sank. I dove down but the water slowed me and I could not reach her. My eyes were open but the water was so muddy I could barely even see my own hands. I kept gasping up and diving down, the sun was sinking into the trees.

She would not show again until dusk, when from the bank I saw her ghost rise from the water and walk into the woods.

The strays tuned up. There was a ringing from the telephone inside the house. It would ring and stop a while. Ring and then stop. The sheriff's car rolled its silent flickering way through the trees. Its lights put a flame in all the whispering leaves. There was a hollow taunting shout from up on the ridge but I paid it no mind.

I once heard at dawn the strangest bird, unnatural, like sweet notes sung through an outdoor PA system, some bullhorn perched in a tree in the woods, and I went outside.

It was coming from east of the house, where the tornado would come through. I walked down a trail, looking up. It got louder. I got to where it had to be, it was all around me in the air, but there was nothing in the trees. A pocket of air had picked up a signal, the way a tooth filling will pick up a radio station.

It rang in my blood, it and me the only living things in that patch of woods, all the creatures fled or dug in deep, and I remember that I felt a strange happiness.

Contributors' Notes

Raised in northern Michigan, author **Doug Allyn** served in Southeast Asia in military intelligence during the Vietnam War, later studied criminal psychology at the University of Michigan, then somehow parlayed those credentials into a twenty-year career in rock music before becoming an author.

From the beginning, critical response to his work has been remarkable. After winning the Robert L. Fish Memorial Award for best first short story, he has won or been nominated for every major award in the mystery field, including the ultimate prize, the Edgar Allan Poe Award.

- "Miracles! Happen!" features R. B. Axton, a composite character based on a number of amiable thugs I met on the fringes of the music business. The moral is straightforward. If you've lived at all, you are scarred. Some marks are visible. But for good or ill, the deepest cuts don't show.

David Beaty was born in Brazil of American parents. A graduate of Columbia University, he earned an MFA in creative writing from Florida International University. He has worked in Greece, England, and Brazil and currently lives in Coral Gables, Florida.

- I once played a version of "Ghosts" — an infinitely more benign and enjoyable version — when I was nine or ten years old. I forgot about it until the day five or six years ago when I looked at my parents and was shocked to see that they'd grown old. And then I remembered the night when, still young, they'd powdered their hair and dressed up in sheets and we played hide-and-seek in our darkened house in Miami.

Tom Berdine was born and raised in Lawrence Park, outside Erie, Pennsylvania, and attended the University of Buffalo. With brief stints in retail sales, textbook editing, construction, and sawmill work, his career has been in the people business, mainly child welfare, from which he retired last year. He is a husband, father of five, grandfather of three.

▪ "Spring Rite," in one form and another, gathered rejection notices for about fifteen years. I worked on it from time to time, feeling it was a good story and motivated to capture, or recapture, the intense feeling of a recalled scene — less than a scene really, an image or two — from a live television drama I saw as a kid. (We go way back with television in our family, our first set being homemade by an engineer rooming in the attic.) A fragment from that old video play, seen in boyhood, installed itself in my mind as a marker for the sexual mystery and outright dangerousness of women. I was able to finish this story when I stopped being preoccupied with plot and recognized that what I was after was an evocation of that dark, ephemeral little nugget: the women here are mainly offstage, taken in only in sideways glances, at a distance, or in the imagination, so powerful are they, and the Fisher woman in particular is intended as the ghost of that phosphorescent creature I gulped from the surface of a ten-inch cathode-ray tube fifty years ago.

The setting for "Spring Rite" is the area in which I have lived for the past twenty or so years, with place names altered so that my neighbors won't think I'm talking about them — something I do not do, vis-à-vis the advisory on gossip contained in "Spring Rite" — even though many of them naturally have stories and family histories more interesting than that of the Kramer brothers. For me, one of those people who can't shut up and has boxes of unfinished novels, the mystery genre is very practical: solve the mystery, that's the end.

Bentley Dadmun was born and raised in Wisconsin and has lived in New Hampshire for the past twenty years. After spending several decades wandering the wrong roads, he now leads the life of the stereotypical hungry writer, and although it is often frustrating, the act of building a story is a joy without equal.

▪ I like to write about protagonists who are somewhat dysfunctional and eccentric but get the job done in spite of themselves — people who, while on their quest, must drag their baggage along with them, for that is how most of us function and that is how most of us live our lives, although few of us engage in worthwhile quests.

Before earning B.A. and M.A. degrees at Northwestern University, **Barbara D'Amato** worked as an assistant surgical orderly, a carpenter for stage magic illusions, an assistant tiger handler, and a criminal law researcher. She is a past president of the Mystery Writers of America and Sisters in Crime. Born in Grand Rapids, Michigan, she now lives in Chicago.

▪ My husband and I drove Route 66 decades ago, when it still more or less existed as a continuous road. It seemed to me to be a bit of America that had seen most of the changes of the twentieth century, so I wanted to explore that in the story of "Motel 66," as well as the effects of time on human beings. The story is also about secrets. We all have secrets. In this case, two people who are close have secrets, but what happens when two long-held secrets suddenly intersect?

Geary Danihy was born in New Haven and grew up in Hamden, Connecticut. He attended Notre Dame High School, spent two and a half years at West Point, requested release, got married, and six months later was back in the army at the Artillery OCS, in Fort Sill, Oklahoma. Discharged in 1970, he attended the University of Idaho to complete his B.A. and then his M.A. in English. After several jobs, he opened his own promotion agency, Culdan, which grew to include an advertising agency that handled the Jordache jeans account for two years. When the agency closed, he and his wife decided to take a chance and make a living "doing what we always wanted to do." For her, that meant creating a company called Binky Botanika, which offers herbs, spices, and handmade bath and facial products. For me, that meant writing.

- "Jumping with Jim," my first published story, is the result of my lifelong interest in the conflict between desire and duty. (I was raised on a steady diet of movies like *High Noon, Beau Geste, Casablanca,* and *Captains Courageous.*) My wife and I disagree over whether Conrad's Lord Jim did the right thing by sacrificing his love for a "higher principle," but we have no disagreement with Frank Taylor's decision.

Jeffery Deaver, a former attorney and folksinger, is a *New York Times* bestselling author of fourteen novels. He has been nominated for four Edgar Awards from the Mystery Writers of America (two for his short stories) and is a two-time recipient of the Ellery Queen Readers' Award for Best Short Story of the Year. His book *A Maiden's Grave* was made into an HBO movie starring James Garner and Marlee Matlin, and his novel *The Bone Collector,* starring Denzel Washington, was a feature release from Universal Pictures. His most recent novels are *The Devil's Teardrop, The Empty Chair,* and *Speaking in Tongues.* He lives in Virginia and California.

- Rarely do I write novels or stories based on actual occurrences, but "Triangle" is one that I did extract from real life. I lived in Manhattan for a number of years, and now that I am a resident of the sort-of South (outside-the-Beltway D.C.), I find myself returning to New York with some frequency. One summer day, en route north, I stood at the United Airlines gate at Dulles Airport and watched a tiny drama unfold — it involved a mother and stepfather seeing off a young boy, flying to the city, presumably to spend the weekend with his natural father. The boy was upset, the mother bored, and the stepfather pleased, possibly looking forward to some time without the youngster at home. A psychologist undoubtedly could find in this sad scenario a number of insights about dysfunctional families and the anger of youth. The mind not being my forte, however, I decided to turn the situation into a story more aligned with one of my specialties: murder.

Edward Falco is the author of the hypertext novel *A Dream with Demons*, the print novel *Winter in Florida*, and the short story collections *Plato at Scratch Daniel's* and *Acid*. *Acid* won the Richard Sullivan Prize and was a finalist for the Patterson Prize. His stories have been widely published in journals, including the *Atlantic Monthly*, the *Missouri Review*, the *Southern Review*, *Playboy*, *Ploughshares*, and *TriQuarterly*. Annual anthologies that have selected his stories include *The Best American Short Stories*, *The Best American Mystery Stories*, *The Best American Erotica*, and *The Pushcart Prize*.

▪ "The Instruments of Peace" is a story that emerges out of the years I spent working with racehorses, first as a farmhand in Wallkill, New York, later as groom in Orlando, Florida, and finally as a trainer at Monticello Raceway in the Catskill Mountains, where my career ended ignominiously after I bought a yearling with bone spurs and my one and only money-maker bowed a tendon. Having failed as a horseman, I retreated to the quiet of academia, where I have since consoled myself with writing.

Tom Franklin won the 1999 Edgar Award for Best Mystery Story for his novella "Poachers," the title piece of his first book, published in 1999. The novella also appeared in *The Best American Mystery Stories 1999* and *The Best American Mystery Stories of the Century*. Franklin, from Dickinson, Alabama, now lives in Galesburg, Illinois, with his wife, the poet Beth Ann Fennelly. He is currently working on a novel, *Hell at the Breech*.

▪ I worked at a plant very much like the one in "Grit" for over four years, frequently on the night shift, during my early twenties. Nowadays, when I tell people about the grit factory, they often think it's *grits*, the kind you eat. I tell them no, no, it's sandblasting grit. At the plant, I ran the front-end loader and the forklift, unloaded slag from railcars, and loaded hundred-pound bags (for which I'm still seeing a chiropractor).

"Grit" is dedicated to the great bunch of guys I knew there: my uncle, D Bradford, who got me the job; Steve Sheffield; Bryan Ward; Roy Simon; Robert Evans; and the plant manager, Jim Seidenfaden. Uncle D, Bryan, and Jim still work at the plant; Robert is out owing to a back injury; and Roy died a few years ago.

David Edgerley Gates grew up in Cambridge, Massachusetts. His earliest influences were Kipling and Stevenson, *Puck of Pook's Hill* and *Treasure Is-*

land, which his father read aloud to him, but what he first read on his own was the Hardy Boys mysteries and Carl Barks's Donald Duck adventures in *Walt Disney's Comics & Stories.* His short fiction has appeared in *Alfred Hitchcock, A Matter of Crime,* and *Story.* An earlier mystery featuring Placido Geist, "Sidewinder," was a Shamus nominee for 1998. Gates lives in Santa Fe.

- "Compass Rose" is the fifth story I've written with Placido Geist. In the first story, he wasn't even introduced until about a third of the way in, and I didn't realize at the time he was going to be the hero. I underestimated him at first appearance, just like everybody else.

The ghost of Sam Peckinpah inhibits these bounty-hunter stories because of the period, and because I'm trying for an elegiac quality but without making it too obtrusive. Placido Geist is himself an unsentimental sort.

Robert Girardi is the author of three novels — *Madeleine's Ghost, The Pirate's Daughter,* and *Vaporetto 13* — and one collection of novellas, *A Vaudeville of Devils: Seven Moral Tales,* from which the selection in this volume is drawn. He is a native of Washington, D.C., but spent a good portion of his youth in Europe, an experience reflected in the international settings of much of his fiction. He lives in Washington with his wife, the poet and mystery writer Linda Girardi, and their two children, Benjamin Oliver and Charlotte Rose. He can be reached at 1girardi@aol.com.

- I've always been amused by the various goofy ways there are to die, and to my mind falling out of or off of a building has always had an element of comic absurdity. I've also long wanted to write an anti-Grisham lawyer story in which the lawyer is not only incompetent but utterly mistaken regarding the guilt or innocence of his client — and I suppose from these two slightly ridiculous impulses "The Defenestration of Aba Sid" was born.

Chad Holley was born and raised in Mississippi and received an MFA from the University of North Carolina at Greensboro in 1999. His stories have begun to appear in such places as the *Chattahoochee Review* and the *Greensboro Review.* He is currently working on a novel and a collection of stories.

- In one of her letters, Flannery O'Connor said something to the effect that too often the stories she fussed over least seemed to be the ones folks liked the most. I want to say that's been true of "The Island in the River," but then maybe it's been long enough now that I've just forgotten the fussing. There is always fussing. The initial ingredients for this story were a terrible dream, a recent hunting trip, and the crackling vinyl soundtrack to *Pat Garrett and Billy the Kid.*

Ex–police officer, ex–army tank gunner, and ex–auto parts salesman, **Edward Lee** is the author of more than a dozen novels, most recently the police procedural *Dahmer's Not Dead* (with Elizabeth Steffen), and the conspiracy thriller *The Stickmen.* Lee has also sold over sixty short stories in the horror and suspense field, plus a number of comic scripts. Currently he lives in Seattle, where he pursues a peculiar hobby: collecting crab shells.

• "ICU" actually went through several phases of revision over the past few years. I wanted to write something hard, fast, and dark, with a payoff ending, but something that also probed fairly deeply into the psyche of a sophisticated modern sociopath. I wanted the trimmings to be real; hence, via a stack of textbooks and some law enforcement journals, I did quite a bit of research involving the technical mechanics of child pornography, its statistics, its distribution, etc. I reworked the piece a number of times, avoiding telling the story from the antagonist's point of view, which seemed *too* dark, but then I just said to hell with it and did it. Lastly, I tweaked the ending at the suggestion of editor Al Sarrantonio and was thrilled to have the piece published in Avon's *999.*

Dennis Lehane considers himself a short story writer who somehow fell into writing novels. He has written five crime novels, including *Gone, Baby, Gone* and *Prayers for Rain,* with the Boston private detectives Patrick Kenzie and Angela Gennaro as the lead characters. His next novel, *Mystic River,* is his first novel not of that series. He lives in Boston with his wife, Sheila, and their two bulldogs, Marlon and Stella.

• I went to college in Florida, and usually I'd drive to or from Boston at the beginning and end of the school year. Sometimes I'd take I-95, and other times I'd spend four or five days driving the back roads through Georgia, the Carolinas, Virginia, and Delaware. For some reason, every time I passed through the Carolinas, the roads were littered with what seemed like a prodigious number of dog corpses. I've never discovered any logical reasons for this, but just the same, time and time again, I'd drive through the Carolinas and see several dead dogs. It stuck in my head, and when I was in graduate school I wrote an early draft of "Running Out of Dog" that was solely about a guy who worries that his best friend has become one of those men who may one day walk into a place of business with a loaded rifle and kill everyone he sees. Five years later, I dusted the story off and decided to open it up. I added several characters (as well as twenty-five manuscript pages), changed the time in which the story was set, and created a far more ambiguous ending. What stayed the same was the basic idea — a guy who shoots dogs for a living and gets an unhealthy taste for it — and the title. Like all my stories, I'm not sure how I feel about it, but it's my wife's favorite. My dogs, however, hate it.

A native of Houston, Texas, **Thomas H. McNeely** has recently received fellowships from the MacDowell Colony and the J. Frank Dobie Memorial Project at the University of Texas at Austin. "Sheep" is his first published work of fiction. He teaches at the Grub Street Writers' Workshops and Emerson College in Boston, where he is currently at work on a collection of linked stories.

▪ The idea for "Sheep" came to me while I was working for a nonprofit law firm in Texas that defended death row cases. At the time, I spent many hours looking at crime scene photos and many hours with the men who committed those crimes. I was struck by my inability to connect what I saw in those pictures with the men I came to know. That moment, and the comparisons it suggested to me about the criminal justice system's inability to consider how the men they sought to execute came to be who they were, formed the kernel of the story.

All of my models for Lloyd, unfortunately, are dead. The story is a tribute to their courage, and the courage of the people who defended them. Many thanks also to James Carroll and Pamela Painter.

Martha Moffett was born at the end of a dirt road in St. Clair County, Alabama, was a student of Hudson Strode's at the University of Alabama, then worked in publishing in New York City (*GQ,* the *American Heritage Dictionary, Ladies' Home Journal*). She wrote her first novel on the subway on the way to work and raised three daughters. She currently lives in Florida, where she recently won a state fellowship and grant for a play. She remembers with gratitude a fellowship at Yaddo, where her lunch was left on the front porch so that she could work all day.

▪ I've always liked to read scary, suspenseful stories, but this is the first story I've written that scared me. I think it works because the reader knows what a bad type Nick is, and feels anxiety for Storey, who doesn't have a clue.

Several readers have commented on the difficulty of writing from a male viewpoint, but there was no difficulty. I've never seen why there should be. Don't we all think about each other, study each other, pretend to be each other, remember all the words spoken in bed? Writing from a male viewpoint is an interesting undertaking.

Patently squeamish when it comes to reading about himself in the third person because of its obituary-like overtones, **Josh Pryor** lives outside Los Angeles, where he is a part-time professor of composition at El Camino College. He has published several pieces of short fiction in both national and regional magazines and is currently at work on a collection of stories and his second novel, *The IT Conspiracy.* He can be reached at joshuapryor@yahoo.com.

▪ I've never really thought of myself as a "mystery writer" per se. My fiction, however, seems to have a mind of its own, often wedding characters to circumstance in suspenseful, typically macabre twists of fate. Usually I'll start out with the best of intentions, but when I sit down to write, something comes over me, and bad things have a way of happening to those unfortunate souls spawned from my imagination.

"Wrong Numbers" was inspired by a friend who actually worked in human resources at Pac Bell. My initial intent was to write a story about a new hire gone wrong. At the time, not even I realized that Karloff was a budding psychopath and how terribly wrongly events would unfold.

Shel Silverstein was born in Chicago in 1930 and is best known for such children's books as *The Giving Tree,* which sold more than five million copies, and *A Light in the Attic,* which remained on the *New York Times* bestseller list for 182 weeks. One of the most versatile and successful artists of our time, he regularly published cartoons and illustrations in *Playboy,* and he wrote the words and music for many popular entertainers, including Lynn Anderson, Jerry Lee Lewis, Dr. Hook, the Brothers Four, and Johnny Cash, including Cash's famous "A Boy Named Sue." The kind and gentle man who brought so much delight to so many millions of children of all ages died on May 10, 1999.

Peter Moore Smith was born in Panama and has lived in Nebraska, Alaska, North Carolina, New York, New Jersey, Virginia, and West Germany. Currently his home is Manhattan, where he lives with his wife, Brigette, a graphic designer. His short fiction has appeared in a number of literary publications, and his story "Oblivion, Nebraska" was selected for the Pushcart Prize 2000 volume. His first novel, *Raveling,* is forthcoming.

▪ There is something about the image of a little girl splashing around in one of those backyard swimming pools and the play of light across the surface of the water that is to me central to my American childhood. I can practically taste the chlorine. There is also something about the idea of losing a sister that I find deeply disturbing. I have two. Losing either one of them would be the worst thing in the world and, to my twisted writer's imagination, well worth writing about.

Brad Watson's collection of stories, *Last Days of the Dog-Men,* won the Sue Kaufman Prize for First Fiction from the American Academy of Arts and Letters and the Great Lakes Colleges Association New Writers Award. He was born in Mississippi, was educated there and in Alabama, worked as a newspaper reporter among other things, and taught at the University of Alabama. He currently is Briggs-Copeland Lecturer in Fiction and director of the creative writing program at Harvard University.

▪ "Water Dog God" began as a major revision of another story, then became its own thing. I first thought of it, though, as a failed revision of the other story, "A Blessing," and put it away in a drawer. Only after *Dog-Men* had come out did I rediscover it and realize it had possibilities. I revised it every six months or so for the next couple of years, and revised it more than once for Marc Smirnoff at the *Oxford American*. It went from very weird to nicely strange. Or at least that's my view. In "A Blessing," a couple expecting a child drive out to get a new dog from the owner of this place on the lake. The couple became, after a fashion, the girl Maeve, and the dog owner became a very different person from the one he was in "A Blessing." The original story was in the third person, from the point of view of the pregnant woman. As far as I can tell, the only things the two stories still share are the setting and the sense of nascent — later delivered — violence about this place. The sorts of things the pregnant woman fears in "A Blessing" are realized in "Water Dog God." Sort of.

Other Distinguished Mystery Stories of 1999

HOWARD, CLARK
  The Global Man. *Ellery Queen's Mystery Magazine*, December

KAMINSKY, STUART M.
  What You Don't Know. *Death by Espionage*, ed. Martin Cruz Smith (Cumberland House)
KELTS, ROLAND
  Hiropon My Heroine. *Zoetrope*, Winter
KLINGER, LESLIE
  The Adventure of the Wooden Box. Mysterious Bookshop
KNIEF, CHARLES
  Hell. *Murder on Route 66*, ed. Carolyn Wheat (Berkley)

LIPPMAN, LAURA
  Orphan's Court. *First Cases*, vol. 3, ed. Robert J. Randisi (Signet)
LUSTBADER, ERIC VAN
  Slow Burn. *Murder and Obsession*, ed. Otto Penzler (Delacorte)

MALONE, MICHAEL
  Invitation to the Ball. *Murder and Obsession*, ed. Otto Penzler (Delacorte)
McPHEE, JENNY
  Mrs. Lange's Party. *Zoetrope*, Winter
MILLHAUSER, STEVEN
  The Disappearance of Elaine Coleman. *The New Yorker*, November 22

OATES, JOYCE CAROL
  In Copland. *Boulevard*, Fall

PEEL, JOHN
  Toccata and Feud. *The Literary Review*, Spring

REDDING, JUDITH M.
  Mud. *Night Shade*, ed. Victoria A. Brownworth and Judith M. Redding (Seal Press)

SaFRANCO, MARK
  The Man in Unit 24. *Hawai'i Review*, Fall/Winter
SALTER, JOHN
  Shoshone Insurance. *Nebraska Review*, Summer
SCHUTZ, BENJAMIN M.
  Expert Opinion. *Diagnosis Dead*, ed. Jonathan Kellerman (Pocket)
STASHOWER, DANIEL
  The Second Treaty. *The New Adventures of Sherlock Holmes*, ed. Martin H. Greenberg, Jon L. Lellenberg, and Carol-Lynn Rossel (Carroll & Graf)

WESTMORELAND, KENT
  A Relatively Small Sum of Money. *Blue Murder*, May